THE PENGUIN CLASSICS

FOUNDER EDITOR (1944–64): E. V. RIEU

LUDOVICO ARIOSTO was born in 1474, the son of an official of the Ferrarese court. He first studied law, but later acquired a sound humanistic training. His adult life was spent in the service of the Ferrarese ducal family. Essentially he was a writer; his lifetime's service as a courtier was a burden imposed on him by economic difficulties. His fame rests on his major work, *Orlando Furioso*. The poem was probably begun about 1505. It was first published in 1516. The most important of Ariosto's minor works are five comedies, written for production in the Ferrarese court.

Ariosto died in 1533.

BARBARA REYNOLDS is Honorary Reader in Italian at Warwick University. A graduate of University College, London, she was for twenty-two years Lecturer in Italian at Cambridge University and from 1966 until 1978 was Reader in Italian Studies at Nottingham University. Her first book was a textual reconstruction of the linguistic writings of Alessandro Manzoni. The General Editor of the *Cambridge Italian Dictionary*, she has been awarded silver medals by the Italian Government and by the Province of Vicenza, and the Edmund Gardner Prize for her services to Italian scholarship and to Anglo-Italian cultural relations. She was appointed Visiting Professor in Italian at the University of California, Berkeley, for 1974–5.

Barbara Reynolds completed and annotated the translation of Dante's *Paradiso* begun by Dorothy L. Sayers and has translated *La Vita Nuova* for Penguin Classics. She was awarded the Monselice International Literary Prize for her translation of Ariosto's *Orlando Furioso*.

ORLANDO FURIOSO
(THE FRENZY OF ORLANDO)

A Romantic Epic by
Ludovico Ariosto

PART ONE

TRANSLATED
WITH AN INTRODUCTION BY
BARBARA REYNOLDS

PENGUIN BOOKS

Penguin Books Ltd, Harmondsworth, Middlesex, England
Penguin Books, 625 Madison Avenue, New York, New York 10022, U.S.A.
Penguin Books Australia Ltd, Ringwood, Victoria, Australia
Penguin Books Canada Ltd, 2801 John Street, Markham, Ontario, Canada L3R 1B4
Penguin Books (N.Z.) Ltd, 182–190 Wairau Road, Auckland 10, New Zealand

—

This translation first published 1975
Reprinted 1977, 1981

—

Introduction, translation and notes copyright © Barbara Reynolds, 1975
All rights reserved

—

Made and printed in Great Britain by
Hazell Watson & Viney Ltd,
Aylesbury, Bucks
Set in Monotype Garamond

FOR
ADRIAN

CONTENTS

... the story is extant, and written in very choice Italian.
Hamlet, III. ii.

INTRODUCTION

I. THE POEM

THE *Orlando Furioso* is above all a poem to be enjoyed; the chief aim of its creator was to give delight. Ariosto succeeded brilliantly, and for centuries his long and varied epic proved a treasure-house of enjoyment, frequented as eagerly in England as in Italy. 'One of the great narrative poems of Europe', writes Graham Hough, 'it has perhaps given more sheer sparkling pleasure to its readers than any other poem on the same scale.'[1]

Yet some cultural adjustments are needed before the modern reader can enter into full enjoyment of this early sixteenth-century romantic epic. The very word 'romantic', associated as it now is with early nineteenth-century art and literature, requires some explanation. A romantic epic is an epic of Romance: that is, of post-classical, medieval legends, especially those relating to the paladins of Charlemagne and the knights of Arthur. Such material has long been out of favour as an inspiration to poetry. So, too, have vast, complicated tapestry-like verse narratives, with their numerous digressions and disconcertingly varied strands. Between Ariosto and the modern reader are a few hurdles to be cleared. Among them are the rules set up by later sixteenth-century theorists: the rigid separation of literary genres, the strict observance of the unities of action, time and place, and the disapproval of abrupt transition in style and tone. It is true that in drama Shakespeare accustomed the English to variety and contrast within a single, unified work, but no English poet achieved or aimed at a comparable diversity for epic.[2] The sheer length

1. Introduction to Sir John Harington's translation, edited by Graham Hough, Centaur Press, 1962, p. vii.

2. Some of the distinctions between Ariosto and Spenser are discussed on pp. 78–81. See also the discussion of Tasso's views on the epic, pp. 78; 80.

(no less than 38,736 lines) and the leisured pace of the poem
may also prove obstacles in a world accustomed to rapid,
often non-verbal, communication.

In an age suspicious of 'escapist' literature, it may be of help
to say at once that Ariosto had a serious-minded as well as a
light-hearted purpose and that his poem shows a deep concern
for the values of Christendom. The *Orlando Furioso*, for all its
many sub-plots, is mainly the story of the defence of Europe
by Charlemagne against Islam and evokes a crucial stage in
the history of western civilization.

Critics are not agreed as to the central, unifying element in
the structure of the poem. Some have seen it in the hopeless
love of Orlando for the Eastern princess, Angelica, daughter
of the Great Khan – a love which brings about his madness.
Others have found it in the theme of the ducal house of Este,
the rulers of Ferrara, Ariosto's patrons, whom he praises
throughout the poem and whose legendary origins he cele-
brates in the marriage of two of the main characters, Brada-
mante and Ruggiero. Still others have seen the unifying factor
not in one of the many themes, not in the concept of chivalry,
not in a regret for the ideals and heroism of a bygone age, but
in a stylistic individuality, an aesthetic harmony, an ironic
detachment.

While the structural importance of such features must be
acknowledged, what gives the work its fundamental unity is
the concept of Europe, seen by Ariosto as the fount of the
creative and civilizing forces of the world. As Virgil was the
poet of Rome, Ariosto is the poet of Europe.

The battle of Poitiers in 732, at which the Frankish leader,
Charles Martel, defeated the Moslems, is said to have been a
decisive victory. Yet his grandson, Charlemagne, found it
necessary to continue the struggle; in the course of fifty-three
campaigns, he defied and overcame the pagan forces encircling
the Christian world: yet even he failed to break the hold of the
Saracens in Spain. The threat of the Infidel remained. The
legends to which the conflict gave rise acquired in consequence
an enduring vitality, to be seen even today in the heroic duels
between paladins and infidels in the puppet-theatres of Liège

and Palermo. A lasting relevance had been ensured by an ever-present danger and an undiminished need for a united Europe.

Ariosto was twenty-four in July 1499 when the Turkish fleet of Bayezid II defeated the Venetians at Lepanto.[1] Bayezid's predecessor, Mohammed II, having taken Constantinople in 1453, subdued Serbia, Walachia, Bosnia and Albania, obliging Venice to surrender Scutari and Kroia and to pay an indemnity of 100,000 ducats; he next conquered the Crimea, bestowing it as a tributary province on the Tartar Khan and, preparatory to his plan of conquering Italy, began to menace Rhodes. A naval expedition was unsuccessful, but a land attack on southern Italy prevailed: Otranto was captured. In 1521, Suleiman marched into Hungary; five years later, at the battle of Mohács, the Hungarians were severely defeated and Budapest was seized. Encouraged by Francis I of France against the Emperor Charles V, Suleiman laid siege to Vienna, and part of the Turkish army marched into Germany as far as Regensburg. In 1532 Suleiman again bore down upon Vienna.[2] In addition to these menaces by land, Moorish pirates, operating from the coast of north Africa, harassed European shipping in the Mediterranean. Khair-ed-Din (better known as Barbarossa) built up Algiers as a stronghold of piracy. So intolerable was this molestation that Charles V enlisted the Genoese admiral Andrea Doria to clear the Mediterranean of Corsair vessels, an achievement for which Ariosto sings his praises.[3]

The *Orlando Furioso* is as deeply concerned with the events and personages of its author's lifetime as it is with the conflict between the Carolingians and the infidels. During the twenty-seven years of its composition the poem underwent a continuous process of development. Its dynamic response to contemporary affairs, what has been well termed its 'mobili-

1. The great victory of the Christian league against Turkey was won at the second, more famous battle of Lepanto in 1571.

2. It is interesting to consider the dates of the three editions of *Orlando Furioso* in relation to these events: 1516, 1521, 1532.

3. XV. 30–35.

ty',[1] has resulted in a stereoscopic effect, showing the reader eighth-century and sixteenth-century Europe in perspectives which relate to each other. An important instance is the relationship of Charlemagne as unifying head of the Christian world to the figure of the Emperor Charles V who, in much the same way as the Emperor Henry VII may be said to have entered the *Divina Commedia*, entered the *Furioso* on succeeding to his vast inheritance in 1519. No Emperor since Charlemagne had mattered so much to Christendom. Of simple and unshakeable faith, he was the last of the Holy Roman Emperors to pursue the medieval ideal of universal empire. He saw clearly the need for Europe to present a united front against the Turkish menace; and as heir to the Spanish throne he had inherited the traditional struggle of the Spanish kings against Islam. That he failed to unite Europe and that he was defeated in his aims as a Catholic monarch by the reforming movement in Germany is not relevant to the poem. What is significant is the light in which Ariosto presents him.

In Canto XV, while Astolfo, the English duke, is sailing westwards across the Indian Ocean, his guide, Andronica, prophesies the voyages of explorers of the fifteenth and sixteenth centuries, reserved by Providence until the coming of Charles V:

> 'God's will it was that in the ancient days
>   This path across the globe should be unknown;
> And seven centuries must run their phase
>   Before the mystery to man is shown,
> For, in the wisdom of the Almighty's ways,
>   He waits until the world shall be made one
> Beneath an Emperor more just and wise
> Than any who since Augustus shall arise.

> 'A prince of Austrian and Spanish blood
>   Born on the Rhine's left bank, behold, I see:
> With valour such as his no valour could
>   Compare, in legend or in history.
> I see Astraea with new power endued,
>   From death restored to life and victory.

1. C. P. Brand, 'Ludovico Ariosto, Poet and Poem in the Italian Renaissance', *Forum for Modern Language Studies*, IV, 1 (1968), p. 101.

> I see the virtues, by the world exiled,
> Return in triumph, and all vice reviled.
>
> 'For valour, whence all other virtues stem,
> God wills not only that this Emperor
> Shall wear upon his brow the diadem
> Which Roman Emperors have worn before,
> But, glittering with many a new gem,
> His sceptre shall encompass many a shore
> Which knows no season but the winter's cold;
> And there shall be one shepherd and one fold.'[1]

In the light of this ideal and of the need for unity, it is not surprising to find Ariosto rebuking other Christian monarchs for their mutual hostility:

> No longer now defenders of the faith,
> With one another Christian knights contend,
> Destroying in their enmity and wrath
> Those few who still believe; make now an end,
> You Spaniards; Frenchmen, choose another path;
> Switzers and Germans, no more armies send.
> For here the territory you would gain
> Belongs to Christ; His kingdom you profane.
>
> If 'the most Christian' rulers you would be,
> And 'Catholic' desire to be reputed,
> Why do you slay Christ's men? Their property
> Why have you sacked, and their belongings looted?
> Why do you leave in dire captivity
> Jerusalem, by infidels polluted?
> Why do you let the unclean Turk command
> Constantinople and the Holy Land?[2]

With the election of Pope Leo X, there was perhaps hope of a change of policy:

> And you, great Leo, bearing on your back
> St Peter's burden, do not still allow
> Fair Italy to sleep in sloth for lack
> Of your strong arm to pull her from the slough.
> You are the Shepherd: from the wolves' attack

1. XV. 24–6.   2. XVII. 74–5.

Defend your flock; stretch forth your right arm now.
Like your proud name, chosen for you by God,
Be leonine and worthy of your rod.[1]

The link between the eighth and sixteenth centuries could
hardly be more clearly pointed than in these stanzas in which
Ariosto interrupts his narrative to rebuke and exhort his
contemporaries. Explicit, too, is the relevance of the poem to
Ariosto's patrons, the Duke of Ferrara, Alfonso I, and his
brother, Cardinal Ippolito, whose origins he traces back to
the House of Troy.[2] Addressed directly to Ippolito, the poem
is offered as a second *Aeneid*, though with becoming modesty
Ariosto laments the inadequacy of his powers in comparison
with Virgil's:

In truth, to sing of all its glorious deeds,
This new Augustan age a Virgil needs.[3]

Ariosto's fulsome praise of the House of Este, on whom he
depended for a livelihood, has been judged distasteful by his
more fastidious readers. In fairness to Ariosto, it must be
conceded that there was much which he could genuinely
praise. This Guelf family, who took their name and titles from
the township and castle of Este, were of Lombard descent and
had connections, dating from the eleventh century, with the
princely houses of Brunswick and Hanover.[4] They first ac-
quired political importance in Ferrara in the twelfth century
through marriage with the Marcheselli family, who were the
leaders of one of the two main factions in the city. The other
faction was led by the Torelli, who remained rivals of the
Estensi until 1240 when Azzo Novello (1205–64), having
been expelled from Ferrara by Salinguerra Torelli, returned to
power with the support of the Guelf League formed by Pope
Gregory IX. The rule of the Estensi over Ferrara was form-
alized after the accession to the head of the family of Obizzo II
(1240–93), who was created perpetual lord by the Ferrarese

1. XVII. 79. The hope was not fulfilled.
2. For the historical and legendary genealogy of the House of Este, see
the tables on pp. 732–4.
3. III. 56. vii–viii.
4. They were thus distantly related to the Duke of Brunswick who in
1714 became George I of England.

and also chosen as lord of Modena and Reggio Emilia. Family disputes arose in which both Venice and the Papacy became involved. Eventually Pope Clement V, who was overlord of Ferrara, prevailed with the help of the Angevins of Naples. In 1317 the Ferrarese rebelled against King Robert of Anjou and called back their former rulers. From then on the Estensi governed Ferrara without interruption for nearly three centuries. Pope John XXII created them papal vicars and Pope Paul II conferred a dukedom on Borso d'Este in 1471.

Ariosto, surveying the creation of this dynasty from its turbulent beginnings to its sixteenth-century glories, must have felt his pulses leap in recognition of an epic theme. The court, one of the most brilliant in Europe, attracted a concourse of poets, scholars and artists. Niccolò II, who ruled from 1361 to 1388, had given hospitality to Petrarch; Alberto (1388–93) founded the University; Niccolò III (1393–1441) was the patron of Guarino da Verona and of Pisanello; Leonello (1441–50) and his brother Borso (1450–71), both patrons of art and learning, made Ferrara illustrious as a centre of culture. The Schifanoia palace, with its frescoes by Francesco Cossa representing the seasons and the months, was one of the glories of Italy. Ercole I (1471–1505), who with the help of the architect, Biagio Rossetti, planned the new district, known after him as the Addizione Ercolea, made Ferrara the first modern city in Europe. The stately symmetry of her streets and squares, laid out in accordance with the principles of Alberti, her monumental palaces in their superb gardens were the admiration of all visitors. The palace of Belriguardo with its frescoed halls, its gardens adorned with fountains and statues, its skilfully designed perspectives, seemed to Ludovico Sforza when he saw it in 1493 to be the most beautiful place in the world. But even the beauty of Belriguardo was surpassed by the palace of Belvedere which Alfonso I (1505–1534) built on an island in the Po: a flight of marble steps led from the riverside to a grassy court surrounded by low-cut box hedges and graced by a central fountain. An imposing villa with a classical portico and colonnade rose on one side of the court. The marble atrium, decorated with nymphs and cupids, opened into frescoed or tapestried apartments. Beyond the duke's private rooms was a chapel; beyond this, a sunken garden, containing rare fruit-trees and adorned with still more fountains, led on towards a menagerie filled with ostriches, elephants and other exotic animals, screened finally by woods and orchards sloping to the water's edge.

The creation of beauty and splendour was looked on in the Renaissance as a noble achievement, worthy of the highest of men's gifts. It would never have occurred to Ariosto to do other than exalt his patrons for fostering such a high level of creativity. It must indeed have seemed, without undue hyperbole, a 'new Augustan age' which they had brought into being. For the magic palaces and enchanted gardens of his narrative it was not necessary for him to indulge in fantasies: he had only to look about him.[1]

Of the grimmer realities of war, intrigue and conspiracy, Ariosto was well aware. In his attitude to his patrons, which is by no means wholly subservient, there is an interesting element of ambivalence. Sometimes he awards lavish praise, as in the following tribute to Ippolito:

> Magnanimous Signor, your every act
> With reason I have praised and still I praise,
> Though my poor style, alas! the power has lacked
> Your glory to its fullest height to raise;
> But, of your virtues which applause attract,
> To one my tongue most heartfelt tribute pays:
> Though many are in audience received,
> Their evidence is not at once believed.
>
> When blame against an absent man is laid,
> I hear you bring excuses to defend him;
> When all accusers all their say have said,
> One ear you keep unprejudiced to lend him;
> And long before a judgement you have made,
> A hearing, face-to-face, you will extend him.
> For days and months and years you may defer
> Before you find against him, lest you err.[2]

1. His description of the realm and garden of Alcina, VI. 20–25, 71–75, tallies closely with reality, as he knew it.
2. XVIII. 1–2.

But Ippolito was not at all the restrained and prudent character he is here represented as being. His rise to ecclesiastical office had been rapid, even for Renaissance times: tonsured at the age of six, at eight he was Apostolic Protonotary, at eleven Archbishop, at fourteen a Cardinal. Since holding ecclesiastical office was for members of princely families a political rather than a priestly function, there was no reason why a cardinalship should place restrictions upon Ippolito's way of life. Nor did he allow it to do so. An episode in which both he and Alfonso were involved shows the brothers in an unpleasing light. It is related that in 1505, when Ippolito was paying court to Angela Borgia, who had come to Ferrara with her cousin, Lucrezia, on the latter's marriage to Alfonso, Angela laughingly remarked that his brother Giulio's eyes were worth more than the Cardinal's whole person. The next day, while out hunting, Giulio was set upon by a band of assassins who blinded him while Ippolito looked on. The doctors later succeeded in saving the sight of one eye. Giulio's demand for justice was disregarded, Alfonso merely sentencing Ippolito to nominal banishment. Giulio then conspired with another brother, Ferrante, to kill Alfonso and put Ferrante in his place. When the plot was discovered, Ferrante knelt at Alfonso's feet to ask forgiveness. Alfonso struck him in the face with a staff, putting out one of his eyes. Both he and Giulio were condemned to death but at the last moment the sentence was commuted to life-imprisonment. In the dungeons below the castle the two half-blinded brothers dragged out their miserable existence, while up above the brilliant life of the court continued. Ferrante died, aged sixty-three, while still imprisoned, but Giulio lived on, to be liberated finally at the age of eighty-one by Alfonso II.

Soon after the conspiracy Ariosto wrote a dramatic eclogue on the subject, for the entertainment of the court. In the *Furioso* he refers to the event again, as part of the prophecy which the sorceress Melissa makes to Bradamante in Merlin's cave concerning her descendants. Having seen two spirits about whom Melissa has told her nothing, Bradamante says:

> 'I noticed two of grim, foreboding look,
> Between Alfonso and Ippolito.
> Something concerning them I'd gladly know.'[1]

Melissa grows pale and bursts out weeping:

> 'Ah! victims both, your happiness destroyed
> By evil men who, evil plans pursuing,
> Brought you, ah, woe is me! to your undoing!'[2]

The 'evil men' are their fellow-conspirators. Of Alfonso and
Ippolito, who were guilty of such cruelty and injustice,
Melissa says, addressing them directly:

> 'O virtuous offspring, worthy of the good
> Duke Ercole, let not their fault dismay you!
> These wretched reprobates are of your blood!
> Compassion then, not justice, here should sway you.'[3]

A cautious plea for mercy; whereas the praise of both Alfonso
and Ippolito by Melissa in earlier stanzas has been fulsome in
the extreme. The greatest debt which Ferrara owes to their
father, Duke Ercole, is to be seen not in the magnificent im-
provements he has made to the city, nor in his resistance to
the Venetians, nor yet in his alliance with the French king,
Charles VIII, by which he spared Ferrara the devastation
which other cities suffered, but in the fact that he has fathered
two such sons:

> 'As deep indebtedness as any State
> Will feel towards its prince, Ferrara's debt
> Will ever be to him, not only that,
> Removed from marsh and bog, she will be set
> In fertile plains, nor that he'll there create
> More amplitude within new walls, nor yet
> That temples, palaces to make her fair
> He'll build, and theatres, and many a square,
>
> 'Nor even that against the avid claws
> Of the wing-bearing Lion he will stand
> Firm and unwavering, nor yet because,
> When the French torch sets all the lovely land

Of Italy ablaze, she'll have no cause
To fear, alone exempt from the demand
For tribute – not for these and not a few
Such benefits her greatest thanks are due,

But for illustrious offspring he'll beget:
The just Alfonso, Ippolito benign.'[1]

Concerning Ippolito, Melissa is given even more hyperbolic praise to utter:

'He on whose reverend head a purple hat
Is poised is the illustrious Cardinal
Ippolito, whom men will designate
Magnanimous, sublime and liberal.
All prose and rhyme would be inadequate
His catalogue of praise to chronicle.'[2]

On the other hand, here, as elsewhere, it is difficult to be sure exactly what Ariosto's intentions were in awarding such extravagant encomium. It is not only faint praise which damns.

In view of Ariosto's care not to offend his patrons, it is remarkable that he should speak out vehemently against the use of artillery. Duke Alfonso is famous in the history of warfare for his use of cannon. He himself designed several pieces of ordnance and superintended their casting, once giving orders for a statue of his enemy Pope Julius II (by Michelangelo) to be melted down and put to more active use. By the time of his death in 1534 he had accumulated about three hundred major pieces. The battle of Ravenna, which was fought on Easter Day, 11 April, 1512, between Spain and the Papacy on one side, and France, allied with Ferrara, on the other, was won by Alfonso, who by a brilliant manoeuvre brought his artillery up on the side of the battlefield, raking the enemy upon the flank just as the French were about to retreat. This was not the first time that artillery had been used in Italy in an important encounter: when Charles VIII invaded Italy in 1494, he brought 43 pieces of ordnance, 14 of which weighed 2,137 kilograms; they were drawn by 23 horses and 100

1. III. 48–9, 50. i–ii.   2. ibid. 56. i–vi.

men; but the battle of Ravenna showed conclusively for the first time that artillery could have a decisive effect upon the result.[1]

Ariosto praises Alfonso for his victory, won at so little cost to his side, in comparison with the expensive victories of the pagan armies in his poem,[2] and he refers admiringly to Alfonso's famous cannons, *Terremoto* and *Diavolo*, to which Ruggiero is compared.[3] Yet his denunciation of artillery is one of the most forceful utterances in the work. When Orlando casts King Cimosco's anachronistic cannon into the North Sea, he shouts:

> 'Accursèd and abominable tool,
> In Tartarean depths devised and forged
> By that Beelzebub beneath whose rule
> The world to its destruction thus is urged,
> I re-consign you to the deepest hole
> Of the Abyss whence you were first disgorged!'[4]

But his noble action is to no avail, for 'in our grandfathers' time, or just before',

> The hellish instrument, which fathoms deep
> (More than a hundred) hidden in the sea
> For years remained, was by vile craftsmanship
> Raised to the top; and first in Germany,
> Where they experimented, step by step,
> To find what sort of engine this might be,
> The devil sharpening their acumen,
> They learned the damage it could do to men.
>
> O hideous invention! By what means
> Did you gain access to the human heart?
> Because of you all glory's fled long since;
> No honour now attaches to the art
> Of soldiering; all valour is pretence;

---

1. cf. Sir Charles Oman, *A History of the Art of War in the Sixteenth Century*, Methuen, 1937, pp. 130–50; F. L. Taylor, *The Art of War in Italy 1494–1527*. It is related that Alfonso's artillery killed as many French as Spaniards and that, on being asked to cease firing, he turned to his gunners and said: 'Keep it up, they are all our enemies.'

2. XIV. 2.   3. XXV. 14 (Vol. II of this translation).
4. IX. 91. i–vi.

Not Good but Evil seems the better part;
Gone is all courage, chivalry is gone,
In combat once the only paragon.

How many lords, alas! how many more
Among the bravest of our cavaliers
Have died and still must perish in this war
By which you brought the world to bitter tears
And Italy left stricken to the core?
This is the worst device, in all the years
Of the inventiveness of humankind,
Which e'er imagined was by evil mind.[1]

Until the development of artillery as a decisive weapon, in which Alfonso played so important a role as pioneer, battles were fought on a comparatively small scale. Mercenary warfare in Italy is no longer believed by military historians to have been as bloodless as Machiavelli made out, but far larger numbers of casualties occurred after 1494.[2] When Ariosto visited the field of Ravenna on 12 April 1512 (the day after the battle), the dead lay so close together that for many miles it was impossible to step without walking on them – a spectacle which he describes in one of his minor poems[3] and which is prophesied by Melissa in the *Furioso* when she foretells Alfonso's victory:

'Such skill he'll show, so masterful a lance
He'll brandish on Romagna's battlefield,
That he'll secure the victory to France,
Forcing Pope Julius and Spain to yield.

---

1. XI. 23, 26–7; cf. Hotspur's scornful reference to a 'certain lord' who said 'that it was great pity, so it was, /This villainous saltpetre should be digged /Out of the bowels of the harmless earth, /Which many a good tall fellow had destroyed /So cowardly, and but for these vile guns /He would himself have been a soldier.' (Shakespeare, *I Henry IV*, I.3, New Penguin Shakespeare, ed. P. H. Davison).

2. cf. Michael Mallett, *Mercenaries and their Masters*, Bodley Head, 1974, pp. 2–3; J. R. Hale, 'Gunpowder and the Renaissance: an Essay in the History of Ideas', *From the Renaissance to the Counter-Reformation: Essays in Honour of Garrett Mattingly*, ed. Charles Carter, Jonathan Cape, 1966, pp. 113–44.

3. *Capitolo* XVI. 37–42.

> The horses, fetlock-deep, can scarce advance
> For human blood which saturates the weald –
> The dead so many, and so small the trench
> For Germans, Spaniards, Greeks, Italians, French.'[1]

Though Melissa has remarkable powers of prevision, they do not enable her to see just what sort of lance it is that Alfonso will brandish on the battlefield of Ravenna; but Ariosto knew, and he had seen the result. His condemnation of such means of slaughter is given expression only in the third and last edition of his poem, occurring in the material which he added between 1521 and 1532. For four years of this period he was living in independent retirement, in his own house, a circumstance which perhaps throws light on the reservations which patronage imposes.

Enough has been said to show that part of Ariosto's purpose was to awaken response to the ideals of Christendom and chivalry. Yet the *Orlando Furioso* is not primarily a work of exhortation (far from it) and to stress such powerful and stirring utterances at the expense of the exuberant vitality of the narrative or of the beauty, elegance and wit of its pleasure-giving stanzas would do disservice to the poem as a whole. Ariosto places all the fertility of his creative genius and all the skill of his poetic art at the disposal of his readers, whom it is his delight to entertain, move and surprise. The apparently random introduction of one story after another, the abrupt transitions, the cliff-hanging ends of cantos, the leaps from the sublime to the grotesque, from tragic to comic, are all part of the enjoyment he desires to provide. Such contrasts are characteristic of other arts of the Renaissance. The tone-colours of sixteenth-century instruments, more varied and less homogeneous than those of the modern symphony orchestra, offered a range of sound that was sometimes sensuous, sometimes austere, sometimes earthy, sometimes bitter-sweet. This was the Renaissance sound, which, like the Renaissance taste, gave pleasure by sharp contrasts. The menus which survive of Renaissance banquets show that sweet, sour and savoury dishes were served in combinations which some modern palates might find strange: stuffed fat geese flavoured with cheese, sugar and cinnamon, for instance, or almonds in garlic sauce. An exuberance of appetite, apparent from sixteenth-century menus, is matched by the gusto with which the cornucopia of Ariosto's creation was poured forth and with which it was relished. The element of surprise, so important an ingredient in Ariosto's art, was also present at the table. In 1532, at a banquet in Venice, a mock pie was prepared which when cut was found to contain a number of live birds which flew out and all about the room.

Like the Renaissance musician and the Renaissance chef, Ariosto contrasts his effects, stimulating the reader's responses and playing upon them with masterly skill. The randomness of the poem's structure is only apparent; its purpose is to offer a rich diversity, a sense of splendour and plenitude, regaling the mind and senses with vivid awareness of the multifariousness of life. Ariosto is firmly in control of all his stage properties, his magic paraphernalia and his immense cast of characters. He remembers who has the magic ring, where the magic shield is and who has won whose helmet. He knows when he intends to move up thousands of troops for the siege of Paris and when to focus on two knights in single combat, when to scatter his protagonists to the farthest corners of the earth and how to bring them back. The entire globe is his stage but even this does not suffice: part of his action spills over on to the moon, that nightmare repository of so many futile actions and vain hopes. Travel is achieved mostly on horses. Some of them have names and are well known to readers of earlier romances: Baiardo, Brigliadoro, Frontino and Rabicano. They create problems of logistics when separated from their riders, but Ariosto is scrupulous in accounting for them. Twice he entrusts a horse to Bradamante's care; there is good stabling at Montalbano. Baiardo, in his concern for his master, Rinaldo, plays a more than equine role. When Orlando has to face the vile king of Frisia's cannon, Ariosto arranges for him to leave his irreplaceable charger, Brigliadoro, safely behind. One manifestation of Orlando's madness is that he leaves him unattended and that he deals savagely with other horses.

Journeys by sea, though less frequent in the poem than

journeys on horseback, are infinitely more perilous, reflecting perhaps the reality of sea travel in Ariosto's day. Almost always the ships are blown off course; hurricanes, whirlwinds and shipwrecks are all part of the repertoire which Fortune commands, tossing the characters now here, now there, diversifying their adventures and extending and complicating the plot. Travel by air is achieved in two ways. Astolfo is taken to the moon and back in a divinely-powered chariot. This is a supernatural means of transport, used for the special purpose of recovering Orlando's wits.[1] The hippogriff, or winged horse, on the other hand, is no magical or mythical creature, but a natural phenomenon, the offspring of a griffin and a mare:

> . . . Such beasts, though rare,
> In the Rhiphaean mountains, far beyond
> The icy waters of the north, are found.[2]

This magnificent mount, whose genealogy may be traced to Pegasus, carries its riders with disdainful ease over the entire globe (on one occasion from the Far East to the Hebrides), thus serving to enlarge the geographical boundaries of the action, yet remaining within the romantic epic's limits of credibility. If the chariot to the moon is fantasy, the hippogriff belongs to science fiction.

Within a firmly-constructed framework of verisimilitude (a technique he has learnt from Dante) Ariosto introduces the unbelievable. This is true especially of the military prowess of the warriors, Orlando, Rinaldo, Ruggiero, Rodomonte and Mandricardo, who perform prodigies of valour and strength on a scale which belongs to mythology rather than to reality. In this they are to be compared with their heroic counterparts in the *Iliad* and the *Aeneid*. Yet the constant, the norm to which everything is ultimately linked, remains the human heart. It is the aspirations, the love, the despair, the rage, the grief of the characters which matter. However fantastic their adventures, however far from reality the descriptions of their deeds, they retain an intimate relationship with the reader by

1. XXXIV. 68 et seq. (Vol. II of this translation).
2. IV. 18. vi–viii.

virtue of emotions which he can share with them. When the ferocious pagan warrior Rodomonte has performed, single-handed, such devastation as would be beyond the strength of an entire army in real life, he leaves Paris, disgusted that he has been unable to destroy it utterly. Almost at once he hears the news that his lady, Doralice, has been captured by Mandricardo, and at once he suffers a piercing pang of jealousy which brings him, mythologically proportioned as he is, within the compass of our own experience:

> Cold as a snake, Dame Jealousy the Moor's
> Fierce heart invaded and embraced straightway.[1]

The torments of Orlando which lead to the overthrow of his sanity are presented step by step with a veracity which belongs to classical drama or to the psychological novel, though the frenzy which then supervenes takes us far beyond normal dimensions. When he has read the fateful verses written on the wall of the cave in which Angelica and Medoro have made love, Orlando stands as though frozen, staring at the lines, searching them for some other meaning which will relieve the agony in his heart. This is an emotion at once measurable and measureless, shared by everyone who reads it, yet unique in its reverberations:

> Three times, four times, six times, he read the script,
> Attempting still, unhappy wretch! in vain
> (For the true meaning he would not accept)
> To change the sense of what was clear and plain.
> Each time he read, an icy hand which gripped
> His heart caused him intolerable pain.
> Then motionless he stood, his eyes and mind
> Fixed on the stone, like stone inert and blind.[2]

This is the letter which says that a love-affair is at an end; which asks the recipient not to communicate again, in any way; or the letter which provides evidence of infidelity. The gaze, as fixed as stone, the icy hand on the heart, the refusal to believe, are instantly and intimately recognized:

> I speak here from experience, in brief.
> Of all the sorrows which the pallid moon
> Surveys, this sorrow offers no relief.[1]

Inflict such grief on a superhuman being and the result is madness on a superhuman scale.

On the subject of love, Ariosto asserts more than once that he speaks with authority:

> Of all the many grievous pains of love
> I have myself endured the greater part.
> So vivid is the recollection of
> My pangs, that on this theme I am expert.[2]

His personal life was conducted with discretion. The only woman he truly loved was Alessandra Benucci, whom he met in Florence in 1513. After the death of her husband, Tito Strozzi, she went to live in Ferrara in a house where Ariosto visited her in secret. Even their marriage, said to have occurred in about 1527, was clandestine, for Ariosto, like the Fellows of Oxford and Cambridge colleges up to the late nineteenth century, was in receipt of certain benefices available only to a celibate. Although the love-affair lasted for twenty years, there are intimations in his writings that Ludovico had suffered the torment of jealousy and cursed himself for a fool. He establishes a link between himself and Orlando in his surrender to the mastery of love:

> Once Love has gained possession of a heart,
> What can this cruel traitor then not do?
> See how he tears Orlando's soul apart:
> So loyal once, now to his lord untrue,
> So wise, so versed in every noble art,
> And of the holy Church defender too,
> A victim now of passion unreturned,
> For God and king no longer he's concerned.
>
> But I excuse him and rejoice to have
> In my defect companionship like his,
> For to such passion likewise I'm a slave,
> While my pursuit of goodness languid is.[3]

1. XXIII. 112. iv–vi.   2. XVI. 1. i–iv.   3. IX. 1, 2. i–iv.

Nor did love relinquish its hold with the passing of the years, though he acknowledged its irrationality:

> Who in Love's snare has stepped, let him recoil
> Ere round his wings the cunning meshes close.
> For what is love but madness after all,
> As every wise man in the wide world knows?
> Though it is true not everyone may fall
> Into Orlando's state, his frenzy shows
> What perils lurk; what sign is there more plain
> Than self-destruction, of a mind insane?
>
> The various effects which from love spring
> By one same madness are brought into play.
> It is a wood of error, menacing,
> Where travellers perforce must lose their way;
> One here, one there, it comes to the same thing.
> To sum the matter up, then, I would say:
> Who in old age the dupe of love remains
> Deserving is of fetters and of chains.
>
> You might well say: 'My friend, you indicate
> The faults of others; yours you do not see.'
> But I reply: 'I see the matter straight
> In this brief moment of lucidity,
> And I intend (if it is not too late)
> To quit the dance and seek tranquillity.
> And yet I fear my vow I cannot keep:
> In me the malady has gone too deep.'[1]

Freely admitting his own shortcomings, Ariosto advises against excess in devotion. This is Orlando's error; it is also Olimpia's, who is held up as a warning to all women. Good and evil are evenly divided between the sexes. The perfidious Polinesso and the treacherous Bireno are balanced by the deceitful Orrigille and the murderous Gabrina (the latter, an embodiment of female wickedness, is moved about the poem like a stage-property, with superb disregard for probability). Passion and desire are shown in a sharply perceptive range of intensity, from gross lust to selfless devotion. It is difficult not

1. XXIV. 1–3 (Vol. II). The first three lines of stanza 3 echo lines 12–14 of Petrarch's sonnet (No. LXXVIII), beginning '*Poi che voi et io più volte abbiam provato*'.

to feel some sympathy for the predicament of the enchantress, Alcina, as Handel evidently did in his opera of that name. Evil though she is meant to be, her horror on realizing that she has lost Ruggiero is dramatically conveyed – her beauty crumpled to an ugly senility, her powers dwindled to a frenzied self-deception. Not all the wonders of Logistilla's realm quite make up for the loss of Alcina's magic garden,

> Where everyone in dance or joyful game
> The festive hours employed from early morn;
> Where of sad thoughts no shadow ever came
> To spoil this rosebed life without a thorn.
> There no discomfort was, no cup was empty,
> But endless bounty from the horn of plenty.[1]

The most idyllic treatment of love is reserved for the central episode which is the cause of Orlando's derangement. Angelica, desired and pursued by the greatest heroes of Christian chivalry, by the greatest warriors and monarchs of the pagan world, indifferent to them all, thinking 'no man deserving her was ever born', rides unconcernedly through a forest one day, unaware of what is to befall her. Coming suddenly upon a wounded soldier bleeding to death on the ground, this cold, self-seeking princess, ever prepared to exploit the devotion of her admirers for her own ends, and giving nothing in return, is stirred unexpectedly by a feeling of compassion. She takes the trouble to search a near-by hillside for some stems of dittany, a plant with curative properties (known also to the mother of Aeneas) which she had learnt to use in the East. Meeting a shepherd on a horse, she persuades him to return with her to where the young man lies. She pounds the precious plant between two stones,

> Then, gathering the juice in her white hands,
> She pours some in his wound, and some, which runs
> Over his chest and belly, she extends,
> Smoothing it to his very thighs. At length
> His blood she staunches and revives his strength.[2]

1. VI. 73. iii–viii.
2. XIX. 24. iv–viii. 'Dittany' is a translation of *dictamnus*, a plant growing on Mount Dicte and Mount Ida. Its juice is used to heal the wound in Aeneas' leg (*Aeneid*, XII. 412). Ariosto is unsure about the herb.

The wounded boy is Medoro, who, with his friend Cloridano, had crept out from the pagan camp under cover of darkness to look for the body of their young king, Dardinello, and give him burial. His body and that of Cloridano lie beside him now and he will not depart with Angelica to the shepherd's house until they have been buried.

In that humble home, where Angelica devotedly tends him, his beauty opens in her heart a wound which grows deeper as his own closes and heals. She is the daughter of the Great Khan, he is a common soldier. The irony of the situation is too much for the poet and he bursts out:

> O Count Orlando, O Circassian,
> Of what avail your prowess and your fame?
> What price your honour, known to every man?
> What good of all your long devotion came?
> Show me one single favour, if you can,
> What recompense, what kindness can you name,
> What gratitude, what mercy has she shown
> For sufferings for her sake undergone?
>
> O Agricane, great and noble king,
> If to our life on earth you were restored,
> How you would suffer now, remembering
> How cruelly your person she abhorred!
> O Ferraù, o thousands I might sing,
> Who vainly served that ingrate, and adored,
> You would be stricken to the core, I vow,
> To see her in those arms enfolded now![1]

Angelica marries her soldier and sets off to Cathay with him, where, since her father and her brother are both dead, she will be queen and Medoro will be king – a fairy tale indeed, but whether or not they live happily ever after we are left to imagine for ourselves. They depart from the poem, glimpsed again only for a fleeting moment as Orlando in his frenzy pursues Angelica like a mad dog, without recognition on either side.[2]

So many pairs of lovers star this firmament that the reader is dazzled by the radiance they shed. Eros is omnipresent and,

1. XIX. 31–2.
2. ibid. 42; XXIX. 58–67 (Vol. II of this translation).

if not omnipotent, he inspires feelings that are forceful in the extreme. The intensity with which they are communicated reveals experience of life as well as verbal craftsmanship. Dalinda, with her foolish passion for Polinesso, expresses a physical ardour which bodes ill for her peace of mind as a nun in Denmark. Isabella, in total surrender to the charm and valour of Zerbino, is prepared to let members of her father's household be killed in order to reach him, and all without remorse:

> '. . . I did not weep.
> No maidenly regrets my transports marred.
> The joy I felt I cannot now express,
> So much I yearned my dear love to possess.'[1]

In her fidelity to Zerbino, Isabella is heroic; the manner of her resistance to Odorico when he tries to rape her is magnificent; her reunion with Zerbino is a memorable moment of tenderness and joy. These qualities of tenderness and heroism continue to be manifested by her to the very end, the pitiful end, of her story. She has the single-mindedness of an early Christian martyr.

King Norandino of Syria and his bride, Lucina, are another devoted couple, but they are drawn with less subtlety, perhaps even with an undercurrent of mockery. The author himself seems hardly to believe in them. They are, to tell the truth, rather stupid, but love binds them none the less heroically in their readiness to die for each other. Lucina's inability to make good her escape from the den, after her husband has taken so much trouble to disguise them both as goats, fills the reader with much the same irritation as the failure of her near-namesake, Lucia, in Manzoni's novel, to utter the few words that will make her Renzo's wife.[2]

Doralice, the promised bride of Rodomonte, while on a journey to meet him, escorted by a militia and a train of attendants, is captured by the valorous Mandricardo. At first Doralice weeps, but, unlike Isabella, she soon succumbs to Mandricardo's expert wooing and seductive charm:

1. XIII. 14. v–viii.
2. *I Promessi Sposi*, chapter VIII.

> She answers him more kindly and with grace,
> His bold appraisal she no longer shuns,
> Allows her eyes to linger on his face,
> And with compassion kindles in response.
> The pagan, who has felt the smarting trace
> Of Cupid's piercing arrow more than once,
> Not only hopes, is sure, the damsel will
> Not always be rebellious to his will.[1]

He is not mistaken; they spend that night together in a shepherd's hut and from then on there is no further mention by Doralice of Rodomonte.

By comparison Bradamante and Ruggiero behave towards each other with almost Victorian propriety. It is true that after searching for each other for many months, when they meet at last,

> Ruggiero clasps the lovely maiden to
> His breast; from rosy pink her blushes spring
> To crimson in her cheeks, and from her lips
> The first sweets of a love so blest he sips.
>
> The happy lovers, locked in an embrace,
> A thousand times each to the other pressed.
> Their joy, depicted in their eyes and face,
> Could scarcely be contained within their breast.[2]

But Bradamante, who has been well brought up, knows where to stop. She suggests that it is time for Ruggiero to present himself formally to her father; in the meantime he must be baptized.

Though love and duty contend in the breasts of the warriors, Christian and infidel alike, it is only Orlando who fails utterly to keep the balance. Rinaldo, though ardently desiring Angelica and bitterly resenting Charlemagne's command to leave Paris (where he thinks she is) and sail immediately for Britain to raise troops, nevertheless obeys orders.[3] True to

1. XIV. 60.   2. XXII. 32. v–viii, 33. i–iv.
3. Whereas Orlando secretly leaves Paris, which is besieged, and goes in search of Angelica. Later, however (XXVII. 8–10), Rinaldo does abandon Charlemagne for the same reason.

his knightly vocation, he finds time also to rescue Ginevra, the
Scottish princess, from a shameful and undeserved death. He
is entirely successful in his military mission, as may be seen
from the vast array of English, Scottish, Welsh and Irish
troops, as well as forces from Sweden, Norway, Thule and
Iceland, who are mustered outside London, waiting to em-
bark for Calais. His deployment of the armies outside the
walls of Paris is masterly, and his speech of exhortation a
model of its kind. The climax of his action in this battle is his
encounter with Dardinello. The young African prince has just
slain Lurcanio, whom his brother, Ariodante, is eager to
avenge. The press of combatants, surging round them both,
prevents their coming together. Dardinello's death is defer-
red: Fortune has other plans. And here occurs one of Ariosto's
breath-taking interruptions. We see Rinaldo coming, his
horse plunging through the fray to the fateful spot:

> Fortune continually blocks the way,
> Unwilling these two cavaliers should meet.
> For one she has another plan that day,
> And seldom does a man escape his fate.
> See now Rinaldo turn and join the fray
> And closer round the victim draw the net.
> See now Rinaldo come, by Fortune led,
> That Dardinel by him shall be struck dead.[1]

At that point, the action is held fixed in an eternal moment,
like Paolo Uccello's painting of the battle of San Romano; and
we go to Damascus to continue the story of Grifone. After
eighty-eight stanzas we return and the picture dissolves into
mobility once more. We see Rinaldo, as we last saw him:

> . . . on Baiard,
> Against Prince Dardinello, spurring hard.[2]

Young Dardinello, courageous and undaunted, is no match
for Rinaldo. His followers know it:

> A shudder ran through all the pagan veins,
> Chilling the very heart within each breast,

> Soon as Rinaldo by the Saracens
> Was seen to grasp Fusberta in his fist. . . .[1]

Rinaldo scarcely feels Dardinello's blow on his helmet. He laughs:

> . . . 'Now let us see
> How well my sword a vital spot can find!'
> Spurring his horse, he lets the reins go free.
> His sword-point with the prince's breast aligned,
> He rides towards the youth so forcibly
> The point impales him and protrudes behind.
> Withdrawn, it let flow blood and soul as well,
> As from its horse the lifeless body fell.[2]

The famous simile which follows, inherited from the *Iliad*,[3] is an example of those moments of classical pathos in which death in battle is treated elegiacally, dignified by remoteness from reality and linked with an ancient tradition of epic imagery:

> As languishing a purple flower lies,
> Its tender stalk cut by the passing plough,
> Or, heavy with the rain of summer skies,
> A poppy of the field its head will bow,
> So, as all colour, draining downward, flies
> From Dardinello's face, he passes now
> From life, and with his passing, passes too
> Such little daring as his followers knew.[4]

The epic power of the first half of the poem begins to swell in volume with the mustering of the British and Northern forces recruited in response to Rinaldo's request for help. The heraldic brilliance of these stanzas,[5] the resounding titles of the captains, their emblem-bearing banners fluttering in the breeze, combine the colour and precision of a military tattoo with the delight of a pretended and detailed authenticity. This parade has a magnificent counterpart in the array of Spanish and African forces in a later canto,[6] their exotic names and

1. XVIII. 151. i–iv. Fusberta is the name of Rinaldo's sword.
2. ibid. 152; cf. *Aeneid*, x. 481 and 487.
3. VIII. 306; cf. also *Aeneid*, IX. 434.
4. XVIII. 153.   5. X. 75–89.   6. XIV. 10–27.

places of origin enriching the tapestry with bold, barbaric hues, chillingly suggestive of an alien savagery.

The siege of Paris,[1] the first large-scale military event in the narrative, is directed and stage-managed with masterly control. It is divided into two phases: the attempt of the infidels to scale the walls before the arrival of the reinforcements from across the Channel, and the battle outside the walls when both sides have been assembled in full strength. This second phase is split into separate encounters between sections of the armies, according to their deployment, and varies between the surging, thronging movements of mêlées and the sharper focus of combat face-to-face. In accordance with epic tradition, supernatural aid is enlisted. In answer to Charlemagne's diplomatically-worded prayer, God sends the Archangel Michael to assist the Christians, and Discord to disrupt the Infidel. But there is nothing supernatural about the measures taken to defend the city:

> Wherever the external wall curves round,
> King Charlemagne has laid his plans with care.
> Culverts are driven deep into the ground,
> And casemates, too, are hidden everywhere.
> Both river-gates by heavy chains are bound
> So that no hostile craft may enter there.
> Defence is made secure at every point,
> At every chink, at every weakest joint.[2]

The enemy, as numerous as the trees on the Apennines, as the waves that bathe the foot of Mount Atlas, or as the stars in heaven, has likewise made realistic plans for breaking through these defences:

> Innumerable ladders for this aim
> King Agramant collected from all hands;
> Trestles and planks from every quarter came,
> And quantities of plaited willow-wands.
> Pontoons and boats he orders for the scheme.
> The first and second army, he commands,
> Shall lead the assault, and he desires to be
> Among the foremost in the day's mêlée.[3]

1. XIV. 65–134; XVIII. 8–58, 146–164.   2. XIV. 106.
3. ibid. 67.

Unaware that the reinforcements, with the help of Silence, are arriving, Agramante gives the signal to begin the assault:

> As the sweet leavings from some country meal,
> Taken al fresco on hot summer days,
> A swarm of importuning flies assail,
> Making with strident wings a buzzing haze,
> As starlings from the purpling tendrils steal
> The ripened grapes, so the besiegers raise
> Resounding shouts which deafen all the skies,
> And leap to take the Christians by surprise.[1]

The Christians are more than ready for them:

> The Christian army, waiting on the wall
> With axes, lances, fire and stones and swords,
> Defends the city, fearing not at all
> The savagery of the barbaric hordes.
> If Death upon some Christian soldier fall,
> Another in his place himself affords.
> The Moors at first abandon the attack,
> By injuries and losses driven back.
>
> Not only steel is used: from towers, blocks
> Are thrown, and crenellated sections of
> The walls are hurled, loosened by frenzied knocks;
> And scalding liquid pouring from above
> Which with intolerable anguish mocks
> The valour of the Moors, who must remove
> Themselves or else endure to lose their sight,
> For Moorish helmets are not watertight.
>
> If these were more injurious than steel,
> What of the clouds of quicklime, or the pitch,
> The turpentine, the sulphur, or the oil,
> Or those incendiary weapons which
> Spin round their targets in a flaming wheel?
> The Saracens fall back into the ditch,
> Vanquished on every side, and many a head
> With whirling fire is harshly garlanded.[2]

1. XIV. 109.   2. ibid. 110–112.

Yet even worse awaits the Infidel. When Rodomonte forces the retreating besiegers back up the scaling-ladders and down into the ditch between the wall and the second parapet,

> Until below so many of them fall,
> The ditch, it seems, can scarce contain them all,[1]

the besieged are undismayed:

> The signal they agreed on they await.[2]

The fearful gully, thirty feet in width, has been lined with kindling-wood, pitch, oil, saltpetre, sulphur and other fuel. At a given signal, the fires are lit:

> Then many single flames form into one.
> From bank to bank the ditch is full of fire.
> Its tongue the pallid bosom of the moon
> Appears to lick, so high it leaps, and higher.
> The pall of smoke obscures the very sun,
> Casting a cloak of darkness, black and dire;
> Cracks, loud enough to split the earth asunder,
> Resound like claps of terrifying thunder.[3]

Rodomonte in the meantime has leapt across the ditch. His attention attracted by the stench, he looks behind him:

> He sees the hellish flames on high ascend,
> He hears the lamentations and the wails,
> And Heaven with his curses he assails.[4]

Eleven thousand and twenty-eight men, their flesh and bones reduced to charred remains,

> Amid that raging holocaust lay dead.[5]

Rodomonte's fury matches the dimensions of the catastrophe.[6] He penetrates the inner defences of the citadel and single-handed, the embodiment of war, wreaks upon Paris such havoc as the Greeks inflicted upon Troy.

1. XIV. 128. vii–viii. 2. ibid. 132. vi. 3. ibid. 133.
4. XV. 5. vi–viii. 5. ibid. 4. ii.
6. The name Rodomonte, invented by Boiardo in the form Rodamonte, has given rise to the word 'rodomontade' in English, meaning extravagant boasting.

In the meantime the forces from Britain, led by Rinaldo, have arrived. He sends 6,000 English archers and 2,000 Welsh cavalry, led by Edward and Herman direct from Calais across Picardy to enter from the north by the gates of St Denis and St Martin. He himself leads Irish, Scottish and the rest of the English troops (and, presumably, their allies from the Far North) round the northern walls towards the east, then south towards the Seine, which they cross by pontoon bridges about three leagues upstream of Paris. After delivering a masterly harangue in which he impresses on the British captains their involvement in the security of Europe, he gives orders for their deployment. The Scottish troops, led by Prince Zerbino, are sent westwards along the left bank of the Seine; the English troops, led by the Duke of Lancaster, are dispatched south-west, with orders to advance towards the Spaniards; the Irish are sent farther south, by a roundabout route, with instructions to occupy the encampments behind the enemy lines. Having given these orders, Rinaldo himself rides westwards along the walls, passing ahead of Zerbino. He arrives to confront troops led by Marbalusto, the giant king of Orano, and the battle begins.[1]

The stanzas which follow are an example of Ariosto's skill in maintaining clarity in the midst of medley. He would have made a superb director of large-scale historical films. The attention is held mainly by the star-performers, who point the pattern of the action as they appear in close-up, moving forward to the attack; alternately, long shots of troops in formation or of the field littered with the bodies of men and horses extend the range of vision with a sweep to which perhaps only the wide-screen cinema could do full justice. With pulse-stirring rapidity the episodes follow one upon the other, each so clearly identified that it would be possible to enact the entire conflict by using the stanzas as stage-directions.[2]

1. There is a sketch-map of Paris, accompanied by an analysis of the siege, on pp. 474–7.
2. The theatrical element in the work was brilliantly captured by Luca Ronconi in his recent production of *Orlando Furioso*. By surrounding and involving the audience as bystanders, he was able to impress on them the immense variety and complexity of the poem. It was performed at the Edinburgh Festival in 1971.

When the African commander-in-chief, Agramante, moves
forward into the centre of the picture, his first decision is to
send a detachment led by the king of Fezzan to attack the
Irish, whose intentions he has now learned. He then moves
northwards, from his position south-west of the walls, to aid
Sobrino, by whom the Scots are being hard pressed. Zerbino
has been unhorsed and only two of his captains, Ariodante
and Lurcanio (who are Italians), remain to support him.
Rinaldo in the nick of time rallies the fleeing Scottish troops
and enables Zerbino to remount. Thus it is that at the very
moment when Agramante and Dardinello arrive, Zerbino is
ready to face them, Rinaldo staying to lend aid.

Meanwhile, the detachments of archers and cavalry led by
Edward and Herman had entered Paris from the north,
welcomed with high hopes by Charlemagne, who was not
then aware of the devastation wrought by Rodomonte in the
citadel.[1] Charlemagne repairs to the scene of the disaster and
when Rodomonte has been driven forth decides to deploy his
forces 'as for checkmate'.[2] Ringing the city with defensive
troops 'from St Germain round to St Victor's gate',[3] he
issues commands that on the plain outside St Marcel all the
other regiments shall gather for the final encounter.[4] He him-
self meanwhile moves his troops round to attack the enemy in
the rear, where the Spaniards are mustered under King
Marsilio. Forth they march in close order, the infantry
flanked by cavalry on either side, to the sound of drums and
trumpets.[5] The Spaniards, seeing them advance, make as if to
flee but are rallied by their captains. Meanwhile, Rinaldo and
the Scottish troops are still in conflict with those of Agra-
mante and Dardinello. It is now that Dardinello is slain. His
death is the turning-point. His followers, demoralized, flee in
all directions:

> As waters, when confined by human skill,
> Swelling in volume, rise but cannot spread,
> But, if the enclosing structure yields, o'erspill
> The dam and with a mighty roar cascade,
> So did those Africans, restrained until

1. XVI. 85.   2. XVIII. 38. viii.   3. ibid. vii.
4. XVIII. 39.   5. ibid. 41.

Their gallant leader, Dardinel, lay dead,
Some here, some there, then scatter and disperse
Soon as they saw him tumble from his horse.[1]

The battle is over. King Marsilio, a shrewd tactician, wisely decides to cut his losses. King Agramante, 'bowed by his disgrace',[2] likewise retreats. When night falls the remnants of the African and Spanish troops are entrenched within their stockade.

The bravura with which Ariosto sustains his description of this multiple encounter (for good measure, he complicates it further by a long and intricate digression) is an instance of the skill and zest for which he is famed. The self-generating energy of the action, the triumph of victory, the pathos of defeat, the courage, the cowardice, the exhilaration and the terror of battle, are here presented with the delight, yet at the same time with the detachment, of creative power fulfilled. Here is the hand of a master, in command.

One secret of the fascination of the *Furioso* lies in the mingling of human and superhuman dimensions, in the transitions from everyday experience to sublime and unattainable states of being. The battle-scenes exceed the human dimension in their ferocity. Not only do heads, arms, and other parts of the body, sometimes whole torsos, fly in all directions: Orlando skewers six warriors on one lance and leaves a seventh dying on the ground, the lance being full; Rodomonte scythes the crowd in Paris as though they were so many cabbage-stalks or turnip-tops. Yet there are moments of anticlimax, deliberately contrived, which reduce the knights to size, as when Ferraù, stooping to drink at a stream, drops his helmet in the water; or when Ferraù and Rinaldo continue to fight, unaware that the prize for whom they contend, namely Angelica, has ridden off and left them; or when Ruggiero, having performed Perseus-like miracles of agility upon the hippogriff in his battle with the sea-monster, cannot get his armour off in time to take advantage of the naked Angelica.

Ariosto's relish for the telling of violence is unmistakable, but it is not a morbid relish; there are times when it resembles

1. XVIII. 154.   2. ibid. 158. i.

rather the rumbustious gusto of an animated cartoon. When
Cloridano and Medoro creep about the battlefield in the dark,
looking for Dardinello, Cloridano takes the opportunity to
slay as many of the sleeping Christians as he can. Among them
is Grillo, who has drunk himself into a stupor, his head
propped on a barrel. As Cloridano cuts his head off,

> Together blood and wine (which had approached
> A vatful) spurted from the tub thus broached.[1]

Two lovers, sleeping in each other's arms, are decapitated at
one blow:

> O happy death! O sweetest destiny!
> I vow, as with their bodies they embraced,
> Their spirits rose to heaven interlaced.[2]

These touches of macabre humour are perhaps among the
ingredients which have the least appeal for serious-minded
readers; but in whatever style Ariosto treats the subject of
death, whether superhuman, grotesque, comic or elegiac, he
does not linger, like Tasso, on the aesthetic effect of drops of
blood like rubies on white flesh. The famous simile of the
death of Dardinello which has already been quoted and a
stanza comparing a vertical sword-wound to a ribbon of red
silk,[3] two exceptions which come to mind, are both imitated
from the *Iliad*. Mandricardo's fascinated contemplation of the
bodies slain by Orlando brings in an alien element, intended
perhaps to point the difference between the pagan and the
Christian character.[4]

A fairy-tale quality, not unlike that of folk-lore, is to be
seen, as well as humour, in Ariosto's handling of ogres and
monsters. Not all of these come creeping forth from the lairs
of Celtic forests; some are from Greece. The land orc, uncon-
vincing in his (its) ambiguity, is a latter-day Polyphemus, but

1. XVIII. 176. vii–viii; for the whole of this episode, cf. *Aeneid*, IX.
314 et seq.

2. XVIII. 179. vi–viii. The Italian '*dama*' in the arms of Duke Labretto
on the battlefield is more likely to be a man than a woman. If so, they are
poetic descendants of the Spartan warrior-lovers who vowed to die
together.

3. XXIV. 66 (Vol. II).   4. XIV. 34–7.

without his primitive sublimity.[1] The sea orc, on the other
hand, is well imagined, a truly formidable monster, a marine
emanation from the unfathomable deep, shapeless and meas-
ureless, which only superhuman powers can overcome.[2]
Erifilla and Alcina's hybrid frontier guards, for all their
allegorical self-importance, are like papier mâché figures in a
carnival.[3] The most successful of all the fee-fo-fi-fummery is
perhaps the circumstantial and compelling narrative in Canto
xv, where Astolfo first subdues the giant, Caligorante, and
then kills the monster, Orrilo.

Caligorante is a hunter whose grisly dwelling is adorned
with the remains of the human beings he has eaten. He is
equipped with a magic net, the same in which Vulcan had
caught Mars and Venus *in flagrante*. This trap, at the slightest
touch, curls round the victim, and has never failed its present
owner, until Astolfo so terrifies him by a blast on his magic
horn that the giant tumbles into it:

> A trapper trapped, he falls into the net,
> Which round his body twists itself and wraps,
> And brings that mighty strength to a collapse.[4]

Next, Astolfo defeats Orrilo, a much more difficult task, for
Orrilo's limbs mend as soon as they are severed; even his
head can be picked up and will join on to his neck. Ariosto
tells this tale with rollicking relish:

> Orrilo's fist is severed, club and all;
> Both arms Astolfo chops, complete with hands.
> Now with a transverse stroke, now vertical,
> He slices and truncates and flying sends
> Orrilo's limbs; but wheresoe'er they fall,
> He picks them up and instantly their ends
> Re-join the parent stump and so once more
> His members function as they did before.[5]

Astolfo cuts off his head and gallops away with it; mean-
while:

> The stupid monster had not understood
> And in the dust was groping for his head. . . .[6]

1. XVII. 29–63.   2. X. 100–110; XI. 37–43.
3. VII. 2–6; VI. 61–7.   4. XV. 54. vi–viii.   5. ibid. 82.
6. ibid. 84. i–ii.

When he realizes that Astolfo has seized it, he rides after him:

> He would have liked to shout: 'Come back! Come back!'
> But of his mouth he felt a grievous lack.[1]

The only way to destroy Orrilo is to cut off a certain magic hair on his head. Unable to distinguish this one hair among the many, Astolfo shaves the scalp with his sword. As he does so, the gruesome head, which he is dangling by the nose, turns pale, its eyes squint, and by every sign it shows 'Orrilo has gone west':[2]

> The torso, following the severed head,
> Had tumbled from the saddle and lay dead.[3]

Humour is not an international commodity; it is not always transferable within the same country from century to century, or even from decade to decade. The grotesque Gabrina is ludicrous tricked out in youthful clothing, but our present attitude to old age no longer allows us to laugh at her. Gabrina is in any case too evil a character to be a figure of fun. The sportive jesting between Marfisa and Zerbino and the imposition of absurd obligations in the name of chivalry, like some heavy-handed game of forfeits, creak with the outworn machinery of a disused merry-go-round. Difficulties of another category are created when humour is introduced in contexts where it now seems to be incongruous. When Angelica, chained naked to a rock off the island of Ebuda, awaits a terrible death, Ariosto asks:

> Who can describe her tears, her sobs, her cries,
> The pleas she utters on each wailing breath,
> Her lamentation reaching to the skies?
> It is a miracle the shore beneath
> Does not divide, as on the rock she lies,
> Chained, helpless, waiting for a hideous death.
> Not I, indeed, who am so grieved, I swear,
> That I must move my narrative elsewhere,

1. xv. 84. vii–viii.
2. A literal translation of the original (ibid. 87. vi).
3. ibid. 87. vii–viii.

> Hoping to make my verses less lugubrious,
> Until my weary spirit has revived.
> No snakes dwelling in regions insalubrious,
> No tigress of her progeny deprived,
> No desert reptile, venomous, opprobrious,
> 'Twixt Red Sea shores and Atlas ever lived
> Which could without compassion contemplate
> The beautiful Angelica's dire fate.[1]

Such disengagement is a measure of the limits within which Ariosto explores the fabulous. His poetic world is situated somewhere between high fantasy and reality, and is made visible by the blending of both or the transition from one to the other. Soon after this abrupt withdrawal from the full dimensions of Angelica's tragedy, which would have been discordant with the harmony of his poem, he writes this exquisite description of her. Ruggiero, flying past on the hippogriff, looks down and sees what he thinks at first is a statue of marble or alabaster:

> He might have thought she was a statue, made
> By skilful and ingenious artistry
> Of alabaster or fine marble, laid
> Upon the rock, but that he chanced to see
> A tear steal down her countenance, amid
> The roses and white lilies, tenderly
> Bedewing the young fruit, so firm and fair,
> And breezes softly lift her golden hair.[2]

Poetic imagination, reassembling the fragments of illusion, deliberately broken, has here created a reality of beauty.

That Ariosto believed he had found a magic formula in such contrasting artistry may be seen from the fact that in the last version of his poem, published sixteen years after the first, he used an identical method in the story of Olimpia.[3] Blown off course when sailing with her husband, Bireno, to Zealand, Olimpia awakes in a tent on an island off Scotland.

1. VIII. 66–7.
2. X. 96.
3. This story was added to the third version of the poem, partly in order to introduce Orlando at an earlier stage.

Reaching out in her half sleep to embrace him, she finds him gone. This is a moment of poignant tragedy:

> . . . her arm she gently moves
> Bireno to embrace whom she so loves . . . .
>
> There's no-one there; her hand again she tends;
> She gropes once more; then, finding no-one still,
> First one and then another leg extends,
> This way and that, but all to no avail.[1]

Here Ariosto has deliberately toppled pathos into bathos. Arm, yes; hand, yes; legs, no: that pushes this Ariadne-evoking episode to the edge of parody.[2] Then he retrieves it, restoring it to a sublime classical height, as in the climax of her grief:

> Again she runs along the sandy shore,
> Hither and thither; not Olimpia
> She seems, but some mad creature by a score
> Of demons driven, or like Hecuba,
> A prey to frenzy when her Polydore
> She found there lying dead; and then afar
> Olimpia gazes seawards, like a stock,
> Standing so still, a rock upon a rock.[3]

And, once again, as in the case of the plight of Angelica, Ariosto instantly drops down to a plane of cheerful realism:

> But let us leave her there, her fate to mourn,
> While now Ruggiero's tale I take in hand.[4]

Having thus disengaged himself and the reader from the full horror of her tragedy, Ariosto returns later to her story and we find her, a successor to Angelica, captive on the same rock, also awaiting death from the sea monster. In his description of her beauty, Ariosto, in the full maturity of his art, surpasses himself in this revelation of the Renaissance ideal of perfect womanhood:

1. x. 20. vii–viii, 21. i–iv.
2. Humour, like beauty, is in the eye of the beholder. Not all readers of this passage will find bathos in it; some may see in Olimpia's searching legs a touch of pathetic realism, strikingly observed or imagined and in tune with the whole episode.
3. x. 34.   4. ibid. 35. i–ii.

Her beauty is indeed beyond compare:
Not only on her brow, her eyes, her nose,
Her cheeks, her mouth, her shoulders and her hair
The observer's glance may with delight repose,
But from her breasts descending, down to where
A gown is wont to cover her, she shows
A miracle of form, so exquisite
None in the world, perhaps, can equal it.

Whiter than snow unstained by the earth's smutch
The perfect lily-whiteness of her skin,
And smoother far than ivory to touch;
Like milky curds but freshly heaped within
Their plaited moulds, her rounded breasts, and such
The gently curving space which lies between,
It calls to mind a valley 'twixt two hills
Which winter with its snowy softness fills.

Her lovely hips, the curving of her thighs,
Her belly, smooth as any looking-glass,
Her ivory limbs, were rounded in such wise
They might have been the work of Phidias.
Those other parts which to conceal she tries
I will, as it behoves, in silence pass,
Content to say that she, from top to toe,
Embodies all of beauty man can know.[1]

This is the art of Titian. Olimpia here might be the Venus painted for Urbino, or Diana turning from Actaeon, to whom she is elsewhere compared:

She turns while speaking, as in paint or stone
We see Diana turn from Actaeon.

As best she can she hides her breast and loins,
Leaving exposed the beauty of her thighs.[2]

Orlando, with delicate concern, is planning to find her some clothing when the king of Ireland arrives, who, behold-

1. xi. 67–9.
2. ibid. 58. vii–viii, 59. i–ii. Ariosto's affinities with Italian painters such as Titian, Tintoretto, Dosso Dossi, Correggio, Paolo Uccello and others have been pointed out by Professor Elio Gianturco in a brilliant series of lectures given in the U.S.A. and Europe.

ing such exquisite beauty, and stirred also by Orlando's
account of her undeserved and piteous sufferings, falls in-
stantly and deeply in love:

> As in an April sky the sun is seen,
> Parting the misty curtain of the rain,
> So was Olimpia's lovely face, wherein
> Her eyes shine through those tears which still remain;
> And, as amid the tender, leafy green
> A songbird sweetly carols once again,
> So Love, his wings refreshing in her tears,
> In beams of light to sun himself appears.
>
> And from those radiant orbs a spark he takes
> To tip his golden shaft, and in the stream
> Which waters the fair blossoms of her cheeks
> He tempers it; then, with unerring aim
> And deadly force, the youth his target makes,
> Whose shield, whose mail, are no defence to him,
> For, gazing on her eyes, her hair, her brow,
> He's wounded in the heart, and knows not how.[1]

These visions, with their promise of an ideal physical love,
rising like a phoenix from the dying embers of the ageing
poet,[2] draw deep on his nurture of classical heritage. This is
the civilized love of the mature, self-confident world of
antiquity, the assurance of an ardour which will not wane:

> *sed sic sic sine fine feriati . . .*
> *hoc iuvit, iuvat et diu iuvabit;*
> *hoc non deficit incipitque semper.*[3]

Ariosto's descriptions of female beauty are for the most part
unlicentious, having the remote voluptuousness of painting or
sculpture. His picture of Angelica being carried out to sea on
horseback is a close verbal rendering of Titian's painting of

1. XI. 65–6.
2. He was 58 when he published the third version of his poem, which
included these stanzas; he died the following year, prematurely worn out
in mind and body.
3. 'But in eternal holiday, /Thus, thus . . . /Here is, was, shall be, all
delightsomeness. /And here no end shall be, /But a beginning everlast-
ingly.' (Petronius, trans. Helen Waddell, *Mediaeval Latin Lyrics*, Penguin
Classics edn, 1952, p. 25.)

Europa on the Bull, enhanced by the exquisite image of the winds hushed at the sight of so much beauty.[1] Alcina's loveliness is described in terms of perfect proportion, as a painter of that period would portray it, as Dosso Dossi portrayed Circe.[2] Even in the context of sexual arousal, as in the bedroom scene with Ruggiero, Alcina's attractions are veiled in the imagery of flowers seen through glass:

> Although no gown, no underskirt she had,
> For only in a silken négligé,
> Over her night apparel, she was clad,
> Soft, white and elegant in every way,
> Beneath his hands this garment she now shed.
> Her nightgown, as transparent as the day,
> Concealed her rounded limbs as little as
> The stems of lilies in a crystal vase.[3]

The pleasure of their consummation is conveyed through associations of twining ivy-tendrils and the perfume of exotic plants, only the final couplet of the following stanza providing anything like a direct statement of their physical union:

> Never did ivy press or cling so close,
> Rooted beside the plant which it embraced,
> As now in love each to the other does;
> And on their lips a sweeter flower they taste
> Than Ind or Araby e'er knew, or those
> Which on the desert air their perfume waste.
> To speak of all their bliss to them belongs,
> Who more than once in one mouth had two tongues.[4]

Ariosto's exuberance, it may be seen, includes the expression of the enjoyment of sex. Dalinda's willingness to comply with Polinesso's request that she should dress herself in

1. VIII. 35-37.
2. VII. 11-15. The painting of Circe by Dosso Dossi, now in the gallery of the Villa Borghese in Rome, was intended for the castle of Ferrara. It is said to have been inspired by Ariosto's description of Alcina. Ariosto mentions both the Dossi brothers, Dosso and Giambattista, in XXXIII. 2 (Vol. II of this translation).
3. VII. 28.
4. ibid. 29. The final couplet, inherited from Boiardo, has the ring of a current quotation, rather like a limerick.

Ginevra's clothes borders on the perverted, but elsewhere his championing of the rights of women to physical passion is uncomplicated and disarmingly frank. Rinaldo, hearing that Ginevra is condemned to be burned to death for unchastity, at once allies himself with her, whether she is guilty or not, declaring that in his view a woman who gives her lover solace deserves praise, not punishment. The women of Greece, left alone without their husbands for the long years of the Trojan War, console themselves with youthful lovers, and are forgiven by their husbands on their return,

> For on long abstinence no woman thrives.[1]

The women of Crete joyously welcome Phalanthus and his band of handsome youths, whom on their departure they try to follow, rather than lose the happiness they have found in their arms. It is on being at last abandoned that they set up a State of their own and take vengeance on the male sex. Such imbalance dooms them to destruction, brought about, significantly, by a woman warrior, Marfisa, a sexless Amazon, happy and fulfilled in combat and deeds of chivalry. The trials of strength, both martial and sexual, to which they submit all men who arrive at their city, are treated with an arch lasciviousness which was probably more to the taste of the sixteenth than of the present century. The precise, uncompromising little sketch of the licentious but impotent hermit who tries to rape Angelica is probably more to the liking of our outspoken age.[2]

Women are seen not only as sexual partners or as inspirations to the men; they exist also as personages in their own right. This is to be expected in a period when Italian women received essentially the same education as men. The daughters of a noble house shared in the same studies as the sons, the New Learning being regarded as among the noblest of earthly pursuits. The attainments of Lady Jane Grey or of the daughter of Sir Thomas More would have occasioned no surprise in Italy, where it had long been customary for the daughters of princely houses to speak and write Latin. Women were expected to strive after complete intellectual and emotional development and were regarded as the equals of men. Caterina Sforza, known as the 'first lady of Italy', had the valour and courage of a heroic cavalier. As the wife and later the widow of Girolamo Riario, lord of Forlì, she gallantly defended his possessions in battle, first against his murderers and later against Cesare Borgia.

In keeping with this early sixteenth-century Italian attitude to women, Bradamante, Rinaldo's sister, is recognized by Charlemagne to be her brother's equal in prowess and has been invested with the governorship of Marseilles. Her first action in the poem is to unhorse Sacripante. Contrasted with Marfisa, whose whole life is devoted to battle, Bradamante's character is shown to be womanly as well as virile. The conflict in her heart between love and duty, her anguish at Ruggiero's absence and infidelity, her eagerness to go to his defence, her filial respect for the wishes of her parents, and many other glimpses of her feelings, combine to form a character study of warmly human appeal.

Melissa's prophecy of the distinguished women of the House of Este[1] balances the array of male descendants revealed to Bradamante in Merlin's cave.[2] The theme of female glory stirs Ariosto's poetic powers to the creation of some of his most epic stanzas:

> The courteous fay replied: 'From you I see
> Mothers of kings and emperors descending,
> Famed for their comeliness and modesty,
> Like mighty caryatides, defending
> Illustrious houses no less worthily
> Than men in armour, in due measure blending
> Compassion, courage, wisdom, continence
> With prudent, womanly intelligence.'[3]

As Melissa utters their names, an illustrious portrait gallery is formed in the mind: Isabella d'Este, her sister Beatrice, Ricciarda (the mother of Duke Ercole), Eleanor of Aragon (the mother of Duke Alfonso and Ippolito), Lucrezia Borgia (Alfonso's second wife), Renée de France (wife of Ercole II), Lippa Ariosti of Bologna, of the poet's own family, who was

1. XIII. 57–73.   2. III. 22–63.   3. XIII. 57.

the mistress of Obizzo III; and many others. The loveliest
stanza of all is reserved for Lucrezia Borgia, whose arrival in
Ferrara as the bride of Alfonso Ariosto had already celebrated
in an eclogue:

> As tin to silver or as brass to gold,
> The poppy of the cornfield to the rose,
> The willow, pale and withered in the cold,
> To the green bay which ever greener grows,
> As painted glass to jewels, thus I hold,
> Compared with her, as yet unborn, all those
> Who hitherto for beauty have been famed,
> Or models of all excellence are named.[1]

Ariosto's admiration for women is expressed in the ringing
tones of a feminist at the beginning of Canto XX, perhaps to
offset the disagreeable and unnatural light in which he is
about to present the women's city-state of Alessandretta. He
also apologizes to all women

> . . . who in loving gracious are
> And with one love alone are each content,
> Though you among so many are most rare,
> For few indeed are chaste and continent . . .[2]

for the story of Gabrina's seduction of Filandro, an episode
which shows female nature at its worst. Further acknowledge-
ment of the achievements of women occurs later in the work,
and at the end it is a group of illustrious women whom
Ariosto places foremost among the friends waiting to welcome
him home from his long journey.

From this brief introduction to some of the qualities of the
first half of the poem it will be seen that a great many aspects
of life are represented in it and explored.[3] It will also have
been noticed that the subject extends a long way beyond the
territory of the Carolingian legends. It is therefore appro-
priate now to examine in some detail the literary strands
which Ariosto chose to interweave in his work.

---

1. XIII. 70.   2. XXII. 1.
3. A consideration of the second half of the poem will be found in
Vol. II of this translation.

II. THE LITERARY ORIGINS OF THE POEM

i. CAROLINGIAN

In its basic content the *Orlando Furioso* is a combination of material derived from three different origins: Carolingian, Celtic, and Classical. Of these three vast sources, the earliest, as regards the romantic epic, are the Carolingian legends, the beginnings of which are traced to the defeat of Charlemagne's rearguard in 778 by the Basques in the Pass of Roncevaux in the Pyrenees. This catastrophe, enshrined in the eleventh-century French epic *La Chanson de Roland*, imbued all subsequent Carolingian narratives with a sublime fatality, echoing as late as the nineteenth century in Alfred de Vigny's famous line:

> *Dieu! que le son du cor est triste au fond des bois!*

Between the *Chanson de Roland* and Ariosto's *Orlando Furioso* there are over four centuries of accretion and transformation. The most significant stages of development are those by which the Roland of history became first the epic hero of the *Chanson* and later the Orlando of the Italian romances. The earliest known record of the name of Roland occurs in a document testifying to the presence of a Count Rotholandus, with Charlemagne, at the palace of Herstal, near Liège, in 772. In 790 the name Rodlan appears on the reverse of a coin. The ninth-century biographer of Charlemagne, Einhard, refers in his *Vita Karoli* to the death in battle of Roland, whom he calls Hruodlandus, a prefect of the Breton Marches. Since this is the earliest account in existence of this seminal event, it is worth quoting in full:

At a time when this war against the Saxons was being waged constantly and with hardly any intermission at all, Charlemagne left garrisons at strategic points along the frontier, and went off himself with the largest force he could muster to invade Spain. He marched over a pass across the Pyrenees, received the surrender of every single town and castle which he attacked and then came back with his army safe and sound, except for the fact that for a brief moment on the return journey, while he was in the Pyrenean mountain range itself, he was given a taste of Basque treachery.

Dense forests, which stretch in all directions, make this spot most suitable for setting ambushes. At the moment when Charlemagne's army was stretched out in a long column of march, as the nature of the local defiles forced it to be, these Basques, who had set their ambush on the very top of one of the mountains, came rushing down on the last part of the baggage train and the troops who were marching in support of the rearguard and so protecting the army which had gone on ahead. The Basques forced them down into the valley beneath, joined battle with them and killed them to the last man. They then snatched up the baggage and, protected as they were by the cover of the darkness, which was just beginning to fall, scattered in all directions without losing a moment. In this feat the Basques were helped by the lightness of their arms, and by the nature of the terrain in which the battle was fought. On the other hand, the heavy nature of their own equipment and the unevenness of the ground completely hampered the Franks in their resistance to the Basques. In this battle died Eggihard, who was in charge of the King's table, Anselm, the Count of the Palace and *Roland, Lord of the Breton Marches*, along with a great number of others.[1]

Two texts which have the same title, *Annales Regum Francorum* (Annals of the Frankish Kings), one dated 778 and anonymous, and the other written about 800 by an author known to us as the pseudo-Einhard, refer to the fatal battle but do not mention Roland by name.

Whether the Count Rotholandus of the document of 772 and Einhard's Lord of the Breton Marches, killed in 778, are the same person is not certain, but scholars regard it as probable. Whatever his origins and identity, Roland entered legend and came ultimately to denote a superhuman personage, at times grossly distorted, yet retaining, according to culture and century, something of the qualities to be found in the Roland of the *Chanson*:

Roland's character is simplicity itself. Rash, arrogant, generous, outspoken to a fault, loyal, affectionate and single-minded, he has all the qualities that endear a captain to his men and a romantic hero to his audience. . . . Beneath all his overweening there is real modesty of heart, and a childlike simplicity of love and loyalty – to God, to the Emperor, to his friend, to his men, to his

1. From the translation by Lewis Thorpe, *Einhard and Notker the Stammerer: Two Lives of Charlemagne*, Penguin Classics, pp. 64–5; my italics.

horse, his horn, his good sword, Durendal. His death-scene is curiously moving.

But the picture that remains most vividly with us is that of gay and unconquerable youth. No other epic hero strikes this note so unerringly.[1]

This valorous Roland is found also in the visual arts, represented for over four hundred years in sculpture, wall paintings, miniatures, mosaics, stained glass, engravings and tapestry.[2] In the age-old symbolism of the 'chevaliers affrontés', of two knights in combat face-to-face, Roland, the embodiment of heroic virtue, finds his place. It is in the role of Defender of the Faith that Roland, sanctified and numinous, reaches his apotheosis in Dante's *Paradiso*. He is first mentioned in *Inferno*, when the entrance of Dante and Virgil into the Circle of the Traitors is heralded by a blast upon a horn, blown by the giant, Nimrod:

> . . . I heard a high horn sound
>
> So loud, it made all thunder seem but hoarse;
>   Whereby to one sole spot my gaze was led,
>   Following the clamour backward to its source.
>
> When Charlemayn, in rout and ruin red,
>   Lost all the peerage of the holy war
>   The horn of Roland sounded not so dread.[3]

Here, at the edge of the Circle of Treachery, Dante recalls the betrayal of Roland by Ganelon, whose soul he is about to see, wedged in the ice between two other traitors; but the note which he sounds finally on this theme of 'the holy war' (*la santa gesta*) is not one of defeat but of victory. In *Paradiso*, in the heaven of Mars, Dante comes into the presence of the Defenders of the Faith. This heaven, the symbol of fortitude,

1. Dorothy L. Sayers, *The Song of Roland*, Penguin Classics, 1957, Introduction, pp. 16–17.

2. For a magnificent assemblage of evidence of this, see Rita Lejeune and Jacques Stiennon, *La Légende de Roland dans l'art du moyen âge*, 2 vols., Brussels, 1966. There are statues of Roland in cities all over Europe, e.g. in Bremen and Dubrovnik.

3. *Inferno*, XXXI. 12–18, translation (*Hell*) by Dorothy L. Sayers, Penguin Classics. If, as seems likely, Dante heard the epic of Roland recited in north Italian towns or in the halls of castles where he stayed in his exile, there may be an echo in these lines of some unknown *cantastorie* chanting in Franco-Veneto.

is under the influence of the angelic order of Virtues, the image of divine strength, the workers of signs and the inspirers of endurance. Among the warrior-martyrs is Dante's own ancestor, Cacciaguida, his great-great-grandfather, who served in the Second Crusade. It is he who calls out the names of eight warriors who flash like rubies across the glittering bands of pure white light which form the image of the Cross:

> . . . I saw a flashing lustre run,
> At Joshua's name, athwart the cross and stop;
> Nor was it sooner said than it was done;
>
> Great Maccabee was named; I saw him drop,
> Spinning as he went, along his fiery lane,
> And gladness was the whip unto the top;
>
> Then Roland on the track of Charlemayne
> Sped, and my keen eye following – as it does
> The flight of one's own falcon – watched the twain;
>
> After, my sight was drawn along the cross
> By William, Reynald and Duke Godfrey – three
> Fires, and a fourth, which Robert Guiscard was.[1]

Here, then, is Roland, in this verbal stained-glass window of Dante's cathedral, as sublime as Chartres, where Roland also is. And here in Paradise he is in the company of Joshua, Judas Maccabeus, Charlemagne, William of Orange,[2] Reynald (the converted Saracen giant, who balances the giants of *Inferno*, those symbols of primitive violence), Godfrey of Bouillon and Robert Guiscard, all Defenders of the Faith. Further in glorification of the Christian warrior, no poet could go. Here the legend is pure, undistorted by engrossments. Dante has concentrated on a single theme, Roland the champion of Christendom, betrayed and killed at Roncevaux and elevated to sainthood among his peers of all ages.

Of the many stories of Charlemagne and his paladins by which generations of *jongleurs*, *Minnesänger*,[3] and *cantastorie* held their audiences entranced in market-squares or along pilgrim

1. *Paradise*, xvIII. 37–45, idem.

2. The hero of the twelfth-century cycle of epics in Old French, also known as William Shortnose.

3. The *Rolandslied* of German literature, parallel in development to the Italian romances, did not directly influence them.

routes, two have particular importance for the later Italian tradition. They are *Renaus* and *Aspremont*. The former, an anonymous poem of some 18,000 lines, relates the adventures of a new hero, Renaus (Renaud, Rinaldo), who is to play a major role in Italian romances. The second of the four sons of Aymon, he is a valorous and ferocious warrior, worthy to be compared with Roland, whose cousin he later becomes. He is shown originally in opposition to Charlemagne, who is fiercely hostile to him. The author of *Renaus* identifies him with St Renaut of Cologne and shows him to be protected by God, who performs a miracle to defend him against conspirators who plot to kill him. Italianized as Rinaldo, he later rivalled Roland (Orlando) in popularity, to the extent that *cantastorie* came to be called Rinaldi.[1]

In *Aspremont*, a poem of 12,000 lines which dates from the beginning of the thirteenth century, later retold in Italian as *Aspromonte*, the story is set in Calabria. The African king, Agolante, has invaded Italy from Sicily. Charlemagne moves south to challenge him and is victorious. With the blessing of the Pope, he founds the kingdom of Sicily and Apulia, the achievements of the Normans in south Italy being thereby attributed to the Franks. King Agolante is accompanied by his son, Almonte, who is slain by Orlando. Charlemagne, who is by now Orlando's uncle, had considered the boy Orlando too young to accompany the army and had instructed him to remain behind. Fortunately for the outcome, Orlando disobeyed and was able to save the Christians by his intervention at a critical moment. By this victory he comes into possession of Almonte's helmet, and of his sword, Durindana (Durendal in the *Chanson*), said to have belonged to Hector.[2]

1. It is Rinaldo's exploits which hold the audience spell-bound in the short story by Salvatore di Giacomo, who describes a *cantastorie* reciting in Naples at the end of the last century. (See *Tredici Novelle Moderne*, ed. K. T. Butler and B. Reynolds, Cambridge University Press, pp. 19–27.)

2. In the French *Aspremont*, Hector is a contemporary and friend of Almonte, to whom he gave his sword. Later versions of the story turn him into the son of Priam. I am indebted to Professor André de Mandach for this suggestion as to how the Trojan Hector came to be regarded as the first owner of the sword.

The existence of manuscript copies of such stories in Italy testifies to their popularity there. In particular, St Mark's Library in Venice has a notable collection of texts in Franco-Veneto. It was the convention that such narratives should be recited in French; this created an impression of authenticity and verisimilitude. The language naturally reveals the local origins of the authors. The *Entrée d'Espagne*, for instance, an important item in the collection, is written in Franco-Paduan. The *Prise de Pampelune* is by a Veronese, probably the same Nicola of Verona who wrote an adaptation of Lucan's *Pharsalia*. His name is hidden in an acrostic. Both authors exhibit some coyness about writing works they know will be distorted by *cantastorie*. The diffusion of such stories in French was prevalent in the north of Italy in the early part of the fourteenth century. Adaptations began to be composed in Tuscan in the following century. In the Laurentian Library in Florence there is a manuscript of a poem in octaves, entitled *Orlando*, in which the hero's adventures receive extensive development. This work was to be an important source of material for the Florentine poet, Luigi Pulci, in his composition of *Morgante*.

An even more important source was the Italian prose vulgate of Carolingian legends, compiled by Andrea da Barberino, himself a *cantastorie*, who lived between 1370 and 1433. His work, entitled *I Reali di Francia* (The Royal House of France), is in the form of a chronicle. Animating it is a unifying concept which goes a long way towards explaining the dynamic power which the Carolingian stories exerted over Italian audiences. Charlemagne and his Twelve Peers, with their ancient genealogies, are the instruments whereby God has chosen to ensure the diffusion of the Christian faith throughout the world; they are the champions of the Church of Rome, for which Rome itself was founded, as Dante himself believed.

There is the authority of tradition, therefore, behind the combination of gravity and fabulous romance which is the feature of the three most important literary examples of the Italian romantic epic, Luigi Pulci's *Morgante*, Matteo Boiardo's *Orlando*

Innamorato and Ludovico Ariosto's *Orlando Furioso.*[1] Thus it was that Pulci could set himself both to entertain the court of the Medici with his racy octaves and to please the devout mother of Lorenzo the Magnificent, Lucrezia Tornabuoni, who, it is said, asked him to undertake the work. He tells again the story of Roland at Roncevaux but, like the author of the poem in the Laurentian Library, he sends him off first on fabulous adventures in the Levant, where he captures Babylon. The poem was popularly christened *Morgante*, after the giant of that name whom Orlando converts and baptizes. Amid the rollicking exuberance of this work there are some serious and solemn touches. The creation of two characters entitles Pulci to consideration as an artist of original genius: the devil Astarotte, a great and proud devil, still trailing clouds of angelic glory, who may have contributed something to Milton's Satan; and a second, smaller giant, Margutte, a prototype of Rabelais' Panurge, a strongly delineated villain, perhaps a caricature of a real person, a glutton, drunkard, liar, thief and blasphemer. His enunciation of his creed in terms of food is among Pulci's many verbal *tours de force.*[2]

Pulci also provides an interesting glimpse of Orlando's potential instability. At the beginning of the story, enraged by Gano's (Ganelon's) deceit and Charlemagne's credulousness, he rushes home to make arrangements for his departure. Out of his wits with fury, he mistakes his wife, Alda, for Gano and attacks her with his sword. Here is the seed of Orlando's madness which develops ultimately into a towering Titanic frenzy in Ariosto's *Orlando Furioso.*

The introduction of women and the influence of love is perhaps the most radical alteration in the Roland legend in its transition from *chanson de geste* to romance. 'La belle Aude' and the regret expressed by Oliver that Roland will never lie

1. The definitive edition of Pulci's epic was published in Florence in 1483. It was entitled *Il Morgante Maggiore* (i.e. the enlarged *Morgante*). Boiardo's epic was unfinished when he died, in 1494; the first two parts were published between 1482 and 1483.

2. See John Addington Symonds, *The Renaissance in Italy*, 1906, *Italian Literature*, II, Part I, p. 479. See also pp. 385–98. Leigh Hunt, who much admired the poem, wrote a shortened prose version of it which he dedicated to Shelley. Byron translated the first canto into verse; cf. p. 84.

in her arms are the only concession in the original *Chanson* to the softer emotions. For love one must look there to the ties of loyalty between vassal and lord and to the comradeship between fighting-men, with its moving tone of grave and formal courtesy: 'Fair sir, companion'.

In romance, on the other hand, love luxuriates like an overgrown plant. Women are everywhere, on horseback as warriors, indistinguishable from the men until their helmets are knocked off and their golden hair streams out, as damsels in distress, requiring to be rescued, continually distracting the knights from their primary responsibilities, as symbols of self-indulgence, as sorceresses, good or evil, or as inspirations to valour. The element of amorousness offered variety of plot and characterization and had, moreover, a respectable ancestry in the *Odyssey* and the *Iliad*. It enabled the poet to show the knights in contrast one with another, constant or inconstant as lovers, sensualist or idealist, capable of reformation or lost for ever in the toils of a seductress.

ii. CELTIC (ARTHURIAN)

The chief source of this element of amorousness, apart from the Greek and Roman epics, is the Arthurian cycle of legends. These were appreciated particularly, though not exclusively, in courtly circles, and Dante appropriately imagines Francesca, the wife of the lord of Rimini, reading the story of Lancelot and Guinevere, the corrupting influence of which led to her undoing.[1] Among the French texts which had most influence are *Palamède* and *Tristan*. Rusticiano of Pisa, who wrote up the memoirs of Marco Polo, refashioned a great deal of the material of these two romances in his work entitled *Meliadus*, which dates from about 1275. In the Arthurian cycle of stories the atmosphere is mystical and mysterious. The knights of the Round Table, more sensual and emotional than the Carolingians, seem more concerned with winning the approval of their ladies than with defeating the infidel, though often the two achievements are combined. Their adventures, being individual, require a different shape

1. *Inferno*, v. 127-38.

of story: instead of battle, there is the duel; instead of the crowd-movements of armies and general mêlées, there is a preference for the wanderings of the lonely knight-errant, in the dream world of the irrational.

An intermingling of Arthurian with Carolingian elements was evident already in Pulci's poem and in others which preceded it. The introduction of sorcerers, monsters and giants, in addition to the perils of enamourment, reinforced the powers of evil ranged against the cavaliers, whose ordeals became ever more fabulous and exotic. It was Boiardo who first consciously and deliberately combined the two cycles of legends, proclaiming the element of amorousness from the outset in the very title of his work, *Orlando Innamorato* (Orlando in Love). He wrote it for the Estensi, following the example of Nicola of Verona, who had dedicated his *Prise de Pampelune* to Niccolò d'Este in 1343. There was thus already a traditional cult of the legends at the court of Ferrara, and it is said that the library contained a fine collection of romances in both French and Italian. The level of art and learning, the interest in chivalry, and the staging of tournaments and pageants made Ferrara a propitious centre for the creation of a masterpiece in this genre. Boiardo was a loyal courtier. He served Duke Ercole I in various capacities and was entrusted with high office. In 1481 he was appointed Governor of Modena and in 1487 Governor of Reggio. He was one of the suite who brought the Duke's bride, Eleanor of Aragon, from Naples to Ferrara. Among his admirers was the Duke's daughter, Isabella d'Este, to whom Ariosto was later to read some of his own epic aloud.

The framework of the action is still Carolingian, and Roland is still the main character; but distant, exotic vistas are at once unfolded. While Charlemagne holds plenary court at Whitsuntide, the son and daughter of the Great Khan, Argalia and Angelica, arrive from Cathay, equipped with supernatural powers and magical weapons, to bring havoc and confusion to the Christians. Angelica's beauty causes such rivalry among the knights that they scatter in pursuit of her, leaving Charlemagne inadequately defended.

The love, or the desire, inspired by Angelica is the thread

which links the main characters of this immense poem. Thus
Boiardo puts sexual love in the place of religion as the supreme,
irradiating force in life, a change which reflects the concentra-
tion on earthly existence which was one of the features of the
Renaissance. Angelica is the reason for the siege of Albracca,
where she has taken refuge to avoid marriage with the
besieger, Agricane, King of Tartary; she is also the reason
why Orlando and Rinaldo hurry back to France to defend the
kingdom of Charlemagne against the invading armies of
Agramante. Intertwined with these two major events are
innumerable episodes, interludes and sub-plots. At any
moment Orlando may wander off to kill a giant or a monster,
to destroy an enchanted garden, or to fall into some enchant-
ment himself from which he needs to be rescued. Yet in the
midst of so much elaborate embroidery, some of the original
threads shine through.

In the final encounter between Orlando and Agricane there
is a glimpse of that endearing simplicity of faith and chivalrous
courtesy which characterize the Roland of the *Chanson*. By
pretending flight, Agricane draws Orlando away from the
battlefield before Albracca to a meadow by a wood, with a
fountain on one side; then he explains that he has done so in
order to give Orlando a chance of saving himself, in return
for courtesy which Orlando has shown to him earlier in the
day. He may escape now if he will withdraw from the fight
before Albracca:

> Orlando answered in a gentle tone,
> Such deep compassion on his spirit fell:
> 'The greater worth and valour you have shown,
> The more I pity you, who know full well
> That you will die and yet have never known
> The faith in Christ, but must be doomed to Hell.
> If you in body and in soul would thrive,
> Then be baptized and hence depart alive.'[1]

But Agricane refuses this kind offer and challenges Orlando
to a duel. When the sun goes down and they can no longer see
to continue the combat, they lie down side by side:

1. I. xviii. 36; translated by J. C. Wordsworth.

> To this accord they came without delay
> And both dismounted and their horses tied,
> And on the grassy sward together lay
> As though in friendship and long peace allied,
> So close in one another's sight were they;
> Orlando nearer to the fountain side,
> And Agrican lay nearer to the wood,
> Where a tall pine with shady branches stood.[1]

Orlando looks up at the sky and says:

> '''Tis a right glorious work that we behold,
> This that the heavenly monarchy has made;
> The moon all silver and the stars all gold,
> The light of day, the sun's far-shining face:
> All this has God made for the human race.'[2]

And Agricane, with the resigned tone of experience in his voice, replies: 'I see you want to talk about religion.' And for a while they do, until Agricane says, 'Sleep now, or else if you must talk, talk of arms or of love.' The duel is resumed the next morning and when Orlando has inflicted a mortal wound on his enemy, Agricane asks to be baptized:

> 'Baptize me in this fountain's water, knight,
> Before the power of speech be wholly passed,
> And if in life I wandered from the right,
> Let me not die as one from God outcast.'[3]

Orlando helps him to dismount, and weeps as he does so:

> Fast down his cheeks the tears of sorrow ran,
> And, leaping from his saddle to the ground,
> He lifted in his arms the dying man
> And set him gently on the stone around
> The fountain; long he wept with Agrican,
> Craving his pardon for that deadly wound,
> Then, humbly praying to the heavenly king
> To grant him grace, baptized him at the spring.[4]

Boiardo's poem is unfinished and it is not known how he would have ended it. He refers in advance to Orlando's destruction of Biserta, the capital of King Agramante, and no

1. I. xviii. 40. 2. ibid. 41. iv–viii.
3. I. xix. 13. i–iv. 4. ibid. 16.

doubt the invaders of France were doomed to defeat; but how Orlando would have fared in his love for Angelica it is difficult to guess. Boiardo seems towards the end to be tiring of this theme and to be more interested in the development of a new love story: that of the woman warrior, Bradamante, whom he creates (adding her to the Montalbano family as a sister of Rinaldo), and the pagan knight, Ruggiero. These two, destined ultimately to marry, are indicated as the progenitors of the House of Este. On this suggestion Ariosto seizes, making it one of the major themes of his poem.

Orlando in love appears towards the end to be evading Boiardo's control. He is scarcely rational at times – as Boiardo admits, saying that love had fired his spirit with madness. Yet at times, Orlando seems almost to forget that he has vowed to win Angelica at all costs. He is easily distracted from this purpose, and by no means faithful to her. He is led astray and deceived by the treacherous Orrigille (who reappears in the *Furioso*, but as the deceitful mistress of Grifone, not of Orlando). She tells Orlando that if he climbs a certain rock and looks down a hole he will see all Hell and Paradise. When he mounts credulously to the top (a credulousness which Ariosto gives to Bradamante in a similar situation), she rides away on his horse, saying she hopes he is good at walking. As he goes on his way he curses all women, then immediately strikes his mouth for uttering such a blasphemy: for the sake of Angelica, all her sex is above reproach. This shows a total lack of judgement on the part of Orlando, for Angelica herself has just sent him on a mission which she hopes will end in his death. It is in this maze of error that Ariosto finds Orlando when he takes up the story.

iii. CLASSICAL

The Classical element in the poem may be considered under two heads: namely, content and form. As regards the first, readers who are familiar with the *Aeneid* will notice the extent to which this grave and solemn epic has been laid under contribution. Ruggiero plays a role comparable to that of Aeneas: he is the ancestor of the Estensi as Aeneas is of

Augustus. The conjuration in Merlin's cave of spirits representing the descendants of Ruggiero and Bradamante corresponds to the vision which Aeneas has of the Julian line in the Elysian fields. Merlin, Melissa and Atlante, although Arthurian in origin or inspiration, are the equivalents of the prophetic and oracular beings in the *Aeneid*. Astolfo transformed into a myrtle is a descendant, via Dante's Pier delle Vigne, of Polydorus. Rodomonte is the Mezentius of the pagans; when he leaps over the defences of Paris he recalls Turnus who penetrates into the camp of the followers of Aeneas. Medoro and Cloridano in their midnight search of the battlefield for the body of Dardinello recall the attempt of Nisus and Euryalus to reach Aeneas. Alcina is another Circe, with a suggestion of Dido in her desperation on Ruggiero's departure. The presence of these august retro-figures lends a venerable aura to the eighth-century story, which in its turn projects its own magnified stature upon events of the early sixteenth century.

Ariosto has drawn plentifully also upon Ovid. Olimpia's lamentations on being deserted by Bireno, echoed by the caves, are themselves an echo of Ariadne's cries on the island of Naxos. Much poetic ornament is derived too from Catullus, Horace and Statius. His indebtedness to all his predecessors, both medieval and ancient, has been exhaustively examined by Pio Rajna in his monumental work, *Le Fonti dell'Orlando Furioso* (The Sources of 'Orlando Furioso'), which leaves no doubt that Ariosto's achievement was one of combining, shaping, transforming, adapting, translating and, in the final analysis, recreating material which already existed.

The influence of the *Iliad* may be seen in certain types of episode. The parades of the British and of the pagan troops recall the review of Greek and Trojan forces; duels between rivals for possession of Angelica have their antecedence in the combat between Paris and Menelaus; Aphrodite's intercession on behalf of Paris is reflected in Atlante's protection of Ruggiero; the search by Medoro and Cloridano has its antecedent not only in the expedition of Nisus and Euryalus but also in the night prowl of Dolon; the battles outside Paris have their prototype in the battle which begins when Pandarus breaks the truce; Strife personified becomes Dame Discord; the love-making of Paris and Helen is the archetype of the many love scenes in which *Orlando Furioso* abounds.

Ariosto's indebtedness to Homer is, however, more one of atmosphere than of incident. Echoes of similes from both the *Odyssey* and the *Iliad* charge the romance with the heroic ferocity of a primitive antiquity. Elemental forces, the dawn, the sea, storms, grief, destiny and death are shown against a vast, Homeric horizon. This was a hazardous dimension to introduce as it might have dwarfed the Carolingian personages and their events. That it does not is due to the wide panorama of the historical issues which are involved. The awe-inspiring vista of Troy, remote, yet linked with the central characters by the mystery of blood relationship, stirs the imagination with its compelling blend of history and archetypal myth.

The presence of classicism in the form of the *Furioso* is to be seen in the skilful shaping of the total material, the balancing and contrasting of its many parts and the achievement of unity, of the famous Ariostean 'harmony', from so vast a variety of episodes and styles. It is to be seen also in the mastery of the octave, a stanza adopted for narrative since the time of Boccaccio, which in Ariosto's hands has earned the epithet of 'golden'. Though not all his octaves are gold and some do not even glitter, serving merely to round off one situation in preparation for the next, they all have form and balance. At its most polished, Ariosto's handling of the octave is worthy of the highest manifestations of Italian Renaissance art.

iv. INTEGRATION OF CAROLINGIAN, CELTIC AND CLASSICAL COMPONENTS IN THE CHARACTER OF ORLANDO

It remains a mystery how such diverse material, Carolingian, Celtic and Classical, could be combined to produce a work of art so relevant to contemporary concerns and so characteristic of the Italian Renaissance. Many critics, notably Croce, have spoken of Ariosto's harmony, but in so doing they have described rather than defined or explained the unity of the poem.

Professor Geoffrey L. Bickersteth comes nearer to defining its *artistic* unity when he speaks of the uniform quality of the poem's tone: 'What is characteristic of Ariosto's incomparable voice is his masterly control of its tones. ... By his irony ... (he) imposes unity on his material and he does it ... by his voice.'[1] The nature of its *structural* unity may perhaps be glimpsed if we consider the implications of bringing together in the central character, Orlando, the three main elements of which the poem has been shown to be composed.

Orlando (Roland) begins in the French *Chanson* as a Carolingian, a Frankish hero of impetuous character who dies in tragic circumstances, the victim of treachery and of his own refusal to summon aid. The influence upon him of the Celtic (Arthurian) world of imagination and the enchantment of the East (Angelica) have a disruptive effect upon his Germanic psyche. His reintegration is achieved by the introduction of the newly formulated ideals of Classical (Greco-Latin) balance, proportion and control, illumined by the Christian revelation. As heir to this three-fold tradition, Orlando might be said to stand for European man; and Ariosto's method of freeing his hero from his predicament might represent his belief in the possibility of creating a Europe true to its varied heritage but unified in a bond of peace and fellowship. This was the ideal of Erasmus. It would seem to be interwoven also in the vision of Ariosto, the poet of Europe.

III. LUDOVICO ARIOSTO AND HIS TIMES (1474–1533)

Ariosto's lifetime coincides with the rule of Henry VII and Henry VIII in England, of Charles VIII, Louis XII and Francis I in France, and of Ferdinand and Isabella, and Joanna the Mad, in Spain. The two Emperors of the period, Maximilian I and Charles V are outnumbered by the eight Popes, Sixtus IV, Innocent VIII, Alexander VI, Pius III, Julius II, Leo X, Adrian VI and Clement VII.

1. *Form, Tone and Rhythm in Italian Poetry* (The Taylorian Lecture), Clarendon Press, 1933, p. 30.

This list of some of the most potent rulers in the history of Europe serves to remind us that this was the period of the highest achievements of the Renaissance and of fundamental changes in western civilization. To recall only the most significant and far-reaching: Ariosto was 18 when Columbus sailed to the New World in 1492; he was 20 when Charles VIII, his head full of dreams of glory from reading chivalrous romances, invaded Italy with thirty thousand troops, thereby bringing to an end forty years of almost unbroken peace in the peninsula and initiating an era in which it was to become the arena of relentless rivalry between France and Spain. In 1513 Machiavelli published *Il Principe*. In 1517 Luther posted on the door of the castle church in Wittenberg his ninety-five theses against the sale of indulgences. This is the age when men's eyes were beholding for the first time the masterpieces of Raphael, Leonardo, Titian and Michelangelo. In 1527, twelve thousand *Landsknechte*, unpaid and spoiling for plunder, sacked Rome, stabling their horses in St Peter's. Pope Clement VII, a virtual prisoner of the Emperor, who was a nephew of Catharine of Aragon, was in no position to grant the request of Henry VIII for a divorce. In 1532 (the year before Ariosto's death), Henry had broken with Rome and married Anne Boleyn.

Ludovico Ariosto, like Boiardo, was descended from a noble family, and like Boiardo, served the Estensi for the greater part of his life. He was born at Reggio Emilia on 8 September 1474, the first of a family of five sons and five daughters. His father, Niccolò Ariosto, of Ferrara, was Governor of the citadel of Reggio under Duke Ercole I; his mother, Daria Malaguzzi Valera, the daughter of a physician who was also a minor poet, came from Reggio, one of the gayest and most pleasant of the cities ruled by the Estensi: 'Joyful Reggio', Ariosto called it. When Boiardo had been Governor there he ordered the bells of the citadel to be rung to celebrate his invention of the name of Rodamonte for the pagan warrior in his poem. Near by are the castle of the Boiardo family at Scandiano and the Villa Malaguzzi of the family of Ariosto's mother.

Between 1481 and 1482 the family moved to Rovigo, where

the father was appointed to command the garrison; but, owing to a war between Ferrara and Venice, Rovigo became too dangerous for the children to remain there, and they were sent back to Reggio. A few years later, between 1485 and 1486, the whole family moved to Ferrara, where Niccolò eventually became chief administrator of the State. From then on Ferrara was Ludovico's home, though he remained attached to Reggio and continued to visit his maternal cousins at Villa Malaguzzi. To oblige his father, he studied law, first at home under a tutor and later at the University; but after five years his father agreed that he should devote himself to a literary career. Accordingly he was placed under the instruction of the Humanist, Gregorio of Spoleto, with whose aid he perfected his knowledge of Latin. He had hoped to study Greek under his tuition, but Gregorio left Ferrara to go to Milan as tutor to Francesco Sforza, the son of Galeazzo Sforza and Isabella of Aragon. In one of his autobiographical poems Ariosto expresses his lasting regret at the departure of this loved master.[1] At the University Ariosto attended lectures on philosophy and gained a sound knowledge of the New Learning. He derived also valuable stimulus from the company of men of letters and artists who frequented Ferrara, where a high level of intellectual life had been inculcated, particularly owing to the influence of the Humanist educator, Battista Guarino, whose more famous father, Guarino of Verona, had turned Lionello d'Este into a model Renaissance prince.

With the death of Ariosto's father in 1500, when Ludovico was twenty-six, this pleasant life of study and freedom came to an end. Finding himself responsible for a large family, he was obliged to seek public employment under the Estensi. In 1502 he accepted appointment as Governor of the citadel of Canossa and in 1503 he entered the service of Cardinal Ippolito, whose brother, Alfonso, succeeded to the dukedom in 1505.

Among the events of his lifetime, those which impinged most vividly and forcibly upon him were the consequences of the Italian wars. In the complicated diplomacy of the Italian rulers, who vied and plotted against one another instead of

1. *Satira* VI. 166–95.

uniting against the danger they shared, Ferrara supported
France. As the dukes held power as papal vicars and as the
Pope was leagued with Spain against France, this was a
perilous tight-rope. Ferrara was also many times involved in
war with the Venetian Republic.

Ariosto had first-hand knowledge of war, beginning with
his experience as a child of seven at Rovigo. When he entered
Ippolito's service he accompanied him not only on diplomatic
but also on military missions. He saw active service in 1509,
when, owing to the strategy of Ippolito and the artillery of
Alfonso, the entire Venetian fleet was destroyed at Polesella
on the river Po. In the same year he witnessed the siege of
Padua by the Emperor Maximilian, in which Alfonso and
Ippolito assisted, without success, as Padua remained under
the control of Venice.[1] His sight of the battlefield of Ravenna
in 1512 made a lasting impression, as has already been
mentioned.[2]

He was continually on horseback in the service of the
Estensi, on journeys to Bologna, Modena, Mantua, Florence
and Rome, journeys which he found uncongenial and incom-
patible with the life of letters he would so greatly have pre-
ferred. In 1507 he went on a pleasant errand to Mantua to
present the congratulations of Alfonso and Ippolito to their
sister Isabella Gonzaga on the birth of a son. It was on this
occasion that he read some of the *Orlando Furioso* aloud to her,
an unusual post-natal therapy. In the same year he accompanied
the Cardinal on a journey to Milan to meet Louis XII. Four
years later, Louis, undeterred by his predecessor's reverses,
having invaded Italy, was defeated at Novara.

In 1509 Ariosto was sent to Rome (as Rinaldo was sent to
Britain) to ask for troops and money from Pope Julius II to
help Ferrara in a war against Venice. The following year he
returned to Rome in an attempt to placate the Pope, who was
infuriated by Alfonso's alliance with the French instead of
with the Holy League; the Pope's response was to threaten to
have Ariosto thrown into the Tiber. In 1512 Alfonso, who
had been excommunicated and whose State had been placed
under an interdict, went to Rome (though not quite in the

1. cf. XVI. 27.   2. See pp. 21–24.

spirit of Henry IV at Canossa) to negotiate a reconciliation. Such was the wrath of Pope Julius that Alfonso, accompanied by Ariosto, was obliged to make his escape in disguise through Umbria and Tuscany. Ariosto has described this adventurous journey in a letter to Ludovico Gonzaga. Writing on 1 October, he says that they have just reached Florence after spending the night in a hut in the open countryside, their ears pricked for every footfall, their hearts pounding. The letter reads for all the world like a draft for one of his stanzas in the *Furioso*.[1]

In 1513, on the election of Pope Leo X, an event which Ariosto heralds in his poem,[2] he accompanied Alfonso and Ippolito when they went to Rome to pay homage. Ariosto hoped for employment with Leo, thinking he might be a less demanding master than Ippolito. In 1517 he declined to follow Ippolito to Hungary on his appointment to the See of Buda. The next year he took service under the Duke, who paid him so irregularly that he often found himself in financial difficulties. In 1522 he accepted the post of Governor of the Garfagnana, a turbulent district in the Apennines, part of which was then under the dominion of Ferrara.[3] (The day after his appointment was confirmed, he made his will.) Here he spent the three most disagreeable years of his life, in a hostile environment where brigands and local potentates ill-treated and exploited the inhabitants. To add to his difficulties, his authority was not adequately supported by the Duke, his letters to whom show zeal and conscientiousness in a thankless task. Writing on 30 January 1524, he entreats Alfonso to recall him rather than leave him in an untenable and humiliating position.

He returned at last to Ferrara in June 1525. In addition to various administrative duties, he was given responsibility for the court theatrical entertainments. In this capacity he was inspired to rewrite in verse two early prose comedies which he had laid aside, *La Cassaria* and *I Suppositi*, and to adapt a

1. Ludovico Ariosto, *Opere Minori*, ed. Cesare Segre, Ricciardi, 1954, pp. 760–61.

2. XVII. 79.

3. Ariosto's headquarters was at Castelnuovo di Garfagnana. Part of the castle still exists and is now known as the Castello Ariostesco.

third, *Il Negromante*, which he had first composed in 1520. He also wrote a new comedy, *La Lena*, which was staged for the first time during the carnival of 1528. A fifth comedy, *Gli Studenti* (or *La Scolastica*), begun in 1520, was later finished by his crippled brother, Gabriele, whom he had taken to live with him on the death of their father and who remained with him to the end.

By this period, as his salary as Governor of Garfagnana had been adequate, he was in a position to realize his fondest dream and buy a house and garden of his own.[1] From 1528 until his death, he lived in retirement with Gabriele and with his illegitimate son, Virginio, whom he made his heir.[2] He died on 6 July 1533 in his fifty-ninth year.

In the midst of the restless and demanding series of his official duties, Ariosto found time and energy to compose, in addition to his early lyrics in Latin, a great number of Italian odes and sonnets, dramatic eclogues, autobiographical poems in *terza rima* and the five comedies to which reference has been made. His *magnum opus*, an absorbing labour of love, occupied him over a period of about twenty-five years. Beginning, it may be, in 1505 or in 1506, he worked at it continuously, taking it with him on his many journeys, submitting his stanzas and the narrative to unceasing revision and alteration. He read it out loud to whoever would listen; the valuable role played in this respect by his household companions, Gabriele and Virginio, is not difficult to surmise. He was responsive to the suggestions of his friends, and is said to have left the manuscript open in a room in his house that callers might make what alterations they wished. The first edition, published at the expense of Ippolito,[3] to whom it was

1. In Via Mirasole, in Ferrara, now renamed Via Ariosto.

2. Virginio's mother was Orsolina Catinelli da Sassomarino. In 1514 she married someone named Malacisio and Ariosto gave her a dowry of six hundred lire. Ariosto had had another son previously by a family servant named Maria. He was brought up by his mother and became a captain of artillery.

3. Ippolito on receiving the published poem is reported to have asked: '*Dove hai trovato tutte queste coglionerie, Messer Ludovico?*' ('Where did you find all this balderdash, Master Ludovico?'). Ariosto's reply is not recorded.

dedicated, appeared in Ferrara in 1516. It was an immediate success, even though, or possibly for the very reason that, Boiardo's *Orlando Innamorato* was still popular. A second edition, slightly revised, was published in 1521, also at Ferrara. The final edition, revised stylistically with the help of Pietro Bembo and enlarged from forty to forty-six cantos, appeared in 1532, again in Ferrara.[1] This is the text which, with minor editorial adaptations, is regarded as approximating to the author's final wishes, though he would probably have revised it further. There remained five cantos, begun probably in 1521, which Ariosto did not in the end include. They were published after his death by Virginio with the simple title of *I Cinque Canti*.

As we catch sight of Ariosto weaving his way amid the intrigue of Ferrarese diplomacy or involved in the vicissitudes of war, it is important also to keep in panoramic view the more distant events and changes which characterized the age in which he lived. As the descendant of a noble family, he had a personal link with renowned figures of his country's past; as a man of action, soldier and diplomat, he played a direct, though minor, part in the shaping of current events; as a scholar and poet he received the full imaginative impact of the rediscovery of the literature, philosophy and art of Greek and Roman antiquity. This revelation, combined with the geographical extension of the world, made the early sixteenth century an era with which no previous age can be compared. Only our own, with its scientific and technological advances and its explorations of space, can stand beside it. The rapid diffusion of knowledge made possible by our new media of communication had its parallel in the invention of printing, by means of which, for the first time in the history of man, new information and new concepts could be immediately and widely disseminated. By the year 1500 there were a hundred printing-houses in Italy. In Ariosto's own lifetime the relationship of an author to his public had been fundamentally and immeasurably changed.

The exhilarating sense of newness, which must have been

1. The printers of these three editions were Giovanni Mazzocchi dal Bondeno, Giovanni Battista dalla Pigna and Francesco Rosso da Valenza.

the most distinguishing experience of Ariosto's age, with its
New Learning and its New World, explains the *modernity* of
the poem. To the three categories of material of which it has
been shown to be composed, Carolingian, Celtic and Classical,
must be added a fourth: Contemporary. The art of perspective,
so recently discovered by the architect Brunelleschi, and
improved and perfected by the foremost Italian painters,
seems to be applied by Ariosto, with new and heightened
awareness of its possibilities, to his vast verbal canvas. As
Leon Battista Alberti proposed human proportions as the
unit of architectural design, so Ariosto places sixteenth-
century European man in the foreground of his construction,
both as measure and observer. Thus, to contemporary eyes
and with contemporary relevance he shows the medieval
figures in the middle ground and, beyond them, the legendary
vista of antiquity, which is projected in its turn upon the new
European mind, so newly made aware of its inheritance and
so alive to its significance. Thus it is that in comparison with
Orlando Furioso all earlier romantic epics seem but two-
dimensional.

IV. THE *ORLANDO FURIOSO* AND ENGLISH LITERATURE

'I can't make much headway with *Orlando Furioso*', a friend
wrote recently, 'it seems so *foreign.*' This is perhaps how the
work now strikes some English readers who come upon it
for the first time; yet in the early nineteenth century William
Roscoe felt able to say: 'On a work so well known, and so
universally read, as the *Orlando Furioso*, any observations
would now be superfluous.'[1]

However remote and unfamiliar Ariosto's poem may now
appear, it has entwined itself with English literature to a
degree exceeded only by Dante's *Divina Commedia* and the
love poetry of Petrarch. The process had already begun when
Marlowe introduced the story of Isabella's death into *Tambur-*

1. *The Life of Leo X*, 1805, Vol. 11, Chapter XVI.

laine.[1] Olympia (whose name is also derived from the Italian poem), mourning the death of her husband, as Isabella mourned Zerbino, induces Theridamas, King of Argier (as Isabella induced Rodomonte, King of Sarza and Algiers) to stab her in the throat, when she has anointed her neck with a magic substance which she says will render her invulnerable. The beheading of Isabella and the triple bounce of the head (evoking the beheading of St Paul) were changed by Marlowe to a mortal stab-wound for obvious reasons of stage-management.

Since Sir John Harington's translation was not published until 1591, Marlowe must have read the story in the original Italian or in Harington's manuscript, or have heard of it from someone else. In 1592, Robert Greene published his drama *The Historie of Orlando Furioso*, an adaptation for the stage of Ariosto's story of Orlando's madness. As in the poem, Orlando sees lovers' knots carved on the bark of trees; next, verses inscribed on a scroll hung on a branch lead him to believe that Angelica has betrayed him with Medoro. His resulting madness echoes the ferocity of the original:

> Orgalio (Orlando's servant, calling for help):
> . . . the Count Orlando is run mad, and taking of a
> shepheard by the heeles, rends him as one would tear a Larke.
> See where he comes with a leg on his necke.'
> Enter Orlando with leg.[2]

Later, Orlando, grown calm and musing on verses for Angelica, has almost a touch of Hamlet about him:

> Then goe thy waies and clime up to the Clowds,
> And tell Apollo that Orlando sits,
> Making of verses for Angelica.
> And if he doo denie to send me downe
> The shirt which Deianyra sent to Hercules,
> To make me brave upon my wedding day,
> Tell him Ile passe the Alpes, and up to Meroe,

1. *Orlando Furioso*, xxix. 3–26 (Vol. ii of this translation); *Tamburlaine*, Part ii, Act iv, Scene 2. This work was registered in Stationers' Hall in 1590.
2. Malone Society edition, ed. W. W. Greg, 1922, p. 153.

> (I know he knowes that watrie lakish hill)
> And pull the harpe out of the minstrelis hands,
> And pawne it unto lovely Proserpine,
> That she may fetch the faire Angelica.[1]

After sundry martial flourishes involving Sacrepant, Marsillus, Mandrecard, Oger, and Brandemart (whom Orlando kills), Angelica is proved faithful after all and Orlando is restored to sanity after drinking a potion given to him by Melissa.

Three years after the publication of Greene's play, the name of Sacrapant is given to a sorcerer in George Peele's *The Old Wives' Tale*, in which also the unfolding of the story within a story is suggestive of the narrative technique of romantic epics.[2]

It is apparent that before the publication of Harington's translation, knowledge of the *Orlando Furioso* was current in England among men of letters. Robert Greene, in an earlier work, *Alcida*, dating probably from 1588, twice recalls how Angelica forsook divers kings for the 'mercenary Souldier, Medor'. His departure in his drama from the story of her indifference to Orlando is therefore a deliberate adaptation. Greene's interpolations in Italian are sufficiently near to the original to show that he knew it at least in part. He seems to have been taken especially with the charming stanza about Chloris, which he transplants into his play, following it more closely than does Harington's translation.[3]

Shakespeare uses the story of Dalinda's impersonation of Ginevra for the situation of Hero in *Much Ado About Nothing*, but is likely to have taken it from Bandello's *novella*, in which a similar story is laid in Messina, or from Spenser's *Faerie Queene*, where the story reappears with a tragic ending.[4] In *As You Like It* Orlando (who has a brother, Oliver) carves

1. idem., pp. 171, 173.   2. Ed. A. H. Bullen, 1888.
3. xv. 57.

4. Book II, Canto iv. Peter Beverley translated the same story, *The historie of Ariodante and Genevra*, entered in the Stationers' Register 1565–66; the complete text is published in C. T. Prouty's *The Sources of Much Ado About Nothing*, Yale University Press, 1950. There was also a version of the story by George Whetstone in his 'Discourse of Rinaldo and Giletta', printed in his collection *The Rocke of Regard*, 1576. (I am indebted to Professor Geoffrey Bullough for these details.)

initials on the bark of trees in the Forest of Arden (the Warwickshire equivalent of the Forest of Ardennes) and hangs verses on the branches:

> O Rosalind, these trees shall be my books
> > And in their barks my thoughts I'll character,
> That every eye which in this forest looks
> > Shall see thy virtue witnessed everywhere.
> Run, run, Orlando; carve on every tree
> > The fair, the chaste, and unexpressive she. . . .

ROSALIND: But are you so much in love as your rhymes speak?

ORLANDO: Neither rhyme nor reason can express how much.

ROSALIND: Love is merely a madness and, I tell you, deserves as well a dark house and a whip as madmen do. . . .[1]

The echoes here, though merry, are distinct.

Though Shakespeare is nearer to Ariosto in spirit, it was Sir John Harington and Edmund Spenser who were the most influential conveyers of *Orlando Furioso* to the English poetic tradition. As it happened, it was not the true Ariostean qualities which they conveyed. Theorists had been at work in Italy in the half century since his death, interpreting the epic as an instrument of moral instruction. Giangiorgio Trissino had held the poem to ridicule and scorn.[2] The subject of his own epic, on which he laboured for twenty years, was drawn not from the Carolingian and Celtic legends, which he considered puerile, but from the Byzantine historian Procopius, the contemporary of Justinian and Belisarius. His *Italia Liberata dai Goti* (Italy Liberated from the Goths), published in 1547, in which Ariosto's golden octaves are replaced by unrhymed hendecasyllables, is a work of monumental dignity and unrelieved dullness. Two years later, Giraldi Cinthio published his *Discorso intorno al comporre dei romanzi* (Discourse on the composition of romances), in which he maintained that the purpose of the romantic epic should be to inculcate good

1. III. 2, New Penguin Shakespeare, ed. H. J. Oliver. The urge to inscribe the name of the beloved on the bark of trees, or in chalk on walls, seems to be part of the conflicting human desires both to proclaim and to conceal love. The phenomenon is still to be observed in, for example, the personal columns of *The Times*.

2. Boccaccio had also scorned the Carolingian legends as fit reading only for idle women.

morals. Tasso, whose public career seems almost a repetition
of Ariosto's, serving as he did first Cardinal Luigi d'Este and
then Duke Alfonso II, took warning from Trissino's failure,
and several leaves from Cinthio's book. His *Discorsi dell'arte
poetica, et in particolare del poema heroico* (Discourses on the art
of poetry and in particular on the heroic epic), written be-
tween 1567 and 1570, reiterate the noble and edifying function
of epic, of which the theme must be Christian. The multiple
actions of *Orlando Furioso* are adversely criticized; a variety of
elements is permissible, but must be closely interwoven so as
not to violate the principle of unity, an essential requirement.
But for the edifying content to be acceptable to the reader, he
must be enticed and beguiled by a story which holds his
attention and pleases his imagination with the beauty of the
descriptions and the marvels of the events.

The high-mindedness which overtook the Italian epic poets
and theorists of the Counter-Reformation affected both Har-
ington and Spenser. The first of these writers found in Ariosto
much more allegory than the poet had intended, and applied
to it a system of interpretation which would have been more
in keeping with the *Divina Commedia*:

> ... men of greatest learning and highest wit in the auncient
> times did of purpose conceale these deepe mysteries of learning and,
> as it were, cover them with the vaile of fables and verse ... that
> they might not be rashly abused by prophane wits in whom science
> is corrupted, like good wine in a bad vessel; ... a principal cause
> of all, is to be able with one kinde of meate and one dish (as I may
> so call it) to feed divers tastes. For the weaker capacities will feede
> themselves with the pleasantness of the historie and sweetness of
> the verse, some that have stronger stomaches will as it were take a
> further taste of the Morall sence, a third sort, more high conceited
> than they, will digest the Allegorie ...[1]

In this, Harington was no doubt influenced by such interpre-
tations as the commentary of Simone Fornari, published in
1549, in which, for example, the brutish monsters which

---

1. Preface to Sir John Harington's translation. Camoens takes a high-
minded tone concerning fiction when he says his epic, *Os Lusiadas*, is
concerned with real deeds, not the dreams and fables of the imaginary
Rodomonte, Ruggiero and Orlando (Canto 1, stanza 2).

confront Ruggiero at the boundary to Alcina's kingdom are identified with dissimulation, adulation, licentiousness, violence, cowardice, pride, gluttony, sloth, and other vices; the hippogriff is seen as an allegory of uncontrolled impulses; Baiardo, Rinaldo's horse, interpreted as representing Rinaldo's desire for Angelica, is unresponsive to Sacripante (appetite cannot be coerced by force), but docile to Angelica, who caresses it with her left hand (the sinister power of amorous allurement).

Ariosto's allegory is more casual than this. It is nearly always explicit, or very transparently veiled, as in the personifications of Discord, Jealousy and Silence, or in the allegorical figures of Logistilla and her attendant ladies. There is no question of carefully inter-related strata or levels of meaning (literal, moral, spiritual and mystical), as in the typology of Christian exegetics and as adopted by the medieval poets who thought and wrote in that tradition. After Ariosto's day, the Counter-Reformation brought about a fundamental change of attitude to literature and art. Books had to be shown to serve morality or else they were in danger of being proscribed on the Index or consigned to the flames. Theologians and scholars thundered against romances of chivalry. The Spanish mystic Malon de Chaide, writing in 1588, said that they were as dangerous as a knife in a madman's hand. Legislation was passed to prevent their introduction into the Spanish-American colonies. That *Orlando Furioso* is among the works which the priest spares from the bonfire in *Don Quixote*[1] is perhaps due to the edifying reputation it had acquired at the hands of allegorizers, though Cervantes himself is not so easily taken in. By Harington's time, the romantic epics had reached a stage at which they must undergo one of three processes: they could be exorcised, satirized or allegorized.

The allegorizing conception of epic poetry is plainly to be seen in Spenser, whose avowed intention was 'to overgo Ariosto'.[2] There is no doubt that he succeeded as far as

1. Part 1, chapter vi.
2. See the Letter to Spenser from Gabriel Harvey:
'I am voyde of all iudgement, if your NINE COMOEDIES ... come not neerer ARIOSTOES COMOEDIES... than that the ELVISH QUEENE doth

allegory was concerned. Influenced by Tasso, who had recommended the history of King Arthur as among the subjects most appropriate for heroic poetry, and who echoed Aristotle's prescription that the epic hero should be a type of virtue, Spenser devised an elaborate construction for his *Faerie Queene*, whereby Arthur and the twelve knights represent between them thirteen virtues. To the four traditional levels of meaning he sometimes adds a fifth, the political. As with Dante, not all the levels are of equal importance in every context, but, again as in Dante, sometimes all the levels are significant in combination. An instance of this has been analysed as follows:

The 11th canto of Book 1 of *The Faerie Queene* describes the fight between the Redcross Knight and the Dragon, who ravages the Kingdom of Una's parents (Eden). *Literally* this is straight fairy-narrative. *Morally* it describes the Christian life as a battle against evil, helped by the sacraments of Baptism (the well into which the Knight falls at the end of the first day and from which he rises refreshed) and the Eucharist (the tree, representing the Cross, whose balm heals his wounds at the end of the second day). *Spiritually*, this is the Church Militant on Earth, battling against the Devil (heresy and error) in defence of the Truth in its care (Una, who watches the battle from a hill top), and preserved by the sacraments entrusted to it. *Mystically*, it is Christ during the three days of His entombment, when He descended into Hell and, as tradition held from the fifth century onward, defeated the Devil on his own ground and released the dead who had hitherto been in his power (including Adam and Eve). To this may be added the *political* level, of the Church and State of England battling against the power of error of the Roman Church. Una is here Queen Elizabeth.[1]

Into this complex system of meaning, so untypical of Ariosto, Spenser introduces material from the *Furioso*, as though to show how much more meaningfully he can use it.

to his ORLANDO FURIOSO, which, notwithstanding, you will needes seeme to emulate, *and hope to ouergo, as you flatly professed* your self in one of your last Letters.' (*Elizabethan Critical Essays*, ed. G. Gregory Smith, Oxford University Press, 1904, Vol. 1, pp. 115–16.

1. Elizabeth A. F. Watson, *Spenser* (Evans, 1967), p. 60.

A striking example is the beginning of Book III, Canto iii, where, as in Ariosto's Canto III (a pretty piece of coincidental effrontery!), Britomart, the woman warrior who is modelled on Bradamante, visits Merlin in his underground dwelling and hears, just as Bradamante does, the prophecy of the illustrious descendants who will spring from her union with Artegall:

> 'Renownèd kings, and sacred Emperours,
> Thy fruitful Offspring, shall from thee descend;
> Brave Captaines, and most mighty warriours,
> That shall their conquests through all lands extend,
> And their decayèd kingdoms shall amend:
> The feeble Britons, broken with long warre,
> They shall upreare, and mightily defend
> Against their forren foe that commes from farre,
> Till universal peace compound all civill jarre.'[1]

Alcina's garden, transferred to Faery, and blended with Armida's from Tasso's *Gerusalemme Liberata*, becomes Acrasia's Bower of Bliss,[2] and the weak-willed and recognizably human Ruggiero is replaced by the personification of Temperance, Sir Guyon. Here Spenser's poetry is much richer and more voluptuous than Ariosto's, as though the uncompromising rejection of pleasure makes it the more alluring. Justly famous as one of the jewels in the crown of English poetry, it was quarried from the *Orlando Furioso*.

Milton, though he had more in common with Tasso, was well acquainted with the romantic epics. His awareness of Pulci has already been mentioned.[3] Boiardo's account of the siege of Albracca has its echo in *Paradise Regained*:

> Such forces met not nor so wide a camp
> When Agrican with all his northern powers
> Besieged Albracca, as romances tell,
> The city of Gallaphrone, from thence to win
> The fairest of her sex, Angelica,
> His daughter, sought by many prowest knights,
> Both paynim and the peers of Charlemagne.[4]

1. *The Faerie Queene*, Book III, Canto iii, 23; cf. *Orlando Furioso*, III. 18.
2. *F.Q.*, Book II, Canto xii, e.g. ll. 77–8.
3. p. 59. He also mentions him in the *Areopagitica*.
4. *Paradise Regained*, III. 337–44.

To Ariosto he pays the supreme compliment of quoting him
at the outset of his mighty enterprise, joining hands with him
in proclaiming the novelty of his theme:

> Sing, heav'nly Muse! . . .
>   I thence
> Invoke thy aid to my advent'rous song,
> That with no middle flight intends to soar
> Above th'Aonian mount, while it pursues
> *Things unattempted yet in prose or rhyme*.[1]

There are reflections, too, of the discoveries of Astolfo on the
moon, that distorting mirror of the world and all its vanities.
Milton translated four lines from this episode:

> Then passed he to a flowery mountain green,
> Which once smelt sweet, now stinks so odiously:
> This was that gift (if you the truth will have)
> That Constantine to good Sylvester gave.[2]

By the middle of the eighteenth century there had been at
least sixty-seven editions of the poem, one of which had been
published in London. Ariosto was so much in fashion that
Handel wrote three operas on subjects taken from the work:
Orlando, *Alcina* and *Ariodante*. The first is on the theme of
Orlando's love for Angelica. In *Alcina*, now the best-known
of the three, the sorceress has a more dramatic, Dido-like
role than in the original. *Ariodante* follows the story of
Ginevra almost exactly. (This opera was successfully revived
recently at Birmingham with Janet Baker in the title role. A
delightful amateur production in the Senate House in Cam-
bridge by David Piper, with Andrew Downes in the part of
Ariodante, captured a great deal of the eighteenth century's
manner of enjoying certain aspects of the poem.[3]) Charles
James Fox, connoisseur and leader of fashion, took 'excessive
delight' in Ariosto, rating him with Homer: 'Homer and

---

1. *Paradise Lost*, I. 6–16; cf. *Orlando Furioso*, I. 2. ii.
2. *Orlando Furioso*, XXXIV. 80, quoted by Milton in *Of Reformation
touching Church of England discipline*.
3. November 1970.

Ariosto have always been my favourites.'[1] Gibbon speaks of
'the boundless variety of the incomparable Ariosto'.[2] Pope
admired and used the *Furioso*; Johnson accorded it his
weighty approbation; even John Wesley, strange as it may
seem, carried it with him on his preaching circuits; Words-
worth took it with him on his walking tour of Switzerland in
1790. Sir Walter Scott is said to have read Ariosto repeatedly
and to have considered him superior to Homer; the greatest
praise he could think of for Goethe was to call him the Ariosto
of Germany. Scott himself, in his turn, was called by Byron
'the Ariosto of the North'.[3] Macaulay took *Orlando Furioso*
with him on his journey to India; Southey read it in his
childhood. Keats, who learnt Italian from it, attempted in
his unfinished poem, *The Cap and Bells*, to emulate Ariosto's
achievement of the epic mood, which seemed to him to come
nearer than the lyric to universal sympathy and penetration.[4]

It was Byron who, above all, possessed an exceptional
capacity for assimilating and recommunicating the spirit of
Ariosto, for capturing his ability to pass from one thing to
another with the greatest ease, to throw out reflections
apparently casual but full of profundity. The light raillery, the
good-natured fun, the tolerant cynicism, the philosophy of
humour are qualities which the mature Byron shares with
Ariosto. T. S. Eliot considered that Byron was at his best
when he was not trying too hard to be poetic.[5] Disengagement
and lightness of touch are among the very qualities which he
could have acquired from reading the *Furioso*. Lines from it
rose easily to his lips, to judge from a well-known anecdote,
according to which, when some acquaintances were expressing
admiration for the Duke of Wellington after the battle of
Waterloo, Byron replied with the quotation:

1. Letter to Lord Holland and Letter to Mr Trotter, *Memorials and
Correspondence of Charles James Fox*, ed. Lord John Russell, Richard Bentley,
Vol. III, p. 102; Vol. IV, p. 444.
2. *Decline and Fall of the Roman Empire*, Bohn edn, Chapter LXX, Vol.
VII, p. 392.
3. *Childe Harold's Pilgrimage*, IV. 40. viii. A somewhat canny Ariosto,
one might say.
4. See Robert Gittings, *The Mask of Keats*, Heinemann, 1956.
5. *Twentieth-Century Interpretation of Don Juan* (New Jersey), 1969.

Fu il vincer sempre mai laudabil cosa,
Vincasi o per fortuna o per ingegno

(To win was always deemed a splendid thing,
Whether it be by fortune or by skill.)[1]

From Byron's spirited translation into verse of the first canto
of Pulci's *Morgante* may be judged how congenial he found the
mixture of levity and gravity which was a feature of the
romantic epics. In his foreword, or 'Advertisement', he
strangely takes Boiardo to task for 'treating too seriously the
narratives of chivalry' (probably because he had read the
Orlando Innamorato in Berni's 'rifacimento', a less lively
version of the work than Boiardo's original) and accords to
Pulci the credit of supplying Ariosto with that element of
gaiety which he finds so judiciously used in the *Furioso*. He
regards all three poets as the inspiration of 'a new style of
poetry very lately sprung up in England'. He refers here in
particular to John Hookham-Frere's *Whistlecraft* and John
Herman Merivale's *Orlando in Roncesvalles*.[2]

As an admirer of Dryden and Pope, Byron had a respect for
well-constructed rhymed verse forms, unlike Milton, who
regarded the use of rhyme for epic as 'trivial, and of no musi-
cal delight'[3] – a trenchant dismissal of the charms of Spenser,
the poet's poet. Byron's awareness of the possibilities of the
octave stanza in English was first awakened by John Hook-
ham-Frere's *The Monks and the Giants*.[4] The Italian romantic
epics themselves, and such eighteenth-century successors as
Forteguerri's *Ricciardetto* and Casti's *Animali Parlanti*, were
to Byron a veritable revelation, showing him the way to a
new medium of satire and burlesque, exactly suited to his
gifts of wit and versatility, and to his taste for anticlimaxes
and incongruities. In *Don Juan*, regarded as the final expression
of Byron's genius, we have the fullest flowering in English

1. XV. I. i–ii.
2. *The Works of Lord Byron*, edited by E. H. Coleridge (John Murray,
1922), Vol. IV, pp. 279–309.
3. Preface to *Paradise Lost*.
4. 1817.

poetry of a spirit traceable ultimately to Ariosto and his pre-
decessors.[1]

Byron's tribute to Ariosto, whom he esteems, with Tasso,
more highly than Petrarch, is contained in *The Prophecy of
Dante*:

> The first will make an epoch of his lyre,
> And fill the earth with feats of Chivalry:
> His Fancy like a rainbow, and his Fire,
> Like that of Heaven, immortal, and his Thought
> Borne onward with a wing that cannot tire;
> Pleasure shall like a butterfly new caught,
> Flutter her lovely pinions o'er his theme,
> And Art itself seem into Nature wrought
> By the transparency of his bright dream.[2]

This was written in 1819. Eleven years later it was shown that
the Italian romantic epics had not only caught the imagination
of English poets but had attracted also serious critical and
scholarly attention. In 1830 Antonio Panizzi, who was by
then living and writing in England, published his *Essay on the
Romantic Narrative Poetry of the Italians*, together with his
editions of *Orlando Innamorato* and *Orlando Furioso*. This was
the first time since the sixteenth century that Boiardo's epic
could be read as he had written it, divested of the classicizing
'improvements' of Francesco Berni.

A hundred years after Byron's tribute to Ariosto, Ernest
Hartley Coleridge, in his edition of Byron's works, com-
mented as follows:

> Historical events may be thrown into the form of prophecy with
> some security, but not so the critical opinions of the *soi-disant*
> prophet. If Byron had lived half a century later, he might have
> placed Ariosto and Tasso after and not before Petrarch.[3]

He might; but then again he might not. Byron was no great
admirer of Petrarch, the poet of unfulfilled love. When
shown his copy of Virgil in the Ambrosian Library in Milan,

1. It was originally Byron's intention to attempt a combination of grave
and gay in *Childe Harold* as he had found it in *Orlando Furioso*. (I am
indebted to the late Professor Geoffrey L. Bickersteth for this observation.)
2. ed. cit., Vol. IV, Canto iii. 110–18.
3. ed. cit., 1922, p. 265, Note 2.

he was more interested in a lock of Lucrezia Borgia's hair. His well-known couplet from *Don Juan* suggests an airy dismissal not only of the likelihood of sustaining love in marriage but also of the melancholy of Petrarch:

> Think you, if Laura had been Petrarch's wife,
> He would have written sonnets all his life ?[1]

Byron's editor is in fact reflecting the dethronement of Ariosto from the height to which he had been elevated a century previously. This change of fortune is commented on by E. W. Edwards, writing in 1924.[2] Although the magnificent critical studies on the Italian Renaissance by John Addington Symonds, and the full-scale biography of Ariosto by Edmund Gardner, *The King of Court Poets*, had long been available,[3] Edwards still found it necessary to account for the comparative indifference to Ariosto in England:

To many people poetry is a substitute for philosophy. Finding formal philosophy too arid or too abstruse, they turn to poetry for the satisfaction of their philosophic questionings, and of that vague, but often powerful, emotion which the spectacle of life and the universe awakens in reflective minds. . . . It is not possible that the *Orlando Furioso* should make any overmastering appeal to such persons. Ariosto's point of view, like every point of view, has its philosophical implications, but the charm and value of his poem depend upon what it is, and not upon what it suggests or implies.[4]

D. S. Carne-Ross, in a sensitive and observant article written thirty years later, comments on the same neglect and suggests similar reasons for it. Ariosto's poetry is not complex

. . . nor is he concerned with elucidating remote and inaccessible areas of experience. No eminent contemporary poet or critic has been attracted to him.[5]

1. *Don Juan*, 111. 8. 7–8.
2. *The Orlando Furioso and its Predecessors*, C.U.P., 1924.
3. Both works were published in 1906. Edmund Gardner also published *Dukes and Poets of Ferrara* in 1904. Symonds calls the *Orlando Furioso* 'this glittering Harlequin of art in the Renaissance, so puzzling to modern critics'.
4. Edwards, op. cit., p. 108.
5. 'Introduction to Ariosto', in *Nine*, published and edited by Peter Russell, Vol. 111, No. 11, Autumn 1951, pp. 113–25.

Carne-Ross is here speaking of English critics, for Bene-detto Croce's essay *Ariosto, Shakespeare e Corneille*[1] exonerates twentieth-century Italians from the charge of indifference. The fourth centenary of Ariosto's death in 1933 had also stimulated the production of a volume of commemorative articles in Italy,[2] but nothing comparable was forthcoming in England. Carne-Ross attributes the lack of interest to a prejudice against Ariosto's material:

... against the paraphernalia of romance epic which is felt to be sadly outmoded. Yet such a prejudice is surely ill-conceived. The creator needs a framework, a body of known material, which he may animate with his vision of life.[3]

In view of the isolation in which he finds himself, Carne-Ross is remarkably percipient concerning the vexed question of Ariosto's so-called 'irony', of which so many critics have made such heavy weather,

... as if he were mainly a humorous or satirical writer (in contrast to 'our sage and serious poet Spenser'). ... 'How entertaining, but how absurd these knight-errants are!' he is pictured as saying. Nothing could be falser. ... Ariosto's 'irony' is not a mocking or cynical scepticism; it is rather what de Gourmont calls *un esprit ouvert à la compréhension multiple des choses*, a certain emotional detachment from the situation in hand. He is never so deeply com-mitted that he cannot withdraw in time from any scene that threatens to get out of hand and so spoil the balance of the poem.[4]

This is an admirable observation, as is also the concluding paragraph in which he sums up the qualities

... by virtue of which Ariosto must be counted a great and truly classical poet: his untroubled objectivity, the complete separation between 'the man who suffers' and 'the mind which creates'; the delighted energy that so tirelessly animates his enormous poem; his power of transmuting the raw material of experience into lucid, harmonious forms. These are qualities that are needed in every age, and never more so than in our own.[5]

1. Laterza, Bari, 1920.   2. *L'Ottava d'Oro*, Mondadori, 1933.
3. Carne-Ross, op. cit., p. 121.   4. idem., op. cit., pp. 121-22.
5. idem., op. cit., p. 125.

Although the *Orlando Furioso* has an honoured place in the syllabus of many an Honours degree in Italian, to those who read for enjoyment and not under compulsion Ariosto is today largely unknown in England. It is hoped that this new translation will convince the general reader how undeserved this long neglect has been.[1]

V. THE TRANSLATION AND ITS PREDECESSORS

Young Mr Francis Osbaldistone, out of favour with his father and anticipating 'some temporary alienation of affection – perhaps a rustication of a few weeks', comforted himself as follows:

. . . I thought [this] would rather please me than otherwise, since it would give me an opportunity of setting about my unfinished version of *Orlando Furioso*, a poem which I longed to render into English verse . . .[2]

As events turned out, he was not able to pursue the experiment for long. Whether his ambition reflected an urge of his creator's is not known, but it was in fact Sir Walter Scott who encouraged his friend William Stewart Rose, the translator of Casti's *Animali Parlanti*, to undertake the task, goading him mercilessly to its completion. It was published between 1823 and 1831 in two volumes. Since that date and the present there have been no other verse translations of *Orlando Furioso* into English.[3]

1. See also *Ariosto, a Preface to 'Orlando Furioso'*, by C. P. Brand, Edinburgh University Press, 1974.
2. Sir Walter Scott, *Rob Roy*, Chapter 11. I am indebted to Mr Adrian Thorpe for drawing my attention to this passage. Others besides Francis Osbaldistone have embarked on a verse rendering but have not continued, among them the explorer and Orientalist Richard Burton. His version of Cantos I, II and the first eighteen stanzas of Canto III is pencilled (very faintly and almost illegibly) on the margins of a copy of the 1883 edition of *Orlando Furioso* illustrated by Gustave Doré. This volume is in the Library of the Royal Anthropological Society, London.
3. A prose translation by A. H. Gilbert was published in 1954 (Duke University Press). A new prose translation by Richard Hodgens is in

The most admired translator of the *Furioso* has long been
Sir John Harington, the Elizabethan courtier, whose version
has recently been re-published in a *de luxe* edition by Robert
McNulty.[1] Lytton Strachey in *Biographical Essays* describes
Harington as

... whimsically Elizabethan, with tossed-back curly hair, a tip-tilted
nose, a tiny point of beard, and a long single ear-ring, falling in
sparkling drops over a ruff of magnificent proportions ... a
courtier, a wit, a scholar, a poet, and a great favourite with the
ladies.

He was Queen Elizabeth's godson; indeed he was a connec-
tion, for his father's first wife was a natural daughter of
Henry VIII.[2] From her, Harington inherited his beautiful
Italian-style house at Kelston in Somersetshire. Queen
Elizabeth once visited him there on her way to Bath, on
which occasion he had felt obliged to rebuild half the house
to do her honour.

It is related that Harington began his translation by render-
ing about seventy stanzas of Canto XXVIII, in which the
landlord of an inn relates a *novella* worthy of Boccaccio at his
bawdiest. The Queen was much put out by what she regarded
as an impudent attempt to corrupt the ladies of her court and
she banished the offender – until he should have translated the
whole poem.

Se non è vero è ben trovato. The first edition of Harington's
translation, dedicated to the Queen, appeared in 1591, just over
half a century after Ariosto's death. 'One can only wonder',

---

process of publication by Pan-Ballantine; Volume 1, containing the story
of Cantos I to XIII, was published in 1973. A complete new prose trans-
lation by Guido Waldman was published by Oxford University Press
in 1974.

1. Clarendon Press, 1972. Mr McNulty takes the view that the *Orlando
Furioso* is 'a very serious work'. In this he is perhaps more influenced by
Harington's introduction and interpretation of the poem than by his
translation, which captures a good deal of the poem's gaiety.

2. His connection with the monarchy was destined to be strengthened
in 1973 by the marriage of his descendant Captain Mark Phillips to
Princess Anne, the daughter of Queen Elizabeth II.

writes Townsend Rich,[1] 'that he, a young and fairly inexperienced poet, could produce such a long work ... in so difficult a verse form and with such apparent ease.' As for the apparent ease, the manuscript shows that Harington revised his translation almost as scrupulously as Ariosto revised the original. It is true he was not an experienced poet. At Eton and at Cambridge almost all the verse he had composed had been in Latin; as a courtier he was esteemed as a witty writer of epigrams.

The success of his translation must in great part be attributed to the qualities of the English language of that period. As Walter Raleigh remarked, 'the speech of that eloquent age ran freely from his tongue, and in the numerous incidental similes and "sentences", or moral aphorisms, he often attains the note of finality'.[2] The material lay to hand, like some gorgeous glittering brocade; it had only to be cut and fashioned to the shape of the original. His rendering of the first stanza, for instance, glows like a tapestry, romance and colour in every word, enhanced by a patina of archaism which lends it for us a particular charm:

> Of Dames, of Knights, of armes, of love's delight,
> Of courtesies, of high attempts I speake,
> Then when the Moores transported all their might
> On Africke seas, the force of France to breake:
> Incited by the youthfull heate and spight
> Of Agramant their king, that vowed to wreake
> The death of King Trayano (lately slaine)
> Upon the Romane Emperor Charlemaine.

Or this, when Ariosto, having described the beauty of Olimpia, naked on the island of Ebuda, says how unworthy any clothing is of her:

> No, not in Florence (though it doth abound
> With rich embroideries of pearle and gold)
> Could any piece of precious stuffe be found
> Of worth to serve to keepe her from the cold. . . .[3]

1. *Harington and Ariosto, a Study in Elizabethan Verse Translation*, Yale U.P., 1940, p. 32.

2. 'Sir John Harington', in *Some Authors*, Oxford, Clarendon, 1923, p. 148.

3. XI. 75.

This is the English which lay ready to Shakespeare's hand for such lines as

> The intertissued robe of gold and pearl.

It is as natural as picking flowers in a garden.

In his letter of dedication to the Queen, Harington offers Her Majesty

... the fruit of the little garden of my slender skill. It hath been the longer in growing and is the lesse worthy the gathering, because my ground is barren and too cold for such dainty Italian fruits, being also perhaps overshaded with trees of some older growth...

Some of those 'dainty Italian fruits' he pruned: his translation is not complete. 'It is true', Walter Raleigh indulgently remarks, 'that Harington, in the right spirit of a poetical translator, omits and alters, compresses and expands.'[1] By this process he has produced a version 728 stanzas shorter than the original; almost every canto has been reduced in length. In spite of this, the level of accuracy is high for his period, when translation was regarded as an extension of the practice of *imitatio*. The changes he made were not only those of compression, however. He sometimes expands, especially in the moralizing passages. He seems to have been less responsive as an artist than Ariosto to the theme of female beauty and to the theme of femininity in general. Wherever Ariosto rails against women, Harington makes his rendering fiercer, more hostile and condemning. The most striking example of his insensitivity to Ariosto's description of female beauty occurs in his translation of the exquisite stanza in which Ruggiero looks down from the sky and sees Angelica chained naked and helpless to the rock, mistaking her at first for a statue.

This stanza, modelled on Ovid's description of Andromeda, is beautifully designed to fit the two pictures: of the statue, lifeless, laid on the unyielding rock, and of the living body, with the moving tears, freshening the lilies and roses of her face, the young fruit of her breasts, and with the breeze stirring her golden tresses – a transition from the inanimate to

1. op. cit., ibid. Harington included fifty stanzas translated by his brother and one by his father.

life, the one contrasted with the other, to the enhancement of both. Here is what Harington does with it:

> Roger at the first had surely thought
> She was some image made of alabaster,
> Or of white marble curiously wrought,
> To show the skilful hand of some great master,
> But viewing nearer he was quickly taught
> She had some parts that were not made of plaster,
> But that her eies did shed such wofull teares,
> And that the wind did wave her golden heares.[1]

Harington was succeeded by William Huggins, whose translation, also in octaves, was published in 1757; by Henry Boyd in 1784; and by John Hoole, whose couplets, published in 1783, earned him Scott's scornful description as 'the noble transmuter of the gold of Ariosto into lead'. This would have been more applicable to Scott's own friend William Stewart Rose, whose accurate translation, in octaves, is curiously flat and lifeless. Curiously so, because he was of the period and the circle which should have enabled him to capture the lively spirit of the original. Byron's translation of the first canto of Pulci's *Morgante*, which had been published six years previously, was a great deal more spirited and engaging. Byron would probably have been the ideal translator of Ariosto. Had he undertaken the task, the *Orlando Furioso* might not have lost its hold on English readers.

To translate it into verse in the present age may seem a rash and thankless enterprise. There are many warning and discouraging voices. J. Shield Nicholson in his *Life and Genius of Ariosto* speaks of the 'impossible task of a verbatim translation in the original octave stanza'.[2] Townsend Rich says that the octave, a verse form well suited to the Italian language, is unsuitable for English, with its masculine endings and paucity of rhyming words. This is like the perennial insistence on the unsuitability of writing *terza rima* (triple rhyme) in English. In itself the octave presents no insuperable difficulties. Indeed, it presents fewer probably than the Spenserian stanza. The contemporary poet James Gordon uses it supremely well as a

1. x. 96.   2. 1914; pp. vi–vii.

medium for such themes as sailing and flying.[1] The Italian hendecasyllable can be perfectly well rendered by the English five-foot heroic line, which has long been the unit of narrative verse, of lyric poetry, of poetic drama.

Although Ariosto at many points in his work raised his art to a very high level of poetry indeed, long passages are sheer, unadorned narrative, made up of everyday Italian. He is often idiomatic and conversational, sometimes even jaunty. He has no hesitation in changing from one tense to another, if it suits him to do so, or in introducing popular or proverbial sayings. It would be a mistake to heighten where he does not heighten, or to make remote from daily usage what he has chosen to make natural and colloquial. At the same time, a certain dignity has to be maintained; there is a minimum indispensable tone of epic; inversions of the spoken word-order, often unavoidable, are sometimes desirable, as lending a recitative tone. But where Ariosto is concrete and factual, using unadorned realism, the modern translator can quite well follow his example by drawing on the sturdy stock of English realistic vocabulary. There is such an instance when Orlando, in the cave where Isabella is held captive by the pirates, seizes a stone table and flings it at the crowd who cower in a corner:

> Within the cave there was a slab, about
> Two palms in thickness, broad as it was long,
> Balanced upon a block, rough-hewn and stout.
> For meals that mob sat round it, twenty strong.
> Not one of them could give a warning shout
> Before the Count Orlando at the throng,
> Packed tightly in the cave, that heavy table
> Had seized and flung as hard as he was able.
>
> It crushes here a breast and there a head.
> It shatters limbs, and paunches splits agape.
> Some of the mob are lamed and some are dead,
> But all who can still walk try to escape.
> As when a heavy boulder on a bed
> Of vipers crashes, leaving in poor shape

1. e.g. *The Battle of Britain* (a forthcoming publication); cf. his sonnet sequence, *Epitaph for a Squadron*, A. H. Stockwell, 1965.

Their writhing bodies, lately preened and sunned,
So were those cowering villains crushed and stunned.[1]

There is nothing about the English language which is inherently inappropriate to the Italian of Ariosto. Other Italian poets are a great deal more difficult to translate: Dante, *par excellence*, or Petrarch, or Leopardi. William Roscoe considered that 'the fertility of [Ariosto's] invention, the liveliness of his imagery, the natural ease and felicity of his diction ... [his] bold and vigorous ideas' made it possible for him to be transfused into another language and to 'bear without injury all change of climate'.[2] This is perhaps too sanguine, especially in view of his opinion that Ariosto's works had 'contributed more than those of any other author to diffuse a true poetical spirit throughout Europe'. Certainly the responsibility is very great, but the English language, infinitely rich in resources, is more than equal to the task.[3] The inheritance from Elizabethan English has provided a fertile admixture of Italian elements, with which the poetic diction of the English Renaissance was vivified. Twentieth-century English also possesses, and is unashamed to use, a direct, unrhetorical vocabulary and style corresponding closely to the unrhetorical elements which are to be found in the *Furioso*. It is the mingling of, the balance between, the artistically wrought, the elaborate, the heightened, and the direct, earthy, homely, colloquial expressiveness which makes the *Furioso* such a vital and human work. The English language, with its dual Anglo-Saxon and Latin heritage, offers a range and flexibility, far beyond that of French or German, for instance, which makes it a justifiable medium in which to try to render Ariosto.

It is true that Italian has a greater number of pure (perfect) rhymes than English, but the real difficulty is the preponderance in English of masculine rhymes which tend to be obtrusive. The translator has to bear this in mind and avoid monotony in the distribution of the main stresses, arranging occasionally for the rhymes to be heard, as it were, in the

1. XIII. 37–8.
2. Roscoe, op. cit., Vol. II.
3. Whether the translator may be, is of course another question.

background, just outlining the structure of the stanza, as in
the following:

> He met two squadrons; leading one of them
> Was Manilard, a white-haired veteran,
> Norizia's king; when sound in wind and limb,
> He was a formidable foe; a man
> More suited now for counsel, he may seem,
> Than action. Next, of all the African
> Commanders, King Alzirdo's held to be
> The very paragon of chivalry.[1]

Ariosto's unadorned and unemphatic stanzas can be matched
in English by words which speak, as his do, for themselves, as
in this simple and tender evocation of the passage from winter
to early spring:

> When timid streams begin once more to flow,
> By gentle warmth released from icy bonds,
> When grasses greener in the meadows grow.
> And bushes clothe themselves in tender fronds . . .[2]

or in this plain understatement of the heroism of Orlando:

> I well believe that all the winter long
> Many a noble deed Orlando did,
> Which I would gladly tell of in my song,
> But to this day all news of them is hid;
> For he was readier to right the wrong
> Than waste his breath in idle talk; indeed,
> His brave exploits were never known about
> Unless some witness gave the tidings out.
>
> He passed the winter months so quietly
> That nothing certain of him then was known;
> But when the Sun once more in company
> With the mild Ram, in March and April, shone,
> And gentle Zephyr imperceptibly
> Led the sweet Spring a few more paces on,
> Orlando's deeds to blossom then were seen
> Amid new flowers and the tender green.[3]

1. XII. 69.   2. ibid. 72. i–iv.   3. XI. 81–2.

It is permissible and, in so demanding a task, only reasonable, to make full use of the wide range of impure rhymes and assonance which the phonology of English provides and of which all our major poets have availed themselves. The following comment made on this matter by Dorothy L. Sayers in the Introduction to her translation of Dante's *Inferno* is very much to the point:

English is 'poor in rhymes' because it is remarkably rich in vowel-sounds. Of these, Italian possesses seven only, all 'pure' and unmodified by the succeeding consonants. For English, on the other hand, the *Shorter O.E.D.* lists no fewer than fifty-two native varieties, shading into one another by imperceptible degrees. This phenomenon results from the fact that most English vowels are diphthongs to start with and nearly all are subtly modified by a following consonant, particularly by a following 'r'. Indeed, in Southern English, this self-effacing consonant when it appears at the end of a word seems to exist for the sole purpose of performing this duty to its vowel, dying without a murmur when its work is done, after the manner of certain male spiders. (In Northern English and in the Celtic dialects the 'r' is more tenacious of life.) In consequence of all this, 'pure' rhymes are scarce in English; but 'impure' rhymes are frequent and legitimate, producing many curious melodic effects which have no parallel in the verse of pure-vowelled languages.[1]

A further difficulty concerning rhyme in modern English (especially perhaps the rhymed couplet) is that in some readers it tends to arouse embarrassment, as though blank verse were respectable and rhyming forms were not. This may be a heritage from Milton, who said that rhyme was 'the invention of a barbarous age, to set off wretched matter and lame metre', and claimed to have released the heroic poem 'from the troublesome and modern bondage of rhyming'.[2] Uncertainty as to the status of rhyme is increased too by the use of it for light verse, sometimes skilful and polished, as in the hands of W. S. Gilbert, Lewis Carroll, Edward Lear, or E. C. Bentley, for instance, but sometimes trivial and plebeian, as in popular limericks and pantomime. Blank verse has no such disconcertingly vulgar relations.

1. *Hell,* Penguin Classics, p. 57, fn. 1.
2. *Paradise Lost,* Preface, 'The Verse'.

But rhymed poetry has venerable antecedents. Expert practitioners in the learned tradition, such as Dryden, Pope, Byron and Tennyson, are spoken of nowadays with renewed respect. The natural, song-like quality of English country rhyme has been miraculously preserved in the unlearned lyrics of John Clare, a poet now held in ever-increasing esteem. Among twentieth-century writers, W. H. Auden was alive to the magical effect of rhyme intermingled with the natural cadences of speech; Dylan Thomas delighted in the intricacies of a complex rhyming pattern;[1] it is propitious also for the re-instatement of rhyme that in the year of the fifth centenary of Ariosto's birth, in honour of which this new rhymed translation is presented, the poet laureate should be Sir John Betjeman, a master-craftsman of rhythm and rhyme.

1. See his poem 'Do not go gentle into that good night', *Collected Poems*, J. M. Dent & Sons, 1952 (1967 reprint, p. 116).

ACKNOWLEDGEMENTS

TOWARDS the end of his long poem Ariosto imagines that friends are standing on the quayside to welcome him home after his long voyage. With the publication of this first part of my translation, I have reached only a half-way port of call; but already, like Ariosto, I am aware how much I owe to the help and encouragement of friends.

First of all, I should like to thank Dr Geoffrey Lee, whose exceptionally wide reading and phenomenal memory have enabled him to be of great assistance to me. With heroic perseverance he has scrutinized the first draft of every canto and has suggested innumerable improvements. Dr George Purkis, my colleague for fourteen years in the compilation of *The Cambridge Italian Dictionary*, has also read the entire work, canto by canto, and has given me most valuable criticism and help. Dr Richard Webster, the neo-Thomist philosopher, one of whose early loves was poetry, has listened to and read several cantos and has saved me from many ineptitudes. The late Professor Geoffrey L. Bickersteth, who gave me such generous help in my task of completing the translation of Dante's *Paradiso* after the death of Dorothy L. Sayers, once again came to my assistance with advice and encouragement. Professor C. P. Brand, whom I am proud to claim as a former pupil at Cambridge University, has, with a nice reversal of roles, advised me about several aspects of the poem, in general and in detail. James Gordon, experienced both in yachting and in the writing of octaves, has rescued me from many misunderstandings of the nautical stanzas. Wilfrid Scott-Giles, Fitzalan, Poursuivant Extraordinary, has guided me through the intricacies of the heraldic array in Canto x; it is to him that I owe the information in the Notes showing the connection between the emblems of the British troops and the actual armorial bearings of the sixteenth century which Ariosto may have had in mind. I am grateful to Elizabeth A. F. Watson for her advice on the influence of Ariosto on English literature and for permission to quote from her book on Spenser; and to Professor Geoffrey Bullough for information regarding the sources of *Much Ado About Nothing*.

There are many celebrated illustrations to the *Orlando Furioso*, from Tiepolo's frescoes of the episode of Angelica and Medoro, to Doré's engravings. For the first time (so far as I know), maps and diagrams are here provided to help the reader to follow the more complicated journeys and, in particular, the siege of Paris. I wish to express my thanks to Mr Arthur Shelley for the skill with which he has drawn all the visual aids. I am also indebted to Professor J. R. Hale for his help in tracing the movements of troops outside the walls of Ariosto's Paris.

Miss Sylvia Bruce, as copy-editor, has given me most generous and valuable help. I am indebted to her for many excellent suggestions. It will be owing to her skill and care, as much as to Astolfo's visit to the moon, that Orlando will eventually emerge sane and co-ordinated at the end of the work. I owe thanks also to Mr James Cochrane for his editorial advice, as well as to Mr Will Sulkin and to Miss Christine Higgins, of Penguin Books. I am grateful as well to Mrs Betty Radice, who first read Canto 1, in an early draft, and encouraged me to proceed; and to Professor Gwyn Griffiths, to whom the final draft of Cantos 1–xxiii was submitted and who gave this new verse rendering his generous approval.

Many of my friends and relations have helped me, more than they perhaps realize, by allowing me to read parts of my translation out loud to them. Of this invited (and sometimes captive) audience, I should like to thank especially Dr Kathleen Wood-Legh, Mrs Judy Rawson, Miss Isabel Hitchman, Miss Audrey Beecham and Dr Catherine Storr. Of my family, I wish to thank my husband, Professor Lewis Thorpe, who as well as listening has advised me on Arthurian matters and allowed me to quote from his translation of Einhard's *Vita Karoli*; my aunt, Edith G. Reynolds, my mother, Barbara Florac, my daughter, Kerstin Lewis, and my son, Adrian

Thorpe, have all patiently listened, advised and sympathized; to them all I offer loving thanks.

To Mrs Gwen Thimann I owe particular thanks for the personal interest she has taken in the unfolding of the tale, as well as for her unfailing help over many years.

I hope that all these generous-minded people will be pleased by the work which they have helped me to bring forth. My aim in undertaking it has been to give pleasure. If I have succeeded in doing so, it will be largely owing to the companionship I have been lucky enough to enjoy, and which is so much needed ... *tantae molis erat.*

Nottingham, Cambridge   BARBARA REYNOLDS
and the Veneto
31 July 1973

That I have all along intended, saved, and vanquished as you shall all at once hear, that is . . . . .

To this Owen Tudenol I owe . . . the thanks for the personal interest he has taken [unclear] . . .

[illegible lines]

. . . self, all the . . . good people will be pleased by the work . . . will bring with it . . .

. . . succeeded in doing so, it will be . . . own . . . . . . have been luck enough to enjoy . . . which . . . so much esteem. I am, your . . .

Wingham Chandlery,   BENJAMIN STADLER
[unclear]
July 1073

CHARACTERS AND DEVICES

The following lists of characters, monsters, horses, weapons and magical devices refer to the first half of the poem, i.e. Cantos I–XXIII. Except for Charlemagne, the names of the chief characters are given in the Italian form used by Ariosto.[1]

For further information see also Index of Proper Names and Notes to the Cantos.

THE PRINCIPAL WARRIORS

CHRISTIANS

Charlemagne, son of Pepin, Emperor of Christendom, King of France and commander-in-chief of the Christian forces

Orlando, his nephew, also called Anglante or the Count

Rinaldo, cousin of Orlando, also called Montalbano or Montaubon

Bradamante, sister of Rinaldo; also called the Maid

Astolfo, son of the King of England

Zerbino, son of the King of Scotland

Dudone

Iroldo

Prasildo

Ariodante, Duke of Albany

Lurcanio, his brother, Earl of Angus

Namo, Duke of Bavaria

Otto, King of England

Brandimarte (Saracen, baptized by Orlando)

1. As regards pronunciation readers may wish to know that in Italian the final e is sounded, e.g. Agricane has four syllables. It is permissible to omit the final vowel or syllable and Ariosto frequently does so, e.g. Brunel(lo), Brigliador(o)

Sansonetto, son of the King of Persia (baptized by Orlando)
Oliver
Grifone, son of Oliver
Aquilante, son of Oliver
Guidone Selvaggio, bastard son of Count Aymon
Salamone, King of Brittany
Ugier, the Dane
Androponos, priest
Leonetto, Duke of Lancaster
Earl of Warwick
Duke of Gloucester
Duke of Clarence
Duke of York
Duke of Norfolk
Earl of Kent
Earl of Pembroke
Duke of Suffolk
Earl of Essex
Earl of Northumberland
Earl of Arundel
Marquess of Berkeley
Earl of March
Earl of Richmond
Earl of Dorset
Earl of Hampton
Earl of Devonshire
Earl of Worcester
Earl of Derby
Earl of Oxfordshire
Bishop of Bath
Duke of Somerset
Duke of Buckingham
Earl of Salisbury
Earl of Abergavenny
Earl of Shrewsbury
Earl of Huntly
Duke of Mar
Alcabrun (?The Cameron)
Duke of Transforth

Earl of Buchan
Earl of Forbes
Earl of Errol
Earl of Kildare
Earl Desmond
Moratto, leader of forces from the Far North

PAGANS[1]

Africans

Agramante, commander-in-chief of pagan forces, son
　of Troiano
Ruggiero, son of Ruggiero II (King of Reggio) and of
　Galaciella (daughter of Agolante of Africa)
Rodomonte, King of Sarza and Algiers, son of Ulieno
Dardinello, son of Almonte and cousin of Agramante
Marfisa, twin sister of Ruggiero
Sobrino
Marbalusto, King of Oran
Arganio
Buraldo
Ormida
Brunello
Farurante
Libanio
Soridano
Dorilone
Puliano
Agricalte
Malabuferso
Finadurro
Balastro
Corineo
Caico
Rimedonte
Balinfronte

　1. The terms pagan, infidel, Saracen and Moor are used for Africans
and Spaniards; the Orientals are called pagans or infidels.

Clarindo
Baliverzo
Prusione
Manilardo
Alzirdo

Spaniards

Marsilio, King of Spain
Falsirone, his brother
Ferraù, nephew of Marsilio, son of Falsirone
Isoliero, brother of Ferraù
Dorifebo
Balugante
Grandonio
Madarasso
Stordilano
Tessira
Baricondo
Serpentino
Matalista
Bianzardino
Balinverno
Malgarino
Morgante
Malzarise
Folicone, bastard son of Marsilio
Archidante
(L)argalifa
Analardo
Doriconte
The Emir
Langhirano
Malagur

Orientals

Sacripante, King of Circassia
Gradasso, King of Sericana
Mandricardo, King of Tartary, son of Agricane

TRAITOR TO THE CHRISTIAN SIDE

Pinabello, nephew of Ganelon (Gano), of the Maganzan family

PRINCIPAL WOMEN

Angelica, daughter of Great Khan of Cathay; loved and pursued by numerous knights, both Christian and pagan; marries Medoro

Bradamante, daughter of Count Aymon of Montalbano; sister of Rinaldo; loves and is loved by Ruggiero, whom she ultimately marries; Christian warrior

Ginevra, daughter of King of Scotland; sister of Zerbino; marries Ariodante

Dalinda, lady-in-waiting to Ginevra; betrayed by Polinesso

Fiordiligi, daughter of King of Lizza; wife of Brandimarte

Olimpia, daughter of Count of Holland; marries Bireno, is abandoned by him; marries King of Ireland

Isabella, daughter of King of Galicia; loves and is loved by Zerbino

Doralice, daughter of King of Granada; betrothed to Rodomonte; seduced by Mandricardo

Lucina, daughter of King of Cyprus; wife of Norandino

Gabrina, wife of Argeo; betrayer of Filandro

Orrigille, loved by Grifone; paramour of Martano

Orontea, Queen of Alessandretta

Marfisa, sister of Ruggiero; pagan warrior

SORCERERS AND SORCERESSES

Evil	*Good*
Atlante	Merlin
Alcina	Melissa
Morgana	Logistilla

SUPERNATURAL BEINGS

God
Archangel Michael
Ghost of Argalia
Demons in semblance of Bradamante's descendants
Sprite conjured by hermit
Demon conjured by hermit
Proteus

PERSONIFICATIONS

Andronica (fortitude)
Fronesia (prudence)
Dicilla (justice)
Sofrosina (temperance)
Discord
Fraud
Jealousy
Pride
Hypocrisy
Sleep
Silence
Sloth
Laziness
Oblivion

MONSTERS

Alcina's frontier guards
Erifilla
Sea orc
Land orc
Caligorante
Orrilo

HORSES

Baiardo

Rinaldo's horse, given to him by Charlemagne when he was dubbed knight. He is enchanted, possesses human intelligence, is of exceptional swiftness and devoted to his master. He is first introduced in the Old French epic *Renaus*, and is to be found also in Pulci's *Morgante* and Boiardo's *Orlando Innamorato*.

Brigliadoro

Orlando's horse, called Veillantif in the *Chanson de Roland* and Vegliantino in the Italian romances, in which he is won by Orlando from Almonte. It was Boiardo who re-named him Brigliadoro.

Frontino

Ruggiero's horse, belonging originally to Sacripante, when he was named Frontalatte. Boiardo relates that he was stolen by Brunello when Sacripante was riding to Albracca and taken to Africa and given to Ruggiero.

Rabicano

Astolfo's horse, belonging originally to Argalia, the brother of Angelica. He is supernatural, his dam and sire being compounded respectively of fire and wind. He appears in Boiardo's epic.

Hippogriff

The winged horse, unnamed, born of a mare and a griffin. Others of his species, though rare, are to be found in the Rhiphaean mountains. Atlante captured him by enchantment and trained and bridled him.

There is a magic winged horse in Boiardo's epic, but Ariosto insists that the hippogriff is a product of nature.

CHIEF WEAPONS
AND ITEMS OF ARMOUR

SWORDS

Balisarda
Ruggiero's sword. Boiardo relates that it was made by enchantment by the fairy Falerina to kill Orlando, who stole it from her. It was then stolen by Brunello, who gave it to Ruggiero.

Durindana
Orlando's sword, first mentioned in the *Chanson de Roland*, where it is named Durendal. Boiardo says that it belonged to Hector and passed into the possession of Almonte, from whom Orlando gained it when he slew him in Aspromonte.

Fusberta
Rinaldo's sword, named Froberge or Floberge in the Old French epic *Renaus*.

HELMETS

Argalia's, retained in breach of faith by Ferraù and lost in a stream

Orlando's, won by him from Almonte and later seized by Ferraù

Rinaldo's, won from Mambrino

Rodomonte's, inherited from Nimrod

Mandricardo's (Hector's), won in Syria

SPURS OF ST GEORGE

Given to Astolfo by Sansonetto, Viceroy of Jerusalem

LANCE

Astolfo's magic lance, which unseats all those it strikes; it belonged originally to Argalia.

ARMOUR

Rodomonte's armour, inherited from Nimrod, is made of dragon's skin.
Marfisa, Serpentino and Grifone wear enchanted armour.
Orlando, invulnerable except in the soles of his feet, wears armour only for form's sake.
Mandricardo wears Hector's armour, won in Syria.
Gradasso's armour is enchanted.

ARTILLERY

Cimosco uses cannon against Olimpia's defenders. Orlando casts it into the North Sea.

MAGIC DEVICES

ATLANTE'S SHIELD

Its beam renders unconscious all those whom it strikes; when not in use it is kept concealed in a silk cloth. It is used first by Atlante against Gradasso and Ruggiero. He tries to use it against Bradamante but is unsuccessful. Ruggiero obtains it and uses it against a servitor of Alcina, against Alcina's fleet, against the sea orc, and, inadvertently, against Aquilante, Grifone and Guidone Selvaggio. Ruggiero then throws it into a well.

THE MAGIC RING

If worn on the finger, it counteracts all other spells; if put into the mouth, it renders invisible the person who thus holds it. Belonging to Angelica, it was stolen from her by Brunello. It is taken from him by Bradamante, who uses it to counteract the spell of Atlante; she gives it to Melissa, who gives it to Ruggiero to enable him to escape from the enchantment of Alcina; he gives it to Angelica to protect her from the beam of the magic shield which he turns upon the sea orc. She uses it to become invisible, to escape from Ruggiero and later from Orlando, Sacripante and Ferraù. She finally uses it to escape from the deranged Orlando.

THE MAGIC HORN

It is given to Astolfo by Logistilla. Its sound renders all hearers helpless with terror. Astolfo uses it against enemies in Arabia, against the giant Caligorante, against the warrior women of Orontea's kingdom, in Atlante's palace of illusions, and against the harpies.

THE MAGIC BOOKS

Melissa's, by means of which she conjures demons
Atlante's book of spells, by means of which he conjures invisible weapons
Hermit's book, by means of which he conjures a sprite
Astolfo's book of counter-spells, given to him by Logistilla, which he consults to defeat Orrilo and to break the spell of Atlante's palace of illusions.

THE MAGIC NET

Made of strands of steel, it wraps itself round its victims at the slightest touch. It was made by Vulcan to capture Mars and Venus. Mercury stole it to catch the nymph Chloris in it. It was then kept in a temple in Egypt, whence it was stolen by the giant Caligorante. He tries to catch Astolfo in it but stumbles into it himself on being terrified by a blast on Astolfo's magic horn. Astolfo afterwards presents it to Sansonetto, the viceroy of Jerusalem.

ANONYMOUS CHARACTERS
IN ORDER OF APPEARANCE

Messenger from Marseilles in search of Bradamante
Hermit who betrays Angelica
Lady loved by Pinabello

Dwarf who accompanies Ruggiero and Gradasso to
  Atlante's castle
Host at an inn
Monks at an abbey in Scotland
Two ruffians who attempt to murder Dalinda
Traveller who sees Ariodante leap into the sea
Hermit who gives shelter to Ariodante
Two damsels who lead Ruggiero into Alcina's palace
Servitor of Alcina who attacks Ruggiero
Three damsels who try to lure Ruggiero back to Alcina
Pilot who brings Ruggiero to Logistilla
Damsel who asks Orlando to combat Ebudans
Old man who leads Orlando to Olimpia
Two youths who help Olimpia to murder Arbante
Daughter of King Cimosco
Pirates who capture Isabella
Messenger who brings Charlemagne news of Rodomonte's
  destruction of Paris
Squire who brings Agramante news of slaughter of
  troops of Norizia and Tremisen
Shepherd who gives shelter to Doralice and Mandricardo
Dwarf sent as messenger by Doralice to Rodomonte
Hermit who advises Astolfo not to approach Caligorante
Two ladies who rescued Grifone and Aquilante as infants
Traveller from Greece who has news of Orrigille
Knight who tells the story of Norandino
Wife of the land orc
Armenian merchant who found Marfisa's arms
Sea captain who gives passage to warriors from Tripoli
  to Luni
Lady who seeks help for Ricciardetto
Old man who warns visitors to Pinabello's castle
Scottish knight who wounds Medoro
Shepherd and his wife who give shelter to Angelica and
  Medoro
Squires, shield-bearers, attendants, soldiers, guards, pilots,
  sailors, merchants, peasants, crowds *passim*

ORLANDO FURIOSO

CANTO I

1

Of ladies, cavaliers, of love and war,
Of courtesies and of brave deeds I sing,
In times of high endeavour when the Moor
Had crossed the sea from Africa to bring
Great harm to France, when Agramante swore
In wrath, being now the youthful Moorish king,
To avenge Troiano, who was lately slain,
Upon the Roman Emperor Charlemagne.

2

And of Orlando I will also tell
Things unattempted yet in prose or rhyme,
Of the mad frenzy that for love befell
One who so wise was held in former time,
If she who my poor talent by her spell
Has so reduced that I resemble him,
Will grant me now sufficient for my task:
The wit to reach the end is all I ask.

3

Most generous and Herculean son,
The ornament and splendour of our age,
Ippolito, pray take as for your own
Your humble servant's gift, that men may gauge
The debt I owe to you, which words alone
Cannot repay, nor ink upon the page.
And let it not be said my gift is small,
For giving this, my lord, I give my all.

4

Among the heroes most deserving praise
Whose catalogue of names I now prepare,
Ruggiero I will bring before your gaze,
The founder of the lineage you bear.
His valiant deeds which time cannot erase
I will make known to you if you'll lend ear
And from your lofty thoughts your mind incline
To grant admittance to this tale of mine.

5

Orlando who for long had loved in vain,
Seeking the fair Angelica to please,
India, Media and the Tartar plain
And all the booty of his victories
Had left, to bring her to the West again
Where, at the foothills of the Pyrenees,
He found the host of France and Germany
Encamped with Charlemagne in company,

6

To make two monarchs bitterly repent
The folly of their arrogant advance:
The African who from his continent
Had mustered every sword and every lance,
And King Marsilio, on havoc bent,
Who rallied Spain to devastate fair France.
Orlando at this point rejoined the fray,
But scarce had done so than he rued the day;

7

For then it was his dearest love he lost.
See now how often human judgement errs!
She whom he championed from coast to coast
In endless combat, meeting no reverse,
Is taken from him now amid a host
Of friends, on his own ground, and, what is worse,
Without a sword being drawn. King Charles the wise
To quench a flame this remedy applies.

8

Some days before, a rivalry arose
Between Rinaldo and his cousin, Count
Orlando, who both languish in the throes
Of love upon Angelica's account;
Than hers no greater beauty either knows.
Charles, to forestall their enmity, the fount
Of the dispute, the fair Angelica,
Consigned to Namo of Bavaria,

9

Pledging that he would grant her in reward
To which of them in the impending fight
More infidels impaled upon his sword,
Excelling thus in prowess and in might.
Events, alas! with prayers did not accord,
For scattered was the Christian host in flight.
The duke, with others, prisoner was taken
And his pavilion in the rout forsaken.

10

Angelica did not prolong her stay.
She, who was promised as a victor's bride,
Into the saddle leapt and straight away,
Choosing her moment well, set out to ride.
She had foreseen the fortune of the day
Would bring disaster to the Christian side.
Along a forest glade she took her course
And met a cavalier without a horse.

11

His helmet on his head, in full cuirass,
Girt with his sword and on his arm a shield,
As swift as if bare-limbed she saw him pass,
Like one who for the red cloak led the field.
No shepherdess who spied amid the grass
A cruel serpent did to terror yield
More than Angelica, who quickly turned
As soon as she the knight on foot discerned.

12

He was a valiant paladin of France,
The son of Aymon, lord of Montaubon,
Whose horse, Baiardo, by a strange mischance,
Had slipped from his restraining hand and gone.
This knight who now approached at the first glance
Had recognized, though from afar, the one
Who with angelic beauty unsurpassed
In amorous enchantment held him fast.

13

The lovely damsel turns her palfrey round
And through the wood full pelt she gallops off.
Whether in clearings or where briars abound,
Not caring if the going's smooth or rough,
She lets her plunging palfrey choose the ground:
She, pale and trembling, scarce has wits enough.
Deep in a savage wood, as in a dream,
She roams, and comes at last upon a stream.

14

Seated upon the bank was Ferraù.
Covered with dust and sweating freely still,
From battle he but recently withdrew.
To rest and quench his thirst had been his will.
This cost him, though, more trouble than he knew,
For, stooping hastily to drink his fill,
He let his helmet tumble in the stream;
Try as he might, it still eluded him.

15

The maiden then arrived upon the scene,
Her shrieks of terror ringing loud and clear.
And at her voice up leapt the Saracen,
Gazing upon her face as she drew near.
Beyond all doubt he recognized her then,
Though she was pallid and distraught with fear.
Of her vicissitudes he had no inkling,
And there she is before him in a twinkling.

16

He was a gallant cavalier, in whom
Love burned no less than in the cousins' breast,
And proved, despite his lack of helm and plume,
A brave defender, equal to the test.
Drawing his sword, he ran with shouts of doom
Where Montaubon, unknowing, onward pressed.
The knights to one another were not strangers.
They'd vied in many trials of strength and dangers.

17

Cruel are then the deadly blows that hail,
Soon as the knights close in with weapons bare,
Piercing the armour and the coats of mail
And sturdy bucklers which no better fare.
Leaving the combatants in dire travail,
To urge her palfrey onwards her sole care,
The damsel claps her heels against his sides
And over hill and dale away she rides.

18

The warriors with long endurance seek
To overcome each other, but in vain.
Each through the other's guard attempts to break,
But neither can for long advantage gain.
Young Montalbano is the first to speak,
Asking a parley of the knight of Spain,
Like one whose heart, on fire with love, will burst
Unless emotion find an outlet first:

19

'You strive to do me harm, but I will prove
That on yourself you also vent your ire;
For if it happens that two rays, as of
The rising sun, have set your heart on fire,
To hinder me will not advance your love.
If I am vanquished or I here expire,
This will not make the lovely damsel yours:
While we delay she takes another course.

20

'If you still love her, would it not be wise
To intercept her path without delay
And, coming thus upon her by surprise,
Detain her ere she gallops far away?
Let her then be awarded as a prize
To which of us by swords shall win the day;
Else no result, as far as I can see,
Will come of our long strife but injury.'

21

The pagan found this offer not displeasing,
And so it was the contest was deferred.
The enmity between the rivals ceasing,
By hate and wrath they were no longer stirred.
The pagan, from a tree his horse releasing,
The son of Aymon, who at first demurred,
Prevailed upon to mount behind him pillion
To search for her who fled the duke's pavilion.

22

O noble chivalry of knights of yore!
Here were two rivals, of opposed belief,
Who from the blows exchanged were bruised and sore,
Aching from head to foot without relief,
Yet to each other no resentment bore.
Through the dark wood and winding paths, as if
Two friends, they go. Against the charger's sides
Four spurs are thrust until the road divides.

23

They gaze all round but cannot tell which way
Angelica has taken, for the mark
Of hoofs in both directions made that day
Seeming identical, they're in the dark.
The cavaliers but a brief time delay:
Along two paths, as Fortune prompts, they hark,
One here, one there. The pagan round about
Meanders and returns where he set out.

24

He came once more upon that very bank
Where he had dropped his helmet from his head.
Hope of Angelica, if he were frank,
Was now remote, so he resolved instead
To try to raise the helm from where it sank;
And, stepping to the edge, began to wade.
Little he knows the work he'll have on hand,
So deep the helm is buried in the sand.

25

First from a tree a branch he pulled and stripped,
Shaping and smoothing it to form a pole,
Which delicately in the stream he dipped,
Poking with care in every nook and hole,
Although with patience he was ill-equipped.
Boredom at last began to try his soul,
When, rising from the stream – a gruesome sight –
He saw the head and shoulders of a knight.

26

In battle-armour he was fully clad,
Save that his head was bare; from his right fist
A helmet swung, the same the pagan had
In all this time been probing for and missed.
To Ferraù he spoke, irate and sad:
'Disloyal knight! How long will you persist?
You leave this helmet here so grudgingly
Which once you promised to restore to me?

27

'Think back to the occasion when you slew
The brother of Angelica, for I
Am he; my arms, you will recall, you threw
Into the stream; ere many days went by
You promised you would throw my helmet too.
If Fortune intervenes to ratify
Your vow, why do you grieve? But if you must,
Grieve only that you failed to keep your trust.

28

'If a fine helmet you aspire to get,
With knightly honour let the deed be done:
Orlando wears a splendid helm, or yet
Rinaldo a perhaps still finer one,
The former from Almonte when he met
His death, the latter from Mambrino, won.
Leave me this helmet, pledged to me by you,
And make your promise in effect come true.'

29

So startled is the Saracen of Spain,
His hair stands up erect and from his face
All vestiges of colour seem to drain.
He tries to speak but can emit no trace
Of sound. That Argalìa, whom he'd slain
Not long ago and in this very place,
Should thus rebuke him for his breach of faith
Sets him ablaze inside and out with wrath.

30

He had no time to think of an excuse.
The truth of what was said must be allowed.
He stood and not a word could he produce.
Pierced to the heart with shame, his head he bowed.
He then and there determined he would use
(And by his mother solemnly he vowed)
No helmet but the one in Aspromonte
Orlando pulled from off the proud Almonte.

31

This vow, to tell the truth, he duly kept;
That this was best, experience now taught him.
Morose and sullen, on his horse he leapt,
To chase the paladin until he caught him.
For many days he scarcely ate or slept,
Now here, now there, now everywhere he sought him.
As for Rinaldo, that's another tale,
For he set off upon a different trail.

32

Rinaldo had not travelled far, when lo!
He saw his charger galloping ahead.
'Baiardo! my Baiardo! ho, there, wo!
Without you weary is the road I tread.'
The horse, a deaf ear turning, did not slow
Its pace, but galloped further off instead.
Rinaldo, fuming, followed from afar;
But let us follow fair Angelica.

33

Through dark and terrifying woods she flees,
In lonely, wild, uncultivated places.
The rustle of the undergrowth, the trees,
Beech, rowan, elm, her terror interlaces,
Weaving an evil dream in which she sees
Of all she most abhors the dreaded traces.
O'er hill and dale, each shadow a reminder,
She seems to feel Rinaldo close behind her;

34

Just like a fallow fawn or new-born roe
Which from its safe and leafy shelter spies
Its dam seized by a leopard and brought low:
With bleeding throat and breast and flank she lies,
And never more the light of day will know;
From wood to wood the orphaned creature flies
And of the cruel pard it seems to feel,
With every bramble-scratch, the jaws of steel.

35

All day and night and half another day
She wandered endlessly, she knew not where.
At last within a grove she chose to stay,
Made fresh and cool by the caressing air.
Two crystal streams flow past, not far away,
Keeping the grasses green and tender there,
And, murmuring among the little stones,
Give forth a dulcet harmony of tones.

36

This seems to her to be a safe retreat
And distant from Rinaldo many miles.
Tired by her ride and by the summer's heat,
Her fear with need for rest she reconciles.
Along a flowered path she moves her feet,
Letting her palfrey freely range the whiles.
To the luxuriant river-bank it passes
And in the water-meadow crops the grasses.

37

Not far away she sees a charming nook
Where flowering thorn with the vermilion red
Of roses is made gay, glassed in the brook,
With shady oak-trees arching overhead.
In its recess, as she draws near to look,
She finds a sheltered space, untenanted.
Branches and leaves together so entwine,
No sunlight can within directly shine.

38

To all who enter, sweet young grasses lend,
To rest inviting, couches soft and deep.
The lovely damsel's tempted to extend
Her weary limbs thereon and falls asleep.
Too soon, alas! her slumber's at an end:
A sound of footsteps makes her pulses leap.
Softly she rises and, from shelter peering,
She sees a cavalier in arms appearing.

39

If he be foe or friend she cannot tell.
Her heart by hope and fear at once is shaken.
Waiting to see if all may yet be well,
Her apprehensions once again awaken.
The knight, meanwhile, passing beyond her dell,
Towards the river-bank his way has taken.
Propped on his elbow, cheek on hand, he rests,
So deep in thought, a statue he suggests.

40

More than an hour, this knight, whom I will dub
The cavalier of grief, like this remained.
I swear, my lord, when he began to sob,
The very stones to pity he constrained,
And might have wooed a tigress from her cub.
The tears along his cheeks so freely rained,
He seemed more like a river, and the fellow's
Chest, heaving and sighing, was like a bellows.

41

'Alas!' he said, 'my heart both burns and freezes,
Now that my love is rendered null and void.
What shall I do? Each hour my grief increases;
I know the fruit is gathered and enjoyed.
While scarce a word or look my anguish eases,
Others are more delightfully employed.
If I am left with neither fruit nor flower,
Why do I pine for her at this late hour?

42

'A virgin may be likened to a rose
Which on its slender stem, by thorns defended,
Within a garden unmolested grows.
To pluck it no despoiling hand's extended.
The morning dew, the breeze that gently blows,
The rain, the earth, its loveliness have tended.
No sweeter pledge young lovers yearn to wear
Upon their breast or to adorn their hair.

43

'But when from the maternal stalk men sever
The rose in bloom, far from its verdant tree,
All nurture of the heaven and earth for ever
Vanish and benisons no more can be.
Even so the flower of maidenhood, whenever
Yielded, loses its cherished purity.
With zeal a virgin should, more than her eyes,
More than her life itself, defend this prize.

44

'On him by whom she's loved let her bestow
This priceless treasure, and all others shun.
Ah! thankless Fortune, why this cruel blow?
While other lovers triumph, I alone,
All joys denied, must empty-handed go.
How can love's labour from defeat be won?
Yet rather would I end my life today
Than the devotion of my heart gainsay.'

45

To anyone who asks me who this man is,
Who waters thus the river with his tears,
I will reply that he no African is,
But Sacripante, who great sorrow bears –
Circassia's monarch; how it all began is
Soon told: he's loved Angelica for years,
And she who is the cause of his sad plight
Has straightway recognized him at first sight.

46

From the Far East, his heart's desire to gain,
He journeyed where the sun sinks down to rest.
He heard in India with grief and pain
She'd gone with Count Orlando to the West,
Then learnt in France how Emperor Charlemagne
To part her from the cousins thought it best,
Pledging her as a prize to which of these
Most ably helped the golden fleur-de-lis.

47

He saw the camp and heard the tidings there
Of the defeat which threw the Christians over.
He sought the lovely damsel everywhere,
But not a trace of her could he discover.
This is the sad and sorrowful affair
Which pierced the anguished bosom of the lover,
Making him moan, lament and utter cries
Which stopped the sun for pity in the skies.

48

While Sacripante lies there sorrowing,
Making a fountain of his streaming eyes,
Saying first one and then another thing
I see no reason to immortalize,
Coincidence his fortune favouring,
His lady overhears these words of his.
Thus in an instant comes to pass what he
Could scarcely hope for in eternity.

49

The lovely maid observes with close attention
The words, the weeping and the air of one
Whose love for her she finds is no invention.
Of his devotion she has long since known,
And yet to help him she has no intention,
Being cold and hard, more than a block of stone.
She holds the world in such contempt and scorn,
No man deserving her was ever born.

50

And yet, here in the woodlands, unescorted,
She is inclined to take him as her guide.
The drowning man who waits to be exhorted
To cry for help must be a man of pride!
Who knows, if to his aid she'd not resorted,
When such a friend would rally to her side?
For long experience by now had taught her
He was the truest of all those who sought her.

51

Yet she has no intention to relieve him
Of the keen anguish which his life destroys,
Or in her fond embraces to receive him,
Still less to yield the sweetest of love's joys,
But by a shrewd evasion to deceive him.
She plots and schemes and all her wits employs,
How, by her charm, her servant she can make him,
And then, ungrateful, afterwards forsake him.

52

So, from the dark recess which shelter gave,
Angelica stepped forth upon the scene,
As when, emerging from a wood or cave,
Dian or Venus on the stage is seen.
'With you be peace,' she greeted him; 'God save
My honour and preserve it ever green;
And from your mind for ever cancelled be
The false opinion which you hold of me.'

53

No mother with such joy and stupor raised
Her eyes to see the face of her lost son
Whom, when his regiment without him blazed
Its homeward way, she mourned as dead and gone,
As when King Sacripant, who stood amazed,
Such grace and noble bearing looked upon,
And in the presence of that priceless treasure
His joy and stupefaction knew no measure.

54

With sweet and amorous affection filled,
His goddess he approached without delay.
She, with her arms about him, cooed and billed –
Something she never ventured in Cathay –
And of returning home began to build
Fresh hopes; for, now she held him in her sway,
Her prospects brightened and some promise showed
That she might gain once more her royal abode.

55

She gives King Sacripante an account
Of what has happened since the day when she
For help and reinforcements bade him mount
And eastward ride to him who holds in fee
The Chinese Nabathees; of how the Count
From death, dishonour and all jeopardy
Defended her, and how she was, in fact,
As when she left her mother's womb, intact.

56

It may be true, but no man in his senses
Would ever credit it; yet possible
It seems to him, for, lacking in defences,
To what is plain, but made invisible,
The king is blind (or with his sight dispenses),
Since what is not, love's power makes credible.
Thus he believes her for, as all men do,
He gives assent to what he hopes is true.

57

'If by ineptitude the Cavalier
Anglante has mishandled thus his lance,
He is the loser by it, for I fear
That Fate will not provide a second chance.'
(These words of his the damsel does not hear.)
'But I will lead my love another dance,
For if this gift of Fortune I neglect
I shall for ever lose my self-respect.

58

'So I will pluck the early-morning rose
Forthwith, lest I by dilly-dallying
The moment of its perfect freshness lose.
Than this, no sweeter or more pleasing thing,
In spite of her reluctance, woman knows,
Though she shed tears at her deflowering.
Thus no repulse or coyness will prevent
The prompt embodiment of my intent.'

59

Such were his thoughts; and now, as he prepares
For sweet assault and in his aim persists,
A clamour sounding through the forest tears
His ear-drums; he reluctantly desists,
And dons his helmet, for he always wears
Full armour, as for battle or the lists.
He finds his horse and bridles it at once,
And, mounting to the saddle, takes his lance.

60

Along the forest soon there rides a knight
Who has the semblance of a valiant man.
The armour which he wears is snowy white,
Likewise his plume. The Tartar sovereign,
Being put out by the unwelcome sight
Of one whose coming has thus foiled his plan,
Such interruption of his pleasure brooks
With anger undisguised and stormy looks.

61

Awaiting his approach, the king defies
The cavalier, thinking to come off best;
But, in comparison of strength and size,
The oncomer, I think, would pass the test.
Cutting the king's boast short, the knight applies
His spurs and quickly puts his lance in rest.
The other, furious, retorts; then both
Full tilt are galloping in all their wrath.

62

No lions run, no bulls advance with rage
In enmity so deadly or so fierce
As these two foemen in the war they wage.
With equal skill each other's shield they pierce.
The mountain trembles, as the knights engage,
From its green base to the bare peak it rears.
And well it is the hauberks stand the test,
Else would each lance be driven through each breast.

63

The chargers ran unswerving on their course.
Like rams colliding head to head they were.
The pagan's failing to withstand the force
Of impact, fell at once and did not stir
(Although so fine a steed). The other horse
Went down, but rose at once, touched by the spur.
The horse of Sacripante lay prostrate,
Its rider pinned beneath its lifeless weight.

64

The unknown champion, who sat erect,
Seeing the other underneath his steed,
Judged he had done sufficient in respect
Of that encounter, and no further need
Was there to fight; a path which ran direct
Ahead he chose and galloped off at speed.
Before one from his tangle could unwind him,
The other put a mile or so behind him.

65

As when a ploughman, dazed with stupefaction,
After a thunderbolt has struck, aghast,
Slowly uprights himself where by its action
Beside his lifeless oxen he was cast,
And views, dismayed, the shrivelling contraction
Of pine-trees stripped and withered by the blast,
So Sacripante rises to his feet,
The damsel having witnessed his defeat.

66

He sighs and groans, but not because a foot
Or arm is broken or is out of place,
But shame alone so makes his colour shoot
That never has he worn so red a face.
Not only has he been defeated, but
Angelica, to add to his disgrace,
Now lifts the heavy burden from his back
And, save for her, all power of speech he'd lack.

67

'O, pray, my lord,' said she, 'be not dismayed:
Your honour's not impugned because you fell;
But rather should the blame be squarely laid
Upon this hack, which served you none too well,
Its jousting days being over. I'd have said
Yon knight gained little glory and, to tell
The truth, he now the victory should yield,
For he, not you, was first to leave the field.'

68

And while the damsel thus consoles the king,
They see, with horn and wallet at his side,
An envoy on a nag come galloping.
Weary he seems, and breathless from his ride.
He has, they find, no messages to bring,
But asks the king if he by chance has spied
On horseback in the forest a brave knight
With armour, shield and helmet-plume of white.

69

The pagan answered: 'Here, as you can see,
He has unhorsed me, and not long ago
He left; and who it was thus dealt with me,
In case we meet again, I fain would know.'
The envoy said: 'In my capacity
I will inform you without more ado:
You have been felled from horseback by a foeman
Who is a valiant and courageous woman.

70

'She is as beautiful as she is brave;
Nor will I hide her celebrated name:
She at whose hands just now you suffered have
Such ignominy and undying shame
Is Bradamante.' Then the envoy gave
His nag its head. The king, his cheeks aflame,
Knows neither what to say nor what to do
In the dishonoured state he's fallen to;

71

For, having failed to fathom what had come
To pass, he recognizes finally
That by a woman he was overcome.
The more he thinks, the worse it seems to be.
He mounts the other horse, morose and dumb;
No word escapes his lips, but silently
He takes the maid, departing at a trot,
Deferring pleasure to some quieter spot.

72

And scarce two miles they go before they hear
Through the encircling wood a deafening sound:
A clamour and a crashing, far and near,
Making the forest tremble all around.
Soon afterwards they see a horse appear.
Its costly harnessing with gold is bound.
It leaps across the streams and over brakes,
And anything that an obstruction makes.

73

'If tangled foliage and dusky air',
The damsel said, 'do not deceive my eyes,
Among those inter-lacing branches there,
That horse which clears its passage hurdle-wise
Must be Baiardo. Yes, I know, I swear
It's he. How well he seems to recognize
That two upon one horse fare ill indeed,
For here he comes to satisfy our need.'

74

The monarch of Circassia dismounts
And to the horse draws near, the rein intending
To lay hold on; at once Baiardo flaunts
His crupper and, as quick as light, up-ending,
Answers with his heels. Were he now to trounce
The hapless king, no prospect of defending
Him there'd be, for Baiardo's in such fettle,
His hoofs could split a mountain-side of metal.

75

But tame and docile near Angelica
With human gentleness he takes his stand.
No dog more welcoming or friskier
Greeted his master home with leaping and
Great joy. Baiardo still remembers her,
For often she would feed him from her hand
When in Albracca for Count Aymon's son
Great love she had, while he for her had none.

76

Her fair left hand the bridle ornaments
And with her right she strokes his chest and neck.
The horse, of marvellous intelligence,
Submissive as an angel, to her beck
And call responds. The pagan, with good sense,
Then mounts Baiardo, holding him in check.
Her palfrey being thus lightened, from its croup
She moves and to the saddle now mounts up.

77

She chances, casting round her glance, to see
A knight on foot, his weapons as he hies
Clashing against his armour. Angrily
Duke Aymon's son her senses recognize.
He loves her more than life itself, but she
Abhors him as a crane from falcons flies.
Once she loved him and he abhorred her worse
Than death; and now their fates are in reverse.

78

Two magic fountains are the cause of this.
They rise in the Ardennes, not far away
One from the other. Who drinks from one is
Filled with amorous longing; those who essay
The second are to all love's joy and bliss
Rendered immune, and cold as ice are they.
Rinaldo tasted one and love prostrates him,
Angelica the other and she hates him.

79

The water, with a secret poison mixed,
So altered her who formerly adored him
On whom her glance with hatred now was fixed,
Her tear-filled eyes becoming more and more dim,
She urged the king, and in a voice betwixt
Forlorn and fearful, anguished she implored him
To wait no longer for the cavalier
Who fast approaches, but to flee with her.

80

'Have you so little trust?' the king replied,
'And do I stand so low in your esteem?
You look on me as useless by your side?
Unable to defend you I now seem?
Do you forget so soon how I defied
Opponents at Albracca? On this theme,
What of the night when I, alone and nude,
King Agrican and all the field withstood?'

81

She does not answer, nor know what to do.
Rinaldo is approaching much too close.
Already he makes threatening gestures to
The Tartar king who on Baiardo goes,
As he can see. The angelic damsel who
Has set his heart ablaze he also knows;
But what between these two proud knights occurred,
In the ensuing canto will be heard.

CANTO II

1

Ah, cruel Love! What is the reason why
You seldom make our longings correspond?
How is it, traitor, you rejoice to spy
Two hearts discordant, one repelled, one fond?
Into the darkest, blindest depths must I
Be drawn, when I might ford a limpid pond?
Towards her who loves, you stifle my desire:
For her who hates, you set my heart on fire.

2

You make Rinaldo love Angelica,
While he is ugly in her eyes; and yet
When he seemed handsome and was loved by her,
He hated her, as much as man can hate.
Now in vain torment and desire for her
He suffers retribution, tit for tat.
She hates him and so fierce a hate he stirs
That death to his devotion she prefers.

3

Rinaldo called to the Circassian
With scorn and wrath: 'Thief, from my horse dismount!
No man shall take what's mine; who dares, I mean
To make him dearly pay for the affront.
And I will take from you this peerless queen.
To leave her in your clutches would amount
To a grave breach of chivalry indeed.
No thief shall claim this lady or this steed.'

4

'Who calls me thief', the Tartar king replies,
Moved by an arrogance of equal force,
'Lies in his teeth! But that man tells no lies
Who calls you thief! Let us then have recourse
To combat, to decide which of us is
More worthy of the lady and the horse.
Thus far with your opinion I agree:
In all the world none is so fair as she.'

5

As when two mastiffs deadly conflict wage,
Stirred by some jealous rivalry or hate,
Baring their fangs, the better to engage,
And, red as fire, their rolling eyes dilate,
As fearsomely they grapple in their rage,
With raucous snarls, their bristles stiff and straight,
So the Circassian and Montaubon
From goads and challenges to swords moved on.

6

One was on foot, the other on the horse.
What vantage do you think the pagan had?
None whatsoever, and his case was worse
Perhaps than if he'd been an untrained lad.
The charger, taking an instinctive course,
Refused to harm its master; and, to add
To its new rider's troubles even more,
It would respond to neither hand nor spur.

7

He tries to urge it on: the horse stops dead.
He tugs the rein: it breaks into a trot;
Then suddenly it checks and ducks its head,
Arches its back and with its hoofs kicks out.
For taming horses like this thoroughbred,
The pagan, seeing plainly this is not
The moment, firmly grasps the saddle-bow
And to the left leaps to the ground below.

8

Thus liberated by a nimble bound
From the encumbrance of a stubborn steed,
The pagan with the paladin is found
To be well matched: a valiant pair indeed.
Sword upon sword, their mighty strokes resound.
The hammer-blows of Vulcan with less speed
Battered the anvil in the smoke-filled cove
Wherein were forged the thunderbolts of Jove.

9

Now with long thrusts and now with feint and ruse,
They show themselves past masters in their art.
Now upright and now crouching low, they choose
When to be covered, when exposed in part.
Now they gain ground a little, now they lose,
Returning blows, or else from blows they dart,
Whirling around; and where the one gives way,
The other presses home without delay.

10

Behold, with sword upraised, Rinaldo run
And all his might against the pagan fling,
Who looks to safety from his shield of bone;
Fine steel, well-tempered, is its armouring.
The blade, Fusberta, severs it in one
Resounding blow, making the forest ring.
Like ice, both steel and bone the impact cracks.
Nerveless, the pagan's arm all feeling lacks.

11

The timid damsel noted with dismay
The dire effect resulting from this shock.
From her fair cheek the colour ebbed away
As when a man condemned surveys the block.
She saw she must depart without delay
Or else accept what Fate now held in stock:
To be the prize of one whom she abhorred
While she by him was ardently adored.

12

Along a narrow track then, turning tail,
She galloped where the forest was most dense.
Behind her many times, her face yet pale,
She glanced, fearing to see in her suspense
Rinaldo close behind upon her trail.
A hermit she encountered not far hence.
His beard, extending half-way down his breast,
And all his air, a saintliness suggest.

13

Bowed down in years, by fasting rendered lean,
He rode astride a donkey, slow and sure.
No man in all the world had ever been
Whose heart appeared so scrupulous and pure.
As soon as the fair damsel he had seen
Approaching him, though weaker than of yore,
That organ, by such tender beauty spurred,
With warmth of feeling and compassion stirred.

14

She asks the hermit to direct her to
The nearest port, for now her only aim
Is to leave France and flee to somewhere new,
Where she will never hear Rinaldo's name.
The hermit, who the arts of magic knew,
At once a friend and counsellor became.
Eager to help the maid in her distress,
He fumbled in the pocket of his dress.

15

He drew a volume forth, to great effect,
For scarcely had he read one page aloud,
A sprite, in servant's livery bedecked,
Sprang forth to ask his master what he would.
The genie hastens, as the rules direct,
To where the knights are fighting in the wood.
(They have not lain at ease since we have seen them.)
With great audacity he steps between them.

16

'I pray you, sirs,' he said, 'explain to me
What will the death of one of you avail?
What will the outcome of your labours be?
Though one of you succeed, you both must fail,
Since Count Orlando, uncontestedly,
Without a blemish on his coat of mail,
This very hour accompanies to Paris
The damsel who the cause of this affair is.

17

'I saw Orlando hence about a mile,
Riding to Paris with Angelica.
They joked about you both with many a smile,
To think how fruitless all your strivings are.
I would advise you now in the meanwhile
To go in trace of them: they can't be far.
Once with his love in Paris he arrives,
You'll see her ne'er again in all your lives.'

18

Would you had seen the combatants' dismay!
On hearing this, they cursed their very eyes
That they had been so blind – the more fools they
To let their rival carry off the prize!
To seek his horse, Rinaldo moved away
And, breathing fire and brimstone with his sighs,
He swore a solemn oath that he would yet
Have Count Orlando's heart when next they met.

19

To where Baiardo waits for him he strides
And, leaping to the saddle, gallops off,
Leaving the king on foot, to whom, besides,
To bid farewell he has not grace enough.
All barriers Baiardo overrides,
Pricked by the spur, and, where the going's rough,
Not rivers, ditches, rocks, nor clumps of gorse,
Suffice to turn the charger from its course.

20

My lord, I would not have you think it strange
The horse Rinaldo vainly sought for days,
When it had kept securely out of range,
Should now obey him without more delays.
This on its part was no capricious change
For, being almost human in its ways,
It led its master where the lady went
For love of whom it heard him oft lament.

21

When from the duke's pavilion she took flight,
The good Baiardo followed from afar.
Rinaldo left the saddle that he might,
Dismounted, face-to-face, and on a par,
Engage in combat with a noble knight
With whom he was well matched in deeds of war.
The horse, thus freed, followed the lady's track,
Eager to help its master win her back.

22

Where'er she went, Baiardo led the hunt;
Rinaldo followed it in hot pursuit;
And always it refused to let him mount,
For fear lest he should take another route.
It found her twice, quite on its own account,
Yet for Rinaldo neither time bore fruit:
He was impeded first by Ferraù,
Then by the king, as you already knew.

23

The sprite, from whom Rinaldo had received
False tidings, duped the horse as well;
And so, Baiardo, being thus deceived,
Stood and submitted to its master's will.
Burning with love, indignant and aggrieved,
Rinaldo heads for Paris' citadel.
His eagerness, however fast they go,
Would make the wind (still more, a horse) seem slow.

24

At night he is unwilling to resort
To sleep, such his impatience to defy
Orlando, such his faith in the report
Of the magician's sprite (which is a lie).
Just as it seems the time is running short,
He sees at last outlined against the sky
The city where the Emperor Charlemagne
Retreated with such forces as remain.

25

To stem the onslaught of the African,
King Charles's first concern is to prepare
For siege; quickly he carries out his plan,
Reviews his army, lays in stores with care,
Digs a dry moat, restores the barbican,
And looks to his defences everywhere.
He means to send to England for fresh troops
And to deploy them later, as he hopes.

26

He plans to lead his army forth anew
And try once more if vengeance might be won.
He sends Rinaldo without more ado
To Britain (renamed England later on).
The paladin was most unwilling to
Set out again; objection he has none
To Britain – he laments that not one day
Is Charlemagne prepared to let him stay.

27

In all his life he never did a thing
Less willingly, for he was then required
To cease a while from his meandering
In search of her by whom his heart was fired.
Nevertheless, obedient to his king,
He started on the journey as desired;
And so to Calais in a few hours' ride,
Then boards the vessel and awaits the tide.

28

Against the will of all the mariners,
Who urgently advise a homeward tack,
Despite the stormy waters he prefers
To put to sea; the heaven now grows black,
The wind, enraged, that nothing yet deters
The rash adventurer, nor turns him back,
Now lashes out and soon the seas pile up
To crash across the ship from prow to poop.

29

By striking sail the mariners restore
The vessel's trim; in every heart awaken
New longings for the safety of the shore,
Which in an evil moment they'd forsaken.
The wind then blusters with an angry roar:
'I'll not condone the liberty you've taken.'
With shrieks and gusts all headway it denies them.
Each time they turn, it threatens to capsize them.

30

Veering from stem to stern, the cruel gale
Grows ever stronger, granting no release.
Now here, now there, they whirl with shortened sail,
At the storm's mercy tossed on angry seas.
But many threads are needed for my tale
And so, to weave my canvas as I please,
I'll leave Rinaldo and the plunging prow,
And turn to talk of Bradamante now.

31

I mean the celebrated Maid; she is
The one who felled the monarch with her lance:
Daughter of Aymon and of Beatrice,
A sister whom Rinaldo proudly flaunts,
Who for her courage, might and expertise
By Charlemagne and all the Peers of France
Is held in no less honour than her brother,
For they are known to equal each the other.

32

The Maid was loved by a brave cavalier
Vowed to the service of the African.
He was the scion of the old Ruggier
By Agolante's daughter who such pain
And sorrow suffered; from no cruel bear
Or lion sprung, the Maid did not disdain
The love of such a knight, although their fate
Once only has permitted them to meet.

33

He shares his father's name and pedigree.
And now in search of him she goes her way,
As safe, though unescorted, as if she
A thousand squadrons had in her array.
When she had fought Circassia's king and he
Had kissed our ancient mother, as men say,
She crossed a wood and afterwards a hill,
Then came at last upon a lovely rill.

34

A stream which through a water-meadow flows,
Where age-old trees provide a grateful shade,
With pleasing murmuring invites all those
Who pass to drink and linger in the glade,
While to the left a hill with terraced rows
Gives shelter from the noon-day sun. The Maid,
Turning her lovely eyes upon the scene,
A cavalier reclining there has seen.

35

Alone and silent, with a pensive brow,
Reposing in a shady grove beside
A green and flowery bank, he watches how
The limpid, crystal waters slowly glide.
His shield and helm are hanging on a bough;
His charger to the tree is also tied.
His eyes are moist with tears, his face held low,
And all his air betokens grief and woe.

36

The longing we all harbour in our heart
To learn about another man's affairs
Urges the Maid to ask him to impart
The reason for his sorrows and his cares.
He willingly relates the whole from start
To finish and his troubles with her shares,
For from her noble bearing at first sight
He takes her for a truly valiant knight.

37

And he began: 'Good sir, as I was leading
My troops of cavalry and foot to where
King Charles was camped, the Moor's advance
    impeding,
And as a lady I escorted there,
For whom, alas! my stricken heart is bleeding,
Close to Rodonnes I noticed in the air
A knight in armour on a horse with wings,
Wheeling in wide and then decreasing rings.

38

'This thief – whether he was a mortal being
Or an infernal fiend I cannot say –
My lovely and belovèd lady seeing,
As when a falcon swoops to seize its prey,
Dropped like a plummet and, the soldiers fleeing,
The startled damsel snatched and bore away.
The whole of this assault escaped my eye
Until I heard her calling from on high.

39

'So the rapacious kite swoops down upon
The helpless chick which flutters near its dam.
For all her squawks and flappings when it's gone,
She cannot call it back, the poor beldam!
Likewise, how can I hope to follow one
Who flies, hemmed in by mountains as I am?
Among such rocky paths my weary horse
With laggard steps plods a reluctant course.

40

'But, like a man who would have suffered less
If from his breast his heart had cruelly
Been torn, I left my army leaderless
To face whatever was its destiny.
By paths less mountainous in their access
I went wherever Love directed me,
Hoping to find where the rapacious thief
Had carried off my lady, to my grief.

41

'For six long days I journeyed, morn till night,
Through desolate and unfrequented places.
There was no path, no track, as far as sight
Could reach, nor evidence of human traces.
At last I came upon a valley, quite
Enclosed by crags and bottomless crevasses,
Where on a rock a castle, strong and bold,
Loomed up to heaven, splendid to behold.

42

'From far away it seemed to glow like flame.
No glaze, no marble, has such radiance.
When nearer to the shining work I came
And saw the marvel of its walls, at once
I knew that demon masons of ill fame
With incense, exhalations and weird chants
Had clad the castle walls with finest steel,
Forged in the fires and chilled in streams of Hell.

43

'The steel of every tower shines so bright,
No rust disfigures it, nor any stain.
The robber scours the country day and night,
Then in his fort immures himself again.
Whatever he desires has no respite.
His victims can but curse him and complain.
And there my lady – nay, my heart – is held,
And to abandon hope I am compelled.

44

'Alas! what else is there that I can do
But gaze upon her prison, as distressed
As when a vixen, hearing from below
A piteous yelping in an eagle's nest,
Locates her stolen cub and to and fro
Irresolutely paces without rest.
So high the castle is, I give my word,
No one can there ascend who's not a bird.

45

'While I yet lingered there, two cavaliers,
Escorted by a dwarf, came into sight.
At this, new hope within my bosom stirs;
But hope and longing are both doomed to blight.
In deeds of derring-do the knights are peers.
Gradasso rules all Sericana's might;
The other, young and strong, Ruggiero named,
Among the host of Africa is famed.

46

'The dwarf began: "These knights have come to try
Their strength against the castle's owner, who,
Clad in full armour, travels through the sky
Astride a bird-like quadruped, a new
Unheard-of means of transport." "Sirs," said I,
"Have pity on my wretched case. When you,
As I devoutly hope, have won the day,
Restore my lady-love to me, I pray."

47

'How she was taken from me I explain,
My flowing eyes attesting to my grief.
They promise many times they will regain
Her for me, and descend the rocky cliff.
To watch the combat, eagerly I crane,
Praying that God may grant they bring relief.
A level space was visible below,
And twice as long, perhaps, as a stone's throw.

48

'When they arrive beneath the rock, they wait.
Both had desired to open combat first,
But now, whether it be a quirk of fate,
Or that the young Ruggiero ceased to thirst
For precedence, the walls reverberate
To the Serican's horn; the portals burst
Asunder, as the haughty challenge brings
The knight in armour on the horse with wings.

49

'Little by little he begins to rise,
Just as a crane from foreign lands will do,
Which, running rapidly at first, then flies,
Leaving the ground about a yard or two;
Then in the freedom of the air it tries
Its wings, faster and faster, till from view
It's lost. So does the necromancer soar
As high as eagle ever flew, and more.

50

'When he thought good, he turned his horse's head.
With pinions closed, it hurtled from above,
As when a well-trained falcon drops like lead
Upon a rising sheldrake or a dove;
And with his lance in rest, inspiring dread,
With horrifying noise the air he clove.
Gradasso this descent had scarce perceived
When on himself the onslaught he received.

51

'"His lance upon him the magician broke.
In vain Gradasso beat the empty air,
For, flying yet, the horse of which I spoke
Had quickly borne aloft the cavalier.
Such was the impact of the mighty stroke,
It forced to earth the haunches of the mare
(For on an Arab mare Gradasso rode,
The finest mare that ever man bestrode).

52

'Up to the stars the flying charger bears
The knight who, in a flash descending, deals
A blow that takes Ruggiero unawares.
Intent upon Gradasso's plight, he reels
Beneath the shock; his horse no better fares,
And backward moves. Then, as Ruggiero steels
Himself to charge full tilt in a reply,
There is his foe above him in the sky.

53

'Now on Gradasso, now Ruggiero, fall
On brow, on breast, on back, redoubled blows.
The strokes they aim avail them not at all,
Such prowess at evading them he shows.
By his gyrations he can soon forestall
Their moves, but what his next is neither knows.
They cannot tell, his dazzling feints so blind them,
If he is now before them or behind them.

54

'Between two earth-bound knights and one who's not,
The combat lasted till the hour that brings
A veil of darkness which extends to blot
The colour from all lovely earthly things.
This is the truth: I added not one jot.
I saw it and I know, and yet it rings
As false as if my tale were inexact.
Here fiction is less marvellous than fact.

55

'In all this time the flying cavalier
Within a silken cloth had draped his shield.
To me, I must confess, it is not clear
Why he had kept it for so long concealed;
Uncovered, it sends forth a light so sheer,
Whoever sees it, then and there must yield,
Falling to earth as a dead body falls,
To languish in the necromancer's walls.

56

'Red as Bohemian garnet was its ray.
No light to equal it has ever shone.
Beholding it, the knights collapsed straightway,
Their vision dazzled, all awareness gone.
I too lost consciousness, though far away,
And reawoke to find myself alone.
No warriors, no dwarf could I remark:
The field, the plain, the mountain – all were dark.

57

'I thought the necromancer by his spell
Both cavaliers had captured in one swoop.
The blazing beam, which is invincible,
Ended their freedom and destroyed my hope.
So to that place I sadly bid farewell,
Where all my heart's desire is now walled up.
Now judge, of reasons for which lovers pine,
If there be any grief to equal mine.'

58

The knight resumed his attitude of woe
When he had thus accounted for its cause.
His name and lineage you now must know:
Count Anselm Altaripa's son, he was
Named Pinabel, of all true knights the foe.
Born a Maganzan, he obeyed no laws
Of chivalry, and of that breed accurst
In acts of treachery he was the worst.

59

With changing looks the Maid in silence heard
The story the Maganzan thus narrated.
The mention of Ruggiero's name had stirred
Great joy, leaving her countenance elated;
But learning then how her dear love had fared,
When by a magic shield he'd been defeated,
She grew distressed and would not rest content
With one account alone of the event.

60

When she had heard the story through and through,
She said: 'Sir knight, I bid you be of cheer.
This day may yet prove fortunate to you
And serviceable my arrival here.
Let both of us at once press onward to
The robber's den which holds all we hold dear.
Not wasted effort will our journey be
If Fortune treats me not unfavourably.'

61

'Is it your will', the cavalier replied,
'That I should travel back again across
These rugged mountains, acting as your guide?
To me, thus to retrace my steps will be no loss,
For I have lost my all and more beside.
To you this journey is most perilous;
But if, despite my warning, you see fit
To risk imprisonment, then so be it.'

62

Thus having spoken, turning, he remounts
His steed and guides the Maid along the course
She's chosen for Ruggiero's sake; she counts
As naught the risk of capture or of worse.
As they pursue their journey, all at once
They hear behind them, shouting himself hoarse,
A messenger who calls to them to wait.
It is the envoy we have seen of late.

63

From Narbonne and Montpellier report
He brings that all the standards of Castile
Have now been raised, with those of Aigues Mortes;
And to the Maid, Marseilles makes an appeal,
In this predicament, for her support,
Giving the envoy orders to reveal
The need they have of her return; and this
The purpose of his expedition is.

64

This city, with the land that lies between
The estuaries of the Var and Rhône,
To Bradamante by King Charles has been
With confidence entrusted as her own,
For, marvelling, the Emperor has seen
How in great deeds of daring she has shone.
Now from Marseilles an envoy, as I said,
Has come to ask assistance of the Maid.

65

Suspended between yes and no, she tries
To choose: should she return again that day?
Towards Marseilles the path of duty lies;
The flames of love urge her another way.
She chooses finally the enterprise
Of rescuing Ruggiero; come what may,
If to the task she should unequal prove,
At least she'll be imprisoned with her love.

66

She quietens, by means of an excuse,
The envoy's fears and leaves him satisfied.
Turning her horse, her journey she pursues
With Pinabello, who can scarcely hide
His furious annoyance at the news:
Deep is his hatred of the Clairmont side,
And many tribulations he foresees
If she should once discover who he is.

67

Between the Clairmont and Maganza House
The enmity was ancient and intense.
Many a time they'd split each other's brows;
The toll of blood between them was immense.
And so in his black heart the villain vows
That on the first occasion Fate presents
He will betray the unsuspecting Maid
And leave her unescorted, without aid.

68

And, concentrating on his evil scheme,
In hate and fear so deeply did he brood,
That he mistook the way, as in a dream,
And woke to find himself in a dark wood.
There in the very centre, facing him,
Its peak a naked flint, a mountain stood.
And she whose father was the Duke Aymon,
Keeping her guide in sight, still followed on.

69

This is the moment, he now thinks, to try
To rid himself of her who seems a knight.
'Before the sun', he said, 'has left the sky,
We ought to seek a shelter for the night.
Beyond this mountain, in a vale near by,
A splendid castle stands, if I am right.
Wait here for me, while to the naked rock
I now ascend, and with my own eyes look.'

70

With this, along the lonely mountain-slope
He pricked his charger to the topmost peak;
And, looking round about him in the hope
Of finding, in that desolate and bleak
Terrain, a corner where there might be scope
To play his cruel game of hide-and-seek,
He came upon a cavern, dark and deep,
For thirty yards descending, sheer and steep.

71

There was a spacious portal far below
Which to a larger chamber access gave.
From the interior shone forth a glow
As if a torch lit up the mountain cave.
But meanwhile Bradamante was not slow
To follow from afar the scheming knave.
Fearing to lose him if she stayed behind him,
She clambered to the cavern's mouth to find him.

72

And when the traitor knew his first design,
For all his careful plans, would be in vain,
To kill or leave her there, or to combine
Two such betrayals, he began again
To weave a strange new scheme; first, to refine
His treachery, he hastened to explain
That in that deep and dark and hollow place
He glimpsed a damsel with a winsome face.

73

From her fair aspect and her costly gown,
She seemed of noble and of high degree;
But by her attitude of grief she'd shown
That she resided there unwillingly.
When, to learn more about her, he'd begun
The steep descent into the cavity,
Her captor from the inner chamber stepped
And forced her back again, for all she wept.

74

Fair Bradamante, who's as credulous
As she is brave, believes his every word.
She longs to be of help, but perilous
She knows descent will be without a cord.
Then on an elm-tree she sees pendulous
A long and leafy branch; with her sharp sword
She quickly cuts it from the parent bole
And lowers it with care into the hole.

75

The severed end she gave to Pinabel
To hold, and, climbing down, herself suspended,
Feet first, into the cavity, until
She dangled at full length, her arms extended.
He, smiling, asked the Maid if she jumped well,
Then flung his hands apart, as he'd intended,
Shouting in triumph: 'Perish all your breed,
And would I might deal thus with all their seed!'

76

The fate of her whom Pinabel thus cursed
Proved other than his traitor's heart had hoped.
Reaching the bottom of the cavern first,
The sturdy branch, though breaking as it dropped,
Softened her fall and saved her from the worst.
Thus his design to kill the Maid was stopped.
Unconscious for a space of time she lay,
And how she later fared I'll later say.

CANTO III

1

Who is there now will give me voice and speech
To suit the noble theme I have to tell,
And to my verse lend wings that it may reach
The lofty region where my fancies dwell?
Diviner far is now the flame with which
My breast must burn if I would honour well
My lord, for it is now my poem sings
The ancient lineage from which he springs:

2

Than which among the illustrious sons of men
Who to command the world predestined are,
Thou, Phoebus, the globe's beacon, ne'er hast seen
A race more glorious in peace and war,
Nor whose nobility prolonged has been
So many ages, and will last as far,
If truth illumines my prophetic soul,
As heaven's eternal motion round the pole.

3

If their true glory I would now display,
Not mine will serve, O Phoebus, but thy lyre
(Whereon, the Titans vanquished, thou didst pay
Homage to heaven's ruler) I require;
And if, endowed with finer tools, I may
In carving noble stone some art acquire,
In sculpture of fair images I will
Devote all my endeavour, all my skill.

4

And with a scalpel all untried meanwhile
I'll cut the first rough flakes and chippings hence,
And hope that later, in more expert style,
I will complete the work with diligence.
But let us turn to him against whose guile
No shield or breastplate can afford defence.
I speak of Pinabel of Gano's line:
To kill the valiant Maid was his design.

5

The traitor never doubted that the Maid
In the precipitous ravine lay dead.
His countenance a pale and sickly shade,
From the contaminated cave he sped
(By him infected). Where his charger stayed
He soon returned; like one who has been bred
For evil, making matters even worse,
He took away fair Bradamante's horse.

6

But let us leave him who, as he thus schemed
Death to another, his own death procured,
And turn to her whom treachery, it seemed,
Both death and burial in one ensured.
Bemused at first and all her senses dimmed
By the fall's impact and the shock endured,
She rose and entered through a door which gave
Into the second and the larger cave:

7

A spacious room, it seemed like a revered
And hallowed church, much sanctified by prayer,
And by the skill of architecture reared
On alabaster columns choice and rare;
And at the very central point appeared
An altar where a lamp burned bright and fair.
So brilliant was the flame with which it glowed,
It shed its light on the entire abode.

8

Moved by devout humility and awe,
The Maid began, with heart as well as lips,
Soon as the sacred edifice she saw,
To offer prayers to God; kneeling, she keeps
Her head and eyes in reverence held low,
When through a creaking door a lady steps;
Ungirt, unshod, her hair unbound, the Maid
She greeted by her name, then these words said:

9

'O valiant Bradamante, not by chance,
But in fulfilment of a will divine,
You have arrived. I had precognizance
Of your predestined journey to this shrine,
For Merlin said, in a prophetic trance,
Your presence here would coincide with mine.
Thus I have waited to disclose to you
What Heaven has ordained that you must do.

10

'This is the ancient, memorable cave
Which Merlin fashioned, the enchanted seer
Of whom some memory perhaps you have.
The Lady of the Lake betrayed him here.
His sepulchre is yonder in the nave.
Therein his flesh decays. He, without fear,
To please her, with her treachery complied:
Alive he laid him in the tomb – and died.

11

'His spirit with his corpse will ever dwell
Until the trumpet on the Day of Doom
Shall summon it to Heaven or to Hell,
When a dove's form, or raven's, it assume.
Alive, too, is his voice. Clear as a bell
You'll hear it issue from the marble tomb,
For always he has answered questionings
Concerning history and future things.

12

'Some days ago, seeking this sanctuary,
I travelled from a distant, foreign land,
That Merlin might expound a mystery
Of magic which I did not understand.
Since you it was my chief desire to see,
I tarried here a month more than I planned,
For Merlin said (whose words are ever true)
This day had predetermined been for you.'

13

Duke Aymon's daughter close attention pays,
Amazed and silent, while the other speaks.
Such marvel fills her heart at all she says,
She knows not if she sleeps or if she wakes.
Her modest, lowered eyes she dare not raise,
But gazing, downward, this reply she makes:
'Dear Lord above, what can my merit be
That prophets thus foreknowledge have of me?'

14

By the strange words the Maid was caught and won
And in the footsteps of the beckoning dame,
Where the remains of Merlin's flesh and bone
Reposed and where his spirit lived, she came.
The sepulchre was made of hardest stone,
Polished and shining and as red as flame.
The cave, although no sunlight entered it,
By the tomb's radiance was ever lit.

15

Whether it be the shimmering striations
Of marble which thus cleave the dusky air,
Or the effect of songs and exhalations,
Or zodiacal signs which glitter there
(The likeliest of all the explanations),
The onlooker, entranced, is made aware
Of sculptured beauty and of colour which
The venerable sanctuary enrich.

16

Scarcely has Bradamante passed the doors
That guard the threshold of the secret room
When the still-living spirit of the corse
Speaks thus in clearest accents from the tomb:
'May Fortune favour every wish of yours,
O chaste and noble maiden, in whose womb
The fertile seed predestined is to spring
Which honour to all Italy will bring.

17

'Since in your veins the ancient blood of Troy
Commingled from two purest strains has been,
From it will bloom the ornament, the joy
Of every lineage the sun has seen
Where Indus, Tagus, Danube, Nile deploy
Their course, or in all lands that lie between
The globe's two poles. Among your progeny
Dukes, marquises and emperors I see.

18

'Thence will come forth the mighty cavaliers
And captains, by whose strategy and sword
The pride and glory of her former years
To valiant Italy will be restored;
Thence princes, whose just rule the world reveres,
As when the wise Octavius was lord,
Or Numa reigned. Beneath the sway they'll hold
Mankind will see renewed the age of gold.

19

'And that the will of Heaven be effected
Concerning you who as Ruggiero's wife
From earliest beginnings were selected,
Follow courageously your path in life.
By no consideration be deflected
From what you now resolve, for, in your strife
With the vile robber who your love immures,
A speedy victory your fate ensures.'

20

Merlin was silent, these words having said.
The sorceress began then to prepare
Her magic arts to conjure for the Maid
The form and semblance of many a future heir.
A vast array she summoned to her aid,
I know not if from Heaven or elsewhere,
To wait her bidding, gathered in one place,
Diverse in raiment and diverse of face.

21

Then, calling Bradamante to the shrine,
Where she described a circle on the floor,
So wide, within it she might well recline
And leave a margin of a palm or more,
Around the Maid she drew a magic sign
To guard her from what peril was in store.
Bidding her watch in silence, next a book
She opened and with conjured demons spoke.

22

Lo! from the outer chamber came straightway
Spirits, to where the magic ring extended;
But if they onward passed, they found their way
Was barred, as though by moat and wall defended.
Filling the inner sanctuary, where lay
The bones of Merlin, his life's journey ended,
They paid due homage to his costly tomb,
Circling three times around the sacred room.

23

'If every name and deed I were to tell',
The sorceress began, ' of all these wise
And valiant souls who, conjured by a spell,
Appear, though yet unborn, before our eyes,
How long we'd tarry I could not foretell.
To list them all, one night would not suffice.
So I will choose, as time allows, first one
And then another, as seems opportune.

24

'Behold near by one who resembles you
In aspect and in face, jocund and fair:
Ruggiero's son whom you'll conceive and who
In Italy will be proclaimed your heir.
Pontiero's soil with a vermilion hue
He'll stain with an avenging hand, for there
His father's enemies by treachery
Will rob him of his sire, as I foresee.

25

'His valiant prowess will at last bring low
King Desiderius the Longobard;
On him the Emperor will then bestow
Este and Calaone in reward.
Hubert, your grandson, is the next I show:
The glory of Italian arms, he'll guard
Our Holy Church and with such valour fight,
He'll keep her safe from the barbarian might.

26

'See Albert, the unvanquished captain: he
The temples will adorn with many spoils;
Hugo, his son, by whom Milan will be
Brought to submission in its viper's coils.
Heir to the marquisate of Lombardy
His brother Azzo is, and to its toils.
Next Albertazzo who, as I foreknow,
King Berengar and son will overthrow.

27

'Otto the Emperor will deign to grant
His daughter Alda to him as his bride.
A second Hugo see. O blest descent,
Whereby a father's valour's verified!
By him the Romans, long grown arrogant,
Will be reduced and humbled in their pride.
Otto the Third, helped by the Holy See,
Will raise the siege and gain supremacy.

28

'Next Folco comes, who'll to his brother give
Every estate he has in Italy,
And far away among the Germans live,
A duke of vast dominions. Saxony,
Menaced upon one frontier, will receive
His timely help. Heir through his mother, he,
His progeny assisting, will maintain
Stability so long as they shall reign.

29

'And now towards us comes a second Azzo,
A lover more of courtesy than war;
Of his two sons, Bertoldo and Albertazzo,
One will defeat the German emperor,
And with a savage butchery combat so,
The sunny plain of Parma runs with gore.
A famous Countess is the other's wife,
Matilda, of so wise and chaste a life.

30

'His virtue makes him worthy of such bliss,
Which at his age is no small praise intended,
For half of Italy her dowry is.
From the first Henry's line she is descended.
His brother Bertold's pledge of love is this:
Rinaldo of your line. To have defended
The Church from Barbarossa of ill fame
Will bring the greatest glory to his name.

31

'Another Azzo see who'll rule Verona
And all her beautiful surrounding plain.
Entitled then the Marquis of Ancona
In Otto's and Honorius's reign,
Of vast dominions he will be the owner.
Long it would take to tell you and explain
How many will bear high the gonfalon,
How many wars for Holy Church be won.

32

'Obizzo, Folco, other Azzos, Hughs,
Two Henrys, son and father, side by side,
Two Guelfs, one of whom Umbria subdues,
And takes Spoleto's dukedom in his stride.
See one who will new joyfulness infuse
In stricken Italy whose wounds gape wide:
I speak of him' (Azzo the Fifth is shown)
'Who'll bring the tyrant Ezzellino down,

33

'That Ezzellin of monstrous tyranny,
Whom men the son of Lucifer will deem,
Who'll wreak such deeds of inhumanity
And devastation that, compared with him,
Caius, Nero, Sulla, Marius, Antony
True paragons of clemency will seem.
Frederick the Second from imperial height
Will also be brought low by Azzo's might.

34

'With kindlier sceptre he will rule the land
Beside whose waters, with a plaintive song,
Phoebus bewailed his son, whose nerveless hand
Could not control the chariot for long,
When tears of sorrow turned to amber, and
In snow-white feathers which to swans belong
Cycnus was clad. For favours he'll dispense
The Holy See will give him recompense.

35

'Young Aldobrandin I must not forget.
To Rome he'll hasten to defend the Pope,
By Otto and by Ghibellines beset.
Of every stronghold thereabouts the scope
He'll circumvent, diminishing the threat
Of Umbria and Picenum. Then, in hope
Of the support which further combat warrants,
For revenue he will apply to Florence.

36

'Having no jewels or more precious gage,
His brother he will leave as surety.
Flying the sacred banners, he will wage
Victorious war against the enemy.
Setting the Church upon its rightful stage,
He'll slay Celano's Count deservedly.
Serving the Pope with loyalty and truth,
He'll perish in the flower of his youth.

37

'His brother Azzo will become his heir:
Ancona he'll inherit, and from Tronto
To Isauro, the cities everywhere
Between the sea and Apennines and on to
Pèsaro; an upright character, more rare
Than gold and jewellery, will be passed on too,
And magnanimity – these, not being gifts
Of Fortune, are not subject to her shifts.

38

'Rinaldo see, in whom no less will shine
The radiance of valour which for long
Exalts the glory of his noble line,
Till death and envious Fortune do him wrong.
Tidings from Naples reach me in this shrine,
How he will die his father's hostage. Young
Obizzo now comes forward – the new prince;
His manly qualities he'll soon evince.

39

'By him the fair domain enlarged will be:
Fierce Modena and smiling Reggio now
Acclaim his valour and supremacy,
And with one voice allegiance to him vow.
Azzo the Sixth, one of his sons, here see:
The standard-bearer of the Cross, he'll bow
To Holy Church; a daughter of Anjou
He'll wed and gain thereby a dukedom too.

40

'Behold four princes of illustrious fame,
A stately group and of congenial mind:
Aldobrandino, Nicholas the Lame,
Obizzo, Albert, merciful and kind.
Long it would take to tell you how they'll claim
Faenza, how with stronger ties they'll bind
To the fair kingdom Adria, which gave
Its dauntless name to the unconquered wave.

41

'Likewise the land where many roses grow,
Whence was derived its pleasing name in Greek;
That city also where, beside the Po,
Menaced by both its mouths, the people seek
The marshy delta and when wild winds blow
Haul in the fish in plenty; I'll not speak
Of Lugo and Argenta, or many a place
Well fortified, of teeming populace.

42

'See Nicholas, whom as a tender boy
The people of his land will make their lord;
He'll render null and void the hostile ploy
Of a Tydeus; in his hand the sword
Will seem a plaything and to him great joy
The turbulence of battle will afford;
And, fresh from study of brave deeds long past,
The seeds of chivalry anew he'll cast.

43

'Of all who plot rebellion he'll discover
The fell design and to their harm will turn it;
All stratagems so quickly he'll uncover,
No sooner is one planned than he'll discern it.
That Otto Terzi who will lord it over
Parma and Reggio will be slow to learn it,
For by such vigilance he will be foiled
And of both life and kingdom be despoiled.

44

'Thus the fair kingdom constantly extends
Its boundaries, yet in due limits stays,
For never any rival it offends,
But all transgressors in like coin repays.
Hence the First Mover, being well pleased, intends
No barrier to set, but in all ways
To aid its increase and prosperity,
Blessing the realm to all eternity.

45

'See Leonello, see the intrepid Prince
Borso, the pride and glory of his age.
Ensconced in peace, he greater triumph wins
Than all who in the feats of war engage;
Mars he imprisons in the dark and pins
Behind his back the frenzied arms of Rage.
This splendid lord's concern will solely be
His people's welfare and serenity.

46

'Next, Ercole, who will reproach his neighbour,
In whose defence he'll earn a limping gait,
Losing a foot when, with a flashing sabre,
At Budrio the troops of this ingrate
He'll rally and, in payment of his labour,
Find himself menaced at Ferrara's gate.
I know not if this lord has greater claim
In deeds of warfare, or of peace, to fame.

47

'Long will Apulians, Calabrians,
Lucanians his glorious deeds recall,
When, serving with the Catalonians,
In single combat he will hazard all
And win; in daring and insouciance,
He'll vie with many a veteran general.
By skill and prowess, thirty years and more,
He'll hold the dukedom, his by right before.

48

'As deep indebtedness as any State
Will feel towards its prince, Ferrara's debt
Will ever be to him, not only that,
Removed from marsh and bog, she will be set
In fertile plains, nor that he'll there create
More amplitude within new walls, nor yet
That temples, palaces to make her fair
He'll build, and theatres, and many a square,

49

'Nor even that against the avid claws
Of the wing-bearing Lion he will stand
Firm and unwavering, nor yet because,
When the French torch sets all the lovely land
Of Italy ablaze, she'll have no cause
To fear, alone exempt from the demand
For tribute – not for these and not a few
Such benefits her greatest thanks are due,

50

'But for illustrious offspring he'll beget:
The just Alfonso, Ippolito benign.
Even as the Heavenly Twins, remembered yet,
Whose mutual love their lives did so entwine,
To guard each other from all mortal threat,
To Hades, where no light of day can shine,
Repaired in turn, so with these two, each brother
Would gladly give his life to save the other.

51

'The deep devotion of this comely pair
Will make the State's defences more secure
Than if her walls, by Vulcan's skill, should wear
A double iron girdle to ensure
Her safety. Alfonso, in whom in rare
Proportion wisdom's joined with goodness, sure
And true will render justice, so that men
Will think Astraea's come to earth again.

52

'Great prudence he must summon by and by
And all his father's valour emulate,
For, unsupported and with no ally,
He'll be assailed by the Venetian State,
And, on the other side, by her whom I
Know not if mother I should designate
Or step-dame: for if mother, scarce more kind
Than Procne or Medea the Church he'll find.

53

'How often, day or night, with loyal scouts
And foragers, he'll reconnoitre forth!
What skirmishes, what memorable routs!
When from Romagna armies test their worth
Against their former friends, see how with gouts
Of blood, as they escape, they stain the earth,
Bounded on one side by Zanniolo,
Here by Santerno, yonder by the Po.

54

'Soon after face him on the same terrain
The Spanish hirelings of the Papacy,
By whom the Governor of Bastia's slain
After surrender; such atrocity
Alfonso, who will take the fort again,
Will punish with a just severity,
Sparing no man of all the garrison
To take to Rome the news of what is done.

55

'Such skill he'll show, so masterful a lance
He'll brandish on Romagna's battlefield,
That he'll secure the victory to France,
Forcing Pope Julius and Spain to yield.
The horses, fetlock-deep, can scarce advance
For human blood which saturates the weald –
The dead so many, and so small the trench
For Germans, Spaniards, Greeks, Italians, French.

56

'He on whose reverend head a purple hat
Is poised is the illustrious Cardinal
Ippolito, whom men will designate
Magnanimous, sublime and liberal.
All prose and rhyme would be inadequate
His catalogue of praise to chronicle.
In truth, to sing of all its glorious deeds,
This new Augustan age a Virgil needs.

57

'His glory will illuminate his race,
As on the fabric of the world the sun
Casts greater radiance in every place
Than moon or stars, for by him is outshone
All other light. I see him, sad of face,
Fearing, for lack of troops, to be undone,
Then, joyful, leading captive to the shore,
Galleys – fifteen – and other craft galore.

58

'See now two Sigismonds and at their side
Alfonso's five belovèd sons, whose fame,
O'erleaping hill and sea, spreads far and wide.
A second Ercole behold, the same
Who takes the French king's daughter for his bride.
Ippolito the Younger now I name
(That you may know them all). Upon his line
(Less than his uncle's, though) his light will shine.

59

'A third Francesco see, another two
Alfonsos. Now, as I have said before,
Were I to name each branch derived from you,
Wherein ancestral valour grows the more,
The sky would many times turn dark anew
E'er I had finished, and its light restore.
So now I think the time at last has come
These spirits to dismiss, and I am dumb.'

60

And so, with the approval of the Maid,
The erudite enchantress closed her book.
The spirits, who such magic spells obeyed,
The holy cavern rapidly forsook.
Speech being granted, Bradamante said:
'I noticed two of grim, foreboding look,
Between Alfonso and Ippolito.
Something concerning them I'd gladly know.

61

'I saw them come towards us, deeply sighing,
Their gaze averted, of all hope devoid.
Their brothers drew away together, trying,
So it appeared, this couple to avoid.'
The sorceress grew pale and burst out, crying:
'Ah! victims both, your happiness destroyed
By evil men who, evil plans pursuing,
Brought you, ah, woe is me! to your undoing!

62

'O virtuous offspring, worthy of the good
Duke Ercole, let not their fault dismay you!
These wretched reprobates are of your blood!
Compassion then, not justice, here should sway you.'
Then, speaking to the Maid, in milder mood
She said: 'Let not this sadden you, I pray you.
Of them I thought it wiser not to treat.
So, leave the bitter and retain the sweet.

63

'Tomorrow you and I at break of day
Will journey towards the castle built of steel
Wherein Ruggiero lies. The shortest way
I will conduct you and a path reveal
Whereby this harsh and evil wood you may
Escape, and your great destiny fulfil.
Then, as we walk together on the coast,
I'll point you out the road – you can't get lost.'

64

The valiant Maid there tarried all the night
And through the greater part of it conversed
With Merlin, who convinced her it was right
To put her duty to Ruggiero first.
Then, when the sky rekindled with new light
And darkness from the world above dispersed,
She left the cavern by a secret route,
Escorted by the sorceress, on foot.

65

Soon they emerged from a ravine, concealed
By mountains inaccessible to man;
And all that day, without a pause, they scaled
High cliffs, or waded deep where torrents ran.
Then, to beguile their way so far afield,
Of pleasurable topics they began
To speak, choosing such sweet discourse that often
The rigours of their irksome path they soften.

66

The most recurrent and engrossing theme
Of all that the enchantress tells the Maid
Is by what strategy or cunning scheme
She can release Ruggiero. 'If', she said,
'You had the prowess of Minerva or, I deem,
Of Mars himself, if you could call to aid
As vast an army as King Charlemagne,
Or even vaster, all would be in vain.

67

'Not only did the necromancer build
His walls of steel, but on a cliff they rise
To such a height, to no assault they yield.
Mounted upon a destrier which flies,
He sallies forth protected by a shield
Which casts a beam so piercing to the eyes
No man can look on it and not succumb,
But as one dead he lies, quite overcome.

68

'And if you think perchance it will avail you
To keep your eyes tight shut in your defence,
How will you know where he will next assail you,
When to make good your thrust and when to fence?
I know a remedy which will not fail you.
All magic it will turn to impotence.
In the whole world there is no other way,
So listen carefully to what I say:

69

'King Agramant of Africa bestowed
A ring, stolen in India from a queen,
Upon Brunello, who along this road
Some miles ahead of us this day has been.
Such virtue in this magic ring is stowed,
Whoever wears it, has a medicine
Against enchantment and all evil spells;
And many are the lies this trickster tells.

70

'For he is so expert and so astute,
That he has been commissioned by his king,
To try if cunning and a mind acute,
With the assistance of the magic ring,
Which often to its wearer has borne fruit,
Can free Ruggiero; and this very thing
He boasted he could do, and to his lord
(Who loves Ruggiero) he has pledged his word.

71

'That your Ruggiero may well understand
It is not Agramant, but you alone
Who'll rescue him from the enchanter's hand,
I will explain to you what must be done:
Three days you'll walk along the yellow sand
Beside the sea (which you will come to soon).
The bearer of the ring on the third day
Will reach a lodging where you too will stay.

72

'A little man – that you may know him truly –
I'd say he was below six palms in size.
His raven hair is matted and unruly.
A pallid face his swarthy skin belies.
His nose is flat, his beard has grown unduly.
From bushy brows he leers with swollen eyes.
His dress, for speed, is short and of close fit.
So now my picture of him is complete.

73

'Of magic spells with him you will converse
Of which we two have spoken by the hour.
Make known (for this is true) you're not averse
From luring the magician from his tower,
But keep as close as money in your purse
Your knowledge of the ring and of its power.
His company and guidance he will proffer
As far as to the castle: take his offer.

74

'Follow his steps until you come to where you
See the castle; here you must kill the man.
Let not compassion or regret deter you
From a swift execution of this plan.
Lest he should read your mind, you must bestir you,
For, ring in mouth, he'll vanish if he can
Into thin air, before your very eyes.
Thus it is best to take him by surprise.'

75

Talking of this and that, they reached the sea
Where the Garonne finds outlet near Bordeaux.
Here the two women parted company,
Not without tears which soon began to flow.
Yet, eager for Ruggiero's liberty,
The daughter of Duke Aymon was not slow
To wend her way, but onward bravely trudged,
And reached the hostel where Brunello lodged.

76

She knows him just as soon as she sets eyes on him
(His aspect being graven on her heart).
Many a ruse and strategy she tries on him,
But with Brunel mendacity's an art.
Knowing full well this trickster has no flies on him,
She in concealment likewise plays her part.
Name, sex, race, family and place of birth
She hides, watching his hands for all she's worth.

77

She keeps his hands in view for a good reason:
That he might steal her wallet is her fear.
Recalling her adviser's word in season,
She's careful not to let him come too near.
And as they stand there, brooding both on treason,
A mighty uproar smites upon the ear.
I'll tell you later on, my lord, the cause,
But now the time has come to make a pause.

CANTO IV

1

Although deceit is mostly disapproved,
Seeming to show a mind malevolent,
Many a time it brings, as has been proved,
Advantages that are self-evident,
And mortal threats and dangers has removed.
Not all we meet with are benevolent
In this our life, so full of envious spite,
And gloomier by far than it is bright.

2

If long experience and labour too
Are indispensable before you find
A friend who's staunch, reliable and true,
To whom you would confide your inmost mind,
What is Ruggiero's lovely Maid to do?
To Brunel's trickery she is not blind.
She knows his villainy for what it is.
Through all his sly pretence, forewarned, she sees.

3

She too dissembles, as the case demands
With one who is the father of all lies,
And on his thieving and rapacious hands,
As I remarked before, she keeps her eyes.
Then suddenly a mighty uproar rends
The air. The Maid exclaims, 'Lord of the skies!
O Virgin Mother! What is all this din?'
And with these words, she rushes from the inn.

4

She sees the host and all his household there,
Some at the windows, others in the street.
Faces up-turned, into the sky they stare,
As if a comet or eclipse to greet.
So marvellous a wonder in the air
The Maid beholds that few will credit it:
A horse with wings and of enormous size,
Which bears a knight in armour as it flies.

5

Its wings were wide and of the strangest hue.
Between them sat a knight, from heel to crest
In shining armour, polished as if new.
Keeping a steady course towards the west,
Beyond the hills he disappeared from view.
This cavalier, the host informed his guest,
Was a magician (here the truth he spoke),
And, far or near, this was the route he took.

6

Sometimes high up among the stars he flies.
At other times close to the ground he'll skim,
And any lovely women whom he spies
He snatches up and carries off with him.
The wretched damsels he so terrifies
That any who are beautiful, or deem
They are (he takes whichever he can get),
Remain indoors until the sun has set.

7

'He has a castle in the Pyrenees,'
The host continued, 'built by magic art
Of shining steel; so beautiful it is,
In the whole world there is no counterpart.
Of all the cavaliers who visit this
Enchanted palace, none, they say, depart.
It's my belief, good sir, I greatly fear,
They're put to death or held as captives there.'

8

Fair Bradamante to his words attends,
And it is well, for sooner now than late
The magic of the ring the Maid intends
To try (and to succeed will be her fate).
'Have you a guide', she asks, 'among your friends?
I must be gone, my longing is so great
To challenge this magician to a fight
And test my strength against his magic might.'

9

'You need not lack a guide,' Brunello said;
'I'll come with you and keep you company.
I have instructions of the road ahead
And other aids of use to you and me.'
He meant the ring, but he left that unsaid
(To speak of it, he thought, unwise would be).
'Gladly,' replies the Maid (her meaning is
The ring will soon be hers, no longer his).

10

What it was good to say she said; on all
That might endanger her she's wisely mum.
The landlord had a charger in his stall,
In battle strong, and roadworthy. The sum
Required she pays, and buys the animal.
And when the light of a new day has come
She takes her way along a narrow vale,
Brunel now at her head, now at her tail.

11

Mounting from hill to hill, from wood to wood,
They climb at last to where the Pyrenees
Reveal, ıf visibility is good,
Both France and Spain, together with both seas,
As on the Apennines whoever stood
Near the Camàldoli could view with ease
Two coastlines. By a harsh and weary route
They clamber downwards to the valley's foot.

12

A massive cliff, its top encircled by
A wall of steel, they gaze at from below.
Towards the heavens it ascends so high,
All near-by peaks, compared with it, seem low.
Those who would visit it need wings, to fly,
Else wasted effort it would be to go.
Brunello said, 'Here's where the sorcerer
Holds cavaliers and ladies prisoner.'

13

The walls on every side as steeply drop
As if by line and plummet built, four-square.
No steps (it seems) give access to the top.
Winged creatures only can inhabit there.
This is the place where they must make their stop.
The hour has come, the valiant Maid's aware,
For her to take possession of the ring
And kill Brunello without dallying.

14

And yet a coward's act to her it seems
To kill a man so lowly, and unarmed.
To take possession of the ring she schemes
And leave Brunello helpless but unharmed.
Of what's in store for him he little dreams.
Before he has the time to feel alarmed,
He's seized and fastened to a giant fir,
The magic ring surrendered up to her.

15

His tears, his groans, his chagrins and his woes
On valiant Bradamante have no power,
And down the mountain path she slowly goes
Till in the plain she stands beneath the tower.
There, a defiance on her horn she blows,
Which brings the necromancer from his bower.
Her challenge sounded, next with many a shout,
With many a threat, she boldly calls him out.

16

Not long the man of sorcery delayed
When he had heard the challenge of the horn.
On his winged horse, towards the warrior Maid,
Whom he believes to be a man, he's borne.
She at first sight of him is not afraid.
Keeping him well in view, she could have sworn
He had no lance, no sword, no club to harm her,
No weapon which could pierce or break her armour.

17

His shield in a vermilion cloth was draped.
In his right hand he held an open book,
Whence marvellous phenomena he shaped:
A lance which hurtled through the air and took
His adversary by surprise, who gaped
At nothingness, with an astonished look;
Or with a dagger or a club he smote
From far away, by a control remote.

18

His horse was not a fiction, but instead
The offspring of a griffin and a mare.
Its plumage, forefeet, muzzle, wings and head
Like those of its paternal parent were.
The rest was from its dam inherited.
It's called a hippogriff. Such beasts, though rare,
In the Rhiphaean mountains, far beyond
The icy waters of the north, are found.

19

By magic arts he brought it to the West.
Then with determination and insistence
He straightway set himself to train the beast.
Within a month, by patience and persistence,
He reined and saddled it. At his behest
It bore him now without the least resistance
On earth and in the air – no magic creature,
But real and true, a prodigy of Nature.

20

The rest of the magician's stock-in-trade,
Unlike the horse, was supernatural.
This mattered little to the valiant Maid.
The ring, she knew, made her invulnerable.
She flashed a cut or two with her good blade
And put her charger through its paces. All
Her feints and thrusts she tried as though she fought,
Obeying the instructions she was taught.

21

When on her charger she had exercised,
The Maid decided to perform, dismounted,
The actions her instructress had advised.
On all his arts the necromancer counted,
But above all the magic shield he prized,
Whose piercing ray had never disappointed.
Thus, of its efficacy being certain,
From its bright surface he removed the curtain.

22

He could straightway have used it on his foe,
But he preferred to hold a knight at bay,
Taking a cruel pleasure in a show
Of swordsmanship and skilful lance-display,
As a sly cat, deliberately slow,
When he has caught a mouse will sometimes play;
Then, when he wills and only when he wills it,
He makes a sudden pounce on it and kills it.

23

The knight the mouse, the sorcerer the cat
Resembled in such contests hitherto;
But now the case was altered, tit for tat,
As valiant Bradamante nearer drew.
Alert, she watched his every move, so that
No vantage he should gain, and when she knew
That he intended to expose the shield,
She shut her eyes and lay stretched on the field.

24

The shining metal had not injured her
As it had injured others who preceded.
Her plan had been to make the sorcerer
Dismount and in that purpose she succeeded.
As soon as she lay down, the hoverer,
Urging his mount as quickly as was needed,
With a yet swifter fluttering of wings
Swooped down to earth in widely-spreading rings.

25

The shield appending to his saddle-bows,
Which in its silken covering he hid,
To the recumbent Maid on foot he goes.
She, like a wolf in ambush for a kid,
Awaits him and, as soon as he is close,
Leaps up and grasps him in a single bid
To overpower him. The wretch, alas !
Has left his book of magic on the grass.

26

With his own chain the valiant Maid belayed him,
Which round his waist the necromancer wore.
She thought no less a fetter would have stayed him
(And often he had used it thus before).
Already helpless on the ground she'd laid him
And quite inert all this affront he bore.
I cannot blame him, helpless, weak and old,
No match for Bradamante, strong and bold.

27

Planning to cut off the magician's head,
Triumphantly she lifted her right arm;
But when she saw his face, all rage she shed.
A poor revenge it seemed to do him harm.
No worthy foe she had undone, instead
A sad, old man who trembled with alarm;
White-haired and wrinkled, in his helplessness
Three score and ten he seemed, or little less.

28

'For God's sake, take my life, young man!' he cried,
In accents both of anger and despair.
Yet, gladly as the old man would have died,
The valiant Maid was loath to grant his prayer.
First, on these points she would be satisfied:
Who was he? And this castle in the air,
Why had he built it in so wild a place?
Why did he prey thus on the human race?

29

'With excellent intentions, woe is me!',
The aged necromancer, weeping, said,
'I built my stronghold yonder, as you see.
Not for my own advantage am I led
To rapine, but to save from jeopardy
A gentle knight, for in the stars I read
That by a traitor's hand he'll meet his death
Ere long, converted to the Christian faith.

30

'The sun, gazing on both the hemispheres,
Sees nowhere else so beautiful a youth.
Ruggiero is his name. From tenderest years
I nurtured him; now Fate, harsh and uncouth,
And thirst for glory bring him where he nears
Disaster, serving Agramant. In truth
I love him more than if he were my son.
All that I do, I do for him alone.

31

'I built the fortress with one aim in view –
To keep Ruggiero safe. I captured him,
Just as today I planned to capture you.
I also caught, to please his every whim,
Brave cavaliers and ladies, not a few,
And men-at-arms, stalwart and strong of limb,
That, though he is deprived of liberty,
He might find solace in their company.

32

'That they may stay contentedly confined,
I make their every need my sole concern.
From every quarter, joys of every kind:
Games, music, clothing, food, at every turn.
All pleasures, all amusements you will find
For which the lips can ask, the heart can yearn.
The seed I sowed was yielding a fine crop,
But now to all my plans you put a stop.

33

'But, if your heart does not your face belie,
Do not divert my purpose from its course.
Accept my magic shield, a gift which I,
Atlante, make to you; take my swift horse
And leave my castle; if you must deny
Me this request, then take without remorse
One or two captives, or take all you meet,
But leave me my Ruggiero, I entreat.

34

'But if to grant this favour you refuse,
Before you take him back to France, I pray,
My soul from its involucre set loose
Wherein it dwells in squalor and decay.'
The valiant Maid thus answered him: 'I choose
To free Ruggiero; nothing you can say
Will alter my resolve. Your shield and horse
I take as mine by right, no longer yours.

35

'But even were they yours to give and take,
It seems to me they would be poor exchange.
You say you hold Ruggiero for his sake,
To save him from his evil stars. How strange!
Either the heavens' portent you mistake,
Else, though you clearly see, you cannot change
His fate. You cannot now foretell your own!
How can another's doom to you be known?

36

'I will not kill you. Vain are all your pleas.
If no one will oblige, the fatal blow
(If you still long to meet with your decease)
You can inflict upon yourself. Now go,
And first, ere your own spirit you release,
Open the doors of all your prisons.' So
The Maid commanded, urging as she spoke
The captive sorcerer towards the rock.

37

So, bound with his own chain, Atlante went,
With the bold warrior-maiden at his back.
She did not trust him, nor did she relent,
Being not convinced by his apparent lack
Of guile. Not far along the gradient
They climbed before they found a hidden crack,
Whence massive stairways spiralled to the top
And to the castle threshold led them up.

38

The necromancer here removes a block,
Inscribed with cabbalistic signs. Below
Are vases which continuously smoke,
Containing hidden fires. With a fell blow
The enchanter breaks them. At this magic stroke
The hill grows desolate and bleak, and lo!
The walls are gone, nowhere a tower is seen,
As if the edifice had never been.

39

The sorcerer that instant from his chain
Escaped, as from a net a thrush will do.
He and his castle went from the terrain
At the same moment, setting free anew
The knights and ladies; some of these (I mean
The ladies) from superb apartments to
The countryside transferred, in no small measure
Were disappointed by such loss of pleasure.

40

Gradasso there is seen, and Sacripante,
Prasildo also, the brave cavalier
Who with Rinaldo, when from the Levant he
Came, had journeyed; Iroldo, too, his peer;
And finally the lovely Bradamante
Finds her Ruggiero whom she holds so dear.
As soon as he is certain it is she,
He rides to welcome her most joyfully.

41

More than his eyes Ruggiero loved her – nay,
More than the life-blood of his very heart.
Long he had sought her ever since the day,
Glimpsing her golden hair, he knew love's smart.
And how she then sought him, 'twere long to say.
Through the dark forest, wandering apart,
They yearned to find each other, but in vain.
And now they have their hearts' desire again.

42

So when at last he sees her and he knows
That it is she alone who freed him, then
His heart with joy and gladness overflows.
Calling himself most fortunate of men,
Along the valley with the Maid he goes,
Where she achieved her recent triumph when
She overcame Atlante. In the field
They find the hippogriff, bearing the shield.

43

Moving towards it, Bradamante tries
To seize the rein; when almost near enough
She has approached, it spreads its wings and flies,
And lands upon a hillside not far off.
She follows it. Again, to her surprise,
It moves away on to another bluff,
Just as a crow will lead a dog a dance,
Now here, now there, and always in advance.

44

Gradasso, Sacripante, all that band
Of knights who with Ruggiero came below,
Scattered about the terrain, took their stand,
Some on the highest points, some on the low,
Wherever each foresaw the horse might land.
It leads them a wild goose chase to and fro,
Down in the valleys, up the mountain-tops.
At last, near where Ruggiero waits, it stops.

45

This is the secret work of the magician,
Who has not yet renounced his cherished scheme
Of rescuing Ruggiero. This ambition
Fills all his thoughts and every waking dream.
It's he who moves the horse to this position,
That out of Europe it may fly with him.
Ruggiero reaches out to take the bridle,
Meaning to lead it, but that thought is idle.

46

So from Frontino he at first dismounts
(For such the name is of Ruggiero's horse),
Then to the other creature's saddle mounts
And, to encourage it, applies the spurs.
It canters for a while, then all at once
It takes the air and lighter far it soars
Than a gerfalcon rises when the hood
Is lifted, as the falconer thinks good.

47

The Maid, seeing Ruggiero on the steed
In mortal peril and so high above,
By this event is horror-struck indeed.
For a long time she cannot speak or move,
And all that she has heard of Ganymede,
Snatched up to heaven by the will of Jove,
She has no doubt Ruggiero's fate will be,
For just as fair as Ganymede is he.

48

She follows him, her steadfast gaze on high.
As far as she can see, she looks her fill;
And when he disappears, in her mind's eye
The valiant Maid pursues his image still.
Her tears, her groans, her deep despair deny
All solace and relief, weep as she will.
Then, since she can no longer see Ruggier,
She turns her glance upon his destrier.

49

And she resolves that she will not abandon it,
But take it with her, hoping by and by
To see its master. With her gentle hand on it,
She leads it off. Ruggiero from the sky
Looks down upon the earth but cannot land on it.
His mount flies on and carries him so high,
And every peak recedes from view so far,
He cannot see where plains or mountains are.

50

He soars so far, he seems the merest dot
To anyone who views him from the ground.
The hippogriff then heads towards a spot
Whereon the sun, when with the Crab it's found,
Beats vertically, mercilessly hot.
It wings its way as smoothly as a sound
Sea-going vessel speeding on its route.
But let us leave him sailing through the skies,
And to Rinaldo once more turn our eyes.

51

Each day Rinaldo's ship ahead had gone,
Though pressed by winds and tossed by tumbling sea,
Now westward and now northward whirled and spun.
All day and night the gale blew ceaselessly.
At last the Scottish coast they draw upon,
Where Caledonia's forest they can see,
Where oftentimes amidst the ancient oaks
Is heard the clash of war and steel-edged strokes.

52

For there the cavaliers of Britain roam,
Valiant in arms, with knights of other lands,
Some from near by, and others far from home:
Norwegian, Frankish and Germanic bands.
Valour is needed by all those who come,
For here a knight his death, not glory, stands
To find; here Tristan, Galahad, Gawain,
Lancelot, Galasso, Arthur foes have slain.

53

And many a brave knight of both the old
And new Round Table here renown has won,
As many a monument to many a bold,
Brave deed, and many trophies have made known.
Taking his horse and weapons from the hold,
Rinaldo gallops inland and is gone,
Commanding first the pilot to make speed
And wait for him at Berwick-upon-Tweed.

54

Having no company, nor squire to bear
His shield, alone he travelled through the wood,
Seeking adventure, turning here and there,
First to the left, then right, as he thought good.
On the first day he reached an abbey where
Largesse by the kind cenobites in food
And shelter in their fair apartments paid is
To any passing cavaliers or ladies.

55

The abbot and the monks do all they can
To make Rinaldo welcome; he enquires
(But not till he restores his inner man
With all the tasty viands he desires)
If any enterprises, such as an
Adventurous young knight always requires,
Are to be found, whence risking death or worse,
He stands to earn renown or the reverse.

56

They said that in the forest thereabout
There was no lack of strange adventurings,
But often, left in darkness and in doubt,
The monks heard little of such happenings.
'Try, therefore,' they advised him, 'to seek out
An enterprise which fame and honour brings,
So that brave deeds of valour are not lost,
But glory is made known and all its cost.

57

'If you would put your valour to the test,
There is a worthy deed awaiting you,
The noblest task that ever knight addressed,
Whether in ancient times or in the new:
The daughter of our monarch is oppressed.
In need of help, she knows not what to do.
An evil lord, Lurcanio by name,
Intends that she shall die a death of shame.

58

'Lurcanio has reported to the king
(Inspired perhaps by hatred more than right)
That by a secret rope he saw her bring
Her lover to her balcony at night.
By law she is condemned for such a thing
To death by burning. Such, then, is her plight,
Unless within a month – and time is short –
A knight arrives to challenge this report.

59

'The law of Scotland, harsh, severe, unjust,
Decrees that every woman who in love
Bestows herself (except in marriage) must
Be put to death, quite irrespective of
Her rank, if she is thus accused of lust;
And the dread sentence no appeal can move,
Unless a knight will come to her defence
And boldly champion her innocence.

60

'The father of Ginevra, in his woe,
(For such the name is of the fair princess)
Has sent this proclamation high and low:
Whoever rescues her from her distress
And gives to calumny a mortal blow,
If he is nobly born, may claim, no less,
Ginevra as his bride, with such estate
As for her dowry is appropriate.

61

'But if within a month no one has come,
Or, having come, is vanquished, she must die.
This enterprise far better will become
You than all random venturing. Thereby
Not only fame and honour, but the plum
Of prizes you may win, than whom the eye
Of Phoebus none more lovely ever sees,
From Indus to the straits of Hercules.

62

'Wealth also will be yours and a domain
Where you will live content your whole life through,
And the king's favour, if but once again
His honour's reinstated thanks to you.
The laws of chivalry a knight constrain
To avenge the honour of a lady who
Is held by all who know her well to be
The very paragon of chastity.'

63

Rinaldo thought a while and then he said:
'A damsel is condemned to death because
She gave her lover solace in her bed
Who with desire for her tormented was?
A curse upon the legislator's head!
And cursed be all who tolerate such laws!
Death rather to such damsels as refuse,
But not to her who loves and life renews.

64

'And in my view it makes no difference
If the report is false or if it's true,
For this does not affect her innocence
(I'd praise her anyway, if no one knew).
I know just what to say in her defence.
So now a trusty guide I ask of you
To lead me to the accuser. I'll not waver,
For, as God is my help, I hope to save her.

65

'I will not say she did not do this deed.
Lest I am wrong, it would be ill-advised;
But I will say that even if she did,
She does not merit to be thus chastised.
And I will say that mad and bad indeed
He was who first this evil law devised,
Which from the statute-book should be erased
And by a wiser measure be replaced.

66

'If the same ardour, if an equal fire
Draws and compels two people ever more
To the sweet consummation of desire
(Which many ignoramuses deplore),
Why should a woman by a fate so dire
Be punished who has done what men a score
Of times will do and never will be blamed,
Nay, rather, will be praised for it and famed?

67

'This inequality in law much wrong
Has done to women. With God's help, I mean
To show that to have suffered it so long
The greatest of iniquities has been.'
Rinaldo's logic carried them along.
The ancient forefathers were justly seen
To be unjust to have consented to it;
Also the king, who could and should undo it.

68

When next the white and crimson light of day
Dispersed the darkness from our hemisphere,
Rinaldo took his weapons and away
He rode, having this time a squire to bear
His arms and to escort him on his way
Through miles and miles of forest, wild and drear,
Towards the city where a damsel's life
Hangs on the outcome of ordeal and strife.

69

Hoping to find a shorter route, they chose
A path which from the main direction veered,
And all at once a piteous cry arose,
Filling the wood with echoes sad and weird.
They spurred their destriers without repose
Until they reached the valley whence they heard
The sound come forth. There, in the custody
Of two rough villains, a fair maid they see.

70

And she was weeping, more than any maid
Or woman ever wept, or any ever could.
The ruffians at her side, with naked blade,
Prepared to stain the meadow with her blood,
And she was pleading with them, to evade
The cruel moment, hoping that they would
Relent. Rinaldo came and, at this sight,
Rode with loud threats to save her from her plight.

71

The ruffians, seeing help was imminent,
Fled down the vale and hid themselves in fear.
Scorning to follow them, Rinaldo went
Towards the lady, curious to hear
For what misconduct to such punishment
She was condemned; and as his squire draws near,
To lose no time, he bids him now take up
The lady pillion on his horse's croup.

72

And when their former path once more they find,
He looks at her more closely and can see
How fair she is, how gracious and refined,
Although much frightened by the danger she
Has just escaped; and when some calm of mind
She has regained, how did she come to be,
He asks, in such a pass? In a low tone
She answers him, as Canto Five makes known.

CANTO V

1

No creatures on the earth, no matter whether
Of peaceful disposition, mild and kind,
Or fierce and merciless as wintry weather,
Are hostile to the females of their kind.
The she-bear and her mate in sport together,
The lion and the lioness, we find;
The she-wolf and the wolf at peace appear;
The heifer from the bull has naught to fear.

2

What dreadful plague, what fury of despair
In our tormented bosoms now holds sway,
That wives and husbands constantly we hear
Wounding each other with the things they say?
With scratching, bruising, tearing out of hair,
Assault and battery, in bitter fray
They drench with scalding tears the marriage-bed,
And not tears only; sometimes blood is shed.

3

Not only a great wrong, but in God's sight
An outrage against Nature he commits
Who with his gentle helpmeet stoops to fight,
Or in her face a lovely woman hits,
Or harms a hair upon her head; but quite
Inhuman is the man who her throat slits,
Or chokes or poisons her; he, in my eyes,
Is not a man, but fiend in human guise.

4

Such were the evil ruffians who fled
Soon as Rinaldo's swift approach was seen.
He rescued the fair damsel whom they led
To the dark valley, where their plan had been
To draw their swords on her and kill her dead.
We left her talking to the paladin,
About to tell him what the reasons were
For her dire fate. I'll take the tale from there.

5

She thus began: 'I will describe to you
A deed more cruel and deliberate
Than ever Argos, Thebes, Mycenae knew,
Or any other place inspiring hate.
The sun, revolving his bright beams all through
The year, comes to this northern region late,
Being reluctant, I believe, to look
On such a cruel and remorseless folk.

6

'Men treat their enemies with cruelty,
And instances of this all ages show;
But to betray and kill ungratefully
A loyal friend is too unjust a blow.
That the full measure of the treachery
Of which I am the victim you may know,
Why in the very flower of my youth
They planned to kill me, I will tell the truth.

7

'Now, you must know, my lord, that while still young,
I was companion to our royal princess.
Together she and I grew up. Among
Her maids-in-waiting I had honoured place.
But Love unkind did me a cruel wrong.
So much he envied me my happiness,
He made the Duke of Albany appear
More handsome far than any cavalier.

8

'Because he seemed consumed with love for me,
With all my heart I loved him in return.
Words one can hear, the face is plain to see:
The inmost heart one seldom can discern.
Loving and trusting him, I planned that we
Might know the bliss for which all lovers yearn.
I chose, unheeding in my eagerness,
A chamber which belonged to the princess.

9

'She left her garments and possessions there,
Since often she preferred to use this room.
It has a balcony, to which no stair
Gives access, not enclosed, and jutting from
The wall. Love, as you know, will all things dare,
And so my lover many times would come
To climb the ladder made of rope, which I
Let down when in his arms I longed to lie.

10

'This opportunity I always took
Whenever the princess enabled me,
For many times that chamber she forsook,
The summer heat or winter cold to flee.
Since on that side no one could overlook
The palace, none our rendezvous could see;
And night and day nobody passes nigh
The houses lying derelict near by.

11

'For many months and days, joys not a few
We shared; in our delight, no amorous game
Was left untried, and, as our pleasure grew,
I seemed on fire with a consuming flame.
Blinded by love for him, I little knew
How much he feigned, how little, to his shame,
He loved me, though his sinister designs
Should have been evident from many signs.

12

'After some time he showed that he aspired
To the princess's hand, and, what is more,
I cannot tell you whether he was fired
With this ambition after or before
The love he feigned for me, but he acquired
Such an ascendancy that this I bore,
And when, unblushing, with no sense of pride,
He asked me to assist him, I complied.

13

'He told me that his love for me was true
And that his love for the princess was feigned.
His sole intention was, he said, to woo
Her as his bride, and if she then but deigned
To look with favour on his suit, he knew
The king would give consent, for, he explained,
No one in all the realm in rank and blood,
The king alone excepted, higher stood.

14

'And he convinces me that if I lend
My help and he the monarch's son-in-law
Becomes (no one, if he achieved this end,
Could rise to greater height, I plainly saw),
I can rely on him as on a friend.
In all his arguments there seemed no flaw
And he persuaded me that all his life
He'd give to me the love he owed a wife.

15

'My every wish and thought was for his sake,
And no desire of his could I gainsay.
In everything which my dear love would make
Contented, there my own contentment lay.
Thus every opportunity I take
To praise him and extol in every way
His virtues to Ginevra so that she
To love my love may be induced by me.

16

'With all my heart and soul I did and said
All that was possible, as in Heaven above
God is my witness, yet no progress made
In the design to make the princess love
My duke, whom I so greatly praised. Instead,
With her whole heart she was enamoured of
A noble, handsome, courteous cavalier,
Who from a distant land had travelled here.

17

'As a young boy, accompanied by his brother,
He came from Italy with us to dwell.
In all of Britain there was not another
To rival him in feats of arms or skill.
Our king esteemed and loved him as no other,
And, by endowing him, as was his will,
With castles, villas, fiefs and all such gifts,
The knight to a baronial rank uplifts.

18

'If the king found him pleasing, the princess,
Responding to the valour of the knight,
Named Ariodante, is drawn to him no less,
Nay more, for well she knew him to requite
Her love and that his heart with an excess
Of ardour burned for her, with flames more bright
Than Etna, Mount Vesuvius or Troy did
When by their strategem the Greeks destroyed it.

19

'The love she bore him with a heart sincere,
The perfect faith to which her soul inclined,
Made the princess reluctant to lend ear
To praises of the duke. Her steadfast mind
I could not change. The more I persevere,
Pleading with her to look on him with kind
Compassion, she, but scorning him the more,
Towards him grows more hostile than before.

'I deemed it best my lover should refrain
(And many, many times I said as much)
From an endeavour which I saw was vain.
There was no hope that he would ever touch
Her heart; as I repeatedly explain,
Her burning love for Ariodant is such,
If all the waters of the ocean drenched
That flame, no single spark of it were quenched.

21

'The duke, whose name is Polinesso, when
He heard my full account and understood,
And with his very eyes had plainly seen
In this vain enterprise how matters stood,
At last concluded that his love had been
Disdained, that by another she was wooed,
Whom she preferred. With injured pride he burned
And all his love to hate and anger turned.

22

'And, planning how to bring disharmony
Between Ginevra and her love, he schemes
An irremediable enmity
Which shall for ever cancel all their dreams:
By his intrigue, of gross unchastity
(Though innocent) Ginevra guilty seems.
He made me party to his fell design,
Nor did he look for other help than mine.

23

'His plan being formed, "Dalinda dear, you know"
(For that's my name), the duke, my lover, said,
"How from its root a sturdy tree will grow,
However many times the axe is laid:
So my ill-starred enamourment, although
By evil chance impeded and gainsaid,
Still burgeons with new longing and desire
And for fulfilment ever I aspire.

24

'"Yet not so much for pleasure, I confess,
I long for her, as to obtain my way.
So, if Ginevra I may not possess,
I'll bring imagination into play.
I want you to observe when the princess
Retires to rest; when she has cast away
Her garments and lies naked in her bed,
Seize them and put them on yourself instead.

25

'"Notice her ornaments and style of hair,
And, taking every detail in your scope,
All her appearance imitate with care.
Then from the balcony let down the rope,
Which I, pretending to be unaware
Of your disguise, will climb, for thus I hope
By self-deception to assuage my pain
And from my longing some relief to gain."

26

'These were his words; and I, my wits dispersed,
My mind and heart distraught, did not perceive
In all the strategy he thus rehearsed
The obvious deceit he planned to weave.
So, putting on Ginevra's clothing first,
Next from the balcony, where I received
My love, I let the hempen ladder fall.
Too late, the damage done, I see it all!

27

'The duke in the meantime, as man to man,
To Ariodante had addressed these words
(Before their rivalry in love began,
They were good friends, nor ever had crossed swords);
"My lord, I am astonished that you can
So ill repay the love which I towards
All those who are my equals, as is due,
Have always shown, and, likewise, shown to you.

28

'"For I am certain that you understand
I've loved Ginevra now for many a year.
This very day I go to ask her hand
In marriage of the king. Though it is clear
Your heart is fruitlessly bestowed, you stand
As an obstruction in my way. I swear
My chivalry would be a shade more fine
If I were in your shoes and you in mine!"

29

'"And I" (thus did bold Ariodant respond)
"Am even more amazed. You greatly err,
For of the fair princess my heart was fond
Long before ever you set eyes on her.
I know you know how ardent is the bond
Of love between us – how our hearts concur.
Her only longing is to be my wife.
I know she never loved you in her life.

30

'"Why do *you*, then, not show *me* the respect
Which you, in friendship's name, demand of me,
Which I would show to you if, in effect,
You were the one she loved? That she will be
My wife, I am entitled to expect
No less than you, although you hold in fee
A vast estate. The king loves me no less,
And I (not you) am loved by the princess."

31

'"Oh!" said the duke, " great error you're committing.
This love of yours has rendered you unstable.
Since of the pudding proof is in the eating,
Let us put all our cards upon the table.
Reveal your hand. I, likewise, as is fitting,
Will make my own as plain as I am able.
Then he whose hand is shown to be the thinner,
Let him declare the other man the winner.

32

'"And I am ready, if you wish, I'll swear
To keep for ever hidden what you say
In confidence to me, if you'll forbear
To make my secrets known in any way."
And so they both agreed in the affair
And on the Gospel placed their hands straightway,
Promising each to each complete discretion.
Then Ariodante first made this confession.

33

'He told with candour and with perfect truth
How things between him and the princess stood,
How in her words and letters she her troth
Had pledged, vowing no other husband would
She have; failing the king's consent, her youth
She would forgo and whosoever wooed
Her later as his lawful wedded wife
She would refuse and live a single life.

34

'He further said he hoped that in reward
For valour, many a time in battle shown,
Which he would gladly show again, to guard
The King of Scotland and the Scottish throne,
He might so earn his sovereign's regard
That as a worthy son-in-law he'd own
Him, and his daughter's happiness thereby
Secure and with her heart's desire comply.

35

'"So this is how I stand, and I believe ",
He said, "no man can rival me or prove
Me wrong; I'm not impatient to receive
A more explicit token of her love,
Being content, till we are wed, to leave
Things as they are, as by our God above
It is decreed. I ask no more. Her virtue
Would anyway gainsay me if I were to."

36

'When Ariodant his case had thus outlined
And the reward which he looked forward to,
The wily Polinesso, who designed
To make his hoped-for bride appear untrue,
Began: "When I have done, my friend, you'll find
I'm more advanced in this affair than you.
To make you own the justice of my claim,
Chapter and verse I'll now proceed to name.

37

'"She is deceiving you. She loves you not.
A diet of false hopes she's feeding you,
For, when with me, she scruples not one jot
To mock you and your love. That this is true
I'll prove – far more than promises I've got,
Or the vain words you are accustomed to;
And under pledge of secrecy I'll show
What it were better none should ever know.

38

'"I can assure you not a month goes by
But on three nights, or four, or six, or ten,
Naked within her loving arms I lie,
Lost in the pleasure which relieves the pain
Of love. With this you know you cannot vie.
Yours are but empty tales. Surrender then,
Or else provide some further proof. Admit
That you have lost the contest, and retreat."

39

'"I don't believe you,' Ariodant retorted.
"I know that what you tell me is untrue.
The truth for your own ends you have distorted,
It may be to dissuade me from my due.
But since such calumny you have reported,
To combat here and now I challenge you:
You are a liar and defame my love;
A traitor too, as I will quickly prove!"

40

'"It would not be good form", the duke replied,
"To have recourse to mortal combat where
The evidence on which we can decide
The issue is as plain as it is clear.
With your own eyes it can be verified."
An icy tremor seized the cavalier,
And if he truly had believed this boast,
He would straightway have given up the ghost.

41

'His face an ashy pale, his heart pierced through,
His mouth awry as with a bitter taste,
With trembling voice, he said: "If this is true,
No longer my devotion will I waste,
But give up every hope of her – to you
So liberal, to me so cold and chaste!
But do not think I will believe your lies,
Unless I see it with these very eyes."

42

'"I will arrange the time," the other said,
And he departed. Scarce two nights had passed,
I think, ere the arrangement we had made
Should bring him to my arms. The time at last
Had come to spring the careful trap he laid.
And so, his rival in despair to cast,
He bade him come that very night and hide
Where houses long had stood unoccupied.

43

'He pointed out a dwelling, opposite
The balcony where he was wont to climb.
At once the other knight suspected it
Might be an ambush where the deadly crime
Of murder Polinesso would commit,
Feigning the while (that he might choose his time)
To prove concerning the princess what he
Knew well was an impossibility.

44

'Yet he resolved to go, but in such guise
That if the duke intended to waylay him,
He would not let him take him by surprise,
Nor yet succeed in the design to slay him.
He had a valiant brother, bold and wise,
Lurcanio by name; none could gainsay him –
The greatest knight-at-arms of all our court –
And as the strength of ten was his support.

45

'He went to seek his help, and bade him take
His weapons and companion him that night.
Not even with his brother did he break
The vow of secrecy, as he deemed right.
A stone's throw from himself, for safety's sake,
He bade him stand: "If I am in dire plight,
I'll shout, but if you care for me at all,
Brother, I beg you, wait until I call."

46

'"Lead on; rely on me," his brother said.
So Ariodant, as bidden previously,
Entered the house which stood, untenanted,
Exactly opposite my balcony.
The vile deceiver, with an eager tread,
Approached to demonstrate the infamy
Of the princess. He duly gives the sign,
And still I'm unaware of his design.

47

'And so, clad in a robe of purest white,
Adorned with golden bands about the waist,
And on my head a golden net, bedight
With crimson tassels, in her style and taste,
Hearing the signal, I stepped forth to sight
On the veranda, and myself so placed
That from the house where Ariodant was hidden
I could be plainly seen, as I was bidden.

48

'Lurcanio, meanwhile, remained in doubt
And, fearful for the safety of his brother,
Or, it may be, desiring to find out
The cause of all the mystery and pother,
Resolved to see what it was all about.
So, in the dark, with stealthy steps, the other
House he entered, coming within a yard
Or two of Ariodant, and there stood guard.

49

'Of these manoeuvres wholly unaware,
I stood on the veranda, in the dress
I have described; thanks to the moonlight there,
Which made me plainly visible, no less
Than to the similarity I bear
In figure and in looks to the princess,
My face for hers being easily mistaken,
Misgivings in her lover's breast awaken.

50

'The more so, as considerable space
Parted the balcony from where he stood
In darkness near his brother in that place;
And thus it was that Polinesso could
Deceive the wretched lover, whose sad case
May be imagined and well understood.
Then Polinesso up the ladder climbs,
As he has done before so many times.

51

'And straight away, as my fond custom is,
I throw my arms about my lover's neck.
His mouth, his face, repeatedly I kiss.
He, in response, his ardour does not check.
Every caress intensifies our bliss.
Dejected, Ariodante sees the wreck
Of all his dearest hopes, as he believes,
And bitter disillusionment receives.

52

'His sorrow is so great that he decides
To take his life; and on the ground his sword,
Its pommel downwards, sets, that his insides
Upon its point the better may be gored.
Lurcanio, amazed, with mighty strides,
Having this fell design observed, toward
His brother leapt. He'd seen the duke's ascent,
But knew not who we were, nor what it meant.

53

'And he forbade him thus to immolate
Himself. (If he had moved more slowly or
Stood farther off, he would have been too late.)
"Brother," he cried, "Why do you thus abhor
Yourself? What has reduced you to this state?
Have you quite lost the wits you had of yore?
You let a woman drive you to your death?"
All this he shouted in a single breath.

54

'"Perish all women! And this faithless jade,
In whom you put your trust, deserves to die.
As once you loved her, do not be afraid
To hate her. For the sake of honour, try
Some worthier cause, and this your trusty blade,
Which now you turn against yourself, put by
To serve you when you bring this deed to light
Before your lord, the king, in lawful fight."

55

'Seeing his brother standing there beside him,
From his harsh plan the elder now desists,
But, unabated, secretly inside him
His desperate intention still persists.
Now that he deems Ginevra's love denied him,
He thinks no reason for his life exists,
Yet to his brother bravely plays the part
Of one who feels no sorrow in his heart.

56

'Next day, without a word to anyone,
Being driven by a mortal desperation,
His purpose even to himself unknown,
He left for an uncertain destination.
The riddle as to why or where he'd gone
Became the topic of much conversation
Among the members of the Scottish court,
Who put forth theories of every sort.

57

'After eight days or more they saw advance
A stranger who the princess came to find.
He brought her tidings of her Ariodant's
Demise: that he was drowned, not by the wind
Capsized, nor had he perished by mischance;
To his own death he had himself consigned.
From a high precipice, dejected, he
Had flung himself head first into the sea.

58

'"Before he did this deed," the stranger said,
"I met him quite by chance upon my way.
At his request, I followed where he led.
«I want you,» he explained to me, «to say
To the princess, on whose account I fled,
That what you are about to see today
I have been driven to because I've seen
Too much. Ah! happier if blind I'd been!»

59

'"We came just then by chance to where there is,
Opposite Ireland, a high promontory,
And from the summit of that precipice
He plunged, as I have said, into the sea.
So, to fulfil that last request of his,
I left him there and set out speedily."
Ginevra, in dismay, turns deathly pale
At the recital of this grievous tale.

60

'How she despaired, alas! and how she cried,
Soon as she gained the refuge of her bed!
She beat her breast, she rent her garments wide,
She tore her golden tresses from her head.
And often she repeated, mystified,
Those last reproachful words which he had said:
That he was driven by his grief to such
A grievous death because he'd seen too much.

61

'Through all the land there travelled the report
Of Ariodante's broken-hearted leap.
Each cavalier, each lady of the court,
The king himself, could scarce forbear to weep.
Lurcanio's sorrow was of such a sort,
The pain in his fraternal heart so deep,
To follow in his brother's steps he yearned
And on himself his sword he all but turned.

62

'Many a time he muttered through clenched teeth:
"By that intrigue of hers Ginevra drove
My brother from his mind and to his death,
Soon as he saw how faithless was her love."
Desire for vengeance grew with every breath.
Anger and grief together in him strove.
For king's and people's wrath he'd little care:
He'd bring to light the truth of the affair.

63

'Before the throne, being careful first to wait
Until the chamber filled with courtiers was,
He said, "My Lord, as you well know, my late
Lamented brother, disregarding laws
Of reason, killed himself. Of his sad fate
Your daughter is the one and only cause,
For by her conduct, faithless and unchaste,
His youth and life she drove him thus to waste.

64

'" He loved her; and as no dishonour stained
His love, to tell you all is my intent.
By virtuous deeds his hope was to have gained
Her as his lawful wife, with your consent.
Alas! while at a distance he remained,
Grateful if he might sometimes breathe the scent
Of foliage, he saw one climb the tree
And pluck the longed-for fruit clandestinely."

65

'Proceeding with his tale, he then related
How he had seen her let the ladder down
To where her paramour below had waited.
This man's identity remained unknown.
He had disguised himself, Lurcanio stated,
With hair concealed and clothing not his own.
He was prepared by means of his good blade
To verify the truth of all he said.

66

'You can imagine then her father's grief
When such an accusation he has heard.
Not only was it passing all belief,
And in his breast a deep amazement stirred,
But well he knew and understood that if
In her defence no champion appeared,
Able to give Lurcanio the lie,
He must condemn the fair princess to die.

67

'I do not doubt that you have heard, kind sir,
Of this our law which thus condemns a maid
Or married woman, who in love may err
Or give herself outside the marriage-bed,
To die, unless a valiant cavalier,
Before a month elapses, offers aid,
Proving her innocent and in the teeth
Of her accuser saving her from death.

68

'The king has sent his heralds far and wide
(For he believes his daughter innocent)
To say he will bestow her as a bride,
And on her make a handsome settlement,
To any knight who rallies to her side
And clears her of this infamy: so went
His proclamation, but response is slow,
So fierce the bearing of Lurcanio.

69

'Her brother, Prince Zerbino, by ill chance
Is absent from the kingdom; for some time
He has been giving proof of his good lance,
Gaining renown in a far distant clime.
If he were near enough he'd come at once,
Or, if the news could be despatched to him,
Within a month; he would not fail his sister,
But in her present peril would assist her.

70

'The king meanwhile attempts to ascertain,
By other proofs than arms, if false or true
The accusation is, and if the pain
Of shameful death his child must undergo.
So, hoping further evidence to gain,
He asked her maids-in-waiting what they knew.
I understood that if he questioned me
The duke and I would be in jeopardy.

71

'Departing from the court that very night,
I hastened where I hoped to find the duke,
And straight away I warned him that I might
Be questioned; but he uttered no rebuke,
Rather he praised me and allayed my fright
With many a kind word and loving look,
And, bidding me take refuge in a fort,
He chose two servitors as an escort.

72

'By many tokens, as you know, my lord,
I proved my passion was sincere, not feigned.
How truly Polinesso I adored,
How much he owed to me, I have explained.
Now hear what I received as a reward,
Now see what my devotion to him gained,
And judge if any woman in return
For love, love's recompense can hope to earn.

73

'Ungrateful, cruel and perfidious,
No pity or remorse he seems to feel,
And, of my loyalty now dubious,
He fears that in the end I may reveal
His whole intrigue, so sly and devious.
Thus, feigning that his aim is to conceal
Me in the fort for safety, he pretends
My welfare, but my death in truth intends.

74

'In secret those two ruffians he instructed
That when they brought me to a certain spot,
Where he designed that I should be abducted,
They were to kill me, and this gruesome plot,
If by my cries you had not been conducted,
Would have succeeded. Such, then is the lot
Of those who truly love!' So ends her tale,
Related as they ride up hill, down dale.

75

Of all adventures which had come his way,
This pleased Rinaldo most; when he had heard
All that the maid-in-waiting had to say,
He was convinced Ginevra had not erred.
Her innocence was now as clear as day,
And if at first Rinaldo was prepared
To be her champion, whether right or wrong,
Now all the more his bold resolve grew strong.

76

Towards St Andrew's city, where the king
And all his courtiers assembled were
To watch the singular event (a thing
More strange than this they'd seldom seen occur),
Rinaldo galloped at full speed to bring
Assistance in the role of challenger,
And on the journey, near the citadel,
He met a squire who had fresh news to tell.

77

A stranger had arrived to champion
Ginevra in her undeserved disgrace.
The markings on his banner were unknown,
Giving no hint of family or race;
Where'er he went, he kept his visor down,
Thus nobody so far had seen his face.
Not his own shield-bearer, who night and day
Attended him, his origin could say.

78

Then on they went and after riding hard
They saw the city walls against the sky.
Dalinda was afraid to pass the ward
But for Rinaldo put misgivings by.
As they approached they saw the gate was barred.
Rinaldo asked: 'What does this signify?'
He was informed that all the populace
Had flocked to where the combat would take place,

79

Between Lurcanio and the unknown knight,
Across the city, on the farther side,
Where on a plain they had begun to fight.
At Montalbano's name the gate flew wide
And straight away behind him was locked tight.
Then with Dalinda having passed inside,
He leaves her at an inn, as she entreats,
Before he gallops off through empty streets.

80

In words of comfort, bidding her adieu,
He promised he would soon return to her,
Then speedily rode off to where he knew
The warriors in deadly combat were.
Much they had given and much taken too,
Both the accuser and the challenger,
The one to prove Ginevra false intending,
The other knight her good repute defending.

81

Six knights attended them in the stockade.
They were on foot, armed only in cuirass.
The Duke of Albany was on parade,
Mounted upon a destrier; he as
High Constable the spectacle surveyed,
That no untoward event might come to pass.
With joy and arrogance his bosom swelled
When the princess in peril he beheld.

82

Between the serried ranks Rinaldo moves,
His good Baiardo scattering the fray;
For at the thunder of his mighty hooves
Not one for long will linger in the way.
In his magnificence Rinaldo proves
The most superb of all that vast array.
Before the king's pavilion he draws rein
And all the multitude flock round again.

83

Then to the king, Rinaldo in this guise
Began his plea: 'My lord, I pray, to this
Dread combat call a halt. Whichever dies
Of the two combatants will die amiss.
One thinks he has just cause, and yet he lies
Unknowingly; his that same error is
Which drove his brother to his tragic leap,
And drives him now a false revenge to reap.

84

'The other knows not if he's wrong or right.
To his bold heart this is of no import;
For that which moves a noble, valiant knight
Is beauty in distress of any sort.
But I to innocence now bring respite;
I bring the opposite of false report.
For God's sake, part these combatants, I pray,
And then lend ear to what I have to say.'

85

By his authority and noble mien
And by his words, the monarch is impressed,
And straightway to the Constable is seen
To give the needed signal to desist.
To knights and barons gathered on the green
And all the company which round him pressed,
Rinaldo then, withholding not one jot,
Revealed in full the villain's evil plot.

86

And next he offers, for he has no fears,
To prove by arms that what he says is true.
They summon Polinesso: he appears,
Perturbed and undecided what to do;
And when Rinaldo his denial hears,
He shouts: 'Let deeds decide 'twixt me and you!'
They are both armed; all's ready for the fray,
The combat can begin without delay.

87

Ah! how the king and all his people longed
That the princess would be proved innocent,
That God would clearly show she had been wronged
By Polinesso with malign intent!
For he was covetous of what belonged
To others, cruel, proud and fraudulent.
That he should perpetrate such vile deception
Appeared in character and no exception.

88

There on the jousting-field he stands, forlorn,
With trembling heart, his cheek an ashen grey.
At the third blast upon the herald's horn
He puts his lance in rest. And straight away
Rinaldo rides headlong in mighty scorn,
Intending with one stroke to win the day.
His expertise is equal to the test:
His weapon pierces his opponent's breast.

89

Fixed in his trunk, it hurls him to the ground
Six yards at least from where his charger stands.
Rinaldo leaves the saddle with one bound
And of the villain's helmet slits the bands.
Further resistance useless now is found.
He sues for mercy at Rinaldo's hands,
And in the hearing of the court and king
Confesses he has done this dreadful thing.

90

He has not time to tell it all; his breath,
His voice, his life, are all at once cut short.
The king, seeing his daughter freed from death
And from the infamy of ill report,
Is overjoyed and more consoled than with
A loss restored to him of any sort,
Even his crown, supposing it were stolen.
With joy and gratitude his heart is swollen.

91

And when he sees the champion remove
His helmet, and Rinaldo stands revealed
(Knowing him as the son of Aymon of
Great valour), he gives thanks that such a shield
As this his daughter's innocence should prove;
Then turns to him whose face is still concealed,
That knight, unknown, who, in Ginevra's aid,
Challenged Lurcanio with lance and blade.

92

Requested by the king to tell his name,
Or let at least his countenance be seen,
That he may be rewarded, as became
A knight who so courageously had been
Inspired with such a noble, gallant aim,
He moves into the centre of the scene
And there at last reveals what I'll make clear
If my next canto you are pleased to hear.

CANTO VI

1

Doomed is the wretch who thinks that he can hide
All traces of the crime he has committed,
For if all else is dumb, it will be cried
Upon the air or from the depths emitted;
And God Himself events will sometimes guide
So that the sinner by the sin's outwitted,
And inadvertently, without being asked,
He gives himself away and is unmasked.

2

That malefactor, Polinesso, thought
He'd covered every vestige of his crime;
And of his one accomplice he had sought
To rid himself for ever in good time.
The second subterfuge it was which brought
To pass the sequel which defeated him.
This might have been avoided, but he spurred
Too eagerly and, thus, his death incurred.

3

Friends, dukedom, life he lost, at one fell blow,
And, what is worse, he died in dire disgrace.
Now, as I said, they cannot wait to know
Who the strange knight may be, whom none can place.
At last he pulls his helmet off, to show,
To everyone's surprise, the well-loved face
Of Ariodante, mourned by every Scot
Who heard the story of his tragic lot,

4

That Ariodant, for whom so many cry,
For whom Ginevra broken-hearted is,
The king, the court, his brother – not an eye
That has not wept for valour such as his –
They wonder: was the traveller's tale a lie?
No, it is true that from a precipice
He saw him make his tragic leap, head first,
And naturally had presumed the worst.

5

As often happens, when a man's despair
So drives him that his mind on death is set,
But when he sees it, harsh and fierce, draw near,
He finds some recompense in living yet,
So Ariodante saw the matter clear.
Once in the sea, his mood changed to regret.
Exerting all his courage as of yore,
He swam with mighty strokes to reach the shore.

6

He now despised the impulse which possessed him.
The urge to end his life he scorned as mad,
And, once on land, where no one could have guessed him,
In his wet clothes – the only ones he had –
He walked until he came where he might rest him.
Finding a hermit in a cell, who bade
Him welcome, for a while incognito
He tarried, for he thought his host might know

7

How the princess the tragic news had taken,
Whether of joy or sadness she gave sign.
Hearing that by such sorrow she was shaken,
Her very life was threatened with decline,
He wondered if perhaps he was mistaken.
This made him the more bitterly repine,
Regretting that his brother had denounced her
Before her father, and unchaste pronounced her.

8

And he conceived for him as deep a hate,
As ardent as his love for the princess.
He did not want him thus to vindicate
His honour by a deed so merciless,
And when he heard that there was none to date
Who offered to defend her in distress
(Since many cavaliers were hesitant
To challenge one so strong and militant,

9

For many held Lurcanio to be
So skilled in single combat that none dared
To place himself in mortal jeopardy,
Or, if his prowess were in doubt, none cared
To take the risk – thus the majority
Of cavaliers this hesitation shared),
He, having in his mind all this revolved,
To fight against his brother then resolved.

10

'Alas!' he thought, 'that the princess should meet
Her end because of my calamities!
How bitter and acute were my regret
If she should die before my own demise!
She is my lady and my goddess yet,
She is the day-spring of my very eyes.
So, right or wrong, I must take up my shield
In her defence and die upon the field.

11

'Shall I defend the wrong? So let it be.
So let me die, since little do I care,
Save that, on my defeat, the penalty
Of death must then be paid by one so fair.
There is this single recompense for me:
That she before the end will be aware
How ill by Polinesso she was loved,
Since to her aid the coward has not moved.

12

'But I, to whom she gave such great offence –
When the encounter ends she will soon know –
Shall have laid down my life in her defence;
And on my brother, by the self-same blow,
I'll be revenged for giving such offence
To one I love so well; because his foe,
Whom he'll have slain to vindicate his brother,
Will be discovered to have been none other.'

13

Thus turning matters over in his mind
(With little common sense, I may as well owe)
Some new accoutrements he means to find:
New arms, new horse, shield bordered green and yellow,
Sable the rest, a surcoat of like kind.
Meeting by chance a squire, he takes the fellow
To attend him and rides off, to all unknown,
To fight against his brother, as I've shown.

14

I told you how the sequel went and how
As Ariodante he is known once more.
The king by this is as delighted now
As by his daughter's rescue just before.
'She could not find a truer love, I vow;
His ardour will not wane, of that I'm sure,'
Thus the king mused, 'for, thinking she'd offended,
Yet her good name in combat he defended.'

15

So, as he loved his daughter tenderly,
He yielded to the pressure of the court
And to Rinaldo's most insistent plea.
He gladly named the champion her consort,
Creating him the Duke of Albany,
Succeeding Polinesso for, in short,
The dukedom falling vacant when he died,
It was bestowed in dowry on the bride.

16

Rinaldo for Dalinda begged for grace,
Since little in this evil plot she'd done,
And, weary of the world and all its ways,
She vowed to seek admission as a nun
Somewhere in Denmark, where she'd end her days,
And very soon from Scotland she was gone.
But let us once again Ruggiero find
Who on the hippogriff flies like the wind.

17

He was a valiant cavalier, I know,
Stalwart and brave; and yet it's my belief,
Although of calm he made an outward show,
Within, his heart was trembling like a leaf.
He'd passed the whole of Europe long ago,
And, heading ever West, the hippogriff,
Beyond the pillars fixed by Hercules,
Had ventured over the forbidden seas.

18

That strange, enormous, wingèd quadruped
On beating pinions bore him on so fast,
The lightning-flash, by summer tempest shed,
By such velocity would be surpassed.
All other birds by it would be outsped,
All creatures racing it would be outclassed.
Scarcely the arrow or the thunderbolt
Hurtles to earth, I think, with swifter jolt.

19

And when the bird, unswerving in its flight,
Had travelled on, traversing many a mile,
Weaving wide circles, weary now of height,
It hovered low at last above an isle,
Just such a place where Arethusa might
Have lingered in concealment for a while,
When she had caused her lover grievous pain
And underneath the sea had passed in vain.

20

No lovelier isle, no pleasanter it knew
In all its many journeys through the air;
Nor, even had it searched the whole world through,
Would the great bird have found a land more fair.
One last wide circle in the sky it drew,
Then with Ruggiero it alighted where,
Mid cultivated plains and rounded hills,
Lush meadows, shadowed banks and sparkling rills,

21

Welcoming groves of laurel, cool and soft,
Of palm, and myrtle, fragrant and most sweet,
And orange-trees and cedar gently waft
Their perfume, as their fruit and flowers meet
In myriad lovely forms which twine aloft
A leafy shelter from the summer's heat.
Among the branches, flying unafraid,
The nightingales a dulcet music made.

22

Among the roses, which cool breezes keep
For ever fresh, and lilies, white as snow,
The hares and conies confidently leap,
And proudly-antlered stags unhurried go,
Fearing no trap or hunter in the deep
Recesses of the wood, or when with slow
And peaceful gaze they ruminate. Goats frisk,
And every creature frolics without risk.

23

While the winged horse had been approaching land,
Ruggiero from a certain height had seen
That it was safe to leave the saddle, and
So found himself on the enamelled green.
He kept the bridle firmly in his hand,
Then to a myrtle, which he found between
A laurel and a pine, he tied the beast,
For to secure it to the earth seemed best.

24

Not far away he saw a spring, set round
With cedars and date-bearing palms. He drew
His helm and gauntlets off and on the ground
Near by set down his shield. Next, on the view
Of sea and hills he gazed in turn. The sound
Of the caressing breeze which gently blew
Released a joyful murmuring and stir
Among the beech-tree tops and those of fir.

25

From time to time, to cool his burning lips,
Over the plashing fountain, clear as glass,
He bends, and from the crystal water sips;
And to subdue the fire which his cuirass
Has kindled in his veins, his hand he dips
And splashes in the pool – no wonder, as,
Without a pause and armed as for a tourney,
Three thousand miles he travelled on his journey.

26

And, as he tarries there, the hippogriff,
Which he has tied among the shady brakes,
Begins to kick and rear and plunge, as if
It shied at some strange, lurking form. It shakes
The myrtle, so that every bough and leaf
Tosses and twists, and, round about, it makes
A carpet of the mutilated fronds;
And even so it cannot break its bonds.

27

As when a log of wood, which once was green,
Of which the pith has shrivelled, leaving spaces
Where sappy softness formerly has been,
Is thrown upon the flames whose warm embraces
Convert to roars and groans the air within,
As through the hollow aperture it races,
So does that injured myrtle moan and shriek,
As through the splitting bark it tries to speak.

28

A plaintive voice, no longer thus confined,
Issued at last, articulate and clear,
And said: 'If you are courteous and kind,
As from your noble aspect you appear,
This creature from my tree, I pray, unbind.
The suffering I undergo is drear
And harsh enough; let it not be increased
By the infliction of this restless beast.'

29

Ruggiero, startled by this anguished cry,
In great astonishment at once turned round,
And on his senses scarcely dared rely.
He scrambled to his feet and with one bound
The hippogriff he hurried to untie.
And when at last the power of speech he found,
'O human soul, or woodland sprite,' he said,
'I pray you, pardon me' – and blushed bright red.

30

'Since I was unaware that you reside,
A living spirit, hidden in this bark,
I tethered my winged charger to your side,
Which on your fronds has sadly left its mark.
But do not leave me thus unsatisfied,
I pray you, do not keep me in the dark,
But tell me who you are, ah! do not fail,
As you may sheltered be from snow and hail.

31

'If now or ever I can make amends
To compensate you for the damage done,
By her who holds my fate in her fair hands
And of my soul is the custodian,
I swear that I will labour to such ends,
You will have cause to bless me.' Whereupon,
As soon as brave Ruggiero ceased to speak,
From tip to root the bush began to shake.

32

Along the rugged bark a moisture oozed,
As when from a green firebrand the sap,
Yielding at last to the fierce heat, is loosed
Through many a tiny orifice and gap,
And, into sound converted, then disclosed
The story of the spirit's sad mishap:
'By words so courteous I am induced
To say by whom and why I'm thus reduced.

33

'Astolfo was my name: a paladin
Of France, and on the battlefield much feared.
Orlando and Rinaldo are my kin.
As cousinly companions we were reared.
After my father, Otto, I was next in
Line as king of England (so it appeared).
Handsome and debonair, by many loved,
My own worst enemy at last I proved.

34

'Returning from that archipelago
Which waters of the Indian ocean lave
Upon the east, where I with Rinaldo
And others were imprisoned in a cave,
Whence we were rescued, as perhaps you know,
By the supreme endeavours of the brave
Orlando, we travelled on towards the West
Along the lands by northern tempests vexed.

35

'Led on our weary way by cruel Fate,
We came one morning to a lovely strand,
Where stood near by the castle and estate
Of fair Alcina, ruler of that land.
She issued at that moment from her gate.
Alone upon the shore we saw her stand.
Without a net, without a hook, she fished,
Making as many catches as she wished.

36

'The dolphins at her call come quickly leaping;
The tunneys flounder, gasping at her feet;
Sperm whales and seals are startled from their sleeping;
Mullet and salmon, pleasurable to eat,
Crowd in their hundreds, high and higher heaping;
Pistrices, with the orcs, swim forth to meet
The physiters, the grampuses, the whales,
In bulk gigantic and with thrashing tails.

37

'We see one mighty whale, larger than all
The whales that ever swam in any sea,
Upon the surface, plainly visible,
Rising at least eleven paces. We,
As to a man, into one error fall,
For, lying motionless, it seems to be
An island, of proportions vast and wide,
As from afar we scan it, side to side.

38

'Alcina drew the fishes from the waters
By words and charms of which she knew the worth.
She and the fay Morgana both were daughters
Of the same parents (whether at one birth
I know not) and both sisters of King Arthur's.
Alcina looked at me and showed no dearth
Of cunning (in such things she's skilled enough)
As from the other knights she cut me off.

39

'She came towards us with a gracious smile,
With courteous manner and disarming speech,
And said: "Brave knights, pray linger here a while.
Allow me to conduct you from this beach.
To my abode I'll take you and beguile
You with my fish menagerie, of which
I have a great variety, as bright
And countless as the myriad stars of night.

40

'"And if a siren some of you would care
To meet, who with sweet singing calms the sea,
Explore that territory over there,
Where at this time of day she's wont to be."
She pointed to the whale; and I, who dare
All enterprises with temerity,
(And I have bitter reason now to rue it)
Without a moment's pause crossed over to it.

41

'Rinaldo and Dudone quickly sign
To me that I should look before I leap.
To no avail, for of her fell design
I'm now a captive, lost upon the deep.
Alcina laughs, her eyes with triumph shine.
The whale, which knows her purpose, does not keep
Her waiting, but swims rapidly away,
Far from the mainland, to my great dismay.

42

'Rinaldo flung himself into the ocean
To try to rescue me; he may have drowned,
For there arose a furious commotion,
Stirred by the wind, and darkness wrapped us round.
So what became of him I have no notion.
Ways of consoling me Alcina found,
And all that day and the ensuing night
She kept me in her company, or sight.

43

'So, speeding on the back of the marauder,
We journey till we reach this island, where
Alcina's sister reigned, as was in order,
She being King Uther's only female heir.
Alcina had not scrupled to defraud her
Although, as many people are aware,
She and Morgana are the fruit of incest.'
To this Ruggiero listened with great interest.

44

'They are as full of vile iniquity
(Being in sin and infamy well matched)
As she, who lives a life of purity,
To all the seven virtues is attached;
And so they mounted a conspiracy
And more than once an army they despatched,
With orders from her island realm to drive her,
And of a hundred fortresses deprive her.

45

'And scarce an inch of land would she possess
(Her name is Logistilla, I should say)
But for a gulf her sisters cannot pass
And rugged mountain peaks which bar the way,
As Cheviot hills and Tweed create impasse
And Scotch and English forces hold at bay.
And still this evil couple never rest
But every stronghold from her seek to wrest.

46

'This guilty couple are so filled with sin
That Logistilla's virtue they both hate.
But, to resume, how from a paladin
A myrtle I became, I will relate.
Alcina in great bliss now held me in
Her toils, and with a love insatiate
She burned, and I enamoured was no less
By every blandishment and sweet caress.

47

'And in her tender limbs I knew such joy
The sum of all delights it seemed to be,
Such as no lovers in this world enjoy,
For bliss to few is granted copiously.
No memories of war my thoughts employ
Or come between her lovely face and me.
Of her and of her only I'm aware;
Naught can I do but on her beauty stare.

48

'And I by her was loved as much, and more,
And presently no need had she of others.
To all her lovers she had shown the door
(Before my time there had been many others).
The office of adviser I soon bore
And I it was gave orders to the others.
In me she trusted and on me relied,
And day and night I never left her side.

49

'Alas! my bleeding wounds why do I probe,
Having no hope of healing medicine?
Why do I bring to mind these memories of
A happiness now vanished, as within
A myrtle-bush I languish in this grove?
Just when I thought the sum of bliss was mine,
Just when it seemed most ardently she burned,
Alcina to another lover turned.

50

'Too late I learn of her inconstancy.
She loves, or she loves not, as suits her book.
Scarcely two months had passed, I think, ere she,
As was her whim, another lover took
And from all confidence excluded me
With many an unfriendly word and look.
I later learned that she had likewise thwarted
A thousand others by whom she'd been courted.

51

'And, lest her disappointed lovers spread
Report of this lascivious life of hers,
She plants them in a very different bed,
Converting them to palm-trees or to firs,
Or olive-trees, or cedars, or instead,
The lesser status of a bush confers,
Or turns them into animals or streams,
Or any form that pleasing to her seems.

52

'Now you, who by some unaccustomed way
Have travelled to this isle of doom, my lord,
On your account some wretched lover may
Be changed to stone or water at her word.
On you Alcina will devolve her sway,
And bliss beyond all mortal joy award;
But, be advised, the time must surely come
When rock or tree or fountain you become.

53

'Such knowledge as I have I've gladly shared,
Although I doubt if it will much avail you.
At least, for what you'll find, you are prepared.
Forewarned's forearmed: she can the less assail you.
Perhaps, since I have told you how I fared,
Your own good sense and prudence will not fail you,
And what a thousand others could not do –
Defend themselves – will be achieved by you.'

54

Ruggiero had long known Astolfo's name,
For he was cousin to the Maid he loved.
He grieved to find him fallen to this shame,
Changed to a sterile plant and far removed
From noble deeds which for a knight win fame.
For Bradamante's sake his heart is moved;
He'd gladly rescue him if he knew how.
All he can do is to console him now.

55

He ministered such comfort as he could,
Then asked if there was any path which led
To Logistilla's realm by which he would
Avoid Alcina; and Astolfo said
There was another route, he understood,
A rough and rugged, rock-strewn way to tread,
A little further on, then to the right,
And up a slope, towards the topmost height.

56

Let him not think, however, he will far
Advance along this path so harsh and steep,
For he will meet an enemy who'll bar
The way and with ferocity will keep
The pass. Alcina's frontier guards they are,
Who bring to book whoever would escape.
Then for the information he imparted
Ruggiero thanked the myrtle and departed.

57

Untethering his mount, he held the rein
And walked the creature slowly after him.
He did not choose to ride on it just then,
Lest it take off with him another time.
The right-hand path his purpose was to gain
And to the land of Logistilla climb.
He was determined to use all his skill
Not to fall captive to Alcina's will.

58

Should he perhaps his wingèd charger take
And cross the mountain peak by means of it?
He was afraid this might be a mistake,
For it responded little to the bit.
So then he thought: 'My way by force I'll make,
If circumstance and destiny permit.'
Soon, two miles from the sea-coast, he beholds
The lovely city which Alcina holds.

59

A line of bastions has caught his eye
Which rings the mighty citadel around.
They are so tall they almost touch the sky,
And from their topmost height down to the ground
They seem to be of solid gold (and I
Am told by some that evidence was found
Of alchemy): however that may be,
They glitter so, they look like gold to me.

60

But when he saw those walls so rich and fair
(In all the world their equal was unknown),
He shunned the broad, unswerving highway which
Towards the portals would have led him on,
And, hoping Logistilla's land to reach,
Turned to the right towards the hill; but soon
A horde of deadly enemies engage
All his attention with their frenzied rage.

61

No stranger band of foes had ever been,
No faces more repellent or distorted;
Some, human downwards from the neck, were seen
With cat or ape-like heads to be ill sorted.
Some, gambolling, made goat-prints on the green,
And prancing centaurs round about cavorted.
Some old and slow, some young, with urchin grins,
Some naked, and some clad in furs or skins.

62

Some on a charger gallop to and fro
Without a rein; or on a donkey amble,
Or on an ox; on centaurs' backs some go;
On eagles, cranes and ostriches some scramble.
Some drink from stirrup-cups, some bugles blow.
Female or male or both, without preamble
All kinds of tools and implements they brandish –
Rope-ladders, pikes and shovels, all outlandish.

63

The monster who was captain of this crew,
His belly swollen and his lips distended,
Upon a turtle rode; with slow and few
Alternate steps, its wrinkled feet extended.
On this side and on that were ruffians who
With kind solicitude on him attended;
For he was drunk: his brow and chin some mopped,
Some fanned, some held him upright when he flopped.

64

One creature with a human trunk and feet,
With canine neck and ears and proboscis,
Bellows and barks to make the knight retreat
Towards the city which behind him is.
He answers: 'I'll surrender to no threat
As long as I have strength to handle this':
He shows his sword and turns the pointed end
Against his foe, his passage to defend.

65

The monster tries to wound him with a lance.
Ruggiero quickly presses the attack.
He drives his weapon through its chest at once —
Six inches it protrudes behind its back —
Then, shield on arm, makes ready to advance.
His foe, alas! for numbers does not lack.
They goad and harass him at every stride.
He slashes, cuts and thrusts on every side.

66

Some to the teeth, some to the chine he cleaves:
Thus the infernal race he decimates.
They have no shields, no helmets and no greaves,
No coats of mail, cuirass, or armour-plates.
And yet, hemmed in, no headway he achieves
In the congestion which the horde creates.
He needs — the enemy's so numerous —
As many arms as had Briareus.

67

If he had been inclined to use the shield
Which to the sorcerer had once belonged,
And which Atlante cunningly would wield
And many a brave knight with it had wronged,
He could have rendered helpless on the field
The brutish mob which round about him thronged.
But it is well perhaps that he refused
The aid of fraud, and only valour used.

68

But, come what may, he'd rather contemplate
His death than fall a victim to this host.
Meanwhile there issue by the city gate,
Forth from those walls which golden splendour boast,
Two damsels who must be of high estate:
So noble is their bearing, of such cost
Is their attire – no shepherdesses these –
But ladies born to lead a life of ease.

69

And each is mounted on a unicorn.
Whiter than ermine these two beasts appear.
The beauty of the garments which adorn
The riders so enhances them, I fear
No man in all the world was ever born
Who with undazzled vision could declare
A judgement on their loveliness, which seems
The embodiment of all our fairest dreams.

70

And now they move towards the meadow grass
Where brave Ruggiero battles with the band.
The ruffians stand aside to let them pass.
Each lady to the knight extends her hand.
And, with a rosy blush upon his face,
He thanks the damsels, who thus put an end
To his ordeal, and gladly he agrees
To pass the golden gate, if they so please.

71

Above the portal was a pediment,
In all its surface sculpted in relief.
No part of it was lacking ornament,
Being encrusted, it is my belief,
With precious jewels from the Orient.
Four pillars give support, as hard as if
In all their girth hewn from the diamond-stone.
No fairer, lovelier gate was ever known.

72

And on the threshold, near the colonnade,
Alluring damsels sported winsomely.
(If more sedate decorum they displayed,
More comely and more lovely still they'd be.)
In garments of bright green they were arrayed,
With coronals of leaves; seductively,
With beckoning gestures and with smiling eyes,
They ushered in the knight to Paradise.

73

Nor would this be too fanciful a name
For the abode where Love, I think, was born,
Where everyone in dance or joyful game
The festive hours employed from early morn;
Where of sad thoughts no shadow ever came
To spoil this rosebed life without a thorn.
There no discomfort was, no cup was empty,
But endless bounty from the horn of plenty.

74

For here, as with serene and radiant brow,
April, it seems, forever sweetly smiles.
Young men and women to each other vow
Their love; one by a fountain sings, one whiles
Away the time beneath a leafy bough,
One on a shady hill the hours beguiles,
And one with a companion draws aside,
His thoughts of love the better to confide.

75

Among the topmost branches of the trees,
Laurels and conifers, tall pine and beech,
Gaily rejoicing in their victories,
Small Cupids flutter, chattering each to each,
And if a heart as yet untouched one sees,
He shoots; or else, if it be out of reach,
He spreads a net. Some to a stream are flown
To temper darts or file them on a stone.

76

They gave Ruggiero a new mount – a bay –
Strong, spirited, though not for battle bred.
With precious gems and finest gold inlay
Its harness was adorned. A stripling led
The hippogriff; accustomed to obey
The sorcerer, it seemed content to heed
The young attendant in that joyful place
And came behind at a slow, stately pace.

77

The damsels who had given timely aid
When he was harassed by the ruffian band,
Which such ferocious opposition made
When he had tried the path on the right hand,
As they rode onwards turned to him and said:
'My lord, your valiant deeds, we understand,
Have earned you much renown, and we would ask
For your assistance in a certain task.

78

'A little further on there is a marsh,
Which you will see divides this plain in two.
There, Erifilla, cunning, fierce and harsh,
Defends the bridge against all comers who
Desire to cross (if any are so rash).
She is a monster and gigantic too.
Her fangs are long, and venomous her bite,
And bear-like claws she uses in her spite.

79

'Not only in our way does she obtrude,
Which would be unencumbered otherwise,
But often in our garden she'll intrude,
Despoiling it before our very eyes.
And you must know that of that multitude
Beyond the gate, who fought you in such guise,
A number she herself has brought to birth,
The vilest offspring ever seen on earth.'

80

Ruggiero said: 'This task I'll undertake,
And hundreds more I am prepared to try.
So of my humble self be pleased to make
What use you will and on my sword rely.
I wear this coat of mail, not for the sake
Of conquest or of plunder, but that I
May honourably serve the good and true,
And, most of all, fair damsels such as you.'

81

The ladies duly thanked the cavalier.
That he was chivalrous there is no doubt.
Conversing in such manner, they draw near
The bridge and marshy tract, where he must rout
A giantess, whose golden trappings were
Adorned with emeralds and sapphires; but
To my next canto I must now postpone
Ruggiero's battle with this evil one.

CANTO VII

1

He who has left his native country sees
– As further off he goes – things far removed
From what he thought to find; and when he is
Recounting them at home may be reproved
For telling lies, since ignoramuses,
Unless with touch and sight they've plainly proved
A thing, will not believe it; thus it comes,
This canto will seem strange to stay-at-homes.

2

However that may be, I have no need
To bear the inexperienced in mind.
To you alone, my lord, do I pay heed,
Who follow clearly all the threads I wind.
And I shall feel well recompensed indeed
If of my labours sweet the fruit you find.
I left you with Ruggiero in the field
Beside the bridge which Erifilla held.

3

Her shining armour is a splendid sight,
Sparkling with gems of many different hues:
Vermilion ruby, yellow chrysolite,
Green emerald, tawny jacinth nothing lose
Of brilliance in the dazzling eastern light.
And for a mount a horse she does not choose,
But sits astride a wolf, alert and keen,
Upon the richest saddle ever seen.

4

I doubt in all Apulia there howls
A wolf so large, in stature like an ox.
No jerking rein with spume has flecked its jowls.
I know not if with gestures or with looks
She spurs or checks it when it runs or prowls.
A sandy-coloured surcoat, like the frocks
Which prelates wear at court, completes the dress
Of this accursèd, monstrous giantess.

5

This gruesome being on her shield and crest
Flaunted a poisonous and swollen toad.
As he prepared to undergo the test,
The damsels to the brave Ruggiero showed
Where she would gallop with her lance in rest
To harass and impede him on his road.
And now with deadly menaces she cries.
His spear in hand, her challenge he defies.

6

With no less readiness her wolf she spurs.
Behind her saddle-bow she crouches close.
Her lance in rest she places in mid course,
Making the terrain thunder as she goes.
Beneath her helmet, with heroic force,
Ruggiero flings his spear and overthrows
Her. And beyond, behind her mount she passes,
Landing six yards away among the grasses.

7

At once he draws the sword with which he's girt,
To cut the head of the proud monster off –
As well he may, for there she lies, inert
Among the flowers and the emerald turf –
But both the damsels call: 'Pray do not hurt
Her further; that she's vanquished is enough.
And so, brave cavalier, put up your sword
And let us cross the bridge.' Without a word,

8

Ruggiero acquiesced. The way they tread
Is rocky, harsh and rough, and through a dark
And gloomy wood, a narrow path they thread.
Then next along a mountain-track they hark;
And when they reach the summit far ahead
They come at last upon a spacious park,
Where a fair palace beautifies the green.
No lovelier in all the world was seen.

9

The fair Alcina from the outer gate
Comes forth to meet the knight. In royal style
She welcomes him and ushers him in state
Within the court where thronging courtiers smile
Upon the cavalier and indicate,
By bowing deeply (scanning him the while),
How they revere him. Scarce more honour could
They pay if God Himself before them stood.

10

The palace, of all palaces most fair,
Excelled in rich adornment less, in truth,
Than for the comely personages there,
All courteous and noble, none uncouth.
To one another, all resemblance bear,
All in their prime, all in the flower of youth.
Alcina's the most beautiful by far,
As by the sun outshone is every star.

11

Her person is as shapely and as fine
As painters at their most inspired can show.
Her long, fair tresses, which in ringlets twine,
More brightly than spun gold appear to glow.
White lilies in her tender cheek refine
The rosy tints which softly come and go.
A brow serene, of polished ivory,
Completes a face of perfect symmetry.

12

Beneath two finely pencilled eyebrows, dark
As are the brilliant eyes they frame, her glance,
Compassionate, will lingeringly mark
The target where Love's arrows, not by chance,
Will accurately strike, until the spark
Becomes a flame, so many he implants;
And down the centre is a nose so sweet,
Envy itself can find no fault with it.

13

Below, her lovely mouth, as if between
Two dimpled vales, is set, which Nature's tints,
As though by cinnabar, incarnadine.
Parting to speak, her lips reveal the glints
Of pearls and, shaping gracious words, they win
All hearts, be they as adamant as flints.
So sweet a smile they form that in this wise
They open, here on earth, a paradise.

14

Her round and shapely neck is white as snow.
Her bosom, pure as milk, is large and full.
Two ivory breasts, firm as young fruit, below
Her bodice move, as when soft breezes pull
The waters at the margin to and fro.
Her other parts would be invisible
Even to Argos with his hundred eyes,
But from the rest their beauty we surmise.

15

Comely proportions her two arms display.
Long, tapering and slender, as is fit,
Her hand is seen to be, and white as whey.
No blemish or defect disfigures it.
And where her dainty person ends, there play
Her elegant and sweetly-modelled feet.
Angelic semblances from Heaven hail
And cannot be concealed by any veil.

16

In every part of her there lurks a snare,
In all her movements, words, or songs, or smiles.
No wonder, then, if the brave cavalier
Enamoured is of one who so beguiles
And so enchants him and, although aware
(Thanks to the myrtle) of her evil wiles,
He cannot now believe that base deceit
Can be concealed behind a smile so sweet.

17

He'd rather now believe that the transfer
To plant-life of Astolfo on the strand
Was a just punishment for deeds that were
So evil that he had been rightly banned.
And he now thinks that all he heard of her
Is false, by a desire for vengeance and
A spiteful envy prompted. In his eyes
Astolfo's story nothing is but lies.

18

The image of the Maid whom he so loved
Was in his heart no longer to be found.
The sorceress by magic has removed
All trace of any former amorous wound.
By her alone the cavalier is moved,
By her his heart engraved. So, on this ground,
Ruggiero must exonerated be
Of any blame for his inconstancy.

19

Within the palace, banqueting in state,
Where harps and lyres and divers instruments
Make all the air with harmony vibrate,
Ladies and cavaliers lend audience
To courtly entertainers who relate
Stories of love and joyful incidents,
And all their art and skill exert to please
With poetry, romance and fantasies.

20

What sumptuous board to feast a victory,
Such as was held by monarchs of Assyria,
Or Cleopatra offered Antony,
Was ever more elaborate or merrier
Than this Alcina caused the knight to see
On entering her palace's interior?
I do not think that such a feast indeed
Was served to Jupiter by Ganymede.

21

When all the viands have been cleared away,
The company assembles in a ring,
And there a merry game begins to play,
Whereby, each to the other whispering,
Mysterious and secret words they say.
And this for lovers is a useful thing:
Not a few couples, by the evening's end,
Agree that they'll the night together spend.

22

Much earlier than usual that night
The game broke up, and guests for bed prepared
In rooms where pages put the dark to flight
By flaming torches which with day compared.
Taking his leave of friends to left and right,
Ruggiero to his resting-place repaired,
A welcoming and sweetly fragrant nest,
Of all those well-appointed rooms the best.

23

And when with fine liqueurs and candied sweets
The hospitality's renewed to some,
And with deep, reverent bows each one retreats,
And everyone at last has gained his room,
Ruggiero slips between the perfumed sheets,
So fine, they're worthy of Arachne's loom,
And to the passing footsteps now lends ear,
Hoping his fair enchantress he may hear.

24

At every little movement which he heard,
Thinking it might be she, he raised his head.
Sometimes there was a sound, sometimes he erred,
And then he sighed. Sometimes he left his bed,
And round the door, holding it open, peered,
But no one could he see. The hoped-for tread
Was not forthcoming, and this long delay
Occasioned disappointment and dismay.

25

Often he murmured: 'Now this must be she',
And in his mind he'd count the steps along
The passage from his room to that whence he
Supposed Alcina would emerge ere long.
And many such conjectures constantly
Did he indulge in, all of which were wrong.
He greatly feared lest 'twixt the cup and lip
There might occur some unexpected slip.

26

But when Alcina, scented with perfume,
Judged that the time was ripe, but not before,
And all at last was silent as the tomb,
Deciding that she need delay no more,
With quiet steps she glided from her room
And, passing down a secret corridor,
Reached the apartment of the cavalier,
His heart in turmoil between hope and fear.

27

When the successor to Astolfo sees
Those radiant and joyful star-like eyes,
With flaming sulphur all his arteries
Are as on fire and he, for all he tries,
The golden moment instantly must seize.
So, leaping from the bed on which he lies,
Her person to himself he closely presses,
And scarcely can he wait till she undresses.

28

Although no gown, no underskirt she had,
For only in a silken négligé,
Over her night apparel, she was clad,
Soft, white and elegant in every way,
Beneath his hands this garment she now shed.
Her nightgown, as transparent as the day,
Concealed her rounded limbs as little as
The stems of lilies in a crystal vase.

29

Never did ivy press or cling so close,
Rooted beside the plant which it embraced,
As now in love each to the other does;
And on their lips a sweeter flower they taste
Than Ind or Araby e'er knew, or those
Which on the desert air their perfume waste.
To speak of all their bliss to them belongs,
Who more than once in one mouth had two tongues.

30

All that takes place between them in their love,
How they beguile the ensuing nights and days,
Is secret, or at least not spoken of,
For lips are readier to blame than praise.
All pay him homage, showing they approve,
For in her palace everyone obeys
Her wishes and behaves as she desires.
Thus all to favour the affair conspires.

31

No lack of pleasure causes them distress,
For in this fair abode all joys they find.
Two or three times a day they change their dress,
For many different purposes designed.
Always they hold themselves in readiness
For banquets, jousts and feasts of every kind.
By shady hills, or where the fountain plays,
They read of lovers in the olden days.

32

Now in deep vales, now over sunny slopes,
They chase the hare, or else with well-trained hounds
They make the pheasant rise from out the copse
By beating bush and stubble with loud sounds,
Now bird-lime spread, and now with plaited ropes,
Where the sweet-smelling juniper abounds,
Lay traps for thrushes; now with nets or hooks
They probe the fishes from their hidden nooks.

33

While by such joys Ruggiero is delayed,
King Charles by Agramante is beset.
Nor would I have you overlook the Maid,
Who her belovèd knight does not forget,
But by his absence from her is dismayed.
For many days she wept and she grieves yet,
To think how he was carried through the air
Along a strange highway, she knows not where.

34

So now of Bradamante I will tell,
Who many days had looked for him in vain,
Through sunny fields and many a shady dell,
In towns and cities, over hill and plain;
But not a trace of him she loved so well
Was anywhere to see, for all her pain.
She mingles with the army of the paynim,
But none can say what obstacles detain him.

35

She asks more than a hundred every day,
But none can give her an opinion.
From camp to camp she slowly makes her way,
To every barrack and pavilion,
Without being hindered – as, of course, she may,
Thanks to the magic ring which she has on.
When in her mouth (I know that it seems risible)
To everyone it renders her invisible.

36

She cannot, will not, say that he is dead.
The tidings of so great a man's demise
From the Hydaspes river would be spread
To where the westering sun at evening hies.
Not the least notion has she in her head
Where he can be on earth or in the skies.
She'll go on seeking him till the world ends,
Her sighs, her tears, her sobs her only friends.

37

She wondered, should she to that cave return
Where lie the prophet Merlin's sacred bones,
And to compassion try to move the stern
Unyielding marble with her piteous tones,
Till from the tomb's responses she might learn
If he still lived, or if a cairn of stones
Now marked his grave? She vowed that she would take
The seer's advice, howe'er her heart might ache.

38

And so, with this resolve, she took the road
Towards the woods in the vicinity
Of Pontiero where the seer's abode
Was hidden in a mountain cavity.
But she who in the cave foreknowledge showed
Of the fair Bradamante's progeny
Has followed her in thought, and since that day
Has been disposed to give what help she may.

39

For that benign and wise enchantress who
Has taken Bradamante to her heart –
Since she would be the ancestress, she knew,
Of heroes, nay, of demi-gods in part –
Ponders each day what she will say and do,
For by the medium of her magic art
She's seen Ruggiero freed, but gone, alack!
To India, whence he has not come back.

40

She's seen him riding on the flying horse,
Which neither by the rein nor with his foot
Can he control. It takes him quite off course,
Along a dangerous and unknown route.
She knows that now in idleness and worse
He lives and all his time in the pursuit
Of pleasure spends, forgetful that his word
Is pledged to both his lady and his lord.

41

So now he wastes the flower of his youth,
And in unending idleness this knight
Would have consumed his soul and body, both;
And that which lingers when the rest is quite
Defunct, the fragrant residue, in truth,
Of all our virtues, which, in death's despite,
Preserve us from the oblivion of the tomb,
Would have dispersed upon the wind like fume.

42

But that kind sorceress, who had more care
Than he had for himself, now planned how she
Might pull him up a hard and rugged stair,
Against his will, to virtue's victory,
Just like a good physician who will dare
To cure with poison, knives and cautery,
And, though in the beginning he gives pain,
The patient thanks him when he's well again.

43

She had no special tenderness for him –
Not like Atlante who was blind with love.
That foolish sorcerer had but one aim:
To keep Ruggiero from all danger of
An early death, or risk to life and limb;
And to this hope tenaciously he clove.
For all the fame Ruggiero might have won,
Of the knight's years he would not barter one.

44

He sent him to the island of Alcina
That he might lose his conscience at her court.
Of many necromancers none was keener
In all the wily practice of his art.
By means of it he'd brought about between her
And Ruggiero an amour of such a sort,
His freedom he would never have achieved
If longer than King Nestor he had lived.

45

But, turning now to her who can foresee
The future, both of persons and events,
She goes directly to the path where she
Anticipates with wondrous prescience
That she will meet the Maid: and instantly
All Bradamante's anguish and suspense
Are turned to hope, but then she hears the truth:
Alcina's magic has enslaved the youth.

46

The Maid is near to death when the kind fay
Has told her the extent of the disaster.
Not only is her love so far away
(And remedy is needed all the faster),
But he is captive to Alcina's sway.
The other where the pain is puts the plaster:
She promises the Maid that she will see
Her dear Ruggiero in two days or three.

47

'Since, Lady,' she began, 'you have with you
The magic ring which every other spell
Can counteract, I know that I can do
What is required to bring to naught her fell
Design and your belovèd from her woo;
You can rely on me to make all well.
I'll start this very evening on my way
And be in India at break of day.'

48

She tells her how she means to keep her troth,
How she will set about her wily plans
To rescue him from decadence and sloth
And bring him safely back once more to France.
The Maid gives up the magic ring, and both
Her heart and soul she'd offer to advance
The scheme, would any sacrifice have made,
If she could lend her dear Ruggiero aid.

49

So to the sorceress she yields the ring
And to her skill entrusts Ruggiero's fate,
And many loving greetings bids her bring;
Then for Provence departs, where she will wait.
The enchantress conjures up a wondrous thing:
A horse, one foot bright red, but black as jet,
In all its other parts; so great her skill,
She summons such phenomena at will.

50

I think it was a sprite or farfarel
Who thus was metamorphosed as a horse.
The fay, bare-footed and ungirt as well,
Her hair dishevelled, started on her course,
And lest the ring should counteract the spell,
She took it off and slipped it in her purse.
Faster she rode than man had ever seen her.
By morn she's on the island of Alcina.

51

And there miraculously she changed form.
Over a palm in stature first she grew.
Her legs and arms she altered to conform
As in proportion to her height was due.
Guessing Atlante's size, she chose the norm
Of all the necromancers whom she knew.
That done, she draped a beard about her chin,
Furrowed her brow and wrinkled all her skin.

52

Her imitation of Atlante's face,
Of his whole aspect, manner, gait and style,
Is so convincing, she could take his place
And raise no smallest doubt. First for a while
She judges it is prudent to efface
Herself and patiently the time beguile;
So in the gardens she resolves to bide
Until Alcina leaves Ruggiero's side.

53

Soon, by good luck, she found him quite alone,
Taking the fresh and limpid morning air,
Along a lovely stream which trickled down
The hillside to a lake serene and clear.
The exquisite attire which he had on
Was soft and sensuous, an idler's wear,
Woven in silk and gold with subtle touch
By her who held him in her evil clutch.

54

A splendid chain he wears about his neck;
Glittering with gems, it reaches to his breast.
Two shining bracelets now his arms bedeck
(Alas! once of all arms the manliest!).
Two little threads of gold his ear-lobes prick,
Forming two rings from which the loveliest
Of pearls are hung, one dangling at each ear,
Finer than Indians or Arabs wear.

55

From curling tresses, scented with pomade,
A costly and delicious fragrance came.
So amorous was every move he made,
It was as though, to his undying shame,
A servile courtship all his life he'd paid
To women of Valencia. His name
Alone remains unaltered, nothing else,
So greatly is he changed by magic spells.

56

The enchantress in Atlante's form appeared,
In face and aspect venerable and grave,
Such as Ruggiero ever had revered.
And just such glances of reproof she gave
As from his boyhood upwards he had feared.
And she began: 'Is it for this I have
Devoted all my energies to you?
Is this the fruit I am entitled to?

57

'Was it for this on marrow-bones I fed you
Of lions and of bears? And, as a child,
Was it for this along ravines I led you,
Hunting for snakes to strangle in the wild?
Was it for this I hardened you and bred you,
To render tigers, boars and panthers mild?
Of all this, do you think the aim alone is
To be Alcina's Attis or Adonis?

58

'Is this the man whose destiny I've seen
In sacred entrails, stars and points combined,
Responses, auguries and dreams and in
All signs by which the future is divined
(In which, alas! my years have squandered been),
For whom courageous deeds of such a kind
Have been predicted since his infancy
That never would his prowess equalled be?

59

'Do you think Alexander sank so low?
Do you believe that this the method is
A Caesar to become, or Scipio?
Who would have thought you capable of this?
You are Alcina's slave; that all may know,
She makes you wear her chain and liveries,
And at her pleasure, everywhere she goes,
Now here, now there, she leads you by the nose.

60

'And if by thoughts of your own fame and by
The noble deeds that are your destiny
You are unmoved, then I will ask you why
You have no scruple for your progeny,
And to that womb how long you will deny
The seed from which a glorious company
Of offspring will descend, a mighty race,
Destined in history to take its place?

61

'Do not prevent the noblest souls which dwell
In Heaven as Ideas eternally
From taking form on earth and, visible,
As your descendants, their true destiny
Achieving; nor impede, I beg as well,
Your sons, your grandsons, your posterity,
Who in grim battles, told in epic stories,
Will Italy restore to her past glories.

62

'Not only do you owe a duty to
The harvest which your fertile tree will bear,
Those many valiant sons and daughters who,
Invincible, illustrious and fair,
Should turn you from your ways, but there are two
Who should alone suffice, a noble pair,
Alfonso and Ippolito, who'll lead
The world in virtue, and all good exceed.

63

'I told you of these brothers many a time
And in my stories set them both apart,
For in their valour they will be sublime.
Of your descendants, they the greatest part
Will have in chronicle and epic rhyme.
My prophecies of them most stirred your heart,
And greatly you rejoiced that there would be
Heroes like those among your progeny.

64

'She whom you make a queen, what has she got
More than a thousand whores, that you're enraptured?
You know full well what is the final lot
Of all those whom this concubine has captured.
That you may clearly see the evil plot
And who it is by whom you are denatured,
Take now this ring and put it on your finger;
Return to her and see how long you'll linger.'

65

Stricken by shame, Ruggiero, as though dumb,
Hung down his head and knew not what to say.
Holding between her finger and her thumb
The magic ring of which she spoke, the fay
Slipped it upon his little finger. Numb
Before, his senses spring to life straightway.
Aware now of his state, he is beside himself,
And longs for a deep hole in which to hide himself.

66

And in a flash the enchantress broke the spell
And reassumed the shape she always wore.
For, now that her design had worked so well,
She did not need Atlante's any more.
The time has come, I think, her name to tell:
Melissa – which I've not divulged before.
A full account she gives Ruggiero now
Of who she is and why she came and how.

67

She tells him she is sent by the fair Maid
Who longs for him and cannot live without him,
To cut the chain by which he's captive made,
Wound by Alcina's magic art about him.
Atlante of Carena's form, to aid
Her in her strategy, she took to rout him.
But now that to his senses he's returned,
She wants the truth by him to be discerned.

68

'That valorous, fair Maid, who loves you so,
And who in all respects deserves your love,
To whom (if you do not forget) you owe
Such freedom as you're not divested of,
Sends you this magic ring which, as you know,
Protects the wearer from all spells. To prove
Her true devotion she would gladly send
Her heart as well, if that would matters mend.'

69

Thus does the sorceress her theme pursue
Of Bradamante's love for him, commending
Her valour as a woman warrior too
(Affection with the truth, perhaps, contending),
Her case, as loyal messengers should do,
With every means at her command defending,
Until at last Ruggiero for Alcina
Conceived such hate, no hatred could be keener.

70

And now, as once he loved her, he abhorred her.
Nor is it strange that he has thus awoken,
Since by her spell it was that he adored her,
Which by the magic ring he wears is broken.
To what she truly is, it has restored her,
Of sorcery annulling every token,
And, from her tresses to her feet and legs,
All beauty's gone and nothing's left but dregs.

71

And as a boy who hides a fruit away
And then goes off, forgetting all about it,
On finding it long afterwards one day
Within a drawer or cupboard where he'd put it,
Astonished at the sight of such decay,
Is more than willing now to do without it,
And takes the putrid thing, with mould encrusted,
And flings it far away from him, disgusted,

72

So did Ruggiero, when his former lover
Was altered by the ring which, when it's worn,
Undoes all other magic spells, discover,
Though to her loveliness he could have sworn,
That underneath her magic mask and cover
(No greater shock he'd had since he was born)
She was an agèd and a hideous crone;
No uglier in all the world was known.

73

In truth, Alcina was, without a quibble,
Wrinkled and frail; her hair was sparse and white,
And from her toothless mouth there ran a dribble.
Scarcely six palms did she attain in height.
Older than Hecuba or Cumae's Sibyl,
She had outlived all other women quite.
By means of artifice unknown to us,
A girl she could appear, and beauteous.

74

She makes herself so young and beautiful
That many, like Ruggiero, she has snared.
But now the ring enables him to pull
Away the mask which has so long impaired
Men's vision. It is, then, no miracle
That brave Ruggiero, who this madness shared,
Is sane again. No magic can avail her,
And all her beauty's remedies now fail her.

75

But as Melissa has advised, he shows
No sign of his emancipation yet,
But to the palace armoury he goes,
His helmet and his harness thence to get.
And when he has rearmed from head to toes,
Alcina's mind and heart at rest to set,
He feigns to try his skill, which he displays
Like one who has not fought for many days.

76

Next his good Balisarda he put on
(Such is the name Ruggiero's sword possessed).
Then took the shield which blinded everyone,
Or with acute bewilderment oppressed
The senses of all those on whom it shone.
Atlante thus his enemies suppressed.
Its dazzling surface silken folds bedeck.
He hangs it, thus concealed, around his neck.

77

Then in the palace stables he commands
The saddling of a horse as black as pitch.
This is the one the sorceress intends.
She knows how it responds to spur and switch.
Its name is Rabicano to its friends.
It once belonged to the sad myrtle which,
A plaything now of winds along the strand,
The giant whale had carried to this land.

78

He did not choose the wingèd destrier
Which close to Rabicano had been tied,
For the enchantress said to him: 'Take care;
That animal is dangerous to ride.'
She promised she would bring it to him where
They might essay some practice flights, and guide
The hippogriff with bridle and with bit,
Until at last he learned to master it.

79

To leave the hippogriff likewise averts
Suspicion from the flight which he prepares.
In all Ruggiero does, the fay exerts
An influence and guides him unawares.
The agèd hag's abode he now deserts,
That soft, unmanly palace without cares.
A gate in the side wall he means to breach,
Whence Logistilla's kingdom he may reach.

80

Approaching the portcullis, he surprised
The guards: he slashed, he thrust, he hit out blind:
Some he had killed, some wounded, he surmised.
Across the bridge he galloped like the wind,
And, long before Alcina was advised,
He left her half a dozen miles behind.
In my next canto I go on to say
How he to Logistilla found the way.

CANTO VIII

1

Enchanters and enchantresses abound,
Plying their artifice among us all,
And many a lover to a face is bound
Which has been changed from plain to beautiful,
Not by the aid which in the stars is found,
Nor by the spirits magic spells recall,
But by dissimulation, fraud and lies
In never-to-be-loosened knots and ties.

2

He who the ring of fair Angelica,
Or, better, who the ring of Reason had,
Could see all countenances as they are,
Not in an artificial beauty clad,
Or masked as virtuous phenomena,
Which ugly are beneath the paint, or bad.
So, for Ruggiero it's a lucky thing
That he has seen the truth, thanks to the ring.

3

By using guile, Ruggiero, as I said,
Has reached the gate on Rabicano's back.
His Balisarda serves him in good stead.
The startled guards all preparation lack.
He wounds a few, and others leaves for dead.
He crashes resolutely through the wrack
And gallops towards a wood; but a short way
He goes, then meets a servant of the fay.

4

Upon his wrist he had a falcon, which,
Delighting in the chase, he daily brought
To fly by ponds or open country, rich
In game of many species which it caught.
Beside him ran a faithful dog, or bitch.
A nag, not much adorned, he rode. He thought,
Seeing Ruggiero ride at such a pace,
He must be of a mind to leave the place.

5

He rode to meet him and with haughty mien
Demanded where he galloped at such speed.
No answer came; so, taking this to mean
In his conjecture he was not misled,
Concerning what Ruggiero's aim had been,
He stretched towards him his left arm and said:
'What say you if I stop you in your tracks?
You've no defences if this bird attacks.'

6

He frees the falcon, which so beats its wings
That Rabicano is outsped by it.
Next from his palfrey the assailant springs
And in that instant has removed the bit.
As through the quivering air an arrow sings,
Straight to the target it will surely hit,
Like fire, or wind, behind the falcon ran
The horse, released, and, after it, the man.

7

The dog has no desire to lag behind,
But chases Rabicano with the same
Rapidity as in a pard you'll find
Pursuing hares. Ruggiero, put to shame,
Turns to the man who's running like the wind,
And has no weapon save a stick to tame
The dog and teach it to obey his word.
Ruggiero thus disdains to draw his sword.

8

The man, approaching, gives him a sharp blow.
The dog, in that same moment, bites his foot.
The horse, unbridled, likewise is not slow
To rear its mighty crupper and lash out,
Three times and more – a formidable foe.
The falcon swooping on him, follows suit,
And with its shriek so terrifies the horse,
It will respond to neither rein nor spurs.

9

Ruggiero then has no alternative
But to unsheathe his sword and with its aid
Such molestation from him try to drive.
And so, now with the point, now with the blade,
He threatens man and beasts, who still contrive
To importune him. On all sides waylaid,
He sees his honour is in jeopardy
If he does not succeed in breaking free.

10

He knows that if obliged thus to delay
He'll have Alcina's army round his ears.
Trumpets and drums and bells, both far away
And close at hand, up hill, down dale, he hears.
Against the man and beasts but small headway
He makes with Balisarda, so he fears
A more effective weapon he must wield:
The sorcerer Atlante's magic shield.

11

He draws aside the crimson draperies
Wherein the shield for many days has lain.
Its shining surface so intensifies
The light, that by a thousand times again
Its power's increased. The huntsman senseless lies,
The dog, the horse, collapse. The bird in vain
Attempts to fly on wings that droop and fold.
Joyful, he leaves them sleeping on the wold.

12

Alcina, who has meanwhile heard the news
Of how Ruggiero forced the outer gate
And killed a number of the guards, reviews,
Dismayed, the desperation of her state.
She rends her clothes; in torrents of abuse
She blames her own stupidity, too late.
Straightway she sounds the signal for alarm
And gives commands for all her host to arm.

13

Into two sections she divides them: one
She sends to catch Ruggiero on his way.
The others to the harbour mole have run,
To embark on sailing-ships without delay.
The azure of the ocean turns to dun
Beneath the spreading canvas. Her dismay
Seems to have robbed Alcina of her senses,
To leave her city thus without defences.

14

As no one watches the abode or grounds,
This gives Melissa, who intends to free
The prisoners in which the place abounds,
Every convenience and facility
Of the fell premises to go the rounds,
Inspecting all devices thoroughly.
Seals, knots, rhombs, spirals, images she finds:
She breaks, she burns, she loosens, she unbinds.

15

This done, across the meadowlands she hastes
Where in their hundreds former lovers wait,
Changed into fountains, rocks or trees or beasts.
She reconverts them to their former state.
Not one of them a single instant wastes.
As soon as they can walk, they emulate
Ruggiero, who to Logistilla flees,
Thence make for Persia, Scythia, India, Greece.

16

To her who thus releases them once more
The thanks they owe can never be repaid.
The first of those her magic powers restore
To human semblance is the duke, who bade
Ruggiero be advised; the one who wore
A myrtle's shape, for whom Ruggiero made
A special plea and, that the fay might bring
Him to his former self, gave her the ring.

17

So with this kind entreaty she complies
And to his former shape the English duke
Restores; and yet Melissa in no wise
Will rest content until by hook or crook
She finds his golden lance which, as it flies,
Unerringly its victim brings to book.
From Argalìa Astolfo won this lance;
For both it earned renown throughout all France.

18

The lance was taken from him by the witch
And in some secret palace-cupboard stowed,
With all Astolfo's other weapons which
Were stolen likewise in that dread abode.
Melissa found them all without a hitch.
Taking Astolfo pillion, off she rode,
And (while Ruggiero an hour's journey still has)
Making good time, she reaches Logistilla's.

19

Among harsh, rugged rocks and thorny brakes,
To gain the kingdom of the virtuous queen
Now this way and now that Ruggiero takes.
No lonelier, wilder landscape has he seen.
After great labour, at long last he makes,
At the day's hottest hour, a shore between
The ocean and the mountain, facing south,
A region of sterility and drouth.

20

The near-by mountain wall in the sun's glare
Throws back a blaze of heat so furious,
It liquefies the sand and turns the air
To fiercer blast than a glass furnace-house.
All birds, in the rare shade, are silent there.
Only the cicadas' monotonous
Refrain, rising where desert plants abound,
Fills hills, dales, sky and sea with deafening sound.

21

Along that sandy, sun-exposed terrain,
The sole companions in his journeying
Ruggiero knew were heat and thirst and pain.
Irksome indeed he found such labouring.
But I must not continue in one strain,
Nor always harp upon the self-same string;
So I will leave Ruggiero in the heat,
To Scotland go and there Rinaldo meet.

22

Seeing that by the king and the princess
And all the land he's held in high esteem,
He judges it is timely to address
The court and to reveal King Charles's scheme
Of raising troops in Scotland and, no less,
In England, to assist in his extreme
Necessity against the Infidel.
Rinaldo pleads the case and pleads it well.

23

The king without delay replies and says
That all the forces under his command
He'll gladly make available; and prays
Rinaldo to report that a large band
Of horse and men-at-arms he'll quickly raise
For the defence of Emperor Charles' land;
And he himself, if not so full of years,
Would joyfully have led the cavaliers.

24

And by old age he would not be dissuaded,
Save that a valiant son he did not lack.
None worthier to lead, he was persuaded,
Shrewd in defence, and forceful in attack.
By him the Emperor would be well aided;
To Scotland he was soon expected back;
And that his son might gain thereby great lustre,
He'd rally all the troops that he could muster.

25

And so his stewards he despatched both far
And wide, through all his land, to levy horse
And men; proud vessels he prepares for war,
Munitions, victuals, and, the public purse
Depleting, settles each particular.
To England then Rinaldo shapes his course.
The king as far as Berwick kindly keeps
Him company and, on departing, weeps.

26

When favouring breezes blew abaft the poop,
Rinaldo went on board and waved farewell.
The pilot, casting off the mooring-rope,
At once set sail and held his course so well
That uneventfully he brought the sloop
Where the fair Thames, meeting the salt sea swell,
Grows brackish. Thence, along a route well tried,
They sailed and rowed to London with the tide.

27

With letters patent to the Prince of Wales,
Rinaldo carries out his embassy.
King Otto whom the foe likewise assails
With Charlemagne, has countersigned the plea,
Which to the prince Rinaldo now retails,
For all the cavaliers and infantry
Which England can provide and send to Calais,
That France against the Infidel may rally.

28

The prince I speak of, who in Otto's place
Remained to occupy the royal throne,
Received the son of Aymon with such grace,
More honour to his king he ne'er had shown.
He pledged such forces as would meet the case,
Recruited not from English soil alone,
But also from the islands round about,
And named the day when they would all set out.

29

My lord, like the good instrumentalist
Who plays on many different strings at will,
And tunes and modulates as he thinks best,
Moving from bass to treble, soft to shrill,
So, as I tell you of Rinaldo's quest,
Thoughts of Angelica I harp on still.
I left her fleeing from him, much upset,
And in her flight a hermit she had met.

30

Her story I'll advance a little more.
I told you that she asked entreatingly
How she might find her way to the sea-shore.
So great her terror was, that she must flee
Not France alone, but Europe, and she swore
That she would die unless she crossed the sea.
The hermit schemed to keep her there at leisure,
For in her company he found much pleasure.

31

Her beauty had inflamed the old man's heart
And warmed the frigid marrow of his bones;
And when he saw her speedily depart,
Paying no heed to his cajoling tones,
With many a prick he made his donkey smart,
Striving to urge it on with shouts and groans;
And yet for all he cudgelled the poor beast,
Trot it would not, not hurry in the least.

32

Since now already she is far away
And very soon he'll lose all trace of her,
He goes to his black cave without delay
And conjures demons straight from Lucifer.
One of this evil horde he bids obey,
Saying to what command it must defer:
To enter and possess, by magic art,
The horse that bears both damsel and his heart.

33

And, like a well-trained hunting-dog, which knows
How best to fox the fox and capture hares,
For when the prey in one direction goes,
He in another instantly repairs,
To scent and trail thus turning up his nose,
Then at the joining of the pathways, there's
The hound, his jowls with fearsome fangs agape –
So did the hermit cut off all escape.

34

His strategy will later be revealed.
She, unsuspecting, on her lonely ride
Continued, and her failing courage steeled.
Day after day, all respite she denied.
Meanwhile, the demon, in the horse concealed,
Awaits his moment, as a fire will bide
Unseen, then leaping with a deadly roar,
Wreaks havoc and destruction all the more.

35

Angelica has kept a steady course
Along the sea-coast road in Gascony.
Now on the beach itself she guides her horse,
Choosing the firmest patches carefully.
The demon then lets loose its evil force
And drives the frenzied charger out to sea.
Distraught and terrified, the only thing
That she can do is to her saddle cling.

36

She tugs the rein but still the creature swims
Far out, in water even deeper yet.
Her dress is gathered high above her limbs
And from the mounting waves she draws her feet.
Her tumbled hair over her shoulder brims
And wanton breezes make on it a sweet
Assault, while all the greater winds are hushed,
By beauty such as hers perhaps abashed.

37

Her lovely face and bosom drenched with tears,
She turns her longing eyes towards land in vain,
Which dwindles as she looks, and disappears.
The horse, still plunging on into the main,
Makes a wide curve, and to the right hand veers,
A distant, solitary coast to gain;
And there, among dark rocks and caves appalling,
He sets her down as shades of night are falling.

38

Finding herself alone in such a place,
Which, even to behold, strikes drear and stark,
And at the hour when Phoebus hides his face
In ocean, leaving earth and heaven dark,
She stood stock still; none any sign might trace,
Nor in her immobility remark
If she a woman were of flesh and bone,
Or else a painted image made of stone.

39

Bemused and motionless, on shifting sands,
Her tumbled tresses in the breezes blowing,
Her lips immobile, with imploring hands,
She fixed her gaze on high as though the All-knowing
Mover she accused; thus a while she stands;
Then, to relieve her grief, her tears sets flowing,
And (though at first her faculties were stunned)
Her sorrow loosens in this doleful sound:

40

'Ah! cruel Fortune, what remains to do
Ere your desire to torture me is sated?
What more can I surrender up to you
Than this my life, so wretched and ill-fated?
Yet you refused to take it and withdrew
Me from the waters where for death I waited,
For you could not forgo or let pass by
This chance to make me suffer ere I die.

41

'I do not see what ill can more be done,
So greatly have you wronged me before now.
By you I'm exiled from my royal throne,
And no return to it will you allow;
And, what is worse, my honour's lost and gone,
For though I have not sinned, and this I vow,
Because I wander homeless, men make haste
To slander me and say I am unchaste.

42

'For what in all the world is left to her
Whose chastity is lost? That I am young,
Or men should think me fair, whether they err,
Or whether, after all, they be not wrong,
This is no benefit the Fates confer.
My ills in origin to this belong:
For this my brother, Argalìa, died,
Pierced through his magic armour to his side.

43

'It is for this the king of Tartary
Slew the Great Khan, my father, ruler of
Cathay and India, whence it comes to be
That to this state I am reduced and rove
From morn till evening, changing hostelry
Each day; if, then, of honour, wealth and love
You robbed me, never ceasing thus to harm me,
By what new torments can you now alarm me?

44

'If drowning was a death too easy for me
To satisfy in full your cruel taste,
Despatch some savage creature to devour me:
I'll not resist, if only it make haste;
Or any other fate to overpower me –
I'll thank you if I die of it at least.'
These were the words the wretched damsel cried,
When suddenly the hermit's at her side.

45

From a high cliff meanwhile he had surveyed
Angelica far down upon the shore,
Whom towering rocks and beetling crags dismayed.
He had arrived about six days before,
By demons through untrodden paths conveyed.
He now approached: a pious air he wore,
More sanctimonious than any saint's
Imaged in marble or in artist's paints.

46

Becoming then aware of him, she took,
Not knowing who he was, some comfort; and,
Although still wan and pallid was her look,
Her fears diminished; when he took his stand
Beside her, all precaution she forsook,
And said: 'Father, behold on what a strand
I am marooned; help me, I beg of you',
And told him, sobbing, what full well he knew.

47

The hermit to console her first essays
With pious arguments, and while he speaks
His sacrilegious hands begins to place
Now on her bosom, now upon her cheeks,
Then, growing bolder, ventures an embrace.
Affronted, to discourage him she seeks,
And with one hand she strikes at him and pushes,
Her countenance suffused with modest blushes.

48

Then from a pocket in his robe, full-skirted,
He drew a bottle, full of magic juice;
And in those orbs whose beams, by Love converted,
So powerful a radiance produce,
A single droplet of this potion squirted,
Enough a heavy slumber to induce.
Angelica at once it stupefies
And on the sand a prey to lust she lies.

49

And, as defenceless in his arms she rests,
Embracing her, he touches her all over,
Kisses her mouth and both her lovely breasts.
The rough and lonely place gives perfect cover,
But in this joust his weary jade resists.
For all he longs to prove himself a lover,
Years having undermined his aptitude,
The more he strives, the less he can make good.

50

Whatever methods he experiments,
His lazy courser simply will not jump;
Nor will it lift its head in consequence
Of any jerking rein, or spur, or thump.
To sleep beside her, then, is less expense.
But Fortune will not leave him there to slump
In such inertia; having ill begun with him,
She schemes, as is her wont, to have more fun with him.

51

Before continuing, I think it best
To tell you what had happened in the seas
Of the far distant North, towards the West,
Beyond Ireland, among the Hebrides.
Now of inhabitants, the emptiest
An island named Ebuda is of these,
For vengeful Proteus there resolved to keep
The orc and other monsters of the deep.

52

The earliest historians aver
(I know not if there's truth in what they say)
That once a mighty king was monarch there.
His daughter, beautiful in every way,
Inspired in Proteus' breast such love for her
That in the sea itself he burned; one day,
When, sporting on the shore, her maids escaped her,
(Thus unattended leaving her) he raped her.

53

This was a grievous and a tragic thing,
For in her womb she bore the sea-god's child.
No plea for mercy could placate the king,
Whose nature was the opposite of mild.
No stay of justice, no remònstrating
Would he permit; and so she died, reviled.
His grandson, too, as sinless as the morn,
Was put to death before he had been born.

54

When Proteus, shepherd of that awesome flock
Which Neptune, ruler of the sea, commands,
Hears how his love has died upon the block,
He in his rage all treaties countermands,
And, letting loose his hordes to run amok
Upon Ebuda's shores, he, gloating, stands
To watch them savage oxen, horses, sheep,
And everywhere ferocious harvest reap.

55

And even to the city gates they swarmed,
Destroying every living thing they found.
On guard both day and night, the people, armed,
Endeavoured all in vain to hold their ground.
Farms were deserted, everyone alarmed.
At last, despairing, they resolved to sound
The oracle, which, asked for its advice,
Gave them these words of counsel in a trice:

56

A damsel they must choose, as beauteous
As she whom sorrow to the scaffold bore;
And, to console the outraged Protëus,
Present her in exchange upon the shore.
If he accepted her, then plenteous
Their recompense would be, for he no more
Would trouble them; but if he's not content,
More damsels, one by one, they must present.

57

And so began the awesome destiny
Of all the maidens in the neighbourhood.
Each day to waiting Proteus, by the sea,
A damsel's offered, but in cruel mood
He spurns them all and passes them with glee
To the fierce orc which gulps them down as food.
This one remained beside the river-mouth
When all the other monsters drifted south.

58

Such is the history that I have read,
But whether true or false I cannot say.
Thus by Ebudans is interpreted
The cruel custom whereby every day
A monstrous orc on woman's flesh is fed,
To which the islanders this tribute pay;
Thus, though a woman's life is everywhere
A burden, it's intolerable there.

59

O wretched maidens whom the Fates transport
To that fell shore where people lie in wait
To catch you for the cruel monster's sport!
Of victims from abroad the score is great,
Yet always there are more to come to port,
To furnish for the orc a living bait;
And if the winds that way should fail to blow,
The cunning hunters seek them high and low.

60

In galleys, privateers, or any boat
The coastal waters eagerly they scour,
Seeking provisions for the monster's throat;
And many lovely women captured are
By whatsoever means success promote:
Force, flattery, or gold; from near and far,
From here, from there, from everywhere they bring them,
And into prisons, dungeons, towers fling them.

61

One of their evil galleys chanced to pass,
Hugging the desolate and lonely strand,
Where, among brakes and briars, on the grass,
The hermit's victim lay, as he had planned.
Hoping to find fresh water and amass
Timber for kindling, rowers put to land
And saw, clasped in the holy father's arms,
The flower of all female grace and charms.

62

O tender spoil, too exquisite and rare,
Too precious for these rough barbarians!
O cruel Fortune, who could be aware
That, ruling us with such insouciance,
You'd offer as an avid monster's fare
That peerless beauty which at Agrican's
Command the Tartars from Caucasia
Came forth to capture once in India?

63

That peerless beauty which before his sword
And all his kingdom Sacripante placed,
That peerless beauty which Anglante's lord
Unhinges and his honour has defaced,
That peerless beauty which with one accord
The East has championed against the West,
Is left alone with no one to befriend it,
And not a word is uttered to defend it.

64

The fair Angelica, in her deep swoon,
Is bound and chained before she can awaken,
And, likewise, to the dismal vessel, strewn
With wailing prisoners, the hermit's taken.
To the dread island making headway soon,
As from the mast the sail once more is shaken,
They reach the fortress where the victims wait
Until their turn arrives to meet their fate.

65

Because so lovely are her form and face
That in her captors sympathy they stir,
Rousing compassion in that savage race,
Her day of doom they constantly defer
By putting other women in her place.
They hope the time will never come for her;
But to the monster she is led at last,
And people weep to see her going past.

66

Who can describe her tears, her sobs, her cries,
The pleas she utters on each wailing breath,
Her lamentation reaching to the skies?
It is a miracle the shore beneath
Does not divide, as on the rock she lies,
Chained, helpless, waiting for a hideous death.
Not I, indeed, who am so grieved, I swear,
That I must move my narrative elsewhere,

67

Hoping to make my verses less lugubrious,
Until my weary spirit has revived.
No snakes dwelling in regions insalubrious,
No tigress of her progeny deprived,
No desert reptile, venomous, opprobrious,
'Twixt Red Sea shores and Atlas ever lived
Which could without compassion contemplate
The beautiful Angelica's dire fate.

68

Ah, if the Count Orlando only knew
The plight of her for whom he sought in Paris!
Or if the tidings reached the other two
Whose understanding from the truth so far is!
Risking a thousand deaths, they would pursue
A noble course, more chivalrous than war is;
But if a message came, how then could they
Their lady rescue who's so far away?

69

Meanwhile in Paris, King Troiano's son
The citadel besieges with success.
(In all the world his prowess is well known.)
To dire extremity reduced, no less,
The Christians now appear to be undone.
But Heaven hears their prayers and in redress
Sends down the rain; else to the pagan lance
The Empire had surrendered, and fair France.

70

For God to Charles's just lament paid heed
And from the conflagration's raging threat
The Christians by a sudden downpour freed.
(The flames might otherwise be burning yet.)
Wise is the man who turns to God in need.
Where else will he find help when he's beset?
This miracle for Charles, who is devout,
Was aid divinely sent, he has no doubt.

71

Orlando that same night lies wide awake,
His thoughts, distracted, rambling here, now there.
He tries to concentrate but cannot make
His troubled conscience settle anywhere,
As on the crystal surface of a lake
The trembling shafts of sunlight mirrored are,
Leaping to roof-top and, at random glancing,
Sparkle and gleam, in all directions dancing.

72

And to his anguished mind his love returns.
Though never absent, now while he's at rest
She kindles him anew and brighter burns
The flame which seemed by day to have quiesced.
Over and over in his thoughts he churns
How he had travelled with her to the West
As far as from Cathay, how at Bordeaux
He lost her and now seeks her high and low.

73

His conduct he repented grievously
And often he reproached himself in vain.
'My love,' he said, 'how reprehensively
I have behaved towards you! To think (what pain!)
I might have had you night and day with me
(If my devotion you did not disdain),
But into Namo's hands instead I gave you,
Not knowing from such outrage how to save you.

74

'Had I not reason to oppose this course?
And Charles perhaps would not have said me nay.
And who against me would have dared use force,
Or who by violence take you away?
And ought not I to arms have had recourse,
My breast presenting to the bitter fray?
In the event, not Charles with all his might
Could have despoiled me of you in fair fight.

75

'Would he had placed her in another's care,
In Paris, or some citadel well guarded!
To Namo he entrusted her, aware
That she'd escape and would not be awarded
To me as guerdon. No one anywhere
Deserved her more, yet I'm thus ill-rewarded.
I'd have protected her; ah, how I rue
That what I could have done I did not do!

76

'O my sweet life, where are you now, alone,
Far from my help, so lovely and so young,
Like a lost lamb which, when the day is flown,
Meanders in a wood, in hopes ere long
The shepherd will locate her bleating tone;
But from afar the wolf has heard among
The plains her voice uplifted in the night,
And all in vain the shepherd mourns her plight.

77

'My hope, where are you now, where can you be?
Alone you wander yet on ways untracked?
Or did the wolves destroy you cruelly
When your Orlando's faithful arm you lacked?
And that sweet flower, the height of bliss, ah me!
Which scrupulously I preserved intact,
Lest I offend a maidenhood so chaste,
By force has now been taken and laid waste?

78

'Alas! what do I long for but to die,
If men have robbed me of that sweetest bliss?
Send down on me, I pray, O God on high,
All other sufferings, but spare me this!
If it be true, I'll end my life with my
Own hands and send my soul to the Abyss.'
Such were the words Orlando uttered, sighing
And weeping, restless on his pallet lying.

79

All creatures on the earth to rest their bones,
Or to refresh their souls, now took their ease,
Some on soft beds and others on hard stones,
Some on the grass, still others in the trees;
But you, Orlando, amid tears and groans,
Your eyelids scarce have closed to gain release.
Those irksome, goading thoughts give no respite,
Not in your sleep, so fitful and so light.

80

In broken slumber thus Orlando dreams:
Upon a bank where flowers his soul refresh,
He gazes upon ivory which seems
By Nature tinted to resemble flesh,
And on two radiant stars, of which the beams
Serve to revive the soul which they enmesh:
I mean her eyes and face (as you have guessed),
By which his heart is riven from his breast.

81

He felt the greatest happiness and joy
That ever a requited lover knew;
When there arose a tempest to destroy
The plants, the trees, the flowers and all that grew.
No winds, the globe around, such force employ
When in their jousts and tourneys they fall to.
He seemed to seek now here, now there, for shelter,
Lost in a desert, running helter-skelter.

82

The unhappy man meanwhile (he knows not how)
Has lost his lady in the darkling air.
He calls her name, now in the forests, now
In open country, echoes everywhere
Awakening. 'What powers', he cries, 'allow
That from a sweetness such as this, so rare,
Poison so bitter comes?' Entreating aid,
Her voice is heard in valley, hill and glade.

83

To left and right, up hill, down dale, in vain
Pursuing her, breathless he seemed to race
Wherever he could hear her voice. The pain
Of fearing that her lovely eyes and face
He'd never in his life behold again
Tortured his anguished heart. From a new place,
A new voice called: 'Confirmed are all your fears!'
Then he awoke, his pillow drenched with tears.

84

Forgetting that in dreams the things we see,
Inspired by fear or longing, are inclined
To be untrue, firmly convinced was he
His lady was in danger, or repined
In degradation and humility,
And from the restless couch where he reclined
He sprang and, taking shield and coat of mail,
He mounted Brigliadoro and made trail.

85

He took no squire, nor, lest dishonour might
Attach to his good name (one of the chief
Concerns of chivalry), his coat of white
And crimson quarterings, in the belief
That dubious paths would beckon (as was right);
But chose instead, in keeping with his grief,
A coat of inky black, which he put on,
A trophy he had from an emir won;

86

And silently, at midnight, stole away.
No courtesy to Charlemagne he showed,
Nor yet to Brandimarte did he say
Farewell, the friend to whom great love he owed;
But when, her golden locks in disarray,
The Dawn had risen from the rich abode
Of her Tithonus, darkness scattering,
His absence was then noticed by the king.

87

With grave displeasure Charlemagne has seen
His nephew has deserted him that night;
The more so, as his duty would have been
To stay and aid his uncle in his plight.
The Emperor cannot contain his spleen,
But utters condemnation of the knight,
And threatens that if he does not return
A bitter lesson he will make him learn.

88

But Brandimarte holds Orlando dear.
Whether he hopes to bring him back again,
Or he is moved to anger thus to hear
The Emperor revile him, is not plain,
But scarcely does he wait till night is near
Before he follows in Orlando's train.
No word to Fiordiligi does he say,
Lest she should lovingly his plan gainsay.

89

She was his lady, whom he greatly loved.
Rare were her charms and beautiful her face,
And seldom from her company he moved,
Such her endowments were of mind and grace.
If now his absence an exception proved,
It was because he hoped within a day's
Duration to complete the task in hand.
Events detained him longer than he planned.

90

After a month, when he had not returned,
Fair Fiordiligi could no longer wait,
Such was the flame of love with which she burned,
But set off unescorted through the gate.
In many lands thereafter she sojourned,
And in due course her story I'll relate,
And of them both will tell you more anon.
Orlando's my concern from this point on.

91

His coat of arms he'd prudently replaced
And to the city's barbican had ridden.
And to the guard who vigilantly paced,
(His world-renowned insignia being hidden)
He whispered low: 'I am the Count.' In haste
The captain let the drawbridge down as bidden.
Where the besiegers were he rode straightway.
What followed, in the following I'll say.

CANTO IX

1

Once Love has gained possession of a heart,
What can this cruel traitor then not do?
See how he tears Orlando's soul apart:
So loyal once, now to his lord untrue,
So wise, so versed in every noble art,
And of the holy Church defender too,
A victim now of passion unreturned,
For God and king no longer he's concerned.

2

But I excuse him and rejoice to have
In my defect companionship like his,
For to such passion likewise I'm a slave,
While my pursuit of goodness languid is.
Attired in black as sombre as the grave,
He leaves the army of the fleur-de-lis,
And soon he finds, ere he has ridden far,
The troops of Spain encamped and Africa,

3

Or rather, not encamped, because the rain
Had driven them for cover here and there.
In desultory groups about the plain
They stand in tens, in trios, or a pair.
Stretched on the ground in weariness or pain,
Some sleep, some, leaning on their elbows, stare.
Their lives Orlando easily could take,
But not one move towards his sword will make.

4

For he is chivalrous, there's no denying.
He'd never stoop to kill a man asleep.
From end to end the camp he searches, trying
Along the path of his dear love to keep.
If any man's awake, he asks him, sighing,
If he perchance has seen her and with deep
Emotion he describes her, saying: 'Please
Direct me if you can to where she is.'

5

When morning brought the scene to light once more,
He searched the Moorish army through and through.
The surcoat of an emir which he wore
Made this less hazardous for him to do,
And in his quest it helped him furthermore
That other languages than French he knew.
He spoke the Arab tongue so fluently
Men deemed him born and bred in Tripoli.

6

Thus the encampment for three days he scoured,
His only object being to find his love.
Then other cities, other towns he toured,
And not of France alone, but also of
Auvergne and Gascony; from many-towered
Fortresses to the last hamlet, creek and cove,
And from Provence to Brittany he seeks,
From Picard plains to Pyrenean peaks.

7

Between October and November, when
The leafy covering of trees grows less,
Till gradually all their limbs are seen
As they stand shivering in nakedness,
When birds, departing hence, fly southwards in
Vast, serried flocks, the Count, in his distress,
Began his search, nor all the winter through
Did he desist, nor when the year was new.

The journeys of Orlando and Olimpia

(Canto IX. 18-end;
Canto X. 15-16)

Miles
0 ————— 100

Orkneys

SCOTLAND

ENGLAND

London
Thames

N.W.storm

St Malo
Couesnon

Note: For the sake of the modern reader, the imaginary journeys are indicated on modern maps

.... Orlando, blown off course when sailing from St Malo to England to rescue Angelica, lands at Antwerp.

-- Orlando sails with Olimpia from Antwerp to Holland; leaving her on board, he rides to Dordrecht.

--- Orlando sails from Holland beyond the tide and throws Cimosco's cannon into the North Sea.

— Olimpia and Bireno, sailing from Holland for Zealand, are blown off course and cast up on an island off Scotland (probably one of the Orkneys).

8

From one town to another, on he rides
And to the margin of a river goes
Which Normandy from Brittany divides
And gently to the sea in summer flows;
But swollen now with rains and flecked besides
With the white residue of melting snows,
It has destroyed and washed the bridge away,
Leaving no means to cross the waterway.

9

Along the river-bank Orlando peered
To see if he could find a boat whereby
(Since he is not a fish, nor yet a bird)
He might cross over, when there caught his eye
A little ship, in his direction steered.
A damsel in the stern he could espy
Who made repeated signals with her hand,
Nor did she cease until the boat touched land.

10

She did not beach the prow, perhaps afraid
That he might board the boat against her will.
Orlando earnestly besought the maid
To help him to pursue his mission still.
'I'll take no cavalier across', she said,
'Who does not promise first that he'll fulfil
An obligation, honourable and just;
In all the world there is no worthier trust.

11

'So now, if you desire to pass, brave knight,
With my assistance to the other shore,
First, my condition is that you must plight
Your word to me, promising that before
Another month goes by you will unite
With Ireland's king who is preparing war
Against that cruel island named Ebuda:
In all the encircling seas there is none cruder.

12

'Beyond the coast of Ireland, to the West,
There lies, men say, an archipelago.
Of all inhabitants the cruellest,
Hunting for women the Ebudans go,
Whom they then feed to a voracious beast.
To claim the dreadful sacrifice they owe,
It waits expectantly upon the shore,
Adding each day a victim to its score.

13

'The trading vessels which those waters ply,
Unloading there the cargoes they collect,
At intervals replenish the supply
Of lovely women, for, if you'll reflect
That one a day is destined thus to die,
A goodly number's needed, in effect.
If pity is no stranger to your heart,
If love you serve, let valour be your part.'

14

With difficulty can Orlando bear
To hear the story out; he plans that he
Among the very first will volunteer,
As brave knights do when evil deeds they see.
He thinks, and by his thought he's moved to fear,
Angelica a prisoner must be
Of the Ebudans, for he's searched all over
And not a trace of her can he discover.

15

Imagining her fate, his feelings throw
His plans into confusion; with all speed
To the vile region he prepares to go
Where they are guilty of this hateful deed.
He boards a ship not far from St Malo.
No sooner from its moorings is it freed,
Than he instructs the crew to cram on sail,
And that same night they pass Mont St Michel.

16

To port they leave Brieuc's and Tréguier's strand;
Hugging the Breton coast, they journey on,
Towards the chalk-white cliffs from which the land
Of England gained the name of Albion.
The south wind drops and from the course they planned
They're driven by a north-west hurricane.
The captain lowers sail and is resigned
To let the ship be driven by the wind.

17

And so, astern the vessel now appears
To slip, and in a single day, alas!
To lose the progress made in four. Then steers
The helmsman seaward lest the galliass
Should strike the rocks; four days the wind now bears
From dead ahead, then drops and lets them pass
Within a river-mouth, safe from the sea,
And so to Antwerp's calm security.

18

The weary pilot had no sooner docked
Than from the city, which on the right hand
The port and estuary overlooked,
A venerable figure neared the strand.
Bowed down in years he seemed, and silver-locked.
Stepping aboard, he proffered greetings and
In courteous words addressed Orlando, who
He thought must be commander of the crew.

19

He begged him on behalf of a fair maid,
Whom he described as noble, gracious, kind,
Not to refuse to rally to her aid,
For bitterly she grieved in soul and mind.
If he preferred to wait on board instead,
Her way to where the vessel lies she'd find.
He trusted that such courtesy he'd grant
As had been shown by other knights-errant.

20

No other cavalier who'd passed that way,
Whether by land he'd travelled, or by sea,
Had shown the least reluctance to obey
Her summons in her dire extremity.
Orlando, hearing this, did not delay.
Leaping ashore, he followed willingly
The footsteps of the agèd messenger,
And wheresoe'er he led, made no demur.

21

The paladin was brought at last to where
In Antwerp's centre a fair dwelling rose.
He enters and on going up the stair
He finds a lady plunged in deepest woes,
As from her face he is at once aware
And as the room, draped as for mourning, shows.
In a soft voice the noble knight she greeted,
With gracious gesture bidding him be seated.

22

'My father was the Count of Holland,' she
Began; 'so dear was I to him, although
He did not lack for other progeny –
I had two brothers—yet he loved me so
That everything I asked he granted me,
His heart's desire being never to say no;
And while I lived in happiness thus blest,
There visited our land a noble guest.

23

'He was the Duke of Zealand, on his way
To Biscay, to take arms against the Moor.
This youth, as lovely as the month of May,
Inspired a love I never felt before,
And quickly I fell captive to his sway.
His look and his demeanour made me sure –
I thought, I think, and think that well I knew,
He loved and loves me with a heart that's true.

24

'A wind, to others contrary, detained
Him here. The forty days went slowly by
For those who waited, and their patience strained;
And yet for me on wings they seemed to fly.
So much by this our mutual ardour gained,
It was agreed that we would ratify
Our love with solemn rites on his return:
And thus he pledged, and I pledged in my turn.

25

'No sooner had Bireno left our land
(For that, as you must know, is my love's name)
Than for his son a monarch sought my hand
Whose kingdom's distance is from us the same
As that which separates the salt sea strand
To which the river flows; not without fame,
As Friesland it is known. To gain consent,
His highest ministers of state he sent.

26

'But I, who gave my promise, nor can break
The faith I've pledged (and even if I could,
Love does not grant that I should thus forsake
My heart's desire in base ingratitude),
Decide that I must resolutely take
Whatever steps this proposition would
Obstruct, with which, ere ever I'd comply,
I told my father, I would sooner die.

27

'My kindly father, who was only pleased
By what pleased me, to spare me such a fate,
Straightway all such negotiations ceased,
Though to withdraw, it was already late;
And this the king of Friesland so displeased,
That he took umbrage and in frenzied hate
Invaded Holland; thus a war began
Which slaughtered my relations to a man.

28

'Not only is he powerful and strong –
Few in our age against him can prevail –
But so astute and cunning in the wrong
He perpetrates, no courage will avail
Against his evil practices for long.
All strength, all strategy must surely fail
Before a strange new weapon he possesses:
Along a metal tube a ball he presses,

29

'And a rare powder; next, a flame applies
To a small hole which scarcely can be seen,
As the physician does to cauterize
And seal the severed ending of a vein.
Ejected by explosion, the ball flies
With a loud noise, so that men think there's been
A mighty tempest in which thunder crashes
And everywhere the lightning burns and flashes.

30

'Twice with this cunning arm he put to flight
Our company and both my brothers slew:
The elder first, his body-armour quite
Fragmented and his valiant heart shot through;
The second perished in the second fight.
As, routed, from the battlefield he flew,
A blow upon his back the weapon cast
And through his breast the deadly ball then passed.

31

'My father, who defending was one day
The only castle left to him of all
His strongholds, in a comparable way
Was done to death by yet another ball.
For, as he came and went, before the fray,
Providing for whatever might befall,
From a safe distance, counting on surprise,
The traitor shot him right between the eyes.

32

'My brothers and my father dead, I'm thus
Sole heiress of this island, I alone.
The king of Friesland, whose desire it was
To gain a footing here, has clearly shown
His true intention, making plain to us
That he will grant us rest and peace as soon
As I consent to break my former vows
And take his son, Arbante, as my spouse.

33

'Moved not so much by hatred, which in fact
I feel for him and all his evil band,
Who killed my brothers and my father, sacked
And burned and pillaged all our lovely land,
As by my deep reluctance to retract
From vows I made to him to whom my hand
Was promised, that I'd wait to be his bride
When he returned from Spain, I thus replied:

34

'"For every ill I've suffered I'd as soon,
Nay sooner, contemplate a hundred more,
A death by burning and my ashes strewn
On the four winds around the globe, before
I'd break my vows." My people importune
Me constantly, some clamour, some implore,
Hoping to turn me from my fixed intent
And further devastation to prevent.

35

'And when they saw that protests were in vain
And that, in spite of pleas, still firm I stand,
They made a pact with Friesland's sovereign,
Surrendering my person and this land.
He, for his part, occasioned me no pain,
Being content to make me understand
That he would spare my kingdom and my life
If I would be his son's, Arbante's, wife.

36

'Seeing my hand thus forced, I am prepared,
In order to evade his grasp, to die;
But if I'm not revenged on one who's dared
Thus to affront and injure me, then I
Will suffer greater anguish still. Ensnared
By cunning, I resolve deceit to try.
I feign that his proposal pleases me
And that Arbante's wife I long to be.

37

'Of all my father's former entourage,
I chose two brothers — brave, intelligent,
And, what is more, their loyalty I gauge
Above suspicion, for at court they spent
Their days in training from a tender age,
And in our household they both came and went.
In every way I can rely on them.
To die for me no sacrifice they'd deem.

38

'Of my design I made them both aware,
And they agreed to give me every aid.
One of them went at once to Flanders, where
A vessel he equipped. The other stayed.
And now, while Dutch and Friesians prepare
The wedding-feast, Bireno, it is said,
Has in the Bay of Biscay raised a fleet
And comes, full sail, my enemy to meet.

39

'For, after the first battle, which had slain
My elder brother, I despatched straightway
A messenger to ride and spare no pain
Until he gave Bireno in Biscay
These grievous tidings; he with might and main
Begins to arm; meanwhile his cruel way
The king has won, but, unaware of this,
Bireno has set out to bring release.

40

'The king of Friesland, hearing of it, leaves
The wedding preparations to his son,
And with his fleet departs, which he believes
Will more than match the duke's oncoming one.
He scuttles it and as a prize receives
The duke (but this to us was then unknown).
The prince meanwhile has wed me and desires
To lie with me as soon as day expires.

41

'I'd placed behind the curtains of the bed
My faithful ally, who remained stock still,
Waiting until he saw the newly-wed
Approach me where I lay, to do his will.
Then, lifting up an axe behind his head,
Not in pretence, but with intent to kill,
With his strong arm a mortal blow he smote,
And, leaping up, I cut Arbante's throat.

42

'As by a single blow an ox is felled,
So did that ill-born prince collapse, despite
Cimosco's wiles – for thus the king is called
Who slew my father and my brothers quite
Without compassion and his son installed
As heir, or so he hoped, by nuptial rite,
To all my land; for what he planned to do,
It's my suspicion, was to kill me too.

43

'We knew full well we had no time to waste.
A casket with my precious jewels I fill
And my companion lowers me in haste
Along a rope which dangles from a sill
To where his brother, in a boat tied fast,
Awaits us down below, for good or ill.
The wind our canvas spreads, we smite the waves,
And Providence in mercy three lives saves.

44

'Which the king felt the more, I cannot say –
Grief for his son or burning wrath for me,
When to his kingdom he returned next day
And tidings learned of the catastrophe.
Leading his navy homeward from the fray,
Proud of his captive, flushed with victory,
To celebrate a wedding he expected,
And found his people gloomy and dejected.

45

'Compassion for his son, the hate he bears
For me gave him no rest by day or night.
But never were the dead revived by tears,
While hatred from revenge gains some respite.
So he renounced his sighs and woes and cares,
Turning instead to thoughts of how he might
Combine his sorrow with the power of hate
And force me to submit to a dire fate.

46

'Those who, he learned, had rallied to my side,
Or had assisted me in any way
To hatch the plot in which his son had died,
He killed, or burned their houses, to repay
Them for conniving at the homicide;
And to inflict on me still more dismay,
Bireno also he desired to kill,
But found another way to work his will.

47

'So now he stipulates a harsh condition,
To which he sets the limit of a year,
That he will put my love to death – perdition
Take the tyrant! – unless he brings to bear
Such influence that of their own volition,
Or yielding to coercion, prisoner
My friends deliver me, my love's release
Being made dependent on my own decease.

48

'Now all that can be done to save my love,
Except surrendering my life, I've done.
Six castles which I once was mistress of
In Flanders – I have sold them every one,
And used the proceeds, hoping to remove
The guards with gold, and a battalion
Of troops to raise against my enemy
Among the English or in Germany.

49

'My agents, whether to betray me they'd
Intended, or their efforts went awry,
Have given me more promises than aid,
And one and all have left me high and dry,
Since now of so much wealth I have been bled;
And, what is worse, the time is drawing nigh
When neither funds nor forces will avail
To save my love from death by dire travail.

50

'My father and my brothers I have lost
On his account; my realm, too, for his sake
I have surrendered, and to meet the cost
Of intermediaries, paid to make
Attempts to rescue him, I am almost
Reduced to penury; I now must take
The only course of action left to me:
Surrender and so let my love go free.

51

'And so, if there is nothing else which I
Can do, and all depends on this alone,
That in exchange for his life I must die,
Then for his life I gladly give my own.
One apprehension I am troubled by:
The difficulty of insisting on
An unequivocable *quid pro quo*
In bargaining with such a treacherous foe.

52

'I am afraid that once he has me caged
And works on me his cruel, savage will,
He may not keep to what he has engaged:
That, thanks to me, Bireno shall live still;
But, breaking faith, by fury so enraged,
My death being insufficient to fulfil
His lust for blood, he will renew his crime
And on my love give vent to it next time.

53

'The only reason why I now confer
With any guest who sojourns here with us,
Or any passing gallant cavalier,
Is that I hope, by taking counsel thus,
To be assured, when I am prisoner
Of one so cruel and so treacherous,
Bireno in his freedom may confide,
Nor will be put to death when I have died.

54

'I have requested many a brave knight
To bear me company when to the king
Of Friesland I surrender, and to plight
His word to me that without faltering
Bireno forth from prison to the light
Of day he'll force the Friesians to bring,
While to the dark and death I gladly go,
My love restored to life content to know.

55

'But not a single champion have I found
Who on his solemn oath will promise me,
When I shall be conducted, chained and bound,
Until they set my love, Bireno, free,
Not to surrender me but stand his ground,
Such is the terror of the weaponry,
Which no defensive armour can withstand,
However strongly or robustly planned.

56

'Now, if your Herculean bearing is
Well matched by prowess, and you think that you
Can circumvent the cruel king in his
Design and, should he fail in what is due,
You can release me, then escort me, please,
For I shall feel no terror if you do,
And on your brave defence I may rely;
But if Bireno dies I twice will die.'

57

And here the lady ended her sad tale,
Which many times with weeping and with sighs
She'd interrupted; scarcely could it fail
To move Orlando, in whose heart there lies
No lame desire to make the good prevail.
Wasting no words (on action he relies)
He promised and upon his oath he swore
That he would do as she had asked, and more.

58

For he has no intention she shall yield
To such an enemy to save her love.
He'll rescue both, as long as he can wield
His trusty sword and his known prowess prove.
The very day that she had thus revealed
Her story, with a wind that northwards drove,
They set to sea; the paladin, in haste
To reach Ebuda, had no time to waste.

59

Now on the one, now on the other tack
The pilot sails mid Zeeland's waterways.
They near and leave behind them in their track
One, then another, island; when three days
Have passed, Orlando, eager to attack
Cimosco, disembarks; the lady stays
On board, offshore from Holland, to await
Orlando's news of King Cimosco's fate.

60

Along the coast he goes, from heel to head
Accoutred, on a charger black and grey,
In Denmark born, in Flanders reared and fed,
Deep-chested, broad and strong in every way,
More for endurance than for lightness bred.
His own he'd left behind upon a quay:
His Brigliador, so spirited and fair;
None, save Baiardo, can with him compare.

61

He gallops to Dordrecht and there he sees
A mighty army marshalled at the gate,
Such as a fearful ruler always is
In need of, and especially a new State,
And indicating also an unease
Occasioned by the rumour that a great
Armada had been sighted near at hand,
Led by Bireno's cousin from Zealand.

62

Orlando to the king at once sends word
To tell him that a passing cavalier
Desires to challenge him with lance and sword,
With this proviso: if the challenger
Should lose, she who his son, her spouse and lord,
Arbante, murdered, who's not far from there,
Shall be delivered up to him to pay
The forfeit of her life that very day.

63

And, for his part, the king must promise too,
If in the combat he should vanquished be,
To pay as penalty the rightful due,
And set his prisoner, Bireno, free.
The soldier with Orlando's message flew,
But, lacking honour and all chivalry,
Cimosco plans (and this is no exception)
To trick the brave Orlando by deception.

64

He thinks that if by fraud he takes the knight
He'll get the lady in his hands as well
(If he has heard the messenger aright).
And so he issues orders to detail
A party, thirty strong, to creep from sight
And make a detour from the citadel.
By a circuitous and hidden track,
They issue forth behind Orlando's back.

65

And when Cimosco hears, as he has willed,
The company has reached the place decreed
And all his orders duly are fulfilled,
He issues from the gate, accompanied
By thirty other men; and as a skilled
And cunning huntsman often may proceed,
Or fishermen who near Volano fling
Their nets in a wide circle, so the king,

66

To circumvent his challenger's escape,
Blocks every avenue upon all sides.
Alive he wants him – in no other shape.
This seems a simple task, so he decides
The weapon with the deadly thunder-clap
He'll not employ, but in a plan confides
Where strategy and treachery combine,
To capture, not to kill, being his design.

67

And, as a fowler prudently will spare
The life of birds among the first he nets,
Since greater booty still he hopes to snare,
And, using those as lure and decoy, sets
His traps anew, so did Cimosco dare
To set his own against Orlando's wits.
But he's no man to take at the first stroke,
And soon the ring encircling him he broke.

68

The Cavalier Anglante, where the row
Of soldiery is thickest, drives his lance.
As if they one and all are made of dough,
In one and then another he implants
His weapon, till he's skewered at one go
No less than six; a seventh, too, he wants
To add, but, as no space for him is found,
He has to leave him, dying, on the ground.

69

Just so the skilful archer strings a line
Of frogs which hide in ditches and canals,
Shooting them through the haunches and the spine,
Until from notch to tip with animals
His arrow is replete; the paladin,
Whose expertise such archery recalls,
His fully-burdened lance now flings away
And plunges, sword in hand, into the fray.

70

With his good sword, which never once in vain
He'd wielded, he struck out with all his might.
With blade or point, he felled in mortal pain
First here a man on foot, and there a knight,
On all sides marking with a crimson stain
Surcoats of blue, green, yellow, black and white.
Cimosco grieved that he had not employed
His deadly fire-device to fill the void.

71

In a loud voice he bellows the command,
And threatens all who dare to disobey,
To bring the weapon forth; but none to hand
He finds: those in the city mean to stay
There, those outside take to their heels, unmanned.
He, too, decides the coward's part to play.
Reaching the inner gate, he tries to wind
The drawbridge up; the Count is close behind.

72

He turns to flee, leaving Orlando master
Of entry to the drawbridge and both gates.
His charger spurring faster and still faster,
He gallops past the fleeing renegades
Who've seen their comrades meet with such disaster.
Orlando scorns them all and concentrates
On capturing the king; but in this race
Cimosco's horse has wings, and flies apace.

73

From one road to the next he disappears
From sight. But not for long does he delay:
The strange, new, hollow weapon now appears,
Which he intends shall now come into play;
And down behind it, as Orlando nears,
He crouches like a huntsman in the lay
Of the wild boar, his boar-spear in his hand,
And dogs, their collars armed, at his command,

74

Who hears the branches and the boulders crash,
And, every time the creature rears its snout,
Thinks, from the noise, that it must surely smash
The forest, and the very hills uproot;
So does the king await Orlando's dash,
Determined he shall pay his final scot.
As he draws near, the hole with fire he touches.
Straightway the force of the explosion such is,

75

The monster, with a flash of lightning, mumbles,
Spewing a charge of metal from its bore.
The walls are seen to tremble, heaven rumbles
With echoes of the terrifying roar.
A deadly shaft, which decimates and crumbles
All it encounters and remits no score,
Whistles and shrieks, just as the king desires;
Yet the assassin's brutal plan misfires.

76

Whether in haste, or over-eagerness,
Thinking Orlando's life was for the taking,
Or, as a consequence of nervousness,
For like a leaf his hands and arms were shaking,
With trembling heart he aimed the blow amiss;
Or, God had no intention of forsaking
One who had served Him well: the horse the blow
Received and, falling, motionless lay low.

77

Both cavalier and steed fell to the ground,
But, while in one all signs of life had ceased,
The other leapt up nimbly with one bound,
As though his strength and vigour were increased.
As Libyan Antaeus ever found
From contact with the earth new might released,
So now Orlando, with redoubled force,
Arose from where he'd fallen with the horse.

78

Whoever witnessed hurtling from the sky
Some deafening thunderbolt of Jupiter's
And, where saltpetre, sulphur, carbon lie
Enclosed together, watches as it nears
And instantly in fragments shoots on high
The walls, the monuments, the marble tiers,
Until not earth alone, or so it seems,
But heaven also is consumed in flames,

79

Let him imagine thus Orlando then,
As from the ground whereon he fell he reared him.
Of such fierce aspect was the paladin
That Mars upon Olympus might have feared him.
The frightened king in panic tugged the rein,
Turning his charger as Orlando neared him.
But faster ran the noble Count behind
Than ever arrow flew upon the wind.

80

And what he did not manage to achieve
On horseback, he will carry through on foot.
No one who had not seen him would believe
That he could move so swiftly in pursuit.
He closes in and lifts his arms to cleave,
With his brave sword, down to the neck-bone's root,
Cimosco's head; the villain down he cast;
By such a fall the right's avenged at last.

81

Within the city then is heard the sound
Of clashing swords and tread of troops unknown.
It is Bireno's cousin, whose renowned
And gallant forces to defend his own
He's rallied; when the city gate he found
Wide open, in he went, whence all had flown,
Reduced to panic by Orlando. Thus
No hindrance was there to his impetus.

82

The fleet-of-foot show no desire to lag,
Or make enquiries who these strangers are;
But some, less nimble, or whose footsteps drag,
Observe their language and insignia.
They sue for peace, displaying a white flag,
And to these neighbours from Zealandia
Declare themselves, and to their commandant,
Willing to do whatever they may want.

83

For hostile to the king they long have been
And to his Friesian followers as well.
Their former ruler he had vilely slain.
Against his impious greed they now rebel.
Orlando being on hand to intervene,
Relations soon are rendered peaceable.
Holland and Zealand, thus united, vow
No Friesian shall escape their vengeance now.

84

The dungeon portals to the ground they raze,
And no concern have they to find the key.
Bireno to the Count his thanks conveys,
Owning his obligation gratefully.
Then to the vessel where Olimpia stays –
Such is the name of her whom destiny
Has heiress made of Holland – they repair
In state to see the end of the affair.

85

She whom Orlando had conducted thither
Cherished no hopes that he so much could do.
She would have been content if by her death her
Love might live: and now her subjects come to
Greet her, she and her love are now together!
Long it would take me to recount to you
How long they linger in each other's arms,
Thanks to Orlando, safe from all alarms.

86

Her people reinstate her on the throne
Of her dead father and allegiance swear.
She, by a knot that ne'er can be undone,
Being linked in love, the countship then and there,
Herself, all her possessions, to her own
Bireno gives; he, by another care
Absorbed, which had concerned him when he was in
Friesland, entrusts all Holland to his cousin.

87

For, to return to Zealand is his plan,
Together with his bride; and thence south-west
To wend his way to Friesland once again,
Where he will put his fortune to the test.
A winning card he holds, by which he can
Impose whatever terms he judges best:
Cimosco's daughter who, with many more,
Was taken prisoner some days before.

88

He wants, he says, to wed her to his brother,
A comely youth, stalwart in every way.
He and the Count take leave then of each other
And both of them set out the self-same day.
Orlando has no wish for any other
Share of the booty from the recent fray,
Except the monster arm of which I've spoken,
Which terror in so many hearts has woken.

89

In taking it, his aim is not to use
The deadly weapon in his own defence,
For cowardly he deems it to abuse
The laws which govern knights' accoutrements.
A place to hide it in he means to choose
So that it never more may give offence.
The balls, the powder and all other parts
He takes, and with them on his journey starts.

90

And so, when he had sailed beyond the tide
And reached the farthest depths of open sea,
And nothing of the coast on either side,
Looking to left or right, could he then see,
Taking the deadly instrument, he cried:
'That never more a cavalier may be
Advantaged by your aid, nor evil gain
What valour has deserved, below remain!

91

'Accursèd and abominable tool,
In Tartarean depths devised and forged
By that Beelzebub beneath whose rule
The world to its destruction thus is urged,
I re-consign you to the deepest hole
Of the Abyss whence you were first disgorged!'
Thus to the deep he flung it; and, meanwhile,
The wind propels him towards the Dreadful Isle.

92

Such longing does Orlando feel to know
If she (whom he so loves that every hour
He spends apart from her is grief and woe)
Waits helpless for the monster to devour
Her, that no slightest wish has he to go
To Ireland, nor to anywhere ashore,
Lest some new knightly challenge may detain
Him and all hope to rescue her be vain.

93

He does not land in England, nor upon
The Irish coast, nor veer towards the east.
But let him go where Cupid drives him on,
Who shot so sharp an arrow in his breast.
Ere I return to him, I must be gone
To Holland once again, where as my guest
I'll take you back, for we'd regret indeed
To miss the chance to see Olimpia wed.

94

The wedding is a sumptuous affair,
But not so sumptuous, I must admit,
As one in Zealand which they now prepare.
But I must ask you not to think of it,
For new disturbances arising there
Will interrupt my story for a bit.
Of all these happenings I'll give you news
If my next canto you will now peruse.

CANTO X

1

Of all the constant hearts, of all the love,
Of all the trust in all recorded time,
Of all the women who as models of
Heroic passion rose to heights sublime,
Olimpia the queen of all would prove
(In spite of what now follows in my rhyme).
In all the new or ancient chroniclers,
No greater love you'll ever find than hers.

2

So many tokens of her loving heart,
So many signs, Bireno has received,
Were she to tear her tender breast apart,
Hoping by this the more to be believed,
No clearer certainty could she impart.
If constant souls, as well may be conceived,
Reciprocal affection justly earn,
Bireno should at least her love return.

3

No other woman should he put before her –
Not she whose beauty launched a thousand ships
(Supposing some magician could restore her);
Such loveliness should all things else eclipse;
More than his very soul he should adore her;
His eyes, his ears, his hands, his tongue, his lips
He should more readily renounce, his life
Itself forgo, than part from such a wife.

4

If he loved her as he by her was loved,
If true he was as she to him was true,
If from her vessel's wake he never moved,
Or if to such devotion, love and to
Fidelity like hers he cruel proved,
It is my purpose to relate to you;
And I will make astonished eyebrows rise
And see lips purse and pucker in surprise.

5

And when Bireno's actions I make known,
By which Olimpia's virtue was rewarded,
Ladies, I trust among you there'll be none
By whom henceforth belief will be accorded
To any lovers who their vows intone.
God's omnipresence being unregarded,
Oaths, promises and pledges are combined
Which afterwards are scattered on the wind,

6

Those promises and vows which are dispersed
Upon the air and wafted by the breeze,
Soon as a lover satisfies the thirst
Which burned and parched him; therefore to his pleas,
Dear ladies, be less credulous at first;
Be not so readily disposed to please,
For Love less likely is to play her false
Who learns at the expense of someone else.

7

Be on your guard against those in the flower
Of ardent youth, whose amorous desires
Blaze up and die away in a brief hour,
Just as a burning straw at once expires.
The hunter, chasing hares, will gladly scour
The land, up hill, down dale, through brakes and briars,
In cold and heat, but, once a hare is caught,
He chases others, for this caring naught.

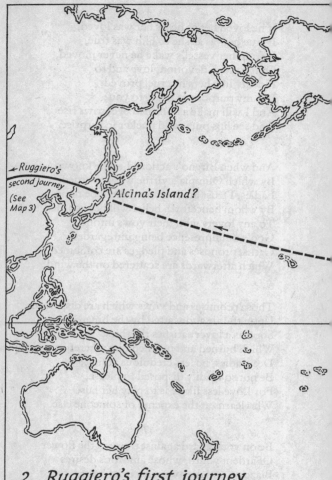

2. *Ruggiero's first journey*

———— *Ruggiero on hippogriff flies from S. France westwards to Alcina's island.*
(Canto VI. 17-21)

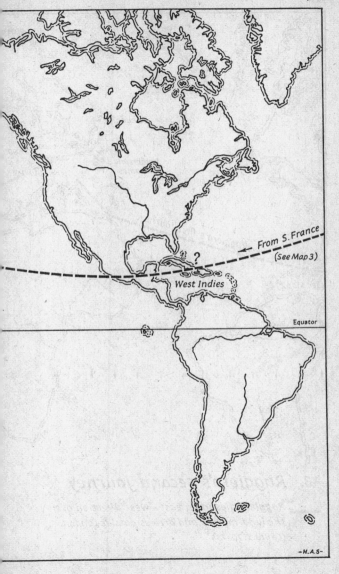

From S. France
(See Map 3)

?

West Indies

Equator

-H.A.S-

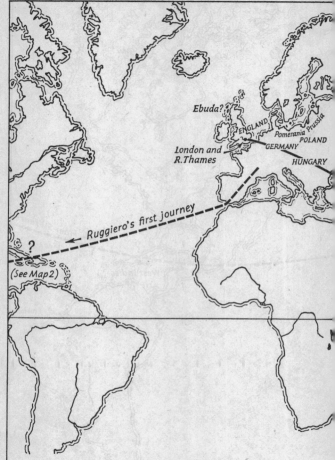

Ebuda?

ENGLAND

Pomerania
Prussia
POLAND

London and
R. Thames

GERMANY

HUNGARY

Ruggiero's first journey

?

(See Map 2)

3. Ruggiero's second journey

Ruggiero flies in an east – west direction over
the land-masses and arrives outside London
(Canto X. 70-73)

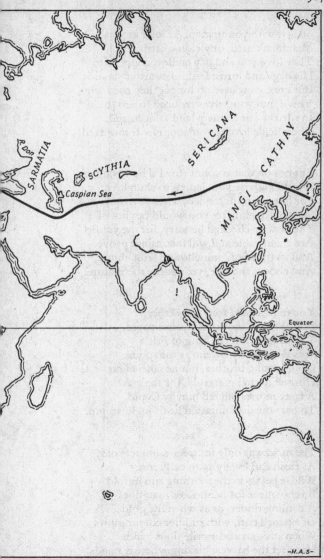

-H.A.S-

8

So is it with young men. As long as you
Maintain a hard, unyielding attitude,
They love you and pay endless court, as to
His liege and lord a faithful courtier should;
But once your love no longer they need woo,
You'll find yourselves reduced to servitude,
In sorrow left to rue what has occurred,
Their fickle love to someone else transferred.

9

But not on that account (for I'd be wrong)
Would I advise you, ladies, to shun love,
For like a vine untended, with no strong
Support to cling to, you would be; but of
The downy-cheeked be wary, for the young
Are changeable and will inconstant prove.
And so the hard, unmellowed fruit abjure,
And choose the ripe, yet not the too mature.

10

You may recall I told you earlier,
Before in my account I made a pause,
The daughter of the king of Frisia
Was destined by Bireno as the spouse
Of his young brother, but he fancied her
Himself, to tell you truly, for she was
A tasty morsel offered him by Cupid.
To pass the dish untasted he thought stupid.

11

The maid was only fourteen summers old,
As fresh and lovely as an early rose
Whose petals to the morning sun unfold.
Bireno burns for her no less than does
A flaming tinder, or as when the gold
Of ripened corn with ruddier colour glows
When envious and sacrilegious hands
Have set the harvest blazing where it stands.

12

Thus with an instant flame for her he burned
And kindled to the marrow of his bones,
When over her dead father, as she mourned,
He saw her weep and heard her piteous tones.
Just as a saucepan from the boil is turned
By adding colder water, so at once
His former ardour, by Olimpia fed,
Quenched by its rival, dwindled and lay dead.

13

Not only was his fever for her sated,
The very sight of her became displeasing,
While for the other, passion now created
An appetite which there was no appeasing.
Until the day drew near for which he waited,
When he would satisfy his longing, pleasing
Olimpia, he feigned, was his sole care,
As though her every wish his also were.

14

And if the maid he fondles, more than once
Exceeding what to innocence is due,
Still there is nobody *qui mal y pense.*
Compassion everyone ascribes it to,
Allowing it his glory to enhance,
That one afflicted, who is blameless too,
He should thus seek to comfort and protect,
For to defend the weak is no defect.

15

O God on high, how often you obscure
Men's vision with an obfuscating mist!
Bireno's motives, held to be so pure,
Were in all truth more worthy of a beast.
So now the sailors, grasping each an oar,
Through brackish waters, sailing north by east,
The duke and his companions gaily carry,
Towards Zealand, there ostensibly to marry

16

The damsel to his brother. Losing sight
Of Holland's coastline, carefully they steered
Away from Friesland, less upon the right
Than on the left-hand tack; and slowly veered
Towards Scotland, when a hurricane, which quite
Re-routed them, out of the north appeared.
Three days it whirled them round, until at last
Upon a lonely island they were cast.

17

When they were beached within a little bay,
Olimpia, unsuspecting, stepped ashore,
Content with her unfaithful spouse to stay.
And when they'd supped together, to restore
Her weary limbs, upon the bed she lay
Within a tent prepared inland before.
The others then returned to board the ship
And, stretched out on their berths, were soon asleep.

18

The travail of the voyage and the fear
Which for three nights had kept her wide awake,
The sense of safety, silence everywhere,
While forest-trees around a refuge make,
Relief from all anxiety, as near
Her husband she reclines, sweet rest to take,
Induce in her a slumber as profound
As in a bear or dormouse may be found.

19

Her faithless lover, whose manoeuvrings
Were keeping him awake, when fast asleep
He saw her, made a bundle of his things
And softly from the tent began to creep.
Gaining the beach, as though he'd sprouted wings,
He raced to wake his crew on board the ship.
Without a sound being heard, without a shout,
The sailors for the open sea set out.

20

The isle was left behind whereon, thus jilted,
Olimpia slumbered sweetly, never waking
Until the frozen dew the Dawn had melted,
Earth's surface with her golden chariot raking,
And halcyon voices o'er the ocean lilted,
Their ancient lamentation ever making.
Then, half asleep, her arm she gently moves
Bireno to embrace whom she so loves.

21

There's no-one there; her hand again she tends;
She gropes once more; then, finding no-one still,
First one and then another leg extends,
This way and that, but all to no avail.
Her somnolence a sudden terror ends.
She gazes round: still no-one; with a chill
Of dire foreboding, from her widowed bed
She starts, leaving the tent with hurried tread.

22

Beside the sea, now certain of her fate,
She tears her face, her hair, she beats her breast.
Along the shore (the moon is setting late)
She looks for signs of life, to east, to west,
In all directions, and, now desperate,
She calls: 'Bireno', and the caves attest
Their sympathy by echoing his name –
'Bireno' – calling every time the same.

23

At the shore's farthest end a cliff arose
Which breakers by their frequent battering
Had hollowed to a structure like a bow's.
It overhung the sea; there clambering,
Olimpia to the very summit goes,
By anguish rendered strong for such a thing,
And from afar the swelling sails she sees
Of her unfaithful, cruel lord who flees.

24

Such is the spectacle which greets her eyes,
Or thus it seems in the uncertain light.
Trembling, she falls upon the ground and lies
Inert, her countenance more cold and white
Than snow; when able once again to rise,
She sends, as best she may in her sad plight,
Her plaintive voice along the vessel's route,
Calling her husband's name in vain pursuit.

25

And when her weary voice grew faint at last,
She wept and beat her palms together, crying:
'Oh, where, Bireno, do you flee so fast?
Too lightly ballasted your vessel's flying.
My soul, without my body, you have cast
Into the hold; add now this weight', and, trying
To hail the vessel, while these words she said,
She waved and with her garments signals made.

26

The winds which bore the ship of the ingrate
Across the water likewise bore away
The voice of poor Olimpia, whose sad fate
Drove her no fewer than three times that day
Her death – so undeserved – to contemplate
By drowning in the eddies of the bay.
From gazing out to sea at last she turned
And to her couch within the tent returned.

27

And, lying prone, confiding to her bed,
Drenching her pillow, she began to mourn:
'Last night to two you gave repose; instead
Not two awake, but only one, forlorn,
Since infamous Bireno now is fled.
Curst be the day that ever I was born!
What shall I do? What can I do alone?
Where shall I look for help when there is none?

28

'I see no man, no handiwork I see
Whence hope of humankind I might derive.
I see no vessel by which I might be
From this dread island taken off alive.
So I must die, with none to bury me,
Or gently close my eyes, or my soul shrive,
My only sepulchre, perhaps, the foul
Devouring maws of savage wolves which prowl.

29

'So here I lie, a victim of alarms,
Fearing to see emerging lions, bears,
Tigers and all such beasts as Nature arms
With fangs and claws; but, whatsoe'er my fears,
You have inflicted on me countless harms
Which more atrocious are than all of theirs,
For one death only they would kill me by,
While you, alas! a thousand make me die.

30

'But even if some pilot here should pass
And, in his mercy, take me on his ship,
That I may circumvent this evil pass
And lions, wolves and tigers may escape,
How can I go to Holland where, alas!
On all the ports and strongholds guard you keep,
My country where I saw the light of day,
Which you by treachery now take away?

31

'You have usurped my kingdom, under guise
Of friendship, claiming kinship's sacred right,
And have installed your henchmen in a trice,
Being careful no resistance to invite.
Shall I return to Flanders? There, likewise,
I am no longer mistress. From your plight
In my attempt to save you, I sold all.
I know not where to go, nor ever shall.

32

'To Frisia, where I have renounced for you
The opportunity to be their queen
(And of my father and my brothers, too,
Unwilling instrument of death have been)?
The sacrifices I have made – not few –
You know as well as I – you too have seen
The consequences I endured, the burden
Of my sorrow – and now behold my guerdon!

33

'Ah! let me not fall prey to a corsair,
Who will abduct and sell me as a slave!
Sooner than that, let come a wolf or bear,
Lion or tiger, any such that have
Fangs strong to crunch, claws sharp to strip and tear,
And let it drag my body to its cave!'
Thus did Olimpia mourn, in her distress
Her golden hair uprooting, tress by tress.

34

Again she runs along the sandy shore,
Hither and thither; not Olimpia
She seems, but some mad creature by a score
Of demons driven, or like Hecuba,
A prey to frenzy when her Polydore
She found there lying dead; and then afar
Olimpia gazes seawards, like a stock,
Standing so still, a rock upon a rock.

35

But let us leave her there, her fate to mourn,
While now Ruggiero's tale I take in hand.
Just when the rays of noon most fiercely burn,
His weary charger plods along the strand.
The sunbeams strike the mountain and return;
Like molten metal is the fine, white sand.
The armour which he wore, as like as not,
Must on his tortured body seem red-hot.

36

Meanwhile his thirst, the weary exercise
Of wading through deep sand, the lonely way
Did little to relieve the enterprise
Or make his journey any the more gay.
An ancient fortress rose before his eyes
Beside the sea, and in its shadow lay
Three ladies of Alcina's court, as he
From their demeanour and attire could see.

37

Upon Egyptian carpets, rare and fine,
In the cool air they sweetly take their ease.
Around them, beakers of refreshing wine
Were spread, with every viand that might please.
And near them, bobbing gently on the brine,
A little skiff was waiting till the breeze
Should fill its idle, lifeless sails again,
For not a breath of wind was stirring then.

38

The damsels, who have watched Ruggiero pace
The shifting sands with slow and painful steps,
See how the sweat is pouring down his face
And thirst is sculpted on his crusted lips;
And they begin sweet words to interlace,
To lure him from the steadfast path he keeps,
And towards the shadow make him turn aside
To rest his weary body from the ride.

39

So, by his stirrup one now takes her stance,
To help him to dismount being her design.
Ruggiero sees another then advance,
Bearing a goblet full of sparkling wine.
But to such music he is loath to dance.
Delaying so, disaster would combine,
Giving Alcina time to come too close,
For she's not far behind, as well he knows.

40

No sulphur or saltpetre ever flashed,
Touched by a flame, nor blazed so furiously,
No raging ocean ever tossed or thrashed,
Tormented by a whirlwind ceaselessly,
As, when they saw Ruggiero, unabashed,
Proceed upon his way unswervingly,
Their beauty (as they deemed it) shunned and scorned,
The last of the three damsels raged and burned:

41

'You're neither courteous nor a cavalier,'
Thus she began Ruggiero to revile;
'That horse is stolen, and the arms you bear
You likewise came by in no honest style.
I'd like to see you hanged for it, I swear,
Burned at the stake, quartered and drawn, you vile
Ungrateful, thieving, ugly miscreant,
Of all the villains the most arrogant!'

42

These were the words the angry damsel said,
With many other insults, all the more
Since he, quite unperturbed, no answer made.
(No glory in such combat he looked for.)
Then with the other two the frenzied maid
Entered the boat which waited by the shore.
With rapid strokes she rowed and level kept
As onward through the sand the charger stepped.

43

Cursing and calling on him every ill,
She finds at every thrust some point of shame.
Nor did she cease from her attack until
At last Ruggiero to the narrows came,
Where to a fairer sorceress he still
Aspired to cross; preceded by his fame,
He is awaited by a little ship
On which the pilot beckons him to step,

44

And joyfully casts off the mooring-rope
To take Ruggiero to a better shore.
If the expression of a face gives scope
To judge the heart, this pilot offers, more
Than many other men, good cause to hope.
Ruggiero, once on board, is grateful for
God's help, and offers thanks; then to the wise
And prudent boatman's words himself applies.

45

He praised Ruggiero for his timeliness
In thus withdrawing from Alcina's clutch
Before she gave him, in her wantonness,
A chalice of a magic potion, such
As rendered all her lovers powerless.
In Logistilla's land, where they'll soon touch,
Virtue and grace and beauty he will find
Which feed, but never satiate, the mind.

46

'This gracious being', said he, 'inculcates
Such reverence and wonder in the soul,
When first her loveliness it contemplates,
All other joys far short of this must fall.
A lover's heart, tormented, vacillates
Between despair and longing, as a rule,
But love for Logistilla asks no more
Than to reflect upon her and adore.

47

'More pleasing aspirations she will teach
Than songs and dances, unguents, baths and food
That, newly oriented, you may pitch
Your higher thoughts towards the highest good
(In loftier flight than ever hawk can reach),
Where bliss in mortal frame may find abode.'
While speaking thus, the pilot sped the boat,
Which from the safer shore was still remote.

48

They saw approaching down the waterway
A fleet of ships, towards them, it seemed, directed.
Alcina, who was ready for the fray,
Her troops to her assistance had collected,
Determined on a single throw to play
All her resources, for her love rejected.
Love was indeed a reason for her course,
Though the affront to pride made matters worse.

49

Not ever since the day when she was born
By such calamity had she been stirred
As by the blow inflicted by his scorn.
The rapid oars across the surface whirred;
To this shore and to that the spray was borne
And thundering echoes all around were heard.
'Ruggiero, take the cover from your shield
Before you perish or your freedom yield!'

50

Such were the boatman's words, who not alone
On words relied, for in an instant he
Detached the silken sheath and forth there shone
The magic beam, of which the potency
Confounded every foe it played upon.
First one and then another blindingly
It dazzles till each man is seen to drop,
Some from the prow, still others from the poop.

51

A soldier who was keeping sentinel
Had seen the coming of Alcina's fleet.
With mighty hammer-clangs he rang the bell
Which summoned the artillery to greet
The foe with fusillades of stones which fell
On whatsoever miscreant saw fit
To seek to harm Ruggiero; thus his life
And freedom were defended in the strife.

52

A group of women gather on the shore,
Sent by Queen Logistilla in all haste;
Andrònica, the bravest of the four,
Fronèsia, with highest wisdom graced,
Dicilla, the most virtuous, and, more
Significant, the radiant and chaste
Sofròsina. The army from the fort
Has issued and is drawn up near the port.

53

Below the citadel, at anchor lay
A fleet of many vessels of great size,
Ready at any time of night or day
At the first sound of bells or warning cries.
Thus fearful and ferocious is the fray
Which on both land and sea will now arise.
Alcina, with no magic to assist her,
Will lose the kingdom taken from her sister.

54

Of how few battles is the outcome plain!
Ah! what surprises Fortune can combine!
Not only did Alcina not regain
Her fleeing lover (as was her design),
But of her fleet, so dense upon the main
Scarce was there room for it to stand in line,
Flames having now consumed all other ships,
Upon one craft, dejected, she escapes.

55

She flees; and her ill-fated company
Have died by burning or are prisoners.
Yet, of them all, the worst calamity
Is that Ruggiero is no longer hers.
By day, by night, she grieves most piteously,
Her loss lamenting, shedding bitter tears,
And many times she longs with her own hand
To all her suffering to put an end.

56

But sorceresses cannot ever die,
Long as the sun revolves and planets tread
In age-long style their pattern through the sky;
Else Clotho had been moved to cut her thread.
Such grief Alcina is tormented by
That she would gladly imitate the deed
Of Dido or the Nile's resplendent queen,
But hers the power to die has never been.

57

But let us leave her to her grief and woe,
And speak of him whose noble deeds have earned
Eternal fame. Ruggiero, as you know,
Was saved. His thanks to God he first returned,
Then from the vessel he prepared to go
On shore. His back now to the sea was turned
And, hastening his steps across dry land,
He reached the citadel close by the strand.

58

No stronger, no more beautiful, was seen
By mortal eye in present times or past.
The walls more precious are than if they'd been
In diamonds or fiery rubies cast.
To try to speak, in our world, of their sheen
And beauty would be time and labour lost,
For in that magic realm, and only there
(Save, it may be, in Heaven) they appear.

59

The gems all others far surpass in this:
That if the shining wall reflect a man,
He sees his soul exactly as it is;
He sees his vices and his virtues plain.
Henceforth no heed he pays to flatteries;
No hostile criticism gives him pain.
Self-knowledge, which derives from such reflection,
Increases his good sense and circumspection.

60

Their radiance, which imitates the sun,
Is of such splendour that eternal day
Created is for all it shines upon,
Regardless of Apollo's yea or nay;
And priceless worth not in the gems alone
Resides, but an observer scarce can say
Which of these two his judgement more enthrals:
The craftsmanship, or substance, of the walls.

61

Above the lofty vaulting on the piers,
Which are so tall they prop the very sky,
The roof a spacious hanging garden bears,
So lovely, to maintain it would defy
The skill of all ground-level gardeners.
Glimpsed through the gleaming battlements, on high
Are fragrant shrubs, ripe fruit and lovely flowers
Which all the year adorn those pleasant bowers.

62

No trees are found of such nobility,
Nowhere such fadeless amaranths are bred,
No roses, lilies, bloom so radiantly,
No violas, in any other bed.
Elsewhere on earth in one same month we see
First burgeon into life and lift its head,
Then droop upon its widowed stalk and die,
A flower subject to the changing sky.

63

But here perpetual the flowers are,
Perpetual the loveliness each wears,
Not because Nature with particular
Indulgence from severity forbears,
But Logistilla's skill extends so far,
Having no need of the supernal spheres
(In earthly gardens an unheard-of thing)
She has created everlasting Spring.

64

Great joy was manifested by the fay
That such a noble knight should visit her,
And she commanded that in every way
He should be honoured as a sojourner.
Astolfo had been there for many a day.
The sight of him rejoiced the newcomer,
And soon all those Melissa had revived
And reinstated as themselves, arrived.

65

When they had rested for a day or two,
Ruggiero, with Astolfo, thought it best
To seek the queen's assistance, for he too
Was eager to depart towards the West.
Melissa for them both resolved to sue,
And humbly she put forward the request
That help, advice, support they might receive
From Logistilla when they took their leave.

66

The fay replied: 'I'll give the matter thought,
And in two days you'll see them duly sped.'
She then considers by what means she ought
To help the knights their homeward path to tread.
First she concludes Ruggiero must be brought
To Aquitaine on the winged quadruped,
And orders the construction of a bit
By which he may control and master it.

67

She demonstrates what he must do if he
Desires the hippogriff to rise on high,
Circle or swoop, or travel rapidly,
Or on raised pinions hover in the sky.
As on the earth a rider one may see
On all his expert horsemanship rely,
So did Ruggiero in this *haute école*
With every twist and turn his mount control.

68

When every detail he was master of,
From his kind benefactress leave he took,
To whom he afterwards was bound in love
Which never in his life his soul forsook.
First I will tell you how he fared, then move
To the adventures of the English duke,
Who hardship still must suffer and great pain
Before he reaches Paris once again.

69

Ruggiero thence set out, but did not take
The route by which he'd come against his will –
Above the ocean, an unending track
Where scarcely any land was visible;
But, now he had the hippogriff in check,
And he could fly it anywhere at will,
He chose to go another way instead,
As when the Magi from King Herod fled.

70

Upon his outward journey, leaving Spain,
He'd come to India in a straight line,
Where eastern waters bathe its coastal plain,
And two enchantresses in battle join.
Now he decides his journey back again
He'll not to Aeolus's realm confine,
But of the global course he has begun
He will complete the circle like the sun.

71

Now on Cathay, to the one side, he cast
His glance, and now on Mangi, near Kinsai.
With Sericana on his right, he crossed
The Himalayas; winging next his way
From northern Scythia to the Caspian, passed
Then to Sarmatia; when below him lay
Two continents divided by the Don,
The Russian wastes Ruggiero first gazed on,

72

Then Prussia and the Pomeranian
Expanse; although he ardently desired
To see his Bradamante once again,
Yet in his wanderlust he still aspired
To visit Polish and Hungarian
And German lands; nor had he yet grown tired
Of the bleak Northern clime before he came
To England, last in distance and in name.

73

But do not think, my lord, that all this while
Ruggiero has remained upon the wing,
For he descends and searches many a mile
Until he finds each night good quartering.
For days, for months, he journeys in this style,
Such is the pleasure his adventures bring.
Then London he approaches one fine morn
And to the river Thames is gently borne.

74

In meadows which lay near the city wall
He watched as men-at-arms and infantry,
Responding to a drum or trumpet-call,
Formed and re-formed in perfect symmetry
Before Rinaldo, the invincible,
The honour and the pride of chivalry,
Whom Charlemagne had sent, you understand,
To gather reinforcements in this land.

75

And just in time Ruggiero fluttered down
To see these forces splendidly arrayed,
As they came pouring forth from London town.
He asked a courteous cavalier, who said:
'These armies, led by captains of renown,
Whose bannerets are proudly thus displayed,
Come from the Scottish, Irish, English host,
Or from the islands round about the coast.

76

'When the parade is done, their way they'll make
Where ships awaiting them at anchor lie.
Across the Channel they will sail, to take
Assistance to the French, beleaguered by
The Infidel. New hopes they'll soon awake
And, at their coming, courage will run high.
That all these armies you may fully know,
I'll point you out the captains as they go.

77

'You see the largest banner over there,
Which leopards with the fleur-de-lis combines?
The commandant who holds it in the air
Is captain-general of all these lines.
Behind him they must follow everywhere.
His name is Leonetto and he shines
In daring and is wise in counselling —
Lancaster's duke, and nephew of the king.

78

'The next, which the wind flutters towards the hill,
Vert, three wings argent, is Count Richard's flag.
He rules all Warwickshire for good or ill.
The Duke of Gloucester comes and does not lag.
His banner is the next in the quadrille:
Two antlers and the muzzle of a stag.
The Duke of Clarence by that torch is known,
And by that tree the Duke of York is shown.

79

'See there a lance which, broken into three,
The Duke of Norfolk's banner signifies.
The Earl of Kent's that thunderbolt you see,
And by the griffin you may recognize
The Earl of Pembroke; scales impartially
The Duke of Suffolk holds; the yoke which ties
Two snakes the Earl of Essex bears; azure,
A garland, is Northumberland's, for sure.

80

'The Earl of Arundel a sinking boat
Displays; next, Berkeley's marquess comes in view;
The Earl of March, the Earl of Richmond, note.
A cleft hill, a hand argent, the first two;
The third, bars undy with a pine, denote.
The Earls of Dorset and of Hampton too
Emblazon on their flags their great renown,
One by a chariot, one by a crown.

81

'The falcon, wings inverted, on its nest
Is borne by Raymond, Earl of Devonshire.
Next, or and sable Worcester, see, attest,
The talbot Derby, Oxfordshire the bear.
That shaft which by a crystal cross is blest
Bath's wealthy prelate holds; the broken chair
Upon a tawny field proclaims the Duke
Of Somerset – you'll see him if you look.

82

'The men-at-arms and archers who ride by
In number forty-and-two thousand are;
But twice as many (and I do not lie)
The total is of those who march to war.
Vert, tawny, or, three banners catch the eye,
Azure and sable, bendy, makes one more:
Godfrey and Henry, in their order, note;
Herman and Edward – captains of the foot.

83

'The Duke of Buckingham parades ahead,
And Henry is the Earl of Salisbury.
Of Abergavenny Herman is the head,
And Edward is the Earl of Shrewsbury.
These are the Welsh and English, as I've said,
But to the west, all Scottish troops you'll see.
They number thirty thousand to a man.
Zerbino, Prince of Scotland, leads the van.

84

'Holding a silver sword between its paws,
A lion 'twixt two unicorns behold –
The King of Scotland's flag; his son, because
The king for active service is too old,
Is here; this prince surpasses Nature's laws,
For, having fashioned him, she broke the mould.
Virtue and grace he has, in him resides
All prowess; he's the Duke of Ross besides.

85

'The Earl of Huntly: azure, a bar or.
The Duke of Mar: a leopard in a trave.
That strange escutcheon yonder, bearing more
Tinctures and charges than the others have,
With many martlets membered on it (or
What birds you will), to Alcabrun the brave
Belongs; no marquess, earl or duke is he,
But chief of clansmen, in the Highlands free.

86

'The ensign of the Duke of Transforth shows
An eagle, proper, gazing at the sun;
See there the Earl of Angus as he goes –
Lurcanio: two wolf-hounds, passant, run
Beside a bull; argent and azure hues
Betoken Albany's proud gonfalon.
The dragon, vert, torn by a bird of prey,
The Earl of Buchan carries to the fray.

87

'The Earl of Forbes is Harman, of great might.
Sable and argent is the flag he bears.
He has the Earl of Errol on his right.
Look: vert, a torch, his name and rank declares.
Now see the Irish coming forth to fight.
They form two squadrons; of the first, Kildare's
The leader, and the other squadron comes,
Led by Earl Desmond, from wild mountain homes.

88

'Kildare's achievement shows a burning pine.
By argent, a pale sanguine, Desmond's known.
Welsh, English, Scots and Irish thus combine
To help King Charles; but they are not alone,
For Sweden, Norway, Thulë, now align;
From distant Iceland, even, troops are gone,
And every land there is in the Far North,
By nature warlike, sends its warriors forth.

89

'From caves they come, from rugged forest-lands,
Horde upon horde; their faces and their chests,
Their sides, their backs, their legs, their arms, their hands,
Are covered with long hair like savage beasts.
The sixteen thousand lances of those bands
Create a forest where their banner rests.
Moratto hopes, who holds it on the plain,
Its whiteness in the blood of Moors to stain.'

90

While on this splendid host, which thus prepares
To aid the French, his gaze Ruggiero turns,
And the insignia each banner bears
And all the British captains' names he learns,
At him one man and then another stares,
As each the rare phenomenon discerns.
In stupefied astonishment they flock
And round him in a circle stand, to look.

91

Ruggiero, to astonish them the more
And to derive amusement from the game,
To his winged quadruped applied the spur
And rose into the air from whence he came.
With slackened rein he let the creature soar,
While those below still more amazed became.
Then, after viewing all the English force,
To Ireland in the west he turned his course,

92

That legendary island where, men tell,
The venerable elder made a cave
Wherein whoever for a space should dwell
Remission from his sins him Heaven gave;
Then, flying farther on, as it befell,
Towards waters which the Breton coastline lave,
Whence, passing to the outer Hebrides,
Angelica chained to the rock he sees,

93

To the bare rock, upon the Isle of Tears
(For thus the savage island now is named),
That isle of inhumanity and fears,
Whose natives for their cruelty are famed,
As in my story earlier appears.
I told you how they forage unashamed
From shore to shore, all lovely women stealing
To feed an orc, voracious and unfeeling.

94

That very morning she'd been brought and bound
To where the orc would swallow her alive.
Such giant monsters in those seas abound
And on such monstrous diet seem to thrive.
I have related how the maid was found
Asleep upon the shore and taken live,
With the enchanter, where the horse had fetched her,
And where the fell magician had bewitched her.

95

The harsh, inhospitable islanders
Exposed the lovely maiden on the strand.
So absolute a nakedness was hers,
She might have issued then from Nature's hand.
No veil or flimsiest of gossamers
Had she to hide her lily whiteness and
Her blushing roses, which ne'er fade nor die,
But in December bloom as in July.

96

He might have thought she was a statue, made
By skilful and ingenious artistry
Of alabaster or fine marble, laid
Upon the rock, but that he chanced to see
A tear steal down her countenance, amid
The roses and white lilies, tenderly
Bedewing the young fruit, so firm and fair,
And breezes softly lift her golden hair.

97

As on her lovely eyes his eyes he fixed,
His dearest Bradamante came to mind.
Love and compassion both his heart transfixed,
Tears he could scarce restrain, and in a kind
And gentle voice, much puzzled and perplexed
(His mount to immobility confined),
'O lady, worthy of no chains', he said,
'Save those in which Love's servitors are led,

98

'Not this, nor any other such abuse
Do you deserve. Who has thus cruelly
Enchained you, marking with a livid bruise
Those lovely hands of polished ivory?'
As craftsmen with a rosy dye suffuse
White ivory, so, at his words, now she,
Her hidden charms uncovered, blushed for shame
And at Ruggiero's gaze abashed became.

99

She'd fain have hid her face, but that her hands
Are fastened to the rock, and so her tears,
Which she is free to weep, she freely sends
To veil her cheeks; her head held low, her fears
And sobs she tries to quell; he understands
At last some syllables which reach his ears
In a low tone; but suddenly she ceases,
Arrested by a roaring, which increases.

100

And there the giant monster can be seen,
One half submerged; as, buffeted in sport
By Auster and Boreas having been,
A long, sea-going vessel comes to port,
So this foul creature, ravenously keen,
Comes for its food. The interval is short.
The damsel in her terror is half dead,
Nor by assurance is she comforted.

101

Ruggiero did not place his lance in rest
But, holding it on high, the orc he smote.
A writhing, twisting mass describes it best.
No other feature can Ruggiero note
By which to recognize it as a beast,
Save head and eyes and tusks and gaping throat.
Upon its front he strikes, between the eyes,
But fails to pierce it, howsoe'er he tries.

102

The first stroke having failed, he smites once more.
The orc the shadow of the beating wings
Perceives, which moves across the ocean floor
Now here, now there, in ever-widening rings.
Leaving its certain prey upon the shore,
It follows after vain imaginings.
Twisting and turning, in pursuit it goes.
Ruggiero swoops and deals it many blows.

103

When from on high an eagle fixes on
A wily serpent gliding through the grass
Or, on a naked rock, coiled in the sun
To preen its glistening, golden carapace,
Not on that side the bird will strike whereon
Its weapons of attack the reptile has,
But, swooping from the rear, the venom misses,
And claws the writhing snake, for all it hisses.

104

Just so Ruggiero with his lance and sword,
Not where the muzzle with sharp fangs was armed,
But where the hateful monster might be gored
To death and he himself escape unharmed,
Struck out and, ever watchful, swooped and soared
As prudence guided him; yet, as though charmed,
The more in these manoeuvres he persisted,
The more the beast, like adamant, resisted.

105

Sometimes a battle such as this a fly
Against a mastiff boldly undertakes
In August, or September, or July,
Those months of dust, of vintage, or of stacks
Of ripened grain, well garnered and laid by.
Stinging his snout and eyes, the insect makes
Unceasing darts and sallies, till, mayhap,
The mastiff is revenged in one fell snap.

106

The monster with its tail the ocean lashes
In frenzy so extreme, it's my belief
The water to the very welkin dashes.
Ruggiero on occasion wonders if
He flies or swims; he is afraid the splashes,
Continuing to drench the hippogriff,
May waterlog its wings, which will in vain
Attempt to lift him from the sea again.

107

So now he thinks he'll try a new attack,
Using that weapon of surprise and shock,
The shield which he keeps hidden in its sack,
Which all opponents senseless seems to knock.
But first, as a precaution, he flies back
To where Angelica lies on the rock
And on the little finger of one hand
He quickly slips the magic, golden band.

108

I mean the ring which Bradamante had,
To free Ruggiero, wrested from Brunel;
To liberate him later from the bad
And sinister Alcina, she did well
To give it to Melissa when she sped
To India; to break that magic spell,
As you'll recall, Melissa did not scorn it;
Ruggiero ever afterwards had worn it.

109

But to Angelica he gives it now,
Lest she be injured by the magic beam,
For loath he is such danger to allow
To those fair eyes of hers which dazzle him.
The monster now approaches and I vow
No vaster creatures in the ocean swim.
Ruggiero bides his time; the veil he raises:
And lo! a second sun in heaven blazes.

110

The magic luminance the monster's eyes
Assails and has its usual effect.
As when a shoal of fish in waters dies
Which mountain fishermen with lime infect,
So on that foaming margin supine lies
The orc, which land and sea alike reject.
Ruggiero strikes it here and there, but no
Impression can he make with any blow.

111

The lovely damsel, during the commotion,
Ruggiero's movements eagerly had followed.
'Fair sir,' she called to him in deep emotion,
Fearing the orc might wake where now it wallowed,
'Release me first, then drown me in the ocean!
Ah! let me by this monster not be swallowed!'
Ruggiero saw the justice of her plea.
Leaving the orc unslain, he set her free.

112

The hippogriff, responding to the spur,
Braces its hoofs and rises in the air;
Away Ruggiero pillion carries her,
Depriving thus the monster of its fare.
It was, indeed, no fitting connoisseur
For this *bonne bouche*, so delicate and rare.
He looks behind and thinks he can surmise
A thousand kisses promised in her eyes.

113

He did not take the course, as he'd intended,
Of circumnavigating all of Spain,
But on a shore near by instead descended,
Where Brittany juts out into the main.
A spot he chose by shady oaks defended,
Where Philomel's lament is heard again,
And where, beside a clearing, is a fountain,
Set round about on both sides by a mountain.

114

The eager cavalier his daring flight
Brought to a halt, and straight away dismounted.
One horse he'd curbed, and yet to a new height
Upon another he would fain have mounted.
One obstacle alone impedes the knight:
His armour – and on this he had not counted –
His armour keeps him back from his desire
And causes him delay, for all his fire.

115

And so, in frantic haste to be without it,
Disorderedly his armour he removed;
And never had he been so long about it,
His tackle tangling as he pulled and shoved.
My canto is too long (I do not doubt it)
And wearisome, my lord, perhaps has proved,
And so this history is now postponed
Until an hour more pleasing shall be found.

CANTO XI

1

Although a rein has often served to check
The impetus of a careering horse,
The curb of reason seldom will turn back
A lover's ardour from its frenzied course
Where pleasure lies to hand; as from its track
A prowling bear the smell of honey lures,
Or from the jar its tongue may catch a drop,
And nothing will induce it then to stop,

2

So now, what reason will the knight deter
From present pleasure of the lovely maid
Whom at his mercy he holds naked there
In that convenient and lonely glade?
No memories of Bradamante stir
His heart and conscience; even if they did
(For many times sweet thoughts of her arise)
He would be mad to forgo such a prize.

3

The harsh Xenòcrates himself that day,
I swear, would have responded to her charms.
His shield and spear already cast away,
Ruggiero struggled to remove his arms
When, lowering her eyes in her dismay
To her bare limbs, now cause of grave alarms,
The damsel saw once more upon her hand,
What she had lost, that priceless golden band.

4

This was the very ring Brunello took,
The ring she'd carried all the way to France,
Escorted by her brother, who to Duke
Astolfo yielded up his magic lance;
With it proud Malagigi's spell she broke
In Merlin's shrine; she'd freed Orlando once,
Together with his peers, from servitude
To Dragontina and her evil brood;

5

And with it she'd escaped, invisible,
From the dread tower where she was left to die.
But to what end these wonders chronicle
To you who know them better far than I?
E'en to Albracca's very citadel,
With Agramante's wishes to comply,
Brunello followed her and by his theft,
Of fortune and of realm she was bereft.

6

Now that she sees it on her hand again,
So filled with stupor and with joy is she
That all appears a dream, or else in vain
Imaginings her sight and touch must be
Deceiving her; drawing it off, at pain
To hide her every movement, furtively
She puts it in her mouth, and is concealed,
As when the sun behind a cloud is veiled.

7

Ruggiero looked about him everywhere,
Turning and twisting like a man deranged,
Until, the ring recalling, to a stare
Of stupefaction his expression changed.
He cursed his inattention then and there,
Railing against her who had thus exchanged
In recompense for all his help and tact
This rude, ungrateful disappearing-act.

8

'O thankless damsel! Is this the reward
You render me', he said, 'for what I've done?
I gave that ring to you, but you preferred
To steal it from me. Why take that alone?
My wingèd horse, my magic shield, my sword,
Myself I give to you, my cruel one.
Do with me what you will, but do not hide
Your lovely face.' She not a word replied.

9

Now by the fountain, now in many a place,
He groped as if he played at blind-man's-buff.
How often did his arms in an embrace
Close on the empty air! She, making off,
Across the country ran at a good pace
Until, beneath a mountain, to a rough
But roomy cave she came, wherein were stored
Supplies of food whence she could be restored.

10

For there a herdsman lived, who many mares
At pasture tended in the vale below,
Among the water-meadows where no tares
Or weeds among the tender grasses grow.
To stalls within the cave the herd repairs
For shelter from the noon-day sun; and so
Angelica her refuge took therein,
At leisure resting and by no-one seen.

11

At last, at evening, when the air was cool,
And she had been restored by ample rest,
Some rustic garments, made of homespun wool,
She draped about her – ah! how strangely dressed,
Compared with the gay robes which as a rule
She chose to wear! But not the lowliest
Of clothing could disguise her noble grace
Of bearing, nor the beauty of her face.

12

No longer, shepherds, sing the praise of Phyllis,
Neæra, or the bashful Galatea;
They'd own one lovelier than Amaryllis,
Could Tityrus and Meliboeus see her!
To choose a mare out of the herd her will is,
Whose speed from all entanglements may free her;
For, having once possession of the beast,
Angelica intends to seek the East.

13

Meanwhile Ruggiero, who had hoped in vain
The lovely damsel to discover near him,
His error saw at last, for it was plain
That she was far away and could not hear him;
And, moving now to mount that horse again
Which equally by land or sky could bear him,
He found the hippogriff had slipped the bit
And soaring high above he spotted it.

14

Thus Fortune deals him yet another blow.
To lose his flying horse is a sad thing,
And grievous, too, it is himself to know
The dupe of female guile; a sharper sting
Than either has inflicted, is the woe
Of having lost the precious magic ring
Which his belovèd Bradamante gave him
From evil sorcery or death to save him.

15

Downcast and melancholy, without hope,
His armour he resumed and hung his shield
About his neck; along a grassy slope,
Leaving the sea, he made towards the weald,
Where a well-trodden pathway seemed to drop
Away from pasture-lands, beyond a field,
Towards the right; there a tall, shady wood
He entered, and a clamour chilled his blood.

16

The clamour was a terrifying sound
Of clashing arms; the brave Ruggiero strode
From tree to tree until at last he found
Two combatants to whom the noise was owed.
What enmity or vengeance held them bound,
I know not, but no mercy either showed.
One was a giant, a ferocious sight;
The other was a bold and valiant knight.

17

The latter with his shield and with his sword,
Leaping now here, now there, himself defends
And a descending cudgel tries to ward
Which by his foe is wielded with both hands.
A horse is lying dead upon the sward.
Looking upon the scene Ruggiero stands,
And soon a hope is kindled in his heart
That the brave knight may play the victor's part.

18

Yet not on that account did he lend aid,
But, standing to one side, all action shunned.
The mighty giant, more robustly made,
The other with one stroke felled to the ground,
Both hands upon the heavy cudgel laid,
And when he saw his victim lie there stunned,
Removed the helmet for the *coup de grâce* –
And then it was Ruggiero saw his face.

19

He sees the dearest, loveliest, most sweet
Belovèd countenance made visible –
For Bradamante's face his eyes now meet,
And she it is the giant means to kill.
Losing no time, Ruggiero rushes fleet
Of foot, sword drawn; but, having had his fill
Of duelling, the giant in a rough
Embrace picks up the Maid and hurries off.

20

He carries her across his shoulder as
A wolf an infant lamb will sometimes fling,
Or as an eagle carries in its claws
A dove or other creature on the wing.
Ruggiero understands there is good cause
To hurry and he runs, a frenzied thing.
The giant moves with strides of such a size
Ruggiero scarce can follow with his eyes.

21

So, as one travels with gigantic tread,
A distant follower the other is,
Along a dark and gloomy path which led
To a broad meadow; but enough of this,
And to Orlando let us turn instead,
Who carried off Cimosco's thunder-piece.
He'd cast it to the bottom of the sea,
That never more discovered it might be.

22

To no avail, because that impious foe
Of humankind who first invented it,
Inspired by thunderbolts which crash below,
Tearing the clouds asunder, then saw fit,
Causing the world an almost equal woe
As by the apple and by Eve's deceit,
To let a wizard seek it out once more
In our grandfathers' time, or just before.

23

The hellish instrument, which fathoms deep
(More than a hundred) hidden in the sea
For years remained, was by vile craftsmanship
Raised to the top; and first in Germany,
Where they experimented, step by step,
To find what sort of engine this might be,
The devil sharpening their acumen,
They learned the damage it could do to men.

24

France, Italy and all the other lands
Have not been slow to learn the cruel skill;
And so, to casting bronze some turn their hands
And hollow forms with molten metal fill;
To bore the iron others give commands.
They make them of what size and form they will.
Bombards or carbines some their weapons name,
Or cannon, light or heavy, of ill fame.

25

Another type is called an arquebus;
Still other names the craftsmen may employ,
Such as a faulcon or a blunderbuss.
Stone walls and iron portals they destroy
And scatter all before them as they pass.
Hand in your weapons, soldier, for alloy,
Even your sword, for, if you'd take the shilling,
To shoulder these new arms you must be willing.

26

O hideous invention! By what means
Did you gain access to the human heart?
Because of you all glory's fled long since;
No honour now attaches to the art
Of soldiering; all valour is pretence;
Not Good but Evil seems the better part;
Gone is all courage, chivalry is gone,
In combat once the only paragon.

27

How many lords, alas! how many more
Among the bravest of our cavaliers
Have died and still must perish in this war
By which you brought the world to bitter tears
And Italy left stricken to the core?
This is the worst device, in all the years
Of the inventiveness of humankind,
Which e'er imagined was by evil mind.

28

And I believe the author of these wrongs
And the unending ill which thence ensued has
Is now consigned by God where he belongs,
In the Abyss beside accursèd Judas.
But let us follow now the knight who longs
To reach in time that coastline of Ebuda's,
Where lovely women, delicate and tender,
The natives to an orc as food surrender.

29

But now the more his haste, the less the wind,
From whatsoever compass-point, would blow.
For signs of wind he searched the hyalined
Horizon, peering from the poop or prow.
At times the lack of headway filled his mind
With deep despair at all the miles to go.
Then by the head so violently it blew,
He had to run before or heave her to.

30

It was God's will that he delayed should be,
The king of Ireland's coming to await,
In order that with more facility
Events might come to pass, which I'll relate.
But when at last the island he could see,
Orlando to his pilot said: 'Here wait;
Give me the landing-craft, which I will row
To yonder rock, for there alone I'll go.

31

'And look me out likewise the strongest cable;
And, next, the largest anchor I will take.
To see why I require them you'll be able
If contact with the monster I can make.'
The skiff was duly lowered and, when stable,
All that he needed for the journey's sake
(No weapons, save his sword) on board was laid,
And for the dreadful rock, alone, he made.

32

Pulling the oars towards his chest, he looks
In the reverse direction from the one
He gains, as from the sea towards the rocks
Or to the shore a crab will sideways run.
It was the hour when Dawn her golden locks
Has shaken loose and flowing in the sun,
Her loveliness half clad, half naked, shown us,
Stirring the jealousy of old Tithonus.

33

As far as a strong arm a stone might throw
The island was when, still approaching it,
He seems to hear, yet not to hear, a low
Lament which breezes fitfully repeat;
And, to the left, he glimpses there below
(The water gently lapping at her feet),
Bound to a tree, a damsel all forlorn,
As naked as the day when she was born.

34

As he is still too far away and she
Her face holds low, he cannot yet discern
It, nor be sure of her identity.
Both oars he plies in eagerness to learn,
When a great roar arises suddenly;
The woods and caves resound, the waters churn,
And lo! the dreadful monster now appears
And half the sea beneath it disappears.

35

As from a gloomy vale a cloud of rain,
Laden with tempest, rises in the air,
The daylight quenching with so dark a stain
That blindest night may not with it compare,
So now the orc approaches, of the main
Enveloping an all-embracing share.
The waters shake; unmoved Orlando stays,
The monster fixing with a haughty gaze.

36

Like one who has resolved what he will do,
With rapid movements, calm and purposeful,
Between the damsel and the orc he drew,
Thus with one stroke to make it possible
To save her and attack the monster too.
His good blade leaving in its scabbard still,
He took the cable, to the anchor mated,
And for the monster, with high courage, waited.

37

The monster, which the paladin soon spied,
Opened its mouth to gulp him down its throat,
Forming a cavern where a man might ride
On horseback; there Orlando entered, boat
And all, if I mistake not; and inside,
The gaping gullet with the anchor smote.
One of the flukes was from its palate hung;
The other was embedded in its tongue.

38

Thus neither jaw the monster can move up
Or down; just so, as further underground
A miner burrows, with a metal prop
He underpins the earth above all round,
Lest, as he works, it should collapse on top
Of him and bury him beneath its mound.
So far apart the anchor's arms extend,
Orlando cannot reach from end to end.

39

Knowing the monster cannot close its jaws,
For he has made the anchor well secure,
His Durindana from its sheath he draws
And lays about him in that cave obscure.
As the besieged will every hindrance cause
To those who in their walls a breach procure,
So every method then of self-defence
The orc employed to spew Orlando hence.

40

Weakened by pain, it thrashed to either hand,
Exposing now its flanks and now its spine,
Or, diving, with its belly stirred the sand,
Which in a shower rose to cloud the brine.
So, judging it was time to make for land
(Or to a watery grave himself resign),
Leaving the monster's gullet thus imbrangled,
He seized the rope which from the anchor dangled.

41

Then he began with rapid strokes to swim
Towards the naked rock, where he sets foot
And gradually hauls in after him
The rope, the anchor and, at last, the brute,
In mortal peril of its life and limb
By virtue of his strength, of world repute,
That strength which with one single tug pulls more
Than any capstan pulled ten times before.

42

As a wild bull, which feels about his horn
The sudden tightening of a hunter's noose,
Will leap and plunge and rear and twist and turn,
In all its vain endeavours to break loose,
So, from its ancient element now torn
By that strong arm, the orc, with many a ruse,
With many a sudden jerk, and many a twist,
The rope in vain attempted to resist.

43

So copiously from its mouth it bled,
Its lashing tail so furiously plied,
The sea that day might well be called the Red,
And might be seen to open and divide.
The tossing waves to such a height are sped,
They reach the welkin, and the sunlight hide.
The woods, the mountains and the distant shores
Re-echo with the savage monster's roars.

44

The ancient Proteus from his grotto came.
He'd seen Orlando enter and then leave
That gaping mouth; then, witnessing its shame,
He'd seen him to the shore the monster heave.
And at this uproar, heedless he became
Of all his flock, and fled; and I believe
That Neptune's dolphins harnessed were that day
To speed to Ethiopia straight away.

45

Ino, all tears, her offspring in her arms,
The Nereids, their tresses loose and flowing,
The followers of Glaucus, all alarms,
The Tritons fled, in all directions going.
Orlando so disables and disarms
The orc, no vestige now of life is showing;
By pain and travail sorely mortified,
Before it reached the water's edge, it died.

46

Quite a few islanders had run to see
The strange event in which the orc was slain.
A deed so holy seems profanity
To those who hold to heathen creeds and vain.
They said it would renew the enmity
Of Proteus, who would send his flock again
To ravage and despoil their island shore,
The ancient quarrel flaring up once more.

47

They judge it will be best to sacrifice
To the offended god ere worse occur,
And, to placate him, deem it will suffice
To cast the body of the warrior
Into the raging sea; as in a trice
A flame is caught from torch to torch, so there
A burning hatred, spread from heart to heart,
Destined Orlando for the victim's part.

48

With bows and arrows, slings and swords and spears,
The natives now descend upon the shore.
From this side and from that a group appears,
Far off, approaching, near, behind, before.
With all this bestial rabble round his ears,
Which threatens to assail him more and more,
Orlando, in astonishment, perceives,
Not thanks, but blows and insults he receives.

49

As when a bear, by Lithuanians led,
Or Russians, who divert the visitors
To fairs, goes by unmoved with plodding tread,
By the shrill insolence of yapping curs
So unperturbed it scarce will turn its head,
So, at this onrush, not a tremor stirs
The paladin, who, with one single breath,
That savage horde could scatter to their death.

50

A space in front of him was quickly made
Where, sword in hand, he turned to face the mob.
The rabble so deluded were and mad,
They thought, because he was divested of
Cuirass, and neither helm nor buckler had,
Without resistance he would let them rob
Him of his life; if only they had known,
From top to toe he was as hard as stone.

51

And what against him others cannot do,
Orlando, for his part, can do full well.
Thirty he kills, with but ten strokes, or few
More, if the truth precisely I must tell.
He turns, thus disencumbered, to undo
The damsel's bonds, when tumult, audible
From yet another quarter, meets his ears
And echoes of it everywhere he hears.

52

For while, upon this side, the paladin
Has held the heathen rabble thus engaged,
The king of Ireland's army has moved in
And, unresisted, through the island raged.
Attacks upon the populace begin;
On every side ferocious war is waged,
A holocaust which no compunction checks,
In which no heed is paid to age or sex.

53

The cruel islanders make no defence,
Partly because they're taken by surprise,
Partly because of poor intelligence
The population is, and small in size.
Thus they submit to fire and violence
And every battlement in ruin lies;
At every home and farmstead troops arrive
And not a single soul is left alive.

54

Orlando all this time remains aloof
To all the tumult and the shrieks he hears.
Thinking by now his foes have had enough,
The rock whereon the damsel waits he nears.
He looks, he seems to know her, and for proof
He draws still closer to the maid in tears:
It is, it is Olimpia indeed,
Betrayed by so iniquitous a deed,

55

Wretched Olimpia, to whom when Love
Had done his worst, relentless, cruel Fate
Had sent a band of pirates to remove
Her to the Isle of Tears, there to await
A dreadful death! Seeing Orlando move
About the rock, she knows him by his gait,
But, naked, and ashamed of her disgrace,
She cannot bear to look him in the face.

56

Orlando asked by what iniquity
To this dread island she had been transferred.
He'd left her in her consort's company,
Serene and joyful; what, then, had occurred?
'I know not if I owe you thanks', said she,
'For saving me from death, which I preferred
To this my wretched life, or if instead
I should reproach you that I am not dead.

57

'For this I thank you, that I have not shared
A death so cruel in the hideous
Vile belly of that monster, where I feared
To make an end so ignominious;
And yet I do not thank you that I'm spared,
For death alone to me is bounteous.
I'll render thanks to you for but one thing,
That sweet release which death alone can bring.'

58

And, weeping bitterly, she told him then
How she had been abandoned by her spouse,
Who left her sleeping on the island when
He had betrayed her and his marriage-vows,
And how brought hence by pirates she had been.
As far as the restricted space allows,
She turns while speaking, as in paint or stone
We see Diana turn from Actaeon.

59

As best she can she hides her breast and loins,
Leaving exposed the beauty of her thighs.
Orlando, who has freed her from her chains,
To bring his drifting boat to harbour tries
(To find some garments for her there he plans);
But now upon the scene Oberto hies,
The king of Ireland, whom the news had reached
How on the shore the deadly orc lay stretched.

60

He'd heard, too, how a cavalier had plugged
The monster's gullet with an anchor and
The creature to the water's edge had lugged,
As sailors pull a boat, hand over hand,
Against the current; some indeed had shrugged
In disbelief, but he had come, as planned,
To verify the rumour, as, meanwhile,
His troops were sacking the barbaric isle.

61

Although Orlando was much stained with blood
And drenched with water beyond recognition –
For owing to the bleeding which ensued
When he had slashed the orc, his own condition
The gory nature of the exploit showed,
The king of Ireland, as by intuition,
Already had deduced and now could see
That no one but Orlando it could be.

62

He knew him well, for he had been a page
Of honour at the court of France, whence he,
His father dying at a goodly age,
Returned to claim the Irish crown, only
A year ago; and often they'd engage
In converse, each the other's company
Desiring; now Orlando to embrace
He ran, the visor raising from his face.

63

The Count is no less pleased to see the king
Than is the king to see the Count again.
Their arms round one another's neck they fling,
Not once, but many times; Orlando then
Resolved to tell Oberto everything.
Olimpia's wrongs he started to explain,
How by Bireno she had been betrayed,
Her spouse on whom a sacred trust was laid.

64

He told him of the tokens of her love,
How, her relations dead, her kingdom gone,
Her deep devotion further still to prove,
Her readiness to die for him she'd shown;
And he himself had been a witness of
A number of the noble deeds she'd done.
While truly thus Orlando testifies,
The tears are flowing from Olimpia's eyes.

65

As in an April sky the sun is seen,
Parting the misty curtain of the rain,
So was Olimpia's lovely face, wherein
Her eyes shine through those tears which still remain;
And, as amid the tender, leafy green
A songbird sweetly carols once again,
So Love, his wings refreshing in her tears,
In beams of light to sun himself appears.

66

And from those radiant orbs a spark he takes
To tip his golden shaft, and in the stream
Which waters the fair blossoms of her cheeks
He tempers it; then, with unerring aim
And deadly force, the youth his target makes,
Whose shield, whose mail, are no defence to him,
For, gazing on her eyes, her hair, her brow,
He's wounded in the heart, and knows not how.

67

Her beauty is indeed beyond compare:
Not only on her brow, her eyes, her nose,
Her cheeks, her mouth, her shoulders and her hair
The observer's glance may with delight repose,
But from her breasts descending, down to where
A gown is wont to cover her, she shows
A miracle of form, so exquisite
None in the world, perhaps, can equal it.

68

Whiter than snow unstained by the earth's smutch
The perfect lily-whiteness of her skin,
And smoother far than ivory to touch;
Like milky curds but freshly heaped within
Their plaited moulds, her rounded breasts, and such
The gently curving space which lies between,
It calls to mind a valley 'twixt two hills
Which winter with its snowy softness fills.

69

Her lovely hips, the curving of her thighs,
Her belly, smooth as any looking-glass,
Her ivory limbs, were rounded in such wise
They might have been the work of Phidias.
Those other parts which to conceal she tries
I will, as it behoves, in silence pass,
Content to say that she, from top to toe,
Embodies all of beauty man can know.

70

If Paris on Mount Ida's slopes had seen
Her beauty, Venus, who so far outshone
The other goddesses, surpassed had been;
And he himself perhaps would not have gone
To Sparta, saying, rather, to the queen:
'Remain with Menelaus, for no one
Do I desire, none other do I love
Save this fair maid I am enamoured of.'

71

If she had lived in ancient Croton when
The painter Zeuxis wished to decorate
The shrine of Juno (that he might attain
Perfection, so historians relate,
He chose five maidens, and elected then
The finest points of each to imitate),
One model only he had then desired:
In her was all the beauty he required.

72

I do not think Bireno ever saw
That lovely body naked, for, if so,
His cruelty had been against the law
Of Nature; King Oberto, you must know,
That to its end her story I may draw,
Is kindled by her with a flame whose glow
Cannot be hid; to comfort her he tries,
And in her tender breast new hopes arise.

73

He promises that he will go with her
To Holland, saying he will ne'er depart
Till he has ousted thence that usurper
And with a dreadful vengeance made him smart;
And all resources, every follower
Which Ireland can supply, he will divert,
If need be, to make good his word. Meanwhile
He sent his underlings about the isle,

74

Among the ruined houses, to seek out
Some women's garments for Olimpia;
And plenty they would find, there is no doubt,
Left by the monster's victims; thus not far
Had they to search, and they returned without
Undue delay, bearing a plethora
Of clothing, of all styles; and one of those,
Unworthy though it be, Oberto chose.

75

The fairest silk, the finest cloth of gold
Which Florentines can weave with all their skill,
All the designs which craftsmen have of old
Embroidered patiently, or ever will,
Unworthy, King Oberto would now hold
Of her whose lovely limbs before him still
He sees – Minerva's skill would scarce be fine
Enough, all goldsmiths' art they would outshine.

76

Orlando is delighted by this turn
In the events; not only will the king
The miscreant Bireno cause to learn
A lesson for his vile manoeuvring,
But he himself, released, can now return
To the main purpose of his wandering:
Not for Olimpia has he travelled here,
But to assist the damsel he holds dear.

77

He'd straight away perceived it was not she
Thus chained upon the rock, but none could say
If she had suffered this iniquity,
For every islander was dead; next day
The troops of King Oberto put to sea,
And to the coast of Ireland made their way.
The paladin goes with them, for his plan
Is to return to France as best he can.

78

Scarcely a day in Ireland he remained;
By no cajoling pleas could he be won,
For love in him such mastery had gained,
Relentlessly it drove him on and on.
So, hoping that his word would be maintained,
He charged the king be faithful, and was gone.
But there was no necessity for this.
The king did more than keep his promises.

79

In a few days he gathered all his host
And with the king of England made alliance,
Likewise with Scotland's king; some on the coast
Of Frisia landed, others to defiance
Zealand roused, or Holland seized; in almost
No time the war is over; full reliance
Olimpia now might feel, for her new lord
Had justly put Bireno to the sword.

80

Oberto took Olimpia as his wife
And from a duchess made her thus a queen.
But let us turn once more to him whose life
So largely spent in wandering has been.
His sails unfurling to the windy strife,
He comes to St Malo, where he was seen
Before; on Brigliadoro once again,
He leaves behind the dangers of the main.

81

I well believe that all the winter long
Many a noble deed Orlando did,
Which I would gladly tell of in my song,
But to this day all news of them is hid;
For he was readier to right the wrong
Than waste his breath in idle talk; indeed,
His brave exploits were never known about
Unless some witness gave the tidings out.

82

He passed the winter months so quietly
That nothing certain of him then was known;
But when the Sun once more in company
With the mild Ram, in March and April, shone,
And gentle Zephyr imperceptibly
Led the sweet Spring a few more paces on,
Orlando's deeds to blossom then were seen
Amid new flowers and the tender green.

83

Up hill, down dale, in country, by the shore,
He travels, filled with sorrow and despair,
When, in a wood where he's not been before,
A piercing shriek of terror smites his ear.
To Brigliadoro he applies the spur
And hurries where a voice he seems to hear.
I'll tell you later on what then ensued;
Till later then, if you will be so good.

CANTO XII

1

Ceres, who hastened from her mother's haunts,
Returning to that lonely valley where
Etna o'er stricken Enceladus vaunts,
Crushing his heaving shoulders buried there,
Finding her daughter gone by evil chance,
Ravaged her eyes, her cheeks, her breast, her hair;
And, failing by these means to gain relief,
Two pines at last uprooted in her grief.

2

At Vulcan's furnace setting them ablaze,
To light her path in either hand she takes
A flame which inextinguishable stays,
And in her chariot, drawn by two snakes,
All woods and fields and plains and hidden ways,
All mountains, valleys, streams and ponds she rakes.
Then, having searched the surface of the globe,
The Tartarean depths descends to probe.

3

If in his power he were equal to
The goddess, as in his desire he is,
To find Angelica, Orlando too
Would search the world, the heaven and the seas,
In every secret corner, through and through,
Descending then to plumb Hell's mysteries;
But as no snakes he has, nor chariot,
He manages as best he can without.

4

He's looked for her in France; now he prepares
To search Italian shores and Germany;
Next, new and old Castile; from Spain, when there's
A ship, to Libya he will cross the sea.
Then, as he ponders on his plans, he hears
A plaintive voice lamenting piteously,
And, pressing forward, he beholds a knight
Advancing on a charger of great height.

5

Upon his saddle-bow, clasped in one arm,
This knight a damsel holds against her will.
Weeping and struggling and in great alarm,
To valorous Orlando in appeal
She calls; to rescue her at once from harm
Is his intent, for, drawing closer still,
He takes her for the one whom night and day
He's sought throughout all France in such dismay.

6

I do not say myself that it was she,
But that she seemed to be the one he loved;
So when his lady and his goddess he
Beheld, as he believed, Orlando, moved
By violent and frenzied agony
Of mind, in a loud voice, as it behoved,
Meaning them as no idle promises,
Challenged the knight with fearful menaces.

7

The villain did not wait, nor answer make,
Upon his priceless booty being intent,
But galloped off through every briar and brake;
Orlando followed but the other went
So fast, the wind he seemed to overtake.
The woods re-echoed with the maid's lament.
Towards a meadow finally they rode,
Where, in its midst, a costly mansion stood.

8

Of inlaid marble, as in days of yore,
The palace walls appeared to be constructed.
The knight drew rein beside a golden door
And entered with the maid he had abducted;
Running not far behind him, Brigliador
His master, fierce and menacing, conducted.
Orlando looked about him when inside,
But neither cavalier nor damsel spied.

9

He straight away dismounts and in a flash
He penetrates the dwelling-rooms within.
Now here, now there, his mighty footsteps crash
Till not a single nook is left unseen.
He takes the curving staircase at a dash,
In every ground-floor chamber having been,
And so upstairs begins his search again,
But all his time and trouble spends in vain.

10

A coverlet of silk or gold adorns
Each bed, and not an inch of wall is bare.
Now this way and now that his steps he turns.
Soft draperies and carpets everywhere
Regale his gaze, but not the sight he burns
To see, the longed-for presence of the fair
Angelica; nor can he find the thief
Within whose grasp he saw her, to his grief.

11

And while in every room he looks in vain,
Cast down with care, not knowing what to do,
In similar bewilderment and pain,
Gradasso, Brandimarte, Ferraù,
And Sacripante the Circassian,
With other cavaliers, go wandering through
The palace as they bitterly reproach
Its owner for evading their approach.

12

They wander looking for him, and each one
A private battle with him seeks to wage:
This knight laments because his horse is gone;
Loss of his lady makes another rage;
Some injury or wrong they all bemoan,
Fixed in their vain regrets as in a cage;
And many who persist in their delusion
For weeks and months remain thus in confusion.

13

When he had searched the palace high and low,
Orlando to himself began to say:
'It will be time and labour lost, I know,
If longer in these premises I stay.
The thief some secret door has not been slow
To find and may by now be far away.'
Thus thinking, to the meadow he went out
Which ringed with green the palace round about.

14

And as he slowly paces the estate,
Fixing his watchful gaze upon the ground,
In case, to left, or right, of the ingrate
The print of recent footsteps may be found,
He seems to hear a voice disconsolate
And recognizes that angelic sound,
Sees that belovèd face which has so changed him,
And from his former self so far estranged him.

15

It is her very voice he seems to hear,
Angelica he hears who calls in grief:
'Help me! My virtue, which I hold more dear
Than life, is threatened; come to my relief!
Ah! While my dear Orlando is so near,
Must it be taken from me by this thief?
Sooner by your own hand would I be killed
Than to such outrage unprotected yield!'

16

These words compel Orlando to return
And search through every chamber once again,
And even twice, for now within him burn
Such hope and passion that he spares no pain.
Her voice sometimes he thinks he can discern
And then he stops and listens, but in vain;
Her voice is heard wherever he is not,
For ever moving as he moves about.

17

Returning to Ruggiero, you recall
He'd followed from a dark and gloomy wood
A giant brutal and immensely tall,
Carrying his lady; now to this abode
(If I can recognize the place at all)
The giant came and through the portals strode;
Ruggiero likewise hurried through the gate,
Pursuing at an undiminished rate.

18

No sooner has Ruggiero stepped inside
The courtyard than he searches for the pair,
And every loggia he inspects beside.
In vain pursuit, he turns now here, now there,
And wanders up and down; each room is tried
For any traces of that Maid so fair:
Without success; he cannot understand
How they can both have vanished out of hand.

19

Four and five times he visits all the rooms,
And every nook and cranny in the place;
Under the stairs he searches, where the brooms
Are kept, and every single inch of space;
Hoping to save her from the fate which looms,
He hurries forth; as in Orlando's case,
A voice recalls him from a near-by grove
And he returns inside to seek his love.

20

The self-same voice, the same phenomenon,
Which for Orlando was Angelica,
Is now Ruggiero's lady of Dordogne
And keeps him of himself a prisoner.
If to Gradasso or to anyone
It calls of those who in the palace are,
He takes it for the thing he most desires,
And longingly, in vain, for it aspires.

21

By this enchantment, hitherto untried,
Atlante of Carena sought to lure
Ruggiero, for he hoped to keep him tied
To that sweet pain and longing, to ensure
His mad ambition he would put aside,
And early death in combat thus abjure.
Alcina and the castle both had failed him,
So now of this new method he availed him.

22

And many others he intended, too,
Of those whose prowess was renowned in France,
Lest they his dear, his loved Ruggiero slew,
To hold for ever in this magic trance.
First one and then another knight he drew
By various means; and for their sustenance
He'd furnished and equipped the place so well
His noble guests with pleasure there might dwell.

23

But let us find Angelica once more.
She has the magic ring, you will recall,
Which on her finger renders her secure
And in her mouth makes her invisible.
Within a mountain cave she's found a store
Of food, a mare, some clothing: in fact, all
She needs; to gain the East is now her plan
And claim once more her kingdom, if she can.

24

She longs to have Orlando's company,
Or Sacripante's; either one would do;
She has no preference, and equally
Their sighs and pleas she is resistant to.
Since on her journey, of necessity,
Towns, cities, garrisons she will pass through,
She needs an escort and a trusty guide,
And well might she in either knight confide.

25

She wandered, looking first for one and then
The other, and through many cities passed,
And regions uninhabited by men;
No sign of them she saw; but, led at last
By Fate, she came where the Circassian,
Orlando, Ferraù, Ruggiero, fast
In strange involvement by Atlante bound,
With many other cavaliers are found.

26

She enters, by the sorcerer unseen,
From all his magic by the ring protected,
And, searching for them both through the demesne,
She finds them vainly seeking her, dejected.
She understands that victims they have been
Of images deceptively projected.
Which of these cavaliers to choose as guide,
She ponders long, unable to decide.

27

She cannot judge which of the two she wants:
The Count Orlando or Circassia's king.
Orlando would the greater valiance
And skill in arms to her protection bring;
But if she chooses him in preference
His very worth may prove embarrassing;
For how will she, when need of him is lacking,
Dismiss so great a knight and send him packing?

28

The other she can manage as she pleases –
Exalt him to the skies, or cast him low.
Of all the pros and cons she ponders, this is
The reason which most weighs with her; and so
The king from his delusion she releases,
And, unintentionally, Ferraù,
Likewise Orlando; thus she is surrounded
By three at once, who gaze at her dumbfounded.

29

And so, by all three cavaliers confronted,
The beautiful Angelica now see.
Through the whole palace, high and low, they've hunted,
Searching in vain for their divinity.
And all around her, too, behold, uncounted,
From their enchantment by the ring set free,
A miscellaneous group of cavaliers
Who bustle, clamouring, about her ears.

30

Two of the cavaliers I now must say
Were clad in armour and were helmeted.
Since entering that palace, night and day
No part of their accoutrement they'd shed.
Each was accustomed to such full array
And scarcely felt the helmet on his head.
But Ferraù, the third, no headpiece wore:
He sought Orlando's, as I said before.

31

He vowed to wear no other till he won
The helmet which the brave Orlando gained
From King Troiano's brother; for the one
Which Ferraù had formerly obtained
Was at the bottom of a stream; unknown
To him, Orlando also was detained
In this enchanted palace, but the spell
Had kept them each to each invisible.

32

Such was the magic of that strange abode,
Of one another they were unaware,
As day and night in full cuirass they strode
With sword and buckler, searching everywhere.
Released from bit and bridle, horses stood,
Still saddled, waiting in a stable where
The mangers were replenished every day
With adequate supplies of oats and hay.

33

Atlante had no power to prevent
The knights from leaping on their saddles once
Again; to follow her was their intent,
Drawn by that rose-and-lily countenance,
That golden hair, and the enravishment
Of those dark eyes. Urging her mare, she runs
O'er hill and dale; she'd take the help of any
One with pleasure: but three are two too many.

34

When long enough she judged the space between
Them and the palace, and no longer feared
Atlante's spell, by which the knights had been
Entranced in a bewitchment strange and weird,
The ring, which had so often helped her, in
Her rosebud mouth she placed, and disappeared,
Quite suddenly, before their very eyes,
To their bewilderment and great surprise.

35

Although at first her plan had been to take
Orlando for her escort, or the king,
When she set out upon her homeward track,
Seeing them thus pursue her in a string,
Such hostile feelings in her breast awake,
To ask their help she finds she cannot bring
Herself, for now to either she is loath
To be obliged: better the ring than both.

36

They turn about the wood, now here, now there,
Their stupefaction written in their faces,
As when a hunting-dog pursues a hare
Or fox, and being close upon its traces,
Loses it suddenly when to its lair
It goes to earth or in the densest places
Of the forest. She sits and watches, mocking,
As helplessly they wander, vainly looking.

37

Because there is one path and only one
Which through the forest leads, so along this
The cavaliers believe her to have gone.
Where else indeed, if only one there is?
Orlando spurs, his rivals follow on,
Their pulses racing equally with his.
She lets them gallop past and does not mind them,
Riding more slowly then, some way behind them.

38

The knights ride on, as far as they can ride,
Until all traces of the path are lost.
They peer among the grass, on every side
And every possibility exhaust.
Then Ferraù, who would surpass in pride
The proudest heart that any age might boast,
Called to the other two in mighty wrath:
'With you I will consent to share no path!

39

'Turn back or take another way instead,
Or else prepare to die here by my hand.
No rivalry in love – be not misled –
I warn you – and all other men – I'll stand.'
Orlando to Circassia's monarch said:
'He scarce could be more bold in his demand
If he'd mistaken us for common riff-raff,
Or timid maidens sitting at their distaff.'

40

And then to Ferraù he said: 'You fool!
But that no helmet I perceive you wear,
And for that reason I am merciful,
How rash you are, I'd make you soon aware.'
The Saracen replied, as cool as cool:
'And if I heed it not, why should you care?
Against you both, no helmet on my head,
I will make good the words which I have said.'

41

'Pray', said the Count to the Circassian,
'Lend him your helmet, to oblige me, while
I castigate the madness in this man,
For such I've never seen'; and in this style
The king replied: 'What greater madness can
There be? But, no offence intended, I'll
Show *you* that I am just as good a tool:
Lend him *your* helmet; I'll chastise the fool!'

42

And Ferraù retorted: '*You* are mad.
If I had cared about a helm, in truth
From one or other of your heads I had
By now snatched one or other helm, or both;
And for your information I will add:
To go without a helm I've sworn an oath
And thus I'll go, until the day I win
The helmet of Orlando, paladin.'

43

'So,' said Orlando, smiling, in response,
'You think that with no helmet on your head,
You'll take that which in Aspromonte once
Orlando from Almonte took? Instead,
I think that when in combat he confronts
You, you will tremble; so, be not misled:
No helmet you will gain, but in dismay
Your arms surrender to him straight away.'

44

The braggart said: 'I've many times before
Orlando pressed so hard that easily
I could have taken all the arms he wore;
If I did not, it was that clemency
Arose within my breast and I forbore.
Now such resolve I feel arise in me
That from all hesitation I am freed.
Next time I have no doubt that I'll succeed.'

45

Orlando lost his patience with him then
And shouted: 'Liar, ugly miscreant!
Where did you fight Orlando? Where and when
Did you perform those exploits which you vaunt?
Anglante's Count, Orlando, paladin,
Stands here before you while you rave and rant,
Thinking him miles away; for I am he.
So, of your boast, the outcome we shall see.

46

'This slight advantage, furthermore, I scorn.'
And with these words his helmet he removed
And hung it on the branches of a thorn;
Then drew his blade, in many a combat proved.
Next, undeterred, the Spaniard, in his turn,
Drew his and stood *en garde*, as it behoved.
Prepared and resolute, his shield held high,
Orlando's blows to parry he would try.

47

Thus the two warriors begin to fight,
Their horses turning, twisting, every way;
And where their armour does not fasten quite,
Or where the steel is thin, there they essay
To drive their pointed swords with all their might.
In all the world, no other pair, I'd say,
Are so well matched in daring and in strength,
And long they keep each other at arm's length.

48

I think, my lord, that you already know
That Ferraù invulnerable was,
Save in that place where, as our bodies show,
The infant in the womb its nurture draws.
Till he was buried in the earth below,
His armour, all his life, where he had cause
For doubt, was reinforced with plates of steel,
In layers seven-fold, and tempered well.

49

Orlando was invulnerable too,
Save in one portion of his mighty frame.
He could be wounded, as perhaps you knew,
In both soles of his feet and rendered lame.
As strong elsewhere as iron, through and through
(If truth is reconcilable with fame),
Like Ferraù, in arms he chose to be
For ornament more than necessity.

50

The battle grows more gruesome at each bout.
The sight of it alarms and terrifies.
The Saracen with every thrust and cut
Strikes home, and all Orlando's blows likewise
The metal plates, or coat of mail, without
Exception, break, unhinge, destroy or slice.
Angelica, invisible, alone,
Considering the combatants, looks on.

51

King Sacripant, meanwhile, in the belief
That the fair maid was riding on ahead,
And since he saw the others locked as if
For many hours, in that direction sped
In which the knights assumed, to their great grief,
The beautiful Angelica had fled
When she had vanished from their view; and thus
The damsel of the fight sole witness was.

52

When she had watched some little time and seen
How horrible and fierce the battle grew,
She judged the danger to both knights was keen.
At last, desiring to see something new,
She planned to take Orlando's helmet then
And watch what the two cavaliers would do,
When they saw gone the bone of their contention;
But not to keep it long was her intention.

53

She means to give it to Orlando soon,
But first intends this trick on him to play.
Plucking the helmet from the branch it's on,
She puts it in her lap and leaves the fray.
Before the knights have noticed it is gone,
She has already ridden far away;
Such is the frenzied rage with which they burn,
To nothing else can they attention turn.

54

But Ferraù, who first perceived the theft,
From battle disengaged himself and said:
'It seems to me that knight who has just left
Has treated us like blockheads, born and bred.
Whichever of us wins will get short shrift,
For we shall both be now unhelmeted.'
Orlando to the thorn-bush turns his eyes
And sees the helmet gone, to his surprise.

55

With Ferraù's opinion he concurred:
The other knight had stolen it; and so
He turned, enraged; his Brigliadoro, spurred,
To leave the place of combat was not slow.
And Ferraù who saw him leave preferred
To follow; thus in single file they go
Till in the grass they see the prints just made
By the Circassian monarch and the maid.

56

Orlando took the left-hand track, the same
The king had chosen, leading to a valley.
The other chose the hillside path and came
Where he desired to be eventually.
Meanwhile the damsel, tiring of her game,
Beside a fountain was disposed to dally,
Where cooling water and the shade of trees
Invite the passer-by to take his ease.

57

The damsel tarries by the crystal stream.
By virtue of the magic ring she wears
She feels secure, and little does she dream
(For she relies on it) that danger nears.
She's hung the helmet on a handy limb
And now she leads her mount to see if there's
A sturdy shrub or tree where she can tie
The animal and let it graze near by.

58

The cavalier of Spain, having pursued
The print of hoofs, now at the fount arrives.
No sooner does she glimpse him from the wood
Than once again to vanish she contrives.
The helmet she must now renounce for good;
She cannot reach it howsoe'er she strives.
The pagan, who had seen her from the fount,
Approached her, full of joy, upon his mount.

59

She vanished (as I said) before his eyes,
As phantoms of our dreams depart with sleep.
To find her in the wood in vain he tries,
Growing more melancholy with each step.
Against Mahound and Termagant he cries,
And all the Prophet's vile discipleship.
Then near the fountain, as it comes to pass,
He sees the helmet fallen on the grass.

60

No sooner has he seen it than he knows,
From lettering inscribed upon the rim,
This is the very helm for which he goes
In search, for it records Orlando's grim
Encounter with Almonte, of all foes
The one who the most sorely tested him.
For all his sorrow that the maid has fled,
He picks it up and puts it on his head.

61

And when the helm is buckled and done up,
He thinks that one thing only lacking is,
Ere filled to overflowing is his cup,
Or he can reach the apogee of bliss:
That is, Angelica; but soon all hope
Of finding the fair maid he must dismiss.
So, wondering what the progress of the war is,
He turns his thoughts towards the camp near Paris.

62

The grief which burned and raged within his breast
For his desire thus left unsatisfied
Was tempered by the pleasure that his quest
Was now fulfilled; nor could it be denied
That Ferraù had done his very best
To keep the oath he'd sworn that day beside
The stream; nor did he go unhelmeted
Until the day Orlando struck him dead.

63

Angelica, invisible, alone,
Went riding on her way with furrowed brow.
Most bitterly she rued what she had done,
For by her haste Orlando's helmet now,
Which she had left behind, was lost and gone.
'I took the helm,' she said, 'but this, I vow,
Was only meant as recompense to him
To whom I am obliged for life and limb.

64

'I only did it for the best, God knows,
Although results have sadly gone amiss.
I took the helmet in the hope that those
Two combatants would call a halt, and this
My only purpose was; now I suppose
That ugly Spaniard wearer of it is.'
Thus she reproached herself in her lament
About Orlando's loss, as on she went.

65

So she continued, angry and distressed.
With careful choice of roads, she made her way
In the desired direction of the East,
Deciding to be visible one day,
Invisible the next, as she thought best.
Then in a wood she saw a youth who lay
Between two dead companions; with a blow
(Unjust) his breast was wounded by a foe.

66

But now about her I will say no more,
Since many things I have to tell you first;
Nor will I speak of Sacripante, nor
Of Ferraù until I have rehearsed
The sorrows which the brave Orlando bore,
Those pains of love by which the Count is cursed,
Those trials and those never-ending woes
Which will torment him wheresoe'er he goes.

67

As soon as he can find a garrison,
Desiring to remain anonymous,
He puts an undistinguished helmet on,
Whether of tempered steel he does not know,
Nor does he care, for he relies upon
His charmed resistance to each thrust and blow.
By day, by night, come sun, come rain, no rest
He takes, as he pursues his endless quest.

68

It was the hour when over Ocean's rim
Apollo drives his horses, wet with dew,
Along the sky where Dawn, ahead of him,
Has sprinkled gold and crimson flowers anew,
And stars, their nightly dance now ended, seem,
Wrapped in their veils, about to bid adieu,
That close to Paris as one day he passed
Orlando proved his prowess unsurpassed.

69

He met two squadrons; leading one of them
Was Manilard, a white-haired veteran,
Norizia's king; when sound in wind and limb,
He was a formidable foe; a man
More suited now for counsel, he may seem,
Than action. Next, of all the African
Commanders, King Alzirdo's held to be
The very paragon of chivalry.

70

He led the second troop; and both had passed
The winter harassing King Charlemagne,
Some of them close to Paris, others fast
By citadels and strongholds in the plain.
When Agramante was convinced at last
All his assaults on Paris were in vain,
He had resolved a siege to authorize,
Finding he could not take it otherwise.

71

And to accomplish this he had a host
Of great proportions and variety:
Not only those he'd rallied by his boast
And those of Spain who'd followed loyally
Their king, Marsilio, but from the coast
Near Arles to Paris and from Gascony
(Except for a few strongholds), he'd subdued
The French and thus his army had renewed.

72

When timid streams begin once more to flow,
By gentle warmth released from icy bonds,
When grasses greener in the meadows grow
And bushes clothe themselves in tender fronds,
King Agramante, who desires to know
How far his present army corresponds
To present needs, has summoned an array
Of all his troops; and so, without delay,

73

The king of Tremisen (Alzirdo) and
Norizia's monarch journeyed towards the place
Where every squadron, regiment or band
Would be inspected; thus it came to pass,
As I have given you to understand,
The two of them encountered face to face
The Count Orlando in his quest for her
Who in Love's fastness held him prisoner.

74

And when Alzirdo saw that Count draw near
Whose valour has no equal among men,
Whose mighty strength and pride make him appear
A second god of war, whose wrathful mien
And haughty resolution chill with fear,
He was amazed and judged him there and then
To be superlative in skills of war;
But to the king's intent this proves no bar.

75

For he was young and filled with arrogance,
Strong and courageous, by his peers esteemed.
His mighty charger spurring to advance,
To be at once victorious he deemed;
But, in encounter with Orlando's lance,
He fell, his heart pierced through; the horse, it seemed,
Was filled with panic as it fled the scene,
No rider on its back to check the rein.

76

A terrifying shout at once arose,
Filling the air for many miles around,
Soon as the youth was seen to fall, of whose
Life-blood a pool was forming on the ground.
Against Orlando rushed a bellicose
Unruly mob: their thrusts and cuts abound,
But from their weapons no such tempest hails
As that by which the Count the horde assails.

77

As when a herd of swine, a savage roar
Emitting, rush stampeding from the plain
Or from the hills, a bear pursuing or
A prowling wolf which left its secret den
To seize a piglet which away it bore,
Its piteous squeals and grunts being all in vain,
So that barbaric rabble set upon him,
Shouting, 'Have at him! Wreak your vengeance on him!'

78

With arrows, lances, swords, his shield they smite.
More than a thousand blows his hauberk bears.
Some strike him with a club with all their might.
On every side they throng about his ears.
But he, whose soul has never harboured fright,
The horde, with all their arms, as little fears
As, when the shades of night the sky suffuse,
A wolf is frightened by a flock of ewes.

79

Bared of its sheath he held that flashing blade
By which he'd slain so many Saracens.
Thus of the total killed, whoever made
An estimate, would have to count in tens.
Already now through streams of blood they wade,
And, strewn in heaps, the slaughtered lie so dense,
The ground, so it appears, can scarcely carry them.
So deadly are his blows that naught can parry them,

80

No cotton quilting which their armour lined,
No swathes of cloth worn coiled about the head.
Not shrieks alone re-echoed on the wind,
But arms and shoulders, legs and top-knots sped
In all directions. Death in every kind
Of guise, all horrible, stalked by and said:
'Orlando's Durindana is more blithe,
A hundred times more useful than my scythe.'

81

Whoever feels one blow finds one enough.
Many remaining scatter through the wood,
Astonished that the combat was so rough;
Because he was alone they thought they could
Soon overpower him; now they make off.
It's *sauve qui peut*, and, while the going's good,
They go, some here, some there, without delay,
Nor are they seen to stop and ask the way.

82

They flee from Courage with her looking-glass,
Which every wrinkle in the soul reveals.
One man alone does not evade this pass,
In whom not cowardice, but age, congeals
The blood; he looks on flight as vile and crass,
Preferring death with honour to all else:
I mean Norizia's king, who put his lance
In rest against the paladin of France.

83

He broke it on the summit of the shield
Borne by the mighty Count, who had not stirred,
But ready stood, his naked sword to wield,
Which to his lance he many times preferred,
And which to stay the onslaught he now held;
But, in his grasp, the sword, descending, veered
So that no cut or thrust was possible.
Fortune thus favouring the king, he fell.

84

Although it is a monarch who lies stunned,
Orlando scorns even to look at him.
Whoever stays, he slashes to the ground,
While all the others flee for life and limb.
As in the air, where space and light abound,
Starlings, a hawk escaping, swerve and stream,
So of that horde, destroyed in a brief hour,
Some gallop off, some fall, and others cower.

85

Nor did Orlando grant his sword repose
Till every living man had fled that day.
And now he hesitates, although he knows
The region well, about the choice of way;
But, whether to the right or left he goes,
His thoughts from where he is are far away.
He fears Angelica, no matter where
He looks for her, is anywhere but there.

86

Enquiring as he went, he chose a route
Sometimes through woods, and sometimes through a plain;
And, as he travelled, wandering in thought,
He wandered from the path and all in vain
Meandered till, arriving at the foot
Of a tall cliff, he saw, as plain as plain,
Pulsating through an opening in the rock
A light, which drew him up at once to look.

87

As in a wood of lowly juniper,
Or in the stubble of an open field,
A hunter will pursue a frightened hare,
And of the paths which intersect the weald
Will make uncertain choice, now here, now there,
Searching whatever bush the prey might yield,
So did Orlando search, in hope to find
The damsel who possessed him, heart and mind.

88

Towards that light which twinkled in the dark
Orlando hastened, and arrived at last
Where through a narrow aperture the spark,
Seeming so distant from the woodland, passed.
Bushes and thorny shrubs the entrance mark,
As round a fortress a defence is cast;
And all who lurk within the cave they hide
From outrage, keeping them secure inside.

89

By day the hiding-place would not be seen.
It was the light which in the dark revealed it.
Orlando thought he knew what it must mean,
And, to discover who it was it shielded,
He tethered Brigliadoro, and between
The thorny branches creeping, which concealed it,
He penetrated to the secret hole
And entered, unannounced, to pay his call.

90

The cavern floor by several steps descended,
Where living people dwelt, as in a tomb.
The roof, rough-hewn, seemed for a vault intended.
Scarce any daylight to the little room
Could pass the thorns by which it was defended,
But fortunately, to relieve the gloom,
There was an aperture towards the right,
A narrow slit which would admit the light.

91

Within, a damsel with a lovely face
The Count observed, seated beside a hearth.
Not more than fifteen years could she retrace
(So judged Orlando) since her day of birth.
So fair she was, she made that savage place
Appear a very paradise on earth,
Although her lovely eyes were filled with tears,
A token of her sorrows and her fears.

92

A grizzled beldam scolded her meanwhile,
As often is the way with womenfolk;
But as he made his way through the defile,
All disputation ceased and neither spoke.
Orlando greeted them in courteous style
(As it behoved) and thus the silence broke.
They rose at once to greet him in reply;
No courteous exchange did they deny.

93

To tell the truth, they turned a little pale
To hear that voice so masterful and strong,
To see that cavalier in coat of mail,
Armed with the weapons which to war belong.
Orlando bade them tell him without fail
What miscreant had done this fearful wrong,
For he must be a cruel, evil knave
Who'd bury thus a damsel in a cave.

94

The maid can scarcely speak, for all she tries.
Her sobs so interrupt her, she is dumb.
Through precious pearls and coral, only sighs
And broken words, in a sweet voice, will come.
Her flower face is watered by her eyes.
Of all those tears she needs must swallow some.
Please hear the rest, my lord, another day.
It is now time to put the book away.

CANTO XIII

1

How fortunate those cavaliers of yore,
Who in their venturings through deep ravines,
Through gloomy forests and in caves obscure,
In serpents' nests, in bears' and lions' dens,
Could find what in proud palaces no more
Are found, nor in the most exalted scenes:
Women who in the very bloom of youth
Can be considered beautiful in truth.

2

I said above how in a squalid cave
Orlando finds a damsel fair of face
And that he asks the maid what villains have
Abducted her to such a dismal place.
By many sobs impeded, yet in brave
And noble accents, sweetly and with grace,
As briefly as she can, in a low tone,
She promises to make her sorrows known.

3

'I know full well, fair knight,' the maid began,
'That if I speak, my woes will be increased.
This agèd crone will soon inform the man
Who brought me here; and yet I am well pleased
To tell the truth to you as best I can,
For, if I die, my anguish will be eased.
What other joy have I to hope for, pray,
Save that my captor grant me death one day?'

4

'My name is Isabella and I was
The only daughter of a king in Spain.
Well did I say "I was", for now, alas!
I am the child of Sorrow and of Pain;
For Love vile treachery committed has.
He is to blame; against him I complain.
Although he gave his aid to me at first,
He secretly contrived to do his worst.

5

'How happy was my former royal estate!
Once I was honoured, rich and young and fair.
Now see to what I am reduced by Fate!
Mine is a wretchedness beyond compare.
First, how it all began I will relate
And trace the steps which led me to despair,
For, if you cannot help me in my plight,
Your sympathy will solace me, fair knight.

6

'My father in Bayona a joust proclaimed,
Twelve months ago I think it now must be,
And many cavaliers, for prowess famed,
Came from afar to test their gallantry.
And, whether Love in this was to be blamed,
Or whether it was true, I seemed to see
One worthy to be praised, and only one,
Zerbino, the great king of Scotland's son.

7

'When, in the field, I saw what deeds he wrought,
Unprecedented proofs of chivalry,
Love of him captured me, though I knew naught
Save that, no more self-owned, he now owned me;
And yet I'm ever aided by the thought
That, by this love o'ermastered though I be,
I lost my heart to no-one void of worth,
But to the fairest, noblest man on earth.

8

'In beauty and in valour far above
All lords Zerbino rose pre-eminent.
He showed and, I believe, he bore me love
Like mine to him, and as sincerely meant.
Nor of our mutual flame lacked one to prove
Interpreter, who oft between us went,
Because in body we were still disjoined;
Though never were we not conjoined in mind.

9

'But when at last the tournament was over,
Zerbino left for Scotland and was gone.
If you know love, the anguish of a lover,
Such as I suffered then, to you is known.
No respite day or night could I discover.
In this I knew that I was not alone,
For, setting now no check on his desires,
Only to have me with him he aspires.

10

'And since our faiths, which each the other banned,
He being a Christian, I a Saracen,
Let him not ask my father for my hand,
By stealth to elope with me he purposed then.
Outside my rich home-town, set on a strand
Amid green fields, beside the azure main,
I had a lovely garden on a height
Whence hills around and sea were all in sight.

11

'Zerbino deemed the place ideal for that
Which our diverse religious creeds forbade;
A scheme he hastened to communicate
He'd formed to make our life thereafter glad.
Near Santa Marta secretly he'd set
A galley, guarded well by men mail-clad,
Captained by Odorico of Biscay,
On sea and land victor in every fray.

12

'Zerbino could not come in person, since
By his old father he had been detained
To succour France's king; and so the prince,
Instead, this Odorico chose to send,
Of all his faithful friends, the one to evince
Himself his faithfullest, most bosom, friend –
He should have been, were benefits but able
Unfailingly to keep a friendship stable.

13

'This man it was, then, who had indicated
At what time he would fetch me, as agreed:
And on the day so eagerly awaited
I let him find me, in my garden hid.
He disembarked, the night which he had stated,
By seamen, armed and brave, accompanied,
Making a river near our town his aim,
Whence, noiselessly, he to my garden came.

14

'Thence I was taken to that well-found ship.
Hearing no warning from the city guard,
The members of our household, roused from sleep,
Were killed, or fled, or captive made on board;
And thus I left my land; I did not weep.
No maidenly regrets my transports marred.
The joy I felt I cannot now express,
So much I yearned my dear love to possess.

15

'Scarce had we rounded Mugia when there rose
A wind from larboard lashing at the sea,
Piling the waves sky-high. A nor-wester blows:
All lost is calm and our serenity.
The furious beam-wind ever stronger grows
Until it reaches such ferocity,
To right the ship no measures are enough,
For all we sail now leeward, or now luff.

16

'It's useless now to think of striking sail,
Unstep the mast or even lighten ship.
To our dismay, approaching La Rochelle,
A line of rocks now bared a jagged lip.
But for the grace of God, what next befell
Had done for us, despite good seamanship:
The tempest blew and on we helpless raced
As if an arrow to its mark we traced.

17

'The captain saw the danger and essayed
A remedy that's very often vain:
A boat was quickly lowered and he made
Me sit in it, with him and two strong men.
The others tried to follow but, afraid
That they would swamp the boat, the captain then
At sword-point held them back and, having cut
The painter, from the foredoomed ship struck out.

18

'We who had taken to the boat were thrown
Shipwrecked, but still alive, upon a bank;
But those we left behind us perished soon,
When with all hands on board the vessel sank.
I bowed my head in prayer and knelt alone,
Eternal Love and Providence to thank,
Who from the fury of the raging sea
For my Zerbino's arms had rescued me.

19

'My jewels and my clothes were left behind
And many precious objects dear to me,
And yet, if hope remained, I did not mind
That they were at the bottom of the sea.
Of paths no trace or vestige could we find,
No habitation and no hostelry.
Only a hill, storm-battered at its peak,
While at its feet the waves their vengeance wreak.

20

'And in that place the cruel tyrant, Love,
Who treacherously every promise breaks,
Who bides his time and watches every move,
And every chance to thwart true lovers takes,
Now with malicious cunning robs me of
My joy, and of good fortune sorrow makes:
The one in whom Zerbino placed his trust,
Now cooled in friendship as he burned in lust.

21

'I cannot tell if his insane desire
Was kindled on board ship and kept from sight,
Or if upon that lonely shore the fire
Which so tormented him was set alight;
His longings now without delay require
Fulfilment of his lustful appetite,
But of one witness he must first be rid
Of those by whom we are accompanied.

22

'He was a Scot, Almonio by name,
Who loyal to Zerbino was and true;
And, as a perfect knight commended, came
To serve the captain and his bidding do.
The traitor said that great would be the shame
If all the way on foot I had to go
To La Rochelle; and sent him off to find
A mount for me or transport of some kind.

23

'Almonio, suspecting nothing, went
Towards a city some six miles away
(All sight of which the woods between prevent);
And Odorico now decides straightway
To tell the other of his vile intent.
He thinks that he can trust him to obey
All his commands, his each and every whim.
(He cannot, anyway, get rid of him.)

24

'This second man of whom I'm speaking now,
Who had remained, to me had long been known:
My childhood friend, Corebo of Bilbao.
On our estate to manhood he had grown.
The traitor thinks it safe to tell him how
He plans to have his will with me alone,
Hoping Corebo in his service would
Be more compliant than to serve the good.

25

'Since he is noble, kind and chivalrous,
He is aghast at Odorico's words.
He calls him base and vile and treacherous,
And with his scorn his bearing well accords.
As neither combatant is timorous,
They mean to have it out with naked swords;
But I am moved to terror at the sight
And through the gloomy forest take my flight.

26

'In every skill of battle trained and bred,
No great display need Odorico make,
And soon Corebo he has left for dead
Upon the ground and follows in my wake.
Love lends him then, if I am not misled,
His very wings wherewith to overtake
Me, and in flattery has schooled him well,
Which renders many women pliable.

27

'But all in vain; my will is fixed and fast.
Rather than yield I am prepared to die.
No vows, no flattery, he sees at last,
No menaces, induce me to comply.
From eloquence to force he has now passed,
And as a suppliant in vain I try,
Recalling how Zerbino, for his part,
Had trusted him, to move his traitor's heart.

28

'And when I knew my pleas were all in vain,
Nor could I look for help from anywhere,
And when that villain, his intention plain,
Towards me lumbered like a ravening bear,
I used my feet and fists with might and main,
My nails to scratch, my teeth to rend and tear;
I ripped his beard, I marked his face with scars,
My shrieks meanwhile ascending to the stars.

29

'Perhaps by chance, or owing to my cries,
Which could be heard a league away, I think,
Or else a band of pirates always plies
Its ghoulish trade when ships are seen to sink,
However it may be, towards us hies
A horde of corsairs from the water's brink.
When Odorico their arrival sees,
He drops the work he has in hand, and flees.

30

'They saved me from that traitor, it is true,
In the same way in which a person can
(The saying, I am sure, is known to you)
Fall out of the proverbial frying-pan
Into the fire; not that they dare renew
Assaults upon my person; not a man
Among them is as villainous as that,
Though this is scarcely to be wondered at.

31

'They keep me here a virgin, well I know,
Thinking that I will fetch a higher price.
Eight months have passed – almost nine months ago
They buried me, like venison on ice.
All hope of my Zerbino I forgo.
I've gathered from their mumblings once or twice
That to a merchant I shall soon be sold,
Then to a Sultan in exchange for gold.'

32

Thus the fair damsel to Orlando spoke,
While many anguished sobs and long-drawn sighs
The smooth narration of her story broke
(Enough to make a viper sympathize).
While thus her woe her words once more evoke,
Or, it may be, her pain she mollifies,
A band of men irrupt into the cave;
Some brandish spikes and others billhooks wave.

33

The first, a man of cruel face, had one
Eye only, swivelling from right to left.
The other eye, nostril and jaw were gone,
Perhaps by some shrewd adversary cleft;
And when his one-eyed glance had fallen on
Orlando, to the others with a swift,
Malicious smile he said: 'See in the net
A bird I hadn't counted on to get!'

34

Then, turning to the Count: 'My dear Sir, I'm
So glad to see you here; good afternoon!
Was it your own idea this rock to climb,
Or did someone suggest how great a boon
Your arms would be to me? For a long time
I've wanted some like yours. Most opportune
Is your arrival here today; indeed
You bring me just exactly what I need.'

35

Orlando, rising, answered with a wry,
Sardonic smile: 'I am prepared to sell,
But let us see if you're prepared to buy.
These are my terms: pray, scrutinize them well.'
And from the hearth, where flames were leaping high,
He seized a brand and flung it (truth to tell)
At random, but it hit the rogue between
The nose and where two eyebrows once had been.

36

Although it struck the villain centrally,
More harm it caused him on the left-hand side,
Blinding the eye through which he still could see;
And not content with this, the brand, beside,
Despatched him to Inferno rapidly,
In Chiron's subdivision, there to bide,
Shot at by arrows and immersed in blood,
With fellow murderers and all that brood.

37

Within the cave there was a slab, about
Two palms in thickness, broad as it was long,
Balanced upon a block, rough-hewn and stout.
For meals that mob sat round it, twenty strong.
Not one of them could give a warning shout
Before the Count Orlando at the throng,
Packed tightly in the cave, that heavy table
Had seized and flung as hard as he was able.

38

It crushes here a breast and there a head.
It shatters limbs, and paunches splits agape.
Some of the mob are lamed and some are dead,
But all who can still walk try to escape.
As when a heavy boulder on a bed
Of vipers crashes, leaving in poor shape
Their writhing bodies, lately preened and sunned,
So were those cowering villains crushed and stunned.

39

Some of the vipers die; some, minus tails,
Go sliding off; some cannot move at all
And no contortion of their coils avails;
And one, on which the boulder did not fall,
Its length uninjured through the grasses trails,
Or slithers to the edge of ditch or wall.
So now Orlando with that fearful blow
Displayed his might and brought those pirates low.

40

Those whom the table missed or scarcely hurt
(Precisely seven, Turpin says) rushed in
A panic to the door; but there, alert,
Ready for action, stood the paladin.
He needed no great effort to exert.
He took them, one and all, to their chagrin.
Their hands behind them with a rope he bound,
Which previously in the cave he'd found.

41

First at the entrance of the cave he bags them;
Then where a gnarled and ancient sorb-tree grows,
Casting a shadow far and wide, he drags them.
He prunes the branches where they seem too close,
Then takes the ruffians by the chin and scrags them,
Hanging them up as nourishment for crows.
He has no need of chains with pointed hooks,
For well enough they dangle from those stocks.

42

The agèd dame, who served the pirate band,
Seeing her former masters now all dead,
Her grizzled tresses tearing with each hand,
Rushed to the wood with cries of grief and fled.
For miles she trudged through harsh, uneven land,
By fear her weary footsteps onward led.
She met a knight beside a stream one day,
But who this was, much later on I'll say.

43

And to that damsel I return who stayed.
She begged the Count not to abandon her;
To the world's end she'd follow him, she said.
His sure defence he offered then and there.
When, crowned with roses, pallid Dawn, arrayed
In purple, as Apollo's harbinger,
Moved down along her customary route,
The Count Orlando and the maid set out.

44

They travelled on for many a day and night,
But nothing worthy of report occurred
Until they chanced to see a gentle knight
Who had been taken captive, they inferred.
To tell now who he was would not be quite
Appropriate, and so I'll say a word
Instead about Count Aymon's daughter, whom
We left dejected and in deepest gloom.

45

The Maid, who all this time has longed in vain
That her Ruggiero might soon be restored,
Was at Marseilles, where havoc, death and pain
Inflicting daily on the pagan horde,
Who in their ravages o'er hill and plain,
Through Languedoc and through Provence had poured,
She well performed the role allotted her,
As captain of her troops and warrior.

46

But many days and weeks and months had gone
And still her dearest love was far away.
She pictured him in peril and, not one,
But thousands of disasters saw; one day,
As she sat sadly weeping all alone,
She saw approach that wise and kindly fay
Who with the ring had made Ruggiero well,
When he was captured by Alcina's spell.

47

Seeing her now return without her lover,
After so long, the Maid grows deathly pale,
And such a trembling seizes her all over,
Her limbs for her support will scarce avail;
But good Melissa knows how to remove her
Doubts and fears; hastening, as though a tale
Of joy to tell, with smiling lips and eyes,
She comforts Bradamante in this wise:

48

'For your Ruggiero have no fear,' she said.
'Alive and well, he loves you as before;
But, by your former enemy misled,
He has been robbed of liberty once more.
Mount now at once upon that thoroughbred,
If you desire Ruggiero to restore;
For, if you will consent to follow me,
I will instruct you how to set him free.'

49

And the good sorceress began to tell
The Maid about the plot Atlante wove,
And how he simulated by his spell
Her image, which appeared the victim of
A giant, and how both invisible
Became, when once they had enticed her love
Into a magic palace, where illusion
Held many knights and damsels in confusion.

50

To all, the sorcerer, as they behold him,
Appears to be their very heart's desire:
Their lady, lord, companion, friend they hold him,
Or anything to which they may aspire;
And in their fruitless longing to enfold him,
They search the palace through and never tire.
Such is the hope of all and such the yearning,
Now here, now there they wander, twisting, turning.

51

'When you arrive in the vicinity',
Melissa said, 'of that enchanted place,
Straightway the cunning sorcerer you'll see,
Wearing Ruggiero's very form and face.
Then he will conjure with his wizardry
An enemy who'll bring him to disgrace.
He means to make you hasten to his aid,
But if you do, he'll capture you, fair Maid.

52

'And that you may not fall into this trap,
Where many knights have fallen, be advised:
For all he seems to be Ruggiero, *cap-*
à-pie, and calls for help, be not surprised.
Stand on your guard and trust him not a rap.
Such evil must be ruthlessly excised.
Despatch him; not Ruggiero will be slain,
But he who thus desires to cause you pain.

53

'It will be difficult, I know full well,
To slay one who appears to be your love;
But do not trust your sight, for by the spell
Impaired, blind to such evil it will prove.
Resolve at once to be inflexible,
And from that resolution do not move.
To kill the wizard is the only course,
Or else Ruggiero never will be yours.'

54

The valiant Maid, fully intending to
Obey Melissa's counsel and to kill
The fraudulent magician, for she knew
That she could trust the fay, with a good will
Took up her arms and followed; travelling through
The woods and fields, Melissa used her skill
The tedium of the journey to allay
By pleasing converse as they made their way.

55

Of all the themes the Maid rejoiced to hear,
To one Melissa many times returned:
The god-like progeny which she would bear
In wedlock to the youth for whom she burned.
As all the secrets of the gods were clear
To her, the sorceress events discerned,
And could predict, which many centuries
Concealed, or which lay hid in mysteries.

56

'Enlightened and illuminating guide,'
So that illustrious Maid began, 'I vow,
Long in advance of time you've prophesied
About my male descendants; tell me now,
I beg of you, about the distaff side.
What valiant women do the Fates allow
To issue from my line? What chronicle
Of virtuous deeds or beauty can you tell?'

57

The courteous fay replied: 'From you I see
Mothers of kings and emperors descending,
Famed for their comeliness and modesty,
Like mighty caryatides, defending
Illustrious houses no less worthily
Than men in armour, in due measure blending
Compassion, courage, wisdom, continence
With prudent, womanly intelligence.

58

'Were I to speak of every one of those
Fair daughters who are worthy of your line,
Much time would I require; of many whose
Renown deserves in this account of mine
Not to be passed in silence, I will choose
But three or four. Ah, why did I confine
Myself to your male offspring in the cave,
Where necromancy visions of them gave?

59

'From your illustrious line there will descend
One who of every noble enterprise
Of art or highest learning is the friend:
Fair Isabella, liberal and wise,
In whom so many rare endowments blend.
This luminary will be seen to rise,
Warming the city where the Mincio flows
And which its name to Ocnus' mother owes.

60

'And there, in honourable rivalry
With her most worthy husband she'll engage
To ascertain which of the two shall be
The greatest host and patron of the age;
And if he claims to rescue Italy
From the invading Gauls' barbaric rage,
She will reply: "Penelope no less is,
By reason of her virtue, than Ulysses."

61

'Great deeds and many in few words I give
Concerning her, and much I leave unsaid,
For in the cave where Merlin still does live,
Though in the sepulchre his bones lie dead,
Much was revealed to me and I believe
Farther than Jason voyaged I should spread
My sails on such a sea; thus I conclude,
She is endowed with all that's true and good.

62

'And there will be her sister, Beatrice,
To whom her name will be appropriate,
Not only for such happiness as is
Permitted to us in our human state,
But for the highest of felicities
Which for the duke, her husband, she'll create,
Who, after she departs this life, will suffer
The keenest woe and anguish Fate can offer.

63

'The name of Sforza and the Snakes will show
Themselves invincible, long as she lives,
From Red Sea shores to hyperborean snow,
From India to the strait which access gives
To your native sea. But once death lays her low,
Them and the Insubrian realm disaster drives
Into subjection to the king of France,
And all her husband's skill is counted chance.

64

'And other Beatrices there will be
Who many years before her will be born;
And one of these, as queen of Hungary,
With a fair crown her tresses will adorn.
Another who the worldly life will flee
And earthly joys and satisfaction scorn,
After her death to sainthood elevated,
With prayers and incense will be venerated.

65

'Others I must omit, for, as I said,
To tell you of them all would take too long,
Though each is worthy to be trumpeted
In story and immortalized in song.
Biancas, Costanzas, and Lucrezias, wed
To dukes or princes, I must leave among
The glories which the future will reveal,
Mothers of heroes, guardians of the weal.

66

'Yours, more than any other lineages,
Good fortune in its womenfolk will know;
For in the partners of their marriages,
As in their daughters, faithfulness will glow.
Concerning two, the many messages
Which Merlin uttered to me there below
He charged me to pass on to you, and I
With his request will gladly now comply.

67

'First I will tell you of Ricciarda, who
All honour and all strength exemplifies.
Widowed while young, she will be faithful to
Her spouse who in the ducal chapel lies.
Her sons, expropriated, wander through
Strange lands, in exile, under alien skies,
Child victims of inexorable foes,
But recompense she'll have for all her woes.

68

'Of the proud line of ancient Aragon,
I'll not omit that wise and splendid queen,
So virtuous that no such paragon
In Roman times or Greek has ever been,
Whom Fortune favours more than anyone
In all the destined futures I've foreseen:
Alfonso and Ippolito she'll bear,
And Isabella, wise as she is fair.

69

'This splendid matriarch, named Eleanor,
Is grafted thus to your life-bearing tree.
What shall I say now of her successor,
Alfonso's second wife, Lucrezia, she
Whose virtue, fame and beauty every hour
Increase, whom fortune and prosperity
Combine to favour, like a plant, no less,
Which fertile soil and rain and sun all bless?

70

'As tin to silver or as brass to gold,
The poppy of the cornfield to the rose,
The willow, pale and withered in the cold,
To the green bay which ever greener grows,
As painted glass to jewels, thus I hold,
Compared with her, as yet unborn, all those
Who hitherto for beauty have been famed,
Or models of all excellence are named.

71

'And by the many who will sing her praise,
Both while she lives and after she is dead,
She'll be esteemed, above all that she'll raise
Those sons so royally whom she'll have bred.
Ercole and his brothers will the bays
Of glorious lustre wear upon their head;
For fragrance is not easily dispersed,
Though later vessels equal not the first.

72

'Nor by my silence would I seem to scorn
The wife of Ercole, Renée de France,
Of the twelfth Louis and of Anna born.
All virtues which the gentle sex enhance,
Or ever have or will, while fires burn,
Or waters flow, or the nine circles dance
In heavenly concord, in this queen I see
Joined and combined in perfect harmony.

73

'Celano's countess, Alda of Salogna,
Both these, and others, I must now omit;
Of Blanche Marie, the fair, of Catalogna,
I fain would speak, but time does not permit;
Likewise of lovely Lippa of Bologna,
And Sicily's princess, as would be fit.
But were I to begin to tell you more,
I'd enter on a sea that has no shore.'

74

Thus having spoken of the greater part
Of the descendants who would spring from her,
Melissa warned her of that magic art
Again, which held her love a prisoner.
Then, coming to a place where to depart
Seemed prudent, for the evil sorcerer
Might see her if still closer she approached,
Or on the threshold of his spell encroached,

75

She left the Maid, first warning her again,
As she had done so many times before,
Against Atlante's image, but in vain;
For, riding scarcely two or three miles more,
The Maid beheld Ruggiero, plain as plain,
Between two cruel giants who so bore
Upon him that his death, or so she deemed,
Was imminent, so true the conflict seemed.

76

And when she sees, in every form and feature,
The very likeness of Ruggiero, caught
By two such ruffians of gigantic stature,
In peril of his life, the Maid, distraught
By anguish of an overwhelming nature,
Forgetful now of all she has been taught,
Believes Melissa hates Ruggiero and
Contrives that he shall die by his love's hand.

77

And to herself she said: 'Is not that he
Who's ever present to my heart and eyes?
And if it's not my love whom I now see,
Whom did I ever see or recognize?
Why should I take another's word to be
The truth, and my own senses thus despise?
Without my eyes, and by my heart alone
The presence of my love to me is known.'

78

While she is thus considering, she hears
What seems to be his voice, imploring aid,
Then sees the phantom, for whose life she fears,
Apply his spurs and gallop through the glade.
Each giant, who his enemy appears,
Pursues him with all speed; at this, the Maid
No longer hesitates but soon is gone
And to the magic palace follows on.

79

And there, no sooner has she passed the gate
Than in that same bewilderment she falls.
Along the alleys, tortuous or straight,
Upstairs and down, through corridors and halls,
She looks for him from early morn till late.
So cunning is the spell that, as she calls,
She seems to see Ruggiero and to hear him,
Yet he does not see her, nor she come near him.

80

But let us leave her there; be not distressed
That she is now bewitched, for from that spell,
When the occasion and the time seem best,
I'll save her and her destined spouse as well.
Now, as a hook must many times be dressed
With change of bait, or else the fish rebel,
So now another path I will explore,
Lest those whom I would entertain, I bore.

81

For many other threads, it seems, I need
To finish such a tapestry as this.
So, may it not displease you to pay heed
To how King Agramant, who captain is
Of all the Moors and pagans of like breed,
While menacing the golden fleur-de-lis,
Gave orders that his forces should parade,
That he might know how many troops he had.

82

For many cavaliers, and footmen too,
Had died or had been wounded in the fray.
Captains were missing – Spaniards not a few,
Libyans and Ethiops the light of day
No longer saw, and soldiers wandered through
Inhospitable lands, or lost their way.
From chaos order hoping now to bring,
Those who remain parade before their king.

83

And to replace the many thousands slain
In battles or in fighting hand-to-hand,
One captain Agramante sent to Spain,
And one to Africa, where many a band
Of raw recruits they undertook to train
And bring to Paris under their command.
But now, my lord, in deference to you,
I will defer the tale of the tattoo.

CANTO XIV

1

In the assaults and cruel conflicts waged
By Africa and Spain against fair France,
The number of the dead could scarce be gauged,
Now wolf's or crow's or eagle's sustenance.
Though these afflictions were in part assuaged
By many a territorial advance,
The infidels had dearly paid the cost
In princes and in nobles whom they'd lost.

2

So bloody were the pagan victories,
Small reason to rejoice the victors had.
If present-day with ancient histories
Can be compared, Alfonso, you, who made
Ravenna so regret your expertise
When, sacked and plundered, she so dearly paid
For help against the Spaniard, represent
Of these reverses the equivalent.

3

For, to assist the French of Picardy,
Artois and Normandy and Aquitaine,
Amid the standards of the enemy
You plunged, and plucked the victory from Spain;
And those who followed with such gallantry
Truly deserved that day, for all their pain,
(Although the triumph was so largely yours)
Their gilded sword-hilts and their gilded spurs.

4

Although hemmed in by enemies untold,
Who on your head unceasing missiles showered,
You felled to earth the acorns of bright gold,
The red and yellow baton overpowered;
But, owing to your thrusts so shrewd and bold,
The lily was not broken or deflowered;
And double is the laurel crown you wear;
Witness to this Fabrizio can bear.

5

This Roman prince, Colonna, whom you saved,
Preserving shaft and capital intact,
Gives you more honour than if you had braved
The whole militia, and in one fell act
The onslaught of as many men had staved
As near Ravenna to the ground were hacked
Or in disorder fled, when all had failed
And neither spikes nor armoured wheels availed.

6

Of greater comfort was that victory
Than gladness, because blighting to our hopes
And joy it is so many deaths to see:
The captain of the French and allied troops
And many princes who in chivalry
Had crossed the formidable Alpine slopes,
Their threatened territories to defend,
Or brother dukes and princes to befriend.

7

Our welfare and our lives by Spain's defeat
Have been preserved; this is the debt we owe.
On us no longer will Jove's tempest beat;
On us no more the winter's blast will blow.
Yet we cannot rejoice at such a feat.
We feel too much the anguish and the woe
Of weeping women garbed in widows' weeds,
The sad young victims of your valiant deeds.

8

King Louis now new captains must provide,
Who for the honour of the fleur-de-lis
Those thieving hands must castigate and chide
Which neither convents spared, nor monasteries,
No mercy showed to mother, daughter, bride,
And, violating sacred mysteries,
The silver tabernacle of the Host
Purloined and on the ground the wafer tossed.

9

Anguished Ravenna! Better had it been
By far, if no resistance you had made,
If Brescia as a warning you had seen,
As you to Rimini now stand displayed
And to Faenza. Louis, to your men
Send good Trivulzio, let by him be said
How many French on havoc bent, and spoil,
Lie dead and buried in Italian soil.

10

As at the present time the king of France
Requires to put more captains in the field,
So then the Spaniards and the Africans,
To organize their forces, have both willed
That all from winter-quarters shall advance
And on the plain in order stand revealed,
That who is missing they may thus perceive
And to each troop a chief or captain give.

11

Marsilio first and Agramante then
Passed in review his forces one by one.
And leading the parade, there came the men
Of Catalonia, with the gonfalon
Of Dorifebo; after them were seen
(Their leader, Folvirant, being dead and gone,
Slain by Rinaldo's hand) the Navarrese.
Isolier now was commandant of these.

12

The army of Leòn obeys the will
Of Balugante; men of Algarvè
Grandonio heads; and those of old Castile
The brother of the king leads to the fray.
The troops of Màlaga and of Seville
Have followed Madarasso all the way
From lands between Cordova and Cadiz
Which Guadalquivir's waters fertilize.

13

Three armies by three captains next are led:
Granàda's men come forth with Stordilan.
The Lisbon troops, Tessira at their head,
Parade; Majorcans follow to a man
Their Baricondo. Larbin being dead,
Tessira, in whose veins the blood royal ran,
Was Lisbon's king; chief of Galicia's side
Was Serpentino; Maricold had died.

14

Toledo's men and Calatrava's too,
Whom Sinagon once led, come forth with those
Who journeyed all the way to the review
From regions where the Guadiana flows.
Their captain's Matalista, brave and true.
Next, with Asturians, Bianzardino goes,
With men of Salamanca and Plasencia,
Of Àvila, Zamora and Palencia.

15

From Saragossa and Marsilio's court
Paraded under Ferraù's command
A well-armed company, with the support
Of Balinverno, Malgarino and
Morgante, Malzarise, who consort
With Ferraù, a formidable band.
Since Fate had driven them from home and realm,
Marsilio to his staff had welcomed them.

16

Among them is the bastard of the king,
The pride of Almerìa, Follicon.
Count Archidant and Largalifa bring
Their troops, with Analard and Doricon;
The Emir, Langhiran the brave, I sing,
And Malagur the shrewd, surpassed by none.
Of these and many more, before the end,
To demonstrate the valour I intend.

17

When thus the military might of Spain
Before King Agramante had passed by,
There mustered then the squadron on the plain
Of Oran's ruler, riding giant-high.
The next which comes laments for Martasin
That he by Bradamante's sword should die,
For bitterly all Garamantes mourn
That by a woman he was overborne.

18

From Marmarica came the third platoon,
Which left Argosto dead in Gascony.
To this a captain must be given soon,
As to the second and fourth company.
The king selected, as was opportune,
(Though captains were not come by easily)
Arganio, Buraldo and Ormida,
Thus giving each of these platoons a leader.

19

Of Libyans Arganio has command.
They mourn the Negro, Dudrinasso, dead.
Brunello leads the Mauretanian band.
His looks are stormy and he hangs his head.
When in the forest, near Atlante's land
(Where he had built a castle, as I said),
He lost the magic ring, to his great cost;
King Agramante's favour too he lost.

20

If Isolier, brother of Ferraù,
Who found him trussed and fastened to a tree,
Had not convinced the king of what was true,
Brunel had dangled from a gallows-tree.
The king, at the last moment yielding to
Entreaties, granted a reprieve, but he
Had warned him he was keeping him in check:
Henceforth he went in danger of his neck.

21

Good cause, then, had Brunello to come there
With head bent down to hide his mournful face.
Next Farivante came; Maurina's were
The horse and foot which followed him apace.
Came then Libanio, just made king, to fare
With whom had Constantina's folk their place,
Since Agramant on him the golden rod
And crown, once Pinadoro's, had bestowed.

22

Next Soridan, from the Hesperides,
And Ceuta's forces follow Dorilon,
Pulian the Nasamones; and after these,
Amonians, by King Agricalt urged on;
Malabuferso Fezzan's leader is,
And Finadurro captains the platoon
Which comes from Teneriffe and from Morocco.
Balastro has replaced the late Tardocco.

23

From Mulga and Arzilla now appear
Two squadrons; since the former's chief is dead,
King Agramant his friend, whom he holds dear,
Brave Corinèo, chooses in his stead.
Of Almansilla's army, who Tanfer-
ion have lost, Caico now is head.
Getulians he gives to Rimedonte.
Then come the Coscan men with Balinfronte.

24

The Bolgan army passes; Clarindo
In Mirabaldo's place is now their king.
Then Baliverzo comes: I'd have you know,
In all that flock no greater rogue I sing.
Of all the troops which there parade on show,
Sobrino's men the greatest promise bring:
No stronger army could there ever be,
No Saracen more circumspect than he.

25

Bellamarina's men pass in review.
Gualciotto, their dead commandant, they mourn.
They're captained now by Rodomonte, who
The heir to Sarza and Algiers was born.
His task in Africa was to renew,
From Sagittarius to Capricorn,
The forces of the Infidel. Three days
Ago he had returned, with no delays.

26

None mightier among the Africans,
Among the Saracens none bolder was.
Before the gates of Paris, in all France
None other was more feared, and greater cause
For fear his prowess was than Agramant's
Or King Marsilio's. Our faith, our laws,
Our paladins this infidel assailed
And in his combats often he prevailed.

27

Prusione now parades, then Dardinel:
The first, the Blessed Isles' king, Zumara's he.
I know not if a hooting owl, or knell
They hear, or whether ravens croakingly
From roof-tops or from leafy boughs foretell
To either prince his awesome destiny,
But for them both the fateful hour is nigh,
And in tomorrow's combat they must die.

28

All were assembled now upon the field,
Except Norizia and Tremisen.
No sign of them did the horizon yield,
Of their insignia or of their men.
While Agramant astonishment concealed
And wondered what their tardiness might mean,
There came a sole survivor who had squired
Alzirdo, who now told what had transpired.

29

He told the king that Manilard lay dead.
Alzirdo too had perished in great pain.
'My lord, that valiant cavalier', he said,
'Who killed our men, your army would have slain
If from the battlefield they had not fled,
As I escaped and lived to fight again.
He deals with infantry and cavaliers
As does a wolf which among sheep appears.'

30

A champion had arrived some days before
To join these forces from across the sea.
In all the West, in all the East, no more
Courageous cavalier there was than he.
The son of Agrican, the successor
And heir he was to realms in Tartary.
King Agramant received him with acclaim
And honour; Mandricardo was his name.

31

For many a glorious deed he was renowned,
And all the world was ringing with his name
For a great exploit, which his glory crowned,
In Syria, where to a tower he came
And, making steel on steel sound and resound,
He won that armour of undying fame
Which the great Hector on his body wore
Defending Troy a thousand years before.

32

He heard the sad narration of the squire
And at his words he lifted up his brow;
For he was filled with an intense desire
To seek this warrior out, he knew not how.
Hiding the thoughts with which he was on fire,
No other knight he trusted with his vow;
Perhaps he deemed it prudent to conceal
His plan, lest someone else his thunder steal.

33

The squire he questioned searchingly as to
The surcoat which that cavalier had worn.
'Black, unrelieved,' was the reply, 'black, too,
His shield and on his helm no crest is borne.'
And this, my lord, as you're aware, was true,
For quartering Orlando had forsworn;
Since inwardly his soul was dark with grief,
In outward sombreness he sought relief.

34

To Mandricard Marsilio once gave
A chestnut steed, jet-black its legs and mane.
In stamina unequalled, swift and brave,
Sired by a fettled roan of southern Spain
On a Flanders mare. Full-armed, determined, grave,
He mounted with one leap; across the plain
He galloped, vowing he would not be back
Till he had found that knight attired in black.

35

Many survivors in his path he crossed
Who from Orlando terrified had fled,
Mourning aghast the sons whom they had lost,
Or brothers who before their eyes fell dead.
Their fear and suffering appeared almost
Engraved upon each face, wherein he read
The havoc they'd endured and all their woe,
As pale and silent through the woods they go.

36

Not far had he progressed before he found
The cruel and inhuman spectacle
Of knights and horses slaughtered on the ground,
Confirming all the story he'd heard tell.
Counting the dead, he cast his eyes around,
And then, dismounting, with his hands as well
Their wounds examined, by this gruesome sight
Moved by strange envy of that unknown knight.

37

As when a wolf or dog, arriving last
Where lies the carcass of a slaughtered bull,
With horns, bones, hoofs must be content, or fast;
While birds and other creatures to the full
Have gorged their hunger on a rich repast,
It sniffs disdainfully at the dry skull;
So did that infidel, like some wild beast,
Rail that he came so late to such a feast.

38

That day and half the next he searched and made
Enquiries as to whether a black knight
Had passed or any wayfarer waylaid.
At length he came upon a pleasing sight:
A little meadow nestling in the shade,
Round which a river formed a loop or bight.
A similar effect, as you may see,
The Tiber makes below Ocrìcoli.

39

On guard along the narrow neck of land·
He sees a group of knights as he draws near.
He asks them who has mustered such a band
And for what purpose it is stationed here.
The captain, being accustomed to command,
Takes him for a distinguished cavalier,
And by his gold and jewelled trappings knows
That an appropriate reply he owes.

40

'We're detailed by Granada's king', he said,
'Our duty being his daughter to escort,
Whom to the king of Sarza he has wed,
Though this is scarcely known outside the court.
And when the cicada has quieted,
And other summer insects of the sort,
We'll bring her to her father in our keeping;
And in the meantime the princess is sleeping.'

41

The pagan, who distrusted all mankind,
Preferred to put this statement to the test.
How they kept guard on her, he meant to find,
And in reply the captain thus addressed:
'I hear she's beautiful and I've a mind
To see her for myself. It would be best
To take me to her or bring her to me.
I pray you, do so, and right speedily.'

42

'Good sir, you must indeed be off your head!',
The captain of the guard at once replied.
Such were his words, and nothing more he said,
For Mandricardo had transfixed his side;
With lowered spear he ran and struck him dead,
Then, making sure the man had really died,
With careful skill he pulled his spear away,
Which he would need to use another day.

43

Since Trojan Hector's armour he had won,
Of weapons he used neither sword nor mace;
For, when he saw that Hector's sword was gone,
He vowed to use no other in its place.
Nor did he vow in vain, and that alone
It was his aim through all the world to trace:
Almonte's sword, now by Orlando worn,
Great Durindana, once by Hector borne.

44

Great is the daring of the Tartar, who
Vastly outnumbered, in defiance calls:
'Now try to stop me, any one of you!',
And, plunging on, to right and left he falls
To smiting them, and nothing they can do
With spear or sword his mighty fury quells.
Already he has culled no small a token
Before he notices his lance is broken.

45

And when he sees that this has come to pass,
In both his hands the butt, which still remains
Intact, he seizes instantly, and as
Ferociously as many blows he rains
As Samson who, the jawbone of an ass
From the ground snatching, slew the Philistines.
Helmets he breaks, and bucklers, too, he smashes,
And with one stroke both horse and rider crashes.

46

They run towards their death as in a race
Athletes prepare to hurdle, leap or jump.
One falls and then another takes his place;
They crowd behind each other in a clump,
For rather would they risk of death embrace
Than be defeated by a broken stump;
And yet such havoc in their midst it makes,
They die beneath its blows like frogs or snakes.

47

When those behind, have seen to their great cost
How cruel death can be in any guise,
And when the greater number have been lost,
A group of them, retreating, vainly tries
To flee; but cruel Mandricard, almost
As if they were his property, denies
To anyone the right to save his life,
And to the bitter end pursues the strife.

48

As 'mid the rustle of a sun-dried marsh
Short-lived is the resistance of the reed,
And as the stubble flies before the harsh
Breath of Borèas, or when flame with speed
Crackles along the furrows, leaving ash
To fertilize the soil for the new seed,
So, fleeing before Mandricardo's ire,
The guards have no defence against such fire.

49

And when at length the entrance-way seems clear,
No living guard being anywhere about,
Along a path where recent prints appear
He seeks the lady of Granada out.
Led by a lamentation he can hear,
He'll soon discover her, he has no doubt.
Between the bodies of the dead he goes,
The loop of river tracing where it flows.

50

Towards her now his steps the pagan bring
(Her name is Doralice, you must know),
Where to an ancient ash he sees her cling,
As though confiding all her grief and woe.
Her tears, descending from a living spring,
Water her lovely bosom as they flow;
And in her face a two-fold fear is shown,
Fear for the fate of others and her own.

51

And when she sees the Tartar drawing nigh,
Blood-stained, with glowering and evil brow,
The shriek she utters splits the very sky,
For turned to panic is her terror now:
Not only guards was she escorted by
(The king, her father, this would not allow),
But maids-in-waiting, counsellors and guides
Had come to keep her company besides.

52

When Mandricardo sees that lovely face
Which has no equal in the whole of Spain,
A web of love, as intricate as lace,
Is woven round his heart, and if in heaven
Or earth he is, or any other place,
He cannot tell; his victory's sole gain,
That captive of his captive he is made,
Such is the beauty of the helpless maid.

53

To her, alas! her tears bring no relief.
King Mandricardo's will she cannot shake,
Although she mourns and weeps, it's my belief,
Making more moan than woman e'er could make;
For, hoping to convert her bitter grief
To keenest joy, he has resolved to take
Her with him, mounted on a snow-white horse,
And in her company resume his course.

54

Ladies and maids-in-waiting and all who
Had formed the retinue of the princess
He sent away with a kind word or two.
'Farewell,' he said; 'I wish you all success.
I'll be her escort, guide and captain, too;
I'll see to all her needs'; and, powerless,
Leaving fair Doralice in his keeping,
The retinue moved off, sighing and weeping,

55

Saying amongst themselves, 'How sad the king
Will be when he hears this! How full of ire
Her spouse will be when people tidings bring
Of the abduction of his bride! What dire
Revenge he'll wreak! Alas! how sad a thing
That of so royal and so great a sire
The daughter should be stolen thus away!
Would that her bridegroom were at hand today!'

56

Content with his great booty, which he owed
To valour and good fortune, now less haste
To find the black-clad cavalier he showed.
Impetuous before, he galloped fast,
But now more slowly and sedately rode.
He pondered meanwhile, lest the time he waste,
Where he might find a lodging for the night,
In hopes to spend the hours in love's delight.

57

And as he went, to comfort the fair maid,
Whose eyes and countenance were wet with tears,
Inventing and embroidering, he said
He'd loved her by repute for many years;
While many left their fatherland, being led
By dreams of glory, and by hopes, or fears,
He'd left his home, not to see Spain or France,
But only to behold her lovely glance.

58

'If love by loving may be earned by man,
Then I have earned your love, for you I love;
Or if by noble birth, King Agrican
My father is; if wealth the heart may move
To fond response, what rival claimant can
Compete with me? To none, save God above,
I yield in power; or if valour serve,
I've shown today that I your love deserve.'

59

These words and many more which Love dictates
The Tartar now addresses to the maid.
Her troubled breast he sweetly thus placates;
Her apprehensions soon begin to fade,
Her fear diminishing, her grief abates,
By which her soul at first was overlaid;
And with more patience she at length lends ear
To the strange wooing of this cavalier.

60

She answers him more kindly and with grace,
His bold appraisal she no longer shuns,
Allows her eyes to linger on his face,
And with compassion kindles in response.
The pagan, who has felt the smarting trace
Of Cupid's piercing arrow more than once,
Not only hopes, is sure, the damsel will
Not always be rebellious to his will.

61

Thus onward in her company he goes,
Wherein he finds such joy and such delight.
Then, towards the hour when refuge and repose
Are sought by creatures from the chill of night,
The pagan spurs his charger, for he knows
The setting sun will soon be out of sight.
Ere long the sound of shepherds' pipes they hear
And smoke from rustic hearths hangs in the air.

62

At one such pastoral abode they knock.
The rooms more homely than adorned appear.
With courtesy the shepherd of the flock
Admits the damsel and the cavalier
And bids them welcome. Do not only look
For gentlefolk in castles: everywhere,
In humble dwellings and in haylofts, too,
The hearts of men are often kind and true.

63

What in the darkness of the night befell
Between the Tartar and the young princess
I cannot, I regret, precisely tell,
So everyone must be content to guess.
I think that they agreed together well
For in the morning they arose no less
But rather more content; and, turning to
Their host, the princess thanked him, as was due.

64

Taking their leave, they wandered here, now there,
And came at last upon a lovely stream,
Which moved so silently that none could hear
It gliding, seaward borne, as in a dream.
The limpid, crystal waters were so clear,
Their furthest depths received the sunlight's beam.
Upon the bank, reclining in the shade,
They found two cavaliers and a fair maid.

65

But soaring fantasy will not allow
Me to pursue one path for long; again
To where the armies are it leads me now.
The son of King Troiano, who was slain,
Threatens to bring the Holy Empire low,
Loud in their roaring are the Moors of Spain,
And Rodomonte, the audacious, boasts
That he will flatten Rome while Paris roasts.

66

King Agramante had received the news
That English troops the Channel now had crossed.
He called, that he might ascertain their views,
The mighty leaders of his mighty host.
Unanimously they advised the use
Of towers and engines at whatever cost,
To bring the citadel of Paris down
Before the reinforcements reached the town.

67

Innumerable ladders for this aim
King Agramant collected from all hands;
Trestles and planks from every quarter came,
And quantities of plaited willow-wands.
Pontoons and boats he orders for the scheme.
The first and second army, he commands,
Shall lead the assault, and he desires to be
Among the foremost in the day's mêlée.

68

The day before the battle, Charlemagne,
Within the threatened walls of Paris, has
Instructed all the priests who there remain
To celebrate the office and say mass;
And that all souls, confessed and free from stain,
Beyond the Stygian flood may safely pass,
He bids them take communion and to fast
As though they thought that day would be their last.

69

Among his nobles and his paladins,
Among his princes and ambassadors,
He goes devoutly to confess his sins.
With folded hands the Almighty he implores,
And humbly his oration thus begins:
'Lord God, though I a sinner am, and worse,
In Thy great mercy, on us pity take:
Let not Thy people suffer for my sake.

70

'Yet, if it is Thy will that we should fail,
In retribution for our sinful ways,
Let not, at least, Thine enemies prevail.
If we, who are Thy servants, and Thy praise
Are known to sing, our dying souls exhale,
Slain by the Infidel, their voice they'll raise
And Thy divine omnipotence deny,
Since thus Thou lettest Thy supporters die.

71

'And where one to Thy will a rebel was,
A hundred henceforth will refuse to bow,
Until at last the false and evil laws
Of Babylon will flourish and bring low
All Thy believers; vindicate the cause
Of these Thy people, who their sacred vow
Fulfilled, to guard Thy Holy Church, and cleanse
Thy sacred sepulchre of Saracens.

72

'Our merits of themselves suffice to pay
No particle of all the debt we owe.
If our offences in the scales we weigh,
For no remission can we hope, I know.
But if Thou add Thy gift of grace, straightway
An equal balance our account will show.
Remembering Thy mercy to all men,
We cannot of Thy help despair. Amen.'

73

Such was the prayer which the Emperor prayed,
Humbly and with contrition in his heart.
He added other prayers too and made
A vow consistent with his royal part.
His fervent worship was not unrepaid:
A guardian angel, waiting to depart,
Gathered his final words and spread his wings
To fly to the Creator of all things.

74

And of such Angels an infinitude
Upon that instant likewise rose above
To bring their messages of prayer to God.
They gazed intently on Eternal Love
And in their holy countenances showed
How they desired that the petition of
The Christian people asking for His aid
Might be fulfilled, as Charlemagne had prayed.

75

And the Ineffable to Whom in vain
No prayer from a believer ever rose,
Lifted His loving eyes and from His train
Of Archangels His faithful Michael chose.
'Go,' He commanded, 'to the Picard plain,
Where Christians disembark to meet their foes,
And bring them softly to the walls of Paris,
So that the pagan army unaware is.

76

'First, seek out Silence: ask him in My name
To come with you upon this enterprise.
He will provide what's needed for the aim
To further which I send you through the skies.
This being done, go quickly to where Dame
Discord sojourns and, bidding her arise,
Tell her to bring her flint and tinder with her
To use among the Moors, and take her thither.

77

'Among the champions of the pagan side
Let her spread mischief and ill-feeling, so
That hate and rivalry, intensified,
Cause them to fight among themselves and foe
Become to those with whom they are allied.
Thus little help their king from them will know.'
The Angel to these words makes no reply
But from that heavenly realm sets out to fly.

78

Wherever Michael flies on outstretched wings,
The clouds disperse, the sky grows clear and bright.
Around his head a golden circle clings,
Like lightning flashing on a summer night.
Musing at first upon celestial things,
He wonders soon where he may best alight
To find that enemy of noise and din
With whom he is commissioned to begin.

79

When on the question he has pondered well,
His reasonings at length in this agree:
Silence he'll find in a monastic cell,
In church, in every aisle and sacristry,
Wherever friar or monk his beads may tell,
Or sleep, or eat, or chant the psalmody,
Where speech has been prohibited to all
And SILENCE is inscribed on every wall.

80

Michael, believing this, began to move
His golden pinions faster on the wind,
For he was sure that Quiet, Peace and Love
In company with Silence he would find;
But, visiting a cloister, notions of
The sort he soon had banished from his mind.
'Silence is gone from here,' the inmates said,
'Save that his name is written overhead.'

81

And neither Piety, Humility,
Nor Quietude, nor Peace did he behold,
Nor Love; though once this was their sanctuary,
They had been driven from the place, of old,
By Greed and Avarice and Cruelty,
By Wrath and Pride, Envy and Sloth; such bold
And ugly upstarts made the Angel stare,
And then he noticed Discord too was there,

82

She whom the Father bade him find as well,
Once he had tracked down Silence to his lair.
He thought he'd have to scour the margins fell
Of the Cocytus, among lost souls there.
Yet now he finds her in this new-made hell
(Who'd credit it?), 'mid office, mass and prayer:
A thing to holy Michael most surprising
And never reckoned with in his surmising.

83

He knew her by her multicoloured dress,
Made of unequal lengths, one up, one down,
Which sometimes covered her, now more, now less,
As the wind blew her tattered, unstitched gown.
Her hair, one tress of which was gold, one tress
Was silver, and another black, or brown,
Was looped in ribbons, or else tightly plaited,
Or hung about her shoulders, loose and matted.

84

Her hands were full of legal documents,
Bundles of charters, hung with seals and bosses,
Counsels' opinions, summonses for rents,
Verbatim records, affidavits, glosses,
Powers of attorney, deeds and instruments,
Which lawyers' pockets line with poor men's losses;
Ready to hand, to illustrate the code,
A group of notaries about her strode.

85

The Angel beckons her and bids her go
And stir the Saracens to bitter strife,
Finding some cause of provocation so
Inflammatory that more and more rife
Their internecine enmity shall grow.
Concerning Silence then, he asks her if
She's seen him in her wanderings up and down,
While setting fires alight from town to town.

86

Discord replies: 'I cannot call to mind
That I have seen him anywhere around.
I've heard him praised, by those who are inclined
To value cunning, for his lack of sound.
But Fraud, whom in our cloister here you'll find,
Can tell you more about him, I'll be bound.
'Tis said she's often in his company,'
And, pointing, cries: 'There yonder, that is she.'

87

She had a pleasing face, a humble gaze;
Of grave demeanour, grave in speech as well,
And modest in her dress, beyond all praise,
She might have been the Angel Gabriel.
And yet deformed and ugly in all ways
Her body is, which ample skirts conceal,
While under them she clutches at her hip
A dagger which is poisoned at the tip.

88

He asks her what advice she has to give
As to the whereabouts of Silence now,
And Fraud replies: 'Once Silence used to live
Among the virtues, nor did he, I vow,
Wish other company; and I believe
He dwelt in abbeys where monks used to bow
To Benedict's and to Elijah's rules,
And in the ancient philosophic schools.

89

'But since Pythagoras and Archytas
And saints like Benedict are now no more,
From honesty and virtue, Silence has
Crossed over to an alien, evil shore.
The nights at first with lovers he would pass,
And then with thieves; not long was it before
He chose, men say, with Treachery to dwell,
And next with Homicide, as I know well.

90

'With coiners of false money he frequents
Locations dark and secret and occult.
He often changes friends and residence;
To find him therefore will be difficult.
Yet be of cheer and full of confidence.
Your hopes of finding him I would not stult.
At midnight to the House of Sleep repair.
You will not fail to find him sleeping there.'

91

Though Fraud tells many lies, these words of hers
Ring true; the Angel leaves the monastery
And, flying slowly, carefully defers
Arrival at the House of Sleep, which he,
As Fraud advised, to come upon prefers
At twelve o'clock, at midnight punctually,
For then he knows that Silence he'll discover
And so at last his mission will be over.

92

In Araby, far from the haunts of men,
A pleasant little valley hidden lies.
With ancient firs and sturdy beech, the glen
All entrance to the sheltered nook denies.
No beams of day can penetrate within,
However hard the noonday sunlight tries;
And such thick foliage the branches have,
The Angel has to enter through a cave.

93

Beneath the black, impenetrable wood
A spacious grotto opens in the rock,
Which tendrils of the twisting ivy hood
And with their clinging love the entrance choke.
Sleep had his residence in this abode,
Lying between two others of his flock:
Sloth dawdled near him, indolent and fat,
And Laziness, inert, beside him sat.

94

Oblivion on the threshold has his seat.
Remembering no face, he turns away
All visitors; no-one will he admit,
No message take, no word of welcome say.
There Silence softly moves on slippered feet,
And with his hand he gestures to convey
To anyone approaching from afar
That callers at this house unwanted are.

95

But Michael comes and whispers in his ear,
'God has a task for you; attend to me:
Rinaldo and his troops will soon draw near
To Paris; make them come so silently
That not a Saracen a sound shall hear.
No shouts, no clash of weapons must there be,
And long ere Rumour her report can spread
Up to the very walls let them be led.'

96

Silence, when he had heard, made no reply,
Save by a nod to indicate assent.
With God's commands being willing to comply,
Obediently to Picardy he went.
There too the Angel Michael chose to fly
And to the squadrons his assistance lent.
Thus they reached Paris in a single day,
Though no one thought it strange in any way.

97

Silence flew here and there and everywhere,
Before, beside the army and behind it,
Raising such obfuscation in the air,
No scout or forager could ever find it
(Though bright and clear the sunshine was elsewhere).
And when he'd blanketed and fleecy-lined it,
So that no trumpet could be heard, *en bref*,
The pagans were as good as blind and deaf.

98

As, benefited by angelic aid,
Rinaldo's troops thus readily advance,
While not a single sound has been betrayed,
Within the pagan camp King Agramant's
Arrangements for a full attack are made,
And with his infantry he waits his chance
To bring the walls of Paris down that day
And to emerge triumphant from the fray.

99

Whoever tried to count the pagan host
Assembled there to menace Charlemagne,
Of counting all the trees as well might boast
Which clothe the Apennines; or of the main
Might count the countless waves which, tempest-tossed,
The foot of Atlas bathe; or likewise feign
To estimate the sum of heaven's eyes
Which midnight deeds of furtive love surprise.

100

The bells are rung with mighty hammer-blows.
Unceasing is the terrifying din.
In every cloister, chapel, choir and close
Hands are upraised, a-wag is every chin.
If God had cared for riches such as those
As in our folly we take pleasure in,
This was the day He might have had in gold
Statues of all his saints, both new and old.

101

Now venerable elders beat their breast,
Survivors of so many former frays,
And envy those whom Fate has laid to rest,
The valiant warriors of olden days.
But the young men, robust and full of zest,
Whom no impending sense of doom dismays,
Run to the walls, unmindful of all warning,
The doleful message of their seniors scorning.

102

They find the nobles and the paladins,
The kings, the dukes, the marquesses, the counts,
The cavaliers, the soldiers, citizens
And foreigners; and as excitement mounts,
In eagerness to slay the Saracens,
They press to have the drawbridge down at once.
While at their zeal the Emperor rejoices,
Yet he resists the clamour of their voices,

103

Preferring to deploy them so as to
Impede the passage of the Infidel.
Here he's content to station but a few;
There, many more stand ready to repel.
Some for incendiaries, some for the new
Defence-machines, he makes responsible,
While he himself much energy expends
As every post he watches and defends.

104

Paris is situated in a plain,
Fair France's navel, nay, her very heart.
Within her walls there flows the river Seine,
Whose waters in a double stream depart,
Forming an island ere they meet again.
This of the city is the safest part,
Although the other two (for there are three)
Both walls and river have as boundary.

105

For many miles the city's girth extends.
Its walls may be attacked from any side.
But one part only Agramant intends
To breach; his strength unwilling to divide,
He aims, in order to attain his ends,
South of the river, towards the west, to bide,
Where, at his back, innumerable lands,
As far as Spain itself, he now commands.

106

Wherever the external wall curves round,
King Charlemagne has laid his plans with care.
Culverts are driven deep into the ground,
And casemates, too, are hidden everywhere.
Both river-gates by heavy chains are bound
So that no hostile craft may enter there.
Defence is made secure at every point,
At every chink, at every weakest joint.

107

King Pepin's son, like Argos, hundred-eyed,
Foresees where Agramante may attack.
Whatever plan by Saracens be tried,
He has a counter-plan to drive them back.
Marsilio, his captains at his side,
For help and reinforcements does not lack:
Isolier, Serpentino, Ferraù,
Grandonio and Balugante, too,

108

And all the others whom he'd brought from Spain;
Sobrino, Falsirone, Dardinel,
Were further to the left towards the Seine –
Puliano and the giant king as well –
Ah! would that I could equal with my pen
The movement of their flashing swords, or tell
How Rodomonte, in his wrath and scorn,
With curses fills the trembling air of morn.

109

As the sweet leavings from some country meal,
Taken al fresco on hot summer days,
A swarm of importuning flies assail,
Making with strident wings a buzzing haze,
As starlings from the purpling tendrils steal
The ripened grapes, so the besiegers raise
Resounding shouts which deafen all the skies,
And leap to take the Christians by surprise.

110

The Christian army, waiting on the wall
With axes, lances, fire and stones and swords,
Defends the city, fearing not at all
The savagery of the barbaric hordes.
If Death upon some Christian soldier fall,
Another in his place himself affords.
The Moors at first abandon the attack,
By injuries and losses driven back.

111

Not only steel is used: from towers, blocks
Are thrown, and crenellated sections of
The walls are hurled, loosened by frenzied knocks;
And scalding liquid pouring from above
Which with intolerable anguish mocks
The valour of the Moors, who must remove
Themselves or else endure to lose their sight,
For Moorish helmets are not watertight.

112

If these were more injurious than steel,
What of the clouds of quicklime, or the pitch,
The turpentine, the sulphur, or the oil,
Or those incendiary weapons which
Spin round their targets in a flaming wheel?
The Saracens fall back into the ditch,
Vanquished on every side, and many a head
With whirling fire is harshly garlanded.

113

The king of Sarza had arrived by then
Beneath the city walls, accompanied
By fresh platoons of officers and men.
Buraldo and Ormida make all speed;
Clarindo also, likewise Soridan,
With Ceuta's king, stand by in case of need.
Morocco's king and Cosca's follow on,
Knowing that here great glory may be won.

114

The banner of King Rodomonte, gules,
A mighty lion on its ground displays.
A lady with a bridle guides and rules
The king of beasts, which at her touch obeys,
For all it roars; and thus his lady schools
The king of Sarza in more temperate ways,
For Doralice is thus figured there,
Whom Rodomonte loves, as you're aware,

115

She whom King Mandricard, not long ago,
Had stolen and seduced, as I have said,
Whom Rodomonte loved and worshipped so,
To whom as her betrothed he had been wed,
As I narrated; little did he know
His promised bride now shared another's bed.
Had he but known, straightway he would have done
What that same day he did, but later on.

116

Up countless ladders now the pagans swarm.
On every rung they're standing two abreast.
The first have scarce the time to feel alarm,
And those below are urging on the rest.
Thus every man with courage now must arm
And willy-nilly undergo this test.
Woe to the ones who hesitate, for they
Are killed by Sarza's king without delay.

117

And so, between the missiles and the fire,
They scale the smoking walls as-best they can,
Ascending where the peril is least dire.
But Rodomonte, like no other man,
Being filled with superhuman rage and ire,
Where the least safety is, leads on the van;
Where greatest danger is, his wrath the worse is;
And while the others pray, he shouts and curses.

118

His armour, made of ancient dragon-skin,
Descended to him from his ancestor
(Who, though remote, was yet his kith and kin)
Who in the plain of Babel built a tower
To reach the starry realms above and in
His pride challenged God's majesty and power.
Sword, shield and helmet, all without a fault,
Had been constructed for this sole result.

119

Proud as was Nimrod Rodomonte is.
No climb for him could ever be too steep.
At dead of night he'd visit the Abyss,
Or scale the starry heights of Heaven's keep.
What does he care? It's no concern of his
If walls are broken, or the ditch is deep.
He wades, he runs, he flies across the moat,
Immersed in mire up to his very throat.

120

Covered with mud and soaking wet, he lands
Where all around him deadly missiles pour,
Just as one sees amid the marshy strands
Of our Mallea many a wild boar,
Which no frail barrier of reeds withstands
Where'er he lumbers up and down the shore.
On high on his left arm his shield is borne
As forth he clambers, holding all in scorn.

121

No sooner is dry land beneath his feet
Than the besieged have cause to know he's near.
Wedged on the bartisans, where no retreat
Is possible, they see him now appear.
Alas! how many Frenchmen's skulls are split,
And larger tonsures cut than friars wear!
Heads fly before the fury of his blows
And down the wall a crimson river flows.

122

Casting his shield, in both his hands he takes
His cruel sword and with a deadly aim
The Duke Arnolfo strikes (from Holland's lakes
And fens, where the Rhine meets the sea, he came).
The unhappy knight as much resistance makes
As sulphur does before a raging flame.
He falls to earth and none his fall can check,
His skull cleft to a palm below his neck.

123

With an oblique manoeuvre of his blade
Two Normans and two Flemings next he slew:
Spinello, Prando, Anselm and Oldrade.
Upon that crowded ledge, in not a few
With one fell stroke his sword such havoc made
That slaughtered limbs in all directions flew.
Next, turning from the four he had thus slain,
Orghetto of Maganza sliced in twain,

124

Cast Andropono down into the moat
(A priest in holy orders); Moschin followed,
Who for religion did not care a groat.
Wine was his god; it's said he sometimes swallowed
Whole barrels at one gulp, and down his throat
No water went; now in the ditch he wallowed.
What irked him most was not that he should die;
Rather, that water he should perish by.

125

He cuts in two Count Louis of Provence
And splits the breast of Arnald of Toulouse,
Four souls from Tours despatches in advance:
Hubert's and Denis's and Claude's and Hugh's;
Next, four Parisians, renowned through France,
Ambaldo, Odo, Walter, Satal lose
Their lives, and many more who likewise fall,
So many that I cannot name them all.

126

A crowd of followers on ladders soon
Swarm up the wall, some here and others there.
Within, the prudent French from sight are gone,
Their first defence being now beyond repair.
They know the Moors will sing another tune
When they discover what awaits them where
Between the wall and second parapet
A deep and fearful gully has been set.

127

Some stay behind to cover the retreat
And shoot at the invaders from below,
While, from the inner mound, new forces meet
Them, and with lances and with arrows show
How they intend such visitors to greet.
The multitude outside they harass so
It might have turned and fled, had it not been
For Sarza's king, the son of Ulien.

128

Some he exhorts and others reprimands;
Against their will he drives them on ahead,
Cleaves with his sword whoever stops and stands
Or, thinking to escape, dares turn his head.
Many he thrusts or pulls with his own hands,
And by the neck or arms or hair has led,
Until below so many of them fall,
The ditch, it seems, can scarce contain them all.

129

While thus the pagans, spilling o'er the rim,
Rush downwards like a river in full spate
And in that dreadful gully, deep and grim,
In vain are struggling to escape their fate,
As though he has a wing on every limb,
The king of Sarza raises his great weight
And, notwithstanding all the armour which
He carries, nimbly leaps across the ditch.

130

It measured scarcely less than thirty feet,
And yet he cleared it like a hunting hound;
And even more amazing was his feat:
He landed on the slope with no more sound
Than if he'd had soft slippers on his feet.
Once more his sword is flashing all around,
Cutting and slitting armour made of steel
As though it were as soft as bark or peel.

131

Meanwhile the Christians, who with care have made
Their plans, along the bottom of the ditch
Bundles of kindling-wood and sticks have laid,
Covered with plentiful supplies of pitch.
No sign of this was anywhere betrayed,
Nor of the many secret vases which
From top to bottom of the fearful trench
Have been embedded by the cunning French,

132

Containing oil, saltpetre, sulphur and
Whatever fuel was appropriate.
For thus it was the Christian allies planned
To make the Saracens repent, too late,
Their arrogance and folly; close at hand,
The signal they agreed on they await,
And while the pagan army now aspires
To clamber from the ditch, they light the fires.

133

Then many single flames form into one.
From bank to bank the ditch is full of fire.
Its tongue the pallid bosom of the moon
Appears to lick, so high it leaps, and higher.
The pall of smoke obscures the very sun,
Casting a cloak of darkness, black and dire;
Cracks, loud enough to split the earth asunder,
Resound like claps of terrifying thunder.

134

Discordant concert and harsh harmony
Of shrieks and wailing, fearful to relate,
Of anguished victims in their agony,
Led by so great a leader to their fate,
Were mingled in a strange cacophony
With raucous roarings of primeval hate.
My lord, this canto has now run its course,
And I must rest awhile, for I am hoarse.

CANTO XV

1

To win was always deemed a splendid thing,
Whether it be by fortune or by skill.
True, bloody victories less honour bring,
While to eternity the praises will
Resound and all the gods the glory sing
Of the commander who forbears to spill
The blood of his own men, but victory
Costless achieves and routs the enemy.

2

Your victory, my lord, deserved all praise,
When both the margins of the river Po,
From Francolino to the stormy seas,
The Lion held and you then tamed him so
That if his mighty roar he still may raise,
When you are there no terror I shall know.
You showed us how to be victorious:
Death to the enemy and life to us.

3

But this the pagan, daring to excess,
Did not achieve; he drove his soldiers on
Into the dreadful ditch where, merciless,
The greedy flames devoured them, sparing none.
The ditch would scarce have held so great a press,
But that the fire reduced them, one by one,
To charred remains and ashes which less space
Need than the flesh and bones which they replace.

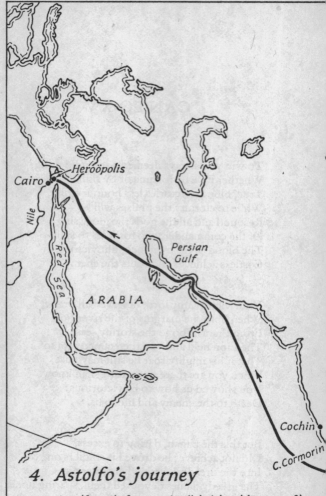

4. Astolfo's journey

Astolfo sails from Logistilla's island (Formosa?)
to the Persian Gulf; then rides through Arabia
to Cairo (Canto XV.12-40)

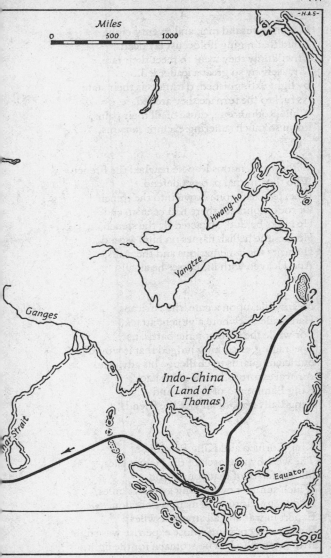

Miles
0   500   1000

-H.A.S-

Hwang-ho

Yangtze

Ganges

Indo-China
(Land of
Thomas)

?

Equator

ar Strait

4

Eleven thousand men and twenty-eight
Amid that raging holocaust lay dead.
Unwillingly they went to meet their fate,
Unwisely by so great a leader led.
By light extinguished, darkness is their state,
As fuel to the furnace they are fed,
While Rodomonte, cause of all their pains,
From so much suffering exempt remains.

5

With a tremendous leap he reached the French
Who the internal parapet defend.
If he, too, had gone down into the trench,
Of rodomontades there had been an end.
He looks behind, attracted by the stench,
He sees the hellish flames on high ascend,
He hears the lamentations and the wails,
And Heaven with his curses he assails.

6

Meanwhile, upon a gate, the Africans
Had made elsewhere a violent attack,
For while the battle on the bartisans
Was raging, their king judged that it would lack
Sufficient guards to challenge his advance.
A royal escort followed at his back:
King Bambirago of Arzilla and
King Baliverzo, of all vice the friend,

7

King Corineo and King Prusion,
The wealthy monarch of the Happy Isles,
Malabuferso, of that country on
Which summer everlasting sweetly smiles,
And many a lord with many a gonfalon,
Expert in war and all strategic wiles;
But some there were whose expertise was slight,
And some who had no stomach for the fight.

8

But the resistance at the gate was more
Than had been looked for by the Africans,
For there, in person, stood the Emperor,
Ugier, the Dane, among his paladins,
King Salamone of the Breton shore,
The Guidos, Gano, both the Angelins,
Duke Namo and his sons: Avolio,
Otto, Avino, Berlingier, who go

9

Together everywhere; of less account,
Innumerable Germans, Lombards, Franks,
Who, in the presence of their monarch, count
To earn his commendation and his thanks.
This battle's outcome elsewhere I'll recount,
For I'm obliged to leave these serried ranks
And hasten back to where the English duke
Now clamours for attention in my book.

10

And that Astolfo may no more be anguished,
I'll take in hand his story once again.
Long in his exile lonely he has languished,
His boon companions yearning to regain;
And Logistilla, who Alcina vanquished,
Thereby once more establishing her reign,
Resolved to send him home without delay
Along the swiftest and the surest way.

11

And to this end a ship was fitted out;
No finer ship had ever sailed the sea.
Queen Logistilla, being in some doubt
Lest he should journey into jeopardy,
Hoping, by this, Alcina's will to flout,
Provided escort and the company
Of temperate Sofròsina and wise
Andrònica, to guide and to advise.

12

Alcina's evil power does not extend
To Persia and Arabia; once there,
Astolfo will be safe; the ship will wend
Along the Scythian shores, then down to where
The Nabateans join the realms of Ind,
Then to the Persian Gulf at last will veer.
The Polar regions being deprived of sun,
This southern route is much the better one.

13

When Logistilla saw that all was well,
She granted the departure of the duke,
But, first of all, before she said farewell,
Some final counselling she undertook
On many things which would be long to tell;
And next, a beautiful and useful book
From all her secret lore she chose and gave him,
Which would henceforth from evil magic save him,

14

Bidding him keep it always at his side
For love of her and for his safety's sake.
The precious volume, written as a guide
Against enchantment, any spell can break.
The cures and counter-spells are classified,
While chapter-headings and the index make
For easy reference. She gives him too
A magic horn, which I'll describe to you.

15

It had so fierce and terrible a sound,
One blast upon it put all men to flight.
No-one in all the world was ever found
Who, having heard it, would then stand and fight.
No tempest's roar, no tremors of the ground,
No thunder could arouse so great a fright.
With many thanks the Englishman then took
His leave, the magic horn and precious book.

16

Leaving the tranquil waters of the port
And with a favourable wind to poop,
He travels on past many a rich resort
And many a busy, teeming city, up
East India's shores where love-sick breezes sport
With the spice-laden air, or languid droop.
A thousand islands stretch to left and right.
At length the land of Thomas comes in sight.

17

Still further north, close to Malacca's coast,
The pilot breasts the Indian ocean's swell;
Hugging those shores, which golden riches boast,
They see the foaming Ganges overspill
Into the main; and to Ceylon almost
They travel and Cape Cormorin as well;
The Mannar Straits and Cochin further on
They see; and soon the Indian coast is gone.

18

Astolfo, with such wisdom at his side,
Then asked what he had long desired to know:
If westward any man had ever tried
Beyond the sunset lands to sail or row,
And reappear upon the eastern side;
And if from India a man might go
By sea and not touch land as much as once
Until in England he arrived, or France.

19

Andrònica this answer gave: 'The seas
Encircle the whole globe in their embrace.
From where the waters boil to where they freeze,
They intermingle and from place to place
They freely ebb and flow without surcease.
But since the continent which we now face
Extends so far beyond the Line, it's said
That Neptune's path is there prohibited.

20

'Thus never vessel from our Indian clime
Set sail for Europe; nor do any say
That mariners, from thence, at any time,
Have dropped their anchor in an eastern bay.
It damps their ardour, howsoe'er sublime,
To find this continent athwart the way;
So long they see it stretching, that they fear
It reaches to the other hemisphere.

21

'But, as the years revolve, behold, I see,
From the far distant regions of the West,
Of Argonauts a brave new company
Who sail along a route as yet unguessed;
Some navigators probe the mystery
Of Africa, and all that coastline test,
Beyond the point of turning, where the sun
Resumes the course six months ago begun.

22

'They travel to the limit of this land
Which makes a single ocean two appear.
They visit every shore and every strand
And all the islands, far away and near.
Still others leave behind, on either hand,
The marks which Hercules set up; from there,
The globe they circle, like the sun, and find
New worlds and new abodes of humankind.

23

'I see the cross raised on the emerald sward;
I see on high the imperial gonfalon.
While some beside the ships remain on guard,
To conquest of the land the rest move on.
Ten from a thousand men claim their reward.
New kingdoms subject are to Aragon.
I see the captains of the Emperor
O'ercoming all, each one a conqueror.

24

'God's will it was that in the ancient days
This path across the globe should be unknown;
And seven centuries must run their phase
Before the mystery to man is shown,
For, in the wisdom of the Almighty's ways,
He waits until the world shall be made one
Beneath an Emperor more just and wise
Than any who since Augustus shall arise.

25

'A prince of Austrian and Spanish blood
Born on the Rhine's left bank, behold, I see:
With valour such as his no valour could
Compare, in legend or in history.
I see Astraea with new power endued,
From death restored to life and victory.
I see the virtues, by the world exiled,
Return in triumph, and all vice reviled.

26

'For valour, whence all other virtues stem,
God wills not only that this Emperor
Shall wear upon his brow the diadem
Which Roman Emperors have worn before,
But, glittering with many a new gem,
His sceptre shall encompass many a shore
Which knows no season but the winter's cold;
And there shall be one shepherd and one fold.

27

'To further His decrees, God will provide
(Decrees ordained to all eternity)
Unconquerable captains at his side,
On land renowned and unsurpassed at sea.
Stout Cortez I behold, who far and wide
New cities under Caesar's majesty
Will bring, and eastern realms so far away,
What realms they are not even we can say.

28

'I see Colonna prosper like his name.
I see the Marquess of Pescara wed
To victory: for Italy they'll claim
A heavy toll of many Frenchmen dead.
And one I see preparing now for fame,
A youth of Vasto, who will race ahead:
The last to leave the starting-post, this horse
Will overtake all others on the course.

29

'So great his zeal, for glory such his lust,
That to Alfonso (for this name he bears)
The Emperor his army will entrust,
Though he is aged but six and twenty years;
Colonna and the marquess being lost,
This youthful captain well with them compares
And under his command the world entire
Will pay obedience to his lord and sire;

30

'Just as, with brave Alfonso's aid on land
His empire Charles will steadfastly augment,
So on that sea he'll gain the upper hand
Which Africa and Europe circumvent.
Andrea Doria, who to every band
Of pirates access yonder will prevent,
Alliance with the Emperor will make
And with imperial might his fortunes stake.

31

'Not Pompey was deserving of such praise.
He cleared that sea of pirates, it is true;
But Roman galleys in those far-off days
Could ram with ease a pirate ship or two.
This Doria in his own strength will raise
Such fear in every caitiff corsair crew,
That from Gibraltar to the river Nile
His name will terror strike in hearts so vile.

32

'I see approaching, under the escort
Of him who thus has earned deserved renown,
The Emperor's ship which safely comes to port,
Whence he will journey to receive the crown.
Andrea spurns reward of any sort,
For when he is presented with the town
Of Genoa, which formerly was free,
He gives his subjects back their liberty.

33

'For the compassion which he thus displays
Much honour and much reverence are due,
For such a deed is worthy of more praise
Than many a glorious battle, old or new,
By Julius Caesar waged in olden days
In France or Spain or in the land where you
Were born, or Africa or Thessaly,
Or by Octavius, or Antony;

34

'For civil war diminishes their fame.
Let all who violate their motherland,
Or liberty enslave, blush red for shame.
With lowered eyelids let them mutely stand
Where men pronounce Andrea Doria's name.
A second gift the Emperor has planned:
Melfi, where Norman barons will hold state
Till all Apulia they dominate.

35

'Not only to this captain will he prove
Magnanimous, but all who serve their lord
With valour and fidelity and love
He will with generosity reward.
The gift of cities, the endowment of
Whole lands to faithful followers afford
More pleasure to this prince, so wise and good,
Than conquest of new empires ever could.'

36

While thus the wise Andrònica foretold
The victories such captains would achieve
When many future ages had unrolled,
Sofròsina her duties did not leave,
But steadfastly the vessel's course controlled.
She'd trim her sails as she could best perceive
The changes in the fluky wind, now east,
Now fresh, now light, but favourable at least.

37

They saw the waters of the Persian bay,
Which from the Maghi took their ancient name,
And, threading through this gulf, without delay,
They entered safely and to harbour came.
Since here the dread Alcina holds no sway,
Astolfo's escort has fulfilled its aim.
He takes his leave of them upon the strand
And on his charger makes his way inland.

38

Through many a field, through many a wood he passed,
Up many a hill, down many a dale, he rode,
And, whether skies were clear or overcast,
Brigands, he knew, were lurking on his road;
Venomous serpents hissed and slithered fast
Across his path, or lions slowly strode;
But every time his magic horn he blew,
His enemies in all directions flew.

39

Felix Arabia his steps explore,
A land of fragrant incense, rich in myrrh,
Which, of all other lands, was chosen for
The phoenix as its home; a sojourner
He there remains till to the Red sea-shore
He comes, where once the waters parted were,
And over Pharaoh and his army closed.
Then Heroöpolis is next disclosed.

40

By the canal of Trajan now he rides
A horse more strange than ever horse has been:
So lightly he steps out, so nimbly strides,
His hoofprints on the sand cannot be seen,
Nor on the grass, nor on the snow besides;
On water he could tread dry-hoofed, and in
His pace, extended, he so swiftly goes,
That lightning, wind, or arrow he outdoes.

41

This is the magic horse which used to bear
Argalìa; of hurricane and flame
Its body is compounded; on pure air
It feeds; and Rabicano is its name.
Astolfo, riding on, arrives at where
Into the Nile the conduit's waters stream.
He has not reached the confluence, when he
Beholds a boat approaching speedily,

42

Steered by a holy hermit in the stern,
Whose silver beard flows half-way down his breast.
Endeavouring to make Astolfo turn
Aside, he calls from far away as best
He can: 'My son, unless you wish to spurn
Your life, if death today is not your quest,
Be pleased to let me ferry you across.
The road you travel leads to mortal loss.

43

'Not more than six miles further on from here,
You'll find a habitation, stained with blood.
A gruesome giant has his dwelling there,
In stature measuring about a rood.
No traveller, nor any cavalier
Alive has ever left that dread abode.
The cruel monster quarters 'em, or strangles 'em,
Or swallows 'em alive, or skins or mangles 'em.

44

'One of his cruel pleasures is a net,
With ingenuity and cunning made.
Close to his evil dwelling it is set
And, hidden in the sand, so subtly laid
That nobody could be aware of it,
Or by more careful steps the trap evade.
Hearing his shouts, his victims run and stumble
And in the dread reticulation tumble.

45

'And with loud roars of glee, the giant then
The draw-strings seizes quickly and pulls tight,
And drags the netted booty to his den.
And whether they be damsel, squire or knight
Of high regard, or simple, common men,
He eats their flesh, their bones casts out of sight,
He relishes their brains and drinks their blood,
And with their pelt adorns his fell abode.

46

'My son, I pray, this other pathway take,
Which will conduct you safely to the sea.'
'Thanks, father, for the offer which you make,'
The cavalier replied courageously,
'But I spurn danger for my honour's sake,
Which dearer than my life I hold to be;
All your persuasions, therefore, are in vain.
The giant's dwelling quickly I must gain.

47

'Myself dishonourably I could save,
But such security I hold in scorn.
Now, if this monster in his lair I brave,
At worst, what many other men have borne
Will be my fate; but, if God's help I have,
And slay the giant and unharmed return,
For thousands I'll have made the way secure.
The benefit outweighs the loss for sure,

48

'If you compare the death of only one
With the security of many more.'
The hermit said: 'Go then in peace, my son.
God send His Michael in support of your
Brave enterprise'; and gave his benison.
Astolfo went his way along the shore
Beside the current of the river Nile,
Trusting his horn more than his sword the while.

49

Between the river and the marshy tract,
Along the sand a little pathway led
Towards a house, which every vestige lacked
Of living inmates, but the balustrade
With many a grisly souvenir was decked:
A naked limb, a torso or a head.
There was no window, battlement or door
That had not, hanging from it, one or more.

50

As in the mountains where snows never melt,
A hunter, who great perils has endured,
Will drape his chalet with a furry pelt,
Or claws or heads of bears he has procured,
Just so this castle where the giant dwelt
Displayed as trophies victims he had lured;
These were the finest specimens; all round,
Blood ran and bones were scattered on the ground.

51

Beside his door Caligorante waits,
For thus the monster, you must know, is called,
Who with the dead his mansion decorates,
As others do with silk, or cloth of gold.
With joy Astolfo's coming he awaits;
For two months now, and nearly three, no bold
And gallant cavalier has passed that way.
The giant thinks this is his lucky day.

52

Towards the marsh which, overgrown with reed,
Stretched dark and menacing beside the track,
Caligorante hurries with all speed,
Intending to emerge behind the back
Of this new victim, as he's done indeed
On previous occasions, when no lack
Of travellers have fallen in his trap,
By Fate drawn on whence there is no escape.

53

Astolfo sees him coming, and his horse
Reins in; his valiant heart is beating fast,
For now he knows that he must choose his course
With care, or in the giant's net be cast.
First to his horn he means to have recourse.
Of this, the sounding of a single blast
Rouses such terror in the monster's heart
That from the marsh he hurries to depart.

54

Astolfo blows his magic horn and tries
To circumvent the trap wherever it
May lie; the fearful sound so terrifies
The giant, on a headlong course now set,
As though, as well as heart, he'd lost his eyes;
A trapper trapped, he falls into the net,
Which round his body twists itself and wraps,
And brings that mighty strength to a collapse.

55

When Duke Astolfo saw that form so vast
Go down inert upon the sandy ground,
Drawing his sword, he galloped up, in haste
To avenge a thousand souls; but when he found
The monster helpless, tied and tethered fast,
The chivalry for which he was renowned
Then stayed his arm: the sight he saw below
So struck him that he could not strike one blow.

56

This was the very net which Vulcan made
Of twisted strands of finest-tempered steel.
No part of it could anyone unbraid,
For every mesh was linked with cunning skill.
A subtle plan, by jealous Vulcan laid
To capture Mars and Venus, it served well:
In flagrant lust he caught the guilty pair,
Bound hand and foot and helpless in the snare.

57

From Vulcan Mercury had stolen it
To catch fair Chloris in Aurora's train,
Who in the early morn comes forth to greet
The sun and scatters the celestial scene
With lilies, roses, violas in sweet
Profusion from her gathered robe; he'd lain
In wait for her until one day he cast
The net upon the air and caught her fast.

58

This capture of the nymph, it seems, occurred
Near where the Nile flows down to meet the sea.
The net was to a temple thence transferred
Where many a sacred rite and mystery
Were solemnized and fervent prayers were heard
To Anubis at Canopus; after three
Millennia were accomplished, with no pity
The giant sacked the temple and the city.

59

He stole the net and made a man-trap, such
That all his prey, of whom there was no lack,
Fell into it; and at the slightest touch
It curled about their feet and arms and neck.
Astolfo seized a chain and in its clutch
He manacled his hands behind his back
And pinioned, too, the monster's arms and chest,
Who could do nothing but the duke's behest.

60

As docile as a maid he stood, the while
Astolfo carefully unwound the net.
His plan is to exhibit him in style
Through every citadel and town; he yet
Desires to keep the snare, for never file
Nor hammer wrought so beautiful a fret.
The giant bows his back, its weight to bear,
Dragged like a captive at a triumph car.

61

Astolfo's shield and helmet too he bore,
As though he were a page; where'er the duke
Appeared, along the road, along the shore,
The joyful crowds of people ran to look.
They knew the dangers now would be no more
Which once poor hapless pilgrims overtook.
Soon now to Memphis, of renown and fame
For all its pyramids, Astolfo came.

62

To teeming Cairo next his steps progress.
The vast proportions of the monster draw
The populace, who round Astolfo press.
'How is it possible,' they ask with awe,
'So large a prisoner and powerless,
The captive of one man?' And all who saw
The cavalier his valour much admired
And paid him homage more than he required.

63

The Cairo of those days was of less size
Than in our times the city's said to be,
When eighteen thousand zones cannot comprise
The populace in its entirety,
When crowded houses, treble-tiered, arise
And, notwithstanding an infinity
Of homeless destitute, the Sultan dwells
In sumptuously furnished marble halls.

64

And all of fifteen thousand servitors
(And every one a Christian renegade)
Are housed beneath one roof, with room for horse,
For kith and kin, to the last man and maid.
Astolfo wants to trace the river's course
As far as to Damietta, where it's said
Whoever is so rash to travel there
Is put to death or taken prisoner.

65

Hard by the estuary of the Nile
A robber has his stronghold in a tower,
And all the people round, for many a mile,
As far as Cairo, victims of his power,
Are terrorized; no one, by force or guile,
This brigand can resist, and every hour
The menace grows; no weapon seems to stay him;
A hundred thousand wounds have failed to slay him.

66

Astolfo's minded to discover if
He can induce the Fate to cut the thread
And put an end to fell Orrilo's life
(For that's his name). He travels towards the dread
Domain, beyond Damietta; on a cliff
Beside the sea it stands, inhabited
By that enchanted offspring of a sprite
And of a fairy, born to do men spite.

67

He finds a cruel battle raging there
Between Orrilo and two warriors.
The robber, single-handed, fights the pair,
Who in the combat seem to come off worse.
Yet for their skill they're famous everywhere,
A reputation which their deeds endorse –
Two cavaliers who valour do not lack,
Grifon the white and Aquilant the black,

68

The sons of Oliver. It's true, their foe
A great advantage had: a savage beast
Of fierce appearance he had brought in tow.
Such animals live only in the East,
Along the banks which border the Nile's flow.
For daily food on human flesh they feast,
And always there's a plentiful supply
Of hapless sailors and of passers-by.

69

This creature near the port was lying dead,
Slain by the brothers on the sandy shore.
With no unchivalry, it must be said,
Can they be charged if two, as heretofore,
Fight against one. They slash his limbs, his head,
But every sword-stroke leaves him as before,
And if an arm or hand or leg he lacks,
He sticks it on again, as it were wax.

70

Down to his teeth Grifone splits his skull
And Aquilante splits it to his chest;
On him such mortal blows are void and null.
He laughs: the sons of Oliver are vexed.
If anyone that silver has seen fall,
Named mercury by the sage alchemist,
And watched its globules hasten to rejoin,
Let him compare it with this tale of mine.

71

Off comes his head: straightway Orrilo bends
And till he's found it he'll not cease to grope.
Now by the nose and now by the hair's ends,
He catches hold of it and picks it up,
And joins it to his neck. Grifone sends
It to the river-bottom with a plop:
Orrilo, like a fish, swims after it
And re-emerges once again complete.

72

Two ladies, elegant and fair to see,
One wearing black, the other dressed in white,
The cause of this ferocious enmity,
Stood looking on at the heroic fight.
The brothers they had reared from infancy,
When by their magic arts from a sad plight
They rescued them as they were borne away,
Clutched in the talons of two birds of prey.

73

From sad Gismonda snatched, they soared on high
And from their native country soon were gone.
But there is no necessity that I
Should here relate a tale that is well known,
Although the author of the story, by
Some strange mischance, I know not how, I own,
Says Ricciardetto and not Oliver
Their father was (but I do not concur).

74

Egypt no longer knew the light of day,
While western regions were still blessed with noon,
And shadows now conspired to hide away
What yet was glimpsed beneath a fitful moon.
Orrilo had already left the fray,
For both the sisters deemed it not too soon
To bring the cruel combat to a close
Until the sun on the horizon rose.

75

The duke had recognized the knights at once
By their insignia and, even more,
The lusty strokes they gave with sword and lance.
He joyfully embraced them on the shore,
And they, for their part, when they saw advance
That baron who the name of Leopard bore
(For thus at court the duke was always known),
No less delight at meeting him had shown.

76

The ladies now conduct the cavaliers
Towards a fair domain where they may rest.
A bevy of attendants soon appears,
With flaming torches, walking four abreast.
Some take their horses, some their swords and spears
(Such courtesy they show to every guest).
Reaching a fountain in a garden, where
A meal awaits them in the open air,

77

Astolfo and the brothers first secure
The captive giant by a second chain
Fixed to an oak-tree, hoping to make sure
That by no means he would break loose again.
A ten-fold guard they manage to procure
For fear, if their precautions prove in vain,
The monster may attack and do them harm
While they repose, suspecting no alarm.

78

Beside the limpid fountain down they sat
To an abundant, sumptuous repast.
The least of all their joys was what they ate.
Their time in pleasurable converse passed.
Orrilo they discussed at length, for that
The topic was which held them first and last.
A miracle to them his exploits seem
And, one and all, they wonder if they dream.

79

Astolfo in his magic book has read
That such enchanted monsters never die
Until one hair is plucked from off their head.
Their souls will then depart, howe'er they try
To battle for their life, and leave them dead.
On this Astolfo knows he can rely,
But yet he wonders how and when and where
To find one fatal strand in so much hair.

80

The victor's palm he savours none the less,
As if already he were crowned with it,
And with one stroke he'd cut the magic tress
And from the monster's trunk his soul had split.
He relishes the task with eagerness,
But first he asks the brothers, as is fit,
If on his shoulders he alone may bear
A weight which proved too heavy for the pair.

81

They willingly resign the task to him,
Convinced his efforts will be all in vain.
The sun had kindled the horizon's rim
When down Orrilo strode on to the plain.
Between him and the duke a combat grim
And terrible began; with might and main,
One with a club, the other with his blade,
More than a thousand deadly thrusts they made.

82

Orrilo's fist is severed, club and all;
Both arms Astolfo chops, complete with hands.
Now with a transverse stroke, now vertical,
He slices and truncates and flying sends
Orrilo's limbs; but whereso'er they fall,
He picks them up and instantly their ends
Re-join the parent stump and so once more
His members function as they did before.

83

The duke, dismounted, after many blows,
Slashes Orrilo through from nape to chin;
And quickly, for he has no time to lose,
He leaps back to the saddle, grasping in
His hand the bloody scalp, on which there grows
The magic hair which he must pluck to win.
He gallops off towards the river Nile,
To stop Orrilo finding it; meanwhile,

84

The stupid monster had not understood
And in the dust was groping for his head;
But when he realized that through the wood
The Duke Astolfo on his horse had sped,
He flung himself as quickly as he could
Upon the saddle of his thoroughbred.
He would have liked to shout: 'Come back! Come back!'
But of his mouth he felt a grievous lack.

85

At least Astolfo has not got his heels,
So to his horse Orrilo claps his spurs;
But Rabicano very soon reveals
A burst of speed which marks a wonder-horse.
Meanwhile Astolfo with his fingers feels
Along the scalp to see if in due course
That single magic hair discerned can be
Which gives Orrilo immortality.

86

Among all those innumerable hairs
There is not one which longer grows or twists.
How can Astolfo find the one which bears
That magic property? Yet he persists
And, since he neither razor has, nor shears
(On which no code of chivalry insists),
He takes his sharp-edged sword and with it cuts,
Nay, rather, shaves those tresses to the roots.

87

The gruesome head he dangles by the nose
And puts his skill at shearing to the test.
By chance he cuts the magic hair which grows
Quite indistinguishable from the rest.
The pallid face, its eyes asquint, now shows
By every sign Orrilo has gone west.
The torso, following the severed head,
Had tumbled from the saddle and lay dead.

88

To where the knights and ladies were the duke
Returned again; Orrilo's head, which bore
Authentic signs of his demise, he took
To show to them, their spirits to restore,
And at the corpse invited them to look
Which lay not far away upon the shore.
On him a smiling face the brothers turned,
But inwardly, perhaps, with envy burned.

89

I do not think the two protectresses
Were pleased to hear the outcome of the fight,
For they were hoping that the war would cease
Before that destiny and tragic plight
Of both the brothers, which from prophecies,
They knew, would be fulfilled, if, as was right,
They went to the defence of Charlemagne,
As now they must, Orrilo being slain.

90

No sooner was Damietta's governor
Assured Orrilo's life was truly fled,
Than he released a feathered messenger
Which bore beneath its wing, secured by thread,
A letter to the Caliph, and from there,
As is their way, a second bird was sped.
Now here, now there, the happy tidings flew
And very soon the whole of Egypt knew.

91

To bring the matter to a fitting end,
The duke exhorted both the noble sons
Of Oliver to come with him and lend
Their strong right arms as loyal champions
Of Holy Church, and valiantly defend
The Roman Empire; they desire at once
To leave the East and win an honoured place
Among the armies of their creed and race.

92

And so the sons of Oliver take leave
Of the two sisters, who with deep regret,
But resignation, their farewells receive.
Their journey on a right-hand course is set,
For they intend to visit, ere they leave
For France, the Holy Places where the feet
Of God Incarnate walked, and humbly pay
Each his devotion where the pilgrims pray.

93

There is a left-hand route to Palestine
Which smoother is and more agreeable,
Hugging the coast in an unbroken line;
But they approached the lofty citadel
Along the right, where many a wild ravine
And rugged impasse lay, for, they'd heard tell,
That route was shorter by six days or so.
Apart from grass and mountain streams that flow,

94

No sustenance can they expect to find.
For this they make provision in advance.
Their bundles on the giant's back they bind.
So great his strength and so robust his stance,
He'd bear the tower of Babel and not mind.
At length the Holy City met their glance,
Where the Supernal Love and Highest Good
Our errors washed with His own precious Blood.

95

Hard by the entrance to the city gate,
They met a knight from Mecca whom they knew.
Still in the flower of youth, named Sansonet,
Prudent beyond his years and famous, too,
For chivalry, to the unfortunate
Great clemency he showed. Orlando to
Our faith converted him, with his own hand
Baptizing him, and brought him to this land.

96

Plans for a fort they find him superintending,
Against the Egyptian Caliph, high and strong.
The Mount of Calvary he was intending
By ramparts to protect some two miles long.
He turned towards the travellers, extending
The courtesy and friendship which belong
To chivalry; himself as their escort,
He bade them welcome in his royal court.

97

He ruled Jerusalem in Charles's stead
And justly kept the Holy Empire's laws.
Caligorante, whom Astolfo led,
Of terror far and wide so long the cause
And now a humble beast of burden made
Which crowds of curious spectators draws,
The duke desires to give to Sansonet
In token of his friendship, with the net.

98

And in return, a baldric, rich and fair,
He gives the duke, his trusty sword to hold,
And, as the custom is, a costly pair
Of spurs, with clasp and rowel of bright gold,
Which the brave dragon-slayer used to wear
Who rescued the princess in days of old.
These treasures Sansonetto had received
When he took Jaffa, so it is believed.

99

Some days in penance in a monastery
They duly spend; then pass to contemplate
Christ's Passion and its every mystery
In all the churches, which the Turks of late,
To our eternal shame and contumely,
With their usurping presence desecrate,
While Europe blazes, everywhere at war,
Except where Christian arms most needed are.

100

While thus their minds on sacred things were set,
On prayers intent and holy thoughts alone,
A traveller from Greece one day they met
Who to the young Grifone was well known.
He gave him news which all his plans upset.
His vows, his aspirations soon were flown,
And such a passion in his bosom kindled,
To nothing all his good intentions dwindled.

101

His heart, alas!, unwisely was bestowed
Upon a lady, Orrigille named,
Who more than any woman else e'er wooed,
Though for her grace and beauty she was famed,
With evil and deceit was so imbued
That nowhere could her equal be acclaimed,
Though numberless explorers you might send
To search the whole world through from end to end.

102

He'd left Constantinople, where she lay
Sick of a fever; there, his duties over,
He'd vowed to visit her again one day.
But little time she needed to recover,
And now to Antioch she'd gone away,
Accompanied by some new rival lover.
For she, a woman in the bloom of youth,
No more could bear to sleep alone, in truth.

103

No sooner had he heard the grievous news
Than day and night Grifone sighed and sighed.
All consolations such as others choose
Failed to relieve his pain or soothe his pride.
Such piercing arrows Love is wont to use,
As all who ever loved have testified.
His keenest woe, the sharpest of them all,
Is that his grief he is ashamed to tell.

104

At least a thousand times and many more
His brother, Aquilante, has reproved him.
He wisely deemed unwise the love he bore
And tried to rid him of it, for he loved him.
To him she seemed no better than a whore;
He duly warned Grifone, as behoved him.
But every time the lover finds excuses,
For passion his discernment thus confuses.

105

And so he planned that he would now depart
And go without a word to Antioch
Whence Orrigille, who had plucked his heart
From out his breast, he now would surely pluck;
And in revenge make her seducer smart
Till all the world with rumour of it rock.
This plan and what its consequences were
To the next canto I must now defer.

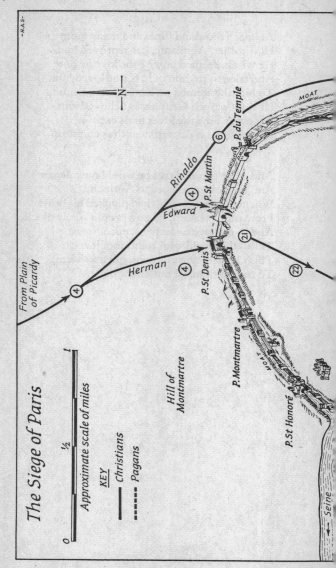

The Siege of Paris

KEY

Christians

Pagans

Approximate scale of miles

0   ½   1

Hill of Montmartre

From Plain of Picardy

Herman

Edward

Rinaldo

P. St Denis

P. St Martin

P. du Temple

MOAT

P. Montmartre

P. St Honoré

MOAT

Seine

475

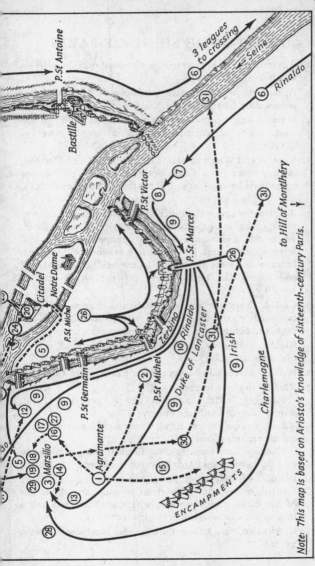

Note: This map is based on Ariosto's knowledge of sixteenth-century Paris.

(See key overleaf.)

KEY TO THE SIEGE OF PARIS

1. Agramante and African troops stationed outside walls on south-west. (xiv. 105)

2. Agramante attacks a gate, probably St Michel, and is repulsed by Charlemagne. (xv. 6–9; xvi. 17)

3. Marsilio and Spanish troops are outside walls, to the west, north of Agramante. Rodomonte is near by. (xiv. 108)

4. English and Welsh troops, led by Edward and Herman, having come from Calais across the Plain of Picardy, enter Paris by the gates of St Martin and St Denis. (xvi. 30)

5. Rodomonte scales the outer walls, plunges into the wet moat, clambers out, drives troops down into inner ditch, where they are burned to death; jumps over ditch and scales inner mound. Having slain a number of defenders, he runs along the river-bank to the bridge of St Michel and enters the citadel. (xiv. 116–30; xv. 3–5; xvi. 19–27)

6. Rinaldo leads the rest of the British forces and allies eastwards round the northern walls, then south. They cross the Seine three leagues upstream. (xvi. 29–31)

7. Rinaldo harangues troops on a knoll of ground, east of the walls. (xvi. 32)

8. Rinaldo moves allied forces closer to the walls. (xvi. 40)

9. Rinaldo deploys forces:
    Zerbino, leading Scottish troops, on right hand, moves west towards the enemy;
    Irish troops, on left hand, move south-west to attack enemy encampments;
    Duke of Lancaster, leading English troops, takes the middle route, westwards towards the enemy. (xvi. 40)

10. Rinaldo himself rides along the route taken by the Scottish troops and passes them, to encounter the forces of Marbalusto and Sobrino, which are stationed half a mile north of the Spanish troops. (xvi. 41)

11. Rinaldo attacks, killing Puliano and Marbalusto. (xvi. 43–50)

12. The pagan vanguard having fled after Rinaldo's attack, Zerbino leads Scottish forces in pursuit. Sobrino and Dardinello lead their forces to halt him. (XVI. 51–4)

13. Duke of Lancaster attacks Spanish forces. (XVI. 66)

14. Ferraù counter-attacks English forces. (XVI. 71)

15. Agramante sends king of Fezzan south to attack Irish forces. (XVI. 76)

16. Agramante leads his troops north to help Sobrino against the Scots. (XVI. 78)

17. Zerbino having been unhorsed, his troops are fleeing. Rinaldo rallies them and enables Zerbino to remount. (XVI. 78–82)

18. Agramante arrives and joins Dardinello in attack against the Scots. (XVI. 83)

19. Rinaldo attacks Agramante and brings down both rider and horse. (XVI. 84)

20. Rodomonte sets fire to the citadel. (XVI. 85)

21. Charlemagne welcomes Edward and Herman, who entered Paris from the north. (XVI. 85)

22. Charlemagne is summoned from the north section of Paris to the citadel. (XVI. 86)

23. Rodomonte is attacked by Charlemagne and Frankish paladins. (XVII. 16)

24. Rodomonte jumps into the Seine at west end of Île de la Cité. (XVIII. 21–3)

25. Rodomonte wades ashore on south-west bank. (XVIII. 24)

26. Charlemagne deploys his forces:
    troops sent to guard the south walls, from Porte St Germain in west to Porte St Victor in east;
    gives orders for regiments to be drawn up on plain outside Porte St Marcel. (XVIII. 38–9)

27. Battle between Agramante and Scots still raging, Rinaldo supporting Zerbino. (XVIII. 40)

28. Charlemagne attacks Spanish forces in rear. (XVIII. 41)

29. Rinaldo slays Dardinello. (XVIII. 146–53)

30. Spanish and Africans retreat to encampments. (XVIII. 156–8)

31. Some enemy troops scatter on plain south of Porte St Marcel; some are drowned in the Seine. (XVIII. 159)

CANTO XVI

1

Of all the many grievous pains of love
I have myself endured the greater part.
So vivid is the recollection of
My pangs, that on this theme I am expert.
So, when I write, as in my verse above,
Or when I speak, of matters of the heart,
Calling some sorrows anguish, others slight,
You may believe my judgement to be right.

2

I say, have said, will say while yet I live,
Whoever in a noble noose is caught,
Although his lady may but ill receive
His ardour and thus render him distraught,
And no reward for his devotion give,
Whence all his time and labour come to naught,
Yet, if his heart be worthily bestowed,
No lamentation to his grief is owed.

3

That lover has good reason to lament
Who falls a captive to the hair and eyes
Of one who in her heart, as hard as flint,
Conceals impurity, deceit and lies.
To flee her is the wretched man's intent,
But like a wounded stag, where'er he flies,
He cannot shake the arrow loose, and feels
Ashamed to own a wound which never heals.

4

This is the young Grifone's very case.
His error he perceives but cannot break.
He knows the object of his love is base,
Who nothing gives, but, thankless, all will take.
No use of reason can his soul release.
His appetite is strong, his will is weak.
Perfidious she is without a doubt,
And yet he is compelled to seek her out.

5

The story now resuming once again,
I say he left the city secretly,
Nor did he tell his brother, who in vain
Had tried to cure him of his malady;
And, turning left, descending to the plain
By a well-trodden route to Rama, he
Approached Damascus, in six days or so,
Then on to Antioch prepared to go.

6

But near Damascus he beheld the knight
Who Orrigille's faithless heart had won.
In all their evil ways these two are quite
Birds of a feather; honour they have none,
In pleasures of the moment they delight,
In nothing can they be relied upon.
And skilfully they mask their perfidy,
All men deceiving by their courtesy.

7

The cavalier I speak of is astride
A splendid charger; Orrigille too
Is mounted on a palfrey at his side,
Wearing a costly robe of gold and blue.
Two pages, bearing shield and helmet, ride
Near by; with so much pomp and retinue
You'd think that very day at least he must
Intend to make his entrance in a joust.

8

Indeed, the king a festive celebration
Has recently announced; all cavaliers,
Clad and accoutred as befits their station,
Have been invited; as Grifone nears,
Great is false Orrigille's consternation.
Reproaches and abuse she rightly fears.
She knows her lover has not strength to match
Grifone, who could soon destroy the wretch.

9

The brazen hussy, cunning as could be,
Though all a-tremble yet from head to foot,
Mastered her voice to speak composedly
And on her face a brave expression put.
No sign of fear could anybody see.
Her plan, agreed beforehand, was astute.
She ran towards Grifone, arms flung wide,
And clasped his neck, and hung upon his side.

10

Then, suiting loving gestures to her words,
With sweet and winsome ways, and weeping too,
She said, 'My lord, are these the just rewards
For one who so adores and worships you?
Your absence of a year but ill accords
With promises you made. What could I do?
For had I waited there for your return
I doubt if I should be alive this morn.

11

'To joust in Nicosia you were gone.
Although my very life hung by a thread,
You left me there to languish all alone,
Sick of a fever, tossing on my bed.
They told me then that you had travelled on
To Syria; all hope, alas! was fled.
Disconsolate, despairing and distressed,
I all but plunged a dagger in my breast.

12

'But Fortune had compassion on my pain,
(You, having none, had left me to lament)
And doubly now her care of me makes plain:
For first my brother to my aid she sent,
And now she brings you back to me again,
Replacing all my longing by content.
I should have died if you had not returned,
So ardently with love for you I burned.'

13

As specious and as cunning as a fox,
She tells a tale as false as it is lame;
And she contrives, so innocent she looks,
To make Grifone think he is to blame.
Her lover, who is party to the hoax,
He takes to be related, of the same
Father even; the lying web she weaves,
As if it were the Gospel, he believes.

14

Not only no reproaches does he make,
Although more treacherous she is than fair,
Not only no just vengeance does he take
Upon his rival, her adulterer;
He has to answer for his honour's sake
The many charges she now brings to bear,
And to the knight all courtesy extends,
As if they truly brothers were and friends.

15

He journeys with him to Damascus gate
And by him, as they ride along, is told
Of the festivity and splendid state
The wealthy king of Syria will hold,
In which all visitors participate.
Whate'er their race, whatever faith they hold,
Whate'er their rank or standing, he requests
While he keeps open court they'll be his guests.

16

No further now this story I'll pursue
Of the false Orrigille's perfidy,
Who to so many lovers proved untrue,
Of her betrayals an infinity
I could recount; but I'll return with you
To Paris and resume the history
Of twice one hundred thousand men-at-arms
Who ring the city round with war's alarms.

17

As numerous as flying sparks they seemed
Arising from a bonfire newly stirred.
You will recall King Agramante deemed
A certain gate (in this his aides concurred)
Would be unguarded, and he little dreamed
To see King Charles in person, as you heard,
With both the Guidos, Otto, Angeliero,
The Angelins, Avino, Berlingiero,

18

Avolio, the leaders of his host.
Both armies, in the presence of their kings,
Desired to show forth to the uttermost
The daring which reward and glory brings.
The pagans, who so many men had lost,
No danger heeded in their reckonings,
But in the folly of their exploits vied
With all the many thousands who had died.

19

The arrows from the ramparts fall like hail
Upon the pagan enemy below,
And piercing shrieks the sky with fear assail,
Arising from the Christians and their foe.
But let both kings now wait upon my tale,
To sing of Rodomonte I must go,
That Moorish Mars, so fierce and terrible,
Who rushes through the stricken citadel.

20

I do not know, my lord, if you recall
This Saracen who menaces the French,
Who led his soldiers from the outer wall
And drove them down into the second trench,
Where they were burned to ashes one and all,
A sight to cause the blackest heart to blench.
I said how he had vaulted with one bound
Across the ditch which ringed the city round.

21

When it is known that Saracen is close
Whose coat of mail is made of dragon's skin,
The sick, the agèd, the less bellicose
To shriek and wail and beat their palms begin,
And so vociferous the clamour grows,
The very stars re-echo with the din,
And all who can escape without delay
In houses, churches, hide themselves away.

22

His cruel sword the Saracen rotates
And few there are he does not leave for dead.
A foot with half a leg he here truncates,
There from a torso spins a severed head.
He splits them to their haunches from their pates,
Or cuts them clean across with transverse blade.
Of all he kills or wounds or seeks to chase,
Not one delays to look him in the face.

23

A hungry tiger leaping at the throats
Of helpless cattle on the Persian plain,
A wolf among a flock of sheep or goats
Upon the mountain under which in vain
Typhoeus struggles, savagery denotes
Equal to his; no serried ranks of men
His victims are, but merest *hoi polloi*,
Unfit a knight's attention to employ.

24

Nobody's face he sees, of all the ones
He kills or wounds; along a road which leads
Towards the bridge of St Michel he runs,
Raging, red-handed from his dreadful deeds,
Whom everyone throughout the city shuns.
His cruel sword no rank or standing heeds.
To man or master no regard he pays,
The just and the unjust alike he slays.

25

No sanctuary now can save the priest,
No innocence protect the little child,
No woman's beauty move him to desist,
No rosy cheeks, no glances sweet and mild;
The old are slain in fury unappeased.
By cruelty his valour is defiled,
For, blind and undiscerning in his rage,
He is deterred by neither sex nor age.

26

Not only people does this fiend destroy,
This chief, this lord, this very king of crimes;
Himself on fire with an unholy joy,
A blaze which to the roofs and steeples climbs
He kindles, till the city burns like Troy,
For it was built of wood in bygone times,
As houses are in Paris to this day,
At least six out of ten, so people say.

27

The flames demolish each and every thing,
But this is not enough to vent his ire.
He clambers up wherever he can cling,
To smash the roof-tops down into the fire.
At Padua you saw besiegers fling
No mortar-bombs so terrible and dire
As Rodomonte is, who with one shake
So long and high and wide a wall can break.

28

While there that cursèd demon havoc made
With fire and sword, if Agramant outside
Had carried through his purpose to invade,
All Christians in the city then had died;
But this catastrophe events forbade,
For Scots and English forces, side by side,
Led by Rinaldo, under Michael's care,
Came up to take the pagans unaware.

29

As God had willed, while in the citadel
Occurred those dread events which I have sung,
By Silence aided, underneath the wall
Rinaldo had assembled all his throng.
Above the city, some three leagues in all,
They'd crossed the Seine and snaked their way along
The left-hand bank from where they would attack;
The river, therefore, would not hold them back.

30

Six thousand archers of the infantry,
Which noble Edward's splendid banner led,
Two or more thousand of light cavalry,
With valiant Herman riding at their head,
By northern routes (which lead through Picardy)
Were previously by Rinaldo sped,
By St Denis' and by St Martin's gate
To bring relief before it was too late.

31

The impedimenta and the baggage-train
He likewise sent along this nearer route,
And all the other forces which remain,
The archers and the horsemen and the foot,
He brought a long way round to cross the Seine,
By pontoon bridges or by ferry-boat.
When all had crossed, the bridges he destroyed,
And Scots and English in their lines deployed.

32

But first he gathered all his captains round
And, moving towards the river bank near by,
He stood upon a knoll of rising ground
Where he could be observed by every eye,
And every word in every heart resound:
'Lift up your hands in thanks to God on high
Who now in a brief hour of toil and sweat
Sublime renown as recompense has set.

33

'By you, two monarchs will be saved, if you
Will enter by those gates and raise the siege:
Your king, to whom your loyalty is due,
Whom to defend and serve, *noblesse oblige*;
Your Emperor, in all the Empire through,
In all the world, your highest lord and liege;
And other kings and dukes and marquesses,
And lords and knights whose fate in peril is.

34

'By rescuing this city from its plight,
Not only will you save its citizens,
Who for their wives and children keener fright
Experience than fear for their own skins,
For to the weak that rabble no respite
Will show when once the massacre begins;
And virgins who have taken sacred vows
Will suffer outrage in God's holy house.

35

'But, rescuing the city, as I said,
You'll save not only the inhabitants
But all who to the citadel have fled.
From all the many provinces of France,
From every town in Christendom are sped,
Fleeing before the Infidel's advance,
So many from so many nations who
Will owe undying gratitude to you.

36

'In ancient times they gave a hero's crown
To whosoever saved the life of one
Of Rome's proud citizens; now what renown
Will you deserve, who'll save not one alone,
But countless multitudes in this one town?
But if this sacred task remains undone,
If cowardice and sloth now hold you back,
Who will be free from danger of attack?

37

'I say not Italy, not Germany,
Nor any Christian country I could name.
Think not because you dwell beyond the sea
You will be safe; your fate will be the same.
Your kingdom also is in jeopardy.
If from Gibraltar Moorish pirates came
To raid your islands in marauding bands,
What will they do once they possess our lands?

38

'But if no honour, no self-interest
Should animate you for this enterprise,
Our duty is to succour when oppressed
Those whom the Church in one cause unifies.
Let no man harbour fear within his breast
That I shall fail to take them by surprise,
For surely I shall rout them easily.
Ill-armed and spiritless they seem to me.'

39

Thus did Rinaldo with much eloquence,
In clear and ringing tones which heavenwards rose,
Stiffen the mettle of the regiments
And make the captains still more bellicose,
Spurring with these and other arguments
A willing charger, as the saying goes;
And when he had concluded his harangue,
Silence, who came to help him (as I sang),

40

Enabled him to move without a sound
His triple army closer to the wall.
Upon Zerbino, on the right-hand ground,
The honour of attacking first would fall.
The Irish to the left, a long way round
He sent, and in between he stationed all
The English troops, led by Lancaster's duke,
Then silently his own position took.

41

Riding along the bank where he had sent
Zerbino to his post beside the Seine,
He passed the Scottish troops and onward went
To where the king of Oran and his train
With King Sobrino's forces were intent,
A half a mile or so from those of Spain,
On keeping careful watch upon that side
O'er all that territory vast and wide.

42

But not a single forager or scout
Had heard the silent troops assemble there.
Eager to put the Infidel to rout,
The Christian army could not now forbear
To burst upon their foe; they raised a shout
And with the sound of trumpets split the air;
And such a pandemonium arose
That in the pagans' bones the marrow froze.

43

Rinaldo spurred his charger on ahead,
His lance in rest, in readiness to strike.
A bowshot's length away he soon was sped,
Such his impatience was, such his dislike
Of all delay; as when the sky o'erspread
With lowering clouds, sends forth a cyclone like
A harbinger of tempest, so the knight,
Spurring Baiardo, heralded the fight.

44

This coming of the paladin of France
Gives warning to the Moors of future woes.
All hands are shaking, trembling every lance;
Feet climb to stirrups, thighs to saddle-bows.
One king alone maintains a haughty glance:
Puliano, who Rinaldo little knows.
Heading towards a combat fell and grim,
He gallops off full pelt to challenge him.

45

He spurs with both his rowels and intense
Over his lance he crouches for the kill,
And from his hands he drops the slackened reins,
Letting his gallant charger have its will.
His valour is, moreover, no pretence,
And neither is the artistry or skill,
Acquired in many jousts and many wars
By Aymon's son, nay, by the son of Mars.

46

It seemed each knight a parity of blows
Delivered then upon the other's head;
But this was not the case, the sequel shows,
For one rode on, the other was struck dead.
The harsh realities of war impose
More searching tests of valour, be it said,
Than grace and style; and fortune too is needed,
Without which valour seldom has succeeded.

47

Rinaldo reacquires his trusty spear
And levels it at Oran's giant king.
Though well endowed in bulk he may appear,
His heart is but a poor and worthless thing.
In prowess he is not Rinaldo's peer,
And yet the deed is worth the chronicling.
A blow upon his shield Rinaldo fetches,
Low down, because his arm no higher reaches.

48

The shield did not withstand the mighty stroke –
Though steel without and toughest wood within –
Which through the giant's massive belly broke.
His soul departed, puny, weak and thin.
The horse, so overburdened, gladly shook
Its haunches free of such a weight, and in
Surprise at its relief, and gratitude,
It would have thanked Rinaldo if it could.

49

His lance being broken, he now turns his horse,
So light of foot on wings it seems to pass,
And where the combat thicker is and worse
He flings himself amid the seething mass,
Staining Fusberta with the blood of Moors,
Shattering weapons as though fragile glass.
No tempered steel resists Rinaldo's slashes,
As into living flesh he hews and gashes.

50

And yet few arms of steel this cutting blade
Clashed with, few metal bucklers could it find,
But shields of oak, or else of leather made,
Gipons, and wrappings such as pagans wind
About their heads; small wonder, as he laid
About him, like the corn before the wind,
Like grass beneath a sickle, down they dropped
As everywhere Rinaldo slashed and lopped.

51

No sooner is the pagan vanguard fled
Than Prince Zerbino and his troops advance.
With pennon fluttering, he rides ahead,
His courage high, in readiness his lance.
His men-at-arms, by such a leader led,
Ride proudly forth on steeds which proudly prance.
Like lions or like wolves they seem which leap
Upon a helpless flock of goats or sheep.

52

Then all together spurred their horses on,
As soon as they drew near, and straight away
The space between opposing ranks was gone.
Both armies then were merged in a mêlée,
The strangest any had set eyes upon:
Only the Scottish troops drew blood that day,
Only the pagans fell, as if their aim
Were dying and such dying were no shame.

53

Colder than ice the Moorish hearts appear,
While every Scot is like a raging flame.
Rinaldo has so frightened them, they fear
That every Christian's arm must be the same;
But King Sobrino brings his forces near,
Not waiting to be heralded by name.
His squadron has more valour than the first,
For glory and revenge a keener thirst.

54

This squadron was the least to be despised
Of all the many troops of Africa.
Next, Dardinello's forces, ill-advised,
Ill-armed and ineffectual in war,
For all the panoply, so greatly prized,
And shining helmet which their leader wore.
The squadron which Isolier led forth
Was, I believe, in size and strength the fourth.

55

Meanwhile Trasone, the good Duke of Mar,
Rejoicing in the noble enterprise,
His knights from combat will no more debar,
Now that he sees before his very eyes
Isolier's ruthless forces from Navarre
Moving apace, and hears their battle-cries.
Then Ariodante, Duke of Albany
(Newly created), moves his company.

56

The clamour of the strident clarions,
The tambours and the Moorish instruments,
The whirr of slings, the clattering of stones,
The twang of bow-strings, divers implements
And war-machines, the catapults, the groans,
The shrieks, the ululation, the laments
Combine to form as deafening a roar
As the Nile's cataracts, or even more.

57

A shadow covers all the sky around,
So dark the cloud of arrows which ascends.
The breath and sweat, combined with dust, compound
A turbid mist which over all impends.
One side moves up, another, losing ground,
Alternately advances and defends,
And where you see one dying soldier lie,
Another he has slain lies stretched near by.

58

As one platoon withdraws, with many dead,
Another in its place at once is seen.
Some, fully armed, move up with heavy tread;
There infantry, here cavaliers close in.
The earth beneath their feet is dappled red;
To crimson now the grass has changed from green;
Where once the plain was starred with blue and gold,
Horses and knights are lying, dead and cold.

59

The Prince Zerbino an example showed
Of prowess marvellous in one so young:
He cut and slashed, he lopped and sliced and mowed,
Thinning the ranks of the opposing throng.
Next, Ariodante with high courage rode,
Newly promoted captain, and among
The forces of Navarre and of Castile
He scattered terror with his flashing steel.

60

Chelind and Mosco, the two bastard sons
Of Calabruno, Aragon's late king,
For skill and daring famed among the Dons,
And young Calamidor, in duelling
The first of Barcelona's paragons,
Had left the standards far behind to fling
Themselves together on Zerbino's horse,
Which fell to earth beneath their three-fold force.

61

The horse, speared by three lances, lifeless falls;
But on his feet Zerbino is not slow
To seek out those who played his steed so false
And punish so unchivalrous a blow.
First Mosco, the incautious, he forestalls,
Who, mounted, fears no danger from below.
Zerbino spears the bastard in mid flight
And flings him from the saddle, cold and white.

62

And when Chelindo sees his brother slain,
By theft thus taken from him, so to say,
He turns towards Zerbino once again,
Resolved this Christian cavalier to slay.
But he the other's charger by the rein
At once has seized, and neither oats nor hay
That horse will eat, nor carry on its back
Its master felled in one swift, fell attack.

63

And when Calamidor that blow has seen,
He thinks it best to turn his horse about
And with all speed make off; but Prince Zerbin
Flings after him a weapon with the shout:
'Wait, traitor, wait!' The cutting edge, so keen,
Misses Calamidor, but not far out.
The crupper of the horse receives the blow
And down to earth it crashes and lies low.

64

The rider creeps away and on all fours
Endeavours to escape, to no avail.
By chance the Duke Trasone on his horse
Tramples upon him in his heavy mail.
Ariodante and Lurcanio course
To follow in the Prince of Scotland's trail.
They find him in a group of knights and counts
Who form a guard until the prince remounts.

65

Ariodante swung his sword around,
As Artalico and Margano knew
(He left them lying wounded on the ground),
As to their cost, two others whom he slew,
Etearco and Casimiro, found.
Lurcanio now shows what he can do:
He strikes, he overturns with all his strength,
Till many a pagan measures his full length.

66

But do not think, my lord, that on the plain
The battle is proceeding with less rage
Or less ferociously than near the Seine.
The Duke of Lancaster moves up to wage
A fierce attack upon the troops of Spain.
With equal strength and skill both sides engage,
For every captain there and every knight
And every foot-soldier knows how to fight.

67

The Dukes of York and Gloucester lead the van,
And Richard, Earl of Warwick, follows on,
With Henry, Duke of Clarence, veteran
Who many a laurel crown has bravely won;
And facing them are Baricondo's clan,
By Matalista flanked and Follicon;
Majorca, Almerìa, Grànada
Respectively their territories are.

68

The tide of battle wavers to and fro
And in the balance hangs the bitter fray.
Forwards and back alternately they go,
Like barley in the fitful winds of May,
Or as the inconstant waters ebb and flow,
Making a mobile margin in their play.
When Fortune for a while both sides had teased,
The Moors at last were vanquished, as she pleased.

69

The Duke of Gloucester wields his heavy spear,
And mighty Matalista is brought low;
The Duke of York's, which is yet heavier,
Reverses Follicone at one blow.
Both infidels are taken prisoner
And hostages among the English go,
While at this very moment of the strife,
Clarence robs Baricondo of his life.

70

At this the pagans all the more take fright.
The Faithful grow more confident and bold.
The former, being now intent on flight,
Break in confusion, all their courage cold.
The latter, pressing forward for the fight,
By gaining ground, consolidate their hold;
And were it not that help is on its way,
The pagan side had lost the field that day.

71

But Ferraù, who up to now had stayed
Beside his lord and king, Marsilio,
When he beheld that splendid banner fled
And half the army broken and brought low,
Had spurred his horse and urged it, unafraid,
Where battle raged, and there Olimpio
Of Serra he had seen, his head split through,
Fall dead and with his brains the terrain strew.

72

This was a youth who by his dulcet song,
Accompanied by strains upon the lyre,
The coldest heart of stone could touch ere long
And to no greater fame did he aspire.
For neither shield nor weapons did he long,
No love of glory set his heart on fire;
Yet, shunning thus both scimitar and lance,
He met his death in war, so young, in France!

73

When Ferraù had seen Olimpio fall –
A youth whom he had loved – he raged and cursed.
This was a greater grief to him than all
The many thousands who had perished first.
And, seeking vengeance dire and terrible,
Upon the knight who cut him down he burst.
His head, his eyes, his face, his breast he slashed,
And to the ground in hate his body dashed.

74

He hurries on, more vengeance yet to wreak.
Helmets he shatters, coats of mail he chops.
He splits a forehead open, slits a cheek,
Cuts off a head, or else a forearm lops.
The life-blood pours and souls from bodies leak.
The pagans' cowardly retreat he stops,
For the ignoble rabble, terrified,
Were fleeing from the plain on every side.

75

Then Agramante into battle came,
Eager to fight and many lives to take,
With Prusion and Soridan who aim,
Like Bambirago and Fàrurant, to make
Great havoc; others too, whom I'll not name,
Who of their blood this day will form a lake.
I might as well attempt to number all
The leaves which from the trees in autumn fall.

76

First Agramant a company detached
Of horse and foot, which under Fezzan's king
Straightway behind the encampments he despatched,
Where he had seen the Irish mustering,
With whom the men of Fezzan were well-matched;
Their squadrons, after long meandering
(Intended to put others off the track),
The pagan camp were planning to attack.

77

And Fezzan's king complied without delay,
For with each hour the peril greater grew.
Next Agramante orders an array,
Divides the troops and without more ado
Despatches them to mingle in the fray.
Towards the Seine he goes, where he can do,
It seems, most good, for from that quarter came
Request for aid in King Sobrino's name.

78

The squadron which he led comprised almost
Half of his army, and their noise alone
Filled with forebodings all the Scottish host.
In chaos and confusion they were thrown,
Their courage and their resolution lost.
In all, three captains only had not flown:
Lurcanio, the Duke of Albany,
And Prince Zerbino, in great jeopardy,

79

For he is still unmounted; but the son
Of Aymon, who by now has put to flight
A hundred banners, ere he hurries on,
Hearing the news of Prince Zerbino's plight,
Left by his own platoon on foot to run
Among the soldiers of Cyrene's might,
Turns round his horse's head, and where he sees
The Scottish troops retreating, rallies these.

80

And with these words he held the cowards back:
'Where are you making for? So soon you yield?
So ill-prepared are you for an attack?
To such a paltry foe you leave the field?
Look round about: of spoils there is no lack,
To adorn your churches and your glory gild.
What exploit, pray, is this, that the king's son
You leave on foot, abandoned and alone?'

81

Then from his shield-bearer he seized a spear
And, seeing Prusion not far away,
He waited till the infidel drew near
And lo! stretched out upon the ground he lay.
Next, Bambirago and Agricalt, his peer,
He kills, then Soridan attempts to slay.
The first are vanquished by Rinaldo's skill,
And yet the third his prowess fails to kill.

82

He grips Fusberta, for his spear is split,
And Serpentino strikes, whose magic arms
Cannot protect him from so shrewd a hit
And down he goes, unhorsed, for all their charms.
Thus does Rinaldo round Zerbino beat
A circle and all challengers disarms,
Allowing him to choose and mount a steed,
Of those whose backs of riders have been freed.

83

He does so in the very nick of time,
For Agramant and Dardinel arrive,
With others I have mentioned in my rhyme
(Else had he not, perhaps, escaped alive);
But, as I said, the prince remounts in time,
And with his lusty sword begins to drive
First one and then another soul to Hell,
With recent news of world affairs to tell.

84

The good Rinaldo, whose concern it is
To bring the most ferocious pagans down,
Turns to attack King Agramant, for his
Exploits in battle, worthy of his crown,
Are equal to the strength and expertise
Of many hundreds (such the king's renown);
Spurring Baiardo hard, to earth he flings
Both horse and rider with the force he brings.

85

While thus a cruel battle raged outside,
And man to man was linked in bitter hate,
Fires lit by Rodomonte raged inside,
Reducing Paris to a sorry state.
Charles, in another quarter occupied,
Knows nothing of the citadel's dire fate;
He welcomes in with joy and highest hopes
Edward and Herman, with their British troops.

86

But to him came a messenger, all pale,
Who scarce could speak at first, or draw his breath;
When he began he told a dismal tale.
'Alas!' he sighed, like one who is near death,
'The Empire's lost and nothing will avail!
His people God abandons here beneath!
The Devil walks among us all today
And from our homes is driving us away!

87

'Satan himself (for who else could it be?)
For our fair city's ruin is to blame.
Look yonder at the sky-line: turn and see
The whirling smoke and the devouring flame.
Can you not hear the cries which piteously
Assail the skies? Believe me, in God's name,
The Evil One it is who thus employs
These evil means and all our homes destroys.'

88

And like a man who, turning a deaf ear,
Ignores the warning of the tolling bell
And all the signs of tumult which appear,
Which to those farther off the worst foretell,
Yet he, to whom calamity is near,
To all such portents is insensible,
So Charles, convinced at last by sound and sight,
Was roused to bring assistance to such plight.

89

Choosing the finest of his paladins,
He leads a splendid army after him
Towards the square, where many citizens
Are fleeing from a destiny so grim.
He hears the noise, he sees the evidence
Of many a torso, many a scattered limb.
But now I'll pause; if any would hear more,
Let him return at some convenient hour.

CANTO XVII

1

Almighty God, when all our many sins
Have passed beyond the point of being remitted,
His justice (and His mercy) to evince,
Our punishment to tyrants has committed.
Thus in the days of ancient Rome, long since,
The rule of monsters often He permitted,
As Sulla, Caius Caesar, Marius,
Or cruel Nero and Tiberius,

2

Domitian and the youngest Antonine,
Or Maximinus, from the people raised
And set on high in the imperial line,
Creon of Thebes, Mezentius, half-crazed,
Terror and scourge of every Agylline,
Who with men's blood the soil of Caere greased;
And Italy in later times has known
The rage of Longobard, of Goth, of Hun.

3

What shall I say of Attila, or of
Vile Ezzellino da Romano's crimes?
Or many hundreds more whom God above
Has sent, in ancient as in recent times,
A clear example of His wrath to prove,
Our evil ways thus punishing betimes;
And to us, sheep-like, futile and unshriven,
Ferocious wolves as guardians has given?

4

Their hunger, it appears, is unabated,
However full of flesh their bellies are,
And ultramontane wolves, likewise unsated,
Come prowling down from forest-lands afar.
The many bones by Trasimene, ill-fated,
Or those at Cannae or at Trebbia,
Less fertile make the soil than those which lie
Where Adda, Mella, Ronco, Tar flow by.

5

Now God consents that we should punished be,
By other races who perhaps are worse,
For all our manifold iniquity.
The time will come when we shall raid their shores
And make them of their errors pay the fee
(If ever we shall learn to mend our course),
When they will suffer as an aftermath
The penalty of the Almighty's wrath.

6

The Christians must have caused by their excesses
A clouding of the Father's countenance.
On every side the Saracen oppresses
With murder, rape and all incontinence;
But worse than all the worst of these distresses
Is Rodomonte's pitiless advance.
The tidings reached King Charles, as I have said,
Who to the rescue with new forces sped.

7

He meets his broken army on the way.
The churches, palaces in ruins lie,
Burning and desolate; from this one may
Deduce that Rodomonte has passed by.
King Charles imperiously bids them stay:
'Where are you going? Whither do you fly?
What other refuge, think you, will be left
If Paris is abandoned and bereft?

8

'One man alone wreaks havoc in your city,
Which walls enclose, whence there is no escape?
You let him slay and slaughter without pity
And on him no revenge you plan to reap?'
Charles was so angered by the shame of it, he
Tongue-lashed his army into better shape,
Then made his way towards his royal court,
Where Rodomonte slew as though for sport.

9

There, terrified, a multitude had flocked
For safety to the palace, for, the age-
old building with munitions being well stocked,
Its massive walls might well withstand a siege.
But all defences Rodomonte mocked.
Unaided, in his arrogance and rage,
He held the forecourt, brandishing his sword
And hurling flaring missiles at the horde.

10

Then of the palace, lofty and sublime,
He hammers on the door with mighty blows.
The inmates to the topmost turrets climb:
A crenellation falls, a column goes.
Having no boiling oil or pitch or lime,
One flings a baluster, another throws
A marble slab, or gilded beams some break,
Sparing no work of art for beauty's sake.

11

Before the door, the monarch of Algiers
Stands in his shining armour, brave and strong;
A gleaming helmet on his head he wears,
As when a snake, shedding its skin among
The undergrowth, rejuvenated rears
Itself in glistening pride, its triple tongue
Vibrating, darting from its eyes such fire,
All other creatures from its path retire.

12

No catapult, no bow, no mangonel,
No balustrade, no beam, no architrave,
No battlement which on the pagan fell,
From his right arm the palace door could save.
He slashed and hewed and battered it so well,
That faces, pale as death, of the enclave
Therein were seen, and saw the press outside,
Through all those apertures now gaping wide.

13

In stately houses women rush apace
From room to room in desperate distress,
Beating their breasts and shrieking, pale of face.
Their loved possessions fervently they kiss,
Flinging their arms as in a last embrace
About those objects which to lawlessness
Must be surrendered. Such the peril was
When Charlemagne rode up. Without a pause

14

He thus addressed the barons at his side,
Who many a time had rallied to his aid:
'Are you not those companions who defied
A hundred thousand men, and by whose blade
Almonte, Agolant, Troiano died
In Aspromonte? Are you now afraid
Of one, a single one of that same brood,
Within whose veins there flows that self-same blood?

15

'Must I now see that valiant prowess fail,
Unequal to the courage I saw then?
Turn on this dog and make him now turn tail,
This snarling dog, unmuzzled, which eats men.
No brave heart at the thought of death will quail,
For death must come, it matters little when,
If it be death with honour; neither fear
Nor doubt have I, provided you are near.'

16

With these concluding words he urged his steed
With lowered lance against the Saracen,
As Namo, Oliver and Ugier did,
Likewise Avolio and bold Avin,
Otto and Berlingier, whose every deed
Together is performed, for they are seen
Together always. Rodomonte's breast
And head and sides they strike. But, for the rest,

17

Let us have done, my lord, for pity's sake,
With talk of wrath, of fury and of death,
And to the city of Damascus make
Our way (spending for now no further breath
Upon the Saracen), where I will take
Grifone's tale in hand. I left him with
Perfidious Orrigille and that other
(Her paramour, of course, and not her brother).

18

Of all the wealthy cities of Levant,
Ornate and populous, Damascus is
Reputed the most fair and opulent.
Set in a plain where corn and fruitful trees
In winter as in spring abundance grant,
A week away from the metropolis,
Jerusalem, it lies. A near-by height
Occludes the early rays of morning light.

19

Two crystal streams which through the city flow
Give water in their branching rivulets
To gardens where in sweet profusion grow
Fronds, ever green, and fragrant flowerets;
And perfumed waters turn the mill-wheels, so
Abundantly the blossoms yield their sweets;
And every passer-by inhales the scent
Wherewith each mansion there is redolent.

20

Now all the high road festive is today
With bunting, pennons, flags and drapery
And many a fragrant garland and bouquet.
Now every portal has its canopy,
And every window-sill is bright and gay
With sumptuous brocades and tapestry,
But more with ladies in their beauty's pride,
Adorned with silks and gems, on every side.

21

Through many a doorway might be glimpsed within
Dancers disporting to a gladsome sound;
And riders too along the road are seen
On horses splendidly caparisoned.
Bevies of noblemen accoutred in
A rich and elegant attire, are found:
With Eastern gems and Erythraean pearls
Adorned, they number vassals, barons, earls.

22

Grifone and his company move on,
Gazing in admiration, left and right,
Until a fair demesne they come upon,
Where they are bidden by a gentle knight.
Therein no courtesy is left undone,
Observed is every hospitable rite.
When they have bathed and are refreshed at last,
He leads them to a sumptuous repast.

23

And of King Norandino he related,
Who ruled Damascus and all Syria,
By whose command a joust had been instated,
To which brave knights had come from near and far,
Who when they had been well and truly fêted
Would on the morrow to the lists repair.
If of the present company the bearing
Was matched by skill, they too might show their daring.

24

Although at first Grifone had not planned
To undergo so rigorous a test,
He felt at once inclined to try his hand.
He judged that this decision was the best.
But first of all he wished to understand
The origin and nature of the feast:
Was it an annual event, or newly
Instituted? The knight informed him duly,

25

Replying in these words: 'This festival
Will be repeated every fourth new moon.
This is the first, the precedent of all.
Never before has such a feast been known.
The day our king was saved we thus recall,
When, in great peril, he had undergone
Four endless months of suffering and grief,
The tale of which surpasses all belief.

26

'To tell you plainly what in truth occurred,
Our king, a victim of the power of love
(His name is Norandino, you have heard),
The beautiful and lovely daughter of
The king of Cyprus had for long adored.
His overtures at last successful prove:
He weds the fair princess and makes for home,
And many lords and ladies with him come.

27

'But, driven off our course, with sails full-spread,
Far from our port, to that deceitful sea
'Twixt Crete and Rhodes by cruel Fortune led,
We met a storm which tossed us cruelly.
Three days and nights obliquely we were sped
By towering waves; the captain finally
Made land; we disembarked, fatigued and wet,
On a green shore, 'mid shady hillocks set.

28

'Pavilions were put up and tents were pitched.
From tree to tree the awnings we had brought,
For shelter we commanded should be stretched.
Soon fires were kindled, provender laid out,
Carpets and tables from on board were fetched.
The king meanwhile amid the woodland sought
For goats or fawns or stags, or any kind
Of game; his bow two servants bore behind.

29

'In pleasant expectation as we sat
Awaiting the return of our brave king,
We saw a fearful sight, a monster, that
Along the sandy shore came lumbering.
God save you, my dear sir, from such a fate,
And grant you never see so vile a thing!
Far better that it be described to you
Than that you see the dreadful beast close to.

30

'No term of length can be compared with it.
Its width is measureless, and vast its girth.
In place of eyes, beneath its brow are set
Bone-like projections; coloured like the earth,
It ambles on towards us where we sit,
As though an alp had yawned and given birth.
Its chest is moist with slobber, long its snout,
Whence tusks or fangs, as on a boar, stick out.

31

'With quickened steps it snuffled at the ground,
As hunting-dogs will do when on the trail
They narrow down their quarry, round and round.
And we who fled, our countenances pale,
Seeing it blind, no crumb of comfort found.
Though lacking eyes, the monster did not fail
To use its nose to lead it to its prey,
And wings were then required to get away.

32

'Some scatter here, some there, but swifter than
The wind it overtakes them, and of all
The company of forty scarcely ten
Are left alive the sorry tale to tell.
Some swim to safety; others in its den
Are destined for a fate more tragical:
Stuffed in the monster's sack, which dangles from
Its side, they're carried to its grisly home.

33

'Such dwelling as the evil monster had
Was in a cliff close to the water's edge,
Carved in the living rock, of marble made,
As pure and white as an unwritten page.
Therein a matron lived, cast-down and sad;
And other women too, of every age,
Of every kind and aspect, it held there.
Some were repulsive, some surpassing fair.

34

'Beside the secret grotto where it dwelt,
Close to the very summit of the rock,
It had another just as large, which held
Of sheep and goats quite an extensive flock.
Winter and summer, as the monster felt
Inclined, the door of this it would unlock
And let them out or drive them in at will,
Its pleasure, more than hunger, to fulfil.

35

'It much prefers the taste of human meat.
To sate this appetite, ere we arrive,
Three of our youths it now proceeds to eat,
Gulping them down, all three of them alive.
Then from the stall, removing first from it
A heavy stone, the flock begins to drive
Into the open. We, now penned inside,
Can hear its bagpipes sounding far and wide.

36

'Our king, meanwhile, returning to the coast,
Looks on the scene with an astonished stare.
He scarce can comprehend what he has lost:
Tents and pavilions empty everywhere,
On every side signs as of holocaust,
While out to sea his mariners prepare
To raise the anchor and to hoist the sails.
Alas! to raise his spirits naught avails.

37

'Perceiving him upon the shore, straightway
They send a boat to bring him safe on board;
But, hearing what the sailors have to say
About the dreadful monster so abhorred,
Upon the instant he decides to stay
And track it to its den, where his adored
Lucina has been carried off; for I
Can swear, without her he would rather die.

38

'He tracks the recent footprints on the sand,
Impelled by haste such as a lover knows.
Now to the right, and now to the left hand,
As far as to the monster's den he goes,
Where we, in dire foreboding, have been penned,
Anticipating death and all its throes.
At every sound we seem to see before us
That evil monster ready to devour us.

39

'Fortune so willed that at its dwelling-place
The king saw not the monster but its wife.
And she, no sooner had she glimpsed his face,
Cried out: "Be gone, my lord! Flee for your life!"
But he replied: "My steps I'll not retrace.
To me I vow it matters little if
I'm caught; no worse my fate would be, for I
Beside my consort am resolved to die."

40

'Continuing, he begs the dame to give
What news she can of captives from the shore.
His fair Lucina, does she still survive?
This is the news he is most eager for.
She tells him that Lucina is alive
And further says, to comfort him still more,
To be devoured will never be her plight;
The orc for females has no appetite.

41

'"And certain evidence of this", said she,
"In my continued presence here you have
And all these women who are here with me.
But any who attempt to leave the cave
It punishes with great severity.
No peace, no consolation then they have:
It buries them, or chains them foot and hand,
Or makes them lie stark naked on the strand.

42

'"Though when it brought your people here today
It did not sort the women from the men,
But in an undiscriminating way
It drove them all into the self-same pen,
Your love will have no reason for dismay.
It knows the sexes by their smell, and when
It sniffs the males there are no ifs and buts.
With four or six a day it stuffs its guts.

43

'"Plans or advice for rescue have I none.
To save her there is nothing you can do.
You must content yourself with this alone,
That as we here survive she will live too.
But for yourself, make haste and flee, my son,
Before the orc return and swallow you.
It will soon sniff you out, inside the house.
It knows who's here, down to the smallest mouse."

44

'The king replied that he would not depart
Till he had seen Lucina once again.
Sooner than live from his dear love apart
He'd rather die with her and share her pain.
When the good matron sees that all her art
And all her protestations are in vain,
His firm resolve she helps him to fulfil
By using all her cunning, all her skill.

45

'Inside the den were many carcasses
Of goats and sheep, some old and others young.
To feed on them the inmates' custom is,
And many a sheepskin from the rafters hung.
The beldam urged the king to use the grease
Of an old goat which round its bowels clung.
He oiled himself from head to foot so well
No vestige was there of his human smell.

46

'And when that evil stench appears to her
Convincing of the normal smell of goat,
She takes a skin and on the visitor
She drapes it like a wide, capacious coat.
Then, covered in this strange involucre,
He crawls along beside her on the route
To where his fair Lucina languishes,
For whom his very soul in anguish is.

47

'Obediently, beside the entrance to
The cave, he waits until the orc is seen
Returning with its flock; and late into
The evening dusk his vigil long has been
Before the sound of pipes is heard anew,
The flocks recalling from their pastures green;
And every day returning thus you'll find them,
The cruel shepherd following behind them.

48

'Imagine how his heart began to race
Soon as he saw the monster drawing near,
And he beheld that evil, cruel face;
And how he truly loved will now appear,
For of pretence his ardour had no trace;
Love for Lucina conquering his fear,
Soon as the monster had removed the block
King Norandino entered with the flock.

49

'When all the goats and sheep have passed inside,
The monster, having first secured the door,
Sniffs at us all in order to decide
Which of the men for supper he'll devour.
It chooses two and eats them, hair and hide.
(When I recall those fangs I shake once more!)
As soon as it departs, the king has cast
His fleece and clasps Lucina to his breast.

50

'No joy she feels in his embrace; instead,
The sight of him affords her keenest sorrow.
She knows that very soon he will be dead
And that his end he may well meet tomorrow.
"In all my suffering", Lucina said,
"This crumb of comfort only could I borrow,
That you, my dearest lord, were far away
When we were captured by the orc today.

51

'"Thought of the dreadful death I must endure,
Concerning which I was disconsolate,
Caused me most bitter grief, but only for
My own misfortune and my own sad fate;
But now, whether I predecease you, or
You die before I do, I shall regret
Your death, my love, more than my own demise."
And she continued sadly in this wise.

52

'The king replied, "I hope to rescue you
And all these others here with you confined,
And I will die if this I cannot do.
You are my sun, without you I am blind.
My way of entering, my exit too
Will be, and yours, if you will come behind,
Disguised, as I am, by this brutish stench,
If such a fetor does not make you blench."

53

'The need for cunning taught us to comply
With the instructions of the kindly dame.
To trick the orc, accustomed to rely
Upon its sense of smell, we used the same
Foul unguent as the king was covered by.
To pass the orc unnoticed was our aim.
Killing a number of the sheep and goats,
The older and more fetid, with thick coats,

54

'We oiled ourselves with intestinal fat,
The foulest, greasiest which could be found
Inside the beasts and, when we had done that,
Fleeces and skins about ourselves we wound,
And thus anointed and attired we sat
And waited for the morning to come round.
As soon as the first rays of dawn appeared,
The grisly shepherd's fluting tones were heard.

55

'It held its hand against the aperture
To keep us from escaping with the flock.
It touched us as we passed, and to make sure
It sniffed at every ewe and every buck.
But with the animals we passed the door,
Women as well as men, and by good luck
Not one of us did it suspect until
Lucina, in great terror, reached the sill.

56

'Perhaps because Lucina did not wish
To smear herself with fat as we had done,
Or by her gait, which was more womanish
Than goat-like, her disguise at once was known,
Or, when it touched her with its ogreish
Appendages, she gave a frightened moan,
Or that her tresses tumbled loose about her —
It held her back, and we passed on without her.

57

'Intent on our escape, we had no eyes
For anything but our own destinies;
But when I heard Lucina's doleful cries
I turned: the orc had stripped her of her fleece
And thrust her in the cave; still in disguise,
Covered in wool or skin and smeared with grease,
Amid green hills and pleasant slopes we creep,
Where'er the shepherd leads its goats and sheep.

58

'And there we waited till the long-nosed orc
Lay sleeping in the shadow of a wood.
We parted then, where branching pathways fork,
Some to the shore and some, as best we could,
Into the hills, there in dark caves to lurk.
Only our king this urge to flee withstood,
Remaining constant to his first intent,
To save his bride or die in the attempt.

59

'When, as he left that prison, he had seen
That she alone a prisoner remained,
By grief distracted, he had almost been
Spontaneously led to make an end
And let himself be mangled there and then
By those foul jaws, but still by hope sustained
Of rescuing her yet, by hook or crook,
He changed his mind and lingered with the flock.

60

'That evening, when the monster brought them back
And knew that we, its provender, had fled,
And understood that supper it would lack,
It blamed Lucina and devised a dread
And fearful punishment, such as its black
And evil heart conceived: high overhead
Upon a rock in chains she was to lie.
King Norandin looks on and longs to die.

61

'Morning and evening the unhappy lover
Observes her as she languishes and weeps,
When, mingled with the flock, he wanders over
The higher slopes and homeward sadly creeps.
With suppliant face she begs that, if he love her,
For God's sake he will flee, for here he reaps
No benefit, but risks his precious life,
Making more wretched yet his wretched wife.

62

'The monster's spouse entreated him likewise,
But likewise vain all her entreaties prove.
The constant lover constantly denies
That he will ever leave without his love.
Passion and pity bind him with their ties
And from his firm resolve he will not move.
But then it chanced that Mandricard one day,
Accompanied by Gradasso, passed that way,

63

'And in their sudden raid they proved so bold
They snatched Lucina from the monster's cave
(Luck helped them more than judgement, I am told).
In eagerness the fair princess to save,
They hurried to the vessel, where her old
And grieving father stood, and there they gave
His daughter to his arms; all this occurred
One morning while the flock was still immured.

64

'And when they issue from the squalid house
And Norandino learns his bride has flown
(He hears the story from the monster's spouse
Who tells him just how the affair has gone),
He renders thanks to God above and vows
That when his way to freedom he has won,
Wherever men may be coerced or bought
By arms or gold the princess will be sought.

65

'Then, filled with joy, he wanders with the band
Of snub-nosed sheep among the pastures green;
And there he waits, while, lying close at hand,
Stretched in the shade the monstrous orc is seen.
After some days he hastens to the strand;
To save his own, he sheds his borrowed skin.
He boards a vessel in Satalia,
And in three months arrives in Syria.

66

'In every citadel and town, in Rhodes,
In Cyprus, Turkey, Egypt, Africa,
Along the thoroughfares, along the roads,
He searched for fair Lucina, near and far,
By sea, by land, up mountains and in woods;
And all this time he had no news of her,
Till from her father tidings came at last
That safe to Nicosia she had passed.

67

'In joy and thankfulness at the good news,
The king prepares a fine and costly feast;
And as each fourth succeeding moon renews
Her face, another will be held, at least
As sumptuous as this, lest he should lose
The memory of when, clad like a beast,
He wandered with the hairy flock. Tomorrow
Four months it is that he escaped such sorrow.

68

'What I have told you, I in part have seen,
In part have heard from one who saw it all
From A to Z: the king himself, I mean.
Four Ides, four Kalends there he stayed, recall,
Till sorrow into joy transformed had been.
This is the truth and if it should befall
That anyone should tell you otherwise,
He has been misinformed, or else he lies.'

69

And thus Grifone came to know the cause
Of that fair feast, and half the night they sat
Discoursing of the monarch's love, which was
Exceptional (they all agreed on that);
And, rising then from table, their repose
They took as guests in the same habitat.
Next day the morning dawns serene and clear
And joyful sounds of revelry they hear.

70

Along the streets, with drum and clarion,
Calling the people to the city-square,
The heralds go; and horses proudly run.
Thronging with life is every thoroughfare.
Grifone puts his shining armour on,
Which precious is and most exceeding rare,
Unyielding and impenetrable made
By the enchantment of a snow-white maid.

71

That miscreant of Antiochia,
Viler than vile, then arms himself likewise.
The hospitable knight his armourer
Instructed had to furnish all supplies,
All chivalrous paraphernalia,
Lances and spears, robust, of every size,
And èquerries, on horseback and on foot,
To serve them well at their disposal put.

72

They reach the square and, drawing to one side,
As yet unseen, they watch the panoply
Of knightly combatants who hither ride,
Alone, or forming groups of two or three.
Some, sad or joyful hearts display with pride,
Combining the bright hues of heraldry,
Or emblems, on a crest or shield designed,
Love represent as cruel or as kind.

73

For you must know, my lord, the Syrians
Had then assumed this custom of the West,
Perhaps because the cavaliers of France,
Of Christian knights the finest and the best,
Of that abode were the custodians
Which God Incarnate with His presence blessed,
Which Christians now, to their undying shame,
Leave in the hands of pagans of ill fame.

74

No longer now defenders of the faith,
With one another Christian knights contend,
Destroying in their enmity and wrath
Those few who still believe; make now an end,
You Spaniards; Frenchmen, choose another path;
Switzers and Germans, no more armies send.
For here the territory you would gain
Belongs to Christ; His kingdom you profane.

75

If 'the most Christian' rulers you would be,
And 'Catholic' desire to be reputed,
Why do you slay Christ's men? Their property
Why have you sacked, and their belongings looted?
Why do you leave in dire captivity
Jerusalem, by infidels polluted?
Why do you let the unclean Turk command
Constantinople and the Holy Land?

76

Spaniards, have you not Africa near by,
Which more than Italy has injured you?
And yet, to ravage *her*, you now deny
Those former noble claims of derring-do?
Ah! wretched Italy, asleep you lie,
In drunken stupor, fallen subject to
This and that other nation who were once
Your slaves, your subjects, your dominions?

77

Switzers, if hunger drives you to invade,
Like famished animals, the Lombard plain,
To beg among us for a crust of bread,
Or end your poverty, in battle slain,
See how the riches of the Turk are spread
Near by: chase him from Europe, from his den
In Greece expel him and your bellies sate,
Or in those regions meet a nobler fate.

78

And to your German neighbours now I say
What I have said to you: look to the East.
The wealth which Constantine once took away
From Rome lies there; he portioned off the best
And the remainder gave into our sway.
The Pactolus and Hermus, rivers blest
With gold, Phrygia and Lydia and that land
Much praised in legend, all lie near at hand.

79

And you, great Leo, bearing on your back
St Peter's burden, do not still allow
Fair Italy to sleep in sloth for lack
Of your strong arm to pull her from the slough.
You are the Shepherd: from the wolves' attack
Defend your flock; stretch forth your right arm now.
Like your proud name, chosen for you by God,
Be leonine and worthy of your rod.

80

From one theme to another now I go,
Leaving the path which previously I strode;
But not so far that yet I do not know
How to regain once more the rightful road.
The Syrians, I said (was it not so?),
Accoutred like the French to battle rode;
And in Damascus festive was that day
The central square with chivalrous array.

81

From their pavilions lovely damsels cast
Bright-coloured flowers on the combatants,
While at the sounding of the herald's blast
These make their horses jump or make them prance.
Each one, in prowess whether first or last,
Desires to meet with an admiring glance.
Some arouse laughter, some inspire esteem,
And some draw shouts of wonder after them.

82

A set of weapons was the victor's prize,
Presented to the king some days before,
Found by a merchant, to his great surprise,
As homeward from Armenia he bore
His caravanserai of merchandise.
The king a surcoat added, what is more,
Adorned with precious gems and pearls and gold,
Of value unsurpassed, of price untold.

83

But if those arms the king had truly known,
Above all else he would have held them dear,
Not as a trophy offered to be won
(Though held as bountiful, both far and near).
Long would it take to tell you of the one
Whose disregard of them must strange appear,
Who left them in the middle of a street,
Where they were spurned and kicked by passing feet.

84

This tale I will recount to you below.
But first Grifone's story I'll advance.
When he arrived, already many a blow
Had been exchanged, and broken many a lance.
Eight cavaliers combined, as you must know,
To challenge one by one all combatants.
Well versed in arms they were, of noble birth,
And loyal to their king, who knew their worth.

85

Thus in the precincts of the city-square
For one whole day all comers are defied.
Lance, sword and mace they wield and do not spare.
Their king looks on at them with joy and pride.
Their coats of mail are pierced, the blows they bear
And give, with deadly skill are multiplied,
As though they fought in earnest, not in jest,
Save that the king cries 'Hold!', if he thinks best.

86

Then he of Antiochia, of sense
Devoid (Martano was the coward's name),
As though accustomed to such tournaments
And strength like young Grifone's he could claim,
Entered the lists with misplaced confidence.
First, to one side he waited, with the aim
Of seeing the conclusion of a fierce
Encounter 'twixt two noble cavaliers.

87

Seleucia's lord, one of the noble band
Of whom I spoke, in combat was engaged
With Count Ombruno, and, as Fate had planned,
When at its height the deadly contest raged,
Struck him a blow which he could scarce withstand.
It pierced him through the brow; his soul, uncaged,
Departed. His untimely death all mourn.
No nobler, better knight was ever born.

88

Martano greatly fears on seeing this
That he will meet a comparable fate.
Reverting to his native cowardice,
He looks about him for escape: too late.
Grifone, next to him, insistent is
That he shall in no wise prevaricate,
Pushing him towards a knight who has emerged,
As if a dog against a wolf he urged,

89

Which, moving backwards ten or twenty steps,
Barks from a distance and the dog defies,
Baring its fangs and curling back its lips,
With fiery hatred burning in its eyes.
Seen by those princes, whose brave deeds eclipse
All other cavaliers, the coward tries
To escape the lance which he cannot withstand,
By turning head and rein to the right hand.

90

For this default you might have blamed the horse,
If as a coward you were loath to brand him;
But with his sword his conduct was far worse –
Demosthenes himself could not defend him.
As though of paper (it was steel, of course)
His armour was, he feared each blow would rend him.
Then breaking through the ranks, he fled, and laughter
From all the crowd arose and followed after.

91

The clapping and the mockery became
So boisterous that, as Martano fled,
Grifone, who remained, was filled with shame,
As though *he* had been guilty of the deed,
And brought dishonour down upon his name;
At his companion's flight he hung his head
And rather would he seek the fire's embrace
Than stay, defiled and tainted, in that place.

92

As inwardly, so outwardly, he burns,
As if his were the shame and only his.
The crowd of onlookers at once discerns,
And longs to see him test, his expertise.
Much on Grifone's skill and courage turns.
Perfection more than ever needful is.
An inch, a fraction of an error will
Appear an even grosser blunder still.

93

Already on his hip his lance was placed,
For seldom in such matters could you fault him.
Riding his horse full tilt, his foe he faced,
Then lifted up his weapon to assault him.
The lord of Sidon fell and was disgraced,
Having expected easily to halt him.
This drew the crowd, astonished, to its feet,
For it expected quite the opposite.

94

Grifone still the self-same weapon held
Which in one piece intact he had retained,
And into three he broke it on the shield
Of him who over Laodicea reigned,
Who three times tottered and a fourth time reeled,
But on the crupper of his mount remained,
Stretched out; at last he lifted up his head
And, turning swiftly, towards Grifone sped.

95

Seeing him upright in the saddle, whence
The impact failed the rider to unfix,
Grifone thinks: 'What at one blow the lance
Could not, the sword will do in five or six.'
He brings it down upon his helmet once,
And twice, and thrice; as if a ton of bricks
Has struck him from above, the knight is stunned
And lies defeated, sprawling on the ground.

96

Two brothers who from Apamìa came,
Accustomed to prevail in feats of war,
Who Thyrsis and Corimbo were by name,
Were vanquished by the son of Oliver:
One by the lance was toppled, to his shame,
One by the sword; soon every spectator
Knew that Grifone would the winner be,
For certain now appeared his victory.

97

Next Salinterno, minister of state,
Entered the lists, the object of all eyes.
The reins of government, his country's fate
He held in his two hands; well versed, likewise,
In feats of arms, he could not suffer that
A foreigner should carry off the prize.
Taking a lance, in readiness he waits
And challenges the youth with many threats.

98

He in reply a heavy lance, the best
Of ten, aimed full at his opponent's shield.
Piercing his body-armour and his chest,
More than Grifone's purpose it fulfilled.
From side to side the cruel weapon passed
And by a palm protruded; thus was killed
That avaricious minister, whose fall
(Save to the king) gave great delight to all.

99

And next Grifone caused to bite the dust
Two of Damascus; one was Ermofil.
Control of the king's army was his trust.
The other, Carmond, was an admiral.
One left his saddle at the lance's thrust.
The heavy charger on the other fell,
Unable to sustain the mighty blow
By which Grifone brought its rider low.

100

Seleucia's lord alone remained upright,
He who the other seven far surpassed.
His horse and arms, as well became his might,
Were choice and perfect, tempered and well-cast.
Now where the helms are open to the light
They aimed their lances as they galloped past.
Grifone's stroke, the stronger of the two,
The other caused to veer, and checked him, too.

101

Casting away the stumps, they turned once more,
Brandishing swords, and with high courage rode.
The pagan the first stroke received, which tore
His shield, revealing bone and leather (it would
Have split an anvil), though from a vast store
Of thousands he had chosen it; his good
Mail-armour, reinforced, his thigh defended,
Checking the heavy blow where it descended.

102

The baron of Seleucia likewise smote
Grifone's visor, and with such a blow,
He would have split it open were it not
By magic, like his other armour, so
Impervious it yielded not one jot.
Yet in the other's armour you must know
Grifone many a slash and rent has made,
As stroke on stroke he parried and repaid.

103

It can be clearly seen by everyone
That in this fight Grifone is on top.
The other champion will perish soon
Unless King Norandino bids them stop.
The herald, at his signal, steps upon
The jousting-ground and makes his baton drop
Between the combatants; their swords are raised,
And for this clement act the king is praised.

104

The eight who had thus challenged all who came
And, in succession, against one had failed
(Their fortune being unworthy of their fame),
Dead or alive, had quit the stricken field.
The others who had hoped to challenge them
Remained, but since Grifone had prevailed,
And victory had won in every fight,
No further test of valour seemed in sight.

105

So short a time the tournament endured,
That all was over in an hour or less;
But Norandino for his guests ensured
A game that before evening should not cease;
And, stepping on the field, a space conjured.
Then, judging their attainments with finesse,
The combatants he coupled two by two,
And set in motion all the joust anew.

106

Grifone had decided to return
To where he lodged; he was so full of rage
And so humiliated by the scorn
Martano stirred, no triumph could assuage
The sting of obloquy. A liar born,
Martano understands just how to gauge
His cunning lies, helped by the meretricious
Orrigille, who is no less judicious.

107

Whether or no the youth believed these two,
He none the less accepted their excuses.
His sole intention there and then was to
Persuade them to be gone lest more abuses
Should at Martano levelled be; and so
Along a secret path which no one uses,
Leaving the city gate that very day,
To the periphery they made their way.

108

Whether Grifone or his horse was tired,
Or both were weary from the many trials,
At the first inn for lodging he enquired,
Though scarcely had they gone above two miles.
He shed the arms with which he was attired,
And saw his horse unsaddled too meanwhiles;
Withdrawing to his chamber, he undressed
And lay down naked on his bed to rest.

109

Grifone had no sooner placed his head
Upon the pillow than he fell asleep.
No dormouse and no badger, be it said,
Enjoyed so sweet a slumber, nor so deep.
Meanwhile Martano Orrigille led
To an adjoining garden; there, to reap
Advantage from discomfiture, they plan
The strangest strategy devised by man.

110

Grifone's horse and clothes and arms he meant
To take and, thus disguised, as though that knight
He were who that day in the tournament
Such proof had given of his skill and might,
To claim the victor's prize was his intent.
He mounted then Grifone's steed, as white
As milk, wearing his armour, crest and shield
And all the weapons he was wont to wield.

111

By squires escorted, and accompanied
By Orrigille, to the square he came
When evening fell, and at the time agreed
Concluded soon was every joust and game.
The king commands his heralds with all speed
To seek that noble cavalier whose name
He knows not but whose crest and horse are white,
And who the victor was in every fight.

112

So, in the armour of another man,
As once the donkey wore the lion's skin,
On being summoned, as had been his plan,
In brave Grifone's place, to Norandin
The villain went. Straightway the king began
To honour him; as if he were his kin
He welcomed him and, not content to praise him,
In every man's esteem desired to raise him.

113

He bids the heralds sound their clarions
And name him victor of the games that day.
Through all the palisades the resonance
Of that base name reverberates. To pay
Him yet more honour, by his side he wants
The vile impostor as they ride away,
And on him as much graciousness confers
As if he had been Hercules or Mars.

114

To sumptuous apartments he was led
And Orrigille too is lodged likewise,
By high-born servitors accompanied
And chamberlains attired in courtly guise.
But of Grifone, now, who on his bed,
Fearing no trick or treacherous surprise,
Had fallen fast asleep, it's time to speak.
Not until evening came did he awake.

115

When he arose and saw the hour was late,
He hastened from his room; there, plain to view,
Were traces of the flight of the ingrate,
Her so-called brother and their retinue.
At first he wondered what might be their fate,
But soon, on looking here and there, he knew.
His armour and his clothing all are gone
And in their place he finds Martano's own.

116

The landlord of the inn describes to him
How they departed several hours ago,
And how the knight, white-clad in every limb,
Was mounted on a horse as white as snow.
To this Grifone listens, stern and grim.
The truth, concealed by love, he now must owe,
And to his grief at last he understands
What has occurred and how the matter stands.

117

In vain he rails at his stupidity,
When he has heard the landlord's story through,
In having been the dupe of trickery
Of one who many times had proved untrue.
Would he had punished her duplicity!
But seeking now revenge upon his foe,
He is obliged to ride his very horse
And even wear his armour, which is worse.

118

Better it were to go unarmed and bare
Than put that evil traitor's garments on,
Or his abominable buckler wear,
His banner flourish or his helmet don;
But in his longing to discover where
The harlot and her paramour have gone,
His reason is o'erswayed; and to the town
He rides an hour before the sun goes down.

119

And as he nears a gate, he sees not far
Upon the left-hand side a splendid pile,
Designed for pleasure rather than for war,
With rooms adorned in fair and costly style.
Therein the king and all his nobles are.
Together with their ladies, they beguile
The hours of evening, banqueting in state,
And the joust's ending fitly celebrate.

120

Beyond the loggia where the feast is laid,
A broad and distant prospect they command.
Before their gaze the cornfields are displayed
And all the many roads on either hand.
Thus as Grifone towards the palace made,
Bearing those arms which bore a coward's brand,
He was observed (of Fortune now the sport)
By Norandino and by all his court.

121

Mistaken for the wretch whose arms he wore,
He moved that company to jeer and jest,
Whereas Martano, who was honoured more
Than any courtier present at the feast,
Was seated by the king, and she who bore
No sisterly resemblance but can best
Be termed his equal sat near by. Their host
Enquired: 'Who is this coward who can boast

122

'So little pride that, after such display
Of craven fear as in the tournament
He made before our eyes this very day,
He comes towards us, bold and impudent?
Why did you make him your companion, pray?
No other would you find in all Levant
To equal him. Perhaps you keep him near,
That braver still in contrast you appear?

123

'But by the gods in heaven above I vow
That were it not for my regard for you
I would have visited this wretch ere now
With public ignominy, as was due;
For never in my realm do I allow
Cowards to go unpunished; this is true.
And so if hence he unrewarded goes
You must believe that this to you he owes.'

124

And he, whose soul contained the sediments
Of every vice, replied: 'O Sire esteemed,
I met this knight upon the road by chance,
Coming from Antiochia; he seemed,
As far as I could judge him at first glance,
A worthy cavalier, and so I deemed,
Having no reason to think otherwise,
Until today, when, to my great surprise

125

'And grave displeasure, he betrayed such fear
And in his timorous retreat persisted.
To teaching him a lesson I was near,
On which there was no need to have insisted;
Yet for your Majesty, whom I revere,
I had respect and therefore I desisted.
But I have no desire he should go free
Because he travelled in my company.

126

'My honour will be stained and on my heart
A grievous burden will for ever weigh
If to the shame of all he now depart
Unpunished and unharmed in any way.
Nay, rather would I see him, for my part,
Hanged from these very battlements today,
For that would be a deed of noble worth,
A warning to all cowards from henceforth.'

127

Martano's words by Orrigille are
At once confirmed, but Norandin replies:
'I do not think we need to go as far
As you suggest; the fault which in him lies
Is not so grave nor so irregular;
But for the punishment I now devise
I wish the people summoned to look on.'
And he gives orders what is to be done.

128

He sends a baron to the city gate.
A group of men-at-arms march at his side.
There by the bridge so silently they wait,
In ambuscade so patiently they hide,
Crouching unseen behind a parapet,
That when they hear that borrowed charger ride
Across the bridge, they leap upon their prey
And hold him prisoner till break of day.

129

The Sun his golden locks no sooner raised
From the sweet bosom of his ancient nurse
And from the mountain slopes the shadows chased,
While peak on peak he rendered clear and terse,
Than vile Martano cunningly appraised
His situation; fearing a reverse,
If brave Grifone's words should undeceive
The king, he bade adieu and took his leave,

130

Finding excuses when the king expressed
The wish that he Grifone's shame should see.
Many a gift upon the wretch was pressed
In token of his (not his) victory.
The highest honours which his realm possessed
The king bestowed upon him gratefully.
So let him now depart: I promise you,
He'll not go far ere he receives his due.

131

Forth from the dungeon cell where he has lain
They drag Grifone to the crowded square.
To make his ignominy the more plain,
No helmet, no cuirass, they let him wear;
As though he went to market to be slain,
Dressed in a doublet, to the public stare
Exposed, upon a common cart they place him,
Harnessed to lean-flanked cattle to disgrace him.

132

Around this vile quadriga there appear
A crowd of harlots and of ancient crones.
Now this one and now that his charioteer
Pretends to be, and urges on with groans
The slowly-pacing cows; but most to fear
He has from bands of children, who fling stones
As well as insults; all restraint they lack
But, by good fortune, elders hold them back.

133

Those arms which were the cause of so much ill
And have misled the judgement of the king,
Are dragged behind the lowly vehicle
And to the dust his reputation bring.
Before a raised tribune the cart stands still,
And there, accompanied by trumpeting,
He hears the recitation to his face
Of deeds which are another man's disgrace.

134

Next, as an object of contempt they show him,
Going the round of churches, workshops, houses,
That for a coward every man may know him.
No jibes, no taunts, no insults, no abuses,
Are anywhere withheld; then forth they throw him,
In final ignominy, as their use is,
Driving him from their midst with cuffs and blows,
For who he is not one among them knows.

135

No sooner were his hands and feet released,
Which till that moment had been tied with thongs,
His buckler and his sword Grifone seized,
Which in the dust had trailed. At last his wrongs
And sufferings, or so it seemed, had ceased.
To my next canto what came next belongs,
For it is time, my lord, to finish this,
Of which the length perhaps excessive is.

CANTO XVIII

1

Magnanimous Signor, your every act
With reason I have praised and still I praise,
Though my poor style, alas! the power has lacked
Your glory to its fullest height to raise;
But, of your virtues which applause attract,
To one my tongue most heartfelt tribute pays:
Though many are in audience received,
Their evidence is not at once believed.

2

When blame against an absent man is laid,
I hear you bring excuses to defend him;
When all accusers all their say have said,
One ear you keep unprejudiced to lend him;
And long before a judgement you have made,
A hearing, face-to-face, you will extend him.
For days and months and years you may defer
Before you find against him, lest you err.

3

If Norandino had but done the same,
No need was there to use Grifone so.
While your procedure has enhanced your fame,
His honour now is blackened and brought low
By many deaths for which he is to blame.
Enraged, Grifone strikes blow after blow;
He cuts, he thrusts, he runs them through the heart
And thirty men lie dead beside the cart.

4

The others scatter and, wherever fear
Suggests, they run, some to the fields, to find
A refuge, others to the streets; some here,
Some there, falling on one another, blind
With terror, near the gate. The cavalier,
Wasting no words, leaves mercy far behind
And lays about him with his deadly sword
In vengeance for the scorn he has endured.

5

The first of those who reach the city gate,
Whose wits are no less nimble than their heels,
Grifone's next intent anticipate.
Pulling the drawbridge up, as quick as eels,
They scurry past in droves, or separate,
Their faces pale, bemoaning all their ills,
And through the streets, on each and every side,
Clamour and shouts are raised and warnings cried.

6

The valorous Grifone seizes two
Whom in the nick of time the bridge forestalls.
The brains of one the near-by meadow strew,
Dashed out against a millstone; next he falls
Upon the other wretch and runs him through,
Then flings him high above the city walls:
A chill through all Damascan veins it sends
To see him thus returning to his friends.

7

Now many feared Grifone would leap back
Across the walls, and no confusion could
Be greater were the Sultan to attack
Damascus and the city be destroyed.
Clatter of armour, tramp of feet, no lack
Of calling by muezzins, high and loud,
Beating of drums, the trumpet's strident cry
Deafened the earth and echoed through the sky.

8

But the conclusion to some other time
I must defer and say now what befell
King Charles, whom I must follow in my rhyme,
And once again of Rodomonte tell
Who slew so many Frenchmen in their prime.
I left the Emperor escorted well
By the great Dane, Namo and Oliver,
Avin, Avolio, Otto, Berlingier.

9

Eight lances, aimed with deadly violence
By eight such warriors, converged upon
The dragon's scales in which the Saracen's
Strong torso well protected was. As on
A ship the mast rears up when canvas thence
Is lowered at the gust of Aquilon,
So sprang up Rodomonte, safe and nimble,
From blows that might have made a mountain tremble.

10

Guido, Riccardo, Salamon, Ranier,
The traitor Ganelon, Turpin the true,
Matthew from St Michel, Mark, Angiolier,
Next Ivo, Angiolino and then Hugh
To threaten the vile Saracen draw near;
And to the eight already known to you
Edward is added, Harriman is well,
Who both now reached the stricken citadel.

11

Never did lofty fortress toss and quake,
Built on the solid rock or mountain side,
When from the north or south the tempests make
The fir-tree forests tremble in their pride,
As now the cruel Moor is seen to shake
In rage and blood-lust still unsatisfied.
As peal and flash conjoin in thundery weather,
So do his wrath and vengeance blaze together.

12

The nearest head he severed at one blow
(Hugh of Dordogne's it proved to be, alas!).
Cleft to the teeth, he tumbled and lay low,
And yet of tempered steel his helmet was.
A shower of blows the Moor received also,
Which on him made as little impact as
A needle on an anvil: against those scales,
A dragon's carapace, no force avails.

13

All strong-points, all redoubts, all garrisons
Are undefended, for all men-at-arms,
Summoned by trumpets and by clarions,
Have rallied to the focus of alarms.
The populace from every quarter runs
And to the centre of the city swarms.
Knowing they cannot flee, they quickly snatch
What weapons they can find, and boldly watch.

14

As sometimes in a cage, securely barred,
Wherein is kept an agèd lioness
In many a grim encounter battle-scarred,
To please a gaping crowd which round it press,
A bull, abstracted from a stable-yard,
Is introduced: the cubs who watch it pace,
Proud and untamed, at those great horns take fright,
And cower in a corner out of sight.

15

But if their dam ferociously attack
And sink her teeth in the intruder's ear,
The cubs, likewise, no longer courage lack,
But, emulating her, draw boldly near.
One bites it in the paunch, one in the back:
Just so the citizens abandon fear,
From roofs and windows, porticoes and doors,
A rain of missiles on the pagan pours.

16

So many are the horse and infantry
Scarce can the square the total force contain;
And of the crowd so vast a quantity
From every street comes flocking in amain;
Dense as the swarm that follows a queen bee,
All hopes to cut them down would be in vain.
Were he to try for twenty days or more,
This task of slaughter would defeat the Moor.

17

Like helpless cabbage-stalks or turnip-tops
Some he beheads, but, weary of this game
(For all he slashes, slices, cuts and chops,
The total number still appears the same),
He sees how useless is such toil, and stops.
To leave while he has breath is now his aim.
Unwounded yet and strong, he thinks he should
Make his departure while the going's good.

18

So, casting round about his cruel eyes,
He sees that all retreat has been cut off
But, carving through that crowd in cruel guise,
He opens up an exit soon enough.
His weapon brandishing, he first defies
The British, seasoned warriors and tough,
Who recently across the Channel sped,
With Harriman and Edward at their head.

19

Whoe'er has watched when through a palisade,
Which served to keep in check a surging throng,
A bull comes crashing, wild and rampant made
By snarling dogs and goaded all day long,
And seen the scattered mob look back, afraid,
While one is gored, another tossed and flung,
Let him imagine now that cruel Moor's
Advance: like such a bull he is, or worse.

20

A sideways slash at ten or twenty men:
As many heads are rolling on the ground –
One stroke for each, and not one stroke in vain,
As if a willow-tree or vine he pruned.
His pagan surcoat purple with the stain
Of Christian blood, and leaving all around
Shoulders and legs and other severed parts
To mark his trail, he finally departs.

21

So arrogantly through the crowd he goes,
So eager still to fight he seems to all,
That what his true intent is no one knows.
Looking for ways to leave the citadel,
He comes at last to where the river flows
Below the island and beyond the wall;
But now the men-at-arms and populace
Reluctant are to let him go in peace.

22

As in Numidian or Massilian woods
You may behold some noble-hearted prey
Which, though retreating, yet unhurried plods
In stately dignity to hide away,
So Rodomonte, facing fearful odds,
Does nothing base or cowardly that day,
But through a forest, formed of swords and spears
And flying darts, the river-bank he nears

23

With slow and steady strides; and three times more
His fury blazes forth and back he turns
And stains his blade anew with Christian gore.
A hundred fall; but now his anger burns,
Assuaged at last, less fiercely than before.
Reason at length a better course discerns:
Desisting from all further thrusts and lunges,
He clambers down the bank and in he plunges.

24

Wearing full armour, through the flood he swam
As though buoyed up by floats of cork. Of all
Your sons, O Africa, not one can claim
Equality with him, not Hannibal,
Nor yet Antaeus. When at length he came
To shore, it irked him that the citadel
Through which unaided and alone he strode
Unconquerable stands and undestroyed.

25

So gnawed was he by mingled wrath and pride,
He thought of storming Paris once again,
And in his very soul he groaned and sighed,
In longing to destroy her; but just then
Coming along the river-bank he spied
One who might cool his wrath and soothe his pain.
I'll tell you who it was without delay,
But first there's something else which I must say.

26

Dame Discord I must speak of, that same wife
To whom the Archangel the task entrusted
Of stirring enmity and bitter strife
Among the leaders Agramant had mustered.
She left the monks before you could say knife,
But first a deputy in whom she trusted
She chose, to keep, while she was gone abroad,
The fires of hate alight: her name was Fraud.

27

But ere she put the monastery behind her,
She thought she would enlist the help of Pride.
Not far, indeed, had she to go to find her:
They lived together always, side by side.
She in her turn unwilling was to bind her
Until a substitute she found, well tried;
So, for the days when she would absent be,
Her locum tenens was Hypocrisy.

28

Discord and Pride set out upon their way
To work their havoc on the pagan band;
And as they went they met that very day
Their sister Jealousy, who also planned
To seek the pagan camp; attired in grey,
She seemed cast-down and sad, and by the hand
She led a dwarf, by Doralice sent
To Sarza's king, for help in the event.

29

For when King Mandricardo kidnapped her
(I told you where and how this came about),
She secretly despatched a messenger –
This dwarf – to seek King Rodomonte out.
The damsel hoped the dreadful news would stir
Her true affianced; she had little doubt
That fearful vengeance he would swiftly take
Upon this interloper for her sake.

30

Dame Jealousy then met him on the road
And when she learned the reason for his quest
Beside him gladly on the way she strode;
Such enterprises always pleased her best.
To Jealousy, her sister Discord owed
Much help in her achievements in the past,
So she rejoiced to see her, for she knew
How she could help in what she planned to do.

31

To stir hostility between the son
Of Agrican and Rodomonte seems
To her a likely plan (another one
She will devise for others); as she schemes,
The left bank of the Seine they come upon
Just as the pagan plunges in and swims;
And in the full regalia of war
They see him wading out upon the shore.

32

As soon as Rodomonte recognized
The dwarf, his anger died, his furrowed brow
Became serene, his joy was undisguised,
His courage rose, and peace, he knew not how,
Filled all his heart; nothing so much surprised
Him as the truth he was to hear, I vow.
He went to greet him, asking joyfully:
'What tidings of our lady? How is she?'

33

The dwarf replied: 'No longer mine or yours
Would I describe her now, for yesterday
A knight whom we encountered on our course
Seized her by violence and made away.'
Cold as a snake, Dame Jealousy the Moor's
Fierce heart invaded and embraced straightway.
The dwarf, continuing, told him the whole,
How but one man his Doralice stole

34

And all her escort killed. Dame Discord took
Her tinder-box and flint; and close to Pride
She set them down; a spark was quickly struck,
The tinder caught, the flame did not subside,
And Rodomonte's soul, thus kindled, shook.
Knowing not where to turn, he groaned and sighed.
His livid features with such fury blazed,
All Heaven and all Nature stood amazed.

35

As when a tigress to her empty lair
Returns at length to find her offspring gone
And, seeking for them vainly here and there,
She senses what some predator has done,
Her fury knows no bounds, and without care
For mountain, river, night or midday sun,
She tracks the malefactor down, come hail,
Come rain, come shine, however long the trail;

36

So does his flame of fury rage and toss.
'Take me to where she is at once,' he said,
And he does not intend to let the moss
Grow underneath his feet; more quickly sped
Than any lizard flickering across
The road when the sun blazes overhead,
He leaves, without a mount of any kind,
Resolved to take the first that he can find.

37

When Discord his intention understood,
She looked at Pride and smiled; then off she went
To send along his route a horse that should
Involve him further yet in more dissent.
To clear the road of others she thought good,
For one and only one Dame Discord meant
Him to encounter; but I'll leave her now
And to King Charles return, if you'll allow.

38

As soon as Rodomonte left the scene,
The many fires, still burning, were put out.
When order once again restored had been,
Troops were despatched to guard some weaker spot,
Or to pursue the fleeing Saracen
And put the remnants of his ranks to rout.
From St Germain round to St Victor's gate,
King Charles his forces placed as for checkmate.

39

He gave instructions that at St Marcel
The regiments should marshal on the plain –
A space both adequate and suitable;
And he exhorted them with might and main
To smite the pagan hard and smite him well,
That echoes of the deed should long remain.
Next, those who bore the standards took them hence
To give the sign for battle to commence.

40

Through thick and thin King Agramant had stayed
Upright upon his saddle, and meanwhile
On Prince Zerbino deadly onslaught made.
Stroke upon clanging stroke, in hammer style,
Sobrino and Lurcanio repaid.
Rinaldo, single-handed, showed his skill
Against a band of pagans; by good luck
Shrewd thrusts he dealt and telling blows he struck.

41

While thus the battle rages to and fro,
King Charles is planning to attack the rear.
The Spaniards under King Marsilio
Around his standard are assembled there.
In close array the valiant Christians go;
Flanked by the cavalry the footmen are.
The sound of drums and trumpets which ascends
Reverberates, it seems, to the world's ends.

42

The Saracens, who saw them thus move on,
Withdrew straightway and made as if to flee.
They would have turned and broken ranks and run
Here and there, scattered irretrievably,
But King Grandonio and Falsiron,
Who both had been in greater jeopardy,
Fierce Serpentino, Balugante too,
Came on the scene in time with Ferraù.

43

'Brothers, companions, valorous and brave,'
The last vociferated, 'do not quail.
Before this fragile spider's web they weave,
Stand firm and in your duty do not fail.
Think of the glory and the gains you'll have,
Which Fortune, if we win, will yield as spoil.
Think of the losses and extreme disgrace,
Which, if we are defeated, we must face.'

44

So saying, he had seized a mighty lance
And rammed it with full force at Berlingier,
Who ceased to harass Argalif at once,
His helmet broken wide from ear to ear.
Next with his cruel sword he felled perchance
Another eight, succeeding everywhere,
For every stroke of his its target found
And knocked at least one Christian to the ground.

45

Meanwhile Rinaldo, fighting somewhere else,
Has killed more Saracens than I could count.
Their ranks he scatters, order he dispels,
Creating space around him and his mount.
Respect likewise Lurcanio compels,
Who, while Zerbino (men will long recount
The deeds of both) the helm of Finadur
Has split, Balastro added to his score.

46

Alzerbe's troops Balastro had commanded,
Which formerly were by Tardocco led.
Those from Morocco, Zamor, Saffi, banded
Together, Finadur had as their head.
Was there no African, I hear demanded,
Of whom it could be reasonably said
That he could wield a lance? In truth, my story
Will overlook no-one deserving glory.

47

Zumara's monarch I will not forget,
The noble Dardinel, Almonte's son,
Who with his lance, Claude of the Wood upset,
Hubert of Mitford, Elio, Dolphin, one
By one, and with his sword, the Earl (ill met)
Of Stamford (Anselm), Raymond, Pinamon,
Of London both; seven in all, that made,
Two merely stunned, one wounded and four dead.

48

And yet, for all the valour he displays,
His men to his example do not rise.
They fall behind, our troops they will not face,
Although inferior our number is,
For we outstrip them in all warlike ways,
In swordsmanship and jousting expertise.
Thus men of Marna, Ceuta, Zumara,
Morocco, the Canaries, routed are.

49

But, most of all, Alzerbe's forces flee,
Whom Dardinello rallied once before,
And whom he now harangues alternately,
Their failing courage hoping to restore,
With prayers, or bitter words of irony:
'If you recall Almonte's deeds of yore,
I shall now know, if you leave me, his son,
To face such jeopardy as this alone.

50

'Stand firm, I beg of you; think of my youth,
In which such hopes you formerly reposed.
If you are taken captive, death uncouth
Awaits you, not escape, as you supposed.
None will see Africa again, in truth.
Let us close ranks, else will all roads be closed.
Too high a rampart and too broad a moat
The mountain and the ocean constitute.

51

'Far better were it here and now to die
Than linger at the mercy of these hounds.
Faithful companions, I entreat you by
Our God above, have faith in my commands.
All other remedies are vain; but why
Should we fear those who have, like us, two hands,
One life, one soul?' With this the strong young prince
Smote Athol's earl and drove his spirit hence.

52

Almonte's memory then kindled so
Those Africans who formerly had fled,
They deemed their hands of use once more, and lo!
They turned to follow where their leader led.
William of Bromwich, as the English go,
Is tall; he tops his fellows by a head,
But Dardinello cuts him down to size.
Next by his hand Herman of Cornwall dies.

53

As Herman fell face-forward from his mount,
His brother ran to help him up again,
But Dardinel, whose weapon was not blunt,
Split him to where the torso splits in twain.
Then Bogio's belly pierced (Vergalle's count),
His promise to his wife thus rendered vain:
Within six months he vowed he would be home
(If still alive); now he will never come.

54

The brave young Dardinello saw near by
Lurcanio approaching, who had slit
Dorchino's throat and flung him down to die,
And Gardo's skull e'en to his teeth had split.
He saw his friend Alteo vainly try
To save himself, but fierce Lurcanio hit
Him on the cervical, a mortal blow,
Which brought, alas! this loved companion low.

55

A lance he seizes – to Mahound he swears,
If vengeance it be granted him to take,
That of the weapons which Lurcanio bears
A votive offering in the mosque he'll make.
Hoping this vow may reach his Prophet's ears,
He rides across at speed and, like a stake,
He drives his weapon through Lurcanio's side,
Bidding his vassals strip him when he's died.

56

You may imagine Ariodante's grief
When to his death his gallant brother fell;
Nor have you any need to ask me if
He longed to send his slayer's soul to Hell.
But the defenders of the true belief,
As well as a vast throng of infidel,
His way so much impeded that he had
To carve his way to vengeance with his blade.

57

He cuts and thrusts and slashes through the lines,
Unhorsing all opponents who come nigh;
And Dardinello, who his plan divines,
With his desire is eager to comply.
But still the throng re-forms and re-combines,
And will not let them meet, howe'er they try,
Though while one decimates the Moorish ranks,
The other slaughters English, Scots and Franks.

58

Fortune continually blocks the way,
Unwilling these two cavaliers should meet.
For one she has another plan that day,
And seldom does a man escape his fate.
See now Rinaldo turn and join the fray
And closer round the victim draw the net.
See now Rinaldo come, by Fortune led,
That Dardinel by him shall be struck dead.

59

But I have said enough, I think, for now
About these deeds of glory in the West,
And I'll return once more, if you'll allow,
To where I left Grifone; in his breast
Such fury burned, such anger blazed, I vow,
That such a terror spread and such unrest
That Norandino hastened to the scene,
Bringing behind more than a thousand men.

60

King Norandino with his armed escort,
Seeing his people in disordered flight,
Reached the portcullis of the outer fort,
Which rose at his command; meanwhile the knight
No opposition met of any sort
(The livers of that mob being lily-white).
Finding discarded armour (not his own)
He picked it up and quickly put it on.

61

Beside a temple, with vast walls and strong,
And by a ditch surrounded, wide and deep,
Upon the bridge he stood, secure and strong,
Where none can circle or behind him creep.
Uttering threats in voices loud and strong,
The army marches forth, but not one step
The brave Grifone stirs; with scornful glance,
Showing no fear, he watches their advance.

62

And when he judged they had come near enough,
He went to meet them on the road below,
And dealt a savage and severe rebuff,
Both hands upon his sword with every blow.
Then, having for the moment called their bluff,
Back to the bridge he went and to and fro
He sallied forth and once again withdrew,
And every time the number slaughtered grew.

63

To right, to left, he flashes his good blade
And overturns now foot, now cavalry.
The populace on every side lend aid,
Converging on him more and more till he,
The valorous Grifone, is afraid
That soon he'll be submerged in such a sea.
Already wounded in the thigh (the left),
And in the shoulder, scarce breath has he left.

64

Valour, which often brings its own reward,
Earns him the admiration of the king,
Who sees the corpses as he hastens toward
The centre of the fight, and, marvelling,
Beholds the injuries which Hector's sword
Might have inflicted; it's a certain thing
That wrongly he has put this knight to shame,
For this must be a cavalier of fame.

65

And as he nearer comes and face-to-face
Beholds the one who killed so many men,
Heaped in a high and horrifying mass,
Reddening the water with a gruesome stain,
He seems to gaze on, in Grifone's place,
Horatius of ancient Rome again,
Who held the bridge against all Tuscany.
His men withdrawing, not reluctantly,

66

His hand he raises, bare and weaponless
(The ancient sign of peace or of a truce),
And says: 'That I was wrong I now confess.
To lack of observation I reduce
My error and to lying tales, no less,
Which served my better judgement to seduce.
I thought that what I did was done, of right,
To the most abject, not the bravest, knight.

67

'Although the outrage and the shame committed
And all the insults heaped on you today,
To which in ignorance you were submitted,
Are equalled and indeed are wiped away
By the heroic vengeance you have meted,
Yet I would compensate you in the way
That you deserve, by gifts of gold or else
By castles, fortresses or citadels.

68

'Take up to half the kingdom which I own,
And gladly with this portion will I part,
For you have earned, in truth, not this alone,
But my devotion: so, accept my heart;
Give me your hand in pledge that from now on
From loyal friendship we shall not depart.'
So saying, from his horse the king descended,
And to Grifone his right hand extended.

69

After these words which Norandin had said,
Grifone saw him come, arms open held.
His weapon and his wrath aside he laid;
Clasping the monarch's legs, he humbly kneeled.
The king, who saw the wounds from which he bled,
Summoned a doctor that they might be healed,
Then to his palace, gently, without haste,
He ordered that the knight be brought to rest.

70

And there Grifone longer than a week
Remained till he could put his armour on.
But now I leave him, and his brother seek
In Palestine; soon as the youth had gone,
Astolfo and Aquilante in every creek
And cove had looked for him, in every one
Of all the Holy City's holy places
And far beyond, but of him found no traces.

71

Neither could guess, and neither could foretell
The whereabouts of young Grifone then;
But the Greek traveller, as it befell,
Arrived to give some clue to what had been.
He said that Orrigil (that Jezebel)
Upon the road to Antioch he'd seen,
Escorted by her latest paramour
Whom she'd conceived a sudden passion for.

72

Then Aquilante of the Greek enquired
Whether Grifone had heard word of this,
And, learning this was so, all he required
To know he knows, and certain now he is
Grifone's heart to follow her was fired,
To take her from his rival being his
Intention, and to bring upon his head
Ferocious vengeance or to strike him dead.

73

It saddens Aquilante and alarms,
To think his brother should set off alone.
Planning to follow him, he takes his arms,
But first requests Astolfo to stay on
Until from Antioch and all its harms
He brings Grifone back, his mission done.
At Jaffa he embarks, for it seems best
To him to go by sea, and speediest.

74

The south-west wind now favourably blew;
It drove him sure and fast, so that next day
Came well-known Tyre and Sarafend in view.
Passing Beirut and Djebeil, on his way
He went; to port the isle of Cyprus too
He saw; from Tripoli to Laodicea,
He passed Tortosa; sailing on from there,
To Alexandretta he chose to steer.

75

So to the east he turns the vessel's prow,
And rides the waters high and swift and light,
And up the Orontes he prepares to go,
Upon the tideway, as he judges right.
Then Aquilante bids the pilot throw
A bridge ashore, and rides, equipped to fight,
Upstream upon his fiery battle-horse
And reaches Antiochia in due course.

76

News of Martano he soon gathers there
And learns that to Damascus he has gone,
Accompanied by Orrigille, where
The king holds open court to everyone.
So to Damascus he must now repair,
Certain his brother will have travelled on.
Accordingly to leave that day he planned,
But this time chose to travel over land.

77

Towards Lydia and Larissa on he rides;
Above Aleppo, rich and populous,
He rests a while; and God, who there too chides
The wicked and rewards the virtuous,
One league from Màmuga, or there besides,
Arranged for him to meet the villainous
Martano, who, enjoying an ovation,
Displayed his stolen prize with ostentation.

78

When first he saw him, Aquilante thought
The cowardly Martano, clad in white,
Must be his brother, whom so long he'd sought.
(The arms the villain wore deceived his sight.)
And to his lips a cry of joy this brought,
But soon his face and tone were altered quite
As he drew closer and could plainly see
This knight was an impostor and not he.

79

Fearing the villain had been helped by her
Who travelled with him, and that they had slain
Grifone, 'Tell me,' he called, 'you who are
Traitor and thief, as from your face is plain,
Where did you get these arms, this destrier?
They are my brother's. Is he dead? Explain
How else it came about (for this I'd know)
His arms you wear and on his horse you go.'

80

When Orrigille heard that angry voice
She tried to turn her palfrey round to flee;
But Aquilante checked her in a trice,
Being quicker off the mark by far than she.
Martano understood he had no choice
But to remain, being seized so suddenly.
All pale, he trembles like an aspen spray
And knows not what to do or what to say.

81

The shouts, continuing, increase their fears.
Holding his sword-point at Martano's throat,
With frenzied fury, Aquilante swears
The heads of both from off their necks he'll cut
Unless the truth, and the whole truth, he hears.
Martano, swallowing and gulping, but
Revolving too the means by which he'll seek
To disculpate himself, begins to speak:

82

'Why, sir, this is my sister,' he replied,
'Born of a good and virtuous family,
Though by Grifone to dishonour tied
And by him forced to live opprobriously.
Such infamy my patience sorely tried,
But feeling I was insufficiently
Equipped to rescue her from him by force,
To ingenuity I had recourse.

83

'So I arranged with her, who long desired
A better and more worthy life to live,
That when Grifone to his rest retired
And fell asleep, she secretly should leave,
And so she did; but first, as was required,
Lest he should follow and our plot unweave,
We took away his armour and his mount.
As you can see, this is a true account.'

84

So versed was he in every cunning ruse
He might have easily convinced the knight
That on Grifone merely the abuse
Of theft he had been guilty of that night;
But he so wished to furbish his excuse
And make his lying soul seem lily-white,
Instead of leaving well alone, the twister
Pretended Orrigille was his sister.

85

In Antiochia Aquilante learned
She had been known with many men to lie.
With all the rage and scorn with which he burned,
He shouted: 'Thief and hypocrite! You lie!'
To draw his sword upon such scum he scorned
But fetched him with his fist a blow whereby
Two teeth went down his throat; then with no word,
He seized his arms and bound him with a cord.

86

And Orrigille likewise next he tied,
Though much in her defence she found to say.
Dragging the wretches at his horse's side,
Through towns and villages he made his way
Towards Damascus, and if multiplied
A thousandfold the road had been which lay
Ahead, still would his plan have been no other
Than hand the villains over to his brother.

87

Their shield-bearers and baggage-horses too
He brought behind, and to Damascus came
Where everywhere about the city flew
The latest tidings of Grifone's fame.
From first to last, all the Damascans knew
How he had wrongfully been put to shame,
How from his rights his rival tried to oust
Him, and then stole the glory of the joust.

88

The populace the vile Martano see
And pointing at him say to one another:
'See there that evil wretch, is not that he
Who plumes himself on the brave deeds of other
Knights, on the unwary pouring infamy?
And did he not pretend to be the brother
Of that ingrate who still beside him stays,
Who helps the wicked and the good betrays?'

89

And others shouted: 'How well matched they are!
Birds of a feather! Tarred with the same brush!'
Some utter curses at them, others roar:
'Hang, burn and quarter them!' and in the crush,
Craning and elbowing to see the more,
Jostling and hurtling, to the square they rush.
The king such joy ne'er knew, nor ever would,
If on him a new realm had been bestowed.

90

Without his retinue, informally,
He hurries forth to greet the cavalier
Who has avenged his brother's infamy,
And to his palace he invites him, where
He honours and receives him graciously,
As he deserves; but first the evil pair,
By his consent, as prisoners are flung
Into a dungeon, where they both belong.

91

They go together to Grifone's room
Where wounds, unhealed, confine him still to bed;
And when Grifone sees his brother come
He knows how much he knows, and turns bright red.
When they have jested for a while, the doom
Of the two traitors they discuss, agreed
At least that for these miscreants they must
Devise a retribution that is just.

92

The king and Aquilante hold stern views
Concerning death by torture and they air them.
Though Orrigille's name he does not use,
Grifone says he would prefer to spare them.
Skill in his choice of arguments he shows.
The others sift and with their own compare them.
At last they settle, when they all draw breath,
Martano shall be flogged, but not to death.

93

Bound (not, like Caesar, among flowers and grass),
Martano has his flogging one fine morn,
And Orrigille further time must pass
In prison till Lucina shall return:
Her judgement, whether mild or merciless,
The others will accept; so let us turn
To Aquilante's plans. Until the day
Grifone's wounds have healed he means to stay.

94

King Norandino, wise and prudent grown,
After an error of such magnitude,
His heart, with grief and penitence o'erflown,
Still longed continually to make good
The outrage and the wrong which he had done;
And so, to make amends, as best he could,
He thought all day and pondered half the night
How he might best content and please the knight.

95

And he decreed that in full view of all
The citizens who had abused him so
He should be reinstated, in his full
Regalia, that everyone might know,
With glory and all ceremonial
That ever king to perfect knight could show.
And so he makes it known that once again
A tourney will be held a month from then.

96

These festive preparations of the king's
Most solemn, sumptuous and splendid are,
And Fame straightway on swiftly-beating wings
Through all Phoenicia and all Syria
And to all Palestine the tidings brings.
They reach Astolfo in particular.
He and the viceroy of Jerusalem
Vow there will be no tourney without them.

97

As a brave warrior of great repute
The chronicles of Sansonetto tell.
Orlando baptized him, and this bore fruit;
For, as I said, the Holy Citadel
He governed for King Charles; along a route
They go where many signs are visible
And tidings of the tourney reach their ears
Which in Damascus Norandin prepares.

98

And as they slowly journeyed at their ease
Towards Damascus from Jerusalem
That they might, unfatigued, such expertise
Display as customary was of them,
A cavalier they met at the cross-ways
Who in attire, in each and every limb,
A man appeared and yet a woman was,
In battle powerful and marvellous.

99

Marfisa is this warrior-maiden's name.
So mighty was her strength that, sword in hand,
She'd made Orlando sweat (and none can blame
Him) and Rinaldo too, I understand.
She went in search of glory and of fame,
In armour day and night through every land,
For in her wanderings she hoped to meet
Knights-errant to combat and to defeat.

100

And seeing Sansonetto and the duke
Coming towards her in full panoply,
She judged them valiant warriors from their look,
For both were tall and fashioned sturdily;
And such delight in duelling she took,
She spurred her charger at them instantly
And challenged them; but, moving closer in,
She saw and recognized the paladin.

101

His presence stirs a recollection of
Their gallant days of combat in Cathay.
His name she calls and, pulling off her glove,
She lifts her visor, wishing to display
Her features, and embraces him with love
(Her usual pride abandoning that day).
Astolfo too an equal readiness
Likewise reveals, his homage to express.

102

They asked each other whither each was bound
And when Astolfo said (he first replied)
That on to Syria their way they wound,
Where in the capital from far and wide
As many valiant knights as could be found
Were summoned to defy and be defied,
Marfisa, ever by such prospects fired,
To bear them company at once desired.

103

The duke and Sansonetto with delight
Accept; reaching Damascus on the day
Before the joust, a lodging for the night
They find outside the city; here they stay
Until Aurora wakens with her light
Her lover, once so fair, who with her lay.
Refreshing and more sweet was their repose
Than if from palace couches they arose.

104

When the new sun its radiance had shed
In shafts of brilliant light upon the scene,
They armed themselves, first having sent ahead
Their messengers, who soon as they had seen
What was afoot returned straightway and said
That in Damascus now King Norandin
Had come to see how lance on lance would clash
And fragments fly of sturdy beech and ash.

105

So they delayed no more but set off then
Along the high road to the city-square.
Awaiting the king's signal to begin,
They see the knights assemble here and there.
The victor of the games that day will win
A precious mace, a sword, a destrier
Such as befits a gallant warrior
Whose worth has tested been in deeds of war.

106

King Norandino firmly in his heart
Believed Grifone, who had won the first,
Would win the second tourney and depart
Triumphant, such brave hopes for him he nursed;
And he resolved that to fulfil his part
No less a prize to such a knight he durst
Present, to tally with the arms, than mace
And sword, and horse of noble breed and race.

107

Those precious arms which were Grifone's due,
Which in the former tourney he had won,
Which had been stolen by Martano who
Impersonated him, the king hung on
The royal palisade and fastened too
The sword likewise, and fixed the mace upon
The horse's saddle-bows, that all might see
These prizes of a dual victory.

108

But in his wheel Marfisa puts a spoke.
As to the city-square they now advance –
Marfisa, Sansonetto and the duke –
As soon as she has cast one single glance
Upon those precious arms of which I spoke,
She knows them for her very own at once,
For hers they are and dearly prized by her
As objects of great excellence and rare,

109

Although she left them lying in the road,
That gallows-rogue, Brunello, to pursue
The faster, being lightened of their load
When, stealing her good sword, away he flew.
But what befell when after him she strode
I do not think I need relate to you.
Let it suffice that I have told you now
That here her weapons had been found, and how.

110

When she had seen them, I will further say,
And seen that they were manifestly hers,
She would not suffer for a single day
For anything in the whole universe,
That empty of her person they should stay,
But instantly, for better or for worse,
She gallops up and, putting forth her hand,
She plucks her armour from the royal stand.

111

Such was her haste that only part she took.
The rest of it she scattered on the ground.
The king, affronted, with a single look
Hostilities declared, and quickly round
Him to avenge the insult many folk
With spears and lances in their hands were found,
Forgetting what they learned a few days back,
That cavaliers are dangerous to attack.

112

No child midst flowers, crimson, gold and blue,
In Spring has ever played with more delight,
No lovely damsel keener pleasure knew,
To strains of music dancing in the night,
Than among noise of arms and horses, through
The criss-cross maze of lances, where the fight
Is thickest, when men die or blood is shed,
She, strong beyond belief, with joy will tread.

113

She spurs her horse, and at the foolish flock,
Impetuous she drives her lowered lance.
Some in the neck, some in the chest, the knock
Receive; now here, now there, the miscreants
She fells, then with her sword proceeds to dock
The head of one, or slices through perchance
The flank of yet another, or else cleaves
A shoulder and the victim armless leaves.

114

Strong Sansonetto and the gallant duke,
Who like Marfisa were in armour clad,
Though this was not the quest they undertook,
Seeing the battle now in earnest had
Begun to rage, their visors closed and struck
The rabble; using lances first, they laid
About them with their cutting swords so well,
The crowd to right and left before them fell.

115

The cavaliers, who come from many lands,
And the commencement of the joust await,
Seeing the trophy in such warlike hands,
And hoped-for pleasure to such grievous state
Reduced (not everybody understands
The reason why the mob is so irate,
Nor what has happened to outrage the king),
Look on perplexed and greatly marvelling.

116

Some went at once to help the multitude
And later were unable to withdraw.
Others made off as quickly as they could,
Damascus being no place for them, they saw.
Reining their horses, others, wiser, stood
To watch the outcome of the strange uproar.
Among them were the sons of Oliver
Who intervention did not long defer.

117

Seeing the king with venom in his eyes,
Which bloodshot are with rage and hate and spleen,
Since of the tumult many now apprise
Them and of what its origin had been,
Grifone, who can rightly claim the prize,
The insult feels no less than Norandin;
So hastily demanding each a lance,
And breathing deadly vengeance, they advance.

118

But, from the other side, on Rabican,
Astolfo, with his magic, golden spear,
Which, when he jousts, unhorses every man,
Rode out in front of all the others there.
Grifone first, and Aquilante then
He smote, in turn disposing of the pair.
They both lay stretched full length upon the field,
Touched by that lance but lightly on the shield.

119

Knights of great valour, tried and tested too,
At Sansonetto's thrusts from saddles fall.
The piazza's exit people hurry to –
This is as bitter to the king as gall.
Taking her arms and helms, both old and new,
Marfisa, when she sees the rabble all
Turn tail and run for safety, helter-skelter,
Sets out triumphant for her lowly shelter.

120

Astolfo and Sansonetto are not slow
To follow her example; soon they leave
And to the city gate together go.
Grifone and Aquilante sorely grieve
That they were vanquished at a single blow.
Pondering how their honour to retrieve,
They hang their heads in their extreme disgrace
And Norandino do not dare to face.

121

No sooner are they mounted on their horses
Than, spurring hard, the strangers they pursue.
The king, whose thirst for vengeance even worse is,
Follows behind with a large retinue.
The foolish crowd shouts: 'Kill them', till it hoarse is,
And out of danger keeps, as cowards do.
Grifone gallops up just as the three
Companions turn to face the enemy.

122

He recognized Astolfo straight away,
Who the same horse was riding and the same
Device and armour bore as on the day
He killed Orrilo of enchanted fame.
He'd not suspected this in any way
When in the square to challenge him he came.
But now he knew him (and he did not err),
And asked him who his two companions were;

123

And why the unknown knight some weapons took
And left the others scattered on the ground,
Affronting thus the king; the English duke
Can truthfully to the first part respond.
As to the arms, for which the tumult broke,
He had no information, but felt bound,
As the companion of the warrior maid,
(With Sansonetto likewise) to lend aid.

124

While thus Grifone holds the paladin
In converse, Aquilante gallops up.
At once he recognizes him and in
An instant all his hostile passions drop;
And many who escorted Norandin
Likewise approach, but farther off they stop.
Seeing the cavaliers negotiate,
They hold their peace and for the outcome wait.

125

Hearing her name, one of them realized
Marfisa the redoubtable was there,
And, riding back in haste, the king advised,
Unless he wished his retinue to share
A fearful fate, it could not be disguised
They must withdraw: no time had they to spare.
Marfisa the invincible it was,
In truth, who of the tumult was the cause.

126

And when that name King Norandino heard
Which many hairs had caused to stand on end,
Which everywhere in the Levant was feared
And even from afar could shivers send
Down every spine, plainly the truth appeared
Of what had just been said; so, to defend
His followers, whose wrath had changed to fright,
He called them back and saved them from their plight.

127

And for their part, the sons of Oliver
With Sansonetto and with Otto's son,
Besought the fierce Marfisa to forbear
And with the cruel conflict now have done.
The warrior-maiden to the king drew near
And proudly said: 'I do not know upon
What grounds, Sire, you intended to present
These arms as trophy in your tournament.

128

'These arms are mine; on the Armenian route
I left them on my journey here one day,
The better to pursue a thief on foot,
Who the presumption had to steal away
My sword; here, see, my emblem has been put,
Which will confirm the truth of what I say.'
On the cuirass she showed him a device
Consisting of a crown divided twice.

129

The king replied: 'I had them, it is true,
From an Armenian merchant some days back.
If you had asked me for them, whether you
Have claim to them, or claim to them you lack,
You could have had them with no more ado,
As sure as white is white and black is black;
Although Grifone won them as a prize,
He would have yielded them, I'll stake my eyes.

130

'To prove that they are yours, there is no need
To show me your device inscribed thereon.
You say they are: that is enough, indeed,
No witness would I more rely upon.
That they are yours I willingly concede.
A finer prize your prowess oft has won.
So keep them: undisputed let them be.
A greater gift Grifone gains from me.'

131

Grifone, who had set but little store
Upon those arms and wished to please the king,
Said: 'Sire, you could not compensate me more
Than by the knowledge that my actions bring
You joy.' Marfisa thinks: 'Such words restore
My honour fully', and, acknowledging
Grifone's claim to them with courtesy,
Accepts the weapons from him finally.

132

So to Damascus they return in peace
And love; the king renews the festival,
The joust begins, the prize is won with ease
By Sansonetto, who defeats them all.
Astolfo, the two brothers, and Marfise
(Whom I the best of the quartet would call)
Like true companions from the joust refrain,
That Sansonetto may this honour gain.

133

Eight or ten days with Norandin they spent
In joyful revels and festivity,
And then, by love of France their hearts being rent
(Their absence adding to her jeopardy),
They took their leave and from Damascus went.
Marfisa also bears them company,
And now at last her long-felt wish begins
To be fulfilled: beside the paladins,

134

To fight and to make trial of their fame
And probe the skill for which they are renowned.
Another regent of Jerusalem
In Sansonetto's place is duly found,
And they depart, the valiant five of them,
A group unequalled all the world around.
Ere long they have arrived at Tripoli
And make their way down to the near-by sea.

135

A cargo-vessel there its anchor trailed
While merchandise was loaded for the West.
To her old captain, who from Luni hailed,
For passage for themselves they made request
And also for their horses. Clear, unveiled,
The sky gave promise that they would be blessed
For many days with tranquil seas; they pull
From shore, and soon the spreading sails are full.

136

And, wafted by a favourable wind,
In Venus' isle the shelter of a port
They reach which harmful is to humankind,
Where metals crumble, and where life is short.
To Famagusta Nature was unkind
To set a swamp near by to do her hurt,
When all the other places on the isle
With pleasant air its visitors beguile.

137

The foul miasma which the swamp exhales
No vessel there induces to remain.
Before a north-east wind they spread their sails
And to the right hand round the island gain
The port of Paphos, where unloading bales
Of merchandise some of the crew begin.
The rest at once explore to left and right
The land of love and languorous delight.

138

Six miles or seven from the sea, they climb
In gradual ascent a gentle hill.
Oranges, myrtle, cedar, laurel, lime
And aromatic shrubs the landscape fill.
Rose, lily, crocus, saffron, marjoram, thyme
Such fragrance from the sweetly-smelling soil
Waft on the winds which from the island blow
That sailors out at sea its perfume know.

139

A stream which serves to irrigate the slope
Flows from a fountain-head which knows no dearth.
Here for her rule the goddess has full scope.
Here is her bower, here she had her birth.
Here are fair women, nor let any hope
To find them equalled anywhere on earth.
Both young and old, they burn with ardour more,
To Venus subject till their dying hour.

140

Here once again they hear Lucina's tale,
Which they have heard in Syria, and how
She plans as soon as possible to sail
From Nicosia, where from stern to bow
Her ship's refitting. At the captain's hail
The sailors quickly come aboard, and now
They weigh their anchor; setting course to west
They start, with all sail drawing at its best.

141

When rose a nor'west wind which the ship steered
To windward, hauling farther out to sea.
Then from south-west, what had at first appeared
A gentle breeze, at evening suddenly
Tremendous waves above the vessel reared.
Loud thunder followed lightning instantly,
Which cracked its fierce refulgence from on high
And wielded fire-pronged brands to split the sky.

142

The shadows now a veil of darkness spread,
Dimming the atmosphere and every star.
The sea below, the heavens overhead,
The wind and storm combine to howl and roar,
While on the crew an icy rain is shed,
And night, its arms extending more and more,
Within its dark embrace the angry sea
Has plunged in deep invisibility.

143

The sailors now their mettle demonstrate
And show the skills for which they are renowned.
The watchful bo'sun pipes a flageolet,
Which carries orders by its piercing sound:
'Stand by', it whistles, and then, 'Ease the sheet';
Now, 'Ready anchor', 'Up helm', 'Wear her round'.
Some hand the sails; some anchor-cables check;
Some lash the spars, and others clear the deck.

144

The violent weather worsened all that night,
As dark as Hades and as black as pitch;
But steadily against the ocean's might
The captain makes for deeper waters, which
He hopes to find less rough. Despite the weight
Of towering seas augmenting roll and pitch,
He'll not despair. He knows that soon or late
All storms outblow their strength, and moderate.

145

But still it blows, nor yet abates, but worse,
It harder blows when day (if this be day)
Returns; for still the dark obscures their course,
And still the gloom's more night than light of day,
And hence they keep the time by counting hours.
The captain lets the ship the winds obey;
His hopes are failing, in his heart there's fear
As they drift helpless to he knows not where.

146

While these at sea a furious storm molests,
I must not leave inactive those on land
Near Paris, where the Saracen contests
With English forces for the upper hand,
And where Rinaldo smites and sorely tests
His enemies and few before him stand.
I left him, you remember, on Baiard,
Against Prince Dardinello, spurring hard.

147

Rinaldo saw the shield with quartering
Which Dardinello carried with such pride.
Astonished that such challenge he should fling
As with that emblem into battle ride,
Thus with the Count Orlando rivalling,
He deemed him brave, a view soon verified
When he beheld near by the piles of dead.
'This is a bud which I must nip,' he said.

148

No matter where Rinaldo turns his glance,
A space in front of him with speed is cleared.
By pagans and, no less, by Christians
His famous sword, Fusberta, is revered;
And against Dardinello his advance
By no one and by nothing is deterred.
He shouts: 'Young sir, a legacy of strife
That quartering will prove, upon my life!

149

'I come to test, if wait for me you dare,
Your courage to defend the red and white,
For if to guard it against me you fear,
Still less against Orlando will you fight.'
The prince replied: 'This emblem which I bear
I will defend, for it is mine by right.
Not strife but glory I inherited
With this, my father's shield of white and red.

150

'Though I am young, yet you'll not make me yield,
And neither will you make me turn and flee,
Nor force me to surrender up the shield,
Unless my life you take. The contrary
God wills, I trust, for on the battlefield
My line will ne'er dishonoured be by me.'
So saying, with his sword he rushed upon
The valiant cavalier of Montaubon.

151

A shudder ran through all the pagan veins,
Chilling the very heart within each breast,
Soon as Rinaldo by the Saracens
Was seen to grasp Fusberta in his fist,
And, like a lion seeing on the plains
A young bull which no pangs of love molest,
Rush on the youth, whose blow, which first he dealt,
Through Mambrin's helm Rinaldo scarcely felt.

152

Rinaldo laughed and said: 'Now let us see
How well my sword a vital spot can find!'
Spurring his horse, he lets the reins go free.
His sword-point with the prince's breast aligned,
He rides towards the youth so forcibly
The point impales him and protrudes behind.
Withdrawn, it let flow blood and soul as well,
As from its horse the lifeless body fell.

153

As languishing a purple flower lies,
Its tender stalk cut by the passing plough,
Or, heavy with the rain of summer skies,
A poppy of the field its head will bow,
So, as all colour, draining downward, flies
From Dardinello's face, he passes now
From life, and with his passing, passes too
Such little daring as his followers knew.

154

As waters, when confined by human skill,
Swelling in volume, rise but cannot spread,
But, if the enclosing structure yields, o'erspill
The dam and with a mighty roar cascade,
So did those Africans, restrained until
Their gallant leader, Dardinel, lay dead,
Some here, some there, then scatter and disperse
Soon as they saw him tumble from his horse.

155

Rinaldo lets the fugitives escape;
Those who delay he threatens to pursue.
Both he and Albany a harvest reap,
For where Rinaldo goes the duke goes too.
Some Leonetto kills and in poor shape
Zerbino others leaves: they spare but few.
As Charles, so Oliver his duty does;
Guy, Salmon, Ugier, Turpin havoc cause.

156

That day the Moors in deadly peril were.
Not one his country might have seen again;
But King Marsilio without demur
His losses wisely cuts; a better plan
He judges this to be than to defer
Retreat and lose such men as still remain.
Better to save one squadron or one troop
Than risk them all by trying to recoup.

157

He sends his ensigns back to the stockades,
Which by a bank and ditch defended are.
Together with three kings and all their aides,
From Portugal, Granàda, Màlaga.
The king of Barbary he next persuades
As best he can his forces to withdraw,
For if his person and the camp that day
He saves, it will be no small victory.

158

King Agramante, bowed by his disgrace,
Who never thought to see Biserta more,
Who never in his life Dame Fortune's face
Had seen so stern and terrible before,
Hearing this counsel, could not but rejoice
To learn some of his forces were secure.
His standard-bearers turned, his army wheeled,
And, sounding the retreat, his trumpets shrilled.

159

Among the fleeing armies only few
Had waited till they heard the trumpets sound.
Great was their terror; some in panic flew,
And many in the river Seine were drowned.
The king tries with Sobrino to pursue
And rally them, touring the battle-ground,
And every gallant captain there lends aid
To bring the fugitives to the stockade.

160

Sobrino and the king do not succeed
And all the gallant captains likewise fail.
For all they threaten or cajole or plead,
Not one in three returns; of no avail
Their efforts are; two out of three are dead
Or have escaped; and of all those who trail
Towards camp, some in the back, some in the chest
Are wounded; battle-worn are all the rest.

161

In terror till they reached their quartering,
The remnants of the army were pursued,
But scarcely it afforded sheltering,
Though they had strengthened it as best they could.
To Fortune's forelock Charles knew how to cling
When favourable to him her face she showed;
But Night at last, who with her shades descended,
The clamour stilled and the day's combat ended,

162

Hastened, perhaps, by the Creator in
Compassion for his creatures here below.
The streams of blood the earth with scarlet stain
And like a river through the landscape flow;
The losses number eighty thousand slain
Who never more their fatherland will know.
Peasants and wolves from lairs and hovels creep,
The bodies to demolish and to strip.

163

To Paris Charles does not return that night,
But near his foe prefers to bivouac.
Many a leaping fire he keeps alight,
And plans the movements of the dawn attack.
The pagans trenches dig without respite.
Of ramparts newly firmed there is no lack.
Keeping the sentrymen on the *qui vive*,
They make their rounds, in arms from helm to greave.

164

Throughout the night, among the habitations
(Though they attempted to disguise their woes)
The sound of weeping, groans and lamentations
Of the defeated Saracens arose.
Some grieved for friends and others for relations
Who on the battlefield lay dead, and those
Who wounded were moaned in their suffering,
But most they grieved for what the morn might bring.

165

Among the Moorish soldiers, two there were,
In Ptolemais born, to fame unknown,
Whose story, instancing a love so rare,
Deserves to be related and made known.
Medoro and Cloridano, as the pair
Were called, whate'er the face by Fortune shown,
Had loved Prince Dardinello loyally
And with him came to France across the sea.

166

A hunter Cloridano his life long
Had been; robust he was, and lithe and tall.
Medoro's cheek, so tender and so young,
The lily and the rose displayed; in all
That host there was no countenance among
Their comely youth that was more beautiful.
His eyes were black, golden his curling hair,
As if a seraph from on high he were.

167

These two with many other sentinels
Upon the ramparts of the camp stand guard,
While with its sleepy eyes the heaven steals
Its covert glances through the midnight shroud.
Medoro, who can speak of little else,
Laments with deep regret that his young lord,
Prince Dardinello, King Almonte's heir,
Should yonder lie without a sepulchre.

168

And to his friend he says: 'O Cloridan,
How sad I am my lord should there repose,
Dishonoured and unburied on the plain,
Too fine a prey, alas, for wolves and crows!
When I recall his kindness, in my pain
It seems, were I my life itself to lose
In honouring his name, all that I owe
Would be but ill repaid, so deep my woe.

169

'But, that he may not stay unburied, I
Will go and search for him among the dead.
God may allow that where the Christians lie,
Unseen, unheard, in secret I may tread.
Do you stay here, for if the Fates deny
That I accomplish now this pious deed,
If death for me is in the stars foreshown,
My loving heart's desire do you make known.'

170

Amazed the other is to find such love,
Such courage and such faith in one so young.
Unrealizable he tries to prove
His noble plan, but all in vain; ere long
He understands that nothing can remove
The grief by which the other's heart is stung.
Medoro is resolved to die that day
Or in a sepulchre his lord to lay.

171

Seeing his mind was fixed inflexibly,
'I will come with you,' Cloridano said;
'Beside you in this task I too will be;
To honourable deeds I too am wed.
Of what advantage will it be to me
If I remain alive when you are dead?
Better with you to die, Medoro mine,
Than by your death be left alone to pine.'

172

Thus they agreed, and, leaving in their place
Two other guards whose turn was imminent,
Beyond the palisades into the space
Across the ditch among our men they went,
In whom, alas! no longer any trace
Of vigilance was found; all fires were spent;
By wine or sleep made deaf to all alarms,
They lay beside their waggons and their arms.

173

And Cloridano paused a while and said,
'Such an occasion must not be passed by.
This horde who struck our Dardinello dead
Deserves the death of dastards here to die.
Keep watch on every side, behind, ahead;
Be constantly alert with ear and eye,
While I now clear with my good sword and true
A pathway through the enemy for you.'

174

His action he then suited to his words;
And where the soothsayer Alfeo slept,
Who for a year at court among the lords
Of Charlemagne had lived, he softly crept.
But little help astrology affords,
Nor all the skills in which he was adept:
His death in his wife's arms he prophesied,
And in old age, but there and then he died.

175

When, moving cautiously, the Saracen
Had drawn his sword along Alfeo's throat,
He stepped across and killed four other men.
No time had they to speak, nor any note
Did Turpin leave of who they were, and in
The mist of years their names are now remote.
Next, Palidon of Moncalier death found,
Sleeping between two horses safe and sound.

176

And, moving on, he comes to where he sees
The head of Grillo on a barrel propped.
The wretch had emptied it and, now half-seas-
over, into a drunken sleep had flopped,
Thinking he there might safely take his ease,
But boldly Cloridano his head lopped.
Together blood and wine (which had approached
A vatful) spurted from the tub thus broached.

177

And next he killed a German and a Greek,
Conrad and Andropono, with two blows.
These two together had rejoiced to take
The air of night; with drinking and with throws
Of dice, they had resolved to stay awake
Till from the Ganges' bed the sun arose.
But Fortune could not work her will with men
If we foresaw the how and where and when.

178

And as a lion, which, long ravenous,
Will leap upon a flock of sheep and tear
And rend and kill, feeding despiteous
To satisfy its hunger, just so there,
As our men dream, the pagan, merciless,
Cuts veins, slits throats and slaughters everywhere;
And neither is Medoro's weapon blunt,
But for no common rabble does he hunt.

179

When Duke Labretto sleeping there he found,
In his belovèd's arms so lovingly
Entwined, their limbs so closely interwound
No air could pass between them, instantly
He severed both their heads without a sound.
O happy death! O sweetest destiny!
I vow, as with their bodies they embraced,
Their spirits rose to heaven interlaced.

180

He killed Malindo and Ardalico, his brother.
They were the Count of Flanders' gallant sons
Whom Charles had newly dubbed, both one and the other,
The lilies adding to their gonfalons
For swords well stained, and pledging yet another
Guerdon: good lands among the Frisians,
To Flemish kingdoms later on to add,
But this, alas! Medoro's sword forbade.

181

And when their furtive steps are close to where,
Tents being duly pitched that in their turn
The royal tent defend, a cavalier
Stands guard throughout the night, each one in turn,
Desisting from all further slaughter there,
The two, just in the nick of time, now turn.
Improbable to them it seems to be
That all are sleeping in that company.

182

Though they might make away with costly spoil,
Let them now save themselves – a richer gain.
Wherever Cloridano thinks to foil
The sleeping Christians scattered on the plain,
He leads, until they come to where the soil,
Littered with weapons, shows a crimson stain,
Where rich and poor, where vassals and where kings
Lie heaped in chaos such as battle brings.

183

The bodies which in grim miscellany
Appear to cover all the countryside
Might have dissuaded from their piety
The two companions who together tried
To pay their lord this final loyalty,
When from behind a cloud Medoro spied
The crescent of the moon, to which he prayed.
Fixing his eyes on it, these words he said:

184

'O sacred goddess, who in times gone by
Hast rightly worshipped been as three in one,
Who on the earth, in hell and in the sky
In triple loveliness thyself hast shown,
Who as a huntress dost in ambush lie
Or footprints follow, hear my orison:
Show me my king among these many dead,
Who in his life by thee was ever led.'

185

The moon at this petition parts the cloud
(Is it by chance, or by Medoro's faith?).
As fair as when she offered herself nude
To Endymion she seems, a silver wraith.
Lit by her light the whole of Paris showed:
Both plains, the hill, with each and every path,
And, from afar, Montmartre and Montlhéry
To right and left, in perfect clarity.

186

Her radiance with greatest splendour shone
Where Dardinello, the young prince, lay dead.
Weeping, Medoro to his lord had gone
Soon as the shield he saw of white and red.
In keenest anguish bitter tears upon
His face in an unending stream he shed.
So sweet his words, so sweet his gestures were,
The very winds might have been hushed to hear.

187

But in a voice which could be scarcely heard
He spoke, to avoid detection, not as though
To lose his life Medoro greatly feared,
(From life, now so abhorred, he longed to go),
But, as completion of his task he neared,
Caution prevailed lest he arouse the foe.
Raising their monarch dead, to shoulder height,
Sharing his weight, they bore him through the night.

188

Thus burdened, the two friends, as best they could,
Left the dread scene and hurried on their way.
Already he who of the light is god
Put out the stars and chased the dark away,
When Prince Zerbino, from whose breast the mood
Of sleep was banished by the bitter fray,
Returns from the pursuit of Saracens
As soon as the first sign of dawn begins.

189

With him are several other cavaliers
Who see the two companions from far off;
And instantly each one towards them veers,
Thinking that here are gains and spoils enough.
'Brother,' says Cloridano, 'it appears
We must set down our burden and be off,
For it would be indeed a foolish plan,
Two living men to lose for one dead man.'

190

He set the body down, thinking for sure
Medoro would be bound to do the same;
But that unhappy youth, who loved him more,
His dear lord hoisted on his slender frame.
And faster went the other than before,
As if his friend behind or with him came.
If to what fate he left him he had known,
He would have risked a thousand deaths, not one.

191

The cavaliers without a doubt intend
To make them both surrender or succumb;
And here and there they scatter to defend
Whatever pathway they might issue from.
More eager still their leader is to lend
A hand, for closer to them he has come
And by their furtive movements surely knows
These two no Christian allies are, but foes.

192

Near by in olden times there was a wood.
Its tangled boughs and labyrinthine twists
Impede the steps of all who dare intrude –
A habitat fit only for wild beasts.
The pagans entered, hoping that it would
Obscurity afford, which flight assists.
If any in my story take delight
Him now to listen later I invite.

CANTO XIX

1

No man can know by whom he's truly loved
When high on Fortune's wheel he sits, serene.
His friends surround him, true and false, unproved,
And the same loyalty in all is seen.
When to catastrophe the wheel is moved
The crowd of flatterers passes from the scene;
But he who loves his lord with all his heart
Remains, nor after death does he depart.

2

If from the face the soul could be discerned,
Some who at court stand high in men's esteem,
And those who by the lord they serve are spurned,
Discovered to be other than they seem,
Would find their fates reversed: the tables turned,
The humble raised, the great dismissed from him.
But let us seek Medoro who adored
In life and death his sovereign and his lord.

3

Through by-ways overgrown and intricate
The unhappy youth attempted now to flee;
But, hampered by so cumbersome a weight,
His efforts ended in futility.
Losing his way, he stumbled and his feet
In brambles tangled were repeatedly.
The other was already far ahead,
His back of such a heavy burden freed.

4

The clamour of pursuit left far behind,
Still he flew on and like the wind he went.
But when, on looking round, he failed to find
Medoro, with deep woe his heart was rent.
'Alas!' he said, 'how could I be so blind?
Alas! how could I be so negligent?
Medoro, why am I without you here?
How did I come to leave you, when and where?'

5

So saying, his own safety he forgets
And through the tangled wood again he goes,
His steps retracing to where death awaits,
Where danger menaces, as he well knows.
He hears the horses' hoofs, he hears the threats,
He hears the hated voices of his foes.
Of his Medoro they are in pursuit,
Many on horseback, he alone on foot.

6

A hundred horsemen block Medoro's path.
Zerbino shouts commands that he be taken.
The wretched boy runs, whirling like a lathe,
Darting now here, now there among the bracken.
Oak, elm, beech, ash defend him from their wrath.
His precious burden he has not forsaken;
He places it upon the grass at length,
To bear it farther lacking further strength.

7

And as a she-bear on the mountains, when,
Beside her helpless offspring keeping guard,
By a bold hunter threatened in her den,
She roars, her heart 'twixt rage and pity shared,
Her natural enmity against all men
Urging attack with fangs and claws well bared,
By love is drawn to turn towards her young
With tender glances, yet by fury stung,

8

So Cloridano, knowing not how best
To help, and ready with Medoro still
To die, though not ere more than one at least
Of his pursuers he found means to kill,
Fitting an arrow to his bow, released
It, from his secret ambush, with such skill
He instantly accounted for a Scot
Who fell from horseback, through the temple shot.

9

The others, all astonished, in the same
Direction turned, for they desired to know
From whom and whence that fatal arrow came.
Meanwhile, to bring a second Christian low,
The pagan once again took careful aim,
And one who shouted: 'Who then drew that bow?'
Fell from his horse, all further utterance cut,
For Cloridano's shaft had pierced his throat.

10

Zerbino, who was captain of the band,
In rage and fury towards Medoro went.
No more of this was he prepared to stand.
He said: 'For these two arrows *you'll* repent!'
Seizing those golden tresses with a hand
As merciless as it was violent,
He pulled him towards him, but that lovely face
Zerbino's vengeful arm in mercy stays.

11

The boy began entreating him and said:
'I beg you, be not cruel, by your God
This favour grant me, for my king is dead:
Let me inter his corpse beneath the sod.
To this sole action now my life is wed,
Which for one purpose only I hold good:
So in compassion this one boon accord,
That I may live to bury my dear lord.

12

'If, Creon-like, your savage nature is
To feed the scavengers of earth and air,
Give them my limbs for a repast, but these
Of King Almonte's son, let me inter.'
Thus did Medoro plead on bended knees
With words which might a rock or mountain stir.
His piteous ways the Scottish prince so move,
His bosom burns with mercy and with love.

13

That moment there drew near a brutal knight
Who cared but little for his lord's behest.
Raising his lance on high, ah, fearful sight!
He brought it down upon that tender breast.
Zerbino, by this cruel act which might
Disgrace a Turk, is angered and distressed,
The more so as the boy, all colour fled,
Now fallen to the ground, lies as one dead.

14

So keen his anger and so deep his woe,
He said: 'Vengeance, I vow, you shall not lack!'
And turned his horse to bring that villain low
Who made the dastard, cowardly attack;
But he his moment watched and was not slow
To make good his retreat along a track.
Then Cloridano, seeing on the ground
His dear Medoro, forward with one bound

15

Leapt from the wood; casting his bow aside,
Enraged he swung his sword among the foe,
Seeking not vengeance from the strokes he plied
But death (no vengeance could be equal to
His wrath), content that in a crimson tide
His life, now ended, from his veins should flow,
Content, when he at length succumbs to all
Those many swords, beside his friend to fall.

16

Through the deep wood the Scots then rode away,
Their leader to support and to surround,
Leaving the two companions where they lay.
One was quite dead; the other, moribund,
Remained untended for so long that day,
Bleeding so freely from his gaping wound,
His life was almost over, but there passed
By chance someone who succoured him at last.

17

There chanced to pass that way a fair young maid,
Clad in the garments of a shepherdess;
And yet a gracious, royal air she had
Which served but to enhance her loveliness.
So long it is since word of her I said,
You may not know her in her humble dress:
She is Angelica, let me now say,
Proud daughter of the ruler of Cathay.

18

Having regained possession of the ring
Which formerly Brunello from her stole,
Her arrogance was such that everything
And everybody she disdained; the whole
World was beneath her and, remembering
The royal suitors at her beck and call,
She goes her queenly way alone, unmoved
To think that by Orlando she is loved.

19

Of all her errors she the most repents
The love which for Rinaldo once she bore.
It now appears to her a grave offence
Thus to have yearned for an inferior.
Such reckless pride the god of love resents.
Resolved that he will suffer it no more,
He waits beside Medoro and with craft
He fixes to his bow a piercing shaft.

20

And when Angelica, who onward pressed,
Beheld the youth left there to die alone,
Who for his king's unhallowed death expressed
More sorrow and regret than for his own,
Compassion, unfamiliar to her breast,
Entered by portals now for long unknown,
Melting therein her heart, so hard and cold,
The more so as she heard his tale unfold.

21

And she began to call to mind her skill
In medicine, which in India she learned,
Where, for their knowledge how to cure and heal,
Doctors deservedly much praise have earned.
Such lore, transmitted by tradition still,
Is not derived from pages searched and turned;
And so she now bethinks her of a juice,
Prepared from herbs, which will his pain reduce.

22

During her journey she had chanced to see a
Herb upon whose efficacy she reflects.
It dittany, or if a panacea
It was, I cannot say, but its effects
Are such it staunches blood, nor can there be a
Wound it does not soothe; straightway she collects
Some samples of it from a near-by rise,
Then hurries back to where Medoro lies.

23

On her return she met a shepherd who
On horseback through the forest rode; he sought
A missing heifer which a day or two
Before had wandered off; him she besought
To come with her to where Medoro grew
So faint with loss of blood, he had been brought
To his last moments, while around him spread
A crimson stain, so copiously he bled.

24

The fair Angelica dismounts at once,
And from his horse the shepherd too descends.
The precious plant she pounds between two stones.
Then, gathering the juice in her white hands,
She pours some in his wound, and some, which runs
Over his chest and belly, she extends,
Smoothing it to his very thighs. At length
His blood she staunches and revives his strength.

25

His vigour now returning, he could mount
The shepherd's horse, and yet he still demurred,
For to depart Medoro did not want
Till both his king and friend had been interred,
Lest wolves and crows those loved remains affront;
And only when he saw this boon conferred
Did he consent to go where she thought best,
And where she tarried as the shepherd's guest.

26

Nor from that humble home would she depart
Until Medoro was restored to health.
Since first she saw him on the ground, her heart
Was filled with pity; stirred now by such wealth
Of grace and loveliness in every part,
She felt her soul invaded as by stealth,
She felt her soul invaded bit by bit
Till burning passion had encompassed it.

27

Both clean and comely is the shepherd's cot,
Set snugly in the woods, between two hills.
He and his wife, contented with their lot,
Raise up their children there in rustic skills.
The convalescence of the youth is not
Delayed; his wound, thanks to the damsel, heals,
But not before there opens in her heart
A deeper wound, causing a keener smart.

28

A wider and a deeper wound by far,
Caused by an arrow which, invisible,
And fashioned from Medoro's golden hair
And handsome eyes, was aimed by Love with skill,
Now tore the bosom of Angelica.
More for his malady than her own ill
She cares, intent alone on healing one
Who pain on her inflicts equal to none.

29

Her wound enlarges and more grievous grows,
Now burning hot, now icy cold, while his
Shrinks ever smaller as the edges close.
He becomes well, the while she languishes.
Daily his comeliness more lovely shows.
She every hour more ill and wasted is
And, like a snowflake on a sunny day,
Consumed by love bids fair to waste away.

30

If of her longing she is not to die,
She must herself ask help without delay;
And well she knows that she cannot rely
On him she loves the needed words to say.
So, all restraint and modesty put by,
Her tongue, no less her eyes, dares now to pray
For mercy; from that blow she begs him save her
Which the fair youth, perhaps unknowing, gave her.

31

O Count Orlando, O Circassian,
Of what avail your prowess and your fame?
What price your honour, known to every man?
What good of all your long devotion came?
Show me one single favour, if you can,
What recompense, what kindness can you name,
What gratitude, what mercy has she shown
For sufferings for her sake undergone?

32

O Agricane, great and noble king,
If to our life on earth you were restored,
How you would suffer now, remembering
How cruelly your person she abhorred!
O Ferraù, o thousands I might sing,
Who vainly served that ingrate, and adored;
You would be stricken to the core, I vow,
To see her in those arms enfolded now!

33

She lets Medoro pluck the morning rose
Which no despoiling hand had ever touched;
No one so fortunate that garden knows,
No one its virgin flowerbeds has smutched.
To make their union permanent they chose
And Hymen's altar solemnly approached.
Love gave his blessing on their married life.
The bride's attendant was the shepherd's wife.

34

And you must know the honeymoon was spent
In royal style beneath that humble roof.
More than a month that happy pair content
Remained and of their joy gave every proof.
No further than his face her glances went,
For of his love she could not have enough.
Unceasingly she hung upon his side,
Yet her desire was never satisfied.

35

Whether in shade or in the open air,
She has the youth beside her night and day.
Morning and eve, together everywhere,
By stream, by field, the lovers make their way.
Within a cave at noontide they repair,
As welcoming perhaps in every way
As one which gave Aeneas and the queen
From storm a shelter and for love a screen.

36

It was their joy, if a tall tree they saw
Shading a fountain or a crystal stream,
With a sharp-pointed knife or pin to draw,
Or on a stone or rock which soft might seem,
Their names entwined, according to love's law.
Indoors as well, on every wall and beam,
Medoro's name was read in divers spots
Linked with Angelica's in lovers' knots.

37

And when she deemed that long enough and more
They'd tarried there, she planned for them to move
To India (named Cathay), there to restore
Her kingdom and bestow it on her love.
A golden bracelet on her arm she wore,
With precious gems adorned, a token of
Orlando's love for her; it gave her pleasure
To wear this beautiful and costly treasure.

38

To Ziliant Morgana gave it once
When she had held him prisoner in the lake,
And to his father, Monodante, hence
He fled, freed by Orlando, who to take
The jewel in reward for valiance
Reluctant was, but wore it for love's sake,
Intending to present it to his queen
(And how she thanked him for it you have seen).

39

Not for the giver's sake the gift she wears,
But for its workmanship and beauty too
She values it beyond the price it bears,
More than with jewels she is wont to do.
She wore it even on the Isle of Tears
(I know not how she was permitted to),
When to the monster she was offered, nude,
By those fierce islanders so coarse and crude.

40

And yet she left the bracelet to reward
The hospitable shepherd and his wife,
Who made them welcome at their humble board,
Who helped to save her dear Medoro's life,
Her gratitude thus wishing to record.
So, bidding then farewell to war and strife,
They took their leave, ascending the terrain
Which the fair land of France divides from Spain.

41

In Barcelona or Valencia
To sojourn for a day or two they planned,
Where vessels, bound for the Levant and far
Beyond, were newly fitted out and manned.
Gerona from the perpendicular
And the wide waters to behold, they stand,
Then clamber down the mountain slope straightway
And with the shore to leftwards, make their way

42

Towards Barcelona; not far had they gone
Before a madman lying on the shore,
His body caked with mud, they came upon.
Filthy he was, no pig was ever more
Encrusted; as a snarling cur will run
At strangers, with a maniacal roar,
He leapt towards them, menacing attack.
But let us to Marfisa now turn back.

43

Of Aquilant, Marfisa and the duke,
Grifone and the rest I now will tell.
In mortal peril as the tempest shook,
They were in peril from the sea as well.
More overwhelming yet, the storm would brook
No opposition to its angry will.
For three days now the hurricane has blown,
And no sign of abating has it shown.

44

Rigging and spars and superstructures crash
Beneath the elements' hostility,
And what remains the sailors hew and slash
To lighten ship, and cast into the sea.
Some to the compass with a lantern dash,
And scan a chart, their whereabouts to see.
With torches down below some sailors bold
Now test the bilge, and hope her timbers hold.

45

One man astern, and one upon the bow
Assess their hourly headway with a glass;
For they, by watching how the sand-grains flow,
Can judge the time and distance as they pass.
Then, gathering around their charts, they show
Their answers to this critical impasse.
When summoned by the captain, one and all
Collect 'midships, obedient to his call.

46

One says: 'We are off Limaçol, I think,
Where on the shoals we'll surely run aground.'
Another says: 'Off Tripoli we'll sink,
On jagged rocks: the waves our ship will pound.'
A third: 'We're lost; from truth we must not shrink:
This is Satalia,' and they sigh all round.
Each mariner says something different,
But by the same misgivings all are rent.

47

On the third day, with a yet fiercer spite,
The wind attacks, the sea more turgid grows.
A wave the foremast carries off with it,
Another helm and helmsman overthrows.
Of steel or marble is the breast which fright
Does not possess or now no terror knows.
Marfisa who till then felt no dismay
Did not deny that she knew fear that day.

48

Now many vows of pilgrimage begin:
To Sinai, Galicia, Cyprus, Rome,
The Holy Sepulchre, Ettino's shrine,
To many a sacred place of martyrdom.
Meanwhile, the vessel tosses on the brine,
Now rising heavenwards, now dropping plumb.
The captain, in a plight so merciless,
Unships the mainmast to relieve the stress.

49

Boxes and bales, all cargo and all weight
Go overboard, nothing the captain saves;
From every storeroom every precious crate
Of merchandise is given to the waves.
Some man the pumps to stem the rising spate,
Whereby the sea once more its own receives.
Some in the hold attempt to mend the gaps
Wherever shifting planks risk worse mishaps.

50

In travail for four days they thus remained.
Defenceless, to no help did they aspire.
Full victory the ocean might have gained,
Save that its fury now began to tire,
And hope of calm arose and was sustained
When on the prow they saw St Elmo's fire.
Their jury rig and sail it glowed upon,
Instead of on a mast, for there was none.

51

When they beheld that miracle of light,
The grateful sailors fell upon their knees.
With eyes that brimmed with tears – a piteous sight –
In trembling voices they intoned their pleas.
The cruel tempest, which without respite
Till then had raged, at once began to ease.
Fierce squalls no longer menacing disaster,
South-westerlies remain the ocean's master.

52

The tyrant has so fierce a mastery,
So forcefully from his black mouth he blows,
So swift the current of the restless sea,
Which at his bidding fast, yet faster flows,
It bears the vessel on more rapidly
Than ever falcon plummeted and rose;
The pilot fears they may be carried on
To the world's end, or otherwise undone.

53

For this the pilot knows a tactic sure:
Fenders and guys he streams aft from the poop
With other gear to trailing warps secure,
To form sea-anchors, and to put a stop
To her unchecked career, and to ensure
Her speed by something like two-thirds will drop.
By using seamen's dodges of this sort
The vessel's saved and onwards sails to port.

54

Not far from Syria a gulf there is,
Laiazzo named, and there they lower sail;
Hugging the shore so close, they view with ease
The bar which at each end two forts curtail.
But when the captain looks about and sees
Where they have reached, his face turns deathly pale,
For now between the devil and the deep
He knows they are, and there is no escape.

55

For they can neither stay upon the main
Nor yet withdraw, their masts and rigging lost;
Timbers and planks are broken by the strain,
All shocked and buffeted and tempest-tossed.
Yet if in harbour they perforce remain,
They risk to do so at too great a cost,
For death or servitude here lies in wait
For all whom error brings or cruel fate.

56

The captain's chief anxiety was this:
That vessels, fully-manned and built of oak,
Might into battle move; he knew that his
In no condition was, as stock he took,
To risk or undergo hostilities;
And while he pondered this, the English duke
Came up to ask the reason for delay
And why they did not disembark straightway.

57

The captain in reply said all that coast
Was ruled by women, enemies of men.
According to their ancient laws, almost
All prisoners were killed, or must remain
As slaves; and freedom only he could boast
Who of the captive males could vanquish ten;
And further labour too was his that night:
Ten women he must serve for their delight.

58

And if a man succeeds in the first test
But to the next unequal proves to be,
He's put to death, and into serfdom pressed
Are all the members of his company.
But if for both he shows a ready zest,
His followers are set at liberty,
Yet not the man himself – he stays behind!
As husband to ten women he's assigned.

59

Astolfo burst out laughing at the tale
Of this strange custom of the near-by town.
Then, Sansonetto moving within hail
With Aquilant, Marfisa and Grifon,
The captain turned to them and did not veil
The cause of the delay. 'I'd rather drown
On the high seas', he said, 'than bear the yoke
Of servitude to this or any folk.'

60

And all the sailors shared their captain's view,
And death by drowning they preferred to brave.
But this the paladins objected to:
The dangers of the shore they'd rather have.
A hundred thousand swords to them were few
Compared with perils on the ocean wave.
It seemed to them the merest bagatelle
To challenge this or any citadel.

61

The warriors now longed to reach the strand,
The English duke most eagerly of all.
To blow a blast upon his horn he planned,
For that, he knew, would clear the citadel.
The mariners reluctant were to land.
The pros and cons in contest rose and fell,
Until the captain with Astolfo's side,
Which won the day, unwillingly complied.

62

Already when the ship had come in sight
The cruel citizens had fitted out
A galley with a crew of slaves packed tight
And mariners who know what they're about.
It sailed towards the stricken vessel, right
To where, still in uncertainty and doubt,
The captain waited; to the lofty prow
The galley's stern was coupled for a tow.

63

Dragged into harbour, and with oars, for lack
Of sail, assisted, on their way they went.
Impossible it was for them to tack,
The cruel wind all canvas having rent.
Their swords in hand, their armour on their back,
The intervening time the warriors spent
Encouraging all those whose spirits droop,
Filling the captain's breast with a new hope.

64

The structure of the port was crescent-shaped.
More than four miles its measure was all round.
Its mouth six hundred paces open gaped.
On both the crescent's horns a fort is found.
From storms protected, by no tempests raped,
Unless the south wind rages, safe and sound,
The city like an amphitheatre lies,
As tier on tier its buildings steeply rise.

65

And as the ship draws near with her escort
(By now all citizens alerted are),
Six thousand women gather at the port,
Armed with their long-bows and attired for war.
All prospects of escaping are cut short
By chains which they have draped across the bar,
Slung from the vessels which they always use
When thus the harbour they desire to close.

66

One of the women warriors, as old
As Cumae's Sibyl or as Hecuba,
Summoned the captain, that he might be told
The choices offered to them all, which are:
To let themselves be put to death, or sold
As slaves, to bow their necks beneath the bar.
One or the other fate: they must be slain
To the last man, or captive must remain.

67

'But if', she said, 'among you there's a man
So strong and valorous as to defy
In combat ten of ours, and if he can
Outdo them all and one by one they die;
And if in one same night no fewer than
Ten women he in bed can satisfy,
He will be chosen as our lawful prince
And you will be permitted to go hence.

68

'As many as desire are free to stay,
But on this understanding, that all those
Who do remain for liberty must pay:
Ten women each must lie with as their spouse.
But if your champion in his affray
With ten opponents in one bout should lose,
Or to the second test should fail to rise,
We take you as our captives and he dies.'

69

Where the old crone anticipated fear,
She met with courage in response instead,
For confident was every cavalier
He would acquit himself as well in bed
As in the combat with a lance or spear.
Marfisa, too, no lack of courage had:
What Nature had omitted to accord,
She would make good, she trusted, with her sword.

70

The captain was commissioned to reply,
When in full council they had all agreed,
That they had men on whom they could rely
To pass the test in battle and in bed.
The chains are lifted and the ship draws nigh,
A warp is fastened to a bollard-head,
A gangway laid; well armed, to show their worth,
The knights emerge and lead their horses forth.

71

Then to the centre of the town they ride
And see the women arrogantly course
In brief attire, about the countryside,
Or battle in the lists like warriors.
All manly weapons are to men denied,
Save for a chosen group of ten, of course,
Who, as an ancient custom has ordained,
Permitted are to fight, as I explained.

72

The others at the distaff and the spindle,
The comb, the needle and the loom are found.
Their strength diminishes, their spirits dwindle.
Their garments are so long they sweep the ground.
No masculine desires their bosoms kindle
As patiently they plough, in fetters bound,
Or guard the flocks; few males there are in all,
Scarce one in ten, within, without, the wall.

73

The knights decided to select by lot
The one who should defeat the group of ten
And later, while his ardour was still hot,
A second ten-fold victory should gain.
Although Marfisa's prowess they could not
Deny, they limited the plan to men,
Since for the second tournament in fact
The arms required for victory she lacked.

74

But she desired to be included too
And on her fell the fateful choice; then she
Declared: 'I must defend my life; then you
Must labour to defend your liberty.
But with this sword' (and to her sword she drew
Their gaze), 'I'll loose these threads, I guarantee
(I will surrender it if I do not),
As Alexander cut the Gordian knot.

75

'No traveller shall ever more complain
Of this dread town, long as the world shall last.'
Thus did Marfisa her intent explain,
And her companions, since the die was cast,
Agreed to let her take her chance to gain
Their lives and freedom; from their midst she passed
And, bearing armour, coat of mail and shield,
She made her way towards the battlefield.

76

An open space which crowned the citadel
Was ringed by seats arranged in rising tiers.
For tournaments and jousts available,
It had been used for these alone for years.
Four portals made of bronze secured it well.
A motley crowd of female armigers
Filled it completely and Marfisa then
The signal soon received to enter in.

77

She enters mounted on a splendid grey.
Dappled with rings and patches is its coat.
Its head is small, its spirit brave and gay.
Both form and action a proud breed denote.
She chose it and apparelled it one day,
The largest, finest horse beyond a doubt
Of many hundreds in Damascus, where
This gift King Norandino made to her.

78

At noon she entered by the southern gate.
In piercing tones the heralds' trumpets cried
And long she heard the sound reverberate,
Resounding through those tiers on every side.
Then through the northern entrance, in due state,
Marfisa saw her ten opponents ride.
The foremost cavalier who forward pressed
In valour seemed to equal all the rest.

79

He sat astride a mighty charger's back.
Its left hind hoof and brow apart, it quite
Exceeded any crow's or raven's black;
Only its hoof and head were flecked with white.
And in his armour too a total lack
Of colour was the feature of this knight,
Which signified his soul was overcast
By sorrow which all gladness far surpassed.

80

The signal being given to commence,
Straightway nine spears are lowered by the nine;
But he in black no such advantage wants
And of participating gives no sign.
To keep, by civil disobedience,
The laws of chivalry is his design.
He stands aside to watch how one sole spear
Jousting against a group of nine will fare.

81

Her charger, with its smooth and perfect pace,
Bore her with speed to where the clash began.
Her lance in rest she did not fail to place –
So heavy was it that no single man
Could carry it – scarce four its weight could brace
(But what they could not do, Marfisa can).
Her fierce demeanour many hearts assails
And every face among those thousands pales.

82

So wide she slit her first opponent's breast,
It was as though he took the field quite nude.
She pierces the cuirass and padded vest,
But first the shield of iron-plated wood.
Behind his back the metal tip at least
A yard is seen quite plainly to protrude.
Transfixed she leaves him lying there behind,
Advancing on the others like the wind.

83

So fierce a jolt she gave the second foe,
So terrible a shock she gave the third,
Their backs were broken and both fell below,
And from this world were instantly transferred:
The encounter was so violent, and so
Close packed together rode that frightened herd.
Artillery, as I have seen, disperses
The enemy as she did, and no worse is.

84

Against her armour spears in pieces fall.
By these attacks she is as little harmed
As in *pallone* the unyielding wall
Is wont to be in any way alarmed
By the repeated bouncing of the ball.
The habergeon which covers her is charmed;
Forged in the fires of Hell and tempered by
Avernus, every blow it can defy.

85

Riding far off, her charger first she reined,
Then turned and rode against them at full tilt.
Her sword with blood repeatedly she stained,
Plunging it deeply to the very hilt.
Here went a head, there but one arm remained.
Circling another, as though with a belt,
She cuts the breast and head and arms away,
While in the saddle legs and belly stay.

86

Right through the middle of his trunk she hacks,
Between the ribs and thighs, so that he seems
A statue which its nether portion lacks,
And incomplete is in respect of limbs,
Of silver made, more often of pure wax,
Which as a votive offering redeems
The pledges of the faithful when their prayers
Are granted or they are relieved of cares.

87

Pursuing one who fled, she was so quick,
Not to the mid-arena did he gain:
His head she so divided from his neck,
No doctor could assemble them again.
She killed them all, each Harry, Tom and Dick,
Or rendered harmless those that were not slain.
In one way or another she ensured
That every one of fighting her was cured.

88

The cavalier who led the company
Still waited to one side, as he thought right.
It seemed to him a vile iniquity
With one on such unequal terms to fight.
Soon as he saw the others mortally
Hors de combat or else defeated quite,
To show his lack of action was not due
To fear but chivalry, towards her he drew.

89

He signalled with his hand that he desired
To parley ere the combat was resumed.
He little thought this virile knight, attired
In armour, was a woman, but assumed
She was a man and said: 'You must be tired,
So many you have slain or have left doomed
To die; if you were challenged now by me,
Sir knight, this would be grave discourtesy.

90

'Repose until tomorrow I concede,
If you will then return to take the field.
No honour will be mine if I succeed
Against one who for weariness must yield.'
Marfisa thus replied: 'There is no need.
I am inured to weapons and can wield
Them long without fatigue, as to your cost,
I'll quickly prove when quickly you have lost.

91

'Your offer is indeed most courteous.
I thank you, but I have no need of rest.
So many hours of day are left to us,
Shameful it were to do as you suggest.'
He answered: 'Would that Fate were bounteous
And granted mine as I grant your request:
Beware, however, lest the light of day
For you be ended sooner than you say.'

92

These were his words; at his command, in haste,
Two lances, nay, two heavy masts they seemed,
Were brought; he let her choose one to her taste
And took that which inferior she deemed.
Now both being ready, no time need they waste.
Soon as the trumpet's voice to heaven screamed,
The joust began; the hoofs of chargers pound,
Shaking the sea, air, earth for miles around.

93

Not a breath was drawn, not a flicker seen
Of eyelids or of lips in all that throng.
You might have heard if someone dropped a pin
As on the outcome eagerly they hung.
Marfisa, lance in rest, resolves to win,
Intending that the black knight shall be flung
Far from his saddle and no more shall rise.
The black knight strength and skill employs likewise.

94

Their lances, more like brittle willow-wands
Than massive lengths of supple Turkey oak,
Were split and splintered to their very hands.
Their chargers felt so violent a shock
It was as though a sickle cut the bands
Of muscle in their legs, and sinews broke.
Down they both fell, at the same moment, but
Both knights were quick to scramble up on foot.

95

Marfisa had unhorsed in mortal strife
Innumerable knights at the first blow,
But she had never fallen in her life
And now she was unseated, as you know.
The shock so startled her it was as if
She had been stunned by her descent below.
And it surprised the cavalier in black
Who did not lightly fall to an attack.

96

Scarce have they touched the ground than up again
They spring and combat straight away renew.
In frenzied rage they cut and thrust amain.
With shield or blade they parry, or with due
And timely leaps, and all the blows they rain
Resound to heaven, be they false or true.
Those habergeons, those shields, those helmets of
Fine-tempered steel than anvils stronger prove.

97

If the fierce damsel has a heavy arm,
The cavalier's, for his part, is not light.
Being well matched in size and strength, the harm
They do each other they can each requite.
Who seeks two heroes to inspire alarm
Or wonder need not look beyond this sight.
No one has seen more prowess or more skill
Than these two represent, nor ever will.

98

The women who for long amazed have watched
The ceaseless interchange of fearsome blows,
Seeing the knights unwearied, though they fetched
Stroke upon stroke, in need of no repose,
Declare them both unequalled and unmatched,
Throughout all lands which Ocean's arms enclose.
It seems to them they should be dead and gone,
But for their strength, from the fatigue alone.

99

Then, speaking to herself, Marfisa said:
'It was as well for me this knight stood still
And did not join those others whom he led,
Else had the outcome of that fight gone ill
For me, and I might very well be dead,
For, as it is, his blows come nigh to kill.'
Thus she reflected, though without a pause
Her sword she wielded and still fighting was.

100

'It was as well', the knight was thinking too,
'I did not let him rest before this fight.
Defend myself is all that I can do;
So if in slumber he had passed the night,
And with fresh vigour, when the day was new,
Had challenged me, what would have been my plight?
It was more fortunate than words can say
That he preferred to fight with me today.'

101

The battle lasted till the evening fell,
Yet which of them had won was still not clear.
Neither, without a lamp, henceforth could tell
When to avoid each other's thrusts, or where.
Then as the dark increased, the knight thought well
To say to her he deemed a cavalier:
'What shall we do now that the shades of night
Descend impartially to stop our fight?

102

'I think it will be better to prolong
Your life until tomorrow dawns at least.
I can allow no more; one night, not long,
I grant by which your days may be increased.
Do not impute this to me as a wrong,
But, rather, lay the blame where it fits best:
On laws, so merciless, which sorely vex
This kingdom governed by the female sex.

103

'If I now grieve for you and for your friends,
He knows to Whom all things are clearly known.
And you must be my guests, to make amends;
With me you will be safe, and there alone:
Because the crowd whose husbands met their ends
Conspiring are that vengeance shall be done.
For every one whom you today have slain,
Of women you have thereby widowed ten.

104

'And thus it is that for such injury
Revenge by ninety women is desired;
So, if you do not wish to lodge with me,
Expect attack tonight when you've retired.'
Marfisa then replied: 'Most willingly
Do I accept, for as I have admired
Your daring and the skill of every thrust,
So now the goodness of your heart I trust.

105

'Yet do not waste regret on my decease,
But save it for the contrary – your own.
You will allow that no less expertise
Than you (no laughing-matter) I have shown.
So, if your wish is to proceed, or cease,
Or by the moon resume, or by the sun,
Whatever you propose, give me a sign,
You'll find me ready with this sword of mine.'

106

And so the fierce encounter was deferred
Till from the Ganges the new dawn should rise,
When heralds would pronounce the final word
And the conclusion far and wide advise.
The cavalier, whose soul was ever stirred
By liberality, moved to apprise
The other knights and begged till the new day
In his abode they might be pleased to stay.

107

Without demur his courteous invitation
The paladins accepted; by the light
Of torches to a royal habitation
They are led, where their apartments for the night
Exceed in splendour every expectation.
Still more astonished are they when the knight
Removes his helmet; as they now can gauge,
He scarce is more than eighteen years of age.

108

Marfisa is amazed that one so young
Such aptitude and skill in combat shows.
The other is amazed, when by her long
Fair tresses now at last her sex he knows.
They ask each other's name and neither tongue
Reluctant is the secret to disclose.
But what the name is of the cavalier
In my next canto you must wait to hear.

CANTO XX

1

Women in ancient times have wondrous things
Performed in arms and in the sacred arts.
Their deeds, their works, their fair imaginings
Resound in glory in all minds and hearts.
Harpàlyce and Camilla Clio sings,
In battle skilled, in strategy experts.
Sappho and Corinna, in whom genius flamed
In splendour shine and are for ever famed.

2

And truly women have excelled indeed
In every art to which they set their hand,
And any who to history pay heed
Their fame will find diffused in every land.
If in some ages they do not succeed,
Their renaissance is not for ever banned.
Envy their merits has perhaps concealed
Or unawareness left them unrevealed.

3

Such talent in this century, I think,
Is seen in women lovely to behold,
That there will be much work for pen and ink
Ere chroniclers the full account unfold,
And envious calumny at last shall sink,
With lies which evil tongues so long have told;
Such praises will be sung as to surpass
Marfisa's fame, when this has come to pass.

4

Returning now to her, the valiant maid
Did not refuse to tell the courteous knight
What he desired to know, for not delayed
His readiness her favour to requite
Would be; the debt she owed she quickly paid,
That he reciprocate the sooner might.
'I am', she said, 'Marfisa', and this name
Sufficed to tell him all, such was her fame.

5

And he, for his part, without more ado,
Although with more preamble, now began:
'I well believe to every one of you
Is known the name of all my race and clan,
For throughout France and Spain, their neighbours too,
India, Ethiopia, Pontus, every man
Clear knowledge has of Clairmont, whence is sprung
Almonte's slayer, of whom praise is sung.

6

'And he who Chiariel has slain and King
Mambrino and their kingdoms overthrown.
By this same blood, where Danube, emptying
Ten mouths, the Black Sea joins, by Duke Aymon,
Who in that region was then sojourning,
My mother fashioned me of flesh and bone.
A year ago I left her sad of mien,
And went to France to seek my kith and kin.

7

'My journey I could not complete, alas!
A wind propelled me here relentlessly.
Ten months ago, or more, I think it was.
I count each hour of my captivity.
Guidon Selvaggio is my name, and as
A knight nobody yet has heard of me.
Here I slew Argilon of Melibea and
The ten who, one by one, fell by my hand.

8

'With credit too I passed the second test.
And now by ten my lust is satisfied;
I chose them as by far the loveliest
Of all who in this citadel reside.
I govern them and rule as I think best;
The others also by my will abide.
Thus do these women honour and obey
All those who by good fortune ten can slay.'

9

The cavaliers enquired of Guido then
Why there was such a scarcity of males,
And why the women subjugate the men,
When in all other lands the man prevails.
'The reason', he replied, 'I will explain.
I've heard it many times; if it regales
You now to hear it, I will do my best
To tell you why the men are here oppressed.

10

'When after twenty years the Greeks returned
From Troy (the siege had lasted ten long years
And for another ten for home they yearned,
Tossed on a stormy sea, a prey to fears)
They found their wives, who long in torment burned,
Had in their husbands' absence dried their tears
And, taking youthful lovers, were consoled,
No longer left in bed alone and cold.

11

'So the Greek husbands found their houses full
Of bastard offspring; they forgave their wives,
Thinking it better to be merciful,
For on long abstinence no woman thrives.
But for the children otherwise they rule:
They must depart and elsewhere live their lives,
For it appears to them a grave offence
That they should nurtured be at their expense.

12

'Some babies were exposed, and some were spared,
Though taken from their mothers and concealed.
In divers groups the older ones repaired,
Some here, some there; the fate of some was sealed
By military service; some preferred
A life of learning, or to till the field.
Some guarded flocks, still others served at court,
However Fortune turned her wheel in sport.

13

'Among those who departed was a lad,
A son of Clytemnestra, that dread queen.
Eighteen years old, a lily-face he had,
Or like a rose that freshly plucked has been.
Arming a vessel, he set out to raid
The near-by shores; a hundred youths were seen,
Chosen throughout all Greece, of his own age,
Forming his company and equipage.

14

'The Cretans at that time had just expelled
Idomeneus, the tyrant, from their land;
Thus, to ensure their safety, being compelled
New forces to recruit, they hired the band
Led by Phalanthus (as the youth was called).
And for substantial wages they demand
That he shall guard Dictaea from attack,
For they anticipate raid, pillage, sack.

15

'Among a hundred fertile towns of Crete,
Dictaea the most rich and pleasing was,
With women, fair and amorous, replete.
From morn till eve joy reigned without a pause.
Accustomed every foreigner to greet
With open arms, the youths they welcomed as
They would have done their brothers, and to some
They freely gave the freedom of their home.

16

'So handsome and so fair is every youth
(The very flower of Greece Phalanthus chose)
That at first sight the women's hearts, in truth,
Are ravished by the promise they disclose;
And to maintain it each one, nothing loath,
In bed his virile vigour gladly shows.
In a few days so ardent have they proved,
Beyond all joy and pleasure they are loved.

17

'When finally the Cretan men agreed
The war which they expected to be waged
No longer threatened and they had no need
To keep Phalanthus and his band engaged,
The youths at once were eager to proceed.
The women's sorrow could not be assuaged;
They wept and sobbed as bitterly as if
For their dead fathers they were plunged in grief.

18

'They pleaded with their lovers not to go,
Entreating and imploring them to stay;
But finding them unmoved by tears of woe,
The women were resolved to run away,
Leaving their fathers, husbands, sons; and no
Restraint or modesty did they display,
But stripped their homes of gold and gems by night
And not a man of Crete knew of their flight.

19

'The wind was so propitious and the hour
Phalanthus chose for their escape likewise
So favourable was that long before
The Cretans to the women's ruse grew wise,
They sailed for many miles; then to this shore,
Fortune assisting in their enterprise,
They were propelled (it then deserted was).
Here they would count their booty, and repose.

20

'Here they enjoyed a sojourn of ten days,
In amorous delights and pleasures passed;
But, as so often are the wanton ways
Of love, the youths were surfeited at last.
And so they all agreed with no delays
To cast the women off, and off they cast.
Than this no burden's graver to endure:
To have a woman one desires no more.

21

'So eager were the youths for loot and gain,
So disinclined their precious hoard to spend,
They saw it would be costly to maintain
So many concubines, whose needs extend
To more than bows and spears; so to the main
They take, abandoning alone on land
The hapless women; laden with their spoil,
Near Tàranto they reach Apulian soil.

22

'The women, seeing they had been betrayed
By lovers whom more faithful they had deemed,
For days were so astonished and dismayed
That lifeless statues on the shore they seemed;
But, knowing there was no one to lend aid,
However long they wept or loud they screamed,
To put their heads together they began,
And in such dire predicament to plan.

23

'So, ceasing then to weep and wring their hands,
Some of them said: "We must return to Crete;
Better by far our fathers' reprimands,
And retribution – though severe – to meet
From our wronged husbands than on these bleak strands,
Or in dark woods, for lack of food to eat,
Or from exposure, to expire." Some said
Sooner than this they'd drown themselves instead.

24

'They added that a lesser ill it were
To go about the world as mendicants
Or slaves or prostitutes than to incur
Such penalties. The wretched miscreants
Among themselves continue to confer.
One this suggests, and that another wants.
At last one rises, Orontea by name
(Direct descent from Minos she can claim).

25

'The youngest of them all and the most fair,
She was the shrewdest and had erred the least.
Phalanthus she had loved beyond compare
And left her father for him, pure and chaste.
Now, showing by her words and in her air
The wrath which blazed in her heroic breast,
The others' lamentations soon she checked;
Then gave her views and put them to effect.

26

'She urged them not to go from these domains.
The soil, she knew, was rich, the air was good.
Watered by limpid streams, its many plains
Were thickly grown with many a green wood.
Harbours and estuaries, she explains,
Offer a refuge if a tempest should
Drive vessels here off course from Africa
Or Egypt, bearing foodstuffs from afar.

27

'Better, she said, to stay and vengeance wreak
Upon all men, who had so ill behaved;
And whatsoever vessel there might seek
A harbour and which tempest long had braved,
They were to raid and ultimately wreck
And burn, and not a man was to be saved.
Thus she decreed and thus it was decided,
And by that law thereafter they abided.

28

'Whenever tempest threatened, they were seen
Brandishing arms and running to the shore,
By Orontea led, who as their queen
Governed implacably, none ever more.
And any ship which driven here had been
They burned (stripping it well of spoils before).
No man was left alive of whom a word
In any quarter afterwards was heard.

29

'Thus independently for a few years
They lived, the bitter enemies of males.
But they are visited at length by fears.
One doubt the peace of mind of all assails:
If no one children propagates and bears,
Their kingdom lapses and their vengeance fails,
For not beyond their lifetime will extend
Dominion which should last till the world's end.

30

'So, tempering their rigour for a space,
Within four years precisely, from all those
Whom wind and storm delivered to this place,
Ten vigorous and handsome knights they chose
Who, as it seemed to them, could stand the pace
Of loving combat with a hundred foes.
There were one hundred women, so the men
Allotted were as husbands, one to ten.

31

'At first a number were beheaded, who
Unequal to the ten-fold tourney proved.
At last a group of ten were found and due
Reward they had; not only were they loved
By all their wives, but they were granted too
A share of government; but it behoved
Them all to swear on oath that they would slay
All other men whom Fortune sent their way.

32

'First pregnant and then giving birth, the wives
Began to be afraid too many boys
Would be produced and once again their lives
Would subjugated be to men; lest joys
Of freedom they should lose, their ruler strives
And all her ingenuity employs
The danger to avoid which they now face,
That men at length the women may replace.

33

'So, to avoid the risk of being subdued
By men, severe and cruel laws compel
Each mother to retain of all her brood
One male child only and the rest to kill
Or to exchange for females, as seems good;
And when they send their agents forth, they tell
Them never to return with empty hands,
But girls or money bring from foreign lands.

34

'Nor would they spare one boy, but that they need
The help of males for the replenishment
And continuity of their fell breed.
Such is their mother love and sentiment,
They deal most cruelly with their own seed;
For other males their law is different,
Since not at random foreigners are slain.
How they proceed with them I will explain:

35

'If ten or twenty landed on this shore
They were imprisoned; one by one each day,
Chosen by lot, they were beheaded, for
It was these women's habit then to slay
Their hapless victims at a shrine, before
Their goddess of Revenge, whom they obey.
One of the men, later to share this fate,
By lot was chosen to officiate.

36

'After long years there landed on this coast,
By chance, a youth, Elbanio by name,
Who proud descent from Hercules could boast,
Valiant in arms and destined for great fame.
He was imprisoned, being seized almost
Before he knew, as fearlessly he came
Along the shore; with others long he lay
In durance vile, as was their cruel way.

37

'His person is so comely and so fair,
So pleasing an effect his manners make,
His voice and discourse are so sweet to hear,
Elbanio could well have charmed a snake.
As of some miracle, sublime and rare,
News of his beauty messengers soon take
To Alessandra, daughter of the queen
(Who burdened by old age now long has been).

38

'Queen Orontea was surviving still,
Though her contemporaries were by then
All dead; the numbers had increased until
The total had been multiplied by ten.
One rod ten engines drove, for ten-fold still
The ratio of women was to men.
Ten cavaliers were likewise kept in trim
To await whoever came and challenge him.

39

'And Alessandra, eager to behold
The youth of whom such praises had been sung,
So pleaded that her mother, who of old
Would not have yielded, granted to the young
Princess what she desired; as I was told,
The damsel felt her heart so pierced and stung,
Her enmity towards all men is shaken
And captive of her prisoner she's taken.

40

'"Lady," he said, "if pity here were known,
As once it was, before it vanished hence,
And as in other lands, where'er the sun
With its bright beams fair nature gilds and tints,
All noble souls the soft emotion own,
By your sweet beauty which itself imprints
On gentle hearts, my life I would entreat,
That I might lay it, gladly, at your feet.

41

'"But since, beyond all reason, hearts are here
Devoid of kindness, pleas would be in vain.
So I will not entreat you to confer
My life on me, since nothing I would gain.
Yet I would ask that as a cavalier,
With sword in hand, I may embrace the pain
Of death, not as a common criminal,
Or like some sacrificial animal."

42

'Kind Alessandra then, whose eyes were wet
With pity for Elbanio's sad plight,
Replied: "You may perhaps have never met
Women more cruel or of greater spite
Towards men than we are in this kingdom, yet
Not every one is a Medea quite;
And even if they were, within my heart
Pity would prompt me now to stand apart.

43

'"And though in years gone by I too have been
As merciless as others are, I own,
Until today no person have I seen
On whose account compassion I have known.
More than a tiger's rage my rage is keen,
More adamant my heart than diamond stone,
But now all anger leaves me when I see
Your courage, comeliness and courtesy.

44

' "Would that our law less rigid were and strong,
Which to all foreigners relentless is.
I would not shrink from death, though I am young,
If I could save your life by my decease;
But no one is empowered, not among
The highest, to secure you a release.
Though modest is the other boon you ask,
To gain it for you is no easy task.

45

' "But I will do the best that I can do,
That you may have this favour ere you die;
Yet will the torment not be worse for you,
Your death more lingering?" And this reply
Elbanio gave: "I would be willing to
Encounter ten, all armed, and I'd defy
Them (such my hope is now) if every one
Unfeeling metal were, not flesh and bone."

46

'No answer to these words of his she made,
Except to sigh; then turned upon her heel,
A thousand wounds, for which there was no aid,
Piercing her heart which now would never heal.
Her mother she was able to persuade;
The queen agreed that if the youth could kill
Ten others single-handed in a fight
To sentence him to death would not be right.

47

'Calling her council, Orontea said:
"It is incumbent on us, as you know,
From all the men who in our midst are bred,
Or whom the winds of Fortune hither blow,
To choose, for combat in or out of bed,
The strongest and the best; these we allow
To guard our ports and shores, testing them first,
Lest we should kill the best and keep the worst.

48

'"It is my view, provided you agree,
That for the future any cavalier
Cast on our shores by a tempestuous sea,
Straightway of these alternatives should hear:
He can elect to perish instantly
Or against ten opponents wield his spear.
If in fair fight he kills them one by one,
Let him command the harbour's garrison.

49

'"I say this, for as prisoner we hold
A youth who offers to combat with ten.
(This chance of glory let us not withhold,
For it is right, by God, to test such men.)
But if it prove that he was over-bold
Or vainly spoke, let him be punished then."
Her speech being at an end, there took the floor
An old and venerable councillor.

50

'"The reason", she began, "why we proposed
Not all male children to exchange or sell
Was not because our kingdom was exposed
To dangers we could not ourselves repel.
Our practice of retaining some is caused
By what we cannot do alone; 'twere well
If we could propagate a female race
And women were sole guardians of this place!

51

'"Since Nature's law has willed it otherwise,
We have agreed to tolerate a few,
Not many, males; our ruling is precise:
One man in ten is the proportion to
Maintain. Their function is to fertilize
Our women; we ourselves the rest can do.
In men one prowess only do we want,
Be they in all things else incompetent.

52

'"To keep so strong a man amongst us here
Runs counter to our principal design.
If ten are vanquished by one cavalier,
How many women will he keep in line?
If ten of ours of such a species were,
To seize our land tomorrow they'd combine.
To arm the strong is not the way to rule.
We learnt that maxim when we went to school.

53

'"Consider, too, if Fortune should assist
Your protégé and he the ten should slay,
How sorely by their wives they will be missed!
How loud will be the shrieks of their dismay!
But if you wish to put him to a test,
Then let us do so in another way:
If to a hundred women he can give
What ten can manage, let the young man live."

54

'Thus Artemìa spoke (such was her name).
Many agreed, and it was touch and go,
For in that cruel temple of ill fame
They all but sacrificed Elbanio;
But Orontea, whose maternal aim
Was to content her daughter, was not slow
To answer these objections one by one
And so by arguments the senate won.

55

'Elbanio's good looks, of which the news
Had spread among the younger senators,
So touched their hearts and influenced their views
That when they heard the older ones discourse
And urge that circumspection they should use
And let their legislation take its course,
They disagreed so fundamentally
They almost would have set Elbanio free.

56

'It was resolved to grant him a reprieve
If ten opponents he could first defeat,
And next ten women (not a hundred) leave
Content (and in one night this task complete).
The order of release his guards receive.
Choosing a horse and arms, he rides to meet
The ten; his prowess they cannot withstand,
And one by one they fall beneath his hand.

57

'That night he underwent the second test,
Left with ten women, naked and alone.
So valorous he proved (I do not jest)
That pleasure he partook of every one.
The queen by such a feat was so impressed
That there and then she named him as her son,
And gave him Alessandra as his bride,
And the other nine by whom he had been tried.

58

'She left him her co-heir to all this land
(Alessandretta later it was named),
And by this law he was obliged to stand,
Likewise whoever else the kingdom claimed.
If any should be cast upon this strand,
By Fate or whatsoever power is blamed,
Of two alternatives he must choose one:
Death, or the chance to fight with ten, alone.

59

'If it should happen that he kills the band,
He must be tested once again that night.
If he continues his heroic stand,
Emerging victor from this second fight,
Then he is recognized throughout the land
As prince and councillor; it is his right
To choose a squad of nine and here remain
Until one stronger comes by whom he's slain.

60

'About two thousand years this impious law
Has been observed and they observe it still,
Few are the days which here I ever saw
That some poor traveller they do not kill.
If any choose the combat, soon a flaw
The ten will find in his defence, and spill
His life upon the ground; and few indeed
Are those who in the second test succeed.

61

'Out of a thousand there perhaps is one
Who passes it; in all, they are so rare
You scarcely need two hands to count them on.
My predecessor in this strange affair,
When, shipwrecked, I arrived, was Argilon.
For ever undisturbed by earthly care
He sleeps; would that I too might do the same,
Rather than live in servitude and shame!

62

'For games and laughter, amorous delight,
Which pleasure give to persons of my age,
The purple robe, the jewels and the right
To precedence, a stately equipage
Have never been sufficient to requite
For lack of freedom; from this gilded cage
Never to be permitted to depart
I reckon servitude, for my own part.

63

'The flower of my youth in vilest shame
Is fading fast away with every morn.
My heart with burning anguish is aflame.
All pleasure and all company I scorn.
My family's renown on wings of fame
Through all the world and to the stars is borne.
In this, some role might yet be played by me,
If only with my brothers I could be!

64

'And badly used by Fate I think I am,
Being chosen for such shameful service here,
Like some old war-horse that is blind or lame,
No longer pleasing to a cavalier,
Since it defective in some way became,
Which wanders out at grass, now here, now there.
Unless by death set free, no hope have I
And so my only longing is to die.'

65

Guidone ended here his tale of woe,
Cursing that day of ten-fold victory
When men, and women, had good cause to know
The full extent of his virility.
Astolfo watched and listened and was slow
To manifest his own identity
Until he could be certain that Guidon
Was truly, as he said, Duke Aymon's son.

66

Then he replied: 'I am the English duke,
Your cousin, named Astolfo', and with love
In courteous embrace the knight he took
And kissed him fondly; nor was he above
The shedding of some tears before he spoke.
'Your mother, my dear kinsman, could not prove
More clearly, had she marked you with some sign,
Than does your sword, that you are of our line.'

67

Guidone, who in any other place
Would have rejoiced to see his kith and kin,
Greeted his cousin with a mournful face,
For sad is the dilemma they are in:
If he survives, Astolfo, in worse case,
A life of slavery must here begin;
And if Astolfo lives, Guidone dies.
The good of one the other's ill implies.

68

It grieves him that if he should win the fight
The other cavaliers must all be slaves;
Nor, if he is defeated, will their plight
Be bettered; nothing from the impasse saves
Them now which stretches to their left and right:
However many blows Marfisa braves,
Her conquest in the lists will be in vain.
They will be slaves, she, by default, be slain.

69

And on the other hand, the tender years,
The courtesy and valour manifest
In the young cavalier had moved to tears
The paladins, and in Marfisa's breast
Compassion had aroused; she and her peers
Their freedom by his death would be distressed
To win; and if she wins it only by
This means, Marfisa too would rather die.

70

'Guidone, come away with us,' she said;
'By force of arms together we'll break free.'
'Alas!' the youth replied, 'be not misled,
For whether I kill you or you kill me,
No one can get away; all hope is fled.'
She answered: 'What's begun must finished be.
There is no safer road on which to ride
Than where my sword I follow as my guide.

71

'Your valour I have come to know so well,
With you beside me, I will all things dare.
Tomorrow when the throngs of women swell
The seats which ring the palisaded square,
Let us attack them from all sides and kill,
And no one, be she bold or craven, spare.
We'll leave their bodies scattered, to be found
By wolves, and burn the city to the ground.'

72

Guidone answered: 'You may count on me
To follow you and perish at your side.
Than this result no other can there be,
Except that vengeance will be satisfied.
Often ten thousand women here I see
Thronging the theatre from side to side;
As many guard the harbour, fort and wall,
So of escape there is no hope at all.'

73

Marfisa said: 'Be they more numerous
Than Xerxes' army in Thermopylae
Or than the host, to God rebellious,
Which fell from Heaven and in darkness lay,
If you are with me and will fight for us,
I will engage to kill them in one day.'
Guidone answered her: 'There is a plan
Which might perhaps succeed, if any can.

74

'The stratagem I will unfold to you:
No man may step outside the citadel,
For only women are permitted to.
So for a woman's help I must appeal,
Someone whom I can trust, whose love is true,
Who serves me loyally, as I know well,
For many times she gave me proof of this
In things more searching than the present is.

75

'No less than I, she also longs to flee
From servitude, if I am at her side.
She hopes, her rivals left behind, with me
To live for ever after as my bride.
Under the cloak of darkness, by the sea
A fleet of little vessels she'll provide,
Which on arrival there your crew will find,
Equipped with requisites of every kind.

76

'Behind me, in formation, in one squad,
Knights, merchants, mariners (whom as my guests
Beneath my roof the honour I have had
Of welcoming), if you but brace your chests,
You'll clear the road ahead if any mad
And hostile mob our right of way contests.
Thus (with the help of our good swords as well)
I'll lead you from the cruel citadel.'

77

Marfisa said: 'You do as you think fit.
In my own strength a passage I shall clear.
More likely am I to perform this feat,
And single-handed slay all women here
Than to be seen escaping thus, or it
Be thought that I display the slightest fear.
I will go forth by day, by force of arms,
For any other means my honour harms.

78

'If it were known that I a woman am,
I should be honoured by these women and
Esteemed, for willingly my help they'd claim
And in their Council foremost I would stand;
But to these shores with trusted friends I came.
I want no favours which to them are banned.
A great wrong it would be if I went free,
Or stayed and left my friends in slavery.'

79

By these and other words Marfisa shows
Of what concern their danger is to her
And what respect to chivalry she owes.
So, lest her act of daring may incur
Still greater peril for them, she forgoes
The memorable onslaught she'd prefer,
And on her friends' account she yields at last
And lets Guidone do as he thinks best.

80

That night Guidone with Alèria spoke
(Such was the name of his most trusted wife).
No need had he his patience to invoke;
Between them on this matter was no strife.
She armed a vessel and on board she took
Her finest clothes (hoping to leave for life),
Pretending that she wished at break of day
To sail with her companions in the bay.

81

First to Guidone's palace she had sent
Lances and swords and shields and coats of mail,
Which for the merchants and the crew were meant,
Who had been stripped half naked by the gale.
Some slept, while others watched the firmament,
Dressed in full armour, waiting for the pale
First light of dawn and to report the least
Suspicion of a reddening in the east.

82

From the harsh face of earth, the golden sun
The dark, obscuring veil had not withdrawn,
And scarcely had Calisto yet begun
To turn the plough which disappears at dawn,
When, eager for the battle to be won,
In the arena women teem and spawn,
As in their thousands more and more arrive,
Clustered like bees about to change their hive.

83

Trumpets and clarions and tambours shook
The earth and startled heaven with their din.
And now the people no delay would brook:
Their champion was summoned to begin.
The sons of Oliver, the English duke,
Guidon, Marfisa, Sansonetto, in
Full armour, waited with their retinue,
Each man prepared to do as best he knew.

84

Between Guidone's palace and the port
The theatre would have to be traversed;
No other route existed, long or short,
And this it was Guidone told them first.
He next proceeded warmly to exhort
Them to remember all they had rehearsed.
Then, where the heralds would expect to find him,
He entered with his company behind him.

85

Urging them on, in haste Guidone rode
Across the lists, towards the other door;
But he was challenged by a multitude
Of sentinels, in arms, who, ready for
Emergencies, round the arena stood.
Seeing him lead his troop across the floor,
They knew at once what his intention was
And, blocking his escape, her bow each draws.

86

Guidone and the other valiant knights
To answer with their weapons are not slow.
And in particular Marfisa smites
With speed and zest and renders blow on blow.
They try to force the gate, but Fortune blights
Their efforts; many round them are brought low,
Wounded or killed by arrows which descend,
In deadly showers pouring without end.

87

And it was well the hauberks were well made;
In peril now was every warrior.
The horse of Sansonetto was shot dead.
Marfisa's likewise fell and was no more.
Astolfo with himself communed and said:
'What better moment am I waiting for?
Since swords and lances are of no avail,
A blast upon my horn may make them quail.'

88

As desperate cases desperate remedies
Require, Astolfo, judging that the hour
Has come, now to his lips the horn applies.
A blast he blows of such tremendous power,
It seems to shake the earth, the very skies.
In terror all the women cringe and cower.
Then from the scene they flood as in a spate
And not a woman's left to man the gate.

89

As from the roof and windows people throw
Themselves in terror, risking injury,
When flames surrounding them more raging grow,
Which, when the household and the family,
Being fast asleep, the danger did not know,
Grew to their present menace gradually,
So, disregarding life and limb, they sped
And from the terrifying clamour fled.

90

A surging mob, in panic, everywhere,
In desperate attempt to get away,
Throngs every exit, corridor and stair.
They trip and fall and block each other's way.
Some in the press collapse for lack of air.
Some fling themselves from windows in dismay.
Heads, arms, and legs and other parts they smash.
Some die, and some are crippled by the crash.

91

The shrieks and lamentations rose on high,
Accompanied by thuds of bodies falling.
The magic horn's intolerable cry
Provoked a frenzy ever more appalling.
But that the wells of courage should run dry
Among that mob, undignified and sprawling,
Occasions no surprise, for in the hare,
By nature timid, bravery is rare.

92

But of Marfisa's heart (so proud), and of
Guidon Selvaggio's, or the daring sons
Of Oliver who have been known to prove
Their lineage by valour more than once,
And who against a hundred thousand strove,
What will you say? For these heroic ones
Now flee like rabbits or a timid flock
Of doves dispersed by sudden noise or shock.

93

On friend and foe alike the magic horn
Has this effect; behind Marfisa now
The others flee, for not a man is born
Who such cacophony can bear, I vow:
And everywhere they run the sound is borne
And not a moment's respite will allow.
Astolfo gallops up and down the plain,
Blowing his horn more loudly yet again.

94

Some to the hills and others to the sea,
Some to the woods escape and block their ears,
Some, without ever looking backward, flee
For ten long days, so pressing are their fears.
Some cross the drawbridge, never more to see
The citadel in all their after years.
Homes are deserted, squares and temples left,
And everywhere is empty and bereft.

95

Marfisa, Guido, Sansonet, the two
Young sons of Oliver, aghast and pale,
All hurried to the sea; there followed too
The mariners and merchants on their trail.
They found Alèria who, as they knew,
Had fitted out a boat with oars and sail.
Scrambling aboard as quickly as they could,
They left that evil, cruel shore for good.

96

Up hill, down dale, the English duke meanwhile
Had scoured the kingdom to its full extent.
No soul was to be seen for many a mile.
The fugitives in all directions went,
Lurking in hiding-places dark and vile,
Wherever, to their shame and detriment,
They thought they might escape the fearful sound;
Or out to sea they swam and there were drowned.

97

To find his friends the duke sets out once more,
Thinking that he will see them on the quay.
He looks in vain along the empty shore.
Not one of his companions can he see.
And then the ship, her sails full spread before
The wind, he spies at last far out to sea.
So he must follow now another route,
For plain it is that he has missed the boat.

98

But let us let him go, and not regret
That he must travel on so far alone.
For in barbaric lands which are beset
By infidels, where nobody has gone
Except in dread, the horn will save him yet.
(How it can do so has been amply shown.)
So let us rather follow up the tale
Of his companions as away they sail.

99

The canvas bellies as they leave behind
The outline of that cruel, blood-stained coast;
And when no more is heard upon the wind
That deadly sound which terrified them most,
An unfamiliar shame, with rage combined,
So pricks them that, their cheeks on fire almost,
They dare not look each other in the eye,
But, silent, hang their heads and sadly sigh.

100

The pilot, on his homeward course intent,
Passed Cyprus and then Rhodes and next the sea
Which laves a hundred islands; on he went,
Rounding Malea in some jeopardy,
Then by a constant wind so far was sent,
The Greek Morea coast he could not see.
Next, having rounded Sicily, once more
He coasted up the fair Italian shore.

101

At last he comes to Luni once again,
Where he has left his family and friends,
And, thanking God the sailing now is plain,
He brings the ship to and the journey ends.
Finding another pilot who, to gain
Good time, to leave for France that day intends,
The knights once more embark, and spreading sails
Soon bring them to the harbour of Marseilles.

102

The valiant Bradamante, governor
Of all the Marseillais, was, as you know,
Detained; else she would offer lodging for
The cavaliers and gracious words bestow.
They disembarked; Marfisa, that same hour,
Of her companions took her leave, to go
Her solitary way, as she thought best,
And for adventures as a knight to quest.

103

It was unworthy of a knight, she said,
To go protected by so large a group.
All birds and animals which are afraid,
Starlings and doves and deer, together troop;
But the proud eagle and brave falcon aid
From other creatures neither seek nor hope.
The tigers, bears and lions walk alone;
Of greater strength than theirs, fear have they none.

104

None of the others her opinion shares
And so she only through the woods departs.
Along strange pathways she alone repairs.
The other four, who have less daring hearts,
Along a route which many hoof-prints bears
Soon found themselves in more frequented parts,
And at a castle they arrived next day
Where they were well received in every way:

105

Received, but not so well as first it seemed,
For soon they felt the contrary effect.
The castle's lord, whom courteous they deemed,
Came forth to welcome them with feigned respect.
That night when on their beds they lay and dreamed
Or soundly slept and nothing could suspect,
He had them seized, nor would he let them go
Till a strange rite they swore to undergo.

106

But I would rather now the warlike maid
Accompany, my lord, than of them speak,
And, with her, rivers cross and torrents wade.
As in the shadow of a sunlit peak
Along a rushing stream her way she made,
She came upon a woman, old and weak,
Who, weary from the long and dusty way,
Dejected seemed and sad in every way.

107

This was the agèd crone who used to serve
The cruel robbers in the mountain cave,
Where they were dealt with as all such deserve,
And put to an ignoble death by brave
Orlando; and events which I reserve
To tell you later on, this woman have
So frightened that for days she fled in fear
Along untrodden by-ways, dark and drear.

108

Taking Marfisa, from her arms and dress,
To be a cavalier from foreign lands,
She does not run away (from many a less
Alarming warrior she's fled) but stands,
Showing no sign of fear, in readiness
Beside the ford towards which Marfisa wends;
And at the very moment of their meeting
The dame is bold enough to give a greeting.

109

She asked politely that she might be borne
Across the water to the other side.
Marfisa from the day when she was born
Was ever courteous, so she complied.
And she agrees to carry the forlorn
Old woman farther, and so on they ride
Until a marshy tract is left behind.
Ere long a knight approaching them they find.

110

He had a costly saddle under him.
In shining armour and fair raiment clad,
He came towards Marfisa and the stream.
Only a damsel and a squire he led.
The damsel was as lovely as a dream,
But a severe and haughty mien she had.
She and the knight in this well-matched appeared
As could be clearly seen as they both neared.

111

His name is Pinabello of Mayence,
The cavalier who several months ago
Betrayed fair Bradamante who by chance
Encountered him when he, in deepest woe,
Bewailed his love who had been carried hence.
This is the lady he lamented so,
She whom the necromancer bore away
And held as prisoner for many a day.

112

But when Atlante's magic castle proved
As insubstantial as thin air and when
Its prisoners, set free, now freely moved,
Thanks to the skill of Bradamante, then
The lady who by Pinabel was loved
Her favours yielded to him once again;
And now together wandering they went
And many a night in many a castle spent.

113

The damsel, being capricious and unkind,
When she beheld Marfisa's agèd dame,
To mock and laugh at her was much inclined,
Putting her escort thus to scorn and shame.
To suffer this Marfisa had no mind,
So she replied, her cheeks with wrath aflame,
As one intending to defend a cause,
The dame more lovely than the damsel was.

114

And she would prove it to the lady's knight
On this arrangement: that her dress and horse
She would surrender if in a fair fight
Her cavalier was vanquished; to this course
Then Pinabello (who can do no right,
Whose words and deeds grow daily ever worse),
Taking his shield and spear, his charger turns
And, ready to attack, with fury burns.

115

Marfisa, for her part, a mighty lance
Has quickly seized and places it in rest.
She knocks him from the saddle and so stuns
Him that he lies stretched out an hour at least.
Marfisa, having won, and not by chance,
To clothes in which his lady-love is dressed
And to her palfrey now lays rightful claim,
Then she presents them to the agèd dame.

116

And in those youthful garments she desired
The crone to dress herself and to adorn
Her person with the jewels; thus attired,
More ugly yet than in the rags she'd worn,
Upon the lady's palfrey thus acquired
The dame was mounted and away was borne.
Three days they journeyed on the route they chose
Before an episode of note arose.

117

On the fourth day a cavalier they met
Who through the forest galloped quite alone.
And if to know his name your heart is set,
He is Zerbin, the king of Scotland's son.
His beauty those who see him ne'er forget;
Of knightly skill he is a paragon.
Pursuing one who his intent impeded,
He fumes with rage that he has not succeeded.

118

In vain he followed through the tangled wood
One who the code of chivalry outraged.
The miscreant made his advantage good,
The moment of escape so well he gauged.
The forest and a mist combined to hood
The morning light and, though Zerbino raged,
The other cavalier got clean away;
No sign of him he saw again that day.

119

Though he is angry, he cannot forbear
To burst out laughing at what meets his eyes.
The youthful garments of the dame appear
To mock at what her ugly face belies;
And to Marfisa, who is riding near,
He says: 'Sir knight, I see that you are wise:
For ladies of so strange a sort you choose,
There is no fear their favours you will lose.'

120

To judge the beldam by her wrinkled skin,
She than a Sibyl older is by half,
And like a monkey seems, which may be seen
Tricked out in finery to raise a laugh;
And uglier she looks now she is in
A temper, for no mockery or chaff
Is pleasing to a woman, young or old,
Nor yet that she is ugly to be told.

121

Marfisa in response deep umbrage feigned
(For to divert herself like this she chose).
'My lady is more lovely', she maintained,
'Than you are courteous, and to abuse
Her thus you are by cowardice constrained.
You think thereby from challenge to excuse
Yourself and to despise her you pretend;
But I her claim to beauty will defend.

122

'What knight is there,' Marfisa then went on,
'So young, so beautiful this damsel is,
Who in the forest finding her alone
Would not at once attempt to make her his?'
'She suits you well,' Zerbino said. 'No one
Will take her from you, I am sure of this.
As for myself, I'll not deprive you of her:
You may continue joyful as her lover.

123

'If on some other matter you desire
To challenge me, I'll show you what I'm worth.
But I am not so blind as to admire
Your lady-love: the thought moves me to mirth.
To fight, some other pretext I require.
I would not part, for anything on earth,
A couple so well-matched as you two are,
For you are just as brave as she is fair.'

124

'Your lack of gallantry', Marfisa said,
'In your despite I challenge and defy.
I hold that having seen so fair a maid
To take her from me you are bound to try.'
Zerbino answered: 'A strange pact you've made:
A winner is but ill rewarded by
A prize he does not want; the loser too
Will stand to lose what he's devoted to.'

125

'If such a pact does not to you seem good,
Here is another you cannot refuse'
(Marfisa answered); 'if by chance I should
Be vanquished, let it be I cannot choose
But keep her; likewise be it understood
You must accept her from me if you lose.
So let us see which one must do without her:
The loser to obey and never flout her.'

126

'So be it,' he replied, and turned his steed
To take the field and on his stirrups rose.
Crouched in his saddle, with a burst of speed,
Aiming his lance with care, he galloped close
And struck her shield full centre; as much heed
She paid as iron rocks to hammer blows.
She touched him on the helm in such a way
That, knocked clean from the saddle, stunned he lay.

127

Zerbino by his fall was much put out.
This never had befallen him before
In all the countless battles he had fought.
He deemed his name he never could restore.
Upon the ground for a long time without
A word he lay; it pained him even more
When he recalled what he had promised first
And with whose company he now was cursed.

128

The winner, who was in her saddle still,
Rode back and laughing said, 'Here is your prize:
My promise the more gladly I fulfil
As she becomes more lovely in my eyes.
You are her champion now for good or ill;
On you for her protection she relies,
And you have pledged that ever at her side,
You'll serve her faithfully and be her guide.'

129

Not waiting for an answer, out of sight
She galloped through the dark and tangled wood.
Zerbino, who mistook her for a knight,
Said to the agèd crone: 'Now be so good
As to inform me of his name,' and right
Away she told him, giving him much food
For thought: 'That blow was dealt you by a maid,
Who has thus knocked you from your horse,' she said;

130

'Her valour many knights puts to the test.
She shatters many a shield and many a lance;
And recently she travelled from the East
To try her skill against the Peers of France.'
This does not please Zerbino in the least.
His cheeks are crimson, he averts his glance,
And almost, from the helmet on his head
Down to his greaves, his armour blushes red.

131

He mounts his charger and himself rebukes
That a firm grip his thighs did not maintain.
The agèd crone laughs up her sleeve and looks
For every chance to cause him further pain,
Reminding him, as fun at him she pokes,
That he is now her escort and her swain.
His head he lowers, like a weary horse
Which cannot but obey the bit and spurs.

132

And sighing he exclaims: 'O unkind Fate!
What is this change which you impose on me?
My lady, whom more beautiful I rate
Than beauty's self, who was my bride-to-be,
You take, and for her loss to compensate
You offer me this hag for company?
My loss, if total, would have been less strange
And harsh than this inadequate exchange.

133

'Her who no equal had nor ever could
In loveliness, in virtue or in grace,
You cast against sharp rocks and to the flood,
Where fish despoil her body and her face;
And her who long ago should have been food
For worms, beyond the span which to our race
Allotted is, you save, and in this way
Yet heavier burdens on my back you lay.'

134

Such were Zerbino's words, and as cast down
He seemed in utterance and aspect by
His new and odious companion
As by the loss of her he loved; the sly
Old dame, who never had set eyes upon
Zerbino, rumbled who he was and why
He was so sad: this is the very prince
Whom Isabella mentioned not long since.

135

If you remember how the story went,
Here was that hag who from the cavern fled
Where Isabella many months had spent
(Whom her dear love, Zerbino, now thought dead),
When captured by the pirates whose intent
Orlando foiled; who many times had said
Why she had left her home and what befell
And how her ship was wrecked off La Rochelle.

136

So many times she had described her love,
His face, his features and his comeliness,
That when she heard him speak and saw him move
The agèd crone quite easily could guess
He was the reason for the anguish of
Fair Isabella, who had suffered less
At being the prisoner of evil men
Than at the absence of her dear Zerbin.

137

And as her escort's anguished words she hears,
She understands that he has been misled,
That he has wept unnecessary tears,
Believing Isabella to be dead.
Although the ugly creature knowledge bears
Which would rejoice his heart, she is so bad,
Malevolent, malicious and perverse,
The better news she hides and tells the worse.

138

'If you but knew, my proud and haughty knight,'
She said, 'who thus despise me and abuse,
The things I know, you would be singing quite
Another tune; but I would still refuse
To tell you if you strangled me; no right
Have you (so rude you are) to hear my news;
But had you been more courteous to me,
I would have told you all most willingly.'

139

As when a mastiff, rushing forth to seize
A thief, from its ferocity relents
If the intruder throws it bread or cheese,
Or calms it with a feigned benevolence,
So does Zerbino from his anger cease,
Eager to know the rest, for the dame hints
That she whom he has mourned as dead and gone
Is still alive; he begs the ugly crone

140

To tell him more; with a more pleasing face,
He prays and he entreats and he implores,
By God above and by the human race,
To give him news of her whom he adores.
'Nothing I say', said she with a grimace,
'Will give you cheer; this lady-love of yours,
Fair Isabella, is not dead, but death
She longs for and invokes with every breath.

141

'During the days you have not heard of her,
She fell into the hands of twenty men
Or more; consider, after that, if e'er
She should return, what sort of flower then
There will be left for you!' (How can you dare,
Ah, cursèd hag!, to tell such lies? For when
They kidnapped the fair maiden, you know well
She was untouched, though in such hands she fell.)

142

Where she last saw her, he demands to know,
But not a word from her can he extract.
The obstinate old woman still says 'No,'
And will not add one other single fact.
Soft words Zerbino tries at first, then to
More threatening ways he moves, devoid of tact.
He says he'll cut her throat, but nothing which
He does will influence the ugly witch.

143

At length Zerbino gives his tongue a rest,
For talking is no use, he sees that well.
Such jealousy arises in his breast,
His heart with anguish seems to burn and swell.
Most eager is he to begin his quest
And would have gone through fire for Isabel.
But where he longs to go he cannot go,
Being bound by what the hag prefers to do.

144

And so along a strange and lonely way,
Wherever she desired, the prince was led.
No heed to one another did they pay,
No glances were exchanged, no word was said;
But as the sun its shoulders at midday
Began to turn, their silence soon was fled,
For on their path they met a cavalier.
What next occurred I'll later on make clear.

CANTO XXI

1

No load so tight is bound by twisted cord,
No wood is joined so firmly by a nail,
As faith a candid soul, true to its word,
For ever in strong bonds will tie and seal;
And holy Faith, in ancient times adored,
Always depicted was in a white veil
Which so enveloped her from head to foot
One speck her perfect purity could blot.

2

No faith, once pledged, should ever be betrayed,
Whether to one, or many, it is sworn,
Whether in wood or cave the words are said,
Far from the homes of men, in haunts forlorn,
Or in the courts where solemn pacts are made,
Witnessed, on parchment, which fair seals adorn.
There is no need for outward sign or token:
Suffice it that a promise has been spoken.

3

Zerbino kept his word, as all knights must
In every enterprise, and clear it is
Of what account he held that bond of trust,
For he departed from his path to please
That ugly crone, for whom he felt disgust
As if he were in contact with disease
Or death itself; but chivalry forbade
Him to refuse what honour promised had.

4

I said of him that, sick at heart, because
A burden so unbearable he bears,
He rages inwardly, without a pause,
But not a word he says, no word he hears;
And as the chariot of the sun withdraws,
(So I went on) a knight-errant appears.
His coming breaks the silence they maintain
And words between them are exchanged again.

5

The hag, who knew him, knew him for no friend.
Ermònide of Holland was his name.
His sable shield displayed a crimson bend
As emblem of his lineage; the dame,
Her proud resentment bringing to an end,
All sweetness and humility became,
Zerbin reminding of the pledge he gave
From ills to guard her and from foes to save.

6

For enemy to her and to her clan
The rider was who down upon them bore.
Her one and only brother he had slain,
Her blameless father having killed before;
And, not content with this, the traitor's plan
Was to seek out her kin and kill yet more.
'As long as I am here,' Zerbino said,
'There is no need for you to feel afraid.'

7

When he has ridden close enough to peer
As if into a mirror at that face
Which he so much abhors, the cavalier
Threatens Zerbino in a haughty voice:
'Either to duel with me now prepare,
Or leave that hag to meet deserved disgrace
And death; but if you champion the wrong
You too will die, and rightly die, ere long!'

8

With courtesy Zerbino then replies
That it is base and evil in his view
And all the rules of chivalry defies
To kill a woman (and an old one too).
Let him first ponder what it signifies,
Then, if to fight he still desires, some new
And nobler purpose let him find that would
Besmirch him less than shedding female blood.

9

These words he spoke, and more, but all in vain;
At last he was obliged to pass to deeds.
From a sufficient distance on the plain
They turn, with slackened bridles, and their steeds,
Their thundering hoofs devouring the terrain,
More rapidly than ever rocket speeds
Shooting to heaven on a festive night,
Towards each other bore them for the fight.

10

Ermònide of Holland, aiming low,
Had hoped to pierce Zerbino's right-hand thigh,
But his weak lance could not withstand a blow
The Prince of Scotland scarce was troubled by.
His thrust, however, did not fail to go
Right through the other's shield, straight as a die,
Nor through his padded shoulder thence to pass,
Tumbling him from his mount upon the grass.

11

And Prince Zerbino, thinking he was dead,
Alighted, filled with pity, from his horse
And ran to lift the helmet from his head.
Awakened as from sleep, pale as a corse,
The knight first gazed in silence and then said:
'At my defeat I need feel no remorse,
For by your aspect you appear to be
The very flower of knight-errantry.

12

'The principal regret which grieves me now
Is that this traitress my undoing is,
Whom you defend, I know not why or how,
For as companions you go much amiss.
And when you know the reason for my vow
To be revenged on her, recalling this,
Your mind and heart with grief will be distraught
That, to defend her, against me you fought.

13

'If I have breath enough (though I fear not)
I will convince you that in every way
This is an evil woman beyond doubt,
To an extreme such as I scarce can say.
I had a brother who, while young, set out
From Holland, where our home is, to obey
Heraclius, the Emperor by right
Of all the Greeks, by whom he was dubbed knight.

14

'There he became the friend and intimate
Of one, a worthy baron of that court,
Whose castle, strongly walled, was situate
In Serbia, in a fair and choice resort.
Argeo (he of whom I now relate)
Of this vile woman was the fond consort.
He loved the miscreant to a degree
Which ill became so true a man as he.

15

'But she, more volatile than a dry leaf
When a cold wind of autumn strips the trees
And, leaving all their branches stark and stiff,
Spirals its booty wheresoe'er it please,
Grew cold towards her once loved spouse, as if
Her wifely duty she might shed with ease,
And on my brother fastened her desire,
For whom she burned with a consuming fire.

16

'Less opposition to the thrashing waves
The Cape of Glossa's thunder-heights present,
The mountain pine with less resistance braves
The fury of Boreas while, unbent,
Its lofty bole as high to heaven it heaves
As deep into the rock its roots are sent,
Than did my brother the advance repel
Of one whose evil heart was formed in Hell.

17

'Now, as it happens when a bold young knight
In search of combat goes, and finds it too,
My brother, being injured in a fight,
To his companion's castle, where he knew
That he was always welcome, day or night,
Whether Argeo present was, or no,
Repaired, intending to remain until
The wounds he had received should close and heal.

18

'And as he rested there, his friend one day
Upon a journey rode for many miles.
No sooner had he left than straight away
This shameless creature with her wanton wiles
Tried to seduce my brother where he lay.
Such infidelity my brother riles.
He seeks in vain (for he has no redress)
An issue from so grievous an impasse.

19

'Of many evils one at last he chose:
Argeo's friendship, which he held so dear,
He must forgo and all its blessings lose,
And where his name she never more would hear
He must depart; this course is hard, he knows,
But it would ill become a cavalier
To yield, or to accuse her to her lord,
Who with his heart and soul his wife adored.

20

'Though he has not recovered from his wounds,
He puts his armour on, and with a stern
Resolve he sadly leaves the castle grounds,
Intending he will never more return:
To no avail – Dame Fortune but confounds
And thwarts his plan with skill at every turn.
The husband now comes home and finds his wife
In floods of tears and sobbing for dear life,

21

'Her hair disordered and bright red her cheeks.
He asks what has occurred to grieve her so,
And many times must ask before she speaks,
For she is pondering what she can do,
Meaning to take, by stratagems and tricks,
Revenge for such a mortifying blow.
Her ingenuity is taxed indeed:
She has to change from love to hate at speed.

22

'"Alas!" she said at last, "of what avail
To hide what happened while you were away?
Although from all the world I might conceal
What I have done, my conscience night and day
Would prick my soul with wounds which never heal.
Such pain, which no repentance can allay,
Exceeds by far whatever suffering
Just punishment upon my flesh might bring,

23

'"If punishment is just for what duress
Enforced; howe'er that be, what has occurred
And all the wrong I did I will confess.
Then from this tarnished body with your sword
Set free my soul unstained and blemishless;
And to my eyes, quenched of all light, afford
This boon, that freed from calumny and blame
I need no longer lower them in shame.

24

'"For your companion has dishonoured me,
My body having forced to do his will.
Fearing I would recount his villainy,
He has made off and taken no farewell."
Hate now replacing all the love which he
Once bore my brother whom he loved so well,
Argeo takes his arms without delay
(Believing all she says) and rides away.

25

'As one acquainted well with the terrain,
He found my brother, who had not gone far,
Since, not yet strong and being still in pain,
He had been riding slowly, unaware
That he would be pursued; and there and then,
Resolved to be revenged in the affair,
Argeo challenged him and no excuse
Would take; nor could my brother well refuse.

26

'One combatant is strong and full of rage;
The other is unwell and ill disposed
With his companion combat thus to wage,
For friend, not enemy, he had supposed
Argeo still. As soon as they engage,
The weakness of Filandro is exposed
(Such was his name); not long can he sustain
The fierce encounter and is prisoner ta'en.

27

'"Please God", Argeo said, "that my just wrath
And your wrong-doing may the cause not be
Of bringing down the penalty of death
On one whom once I loved and who loved me,
Though you deserve no less an aftermath.
Your life I spare, that all the world may see,
As once you were surpassed by me in love,
How high in hatred now I stand above.

28

'"More of your blood I will forbear to shed.
Your punishment shall be another kind."
So saying, on the horse Argeo bade
His squire green branches interlace and bind.
Placing him on this makeshift bier, half dead,
He brought him to a cell where he confined
And to perpetual imprisonment
Condemned my brother, who was innocent.

29

'But nothing in his prison did he lack
Except the liberty to come and go.
Like a free man, obedient to his beck
And call, he had a well-trained retinue.
But she, whose scheming soul is inky black,
Determined still her purpose to pursue
And on most days my brother went to see,
Entering his cell, to which she had the key.

30

'And her assault upon him she renewed
With greater guile and boldness than before.
"Of loyalty", she said, "what is the good,
If people deem you now my paramour?
What glory you have won! What plenitude
Of spoils! Of booty what a splendid store!
And to a name what benefit results,
Which every man abuses and insults?

31

'"How much it would have benefited you
If only you had yielded what I wanted!
See what your stubborn pride has brought you to –
Branded a traitor and in prison planted!
You'll not escape from here, I tell you true.
Soften the rigour you have vainly flaunted
And if you give me pleasure, I will aim
To give you back your freedom and your fame."

32

'"No, no! It cannot be," Filandro said;
"What you desire my loyalty prevents.
All that is due to honour shall be paid,
However harsh may be my recompense.
Whatever calumny on me be shed,
He who sees all will see my innocence;
He will reward me with eternal grace
When I at last shall see Him face to face.

33

'"If it is not enough that in this cell
Argeo keeps me as a prisoner,
Then let him take my wretched life as well.
My loyalty, so little valued here,
May find reward in Heaven. Who can tell,
When I am dead, the truth may yet appear,
And he will know that faithful to the end
I served him well and he will mourn his friend!"

34

'Thus many times the shameless harridan
Tries to entice him, but to no avail.
Upon her blind desires she sets no ban
And in her lechery she does not fail
To conjure all the evil thoughts she can
Of lust and vice, omitting no detail,
As though a book of images she fingers,
Looking them through before on one she lingers.

35

'In peace for half a year she leaves him then
And in his prison never once sets foot.
My wretched brother hopes that this may mean
Her need for him has now diminished, but
Dame Fortune, the opponent of good men
And ever ready evil to promote,
Provides this wicked woman with the chance
To gratify her blind and lustful wants.

36

'Her husband had an enemy of old,
Baron Morando, also named the Fair,
Who in Argeo's absence would make bold
Incursions on his lands and even dare
To raid his castle; but his courage cooled
Soon as he knew Argeo would be there;
Within ten miles he would not venture then.
To trick Morando, he resolves to feign

37

'A journey to Jerusalem; he goes,
And tidings of his going soon are spread,
And yet his true intention no one knows,
Except his wife, to whom the truth he said,
For every evening when the shadows close
In secret he returns; and from his bed
At dawn he rises and once more is gone,
Under false colours, till the day is done.

38

'In all directions he goes wandering,
Touring his castle-grounds incessantly,
On the look-out in case his ruse should bring
Morando where he has no right to be.
He stayed concealed until the sun's bright ring
Had dipped behind the curtain of the sea,
Then hurried home and by a secret door
He was admitted by his wife (this whore).

39

'And all believed, except his evil spouse,
Argeo to be many miles away.
With cunning guile her moment well she chose
And to my brother's prison went one day.
The stream of tears which down her bosom flows
She brings, as it best suits her, into play.
"Ah, who is there will rally to my side
To save my honour from disgrace?" she cried,

40

'"And with my own, my husband's honour too?
All would be well, if only he were here!
Instead Morando, who is known to you,
Since neither God nor man he holds in fear
(Except Argeo), every day with new
Entreaties or with threats, see now appear!
And all my servants he has bribed as well,
Compliance being determined to compel.

41

'"For having heard my husband is away
And on a long and distant journey gone,
Into my court he boldly comes straightway;
No pretext or excuse he has, not one.
Yet if by chance my lord were here today,
Not only would Morando not have done
So rash a thing – within three miles, I swear,
To approach the castle walls he would not dare.

42

'"And what by messengers he first conveyed
He has today requested face-to-face,
In such a way that I was much afraid
That I would suffer outrage and disgrace.
His ardour with a feigned response I stayed;
With honeyed words I bade him go in peace,
Lest he should take, inflamed and violent,
What he now hopes to gain by my consent.

43

'"I promised but my promise mean to break,
For vows made under stress are null and void.
My aim being to preserve what he would take
By force, this strategy I have employed.
As you can see my honour is at stake
And my Argeo's too; having enjoyed
His love and friendship, which you hold so dear,
You must assist me, my fine cavalier.

44

'"If you refuse, your honour I'll defame:
I'll say that you are not what you pretend,
That cruelty alone has been your aim,
That the good faith which you professed was feigned,
Though you repulsed me every time I came,
You used this shield to gain some other end.
Matters between us might have been discreet;
Now open infamy must be my fate."

45

'Filandro then replied, "There is no need
For such a prologue, since to serve my lord
Is my intention in my every deed.
How I can help him, tell me in a word.
That he thus deals with me I little heed,
I blame him not, I ask for no reward.
To die for him I am prepared, although
My fate and all the world against me go."

46

'She said: "I want you to destroy the man
Who menaces the honour of our house;
I do not fear that any danger can
Result, or for misgivings give you cause.
He will return, according to my plan,
At the third hour of night, when not a mouse
Is stirring; when I hear him give the knock
We have agreed, I will undo the lock.

47

'"Until then, bide your time without alarm
In my apartment, which will be unlit.
First I will help him quickly to disarm
And strip; then you leap out on him and hit."
So did this loving wife her husband's harm
Contrive, and lead him to her cruel pit,
If wife by any right she can be named,
Rather than fury in Inferno framed.

48

'That night this evil woman came and led
My brother, with his weapon in his hand,
To her dire chamber where no light was shed.
The unhappy master gave the signal and
As usual prepared to go to bed.
How rarely evil does not go as planned!
Filandro struck Argeo a fell blow,
Thinking he was Morando, as you know.

49

'With one fell stroke he splits both neck and skull,
Which, bare of helmet, nothing can defend.
Argeo's life by this unmerciful
Attack is brought thus to a bitter end.
O rare event! O case incredible!
Filandro's hope had been to help his friend,
Yet he had slain him with a savagery
He would not visit on an enemy.

50

'And while Argeo lies unrecognized
My brother gives Gabrina back the sword,
For such her name is (you are now apprised).
She, born for treachery, by every word
Has up to then the truth from him disguised;
But eager now to give him his reward,
She takes a lantern and the body shows him
Of his companion – and Filandro knows him.

51

'She threatens that if he does not relent
And to her unrequited passion yield,
She will inform the guards of the event
And what he did will be to all revealed;
And to the gallows she will have him sent,
And shamefully as an assassin killed.
And she reminds him that if *life* he scorns,
No cavalier his *reputation* spurns.

52

'Filandro, filled with sorrow and with fear,
When he perceived the error he had made,
Was almost on the point of killing *her*,
By such a frenzy were his feelings swayed.
Remembering he was a prisoner,
By foes beset, his reason he obeyed,
Else, lacking weapons, with his very teeth,
He would have torn and mangled her to death.

53

'As by two winds a ship is sometimes tossed
And helpless whirls, far out upon the main,
While, alternating, their directions crossed,
One sends it forward, and one back again,
Poop spun to prow and prow to poop almost,
Till mastered by the stronger of the twain,
So now Filandro, driven from two sides,
On the less evil of two thoughts decides.

54

'His reason shows that great the danger is,
Not of death only, but of infamy,
If all is known throughout the premises.
His time for thinking is cut short, so he
The bitter cup must swallow to the lees,
Whether he will or no; and finally,
Although he knew that neither course was good,
His fear did more than obstinacy could.

55

'A traitor's death he deemed so horrible,
The shame of it was so abhorrent that
He promised he would do Gabrina's will
If she would keep her bargain, tit for tat;
And so he plucked, perforce, the fruit of ill-
omened desire, then through the castle-gate
Departed and at length came home to us,
Leaving a name despised and infamous.

56

'And in his heart indelible he bore
The image of his friend whom he thus slew
So foolishly, to do her will who more
Than Procne or Medea, or the two
Together, cruel was; that he forbore
To kill her also was a tribute to
The promise he had given, but in hate
He held her, with a hatred deep and great.

57

'From that time on he never smiled again
And all his words were melancholy; from
His bosom sighs of sorrow poured in vain.
A new Orestes now he had become
Who, the accursed Aegisthus having slain,
Was party also to his mother's doom.
Unceasingly tormented by his grief,
No rest by day or night gave him relief.

58

'This harlot to herself admits at last
How little he whom she desires desires her.
Her ardour for Filandro now is past;
Instead a raging flame of hatred fires her.
She feels for him hostility as vast
As for Argeo, and one thought inspires her:
How to despatch from life (the fiend accursed!)
Her second husband, as she did her first.

59

'She found a doctor full of guile and spite –
The very man to carry out her aim –
Who poisoner should have been called by right,
Rather than healer of the sick and lame.
She undertook his service to requite
If he agreed to play her cunning game:
To rid her by a death-dispensing potion
Of one she now abhorred – such was her notion.

60

'And in my presence and in many others',
Bearing the poisoned potion in his hand,
The agèd evil-doer by my brother's
Bed took his insinuating stand.
'Twould be as good for him, he said, as mother's
Milk is for a baby; but Gabrina planned
Before the medicine killed the invalid
Of this unwelcome witness to be rid,

61

'Or it may be she did not want to pay
The hypocrite the price which she had offered.
With ready skill she caught his hand midway
Just at the moment when the cup he proffered
To which the poison had been added. "Pray",
Said she, "be not put out if I who suffered
Much for my dear love ask you first to taste
This beverage – please grant me this request."

62

'How do you think, fair sir, the wretched man
Felt then? He was confused and horrified.
He has no time to formulate a plan.
Fear of suspicion moves him to decide
To sip the cup as quickly as he can.
The patient, reassured and satisfied
By such a demonstration of good faith,
Swallows the medicine in one single breath.

63

'As when a sparrow-hawk, which in its claws
Clutches a partridge and to eat prepares,
Is by a hound betrayed, which with its jaws
Both predator and booty rends and tears,
So he, the prize dashed from his avid paws,
Where he most looks for help, most badly fares:
A striking instance of the biter bit.
Let all who covet be forewarned by it.

64

'The agèd doctor, his work done, set out
At once towards his private room, where his
Intention was to take some antidote
Which against poison efficacious is;
But still Gabrina is resolved to flout
The hapless man and hinders him in this,
Saying he must remain till all could see
What the effect of what he drank would be.

65

'All his entreaties are of no avail.
She will on no account let him depart.
His strength and faculties begin to fail.
Knowing his death is certain and no art
Can save him, he decides now to reveal
The truth and every detail to impart.
So, what to many others he had done
The doctor to himself did – and was gone,

66

'His spirit following my brother's soul,
Which had, alas! already gone ahead.
We who by now had seen and heard the whole,
And what that charlatan had done and said,
Who, empty-handed, failed to reach his goal,
Seized this abominable beast, more dread
Than any to be found in any wood,
For whom a death by burning was too good.'

67

Ermònide his story ended here.
He would have said what else had come to pass
And how she had escaped, but could not bear
The pain, and fell back faint upon the grass.
Meanwhile two shield-bearers had formed a bier
Of sturdy branches – the sole means, alas!
By which the wounded knight could be conveyed;
To lie on this their lord they now persuade.

68

Zerbino to the knight apologized
And his regret expressed for such offence,
For he saw well he had been ill-advised
To take this creature under his defence.
His honour, which above all else he prized,
And which, unstained, no broken faith consents,
Obliged him to his utmost to defend her
Against whoever threatened to offend her.

69

If he could serve him now in any way
He'd gladly do whatever was his will.
The knight replied he must be rid straightway
Of her who would contrive to do him ill,
And said that he would sorely rue the day
If he continued to defend her still.
Gabrina kept her eyes upon the ground,
For to the truth no answer can be found.

70

Zerbino with Gabrina then set off
Upon the promised journey, as was due.
All day he could not curse the crone enough
Who caused him such a knight such harm to do.
These revelations had now called her bluff.
Now that the truth of the affair he knew,
While he abhorred and hated her before,
He loathed her and detested her still more.

71

She, who Zerbino's hatred fully knows,
In animosity will not give place.
Hers matches his, not one inch less it shows.
He plays his highest card, she trumps his ace.
Her evil heart with venom overflows,
Though this is not depicted in her face;
And thus in hostile harmony they ride,
Competing neck and neck and side by side.

72

Then, as the sun declined towards the west,
A sound of clashing and of shrieks was heard,
Of blows exchanged with vigour and with zest,
From which a fight near by could be inferred.
The strength of this hypothesis to test,
Zerbino towards the source of clamour spurred.
To follow him Gabrina was not slow,
And what next happened in my next you'll know.

CANTO XXII

1

Sweet ladies, who in loving gracious are
And with one love alone are each content,
Though you among so many are most rare,
For few indeed are chaste and continent,
Let it not irk you if I rancour bear
Against Gabrina, and my wrath have spent,
And will again, resuming now my verse,
Cry out upon a nature so perverse.

2

For such hers was; and I have been constrained,
By one whom I obey, not to obscure
The truth; the honour is not thereby stained
Of this one or of that whose heart is pure;
Nor Judas for the thirty pieces gained
Makes John's or Peter's claims to glory fewer;
Nor is the fame of Hypermnestra less
Because her sisters were so pitiless.

3

For one whom I have ventured thus to blame,
As fits the structure of this tale of mine,
A hundred other women I could name
Whose virtues like the sun in heaven shine.
Once more the work resuming, which I aim
To vary as I weave it line by line,
I'll follow first the knight of Scotland's thread,
Who heard a sound of combat, as I said.

4

Between two mountains whence such noises hail
Zerbino enters and not far has gone,
When there before him in a narrow vale
A knight is lying dead, and further on
I'll tell you who he is; just now my tale
Must find Astolfo, whom I left alone
In the Levant and who had thought it best
To make his way at length towards the West.

5

I left him in the cruel citadel
Which at the shrilling of his magic horn
Was emptied wholly of the infidel
And wanton women, of all courage shorn,
And his companions scattered had as well,
Across the sea by spreading canvas borne.
Now let us follow the Armenian road
With him who left that evil land for good.

6

After some days in Anatolia
He reaches Prusa in his wanderings.
Across the sea a vessel from afar
The intrepid paladin to Thrace now brings.
Along the Danube through Hungaria
He rides and thence, as if his horse had wings,
In less than twenty days he crossed the Rhine
And said farewell to lands of '*Ja*' and '*Nein*'.

7

Through the Ardennes he rode to Aquisgrane,
Thence to Brabant; in Flanders he at last
Took ship to go to England once again.
The south wind filled the foresail with its gust.
By noon he saw the cliffs of Dover plain.
A bridge was thrown and to the shore he passed.
He leapt into the saddle and so spurred
He came to London before night, and heard

8

His father, Otto, had been gone long since
To Paris and not soon would he be back,
And almost every baron, every prince,
Had followed in his venerable track.
These tidings the brave paladin convince
That he must follow them, and with no lack
Of haste the port of London reaching now,
To Calais bids the pilot turn the prow.

9

A little breeze upon the port bow blew,
Tempting the vessel out on to the wave,
Which gradually strong and stronger grew
And to the pilot anxious moments gave.
To windward finally the poop he drew,
The vessel from capsizing thus to save,
And down the Channel's length his course he wended,
A different journey from the one intended.

10

To east, to west, he tacks as best he can,
Where the wind drives, and comes at last to port.
No sooner have they docked at Rouen than
Astolfo, stepping forth at this resort,
Commands his squire to saddle Rabican.
He arms himself in haste, for time is short,
And journeys on; that horn he carries still,
More than a thousand men more terrible.

11

And as Astolfo travelled through a wood,
At a hill's foot he found a limpid spring
When overhead the sun in heaven stood
And sheep, their grazing-grounds abandoning,
Sheltered in huts or caves in drowsy mood.
Both heat and thirst the paladin now bring
To a brief halt, and where the shade is cool
He ties his horse and moves towards the pool.

12

He stooped to drink but had not wet his lips
Before a peasant, hiding there near by,
Springs from a bush and on his charger leaps.
Astolfo lifts his head, much startled by
The noise; his thirst being gone, though by no sips
Has it been quenched and still his mouth is dry,
He leaves the pool, and when his loss he sees,
Fast as he can he sets off through the trees.

13

Lest he should disappear at once from sight,
The thief does not at first extend his pace.
His grasp upon the reins now slack, now tight,
He keeps an even distance in the race,
First trotting and then galloping outright.
Leaving the wood behind, they reach the place
Where many noble lords as prisoners
Still languish in a prison without bars.

14

Into the palace now the peasant rides
On Rabicano who goes like the wind.
By shield and helm and all his arms besides,
The duke, impeded, follows far behind.
At last he too arrives with mighty strides,
But now no further trace of them can find;
There being now no sign of thief or horse,
He gazes round, uncertain of his course.

15

With hurried steps he searches here and there
In every loggia, vestibule and room,
But cannot find the peasant anywhere;
Of all his labour no result has come,
Nor does he know (and this is hard to bear)
Where Rabican is hidden; in deep gloom
He spent that livelong day in vain pursuit,
In and around, up, down, all without fruit.

16

Weary with wandering, the English duke
Perceived the palace was bewitched at last
And he bethought him of the little book
Which Logistilla gave him when he passed
From India and which he always took
With him on journeys lest some spell be cast.
He thumbed the index through and quickly traced
The pages where the remedy was placed.

17

Enchanted castles many pages filled,
Together with instructions as to ways
To thwart the enchanter, and to open sealed
Apartments and the prisoners release.
Under the threshold was a sprite concealed
Who tricks of fraudulent illusion plays,
And if the stone Astolfo raised and broke,
The edifice would disappear in smoke.

18

Eager to bring to a triumphant close
So glorious a deed, the paladin
To test its weight no hesitation shows,
But stoops towards the marble to begin;
But when Atlante sees those hands so close,
Ready to render his enchantment vain,
Afraid of what will come to pass, he plots
To bind him fast by other magic knots.

19

Using a subterfuge of devilry,
Atlante caused Astolfo to assume
Fictitious forms, so that he seemed to be
A giant or a labourer to some;
An evil cavalier still others see.
He makes the duke those many shapes become
Which in the wood he took. The prisoners
Turn on Astolfo now to claim what's theirs.

20

Ruggier, Gradasso, Bradamante and
Iroldo, with Prasildo, Brandimart
And other warriors, in a fierce band,
Determine now to make Astolfo smart;
But in the nick of time he takes his stand
And blows upon his horn – and they depart.
Had he not saved himself by its shrill blast,
That moment would have been Astolfo's last.

21

Soon as his lips have touched the magic horn,
Filling the air with terrifying sound,
As a gun startles pigeons from the corn,
So did the knights now scatter all around.
The necromancer too, his pride and scorn
Abandoning, crept out from under ground,
All pale and trembling, and soon fled to where
The shrilling could no longer strike his ear.

22

Jailer and jail-birds fled as in one troop;
Likewise the horses, tethered there, stampeded.
More than a stable-door and more than rope
To keep them from escaping now was needed.
No cat, no mouse was there but flew the coop,
So thoroughly the deadly noise succeeded,
And Rabicano would have fled, no doubt,
Had not the duke been there as he came out.

23

Astolfo, now the sorcerer is gone,
Proceeds to lift the heavy slab away.
He finds a talisman beneath the stone,
And other things which I forbear to say.
Being eager for the spell to be undone,
He breaks all that he finds without delay,
Obeying the instructions in his book.
The palace vanishes in mist and smoke.

24

He found Ruggiero's horse was tethered by
A golden chain – I mean that mount on which
Atlante had arranged that he should fly
To the enchanted garden of the witch,
Alcina; Logistilla by and by
Had made a bridle for it, fair and rich.
From India to England he had flown,
Along the right-hand route, as I have shown.

25

I do not know if you recall the day
When Galafrone's daughter, nude and fair,
Duping Ruggiero, vanished clean away.
And the winged charger rose into the air,
Shaking its bridle free, to his dismay?
To the surprise of all, it flew to where
Its master was and stayed with him until
The day Astolfo broke the evil spell.

26

No outcome of the enterprise could please
The Duke Astolfo or delight him more,
Since there were many lands and many seas
He had in mind to visit and explore;
He could now circle all the globe with ease –
This being what the hippogriff was for;
On his resolve he had no fear to act,
For he had practised riding it, in fact,

27

And on it had acquired some mastery
That day on the enchanted island when
The wise Melissa set the creature free
From her who had seduced so many men
And changed Astolfo to a myrtle-tree.
He clearly saw how Logistilla then
Controlled it with a bridle, and with care
Had watched Ruggiero's lessons in the air.

28

Resolved to ride the hippogriff away,
Finding its saddle near, he saddled it;
Then he selected, from a large array
Of bridles, one of which he judged the bit
Would best constrain the creature to obey.
One thought alone detained Astolfo yet:
Concern for Rabicano made him pause
Before on high into the air he rose.

29

He had good reason to be fond of him:
No better horse for fighting with the lance
Than Rabican, and from the utmost rim
Of India he'd borne the duke to France.
He ponders long, reluctant to the whim
Of passers-by to leave him, or to chance.
He thinks for a long time and in the end
He thinks it best to give him to a friend.

30

He looked about him, hoping he might see
A hunter or some peasant in the wood,
To whom his charger might entrusted be
And led to some near town, as he thought good.
Till the next dawn he watched, but uselessly,
For no one came to break his solitude;
But the next morning, when it scarce was light,
Approaching through the wood he glimpsed a knight.

31

But if I am to tell you all my tale,
I must now find Ruggiero and the Maid.
When the horn's shrilling clamour silent fell,
And the fair couple some way off had fled,
Ruggiero looked, and this time did not fail
To recognize her whom Atlante had
Until this moment by his art concealed,
Each being of each in unawareness held.

32

Ruggiero looks at Bradamante, who
Looks at Ruggiero, greatly marvelling
That for so long her love she never knew –
Such the illusion evil spells can bring.
Ruggiero clasps the lovely maiden to
His breast; from rosy pink her blushes spring
To crimson in her cheeks, and from her lips
The first sweets of a love so blest he sips.

33

The happy lovers, locked in an embrace,
A thousand times each to the other pressed.
Their joy, depicted in their eyes and face,
Could scarcely be contained within their breast.
It grieves them much that for so long a space
They lingered, their proximity unguessed,
Beneath that self-same roof and, to their cost,
So many days of happiness were lost.

34

All pleasures which become a prudent maid,
And on her lover she may well bestow,
Without dishonour Bradamante paid
Ruggiero in return for all his woe,
But must withhold that sweetest fruit, she said,
Till to her father, Aymon, he could go
And in due form their rites be solemnized;
But in the meantime let him be baptized.

35

Ruggiero, who not only for her sake
The Christian life and all that it implied
Most willing was straightway to undertake
(His father, grandfather and all that side
Of his great race were Christians), but to make
Her happy would lay down his life, replied:
'Not only in the water, but in fire
I'll place my head if such is your desire.'

36

And so, to be baptized, and thence to claim
Fair Bradamante as his spouse, he led
The way to Vallombrosa; of this name
There was an abbey whose fair lands were fed
By teeming springs, and where to all who came
The monks were courteous; at a good pace
They reached the forest's edge and in that place
They met a lady, woe-begone of face.

37

Ruggiero, ever courteous and kind
To everyone, to women most of all,
Seeing the rivulets of tears which lined
Her face, so delicate and beautiful,
Was moved by pity and his eager mind
Desired to learn at once what tragical
Event had caused the lady such distress,
And so, first greeting her with gentleness,

38

He asked her why she wept; her lovely eyes
All wet with tears, she raises to his face
And with the utmost courtesy replies,
Telling Ruggiero what has taken place.
'Kind sir,' she said, 'you will feel no surprise
That tears thus down my cheeks a pathway trace,
When you have heard the reason for my sorrow:
A youth who will be slain before tomorrow.

39

'He loved a gentle maiden, sweet and fair
(The daughter of Marsilio, King of Spain).
In a white veil and clad in woman's wear,
Changing his voice and glance, a girl's to feign,
He slept with her each night, and unaware
Her parents and the household long remain;
But so secretive nobody can be
That someone does not notice finally.

40

'One who had seen them, with two others spoke.
They also talked and to the king news spread.
Two days ago he sent a spy, who took
The lovers as they lay asleep in bed.
Alas! They lie apart now, under lock
And key, within our fortress vile and dread.
I greatly fear the youth, before today
Has ended, a dire penalty will pay.

41

'I cannot bear to watch such cruelty
(He will be burned alive) for nothing can
In all my life cause greater grief to me
Than such a death of such a fair young man.
All pleasure I shall ever know will be
Henceforth at once transmuted into pain
Whenever I recall the cruel flame
Which burned that beautiful and tender frame.'

42

When Bradamante these sad tidings hears,
Her heart by strange misgivings is oppressed.
As if he were her brother, anguished fears
For the condemned young man torment her breast
(Nor is this quite as strange as it appears,
As you will know when I relate the rest).
Turning towards Ruggiero first, she said,
'This youth, I think, deserves our utmost aid.'

43

Then to the weeping lady next she turned
And said, 'Lead us within those walls, I pray,
For if the youth is not already burned,
He will go free; trust now to what I say.'
Ruggiero, who the kind heart had discerned
Which in his lady's valiant bosom lay,
Was kindled with desire to save the youth,
As if he were on fire himself, in truth.

44

And to the lady from whose eyes a stream
Of tears descends, 'What are we waiting for?'
He says, 'Weeping will be no use to him.
If you will straightway lead us to the poor
Young man we pledge (our word we will redeem)
To save him from a thousand swords or more;
But hurry, lest our rescue be too slow
And flames, already kindled, fiercer grow.'

45

Such noble words, so fierce and bold the air
Of the proud couple without paragon,
The lady's heart released from her despair,
Renewing hope whence hope had wholly gone;
But for a while she pondered, to compare
Two disadvantages and perils: one
(Which she feared less), to go the long way round,
Or take a route where danger could be found.

46

At last she spoke: 'If we could take the way
Which leads directly to that grievous spot,
I think we should arrive in time today
Before the fire is kindled; but the route
Which we must follow will so twist and stray,
Sending us on a path so round about,
That scarce twelve hours suffice to bring us there,
When we shall find the young man dead, I fear.'

47

To this the bold Ruggiero soon replies:
'Why don't we take the shorter way?'; and she:
'Because along that path a castle lies
Belonging to the Ponthieu family
And scarce three days ago, as I surmise,
All who passed by on quests of chivalry,
To shameful tasks and tests have been coerced,
By Pinabello, of all men the worst.

48

'He is Anselmo Altaripa's son.
There every knight or lady who perchance
Rides by must pay the forfeit; from each one
He takes his horse; all his accoutrements,
A knight, and all the clothes which she has on,
A lady, must surrender; in all France
No braver knight ere tilted than the four
Who to obey this shameful custom swore.

49

'How it began (only three days ago
The custom was imposed) I will now say,
That the iniquity you both may know
Of the vile law they promised to obey:
This Pinabello has a lady, so
Debased she has no equal, and one day
While riding forth with him, I know not where,
She was insulted by a cavalier.

50

'The knight, first mocked by her, because he bore
An agèd crone upon his crupper, fought
With Pinabello (who was gifted more
With arrogance than strength), and quickly brought
Him low; he made her then dismount and for
Her mockery this lesson she was taught:
For he obliged her to take off her dress
And robe the agèd hag in it, no less.

51

'She who remained on foot for vengeance burned
And nothing could assuage her raging thirst;
And Pinabello also, who has earned
An evil reputation as the worst
Of men, when to the castle they returned
This method of revenge with her rehearsed,
That she might once more smile and sleep o' nights,
To rob a thousand ladies and their knights.

52

'And then four cavaliers, as it befell,
Arrived that very day at his abode,
Who from a distant land, as I heard tell,
But recently had travelled, and who showed
Such valour that all others they excel
Who in our lifetime forth to battle rode:
Grifone, Sansonetto, Aquilant
They are and Guy, a younger knight-errant.

53

'And Pinabello in most courteous guise
Welcomed them to the castle, and that night
As in their beds they slumbered, by surprise
He seized them all and gave them no respite
Until they promised him that they likewise
For thirteen months (which was the term he set)
Would seize and dispossess whoever came –
Ladies of rank and cavaliers of fame.

54

'They were to strip the knights of lance and sword,
The ladies of such dresses as they had,
And of their horses; thus they pledged their word.
Though, I have heard, to do so makes them sad,
To keep it they resolved with one accord.
Till now they have unhorsed all who essayed
To joust with them, and many now have left,
Of horse, of arms, of dignity bereft.

55

'They have agreed whoever first by chance
Rides forth, shall fight the newcomer alone.
If the opponent proves so strong a lance
As to remain upright, and *he* is thrown,
The others are obliged to help at once
And fling themselves into the fight as one.
If each alone can many victims take,
Think what a formidable band they make!

56

'Our mission is so urgent, no delays
Can it allow, however gallantly
So great a challenge you may wish to face;
Supposing that you gain the victory,
As from your bearing seems to be the case,
So great a task will scarce accomplished be
In a brief hour; the youth will burn, I fear,
If we expend all day in getting there.'

57

'Let us not be deterred,' was his reply,
And he continued, 'let us do our best,
And to the Ruler of the starry sky,
Or to Dame Fortune, let us leave the rest.
When we begin to joust, you may judge by
Our expertise if to this youth oppressed,
For such a slight offence, as you have said,
Condemned to die today, we can bring aid.'

58

Straightway fair Bradamante led them on,
Choosing the shorter route; when not above
Three miles the three together had been gone,
They found themselves before the portals of
The castle where one cavalier alone,
Or four, the arms, the horse, the clothes remove
From every knight and lady; drawing near,
Two strokes upon a bell within they hear.

59

Next, an old man came trotting through the gate
Upon a nag as fast as he could go,
And as he came he shouted, 'Wait there, wait!
A forfeit you must pay; if you don't know
The custom of the castle, I'll relate
The details and explain what you must do';
And the old man began at once to tell
Them of the law decreed by Pinabel.

60

Then he continued, giving them advice,
As was his way with every cavalier:
'My sons, I would not think about it twice.
Undress the lady, leave your horses here,
Put down your weapons, do not pay the price
Of combat with these four, which is too dear.
Of garments, steeds, and arms there's always more,
But life, once forfeit, nothing can restore.'

61

'Enough,' Ruggiero said, 'enough, I pray,
For I am well informed and hither came
To test my prowess and my strength today,
And see if deeds can match my self-esteem;
No dress, no horse, no arms I'll give away,
If menaces are all I hear: the same
Applies, I know, to my companion too,
Who'll not surrender without more ado.

62

'So, in God's name, let me come face-to-face
With him who claims our horses, arms and clothes,
For we have still to journey for a space
Beyond that hill and have no time to lose.'
The old man answered, 'Here one comes apace
Who means to challenge you when he draws close.'
Across the bridge there rode, in truth, a knight,
His crimson surcoat damasked all in white.

63

Fair Bradamante many times implores
Ruggiero to reserve for her the task
Of combating and throwing from his horse
The knight with the embroidered coat; to ask
Is vain, nothing will turn him from his course.
She is obliged to wear the passive mask
Of onlooker; the enterprise he must
Assume, while she stands by to watch him joust.

64

'Who is this knight,' Ruggiero asked the guide,
'Who through the castle gateway first appears?'
'He is called Sansonetto,' he replied,
'I know him by the crimson coat he wears,
Embroidered with white flowers.' At once they ride,
Without a word, far off, apart; their spears
With deadly and unerring aim held low,
They spur their steeds as fast as they will go.

65

And in the meantime, forth with Pinabel,
The infantry came pouring from the fort
To seize the weapons when the victims fell,
For many were the pickings of this sort;
But the two knights, their horses going well,
Bore down upon each other, not in sport,
Couching their lances, which, of mountain oak,
Were two palms thick, from metal tip to stock.

66

And of such mighty lances more than ten
From well-grown timber in a near-by wood,
Young Sansonet had ordered to be hewn.
Of these he had brought two, as he thought good.
A shield of adamant was needed then,
And breast-plate which the strongest blows withstood.
When he arrived, one lance, at his command,
Ruggiero had, the other he retained.

67

They could have pierced an anvil, I expect.
Half-way along their course the riders met,
The shield of each receiving the impact;
But on that one which had made devils sweat
In Hell, the blow had but a slight effect –
Despite the expertise of Sansonet –
I mean, of course, the shield Atlante made,
Of strange and mighty powers, as I said.

68

I have already told you how its ray
With magic power strikes a victim's eyes:
As soon as the silk veil is drawn away,
Dazzled and helpless on the ground he lies.
Ruggiero thus the shield does not display
Unless some urgent need of it arise.
It was impenetrable too, I judge,
Since this encounter did not make it budge.

69

The second shield, forged by a lesser smith,
Failed to resist the force of such a blow.
As if Jove's thunder it were smitten with,
It cracked, and let the metal point pass through
Until it penetrated underneath
The armpit where the coat of mail gives no
Protection; Sansonetto, wounded, fell,
Surprised, enraged, and mortified as well.

70

He was the first of the four friends who swore
To keep the hateful rule of Pinabel,
Who failed to win the arms the strangers bore,
Who in that jousting from the saddle fell.
(For one who laughs, tears also are in store.)
A second time the traitor rang the bell.
The other three rode forth and stood to hear
The words he spoke to them as he drew near.

71

Then Pinabello, who desired to know
The name of him who with such force and skill
The champion of the fortress had brought low,
Towards Bradamante moved, and to fulfil
God's plan, that he should not unpunished go,
He rode the very horse (he had it still)
Which he had stolen from the valiant Maid
By means of the deceitful trick he played.

72

It was eight months precisely to the day
Since this true son of the Maganza line,
While he and Bradamante made their way
(As I have told you in this tale of mine),
Had thrown her down the cave where Merlin lay
(The branch she clung to saved her by divine
Coincidence), and, thinking she was dead
And buried, had removed her thoroughbred.

73

The Maid has recognized her horse and knows
That evil count who rides upon it too.
When she has heard his voice and seen him close,
'This is,' she says, 'that very traitor who
Did me such grievous wrong, and I propose
To pay him now, with interest, what is due.
His evil deeds have led him here to meet
His just reward, which he shall have, complete.'

74

To challenge and to draw her sword was one
And the same action, likewise to attack.
She first cut his retreat; when that was done,
And to the castle he could not get back,
No hope had foxy Pinabel to run
To earth; with a loud shriek, along a track
Which deep into the tangled forest led,
Not stopping to defend himself, he fled.

75

White as a sheet and terrified, he spurs.
The only hope he looks for is in flight,
And yet his pace does not compare with hers.
That valiant damsel of Dordogne, now quite
Within a lance's distance or a spear's,
Presses behind the wretch without respite.
The din re-echoes through the woods around,
Yet no one heeds it from the castle-ground.

76

All eyes are on Ruggiero there; meanwhile
The other three ride forth to face the fray,
With Pinabello's paramour, that vile
And cruel jade, whose rule they must obey.
Since victory they cannot reconcile
With honour, they would sooner die that day.
Their faces burn with shame, their hearts with grief,
For such dishonour passes all belief.

77

That cruel whore, the vilest ever born,
Deviser of the law of which I told,
Reminds them of the promise they have sworn
To reap revenge for her a thousandfold.
'If my own lance suffices to bring scorn
And shame on him, must I', so speaks the bold
Guidon Selvaggio, 'be assisted by
These others? If I fail, let me then die.'

78

Thus too the reasoning of the brothers ran:
Rather than reap unchivalrous rewards
In triple combat with a single man,
They would prefer, as with their code accords,
To yield or die; but the vile harridan
Replies: 'Why are we wasting time on words?
His arms and horse I brought you here to take,
Not new agreements and new laws to make.

79

'When you were prisoners, that was the time
For such excuses; now it is too late.
Now you must make your resolution rhyme
With your avowed intent, not with a spate
Of empty, lying words.' In the meantime
Ruggiero challenged them, 'Why do we wait?
Here is my horse, newly caparisoned,
Here are my arms, here is the lady, gowned.'

80

The châtelaine thus urges from one side,
Ruggiero from the other does the same.
At last the challenge cannot be denied.
Although their faces are ablaze with shame,
Reluctant to do battle, forth they ride,
In front, the sons of Oliver, whose fame
Is prized in Burgundy; the destrier
Guidone follows on is heavier.

81

Bearing the lance which Sansonetto felled,
Ruggiero rides towards his triple foe.
In front of him that covering is held
Which formerly Atlante, as you know,
Was wont to use – I mean that magic shield
(No human vision can endure its glow)
To which Ruggiero, as a last resource,
In the most grievous peril has recourse.

82

And three times only has he bared its light,
And every time his peril was most grave:
Twice when Alcina would have checked his flight
From her unmanly kingdom; then, to save
From the devouring fangs – ah, fearful sight! –
Of the sea orc, foiled in the foaming wave,
Those lovely limbs (though little joy he gains,
For he is ill-rewarded for his pains).

83

Apart from these three times, he always hid
The magic shield beneath its silken shroud,
Which he could soon remove in case of need,
And if he judged the circumstance allowed.
So now, protected by it, as I said,
Eager for the encounter, forth he rode,
Feeling less apprehension of the three
Than if they were but yet in infancy.

84

Just where the topmost tip and visor meet,
Ruggiero aims at one opponent's shield.
Grifone sways and totters in his seat.
Falling at last, he sprawls upon the field,
Far from his horse; his weapon first had hit
Ruggiero's buckler sideways and revealed
In part its surface, shining, smooth and terse –
Not the result desired, but the reverse.

85

Grifone had already made one rent
In the silk cover which concealed the ray
Whose magic splendour nothing could prevent
(But all before it blind and helpless lay);
Next, Aquilant, who level with him went,
The part which still remained now tore away:
The splendour struck both brothers in the eyes,
And struck Guidon, who rode behind, likewise.

86

One here, another there, falls to the ground.
The shield not only blinds: it renders too
All other senses lifeless, as though stunned.
Ruggiero, who is eager to renew
Hostilities, now turns his charger round,
And as he turns he grasps his sword, so true
And sharp – not one opponent meets his sight:
All three have fallen in so brief a fight.

87

The cavaliers and all their èquerries,
The ladies too, who had been standing by,
The horses I must not forget – all these,
As if they were as dead as mutton, lie.
At first he is amazed and then he sees
The veil which to the left hangs all awry,
I mean that silk in which his custom was
To veil the light, of this collapse the cause.

88

He turns away and, as he turns, his eyes
Search here and there for his belovèd Maid.
Riding in quest of her, in vain he tries
The corner of the field where she had stayed
To watch the first encounter; his surmise
Is that she has departed thence to aid
The youth, fearing perhaps that while they fight
He may already have been set alight.

89

Lying among the others he espied
The very lady who had brought him there.
He picked her up and, as one stupefied,
She lay across his saddle; with an air
Of grave displeasure he set forth to ride;
Her mantle, such as, travelling, ladies wear,
He used to cover up the shield, and she
Her senses then recovered instantly.

90

They travel on. Ruggiero's face is red.
He dare not raise his eyes for very shame,
For clearly he anticipates with dread
His victory will win rebuke, not fame.
'What can I do' (thus to himself he said),
'To make amends and clear my tarnished name?
Now all the victories which I have won
Will be ascribed to spells by everyone.'

91

And as he journeyed onwards, deep in thought,
Of his profound dilemma, it befell,
To the desired solution he was brought:
Midway along his path was a deep well,
By cattle in the summer noondays sought
When on their pastures they have grazed their fill.
Ruggiero said: 'This is the very place,
O shield, to put an end to my disgrace.

92

'No longer will you bear me company.
This is the last disgrace I'll owe to you.'
So saying, he dismounted near a tree.
Taking a heavy stone, he tied it to
The shield, ran to the well and instantly
Buckler and boulder to the bottom threw,
And said, 'Lie there for ever, cursèd shield,
And my dishonour with you lie concealed.'

93

The well is filled with water to the brim;
The shield is heavy, heavy too the stone.
At once they sink (such objects do not swim);
The parted waters close again as one.
The noble deed his valour did not dim.
Nay, rather on Fame's trumpet it is blown:
In France and Spain and all the provinces
Ruggiero's action divulgated is.

94

From mouth to mouth the tidings quickly spread.
Soon everyone the strange adventure heard
And warriors from far and near were led
To seek the magic shield (in which they erred,
For there were many better quests instead).
The forest where the episode occurred
The lady who divulged the deed declined
To name, lest anyone the well should find.

95

Until Ruggiero left the castle-grounds
Where he had won a battle, as you saw,
Losing no blood and suffering no wounds,
Four champions lay stretched like men of straw.
But when the shield which dazzles and confounds
Had been removed, in wonderment and awe,
Though like so many corpses they had lain,
They came to life and stood upright again.

96

And all that day among themselves they speak
Of nothing else but of that strange event:
How can it be that they were rendered weak
And helpless by a beam so violent?
And while the answer still in vain they seek,
They hear that Pinabello's life is spent;
So far they only know that he is dead,
For who has killed him nobody has said.

97

The valiant Bradamante had meanwhile
Caught Pinabello in a narrow pass.
Her sword a hundred times in scornful style
Pierced through his body-armour and cuirass.
She rid the world of filth and stench so vile,
Which France for miles around infected has,
Then left the wood, of this event the sole
Witness, and took the horse the villain stole.

98

She wanted to return at once to find
Ruggiero, but she did not know the way.
Up hill, down dale, and where the rivers wind
She seeks her dear Ruggiero all that day;
But Fortune to the lovers is unkind.
Their paths divergent and divided stay.
All those who in my story still find pleasure,
Pray hear the sequel later at your leisure.

CANTO XXIII

1

Let us help one another, if we can,
For rarely do good deeds go unrewarded.
Or if so, to be loved is better than
To suffer vengeance at the end, unguarded.
If anyone should harm his fellow-man,
The debt to pay will not be unregarded.
Men seek each other out, the proverb says,
The mountain, motionless, unchanging stays.

2

Take Pinabello as an instance now:
He has been brought for his iniquities
To a just end at last: consider how
Precise the balance of the payment is;
And God, who many times does not allow
The innocent to suffer, when He sees
A way to save them, as He saved the Maid,
Will ever to the blameless grant His aid.

3

That villain, Pinabello, really thought
The Maid was dead and buried where she lay.
He never dreamt he would be chased and caught
And for his evil-doing made to pay;
Nor did it, in his plight, avail him aught
That Altaripa was not far away:
His father's mountain fortress, which is near
The territory of the Ponthier.

4

The Count of Altaripa, old and frail,
Is named Anselmo; of his evil seed
That evil fruit was born, named Pinabel,
By friends deserted in his hour of need.
The Clairmont Maid (I told you in my tale)
Ended his worthless life with ease and speed.
No help he found in his extremity,
For all he shrieked and begged for clemency.

5

When she had slain that traitor-cavalier
Whom she had long desired to put to death,
She turned back where she hoped to find Ruggier,
But Fate, sending her down a winding path,
Did not consent to this; now here, now there,
Where branches twined above and underneath,
She wandered ever deeper through the wood,
While all our hemisphere in darkness stood.

6

Knowing no other place to spend the night,
On the young grass, beneath the boughs, she lies.
Sometimes she sleeps, or contemplates the sight
Of Jove or Saturn moving through the skies,
Or Mars or Venus watches with delight,
Or other planets follows with her eyes,
But whether she's awake or if she sleeps,
Ruggiero's image in her mind she keeps.

7

Many a sigh she heaves from her deep heart,
Long sighs of grief, compounded with remorse
That in her soul wrath played a greater part
Than love; her lack of foresight she deplores
Which from Ruggiero keeps her now apart:
'I should have blazed a trail upon my course
To help me to return to whence I came;
My eyes and memory are much to blame.'

8

Such words as these and many more she spoke;
Her self-reproaches gave her no relief.
Sighs from her bosom like a tempest broke;
Unending tears poured in a rain of grief.
At last the long-awaited dawn awoke.
The hours of dark for her had not been brief.
Taking her horse, which grazed not far away,
She mounted and rode forth to greet the day.

9

Quite soon she reached the exit of the wood,
Issuing thence just where, till recently,
Atlante's magic edifice had stood
Where she had long been tricked by wizardry.
She found Astolfo there in pensive mood.
The hippogriff he'd bridled easily,
But still he did not know whom he could trust
With Rabicano: find someone he must.

10

By chance it happened that the paladin,
Just at the moment when the Maid rode out,
Had doffed his helmet, and she thus had seen
And recognized her cousin beyond doubt.
Eager to clasp her long-lost kith and kin,
She rode to greet him with a joyful shout,
And spoke her name and raised her visor high,
That he might recognize her too thereby.

11

No one more suitable could he have found
Whom he could trust to see his horse well shod,
And put to pasture in good grazing-ground,
And give it back to him when Fate allowed,
Than Aymon's daughter, valiant and renowned:
It seemed to him she had been sent by God.
To see her always gave him joy, not least
That day, when need of her his joy increased.

12

When twice or thrice the cousins had embraced
With warm affection, as between two brothers,
And their adventures each to each had traced,
Listening attentively to one another's,
Astolfo said, 'More time I must not waste:
This sky I must explore and many others',
And, telling her what he desired to do,
He showed the valiant Maid the horse which flew.

13

But it occasions her no great surprise
To see the creature spread its mighty wings,
For once before she saw it in the skies
Bearing Atlante on its back; it brings
New tears of grief to Bradamante's eyes
As in her heart the recollection springs
Of how it bore Ruggiero out of range
Along a route so distant and so strange.

14

Astolfo said he would entrust to her
His charger, Rabican, who ran so fast
No arrow from the bow was speedier;
Likewise his weapons to the Maid he passed,
To Montalbano meanwhile to transfer,
There to be kept till he should come at last
To claim them once again; he had no need
Of arms, he thought, upon the wingèd steed;

15

And, if he is to travel through the sky,
He deems it wise to keep his luggage light.
Both sword and horn he holds, though with its cry
The horn would rescue him from any plight.
The lance he hands the Maid was carried by
The son of Galafrone once by right,
That lance which every cavalier unseats
And ignominiously thus defeats.

16

Mounted upon the hippogriff, the duke,
Moving with caution, slowly tried the air.
Then, gaining height and courage, off he took
And in an instant was no longer there.
Just so a ship, avoiding every rock,
Towed by a pilot slowly and with care,
Once having left behind both port and shore,
Spreading all sails, the wind will run before.

17

When Bradamante saw the duke depart
She suffered deep perplexity of mind.
She knew not where to turn or where to start
To carry out the task he had assigned.
An ardent longing, gnawing at her heart,
Is urging her to where she hopes to find
Ruggiero, at the shrine where they arranged
To meet, when they their loving vows exchanged.

18

While undecided Bradamante stands,
She sees by chance a peasant drawing near,
To whom she gives instructions and commands,
Bidding him load the weapons then and there
On Rabicano's back; he understands,
And follows with two horses in the rear,
For she had two: her charger and, as well,
The horse she had reclaimed from Pinabel.

19

She planned to take the Vallombrosa road,
For there she hoped once more to see her love;
But still some hesitation yet she showed:
Which was the shortest way and which would prove
The most convenient? She understood
The peasant had but little knowledge of
The district round about and so she chose
At random where she thought the abbey was.

20

Now here, now there, about the wood she turns.
No one she meets of whom to ask the way
To bring her to her love for whom she yearns.
Leaving the wood at the ninth hour of day,
Upon a hill a castle she discerns,
But whose it is at first she cannot say;
Then looks, and Montalbano she perceives,
Where with her younger sons her mother lives.

21

When she is truly sure she knows the place,
The sense of grief redoubles in her heart,
For she will be discovered if she stays,
Will no more be permitted to depart.
Yet she so longs to see Ruggiero's face,
The fires of love inflict so keen a smart,
That she will die if what they planned, alas!
Does not at Vallombrosa come to pass.

22

She ponders deeply; then away she rides,
Turning her back on Montalbano, and
Facing the abbey where her hope resides,
Where love awaits her at her journey's end;
But destiny, for good or ill, decides,
Ere she departs from her paternal land,
Alard, one of her brothers, she shall meet,
Nor has she time to hide or to retreat.

23

Alardo recently his days had passed
In finding billets for the horse and foot,
Which at the Emperor Charlemagne's behest
Were levied from the cities round about.
Each clasped the other fondly, breast to breast.
No joyful words of welcome were left out.
Then, neck and neck, they ride and, turn by turn
Exchanging news, to Montalban return.

24

The Maid re-entered her ancestral home,
Where Beatrice, her mother, day and night
Had wept, and messengers had sent to comb
All France for news of her. Alas! now quite
Insipid to the Maid and wearisome
Are kisses and fond handclasps, right with right,
Compared with her Ruggiero's fond embraces,
Which on her soul have left eternal traces.

25

Unable now to go herself, she means
To send an envoy in her name straightway
To Vallombrosa, who what cause detains
Her shall make known; and she will also pray
Her love (if any need for prayer remains)
For love of her to be baptized that day,
Then, in due form, as they had both agreed,
To ask her hand, that they may soon be wed.

26

By the same messenger she plans to send
Ruggiero's charger, swift and beautiful.
Dearly Ruggiero loved his equine friend,
And it is true no finer horse in all
The world, not if you searched from end to end
The territories ruled by Charles de Gaulle,
Or by the Saracen, could e'er be found,
Save only those the valiant cousins owned.

27

The day her dear Ruggiero, rash and bold,
Rose on the hippogriff into the sky,
He left Frontino, as his horse is called;
And Bradamante, who was standing by,
Drew near, and on the charger's rein laid hold.
To Montalbano, where she could rely
Upon good stabling, she had sent him then.
Now sleek and fat she found him once again.

28

First, all her handmaidens she set to work
To ply their needles with a ready will.
On snow-white silk, or on a silk as dark
As wine, they traced with a consummate skill,
As worthy as Arachne's of remark,
In thread of finest gold a suitable
And exquisite design; the saddle's bows
And reins thus ornamented, she then chose

29

Of all their number, one, the daughter of
Her nurse Callitrefia; she it was
To whom she many times had told her love
And whom for long she had regarded as
Her confidante, whom she could trust above
All others; to her, Bradamante says:
'Of your discreet assistance I have need;
No better envoy could I find indeed.

30

'Be my ambassador, Ippalca, pray'
(Such was the damsel's name); and with great care
She told the maiden how to find her way
And bade her give her dearest love Ruggier
His Bradamante's greetings, and then say
It was no breach of faith detained her there;
For Fortune, who with us more mighty is
Than we ourselves, she had to blame for this.

31

She bids her mount upon a steed and take
Frontino's costly bridle in her hand.
If anyone she meets shall undertake
To steal it from her, let him understand
Whose horse it is; that single word will make
All comers tremble, for throughout the land,
In all the world, there is no valiant knight
Who at that name does not succumb to fright.

32

She gave her much advice, and for her dear
Charged her with messages time and again.
To all of them Ippalça lent an ear,
And then set out, holding Frontino's rein.
Through roads and fields and forests, dark and drear,
For many miles she journeyed, more than ten,
And not a soul had she been troubled by
Or questioned as to where she went, and why.

33

At noon, as she was riding down a hill
Along a narrow path, she chanced to see
The pagan Rodomonte (whom you will
Recall), accoutred in full panoply,
Led by a dwarf; glowering he looks his fill
And swears by the angelic hierarchy
That such a horse, so splendidly arrayed,
No cavalier has owned, still less a maid.

34

Now, he had sworn an oath to take by force
Whatever mount he should first come upon.
This is the first; it is a splendid horse,
He could not hope to find a better one.
To take it from a damsel is a course
He does not relish and would fain disown.
He contemplates the steed in every limb
And says, 'Ah! would his owner were with him!'

35

'Would that he were!' the fair Ippalca cried,
'He would soon make you change your mind, I know;
Greater than any cavaliers who ride,
Than any pagans who on horseback go,
Is he who owns this horse.' And he replied,
'Who is it who all men surpasses so?'
'Ruggiero' was the answer. 'In that case
I'll take his horse and ride it in his place.

36

'If as you say he is so brave and strong
And far exceeds the fame of every knight,
This charger he can claim from me ere long,
And charge me for it too, if he thinks right.
Tell him I'm Rodomonte; if such wrong
He would avenge, he'll find me, for the light
Of my renown, which everywhere I go
Illumines me, my whereabouts will show.

37

'Where'er I pass, in mountains, valleys, plains,
I leave more devastation in my track
Than does a thunderbolt.' The gilded reins
He turns meanwhile, and on the charger's back
He leaps. Ippalca desolate remains.
Stung by despair, she flings at him no lack
Of menaces and insults and abuse.
He pays no heed, but up the mountain goes;

38

Then by the dwarf along a route he's led
To seek his lady-love and Mandricard.
Ippalca follows, calling on his head
The vengeance of the gods, and cursing hard.
What happened next will later on be said.
Here Turpin, whom I follow as my bard,
Makes a digression and returns again
Where the Maganza miscreant was slain.

39

Scarcely had Aymon's daughter left the scene
To hurry back (she thought) to her Ruggier,
When by another path arrived Zerbin
Who with the hateful hag had still to bear.
He greatly wondered who the knight had been
Whose body in the vale was lying there.
Being compassionate and merciful,
He felt a wave of pity fill his soul.

40

Count Pinabello on the ground lay dead,
For treachery his soul to Hell consigned.
Through countless wounds his life-blood had been shed,
As if a hundred weapons had combined
To bring him to his death; Zerbino sped
Along a recent trail, to try to find
The perpetrator of this homicide,
And to discover who it was that died.

41

He told Gabrina he would soon return
And bade her wait for him until he came.
She quickly scans the body to discern
If there are any gems which she can claim,
With which her ugly person to adorn;
To waste them on a corpse she deems a shame.
Gabrina is unequalled in her greed,
The daughter of an avaricious breed.

42

If there had been some hope of secrecy
She would, I vow, have stolen first of all
His richly broidered surcoat, fair to see,
And all the splendid arms he bore as well;
But that which can be hidden easily
She takes (to leave the rest for her is gall).
A costly belt with which the corpse is girt
She fastens round her waist beneath her skirt.

43

Soon afterwards Zerbino galloped back.
In vain he'd followed Bradamante's traces
Along a tortuous and tangled track,
Where branch with branch entwines and interlaces.
The daylight waned and ere the night grew black
They needs must flee these lonely, rocky places.
Some shelter now the prince sets out to find,
And leaves the vale, but not the hag, behind.

44

And soon they saw, about two miles away,
A castle on a lofty mountain height,
Called Altaripa; here they asked to stay
And both were granted lodging for the night.
But not for long in sweet repose they lay:
The sound of many folk in piteous plight,
Bitterly weeping, soon assaults their ears,
For all the castle's inmates are in tears.

45

Zerbino asks the reason; they explain
That Count Anselmo has received the news
That in a mountain pass his son lies slain.
Zerbino bows his head; lest they accuse
Him of the deed, he thinks it best to feign
Surprise, but in an instant he construes
The indications which he hears to mean
The son must be the body he has seen.

46

Amid the pomp of torches and of flares
The funeral bier is slowly borne along.
The noise of palm on palm affronts the stars;
Still louder swell the voices of the throng.
Their cheeks are inundated by their tears
As endless moisture from their eyes is wrung.
Of all the mourners there, the darkest brow
The grieving father's was that night, I vow.

47

While solemn preparations went ahead
For burial and rites of every sort
By means of which in early times the dead
Were honoured, as the chroniclers report,
A proclamation, from the father read,
Soon cut the people's lamentation short:
It promises a prize to anyone
Who knows the killer of Anselmo's son.

48

From mouth to mouth, from ear to ear, word passed
Of the fine sum of money offered by
The lord; it reached that harridan at last
Whose bestial ferocity could vie
With tigresses, and even bears surpassed.
She plans Zerbino's ruin: he must die –
For spite, or greed, or else the miscreant
Her inhumanity desires to vaunt.

49

Gabrina begged an audience of the lord.
With a preamble, meaning to mislead,
She opened (it was false in every word),
Then told him that Zerbino did the deed,
And from her waist she drew the belt she'd stored,
Which made the father's heart still further bleed.
The evidence and testimony of
The hateful harridan he takes as proof.

50

Weeping and raising both his hands on high,
He swore his son should not go unavenged.
The lodging where Zerbino slept near by
To be at once surrounded, he arranged.
Zerbino little dreamt that foes were nigh
Who clamoured for his blood as though deranged.
As unaware in his first sleep he rested,
The innocent Zerbino was arrested.

51

And that same night they cast him into jail,
In heavy chains and fettered hand and foot.
The sun had not withdrawn the night's dark veil
When sentence had been passed on him: they vote
That he shall be dismembered in the vale
Where the misdeed took place which they impute
To him; no further evidence being brought,
They deem conclusive what the father thought.

52

When fair Aurora streaks the morning sky
With brilliant shafts of white and red and gold,
Accompanied by shouts of 'He must die!',
To pay for what he has not done, behold
The prince; on foot, on horseback, wildly rushes by
A foolish horde of people, young and old.
The Scottish knight, his eyes fixed on the ground,
Humiliated, on a nag is bound.

53

But God, Who often helps the innocent,
As those who trust in Him have cause to say,
Already in this case His aid has sent:
Zerbino will not meet his death today.
Orlando had arrived; his coming meant
The prince would be released without delay.
Orlando saw that motley crowd appear,
Leading to death the hapless cavalier.

54

He was accompanied by the young maid
Whom he had rescued from the mountain cave,
The daughter of Galicia's king, betrayed
And captured by the pirates as a slave
(Her name was Isabella, as I said),
When buffeted by storms, beneath the wave
Her ship had sunk, she who Zerbino loved
More than her very life, as she had proved.

55

Escorted by Orlando she had been,
Beginning from the day he rescued her.
When all those crowds of people she had seen,
She asked the Count Orlando who they were.
'I do not know,' he said, and to the plain
Was gone, leaving her on the mountain there.
Then, looking at Zerbino, at first sight
He knew him for a valiant, noble knight;

56

And for what cause and whither he was led
Thus bound and captive, he desired to know.
The grieving cavalier had raised his head
When he approached, and now he gave him so
Convincing an account that all he said
The Count believed and knew that it was true.
He had no doubt about his innocence.
Here was a case deserving his defence.

57

And when he learned that this had been decreed
By Count Anselmo, Altaripa's lord,
He knew that here was something wrong indeed,
For naught but ill derived from every word
And every action of that evil breed,
Who the undying hatred had incurred
Of all the Clairmonts, of untarnished fame,
Whom to destroy was the Maganzans' aim.

58

'Untie that cavalier, you rabble!' cried
The Count, drawing his sword on the riff-raff.
'Who may this loud-mouthed braggart be?' replied
A spokesman who appeared of sterner stuff;
'No better spark, I think, could be applied,
If he were flame and we were wax or chaff.'
He moved towards the paladin of France.
Orlando in response now couched his lance.

59

The shining armour of the reprobate,
Which he that night had stolen from Zerbin,
Did little to protect him from his fate
In this encounter with the paladin.
Orlando aimed his weapon true and straight
At his right cheek; it did not pass within
(The helm resisted), but the mighty stroke
Sufficed to kill him, for his neck it broke.

60

The Count rode on, keeping his lance in rest,
And in the self-same movement, as it seemed,
He quickly ran another through the chest.
He left his lance in him because he deemed
That Durindana would now suit him best.
Some heads he split in two, some torsos trimmed,
And many throats he cut; and those who fled
Totalled at least a hundred with the dead.

61

More than a third he kills; the rest he chases.
He cuts, he thrusts, he slices, he truncates.
Some scatter shields or helmets in their traces,
Or fling away their spikes or other weights.
One in the forest hides, another races
To a cave. Only a few escape their fates.
Orlando no compassion has that day.
Every man jack of them he tries to slay.

62

Of twenty-and-a-hundred, eighty died
(So forty fled, if Turpin has it right).
At last Orlando to Zerbino's side
Returns; the full extent of his delight
When the young prince has seen him turn and ride,
No poet e'er could sing, no pen could write.
To honour him he'd gladly kiss the ground,
But that upon the nag he is still bound.

63

And while Orlando, who untied his bonds,
Assisted him to gather up his arms
(The property with which a thief absconds
To dust and ashes Fate sometimes transforms),
Zerbino turned his eyes: a sight confounds
His very reason – safe from all alarms,
His love, seeing that now the fight had ended,
In all her beauty from the hill descended.

64

And when Zerbino sees that lovely maid
Whom he has loved so dearly for so long,
That lovely damsel who had been betrayed,
Who, he believed, was fathoms deep among
The waves, for whom so many tears he shed,
He freezes as though ice, his heart is wrung,
His body shakes and trembles; then he burns,
As cold at once to ardent longing turns.

65

Respect for Count Orlando kept him yet
From taking her in his embrace; he thought
(And by this thought the prince was much upset)
Orlando was her lover, and this brought
Distress and pain such as he'd ne'er forget,
And all his former joy was turned to naught.
To see her now another's is his dread,
Greater than when he thought his love was dead.

66

It grieves him even more his love should be
Beloved of one to whom so much he owes.
He could not win her from him easily,
Nor would the undertaking, if he chose
To try, be honourable; although he
To no one else would be prepared to lose
His lady, yet his debt towards the Count
Requires that he shall bravely bear the brunt.

67

They rode in silence to a crystal spring,
Where they dismounted for a moment's ease.
The Count drew off his helmet; the same thing
Zerbino does, and Isabella sees
Her lover face-to-face, and, marvelling,
With sudden happiness her colour flees,
Then floods her like a flower, drenched by rain,
Which blooms in glory in the sun again.

68

She runs without delay, without restraint,
To clasp her dear Zerbino round the neck.
She cannot speak a word, her voice is faint,
A flood of happy tears flows down her cheek.
All this Orlando finds significant.
No further indications need he seek,
For clearly he has understood that he
Zerbino is and no one else can be.

69

When Isabella finds her voice again,
And with her cheeks still wet with happy tears,
She tells her prince, dispelling all his pain,
How Count Orlando honours and reveres
A damsel in distress; he, who in vain
The balance 'twixt his life and love compares
(They are the same), has knelt down to adore
One who two lives thus gives him in one hour.

70

The courteous exchanges oft renewed
Between the knights had lasted for some time,
When sudden clamour from the near-by wood,
Of intertwining branches dark and grim,
Brought to an end this pleasant interlude.
Their helms they don and to their saddles climb.
Scarce have they done so when a cavalier
And with him, too, a damsel now appear.

71

The knight was Mandricardo, who set out
In search of Count Orlando, to avenge
Both Manilardo and Alzirdo, cut
Down in their prime; nor did his purpose change.
Steadfast, he had continued his pursuit,
Whence nothing could deflect him or estrange,
Not even she, whom with a shaft of oak
Despite a hundred warriors he took.

72

The Saracen, in truth, does not yet know
It is the Count to whom he now draws near,
But all the signs and indications show
This is a valiant, noble cavalier.
Only the briefest glance did he bestow
Upon Zerbino, but upon the Peer
Of France he gazed and his insignia read.
'You are the one I'm looking for,' he said.

73

'For ten days now,' he added, 'I have sought
To follow in your tracks, so great the fame
Of your exploit which a survivor brought
When, gravely wounded, to our camp he came.
He told how, single-handed, you had fought
And killed or routed, like a raging flame,
Not only all of Manilardo's men
But all Alzirdo's too from Tremisen.

74

'I was not slow to seek you when I heard,
Eager to put your prowess to the test.
I know that you are he, I have not erred,
I know your surcoat and I know your crest.
Even without this knowledge, undeterred,
Your true identity I should have guessed.
Your aspect, in a hundred, would declare
Beyond a doubt: that cavalier you are.'

75

'It cannot be', Orlando said, 'denied
That you must be a very valiant knight.
Magnanimous desires do not reside
In humble hearts; however, if the sight
Of me is what you seek, let me inside
And out display; so, I will now requite
This valorous request of yours in full.
Behold, my helmet from my head I pull.

76

'When you have looked me squarely in the face,
With your next longing let me then comply;
That same desire which made you come in trace
Of me, I am disposed to satisfy,
And you shall then decide if I disgrace
This proud exterior you know me by.'
'Proceed', the pagan said, 'to the next stage:
My second longing let me now assuage.'

77

Meanwhile, from head to foot, most carefully,
Orlando raked the pagan with his glance.
He gazes at both flanks, but cannot see
(Nor yet upon the saddle-bows, by chance)
A sword or any short-arm weaponry.
He asks him what he uses if his lance
Should miss. 'You may be sure', the pagan said,
'E'en so I give good cause to be afraid.

78

'I swore that I would never wear a sword
Till I won Durindana from the Count,
And every path since then I have explored
That with him I might settle my account.
And (if it interests you) I pledged my word
On the first day this helm enclosed my front,
Which, like these other arms my person bears,
Belonged to Hector, dead these thousand years.

79

'I have them all, save for the sword alone.
Who stole it, when and how, I cannot say.
The paladin now bears it as his own,
Which makes him bold and brave in every way.
If I encounter him, that precious loan
With interest I will force him to repay.
I seek him everywhere, for I desire
To avenge the death of Agrican, my sire.

80

'Orlando killed him by vile treachery,
For ne'er could he have slain him otherwise.'
Orlando could no longer silent be.
Loudly he cried: 'Whoever says so, lies!
But you have sought, and found, your destiny.
I am Orlando; just was the demise
Of Agricane. Let this sword be yours
If against mine your strength the more endures.

81

'Although the sword belongs to me by right,
Let us contend for it as cavaliers.
Let neither of us use it in this fight,
But hang it on a tree; if it transpires
That I am captured, killed or put to flight,
Take Durindana freely, have no fear.'
And with these words, Orlando took the sword
And to a tree attached it with a cord.

82

Already both have galloped off, as far
Apart, perhaps, as half an arrow-fall.
Already both their gallant chargers spur,
Holding their slackened bridles scarce at all.
Already within striking-range they are;
The helmet's sights of each they both assail.
The lances at such impact break like ice.
A thousand splinters fly up in a trice.

83

One and the other lance perforce must break,
For neither combatant desires to yield.
The cavaliers their new positions take,
The remnants of their spears prepared to wield.
The cavaliers the arms of knights forsake.
Like yokels quarrelling about a field,
Or where an irrigation-ditch to fix,
They strive in bitter conflict, armed with sticks.

84

But neither stump withstands the first four blows,
Neither the frenzy of the fray resists.
The struggle on each side more heated grows.
Soon they have nothing left to use but fists.
One tears the other's tassets, or undoes
His rivets, while the other pulls and twists
The links of mail: no hammers heavier,
No pincers more tenacious, ever were.

85

How can the Saracen contrive to end
With honour to himself this fierce affray?
It would be madness further time to spend
In striking more such blows which ill repay.
The pagan grasps Orlando, not as friend
Embraces friend, but quite another way:
He hopes to crush the Count as Hercules
Once held Antaeus in his deadly squeeze.

86

He seizes him with force about the waist,
He pushes him and pulls him to and fro.
Unwary in his rage and frenzied haste,
He does not see what happens down below.
Orlando does not yield, nor does he waste
His strength; waiting to see how things will go,
He puts his hand out to the pagan's horse
And deftly slips its rein off in due course.

87

The Saracen attempts with all his might
To choke him or to lift him from his steed;
The Count Orlando keeps his knees clamped tight
And in his aim so well does he succeed,
The girth (of which the straps are fastened right
Beneath his charger's belly) is thence freed.
Orlando is unhorsed, but scarcely knows
It, still in stirrups, with his thighs held close.

88

The bang with which a sack of armour clangs
On falling to the ground, the Count now makes.
The other's horse, whose bridle dangling hangs,
Freed from the bit, into a gallop breaks,
And through the wood, where overhead there hangs
Dense foliage, a madcap course it takes.
Not heeding where it went and blind with fear,
It bore its rider wildly here and there.

89

When Doralice saw her lover gone,
And so precipitately, well she knew
That escort and defender she had none.
Spurring her palfrey, in his track she flew.
The Saracen in fury, still borne on,
Shouts at his charger, kicks and beats it too.
As though it were a man and not a beast,
He threatens it; it heeds him not the least.

90

The skittish animal, which often shied
For less good reason than it had that day,
Three miles had run, and, being terrified,
Would have run on but by a ditch its way
Was barred; though with no feather-bed supplied,
It welcomed horse and rider in as they
Pitched headlong on impacted earth and stone,
But Mandricardo did not break one bone.

91

And so the charger came to rest at last;
But how could it be guided, lacking rein?
The Tartar mounted, angry and nonplussed.
He did not relish clinging to its mane.
His Doralice, who had followed fast,
Perceiving his dilemma, thus began:
'Pray take my bridle, you have need of it.
My palfrey goes quite well without a bit.'

92

The pagan deemed it was unchivalrous
To take advantage of this kindly thought;
But Fortune to his need proved bounteous
And in his path the vile Gabrina brought.
She, having done her worst, the treacherous
Old harridan, now her own safety sought,
Like a she-wolf which hears from far away
The hunt hallooing and the hounds that bay.

93

A youthful dress and ornaments she wore
Which had been taken, as you will recall,
From Pinabello's lady; what is more,
She rode her palfrey also, which in all
Its points was much too good for such a whore.
Approaching, unaware what would befall,
Before she knew, that evil harridan
Was in the presence of the Saracen.

94

The style of dress in which the hag is clad
Makes Doralice and her lover laugh.
No monkey, no baboon, has ever had
A face as ludicrous as hers by half.
No chivalry the Saracen forbade:
His plan is now to take the bridle off
Her palfrey's head; he does so, then he routs
The frightened horse with menaces and shouts.

95

It gallops through the wood; the evil crone
Is carried helpless, nearly dead with fear.
Up hill, down dale, the palfrey dashes on,
At random, turning here, there, everywhere.
But less concern for her I feel, I own,
Than for Orlando, France's peerless Peer.
His saddle he had easily repaired
And now for further combat was prepared.

96

He paused, when on his charger once again,
To see if Mandricardo would come back.
When he had waited for a while in vain
He planned to follow in the pagan's track.
But first of the two lovers who remain
(Since *savoir-faire* Orlando did not lack)
With gracious courtesy he takes his leave.
When he departs they cannot help but grieve.

97

Zerbino saw him go with deep regret,
At his departure Isabella mourned.
Despite their grief Orlando would not let
Them keep him company, for, as he warned,
The laws of knighthood they must not forget;
For greatly would a cavalier be scorned
Who, seeking battle with a deadly foe,
Escorted by another knight should go.

98

If they should meet the Saracen before
He does, he will remain, he bids them say,
In the vicinity for three days more;
But then he will depart and make his way
Where Christians gather for the holy war,
His homage to the Emperor to pay,
And to defend the golden fleur-de-lis;
Thus Mandricardo will know where he is.

99

And this they promised readily to do,
And in all things comply with his command.
Their pathway now divided into two.
The cavaliers must part, as he had planned.
Before he goes Orlando takes anew
His trusty Durindana in his hand,
Then, where he thinks the Saracen may be,
He moves his gallant charger speedily.

100

In frenzied flight the pagan's horse had run
Along the trackless wood of which I spoke.
Orlando for two days had wandered on
In vain; knowing no longer where to look,
He reached a stream which clear as crystal shone.
The verdant margins bordering the brook
Are painted gay with Nature's vivid hues,
And many stately trees the scene enclose.

101

A gentle breeze the noon was tempering
To summer-weary cattle, which their hinds,
Half-clad, to graze in water-meadows bring.
His armour, helm and shield Orlando finds
Less irksome as, to rest beside the spring,
Amid this rustic scene he gently winds,
Where torment lurks, more dread than I can say,
That inauspicious and ill-omened day.

102

As he gazed round, some letters caught his eye,
Carved on the trees which cast a grateful shade;
He stopped and stared; at once he knew that by
The hand of his belovèd they were made.
This was a place, among the many I
Described, where with Medoro oft had strayed,
Leaving the shepherd's house not far away,
The lady who was Queen of all Cathay.

103

A hundred times the lovers' names are seen,
'Angelica', 'Medoro', intertwined.
Each letter is a knife which, sharp and keen,
Pierces his bleeding heart; his tortured mind,
Rejecting what it knows these carvings mean,
A thousand explanations tries to find:
Some other maiden may have left her mark,
Writing 'Angelica' upon the bark.

104

And then he says: 'I know this writing well.
I've seen and read it many times of yore.
In fond imagination – who can tell? –
Perhaps she calls me by this name, Medore.'
By means of notions so improbable,
And from the truth departing more and more,
Although for comfort he has little scope,
The unhappy Count contrives to build false hope.

105

But ever brighter burns and leaps afresh
The flame of jealousy he would put out:
As when a bird, entangled in a mesh
Or lime, in vain will beat its wings about
In frantic efforts; so in feverish
Delusions, tighter yet the Count is caught.
To where the mountain like an archway passed
Across the crystal stream he came at last.

106

A grotto was thus formed, inside adorned
By ivy tendrils and by vines which traced
Their twisted paths; here from the sun which burned
At noon, the happy pair would lie embraced,
And all around, where'er the gaze was turned,
Their names in lovers' knots they interlaced,
With chalk or charcoal or a pointed knife,
In token of their blissful married life.

107

Downcast, the Count dismounted here to rest.
As he draws near the entrance to the cave,
Words which Medoro wrote his glance arrest.
Thanking the grotto for the joy it gave,
These sentiments in verse he had expressed
(The letters still a pristine freshness have),
Which in his tongue are more elaborate,
I think, than in our own I can translate:

108

'O happy plants, green grass and limpid stream,
O cave so cool and generous of shade,
Wherein Angelica of whom men dream,
To whom so many hopeless suit have paid,
Lay naked in these arms, pressed limb to limb,
Where in sweet dalliance we oft delayed,
Humble Medoro here his tribute pays,
Though he has naught to offer you but praise,

109

'Begging all lovers who shall pass this way,
Ladies or cavaliers or rustic swains,
Or travellers whom choice or Fortune may
Bring hither, here to ease a while their pains,
To bless these plants, this cave, this stream and say:
"O choir of nymphs sing here your sweetest strains,
O sun and moon shine kindly on this place,
These hallowed precincts let no flocks deface."'

110

These verses were in Arabic, a tongue
Which the Count knew as if it were his own.
Of those which he had learnt when he was young,
The language of the Arabs had been one.
This saved him much dishonour when among
The Saracens he found himself; but gone
Are all such benefits he e'er might boast.
His knowledge now he rues with bitter cost.

111

Three times, four times, six times, he read the script,
Attempting still, unhappy wretch! in vain
(For the true meaning he would not accept)
To change the sense of what was clear and plain.
Each time he read, an icy hand which gripped
His heart caused him intolerable pain.
Then motionless he stood, his eyes and mind
Fixed on the stone, like stone inert and blind.

112

He seemed at last as if about to swoon,
So nearly was he vanquished by his grief.
Do not dismiss the truth of this too soon:
I speak here from experience, in brief.
Of all the sorrows which the pallid moon
Surveys, this sorrow offers no relief.
He stands dejected, brow and chin held low,
His grief obstructs his words, no tears can flow.

113

A flood of sorrow in his bosom stays,
And by its very impetus is checked:
As we may sometimes notice in a vase,
Broad-bellied in its shape and narrow-necked,
When someone has too fast upturned the base,
The liquid in the outlet will collect,
And there, in too great haste to issue, stop,
With difficulty dripping, drop by drop.

114

He comes then to himself, and thinks again
How he might prove the truth to be untrue:
Supposing somebody these words should feign
To slander his belovèd's name, or to
Torment him with such jealousy, the pain
Of which would bring him to his death, and who
This dastardly deceit to perpetrate
His lady's handwriting would imitate.

115

Upon such frail and slender premises
His spirits he contrives somewhat to rouse,
Then presses Brigliadoro with his knees,
For now the sister of Apollo was
Replacing him on high; and soon he sees
Smoke rising from the chimneys of each house,
He hears dogs bark, the homing cattle low,
And for a lodging yonder means to go.

116

He wearily dismounts and gives his horse
Into the care of a young stable lad.
One takes his arms and one his golden spurs,
And one to polish his cuirass is bade.
This was the shepherd's house, wherein, of course,
Medoro lay and his good fortune had.
The Count requests a bed but will not eat.
Sated with grief, he wants no other meat.

117

Longing at last into a sleep to fall,
He is tormented by his pain the more.
The hated writing is on every wall,
On every window-frame, on every door.
Tempted to ask the reason for it all,
He hesitates, unwilling to be sure.
The truth, too clear, he shrouds in mistiness,
For thus he hopes that it will pain him less.

118

Now self-deception is of no avail:
Informant he is both and questioner.
The shepherd greatly wonders what can ail
The knight, so full of grief he seems and care.
He undertakes to tell the Count the tale
Of the two lovers who had sojourned there,
Which many folk with pleasure listened to
And which he hopes the knight some good may do.

119

So first he tells him how a lovely maid
Had begged him to convey Medoro home.
With precious herbs his bleeding she had stayed.
In a few days his wounds had healed; but from
His health a deeper wound in her Love made.
A spark an eager flame had soon become,
Which now consumed her with so fierce a fire,
She yearned for him with amorous desire.

120

Regardless of her royal status as
The daughter of the greatest of all kings
Of the Levant, although Medoro has
The rank of common soldier, yet she clings
To him and wants him only for her spouse.
When to its end the narrative he brings,
The shepherd shows the Count the precious gem
Which fair Angelica had given him.

121

This was the axe which at one final blow
His head then severed from Orlando's neck,
For Love the Slaughterer was sated now
With endless batterings; though at this wreck
Of all his hopes Orlando, not to show
His grief, all signs of it attempts to check,
Yet willy-nilly from his mouth and eyes
Sorrow comes flooding forth in tears and sighs.

122

When he can give his sorrow fuller rein,
Fleeing all others, in his room alone,
The tears run streaming down his cheeks like rain.
Sigh follows upon sigh and groan on groan.
Fumbling and groping for his bed, in vain
He seeks relief; harder than any stone,
Sharper than nettles, is that downy nest
Whereon Orlando never can find rest.

123

Then in his travail suddenly he knows
That in this very bed on which he lies
His love has lain, and often, in the close
Embrace that nothing of herself denies.
No less abhorrence now Orlando shows
And no less quickly from that couch he flies
Than we may see a startled peasant leap
Who spies a snake where he lay down to sleep.

124

The bed, the house, the shepherd he now hated.
His one desire was but to get away.
Not for the moon, not for the dawn he waited,
Not for the streaks of white which herald day.
His arms, his horse he first appropriated
And where the forest's heart of darkness lay
Shrouded in densest foliage, he rode
And to his grief gave vent in solitude.

125

His tears, his groans, his sobbings never cease.
All night, all day, in anguish and in pain,
Fleeing all habitats, he finds no peace.
Lying unsheltered on the hard terrain,
He marvels at the fount his eyes release,
That such a living spring they should contain.
His sighing too an endless rhythm keeps
And to himself he muses as he weeps.

126

'These are no longer tears I weep,' he said,
'Streaming so copiously from my eyes.
The tears were insufficient which I shed
To stay my grief, which all relief defies.
The vital humours, now by passion sped,
Through secret conduits to my orbs arise,
And thence these now exude, and with them pours
My life, thus ebbing to its final hours.

127

'These tokens which my torment manifest,
These are not sighs, no sighs resemble these,
For veritable sighs allow some rest.
But when these gusts come forth I feel no ease,
For Love, who burns my heart within my breast,
Fanning it with his wings, creates this breeze.
Love, by what miracle do you contrive
To burn my heart and keep it yet alive?

128

'I am not he, I am not he I seem.
He who Orlando was is dead and gone,
Slain by his lady, so untrue to him,
By her ingratitude, alas! undone.
I am his spirit whom the Fates condemn
To suffer in this dread infernal zone,
No body, but a shadow which must rove,
A warning to all those who trust in love.'

129

He wandered through the forest all that night.
At length his cruel destiny decreed,
At the first glimmerings of morning light,
He should return to where Medoro's screed
Was sculpted on the rock; and at the sight
Of his great wrongs, blazoned for all to read,
No dram of all his blood was not on fire
With hatred, fury, rage and wrath and ire.

130

Drawing his sword, he slashed the offending rock,
And heavenwards the splintered fragments flew.
The cave, the trees, each bole or stem or stock
He hacked, whereon those names still met his view.
From that day forth no shepherd with his flock
Their grateful shade or pleasant coolness knew.
The very spring, so crystalline and pure,
From onslaught such as this was scarce secure.

131

With tree-trunks, branches, stones, and clods of earth
He sullies the fair waters of the stream,
Choking and clouding them for all he's worth.
From top to bottom, murky now and dim,
For ever fouled the fount which gave them birth,
Their purity has vanished, thanks to him.
Wearied at length, upon the ground he lies,
His force, but not his fury, spent, and sighs.

132

Soaked with his sweat, he falls upon the grass
And gazes at the sky without a word.
He neither sleeps nor eats; though three days pass,
Three times the dark descends, he has not stirred.
His grief so swells, his sorrows so amass
That madness clouds him, in which long he erred.
On the fourth day, by fury roused once more,
The mail and armour from his back he tore.

133

His shield and helmet lie, one here, one there,
His hauberk somewhere else; all through the wood
His scattered arms mute testimony bear
To his unhinged and catastrophic mood.
Then next his clothing he begins to tear,
Laying his matted paunch and torso nude,
And that horrendous madness then began,
Not fully to be grasped by any man.

134

His rage and fury mount to such a pitch
They obfuscate and darken all his senses.
Even his sword he leaves behind, from which
It may be judged the mist of madness dense is.
But neither sword nor scramasaxe so rich
A crop could scythe; unarmed his strength immense is.
Barehanded, he uproots at the first blow
A tall and noble pine and lays it low.

135

And other pines, after the first, he pulls,
As if so many fennel-stalks they were.
Tall oak and seasoned elm likewise he culls,
And beech and mountain ash and larch and fir.
As a bird-catcher who, before he gulls
His prey with cunning nets, the ground will clear
Of stubble, nettles, reeds, so now the Count
Rips forests up as if of no account.

136

The shepherds, who have heard the fearful sound,
Anticipating some calamity,
Their sheep abandon, scattered all around,
And at top speed come running out to see.
But if this point today I go beyond,
Too tedious perhaps my tale will be,
And I would rather now cut short my song
Than weary you by making it too long.

NOTES

CANTO I

1. Ariosto takes up the action of Boiardo's *Orlando Innamorato* at the point where Agramante, King of Africa, at the age of 22, vows to avenge his father, Troiano, whom Orlando slew in Burgundy. He calls a council of thirty-two other African rulers and they decide to mount an offensive against Charlemagne.

2. l. 2. cf. Milton, *Paradise Lost*, line 16, which is a translation of Ariosto's original line.

   l. 5. The lady referred to is believed to be Alessandra Benucci, a Florentine, widow of Tito Strozzi of Ferrara. Ariosto first met her in Florence in June 1513. Since the poem was begun in 1505 or 1506, it would seem that this stanza was added or adapted in the course of composition. Ariosto, who was in receipt of ecclesiastical benefices allowable only to a celibate, is said to have married Alessandra secretly between 1526 and 1530.

3. ll. 1–8. *Herculean son*. Cardinal Ippolito was the son of Duke Ercole I. Ariosto was still in his service in 1516, the year of publication of the first edition of the poem. The work is addressed to him throughout, though some of the perorations have a more general application.

4. Ruggiero had already been indicated by Boiardo as the ancestor of the House of Este (see Table, p. 734).

5. l. 3. These regions stand collectively for the East. India represents the whole of Asia, Media the region south of the Caspian Sea, and Tartary the region west of Cathay.

8. l. 8. *Namo of Bavaria*. Namo, Duke of Bavaria, son of Aquilone, is a contemporary and counsellor of Charlemagne. Being elderly, he is judged to be a fit protector for Angelica.

11. l. 4. This is an allusion to the *pallio*, a race held at Ferrara, of which the prize was a red cloak (cf. Dante, *Inferno*, XV. 122, where there is a reference to a foot-race at Verona, of which the prize was a green cloak). Certain frescoes in the Palazzo Schifanoia in Ferrara show the races, both foot and horse, which were held at the time of the Estensi.

12. In Boiardo's poem *Orlando Innamorato*, Rinaldo had dismounted from Baiardo in order to fight on equal terms with Ruggiero, who was on foot. When Rinaldo tried to take hold of the bridle again, his horse made off (*Orlando Innamorato*, III. iv. 29–40).

14. l. 1. Ferraù is the nephew of Marsilio, King of Spain; he killed Angelica's brother Argalia. Like Orlando and Rinaldo, he too is in love with Angelica.

19. l. 3. *two rays*. the eyes of Angelica.

21. l. 6. *The son of Aymon*. Rinaldo.
    l. 8. *the duke's pavilion*. i.e. of the Duke of Bavaria, Namo.

27. Argalia, the brother of Angelica, here reminds Ferraù of the day when, filled with passion for Angelica, he killed him in a duel and threw his body and weapons in a river. He promised to throw the helmet into the water also, after wearing it as a trophy for a few days, but he has not done so. This event is related by Boiardo (*Orlando Innamorato*, I. iii. 60–66).

28. ll. 5–6. Orlando had slain Almonte, the brother of Troiano, at Aspromonte and had taken his helmet and his sword, Durindana, which once belonged to Hector. In earlier romances concerning Rinaldo, Mambrino was a pagan king who made war on Charlemagne and whom Rinaldo killed, taking his helmet.

30. l. 6. Ferraù's mother is Lanfusa, the wife of Falsirone. In the epic entitled *La Spagna*, her cruelty to defeated Christians is mentioned (cf. XXV. 74, Vol. II of the present translation).

31. l. 1. cf. XII. 59–62.

42–3. These two stanzas are modelled on Catullus, LXII, 39–47.

45. l. 4. Sacripante, King of Circassia, is mentioned by Boiardo among those enamoured of Angelica (*Orlando Innamorato*, I. ix. 38 et seq.).

54. l. 8. *her royal abode*. Angelica's palace in Cathay, of which she is now queen after the death of her father Galafrone and her brother Argalia.

55. ll. 4–5. *him who holds in fee/The Chinese Nabathees*. Gradasso, King of Sericana, a region which Ariosto places east of Cathay. The Nabathees were identified by ancient writers as a people of Arabia, but the term was later extended to signify people from the Far East.

56. *It may be true*. Ariosto keeps the reader in doubt as to Angelica's virginity until XIX. 33.

57. ll. 1–2. *the Cavalier/Anglante*. Orlando. His father Milone, was 'Milo de Angleriis', i.e. of Angers (or Anglante), where his castle was said to be situated.

65. This simile echoes Ovid, *Tristia*, I. iii. 11–12.

70. Bradamante (the Maid), the heroic woman warrior and sister of Rinaldo, is the destined bride of Ruggiero and ancestress of the House of Este (Table, p. 735).

75. ll. 6–8. In Boiardo's epic, Rinaldo's horse was sent by Orlando for safe-keeping to Albracca, where Angelica was besieged by Agricane. Count Aymon's son (Rinaldo) was at that time loved by Angelica, but he did not love her (cf. stanzas 77–9).

78. *Two magic fountains*. Said by Boiardo to rise in the Ardennes; one has the effect of enamouring, the other of disenamouring whoever drinks from it. The forest of the Ardennes was part of the scenery of romantic epics.

80. ll. 7–8. Boiardo relates that during the siege of Albracca, Agricane one night broke into the fortress where Angelica was hiding. Sacripante, although in bed, recovering from a wound, rose up and, naked, repelled the invaders with his sword (cf. *Orlando Innamorato*, I. x. 145, xi. 41).

CANTO II

12. ll. 6–8. We meet this hermit again in VIII. 30–33, 44–50.

21. ll. 3–6. This refers to an encounter between Rinaldo and Ruggiero, related by Boiardo, *Orlando Innamorato*, III. iv. 29–40.

32. l. 4. *Agolante's daughter*. Galaciella, who was converted to Christianity on her marriage to Ruggiero II. In retaliation, her brothers left her to perish in an open boat on a stormy sea while she was carrying Ruggiero III in her womb (cf. *Orlando Innamorato*, III. v. 20 et seq.).

33. l. 6. i.e. had fallen to the earth.

34. l. 8. *A cavalier*. Pinabello; cf. stanza 58.

37. ll. 2–3. This is a reference to Charlemagne's sortie against Marsilio, who was on the heights of Montalbano, as related by Boiardo (*Orlando Innamorato*, II. xxii. 61; xxiii. 15).

l. 4. This lady, whom we meet again (cf. xx. 110–15, xxII. 49–51) remains anonymous.

l. 6. *Rodonnes*. Rhodumna, a city on the Rhône, is mentioned by Ptolemy. It is possible that Ariosto is referring to Rodez, which is nearer to Montalbano.

l. 7. *a horse with wings*. The hippogriff, half horse, half griffin, which the magician Atlante, who is here riding it, has captured and tamed; cf. IV. 19. It is derived from the winged horse of classical mythology, Pegasus, and appears to symbolize uncontrolled primitive forces which Ruggiero and Astolfo, who both ride it, have to learn to control.

39. l. 6. *hemmed in by mountains*. Possibly the Cevennes.

45. Ariosto here picks up the thread of a story begun by Boiardo, *Orl. Inn.*, III. vii, in which a dwarf asks Ruggiero and Gradasso to avenge a wrong and leads them to a tower which they must destroy.

55–6. Atlante's magic shield, which is Ariosto's invention (a prototype of the laser beam) is reminiscent of the shield which enabled Perseus to kill Medusa. It also recalls Medusa's head which he used to petrify his enemies, notably the sea-monster sent to devour Andromeda.

58. Pinabel(lo), the nephew of Gano (Ganelon), is derived from a character in the *Chanson de Roland*. The House of Maganza, to which he belongs, was traditionally hostile to the Clairmont line, of which Bradamante is a descendant. All Maganzans are traitors.

61. l. 3. *These rugged mountains*. The Pyrenees.

62. l. 8. cf. Canto 1. 68–70.

66. l. 6. *the Clairmont side*. This family was founded by Clairmont (Chiaramonte). From his brother Bernardo there descended Milone, the father of Orlando; Otto, King of England, the father of Astolfo; and Aymon, the father of Rinaldo, Bradamante, Ricciardo, Ricciardetto, Alardo and Guiscardo; also of Guidone. (See Table, p. 735.)

68. l. 4. This line echoes Dante, *Inferno*, 1. 2.

CANTO III

1. In this stanza Ariosto introduces the theme of the ancestry of the House of Este. Historically, the origins of this family, known as Estensi, can be traced to the tenth century. Ariosto, following Boiardo, extends their line, through Ruggiero, to the Trojans, since he is descended from Astyanax, the son of Hector. (See Table, p. 734.)

2. ll. 6–8. This prophecy was not fulfilled. With the death of Duke Alfonso II in 1597, Pope Clement VIII laid claim to Ferrara, as Alfonso had no issue and Clement refused to acknowledge the validity of Alfonso's bequest of the dukedom to his cousin, Cesare d'Este, a descendant of an illegitimate son of Alfonso I. By 1598, direct papal rule was established in Ferrara. Cesare d'Este became Duke of Modena and Reggio, and thereafter the

THE HOUSE OF ESTE
HISTORICAL (I. Ferrara)[1]

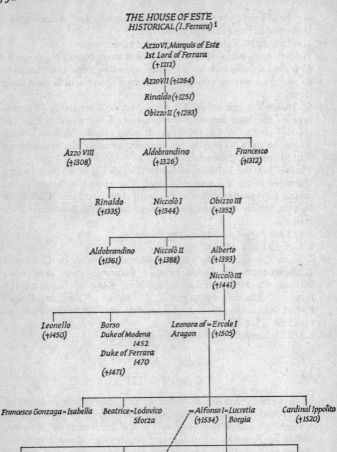

Azzo VI, Marquis of Este
1st Lord of Ferrara
(†1212)

Azzo VII (†1264)

Rinaldo (†1251)

Obizzo II (†1293)

Azzo VIII (†1308)   Aldobrandino (†1326)   Francesco (†1312)

Rinaldo (†1335)   Niccolò I (†1344)   Obizzo III (†1352)

Aldobrandino (†1361)   Niccolò II (†1388)   Alberto (†1393)

Niccolò III (†1441)

Leonello (†1450)   Borso Duke of Modena 1452 Duke of Ferrara 1470 (†1471)   Leonora of Aragon = Ercole I (†1505)

Francesco Gonzaga = Isabella   Beatrice = Lodovico Sforza   = Alfonso I = Lucretia (†1534) Borgia   Cardinal Ippolito (†1520)

Ercole II = Renée de France (†1558)   Eleonora   Cardinal Ippolito (†1572)   Francesco

Alfonso II (†1597)   [Cesare][2] d'Este   Bradamante   Marfisa

1. In 1597 Ferrara was seized by the Papacy. The House of Este continued at Modena.
2. Dotted lines signify illegitimate descent.

Table I. 1

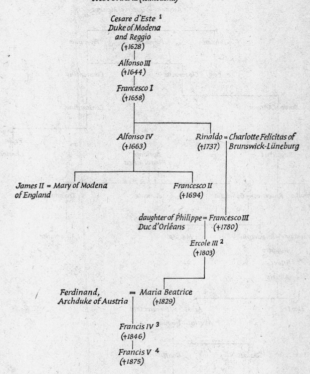

THE HOUSE OF ESTE
HISTORICAL (II.Modena)

Cesare d'Este [1]
Duke of Modena
and Reggio
(†1628)

Alfonso III
(†1644)

Francesco I
(†1658)

Alfonso IV   Rinaldo = Charlotte Felicitas of
(†1663)   (†1737)   Brunswick-Lüneburg

James II = Mary of Modena   Francesco II
of England   (†1694)

daughter of Philippe = Francesco III
Duc d'Orléans   (†1780)

Ercole III [2]
(†1803)

Ferdinand,   = Maria Beatrice
Archduke of Austria (†1829)

Francis IV [3]
(†1846)

Francis V [4]
(†1875)

1. Descendant of illegitimate son of Alfonso I, cousin of Alfonso II.
2. With the death of Ercole III the male line of the Estensi comes to an end.
3. The first of the Austria-Este line. He became Duke of Modena in 1814.
4. He lost the Duchy of Modena when Modena was annexed to Sardinia-Piedmont in 1859.
   He bequeathed his titles to Archduke Francis Ferdinand (1863-1914), owing to whose morganatic
   marriage with Sophia Kotech the Austria-Este line became extinct.

Table I. ii

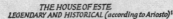

THE HOUSE OF ESTE
LEGENDARY AND HISTORICAL (according to Ariosto)[1]

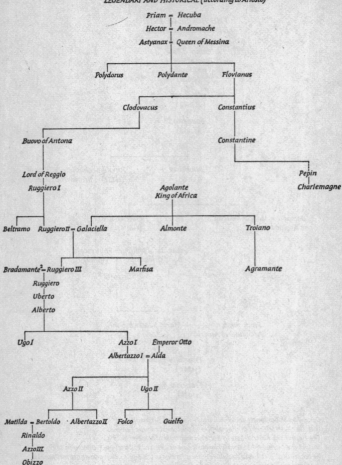

1. *This genealogical tree is based mainly on Canto III. After the mention of Obizzo in Stanza 32, the indication of the generations between him and the historical Azzo VI is confused. In Stanza 38, Ariosto refers to the historical Rinaldo who died in 1251. From here onwards see The House of Este, Historical (I. Ferrara), p.732 and Notes to Canto III.*

2. *For Bradamante's origins, see Genealogical Table of Buovo d'Antona.*

Table 2

735

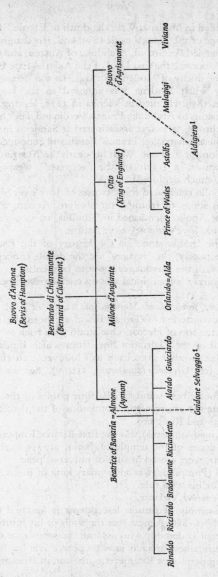

LEGENDARY ORIGINS OF ORLANDO AND OTHER CAROLINGIANS

Table 3

1. Dotted lines signify illegitimate descent.

family resided in Modena. With the death of Ercole III in 1803, the male line of the Estensi came to an end. His daughter Maria Beatrice married Ferdinand, Archduke of Austria, and their son, Francis IV, became the first head of the Austria–Este House; he received the duchy of Modena in 1814. His son, Francis V, lost the duchy when Modena was annexed to the kingdom of Sardinia in 1859. He died in Vienna in 1875, leaving his titles and possessions to Archduke Francis Ferdinand, later heir to the Austrian throne, who was assassinated at Sarajevo in 1914. By his morganatic marriage, Francis Ferdinand renounced claims of succession for his issue. With his death the Austria–Este line became extinct, a result of the 'accursèd' weapon which Ariosto so much deplored!

3. ll. 1–4. Apollo celebrated the victories of Jove over his enemies by playing songs of triumph on his lyre. Ariosto found this function of Apollo mentioned in Tibullus, II. v. 9–10, in connection with Jove's victory over Saturn.

ll. 5–8. The 'noble stone' is the history of the Estensi, the 'tools' are poetry, the 'images' are the details concerning the Este family, or the personages about to be identified.

8. ll. 7–8. Disarray is traditional among enchantresses performing magic.

12. l. 2. *a distant, foreign land.* Mantua (cf. XLIII. 11 [Vol. II]).

17. l. 2. The two strains of Trojan blood are both derived from Astyanax, the son of Hector. One strain goes back to Costante, an ancestor of the Clairmont line, from which Bradamante is descended; the other goes back to Clodovaco, an ancestor of Ruggiero (cf. *Orlando Innamorato*, III. v). See also Tables, pp. 734–5.

l. 5. The four rivers stand for the four points of the compass, and indicate the extent of the dominions of the descendants of Bradamante and Ruggiero.

18. l. 6. Octavius (Augustus) was the first Roman Emperor. In his reign the doors of the temple of Janus, always kept open in time of war, were closed in sign of universal peace.

l. 7. Numa (Pompilius) was a legendary king of Rome, famed in tradition for his wise rule.

19. l. 7. *the vile robber.* Atlante.

20–22. The assembly of future descendants is imitated from the *Aeneid*, VI. 756–886. Aeneas sees the souls of his future descendants; here it is demons who assume the semblance of Bradamante's heirs, since sorcerers have no power over human spirits.

24. This is Ruggierino, or Ruggieretto, the son of Bradamante and

Ruggiero. Pontiero, or Ponthieu, is the region in France where the treacherous Maganzans have their castle.

25. ll. 1–2. Desiderius, the last king of the Longobards, attempted to assert his territorial claims against Pope Adrian I. Threatened with a siege of Rome, the Pope appealed to Charlemagne, who crossed the Alps in 773 and besieged Pavia. Desiderius capitulated in June 774. Ariosto attributes this victory to the son of Ruggiero.

l. 5. Hubert is not historical. Ariosto may have confused him with Oberto I.

26. l. 1. Albert is not historical. Ariosto may have confused him with Oberto II.

l. 3–4. Hugo, son of Oberto II, was Count of Milan in 1021. He died in 1039 or 1040. The viper is the emblem of Milan.

ll. 5–6. This is not historically exact. Hugo was succeeded, not by his brother, but by his brother's son, Albertazzo II, who died *c.* 1044.

26–7. *Next Albertazzo.* Berengarius died seventy-eight years before Albertazzo, in 966. There is no historical confirmation of his marriage to the Emperor Otto's daughter Alda.

27. l. 3. *A second Hugo.* These events attributed to him occurred during the papacy of Gregory V (996–999). Gregory, defeated by the Roman Consul, Crescentius, took refuge in Pavia. Assisted by the Emperor Otto III, he regained possession of Rome. Ariosto here alleges that Hugo, Count of Maine, who died in 997, lent aid to Gregory and Otto.

28. Ariosto has here confused Folco with his brother, Guelfo IV, who became Duke of Bavaria. Folco, historically the head of the Estense line, died in 1136.

ll. 6–8. *his mother.* Alda, daughter of Emperor Otto (cf. 27).

29. l. 1. *a second Azzo.* It is Azzo, not his sons, who fought against the Emperor Henry IV at Parma. He married a Countess Matilda, sister of Guglielmo, Bishop of Pavia (not the famous Matilda, Countess of Tuscany, as at lines 7–8 stated).

29–30. Matilda, Countess of Tuscany, did marry a member of the Estense family, Guelfo V, Duke of Bavaria (not Azzo II).

29. l. 3. *Bertoldo and Albertazzo.* The Ferrarese historian Ricobaldo mentions these two personages and says that Bertoldo defended the Church against Henry IV and had a son, Rinaldo. This may have been Ariosto's source.

30. l. 2. *at his age.* Guelfo V was 18 when he married Matilda, who was then aged 43. Ariosto attributes this disparity in age to Azzo II.

30. ll. 3–4. Matilda's dominions were Tuscany, Piacenza, Parma, Modena, Mantua, Ferrara, part of Umbria and the duchy of Spoleto. She was believed to be the niece of Henry III (the first of the House of Franconia) but genealogists now maintain that she was his first cousin once removed.

31. l. 1. *Another Azzo.* He is unknown to historians. The ruler of Verona was Azzo IV (mentioned later), who also became Marquess of Ancona in 1208. It was Azzo VII who received the investiture from Honorius III.

l. 4. The reference is to Emperor Otto IV and Pope Honorius II.

32. Obizzo is known to have had the following sons: Azzo, Bonifazio, Obizzo, Folco, Alberto. The 'two Henrys' are perhaps Henry the Black (d. 1126), son of Guelfo IV, and Henry the Proud (d. 1139), the former's son. The 'two Guelfs' are Guelfo VI, son of Henry the Black, who became Duke of Spoleto, and his son Guelfo VII.

32–3. Ariosto attributes to Azzo V, son of Obizzo I, who predeceased his father as prisoner of the Veronese, the achievements of Azzo VII.

33. l. 5. Ariosto's notion of Mark Antony's cruelty is probably derived from the latter's proscription of the supporters of Brutus and Cassius, his most notable victim being Cicero.

ll. 7–8. Frederick II, hearing that Parma, formerly held by his Ghibelline forces, had been besieged by the Guelfs, came to its assistance, but was defeated (1248) by the allies, among whom was Azzo d'Este.

34. l. 1. The land referred to here is Ferrara. The first of the Estensi to rule over this region was Azzo VI (not Azzo V). There being little resistance to their rule, their sceptre was 'kindlier'.

ll. 2–7. Phaethon, struck by Jove's thunderbolt, fell into the river Po and was mourned by Phoebus, his father, and by his sisters, who were changed into poplars, and their tears into amber. Cycnus, the king of Liguria, and related to Phaethon, also mourned him and was turned into a swan.

ll. 7–8. Ferrara was regarded by the Papacy as under its dominion, as part of the donation of Pepin or of the legacy of Matilda. The Estensi were invested as rulers of Ferrara by the Pope.

35–6. To assist Pope Innocent III against Otto IV and Frederick II, Aldobrandino raised money from Florentine bankers, leaving them his brother Azzo as surety, who died of poison. Aldobrandino, further at the request of Innocent III, undertook to recapture Ancona, where the Counts of Celano, supporters of

Otto IV, had raised a rebellion. Gualtieri of Celano was slain. Aldobrandino died in 1215.

37. l. 2. *Tronto*. River dividing the March of Ancona from the Abruzzi.

38. Rinaldo was held hostage by Frederick II in Naples and died in 1251 by poisoning. His son was Obizzo II, legitimized by his grandfather, Azzo VII.

39. ll. 1–4. Modena and Reggio offered allegiance to Obizzo in 1288–9.

l. 5. *Azzo the Sixth*. This is historically Azzo VIII. He married Beatrice, daughter of Charles II of Anjou, gaining thereby the title of Count (not Duke) of Andria.

40. l. 6. *with stronger ties*. Faenza was lost (to the Visconti) soon after coming under the dominion of the Estensi.

ll. 7–8. Adria, a city east of Rovigo and south of Chioggia, is the origin of the name Adriatic.

41. ll. 1–2. This is a reference to Rovigo, a city to the north of Ferrara. Its Latin name, Rhodigium, was thought to be derived from the Greek *rhodon*, meaning rose. Rovigo, among the earliest of the Estense dominions, was ceded to the Venetian Republic by Nicholas III and then recovered in 1438.

ll. 3–6. This is a reference to Comacchio, situated between the two mouths of the Po, Primaro and Volano. It yielded to Azzo VIII and confirmed its allegiance to Obizzo III in 1325.

42. l. 1. Nicholas III succeeded at the age of 9.

ll. 3–4. Tydeus, the father of Diomedes, was famed for his rage in his attack on Thebes. The 'hostile ploy' may be a reference to the attack on Nicholas by a distant kinsman, Azzo, or by a Count di Conio, mentioned by commentators, but otherwise unknown.

43. ll. 1–2. Many Ferrarese towns were roused to rebellion by Azzo but quelled by Nicholas.

ll. 5–6. Ottobono Terzi, *condottiere* and tyrant of Parma and Reggio, plotted to kill Nicholas, who had him assassinated.

44. This stanza refers to additions to the domains of the Estensi, especially under Ercole I, who gained Cento, Pieve, Cotignola and half the principality of Carpi.

45. Leonello and Borso, the illegitimate sons of Nicholas III by Stella dei Tolomei, were given preference in the succession over his legitimate sons, Ercole and Sigismondo. Both Leonello and Borso were men of peace and lovers of the arts.

l. 3. *greater triumph wins*. Borso was created Duke of Modena and Reggio by Frederick III and of Ferrara by the Pope.

46. In 1492 the neighbouring Venetian Republic declared war on Ercole, although in 1467 he had valiantly led the Venetian forces in the battle of Molinella, near Budrio in the region of Bologna, when he was permanently injured in the right foot.

47. In his youth Ercole fought under Alfonso I of Naples, King of Aragon and Catalonia. During that period he fought a duel with Galeazzo Pandone and won great glory. Other commentators suggest that this stanza may refer to Ercole's service under John of Anjou against Ferdinand, the successor of Alfonso I. In this case, the 'single combat' would refer to the encounter with King Ferdinand in 1460, whom he almost slew.

    l. 2. *Lucanians*. Lucania was the ancient name of the region in south Italy between the Gulf of Taranto and the Tyrrhenian Sea.

49. l. 4. *the French torch*. Charles VIII, who invaded Italy in 1494.

50. ll. 3–7. Pollux, born of the egg fertilized by Jove, was immortal, but Castor, born of the egg fertilized by Leda's husband, Tyndareos, was mortal. Pollux, out of love for Castor, obtained the right to alternate with him every six months, so that each lived half a year in Heaven and half a year in Hades.

51. l. 8. Astraea is the goddess of justice.

52. ll. 1–4. Venice, jealous of Ferrara's power, attacked Alfonso several times, especially by ship along the river Po.

    ll. 5–8. The Papacy, especially during the pontificate of the warrior-Pope, Julius II, was particularly hostile to Alfonso. Procne, who killed her son and served his body as a dish to her husband in revenge for his infidelity, and Medea, who killed her sons when Jason abandoned her, are cited as instances of cruel mothers.

53. Ariosto refers here to the battle in 1511 between Papal forces, allied with Spanish, and those of Alfonso. Forces from Romagna also joined against Alfonso, their former ally, who defeated them all in a triangular area, near the fortress of Bastia, bounded by the Po, the Santerno (on which Imola stands) and the Zanniolo Canal, which discharges into the Po near Bastia.

54. In the same year (1511) the captain of the Spanish forces, in the service of the Papacy, recaptured the fort of Bastia, which was held by Vestidello Pagano of Milan, on behalf of Alfonso. Contrary to the pact of surrender, Vestidello was put to death. In January 1512, Alfonso recaptured the fort and the Spanish garrison was executed.

55. This is a reference to the battle of Ravenna (1512), at which the Papacy and the Spaniards were defeated by France, largely

owing to the artillery of Alfonso, allied to France. It was this battle which convinced military strategists as to the decisive use which could be made of artillery.

57. At the battle of Polesella (1509), the Venetian armada was destroyed in the Po, largely owing to the skill and strategy of Ippolito.

58. Of the two Sigismonds, one is a brother of Duke Ercole I (d. 1507), the other is a son (d. 1524). The five sons of Duke Alfonso I were Duke Ercole II, Cardinal Ippolito II, Francesco (by his wife, Lucrezia Borgia), Alfonso and Alfonsino (by his mistress, Laura Dianti).

l. 5. *the French king's daughter*. Renée de France.

l. 8. *his uncle's*. Cardinal Ippolito's.

60–62. *two of grim, foreboding look*. These are Giulio and Ferrante, who conspired against their brothers Alfonso and Ippolito, in 1506. Condemned to death, they were reprieved, and imprisoned for life. Ferrante died in 1540; Giulio, liberated in 1559, died in 1561. The story is told that Ippolito, jealous of Giulio, who rivalled him in love, had his eyes put out, and that Giulio then plotted with Ferrante to overthrow Alfonso and Ippolito. Ariosto seems here to be asking for compassion on their behalf, at the same time being careful not to reproach his patrons for their inhumanity.

61. ll. 7–8. *evil men*. Their fellow-conspirators, named in Ferrarese history as Albertino Boschetti, Gherardo Roberti, Franceschino Boccacio, and a priest, Gianni di Guascogna. Ariosto wrote a dramatic eclogue on the subject of the conspiracy soon after it was discovered. The story is unfolded in a dialogue between two shepherds, Tirsi and Melibeo, whose names are taken from Virgil, *Eclogue* VII.

69. In this stanza, Ariosto continues the indications of Boiardo, *Orlando Innamorato*, II. iii. 27 et seq. King Agramante, advised that he cannot wage war successfully against the Christians without the help of Ruggiero, commissions a thief, Brunello, to steal a magic ring from Angelica in Albracca. By means of this ring, Atlante's spell can be broken and Ruggiero freed.

72. This description of Brunello is derived from Boiardo, op. cit. II. iii. 40. His name means 'little dark one'.

CANTO IV

1. This stanza may be intended as a humorous comment on the recommendations of Machiavelli in *The Prince*. cf. IX. 61.

10. ll. 3–5. Bradamante's own horse has been stolen by Pinabello; cf. III. 4–5.

11. l. 4. *both seas*. The Atlantic and the Mediterranean.

18. ll. 1–6. Ariosto here refutes Virgil's statement that such a union would be incredible (cf. *Eclogue* VIII, 26–8).
    l. 7. *Rhiphaean mountains*. Imagined from Homer onwards to exist north of the known parts of Europe. Ptolemy located them in Russia, between rivers flowing into the Baltic and the Euxine.

29. ll. 7–8. Atlante correctly foresees Ruggiero's destiny. His death by treachery has already been foretold by Melissa; cf. III. 24. Atlante also foresees his conversion to the Christian faith. Both these events were forecast by Boiardo, *Orlando Innamorato*, II. xvi. 35, 53.

40. ll. 1–4. Ariosto does not explain how Sacripante reached Atlante's castle. He was last seen in Canto II, contesting with Rinaldo, who left him abruptly to set off for Paris; cf. stanza 19. In Boiardo's epic, Iroldo and Prasildo were liberated and baptized by Rinaldo and followed him to France (*Orl. Inn.*, I, xiii. 5; xvii. 12, et seq.).

41. ll. 3–4. In Boiardo's story, Bradamante had drawn off her helmet to reveal her face to Ruggiero. Attacked by a band of Saracens, she set off in pursuit of one who wounded her and has not seen Ruggiero since that day (op. cit. III. v).

46. ll. 1–2. Frontino first belonged to Sacripante and was named Frontalatte. Brunello stole him and gave him to Ruggiero, who changed his name (Boiardo, *Orl. Inn.*, II. xvi. 56).

51. ll. 6–52. *Caledonia's forest*. This reference goes back ultimately to the seventh of the historical Arthur's twelve battles, as listed by Nennius, in the *Historia Brittonum*, Chapter 56. Ariosto enlarges the sense to mean the Scottish forests in general and he lists the literary Arthurian heroes whom he imagines to have fought there.

53. ll. 1–2. *the old/ And new Round Table*. Explained by commentators as the fraternity of the knights serving Arthur's father, Utherpendragon (the 'old Round Table'), and of those who served King Arthur himself (the 'new Round Table'). This distinction is not found in the original Arthurian texts. The Round Table

first appears in connection with King Arthur in Robert Wace's *Le roman de Brut*, c. 1155.

57. l. 5. *The daughter of our monarch*. Ginevra, sister of Zerbino. Her name is the Italian form of Guinevere and her story is in part that of King Arthur's wife who, accused of adultery, is defended by Lancelot.

58–9. In *Amadis of Gaul*, Book I, I, there is a reference to laws comparable with those described here.

61. l. 8. i.e. from the Far East to the extremity of the Western inhabited world.

CANTO V

4. l. 3. *the fair damsel*. This is Dalinda, who is derived from Bragane, the lady-in-waiting of Isolde, who sacrificed her honour to defend that of the queen, who gives instructions for her to be slain lest she reveal the truth. She is left tied to a tree and is rescued by Palamides, who takes her to a convent (*Romance of Tristan*). The story of Dalinda's impersonation of Ginevra was adapted (indirectly) by Shakespeare in *Much Ado About Nothing*.

5. l. 3. Thebes, Argos and Mycenae were famed for deeds of violence and cruelty; Thebes is associated with the inhumanity of Creon, and of Eteocles and Polynices, Argos with the daughters of Danaus who slew their husbands, and Mycenae with the deaths of Iphigenia, Agamemnon and Clytemnestra.

13. l. 8. Zerbino; the son of the King of Scotland, stands next to him in rank, but the Duke of Albany is among the most eligible suitors for Ginevra's hand and if he married her no one but the king would stand higher. The implication perhaps is that he might even rival Zerbino for the throne.

16. The story of Ariodante is the subject of an opera by Handel.

25–6. Dalinda's readiness to comply with Polinesso in this disguise is not convincing, as Ariosto seems himself aware. In adapting the Spanish romance *Tirante el Blanco*, he has rendered the character of Dalinda less villainous, thereby lessening the verisimilitude of her actions.

69. Zerbino is at a joust at Bayona (cf. XIII. 6).

81. l. 1. *Six knights*. In attendance on Lurcanio.

l. 5. *High Constable*. A constable (*comes stabuli*), originally a shield-bearer of a prince, later became an officer of high rank. The Duke of Albany as High Constable has the duty of maintaining good order and of giving the signal to cease combat (stanza 85).

88. l. 3. *At the third blast.* In public duels the herald gave three signals; at the third the combatants, from opposite ends of the stockade, charged for the encounter.

89. If one combatant in a duel was thrown, it was permissible for the other to finish him off by stabbing him in the face. If he confessed or asked for mercy, he was spared. In Polinesso's case, he has already received a mortal wound.

CANTO VI

1. This moralizing prelude echoes a passage in Cicero's *De Finibus*, Book II, where the same warning is conveyed.

2. By adding to the first crime of inculpating the innocent Ginevra the second crime of trying to do away with Dalinda, Polinesso was unmasked.

13. l. 4. The green and yellow border of the shield symbolizes hope, which is not quite dead in Ariodante's heart.

16. l. 5. *Denmark.* This is Dazia in the original and could be either Dacia (the region corresponding to Romania) or Denmark (known both as Dania and Dacia). It is more likely that Dalinda would take refuge in Denmark from Scotland.

17. ll. 7–8. The 'pillars fixed by Hercules' are the Straits of Gibraltar, which were believed by the ancients to mark the limit of the navigable seas. The pillars or columns placed by Hercules are the two mountains Abyla and Calpe.

19. l. 4. *an isle.* Ariosto may imagine this to be in the Atlantic Ocean, near the New World, probably one of the West Indies. Some commentators, however, have identified it as Japan (vaguely known to Europeans from Marco Polo's *Travels*). In this case, the statement in stanza 25 that Ruggiero has travelled west three thousand miles is not to be understood literally.

ll. 5–8. The island resembles Sicily, where the nymph Arethusa, transformed into a river by Diana, flowed underground to evade her lover, Alphaeus, and re-emerged at Ortygia; but Alphaeus, also transformed into a river, mingled his waters with hers below ground. Hence all her efforts at evasion were in vain.

27. This stanza and stanza 32 recall Dante's description of the voice of Pier delle Vigne speaking through the broken frond of the

tree in which his soul is imprisoned (*Inferno*, XIII. 40–45). Both descriptions have their antecedence in Virgil, *Aeneid*, III. 22 et seq.

34–46. Ariosto is here poking fun at Dante, exaggerating the description. He here picks up the thread of Astolfo's adventures as related by Boiardo. Leaving Albracca in the company of Rinaldo, he was captured by Monodante, King of Demogir, in the Indian Ocean. Among his fellow-prisoners were Prasildo, Iroldo (cf. IV. 40) and Dudone. They were rescued by Orlando (cf. Boiardo, *Orlando Innamorato*, II. xii, xiii).

34. ll. 7–8. Leaving Demogir, Astolfo travelled west across the China Sea.

35. l. 4. *Alcina*. She is Boiardo's invention; cf. *Orlando Innamorato*, II. xiii et seq.

37. Boiardo's story of Astolfo ended with his being carried off by a whale (*Orl. Inn.*, II. xiv. 3 et seq.).

38. *both sisters of King Arthur's*. In the Arthurian legends, there is only one sister, Morgan la fée (Morgana).

43–5. *Logistilla*. She is Ariosto's invention, and the third sister of Arthur. The three sisters represent sensuality (Alcina), acquisitiveness (Morgana), and reason (Logistilla).

44. l. 4. The seven virtues are: justice, prudence, temperance and fortitude (the four cardinal virtues), and faith, hope and charity (the three theological virtues).

48. The same word, *altri*, is used three times by Ariosto in the rhyme position in this stanza, to stress the warning: there are *others*.

58. l. 4. Ruggiero is later taught by Logistilla how to control the hippogriff (x. 66–8).

61. The cat-like creatures have been said to symbolize dissimulation; the monkey-headed, adulation; the goat-footed, licentiousness; the centaurs, violence.

62. This stanza has been interpreted as representing various manifestations of evil: violence, cowardice, pride, vainglory, gluttony, unnatural vice, etc.

63. The captain has been said to symbolize sloth and is described in terms recalling classical representations of the god Silenus.

64. This creature has been thought to symbolize malice and false rumour.

66. l. 8. Briareus, one of the Titans, had a hundred arms and hands.

67. The magic shield had been left attached to the saddle of the hippogriff by Atlante (IV. 25).

70. ll. 5–8. Though he resists the brutish horde, Ruggiero yields to the more subtle allurements of evil symbolized by the two damsels.

73. Alcina's garden symbolizes a life of ease and pleasure, devoid of all moral responsibility.

76. The hippogriff obeys enchantment.

78. l. 3. *Erifilla.* This monster symbolizes avarice, that is, cupidity. Her name may be an adaptation of Eryphile, who brought about the death of her husband, Amphiaraus, for a bribe of a necklace.

CANTO VII

3. l. 7. The wolf is a symbol of avarice (cf. Dante, *Inferno*, I).

4–5. The colour of sand and the poisonous toad are also symbols of avarice.

16. l. 6. *the myrtle.* Astolfo.

18. In this stanza Ariosto implies that supernatural forces have the power of robbing the individual of freedom of will.

20. ll. 1–2. The monarchs of Assyria, especially Semiramis and Sardanapalus, were famed for their luxurious living.
   l. 3. The banquets offered by Cleopatra to Mark Antony are described by Plutarch and Pliny.

21–3. These rather sly stanzas may be intended as a humorous comment on the social life of the Estense court.

24–5. There are echoes here of the torment of Hero waiting for Leander (cf. Ovid, *Heroides*, I. 47–51, 54–6), but Ariosto's touch is lighter.

29. This stanza, imitated from Boiardo, has its antecedent also in Horace, *Epodes* XV. 5–6.

32. The allusion to hunting, snaring and fishing appears inconsistent with the statement in VI. 22 that the animals on the island have no fear.

33. ll. 1–2. Ruggiero's presence at the siege of Paris might have led to its capture by Agramante. His absence is providential for the Christians, while his yielding to sin and his later rejection of it are a necessary part of his moral progress and eventual conversion.

35. l. 6. *the magic ring.* Which she has taken from Brunello (IV. 14).

36. l. 3. The Hydaspes is the Ghelum, a river of the Punjab.

55. ll. 4–6. Valencia is said to have had a reputation for silken dalliance.

61. Melissa, disguised as Atlante, here expresses herself in terms of
    Platonic philosophy, according to which souls exist in a heaven
    of Ideas and precede the bodies they are destined to occupy.
    There is a contradiction between Melissa's reproaches (stanzas
    57–64) and Atlante's recent anxiety about Ruggiero's safety. It
    appears that Atlante reared Ruggiero for heroic deeds until he
    foresaw his death. Melissa assumes the role of Atlante as
    Ruggiero remembers him from his boyhood (line stanza).

66. l. 6. *Melissa*. Ariosto here for the first time reveals the name of
    this benevolent sorceress who will continue to assist Ruggiero
    and Bradamante.

67. l. 5. *Atlante of Carena*. Atlante is said by Boiardo to have an
    enchanted garden in the mountains of Carena, a northern ridge
    of the Atlas Mountains.

73. l. 5. Hecuba, the wife of Priam and mother of fifty sons, out-
    lived all her line. Cumae's Sibyl lived for a thousand years.

76. l. 1. *Balisarda*. This name was invented by Boiardo for the magic
    sword made by Falerina and taken from her by Orlando. It was
    then stolen by Brunello and given to Ruggiero (*Orl. Inn.*, II.
    iv. 26 et seq.; XI. 60; XVI. 2, 12).

77. l. 5. Rabicano originally belonged to Argalia, the brother of
    Angelica. Its dam was compounded of fire, its sire of wind. It
    came into the possession of Astolfo, who brought it to Alcina's
    island. How it reached her stables is not explained, since he was
    carried to her palace on a whale (VI. 40–41).

78. ll. 5–8. It is Logistilla who later gives Ruggiero instruction in
    mastering the hippogriff (x. 66–8).

CANTO VIII

5. l. 6. The falcon is on his left wrist.

6–8. The servitor, the dog, the horse and the falcon symbolize the
    remaining allurements of sensuality which Ruggiero is able to
    resist only with supernatural aid.

14. ll. 7–8. These are magical devices, wax or terracotta images,
    imprints of constellations on metal or stone, knotted threads of
    different colours, etc., by means of which spells were cast.

15. l. 8. *Scythia*. An indeterminate region, roughly corresponding
    to the area between the river Don in the west, the north-west
    extremity of China, and the south of India.

27. l. 1. *the Prince of Wales*. This title was not conferred on the
    hereditary prince of England until 1301. Ariosto does not say

explicitly that this prince was Otto's son, but that he replaces
him in his absence. Astolfo in VI. 33 says that *he* was the heir,
implying that his rash adventures had displaced him from his
inheritance. It is left uncertain as to whether Astolfo and this
prince are brothers.

42. ll. 7–8. Argalia was slain by Ferraù, who pierced him in the
groin where his magic armour did not cover him.

43. ll. 1–3. *the king of Tartary*. Agricane, who killed Angelica's
father Galafrone, the Great Khan of northern China and India.

51. ll. 7–8. Proteus, a sea-god, subject to Poseidon, was the guardian
of his flock. The orc is here a sea-monster, whereas the orc in
Boiardo's *Orlando Innamorato* lived on land.

62. ll. 6–8. Angelica's beauty drew Agricane, King of Tartary, and
half his forces, to fight to the death at Albracca.

64. l. 4. No more is heard of the hermit.

68. l. 3. *the other two*. i.e. Rinaldo and Ferraù.

69. l. 1. *King Troiano's son*. Agramante.

71. ll. 5–8. This simile is taken from Virgil, *Aeneid*, VIII. 22–5.

85. ll. 3–4. *his coat of white/And crimson quarterings*. These armorial
bearings belonged formerly to Almonte. Orlando took them, as
well as his sword, helmet and horse, when he killed him at
Aspromonte (cf. XVIII. 148–50).

86. l. 3, 88–90. Brandimarte, son of Monodante, the king of Dem-
ogir, was stolen as a child and brought up as a slave at Rocca
Silvana. Fiordiligi, daughter of Dolistone, the king of Lizza,
had also been sold into slavery in the same castle. They grew up
together, fell in love and married. Brandimarte was converted
by Orlando and became his boon companion. Fiordiligi was
baptized at the behest of Rinaldo (*Orl. Inn.*, II. xiii. 10; xii.
11; xxvii. 26).

CANTO IX

8–94. These stanzas and stanzas 1–34 of Canto X were inserted by
Ariosto in the third edition of 1532.

8. ll. 2–4. The river is the Couesnon, which flows into the Gulf of
St Malo.

17. ll. 7–8. Antwerp is on the Scheldt, which flows into the North
Sea. It is thought of here as being in Flanders, formerly identi-
fied with territory now divided between the French *département
Nord*, the Belgian provinces of East and West Flanders, and the
Dutch province of Zeeland.

25. ll. 3–8. Cimosco (whose name is revealed in stanza 42), King of Friesland or Frisia, seeks the hand of Olimpia for his son Arbante. Olimpia says that Holland is separated from Friesland by a distance equal to the width of the river (the Old Rhine) at its estuary. The ancient Friesians occupied not only modern Friesland, but also part of Northern Holland, as far as Leyden, on the Old Rhine. In the thirteenth century the Zuider Zee was formed and the name of Friesland was associated thereafter only with the area to the north-east of this expanse of water.

27. l. 7. *Invaded Holland.* Cimosco has captured Dordrecht (stanza 61).

28. l. 7. *a strange new weapon.* Duke Alfonso I used artillery and fire-arms in 1509 against the Venetian fleet which had proceeded up the Po to Polesella, within a short distance of Ferrara. The fleet was destroyed, an achievement which much increased the prestige of artillery. Alfonso again used artillery to defeat the Spanish army at the battle of Ravenna in 1512 (XIV. 2–3). The duke, who personally superintended the casting of two guns of tremendous size, was well to the fore in his enthusiasm for these new weapons. Ariosto, though praising Alfonso in all other ways, expresses vehement disapproval of the use of cannon, which he regards as the negation of chivalry (stanzas 88–91 and XI. 21–8).

59. Orlando leaves Antwerp, in Flanders, taking Olimpia with him. They sail along the Scheldt, in the direction of Holland, passing among the islands of Zeeland.

61. ll. 3–4. Ariosto seems to be echoing Machiavelli's *Prince.* cf. IV. I.

65. ll. 7–8. At Volano, one of the two estuaries of the river Po, fish used to be abundant and were caught by fishermen using a long, wide net called a *tratta.*

77. ll. 5–6. The Libyan giant, Antaeus, offspring of Neptune and Gaea (the Earth), could not be killed as long as he was in contact with the earth. Hercules killed him by strangling him in mid air.

90. l. 3. *the coast.* Of Holland.

94. The wedding in Zealand for which preparations are being made is the intended marriage between Bireno's brother and Cimosco's daughter.

CANTO X

15. ll. 5–8. Bireno and company set sail from Holland.

16. ll. 1–6. They intend to round the northern tip of Denmark to reach the island of Zealand and to do this they at first veer west,

in the direction of Scotland. The island on which they land may be one of the Orkneys.

20–35. Olimpia's realization that Bireno has deserted her, and her expression of despair, are closely modelled on the lament of Ariadne, abandoned on the island of Naxos by Theseus in Ovid's *Heroides*, x.

20. ll. 5–6. Alcyone, the wife of Ceyx, who was drowned, lamented him so pitifully that she was changed into a bird, the halcyon, usually identified with the kingfisher, which has a mournful cry.

29–30. Lions and tigers, unlikely fauna to encounter on an island off Scotland, have been imported from Ovid's Naxos.

34. ll. 4–6. Polydorus, the son of Hecuba and Priam, was killed by Polymnestor and his body cast into the sea. It was washed up on the coast and his mother, recognizing it, took vengeance on Polymnestor by killing his two children and putting out his eyes.

35. l. 1. In the two earlier editions Ariosto had written 'But let us leave *him* there . . .' (Ma lascianlo doler . . .), referring to Orlando (cf. Canto IX. 7).

52. The four ladies represent the four cardinal virtues: fortitude (Andronica), prudence (Fronesia), justice (Dicilla), temperance (Sofrosina).

61. The hanging garden of Logistilla's palace is inspired by the tradition of the hanging gardens of Babylon, one of the seven wonders of the world. Since those are no longer to be seen, the reader may recapture the impression intended here by visiting the beautiful roof garden in memory of Florence Ollerenshaw on the Royal Northern College of Music, Manchester.

70. l. 1. *leaving Spain*. Ruggiero had set out from the Pyrenees, where Atlante's castle had been and where he had mounted the hippogriff (IV. 46).

l. 2. *India*. A generic term for the Far East, applied also to the West Indies, at first believed to be in the East.

l. 4. *two enchantresses*. Alcina and Logistilla.

ll. 6–8. *Aeolus's realm*. The oceans. Ruggiero decides to fly back over the land masses of the globe in an east–west direction.

71. Ruggiero flies over China, divided into Cathay to the north (on his right), and Mangi to the south (on his left). Mangi is Marco Polo's name for the region known also as Ma-ci. Kinsai is Marco Polo's name for Nanking, the capital of Chekiang. Sericana, so called for its silk industry, is the kingdom in China ruled over by Gradasso. Northern Scythia perhaps corresponds to Siberia. There was a European and an Asiatic Sarmatia. The

part mentioned here is the Asiatic. The Don was regarded by the ancients as a boundary between Asia and Europe.

75-6. It is remarkable how willing the 'courteous cavalier' is to give Ruggiero (an unknown warrior) so much valuable information about the troops, and even more remarkable how little urgency Ruggiero feels to pass the information on to his fellow pagans, especially in view of what he is told in stanza 76.

77. Leopards and fleurs-de-lis clearly refer to the fleurs-de-lis of France and the leopards of England borne (quarterly) with a label ermine by John of Gaunt, created Duke of Lancaster 1362, d. 1399, son (not 'nephew') of Edward III. After him there was effectively no Duke of Lancaster, as his son, Henry IV, no sooner became duke than he seized the throne, and the latter's son, Henry V, was already Prince of Wales when he was given the duchy of Lancaster.

78. ll. 1-3. *Count Richard* could be either Richard Beauchamp, who succeeded as earl in 1401, and died 1439, or Richard Neville, created earl 1449, succ. as Earl of Salisbury 1460, d. 1471. As Ariosto introduces the Earl of Salisbury separately (stanza 83. 2) his Warwick must be Richard Beauchamp; but no Earl of Warwick bore Vert three wings argent.

ll. 4-6. *The Duke of Gloucester* is either Thomas Woodstock, son of Edward III, created duke 1385, d. 1397, or Humphrey of Lancaster, son of Henry IV, created duke 1414, d. 1446. Neither bore a stag's head affronté. This was a Stanley badge and had been better given to Derby.

l. 7. *The Duke of Clarence* is either Lionel, son of Edward III, created duke 1362, d. 1368; or Thomas, son of Henry IV, created duke 1412, d. 1421. Neither used a torch as a badge. Ariosto assigned this emblem – a source of *chiarezza*, as a play on the name *Chiarenza*.

l. 8. *The Duke of York* is either Edmund, son of Edward III, created duke 1385, d. 1402; or Edward his son, succeeded 1402, slain at Agincourt 1415. Neither used a tree, and Ariosto probably selected *arbore* as playing on *Eborace*.

79. ll. 1-2. *The Duke of Norfolk* is probably one of the three Mowbray dukes covering the period 1397-1476. None of them used the device described by Ariosto, but a badge of Thomas, Lord Darcy (1467-1537), consisted of three parts of a broken lance, the point erect and the pieces of the shaft crosswise.

l. 3. *The Earl of Kent* is probably one of the three Grey earls, 1465-1524. Their badge was a black ragged staff. This may have suggested the thunderbolt to Ariosto.

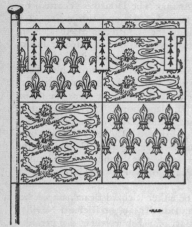

1. Banner of John of Gaunt ('Leonetto'), Duke of Lancaster. (Canto X 77)

2. Badge of Lord Darcy attributed by Ariosto to the Duke of Norfolk. (Canto X 79 ll. 1–2)

3. Water budget and 'Bourchier Knot' of the Bourchier Earls of Essex, described by Ariosto as a yoke and two snakes. (Canto X 79 ll. 6–7)

4. Crest of Berkeley: a mitre charged with the arms – mistaken by Ariosto for a cleft hill. (Canto X 80 ll. 2, 4)

79. l. 5. *The Earl of Pembroke* is perhaps Jasper Tudor, created earl 1453, Duke of Bedford 1485, d. 1495. His crest was a dragon or wyvern with wings raised.

ll. 5–6. *The Duke of Suffolk.* None of the three De la Pole dukes, 1448–93, had a balance or scales in his heraldry. It seems likely that Ariosto chose *bilancia* to rhyme with *Cancia.*

l. 7. *The Earl of Essex.* Henry Bourchier, created earl 1461, d. 1483, and grandson William Henry, succ. 1483, d. 1540, both used as badges a water budget (from the Bourchier arms) and two intertwined cords called the 'Bourchier Knot'; these badges are often found together. Without doubt Ariosto had seen them, but took the water budget to be a yoke and the knot to be two snakes.

l. 8. *Northumberland.* There is no garland in the heraldry of the Percy earls. Their best known badge was a crescent (sometimes found on a blue ground), and it looks as if Ariosto turned this into a garland for the sake of a rhyme (*ghirlanda/Norbelanda*).

80. ll. 1–2. *The Earl of Arundel.* A ship is not found in the heraldry of the Fitzalan earls of Arundel, but William, fifth earl, d. 1487, was Constable of Dover Castle and Lord Warden of the Cinque Ports. Ariosto may have seen, and connected with him, a seal of Dover with the device of a ship. The boat is sinking (*s'affonda*) because Ariosto needed a rhyme with *Ritmonda.*

l. 2. *Berkeley* is identifiable because there was only one marquess: William, succeeded as twelfth baron 1463, created viscount 1481, Earl of Nottingham 1483, Marquess of Berkeley 1489, d. 1492. Ariosto gives him a cleft hill. This looks as if he had seen, but misunderstood, the Berkeley crest of a mitre charged with the arms: Gules a chevron between nine crosslets paty argent.

l. 3. *The Earl of March.* Presumably one of the Mortimer earls. They were also Earls of Ulster. Assigning him a hand, Ariosto may have had in mind the red hand of the O'Neils, which was the badge of the province of Ulster, though it does not appear in the heraldry of the earls.

The Earl of Richmond. None of the earls – Montfort, Neville and Plantagenet – had a pine among their devices.

ll. 6–8. *Dorset.* Presumably one of the Beaufort earls, 1412–48 (when the then earl became Duke of Somerset). There is no chariot in their heraldry.

Hampton. Probably the legendary Sir Bevis of Hampton (or Hamtoun). There is no crown in the arms attributed to him.

81. ll. 1–2. *Raymond, Earl of Devonshire.* Henry Courtenay, who

succeeded as Earl of Devonshire 1511, was created Marquess of Exeter 1525, had as a second crest, or perhaps a badge, a falcon rising from a billet of wood raguly or – very near Ariosto's description.

81. l. 3. *Worcester*. Probably either Charles Somerset, created Earl of Worcester 1514, ambassador to France and the Emperor, d. 1526, or his son Henry. Their colours were not or and sable.

l. 4. *Derby*. Presumably one of the Stanley earls; there is no dog in their heraldry. They had a stag's head affronté, which Ariosto gives to Gloucester (stanza 78).

Oxfordshire. There is no bear in the heraldry of the De Vere earls of Oxford. Ariosto probably gave them *un orso* as a play on *Osonia*. It would have been preferable to give the bear to Warwick.

ll. 5–6. *Bath's wealthy prelate*. The prelate appears to carry a sort of processional cross, consisting of a long shaft surmounted by a cross, either of cut glass or of metal set with crystals. It is interesting to consider why, of all the English prelates, Ariosto should single out him of Bath for special mention. It may be because Ariosto knew something about him. The bishop at that time was Adrian de Castello, an Italian collector of Peter's pence in England. He was ambassador in Rome and clerk to the papal treasury, 1492, created Bishop of Bath and Wells, 1504; he never visited the diocese, and was deprived in 1508.

ll. 6–8. *the Duke/Of Somerset*. There is nothing like a broken chair among the devices of the dukes of Somerset. Ariosto may have chosen *sedia* as a play on *Sormosedia*. He perhaps broke the chair because of the last three Beaufort dukes one was killed in battle and two were beheaded.

82. ll. 5–8, 83. ll. 1–4. *Godfrey* (*Duke of Buckingham*), *Henry* (*Earl of Salisbury*), *Herman* (*Lord of Abergavenny*), *Edward* (*Earl of Shrewsbury*). The colours of their standards are not in accordance with their heraldry.

83. l. 8, 84. ll. 1–8. *Zerbino*, son of the King of the Scots and Duke of Ross; James III of Scotland, 1460–88, had two sons both named James, and a third, John, who became Earl of Mar (stanza 85). The eldest son, Duke of Rothesay, succeeded as James IV. The second son, whom Ariosto is said to have seen in Rome (*Dictionary of National Biography*) and whom he introduces here as Zerbino, was made Marquess of Ormonde at birth and Duke of Ross in 1488. He became Archbishop of St Andrew's and Chancellor of Scotland. A single unicorn appears on the coinage of James III. Two unicorns were first used as

supporters of the Scottish royal arms in the reign of James IV
(Zerbino's brother), so Ariosto was up to date with his infor-
mation. The lion in the Scottish shield does not bear a sword,
but that in the royal crest (which appeared later) bears both a
sword and a sceptre.

85. l. 1. *The Earl of Huntly*. The Gordon earls of Huntly did not
bear anything resembling Azure a bar or.

l. 2. *The Duke of Mar*. Probably John, third son of James III of
Scotland, created Earl of Mar 1486, d. 1503. He bore a differ-
enced form of the Scottish royal arms – a lion rampant within
the tressure of fleurs-de-lis. It is possible that Ariosto thought
of the lion as confined and controlled by the framework of the
tressure, and that this suggested the trave (*travaglio*) to him.

l. 3–8. *Alcabrun*. Ariosto may have seen a Highland chieftain in
his tartan – hence the many colours. There was a sept bearing
the name Cameron, derived from the village so named in Fife-
shire, and formerly called Cambrun. As far back as Bruce's reign
the Cambruns, or Camerons, appear in the records of the
counties of Aberdeen and Perth. It is tempting to regard
Ariosto's Alcabrun as a chieftain of the Cambruns. The initial
syllable 'Al' may represent 'the', as in 'the Cabrun', as the
chief would be called.

86. ll. 1–2. *The Duke of Transforth*. This name has been applied to a
district of Scotland, though not a dukedom or other lordship.
The arms are imaginary.

ll. 3–5. *The Earl of Angus*. There is nothing in the heraldry of
the Douglas earls of Angus resembling a bull flanked by hounds.
Lurcanio is the Italian cavalier, brother of Ariodante, whom the
King of Scotland has endowed with the earldom of Angus
(v. 17).

ll. 5–6. *Albany*. Argent and azure occur in the Stewart arms: Or
a fesse checky azure and argent; but the Stewart dukes of Albany
bore the royal arms of Scotland with quarterings which did not
include Stewart. The Duke of Albany, formerly Polinesso, is
now Ariodante (vi. 15).

ll. 7–8. *The Earl of Buchan*. The Stewart earls of Buchan did not
bear anything resembling a vulture tearing a green dragon.

87. ll. 1–2. *The Earl of Forbes*. His colours were not white and black.

ll. 3–4. *The Earl of Errol*. There is no torch or similar object in
his heraldry.

88. ll. 1–2. *Kildare. . . Desmond*. Both Fitzgerald. There is no burning
pine in their heraldry. Kildare bore Argent a saltire gules;
Desmond, Ermine a saltire gules.

88. l. 5. Thule is usually identified with Iceland, the Faroes, the Shetlands or the north of Norway.
92. ll. 1–4. The 'venerable elder' is St Patrick. His 'cave' is a cavern with a holy well on an island in Lough Dearg.
   ll. 6–8. It is not clear how Ruggiero, heading for Brittany from Ireland, could see Angelica chained to a rock in the Hebrides.
96–99. These stanzas recall Ovid's description of Andromeda chained to a rock and seen by Perseus (*Metamorphoses*, IV. 673 et seq.).
113. l. 6. Philomel, daughter of the king of Athens, was violated by Tereus. She and her sister Procne, Tereus' wife, killed his son Itys. In punishment, the gods changed Philomel into a nightingale, Procne into a swallow, and Tereus into a hoopoe.

CANTO XI

3. l. 1. *Xenocrates*. The Greek philosopher, renowned for the austerity of his morals, who was able to resist the seductions of the courtesan Phryne. Ruggiero, having parted with the ring, has no defences against the allurements of Angelica.
4–5. Ariosto refers here to events related by Boiardo: the theft of the magic ring by Brunello; her brother Argalia's loss of the magic lance to Astolfo and Angelica's defeat of the good sorcerer Malagigi; her liberation of Orlando from the sorceress Dragontina; and her escape from a tower where she had been imprisoned.
12. ll. 1–4. The nymphs and shepherds here named figure in Virgil's *Eclogues*.
21. ll. 5–8. cf. IX. 89–91.
22. l. 7. *a wizard*. This may be a reference to Berthold Schwartz (fourteenth century), believed in Ariosto's time to be the inventor of gunpowder for artillery.
27. The war referred to is the struggle between Charles V and Francis I for supremacy in Europe.
32. l. 8. Tithonus was the lover of Aurora, at whose entreaty the gods granted him immortality, but not eternal youth.
44. l. 1. cf. VIII. 52 et seq.
   l. 8. Ethiopia is mentioned by Homer as a resort of the sea-gods (*Odyssey*, V. 282; *Iliad*, I. 423).
45. l. 1. Ino, the wife of Athamas, sprang into the sea with her son in her arms to escape from her husband's frenzy. They were changed into the sea-gods Leucothea and Palaemon.

45. ll. 2–4. Nereids, Tritons, Glaucus and his followers are all sea-gods or immortal beings in the service of Neptune.

50. ll. 7–8. Orlando is invulnerable except in the soles of his feet (XII. 49).

54. ll. 7–8. cf. Canto IX.

58. ll. 7–8. Diana, surprised by the hunter Actaeon while she was bathing, turned him into a stag, and he was torn to pieces by his own hounds. Ariosto had seen the painting of this subject by Titian.

69. l. 4. Phidias, the Greek sculptor, made statues in ivory which were turned on a lathe.

70. l. 3. The other goddesses were Juno and Minerva.
    l. 5. *the queen*. Helen.

71. Croton (modern Crotone) became an Achaean colony in the eighth century B.C. It is situated in the toe of Italy. Zeuxis of Heraclea in Lucania is said by Pliny to have lived at the end of the fourth century B.C. At Croton he painted an ideal picture of Helen compiled from several models.

73. ll. 5–6. Ariosto seems to have forgotten that most of the Irish forces have gone to France (x. 87–8).

79. l. 2. The king of England is in Paris (VIII. 27–8).

80. ll. 7–8. Orlando had left Brigliadoro at St Malo rather than risk his life against the Ebudans (IX. 60).

83. l. 4. This is the illusory voice of Angelica (XII. 4 et seq.).

CANTO XII

1. l. 1. *her mother's haunts*. Mount Ida. Ceres' mother is Cybele.
   ll. 2–3. The giant Enceladus, struck by Jove's thunderbolt, is buried beneath Mount Etna.

1–2. This description of Ceres' grief and search for her daughter Persephone (Proserpina) is inspired by Claudian's *De raptu Proserpinae*, I. 138 et seq. and by Ovid's *Metamorphoses*, V. The madness of Orlando seems here to be anticipated.

11. It is not explained how Gradasso, Brandimarte, Ferraù and Sacripante have been lured to the palace, but Atlante's reason for keeping them captive there is made plain in stanza 22.

20. l. 3. Bradamante's castle is on the river Dordogne.

31. l. 3. *King Troiano's brother*. Almonte.

48. The invulnerability of Ferraù, except in his navel, is already established in Boiardo and in the Chronicle of the Pseudo-Turpin.

49. The invulnerability of Orlando, who can be wounded only in the soles of his feet, is reminiscent of that of Achilles, vulnerable only in the heel.

54. This situation of the knights fighting for a trophy that has gone echoes the similar situation between Ferraù and Rinaldo in 1. 19–20. On both occasions Angelica is involved.

59. ll. 5–6. Ferraù, being a Saracen, curses in the name of Mahomet (Mahound) and of Termagant, an imaginary deity, held in medieval times to be worshipped by Mahommedans.

62. l. 8. In Pulci's *Morgante*, and in the epic *La Spagna*, Ferraù is killed by Orlando on a bridge.

63. Angelica, for the first time, feels regret on someone else's behalf. This perhaps anticipates the change that is about to come over her.

64. l. 6. The tradition of Ferraù's ugliness is found also in Boiardo.

69. Both Manilardo and Alzirdo exist already in Boiardo. Norizia may be Nigrizia (the Sudan); Boiardo says it is a thousand miles from Ceuta. Tremisen (cf. stanza 73) is perhaps Tlemcen in Algeria; cf. Chaucer, *Canterbury Tales*, *Prologue*, ll. 61–3.

92. l. 1. *A grizzled beldam*. This is Gabrina, who is not named until XXI. 50.

93. Isabella's situation in the cave is inspired by a similar story by Apuleius in his *Golden Ass*, IV.

CANTO XIII

4. ll. 1–2. Isabella's father was Maricoldo, King of Galicia. In Boiardo's poem he was killed by Orlando, but this event is not included in the present work. (*Orl. Inn.*, II. xxiii. 6, 61). He is mentioned in XIV. 13 as having been replaced by Serpentino.

11. l. 5. *Santa Marta*. There is a bay of this name in Galicia. It is long and narrow, and this is no doubt why Zerbino had arranged for the galley to be hidden there.

15. l. 1. *Mugia*. A village in Galicia between Finisterre and Corunna.

36. l. 6. *Chiron's subdivision*. In Dante's *Inferno* the centaur Chiron and his fellow-centaurs Nessus and Pholus guard the souls of those who have committed violence against others. By shooting arrows at them, they compel them to remain immersed in the river of boiling blood which forms the first division of the seventh circle of Hell (*Inferno*, XII).

40. l. 2. *Turpin*. The historical Turpin was Archbishop of Reims at the time of Charlemagne. In the *Chanson de Roland* he is a

warrior-bishop and dies at Roncesvalles. A chronicle was attributed to him, the first five chapters of which were written by an eleventh-century monk of Compostella, the remainder between 1109 and 1119 by a monk of Vienna. It was the custom of authors of Carolingian epics to refer to Turpin as their source, to lend authority to their narrations. Boiardo and Ariosto continue to do so in jest.

42. ll. 7–8. The knight is Marfisa. The meeting occurs in xx. 106.

44. ll. 2–4. The captive knight is Zerbino (xxiii. 53).

45. l. 6. *Languedoc*. A region of southern France, west of Provence, between the Rhône and the Pyrenees, so called from the dialect of French spoken there.

59. l. 4. *Fair Isabella*. This is Isabella d'Este, the daughter of Ercole I and Eleanor of Aragon (1474–1539), an exact contemporary of Ariosto. She married Francesco Gonzaga, Marquess of Mantua. She was celebrated for her knowledge of literature and the arts and as a patron of artists and writers. For thirty years she helped to guide Mantua through the difficulties and dangers which beset her husband's rule. Her court at Mantua was a brilliant centre of culture. Ariosto read cantos of his poem aloud to her when he visited her there, bringing congratulations from her brother Alfonso on the birth of her first son.

ll. 7–8. Mantua stands on the river Mincio. Its name was said to derive from the prophetess Manto, the wife of Tiresias and mother of Ocnus (Virgil, *Aeneid*, x. 198–200).

60. l. 2. *her most worthy husband*. Francesco Gonzaga, Marquess of Mantua.

62. ll. 1–2. *Beatrice*. This is Beatrice d'Este (1475–97), the sister of Isabella, who in 1491 married Ludovico Sforza (1451–1508), first Regent, and later Duke, of Milan. She died in childbirth, aged 22. 'Beatrice' in Italian means she who blesses or gives beatitude.

63. The Snakes, originally an emblem of the Visconti family, became the symbol of Milan. The six years of Ludovico's marriage to Beatrice (1491–7) coincided with a period of fame and success for the Sforza rule. The brilliance of Ludovico's court, his patronage of Leonardo da Vinci, the presence of the talented and ambitious Beatrice, combined to make the duchy of Milan renowned all over Europe. Ludovico, who had acted as regent since 1480 on behalf of his nephew, Gian Galeazzo, was secretly invested with the dukedom in 1494 by the Emperor Maximilian I. That same year his nephew died and he was cho-

sen duke by the Milanese. Two years after the death of Beatrice he was driven from power by Louis XII and, though reinstated for a short time by the Swiss, he was delivered by them to the French in 1500 and died a prisoner eight years later in the castle of Loches.

63. l. 4. *the strait*. The Straits of Gibraltar.

l. 5. *your native sea*. The Mediterranean.

l. 7. *the king of France*. Louis XII.

64. l. 1. *other Beatrices*. The two Beatrices mentioned here are (1) the daughter of Aldobrandino III, who married Andrew II, King of Hungary in 1234, and (2) probably the daughter of Azzo Novello, who entered the convent of St Anthony in Ferrara. She was beatified in memory of her generosity to the convent.

67. *Ricciarda*. This is the daughter of Tommaso, Marquess of Saluzzo, who married Nicholas III and who died in 1474. Her sons Ercole and Sigismondo were disinherited in favour of Leonello and Borso, her husband's illegitimate sons by Stella dei Tolomei, and sent to the court of Aragon. On the death of Borso, Ricciarda saw the legitimate line re-established with the succession of her son Ercole.

68–9. Eleanor of Aragon, the daughter of Ferdinand I of Aragon, King of Naples, was the wife of Ercole I and mother of Alfonso I, Ippolito and Isabella. Ariosto, aged 19, composed a lament in *terza rima* for her death, which occurred in 1493.

69–71. Lucrezia Borgia (1480–1519) was the daughter of Pope Alexander VI and the second wife of Alfonso d'Este, whom she married in 1501 after the death of Anna Sforza. She had been previously married to Giovanni Sforza, lord of Pesaro. This marriage was annulled and in 1494 she married Alfonso of Aragon, Duke of Bisceglie, who was assassinated in 1500. Alfonso was thus her third husband; she bore him seven children.

70. This stanza echoes lines from an eclogue written by Ariosto on the conspiracy of Giulio and Ferrante against Alfonso and Ippolito (111. 60–62). Referring to the arrival in Ferrara of Lucrezia, Tirsi, a shepherd in the eclogue, says that she outshone all other brides as silver surpasses pewter, gold surpasses copper, the rose the wild poppy, the ever-green laurel the pale willow.

71. l. 5. Lucrezia died when her eldest son, Ercole, was 11 years old.

72. Renée de France, the daughter of Louis XII and Anne of Brittany, married Ercole II in 1528. She inclined towards

Calvinism, and adherents to the Reformed religion gathered at her court. Of these the best-known are Calvin himself, under an assumed name, and the French poet Clément Marot. She was obliged to withdraw to a convent in 1554, and died in France in 1575. She was admired for her qualities of mind and character. Her leanings towards Calvinism may not have been known to Ariosto.

73. l. 1. *Celano's countess.* She may be the daughter of Ferdinand I d'Este who married the Count of Celano.

Alda of Salogna. It is not known who she was.

l. 3. *Blanche Marie.* The daughter of Alfonso of Aragon, King of Naples, and wife of Leonello d'Este.

Catalogna. Catalonia.

l. 5. *Lippa of Bologna.* Lippa Ariosti, of the poet's own family, famed for her beauty, mistress of Obizzo III, by whom she had eleven children. He is said to have married her on his death-bed in order to legitimize them.

l. 6. *Sicily's princess.* Beatrice, daughter of Charles II of Anjou, the king of Sicily. She married Azzo VIII in 1305.

CANTO XIV

2. This is a reference to the battle of Ravenna (11 April 1512) at which the French defeated the Spanish, largely owing to the skill with which Alfonso deployed his artillery. Ariosto visited the scene of the battle, and was present at the sack of Ravenna by the French, which occurred the following day. He refers to the cruelty he witnessed there in a minor poem, *Capitolo*, XVI.

3. ll. 3–4. Alfonso advanced his artillery and attacked the Spaniards on the flank just as the French were about to be driven back.

ll. 5–8. Alfonso had a hundred men-at-arms and two hundred light cavalry. Some of them were knighted for gallantry after the battle.

4. l. 3. An oak with golden acorns was the emblem of Pope Julius II, an ally of the Spaniards.

l. 4. Red and yellow were the colours of the Spanish banners.

l. 6. The lily is the emblem of France.

l. 8. *Fabrizio.* This is Fabrizio Colonna, commander of the papal troops. (His name, Colonna, means column.)

5. ll. 1–4. Alfonso took Fabrizio Colonna prisoner and then liberated him and restored him to Rome.

ll. 6–8. The Spaniards fled in disorder before the French attack, despite the use of thirty vehicles with armoured or spiked wheels.

6. l. 4. *The captain of the French.* Gaston de Foix, who was killed while pursuing the Spaniards.

l. 8. *brother dukes.* e.g. Duke Alfonso.

7. l. 3. *Jove's tempest.* This is a reference to Pope Julius II, who would have made the Estensi pay dearly for their alliance with the French if the victory had gone the other way.

8. l. 1. *King Louis.* Louis XII.

ll. 3–8. Ariosto alludes here to excesses committed by the French troops during the sack of Ravenna.

9. ll. 1–3. Ravenna ought to have taken warning from the sack of Brescia, which took place on 19 February 1512.

ll. 4–5. Rimini and Faenza surrendered to the French without resistance.

l. 6. *Trivulzio.* Giangiacomo Trivulzio (1436–1515) was a general in the service of the Estensi in 1511 against the Pope. He was Governor of Milan from 1499 to 1500.

11–27. The names of Spanish and African captains are taken mainly from Boiardo, who derived them from the romantic epic tradition. (See also Index.)

12. ll. 4–5. *The brother of the king.* This is Falsirone, the brother of Marsilio.

15. ll. 5–8. Morgante is the giant in Pulci's epic of that name. Boiardo makes him a noble at the court of Marsilio with the title of king. Ariosto makes him an exiled king, like Malzarise.

17. ll. 5–8. Martasino, King of the Garamantes, an ancient people of central Africa, had been killed by Bradamante.

20. ll. 1–2. The brother of Ferraù is Isoliero. Brunello had been left tied to a tree by Bradamante when she took the magic ring from him. Disobeying Melissa's instructions, she spared his life (IV. 13–15).

25–26. Rodomonte, son of Ulieno and descendant of Nimrod, whose armour he wears, is the king of Sarza, in Algeria. His strength and prowess are superhuman. From his name is derived the word 'rodomontade'.

27. The death of Dardinello, son of Almonte, gives rise to the famous episode in which Medoro and Cloridano search the battlefield for his body (XVIII. 172–87).

30. Mandricardo, the son of Agricane, is in search of Orlando to avenge his father. His prowess is such that he has won the arms of Hector, all except his sword, Durindana, which is in the possession of Orlando. Mandricardo and Rodomonte are the

two most powerful warriors on the pagan side and they become rivals for the love of Doralice, thus balancing Orlando and Rinaldo.

32. l. 4. The warrior is Orlando, who is disguised by black armour (VIII. 85, 91).

38. ll. 7–8. At Otricoli, near Terni, there was formerly a small peninsula formed by a loop made by the Tiber.

40. ll. 5–6. Ariosto has moved from spring to summer with un-expected speed (XII. 72).

50. l. 2. The name of Doralice and a brief indication of Rodomonte's love for her are found in Boiardo's *Orlando Innamorato*. In the episode related here some commentators have seen an allusion to an actual event, namely the abduction of a lady-in-waiting at the court of Urbino, the promised bride of Giambattista Caracciolo of Naples, by Cesare Borgia. There are also literary antecedents for the development of the story (e.g. *Guiron le Courtois* and *Decamerone*, II, 7).

61–3. The night spent by Mandricardo and Doralice in the shep-herd's hut anticipates the episode of Angelica and Medoro.

64. ll. 7–8. They are Orlando, Zerbino and Isabella.

65. The story of Mandricardo and Doralice is resumed in XXIII. 70.

71. ll. 6–8. Charlemagne refers here to a crusade in his time (legen-dary) and to his defence of the Pope against the Longobards.

88. St Benedict, regarded as the founder of Western monasticism, lived from A.D. 480 to 543. In medieval Christian belief, the prophet Elijah (ninth century B.C.) was regarded as the founder of monasticism in general and of the Carmelite order in par-ticular.

89. l. 1. *Pythagoras*, the Greek philosopher (582–500 B.C.), imposed a ban of silence of five years on his scholars. *Archytas* (*c.* 400 B.C.) was a Pythagorean philosopher of Taranto.

92–4. The description of the house of Sleep is based on Ovid's *Metamorphoses*, XI. 592 et seq.

106. l. 5. *Both river-gates*. Where the Seine enters and leaves Paris.

120. l. 4. Mallea is a low-lying, marshy district to the left of Volano, one of the two mouths of the Po, where wild boar abounded.

122. ll. 3–4. i.e. the Gulf of the North Sea.

124. ll. 2–8. Moschino was the nickname of Antonio Magnanimo, a drunkard at the court of the Estensi and a boon companion of students.

CANTO XV

2. Ariosto alludes here to Alfonso's victory over the Venetians on the river Po at the battle of Polesella in 1509. Francolino is about ten kilometres from Ferrara.

6. l. 1. *a gate*. To the south-west (XIV. 105).

16. l. 5. East India does not refer to India but the East generally.

l. 8. *the land of Thomas*. The apostle Thomas was martyred at Maliapur in Maabar (near Madras) which was called St Thomas' land. In the maps of the sixteenth century, Maabar is identified with the peninsula of Indochina, which is shown extended south of the Malay peninsula.

18. Stanzas 18 to 36 were added to the 1532 edition of the poem, possibly to please Charles V, with whom the Estensi were at that time on good terms.

19. l. 6. *the continent*. Africa.

20. In XXVII. 55 (Vol. II of this translation) Ariosto says that Gradasso sails round Africa to reach France.

21. Andronica begins her prophecy of the explorations of Spanish and Portuguese navigators.

ll. 6–8. She refers here to the rounding of the Cape of Good Hope by Vasco da Gama in 1497. The Cape is south of the Tropic of Capricorn.

22. ll. 1–2. The navigators discover that the Atlantic and the Indian Ocean are not divided.

ll. 5–8. Andronica alludes here to the voyages of Columbus and Vespucci.

23. The banner of Charles V was raised by Cortés in Mexico.

24. ll. 7–8. It has been said that Charles V was so gratified by Ariosto's praise of him in stanzas 24–7 that he issued him a diploma of poet laureate.

25. Charles V was born at Ghent on the Rhine on 24 Febuary 1500, the son of the Archduke Philip of Austria and of Joan of Aragon, Queen of Castile.

26. l. 8. This line echoes '*Et fiat unum ovile et unus pastor*' (John, x. 16).

27. l. 5. This is a reference to the conquest of Mexico by Hernando Cortés.

28. l. 1. Prospero Colonna, a Roman prince, was a cousin of Fabrizio (XIV. 4). He was a condottiere who fought first for the French and then for Charles V.

28. ll. 2-3. Francesco d'Avalos, Marquess of Pescara, Spanish captain, married Vittoria Colonna.

l. 6. *A youth of Vasto.* Alfonso d'Avalos, Marquess of Vasto and Pescara, who became captain of the Spanish army. It is thought that this and the following stanza were written after 1531 when Ariosto was sent on an embassy to Alfonso d'Avalos, who commanded the imperial troops at Mantua, to seek help against Pope Clement VII. Alfonso received him graciously and granted him a pension.

29. ll. 5-6. Prospero Colonna and the Marquess of Pescara being dead, Alfonso d'Avalos was appointed captain-general at the age of 26.

30. ll. 5-8. Andrea Doria cleared the Mediterranean of pirates. He fought first for the French, then for the Spaniards, when he expelled the French from Genoa and Naples.

31. ll. 1-4. Pompey cleared the Mediterranean of pirates by order of the Roman Senate.

32. In 1529 Charles V set out from Barcelona for Bologna to receive the crown. He disembarked at Genoa, having been escorted by Andrea Doria. The Emperor invested him with the dominion of Genoa but Andrea Doria restored the city to the people, who reconstituted it a republic.

34. ll. 7-8. Melfi in Basilicata was the stronghold whence the Normans gained control of all Apulia.

37. ll. 1-2. The Persian Gulf was called by the ancients 'Magorum sinus'.

39. l. 8. *Heroopolis.* City of ancient Egypt in the Gulf of Suez.

40. l. 1. *canal of Trajan.* Built by the Pharaohs and restored by Trajan, it connected the Nile with the Red Sea.

41. ll. 1-4. Ruggiero rode Rabicano to Logistilla's kingdom and left on the hippogriff. Astolfo took Rabicano when he departed.

50. The dwelling of Caligorante recalls that of Cacus in the *Aeneid*, VIII. 190-97.

56. Ariosto here echoes Homer, *Odyssey*, VIII. 272-366.

57. The story of Chloris appears to be Ariosto's own invention.

64. ll. 1-4. Ariosto here refers to the Mamelukes, who constituted a bodyguard of the Sultan of Egypt. They were instituted in the thirteenth century.

67. l. 8. The white and black, associated respectively with Grifone and Aquilante, refer to the dresses of their two protectresses (stanza 72). The story of these two sons of Oliver and their battle against Orrilo and a crocodile is continued from Boiardo's narrative.

72. ll. 7–8. *two birds of prey*. An eagle and a griffin (hence their names).
73. l. 1. *Gismonda*. Their mother.

 l. 5. Ariosto refers to the author of *Uggeri il Danese*, in which Aquilante and Grifone are said to be the sons of Ricciardetto, not of Oliver, as in Boiardo.

75. l. 6. Astolfo, as the son of the king of England, has the leopard on his ensign.
97. ll. 1–2. The legend of Charlemagne's conquest of Palestine is apparently founded on a gift of the keys of the Holy Sepulchre and of Mount Calvary from the Patriarch of Jerusalem in 800. Einhard, *Vita Karoli*, Chapter 16, asserts that the Caliph Harun al Rashid agreed to place the Holy Sepulchre under Charlemagne's jurisdiction. The monk of St Gall, *De Carlo Magno*, Book 11, Chapter 9, improves further upon the story.

CANTO XVI

4. Orrigille, the 'base object' of Grifone's love, appears in Boiardo (*Orl. Inn.* I. xxviii. 52; II. xx. 7) where she tricks Orlando who is also in love with her. She becomes enamoured of Grifone, but, falling ill, is unable to accompany him to Cyprus when he goes there to joust. Ariosto picks up the story from this point.
6. Grifone's rival is Martano of Antioch.
8. The king of Damascus is Norandino (cf. XVII. 23 et seq.).
17. ll. 3–4. cf. XV. 6–9.

 l. 7. *both the Guidos*. Guido of Burgundy and Guido of Montfort.
18. l. 5. *who so many men had lost*. 11,028 precisely (XV. 4); they still have 200,000 left (stanza 16, line 7).
20. cf. XIV. 121–30.
21. l. 2. Rodomonte has inherited his armour from Nimrod, his ancestor (XIV, 118–19).
23. ll. 1–2. The simile of the tiger echoes *Aeneid*, IX. 730.

 l. 4. *the mountain*. Epomeo, on Ischia (cf. XXVI. 52), not Etna, in Ariosto's version of the legend.
27. ll. 5–6. Cardinal Ippolito was present at the siege of Padua in 1509 when the Emperor Maximilian's troops used bombards.
28. l. 7. *Michael*. The Archangel Michael (XIV. 96).
30. ll. 7–8. These gates are on the north of Paris and on the right of the Seine.
33. l. 3. *Your king*. Otto of England, who is in Paris.
46. l. 4. Puliano, here struck dead, appears to be resurrected in XL. 73.

67. ll. 7–8. Ariosto distributed these territories differently in XIV. 13, 15.
81. ll. 5–6. Bambirago and Agricalte are resurrected in XL. 73.
85. ll. 7–8. Edward and Herman arrived at Paris from the north-east, entering through the gates of St Denis and St Martin.

CANTO XVII

1. ll. 7–8. Of the five examples of cruel tyrants mentioned here, four are also cited in III. 33.
2. l. 1. *the youngest Antonine*. Ariosto may mean Commodus (Emperor 180–192), the last of the Antonine dynasty, or Eliogabalus (Emperor 218–222), who assumed the name of Marcus Aurelius Antoninus.

   l. 2. Maximinus (Emperor 235–238) was the son of a shepherd.

   l. 4. Creon, legendary king of Thebes, sentenced Antigone to be buried alive because she gave burial to her brother Polynices.

   ll. 4–6. Mezentius, King of Caere (Cervetri) or Agylla (Etruria), was notorious for his cruelty. Ariosto read of him in Virgil, *Aeneid*, VIII. 478–88.
3. l. 1. Attila, King (or chieftain) of the Huns (433–53), was called the Scourge of God for his atrocities. He made himself master of all the peoples of Germany and Scythia and overran Illyria, Thrace, Macedon and Greece. In 452 he invaded Italy and devastated Aquileia, Milan, Padua and other regions.

   l. 2. Ezzellino III da Romano (1194–1259), a Ghibelline noble, son-in-law of Emperor Frederick II and Imperial Vicar in the Marca Trevigiana, was notorious for his cruelty, especially for his massacre of the citizens of Padua.

   ll. 5–8. The slaughter after Hannibal's battles at Lake Trasimene, Cannae or Trebbia is less than that which resulted from the battle of Agnadello on the river Adda in 1509 (when the French defeated the Venetians), of Brescia on the Mella in 1512 (followed by the sack of the city by the French), of Ravenna on the Ronco in 1512 (when the French with the help of the Estensi defeated the Spaniards and afterwards sacked the city), or of Fornovo on the Taro in 1495, won by Charles VIII (XIV. 1–9).

   l. 8. The wolves probably signify the foreign powers which invade Italy.

7–8. The rallying words of Charlemagne to his fleeing army echo the words of Mnestheus to the Trojans fleeing before Turnus in the *Aenid*, ix. 781–7.

9–13. These stanzas are modelled on the attack of Pyrrhus upon the palace of Priam in the *Aeneid*, ii. 445–52; 469–75.

11. Rodomonte's armour, caked with mud in xiv. 120, has here regained its pristine gleam.

19. l. 1. *Two crystal streams*. The Barada and the Avai. cf. Robin Fedden, *Syria and the Lebanon*, John Murray, 1965, pp. 16–17; cf. also 2 Kings v, 12.

22. l. 4. *a gentle knight*. This knight is never named.

23. The story of Norandino and Lucina is continued from Boiardo's *Orlando Innamorato* (ii. xix. 56).

26. l. 5. The king of Cyprus is named Tibiano in Boiardo's epic.

27. l. 2. *that deceitful sea*. i.e. the sea of Crete.

29. This monster, or land orc, is based partly on Homer's and partly on Virgil's description of Polyphemus, cf. *Odyssey*, ix, *Aeneid*, iii.

40. l. 8. In a letter to Lorenzo dei Medici, Amerigo Vespucci reported that he had heard of cannibals who eat only the flesh of males. Ariosto may have known of this.

63. l. 3. In Boiardo's version of the story, the blind orc fell into a hole while pursuing Mandricardo.

65. l. 7. *Satalia*. The Gulf of Adalia, north-west of Cyprus.

70. l. 8. *a snow-white maid*. The protectress of Grifone, clad in white (xv. 67, 72).

72–3. The use of blazonry by the Saracens is briefly mentioned by Joinville in his memoirs of the crusade of St Louis, 1245–50. In *Saracenic Heraldry* (1933), Dr L. A. Mayer shows that the devices used by Muslims of amirial rank in Syria, Palestine and Egypt consisted basically of emblems denoting various offices, e.g. a cup for a cup-bearer, a pen-box for a secretary, and a sword for an armour-bearer. Such devices had not the importance and significance attached to a coat-of-arms in the western countries, and did not develop into a lasting system of heraldry. cf. xiv. 114; xviii. 147, 149.

75. ll. 1–2. '*the most Christian*'. 'Christianissimus' was the title of the King of France in 1469. 'Catholic' was the title of the King of Spain from the time of the expulsion of the Moors from Granada.

ll. 5–6. Jerusalem was freed from the Infidel in 1099 by Geoffrey of Bouillon (First Crusade) and re-taken in 1187.

76. ll. 1–4. The Moors began their conquest of Spain in the eighth

century and continued to harass the country down to the fifteenth. They were expelled from Spain in 1492. Now, says Ariosto, instead of attacking Africa, the Spaniards ravage Italy.

77. l. 1. *Switzers*. The Swiss mercenaries.

ll. 5–8. The Turks had extended their conquests as far as Greece after taking Constantinople in 1453.

78. ll. 4–5. Ariosto refers here to the Donation of Constantine which purported to entitle the Papacy to control the western portion of Constantine's empire.

ll. 6–8. *The Pactolus and Hermus*. Two rivers in Lydia, Asia Minor, said to be rich in auriferous sand. *That land*. Probably Persia or Armenia.

79. l. 1. *great Leo*. This is Pope Leo X (Giovanni dei Medici), elected to the Papacy in 1513. This stanza must have been added as one of the finishing touches to the first edition of the poem.

82. These arms belong to Marfisa, who in Boiardo's epic had left them aside to pursue Brunello, who had stolen her sword (XVIII. 108–9).

129. l. 2. The 'ancient nurse' of the sun is Tethys, the sea.

CANTO XVIII

1–2. These stanzas are an example of Ariosto's fulsome and flattering praise of his patron. Cardinal Ippolito was not celebrated for his magnanimity or justice. (They may be ironic.)

10. l. 1. *Guido*. Either Guido of Burgundy or Guido of Montfort.

12. ll. 7–8. cf. XIV. 118–19.

22. The withdrawal of Rodomonte is reminiscent of that of Ajax in the *Iliad*, XI. 547–55 and of Turnus in the *Aeneid*, IX. 789–818.

26. l. 1. *Dame Discord*. cf. XIV. 76 et seq.

l. 2. *the Archangel*. Michael (XIV. 81–6).

29. l. 2. cf. XIV. 52 et seq.

35. This simile, based on *Iliad*, XVIII. 318–22, was imitated by Statius in *Thebaid*, IV. 315–16 and by Poliziano in *Stanze*, I. 39.

36. ll. 4–6. Ariosto here echoes Dante, *Inferno*, XXV, 79–81.

38. ll. 7–8. The gate of St Germain is to the west, that of St Victor to the south-east.

39. l. 1. The gate of St Marcel is to the south.

53. l. 5. i.e. Bogio is the count of Vergalle.

59. l. 4. i.e. in Damascus.

65. ll. 6–7. Horatius Cocles held the bridge in Rome against the

advancing Etruscans, led by Lars Porsenna. Ariosto has in mind Petrarch's evocation of this heroic feat in his *Trionfo della Fama*, 41.

93. l. 1. Ariosto here echoes Petrarch's reference to Caesar in Egypt 'bound by Cleopatra among flowers and grass' in *Trionfo dell'Amore*, 1, 89–90.

ll. 4–6. Lucina has not yet returned from Nicosia. Ariosto does not complete this story.

98–9. This is the first appearance in this work of Marfisa, the woman warrior who balances Bradamante on the pagan side. She exists already in Boiardo, who makes her a twin sister of Ruggiero (I. xvii. 58; II. i. 70).

101. ll. 1–2. i.e. at the siege of Albracca, as narrated by Boiardo.

103. l. 6. *Her lover*. Tithonus.

106. l. 2. *the first*. The trophy won by Grifone in the first tourney, which consisted partly of Marfisa's arms (XVII. 82).

109. The theft of Marfisa's sword by Brunello and her pursuit of him are related by Boiardo, loc. cit.

122. l. 4. *Orrilo*. cf. XV. 65 et seq.

135. l. 3. *Luni*. An ancient port of Tuscany on the mouth of the river Magra.

136. l. 2. *Venus' isle*. Cyprus.

140. This is the last mention of Lucina.

147. Dardinello bears his father Almonte's heraldic colours, which Orlando, who slew him, has adopted as his own.

151. l. 8. *Mambrin's helm*. Rinaldo took the helmet of Mambrino when he slew him (I. 28).

153. This stanza is modelled on the *Iliad*, VIII. 306–8 and on the *Aeneid*, IX. 434–7.

155. l. 8. *Guy*. Either Guido of Burgundy or Guido of Montfort (cf. 10. l. 1).

161. l. 5. There is a proverbial saying that Fortune wears a forelock but is bald behind, related to the expression 'to seize Time by the forelock'.

165. The literary antecedents of the episode of Medoro and Cloridano are the *Aeneid*, IX. 176–449 (the story of Euryalus and Nisus), and Statius, *Thebaid*, X. 347–448 (the story of Hopleus and Dymas).

174. l. 2. *Alfeo*. This may be an allusion to Luca Gaurico, a Neapolitan astrologer and astronomer, who became Bishop of Cividale and was known at the court of Ferrara; or to Pietro di Pisa, a scientist at the court of Charlemagne credited with occult powers.

177. l. 2. Andropono, a priest, was killed in XIV. 124.
180. l. 4. The fleurs-de-lis of the banner of France were granted as an emblem in reward for exceptional courage.
181. In the original, the word *volta* is used three times in the rhyme position.
184. l. 2. *as three in one*. As Diana, Hecate and Selene.
185. ll. 3–4. Endymion was the lover of Selene.

l. 7. Montmartre is to the north-west of Paris; Montlhéry is due south. Medoro and Cloridano were evidently facing west.

CANTO XIX

12. l. 1. Creon, tyrant of Thebes, prohibited the burial of the Greeks killed outside the city wall, among whom was Polynices.

l. 4. *King Almonte's son*. Dardinello.
17. In XII. 65 Angelica, entering a forest, found a young man lying wounded between two dead companions. It is now revealed that this is Medoro, lying between the bodies of Dardinello and Cloridano.
18. l. 1. Ruggiero gave Angelica the magic ring to protect her from the light of the shield which he used against the sea monster (X. 107–8).
19. l. 2. cf. I. 77–9.
22. l. 3. *dittany*. This is *dictamnum*, a plant believed by the ancients to have curative properties. Aeneas is cured by Venus by means of it (*Aeneid*, XII. 411 – 15).
31. l. 1. *Circassian*. Sacripante, King of Circassia.
35. ll. 7–8. The love of Dido and Aeneas was first consummated in a cave where they took shelter from a storm (*Aeneid*, IV. 160–172).
37. l. 3. *India (named Cathay)*. The region of the Far East named Cathay.
38. Ariosto refers here to an episode in *Orl. Inn.*, II, xi. 48 et seq., in which the brother of Brandimarte, Ziliante, imprisoned by Morgana, is set free by Orlando. The gift of the bracelet is Ariosto's invention.
39. l. 5. *the Isle of Tears*. Ebuda; cf. X. 93 et seq.
40. ll. 7–8. i.e. the Pyrenees.
42. The madman is Orlando.
48. l. 3. Ettino has not been firmly identified. It has been suggested to be Tines in Crete or Udine (Utinum) in Friuli.

50. l. 6. *St Elmo's fire*. An electrical phenomenon which appears on the mast when a storm reaches its end.

52. l. 2. *his black mouth*. Because the south-west wind blows from Africa.

54. l. 2. *Laiazzo*. Aiazzo, in the Gulf of Alessandretta.

61. l. 3. *his horn*. This is the magic horn given to Astolfo by Logistilla (xv. 14–15).

84. l. 3. *pallone*. A game in which the ball is battered continually against the wall, as in Fives or Squash.
    ll. 6–8. Ariosto here reveals that Marfisa's arms are magic. This was the case also in Boiardo's epic.

CANTO XX

1. l. 5. *Harpalyce*. The daughter of Harpalycus, King of Thrace, who defended her country against Neoptolomus, son of Achilles (*Aeneid*, I. 316–17).
   Camilla. The woman warrior of the *Aeneid*, VII. 803, XI. 539–828. She was the daughter of the king of the Volsci and allied with Turnus.
   Clio. The Muse of history.
   l. 7. *Sappho* and *Corinna*. Greek poets.

5. l. 6. *Pontus*. A region of Asia Minor in which, according to Carolingian romances, Rinaldo and the other paladins achieved fame.
   l. 7. *Clairmont*. The ancestral line of Orlando and Rinaldo (see Table, p. 735).
   l. 8. *Almonte's slayer*. Orlando.

6. ll. 1–2. i.e. Rinaldo. It is not known who Chiariello was.
   ll. 4–5. In earlier romances Guidone is the son of Rinaldo by Costanza of Dacia. Ariosto here makes him Rinaldo's half-brother.

7. l. 7. *Melibea*. Ancient city of Thessaly, situated between Mounts Ossa and Pelion. Argilone was Guidone's predecessor in Alessandretta (stanza 61).

13. The story of Phalanthus is told by Justinus (*Historiae Philippicae* III, iv). He is the legendary founder of Taranto. Ariosto adds many details of his own invention (e.g. that he is the son of Clytemnestra) and changes the setting of the story from Sparta to Crete.

14. l. 2. *Idomeneus*. Descended from Minos, tyrant of Crete; he sacrificed his son to Neptune in accordance with a vow.

24. l. 7. *Orontea*. Her name, a symbol of a woman who has re-nounced love, is the title of an opera by the seventeenth-century composer, Cesti. It has been edited by Victor Crowther and performed in an English version (libretto translated by Barbara Reynolds).

42. l. 6. *Medea*. A symbol of cruelty. She killed her children when she was abandoned by Jason.

60. l. 1. *About two thousand years*. This would roughly represent the time from the Trojan War (*c.* 1200 B.C.) to Charlemagne in the eighth century A.D.

66. l. 2. Astolfo's father, Otto, King of England, is the brother of Aymon, Guido's father. Hence Astolfo and Guido are cousins.

76. l. 2. The merchants and mariners were on board with the paladins.

82. l. 3. *Calisto*. Seduced by Jove, she was changed by Juno into the constellation of the Bear or Plough.

100. l. 4. *Malea*. Now Malia, a promontory in the Peloponnese.
l. 6. *The Greek Morea coast*. Of the Peloponnese.

102. ll. 1–3. Bradamante is in Atlante's magic palace of illusions (XIII. 79).

105. l. 3. *The castle's lord*. Pinabello (XXII. 52 et seq.).

107. l. 1. *the agèd crone*. Gabrina, the guardian of Isabella in the pirates' cave, who fled when Orlando killed them (XIII. 42).

111. cf. II. 69–76.

112. cf. IV. 38.

117–18. Zerbino has failed to find the knight who wounded Medoro (XIX. 13–14).

135. cf. XII. 91–2.

CANTO XXI

5. l. 2. *Ermonide of Holland*. A new character, invented by Ariosto.

13. l. 7. *Heraclius*. Emperor of Constantinople from 610 to 641, more than a century before Charlemagne.

16. l. 2. *Cape of Glossa*. Cape Chimera, a promontory of Epirus, known to the ancients as Acroceraunus ('thunder heights'). The simile is modelled on Virgil's *Aeneid*, IV. 445–6. The story of Gabrina's plot to seduce Filandro is taken partly from the romance *Girone il Cortese* and partly from Apuleius' *Golden Ass*, x.

57. ll. 4–6. Orestes, the son of Agamemnon, killed his mother Clytemnestra, and her lover Aegisthus, to avenge his father, and was then tormented by remorse.

CANTO XXII

2. ll. 1–3. It has been said that Cardinal Ippolito, Duke Alfonso
and Isabella, Marchioness of Mantua, insisted that the story of
Gabrina and Filandro should be included, as it was based on an
actual occurrence.

ll. 7–8. *Hypermnestra.* The only one of the fifty daughters of
Danaus who did not kill her husband on his wedding-night in
obedience to their father's command.

4. l. 4. The dead knight is Pinabello; cf. stanza 97, and XXIII. 39.

l. 7. *In the Levant.* In Alessandretta (XX. 88 et seq.).

6. l. 2. *Prusa.* The capital of Bithynia, now Bursia.

l. 3. *the sea.* The Dardanelles.

10. l. 3. *Rouen.* Astolfo, blown somewhat off course, lands at Rouen,
instead of at Calais as he had intended.

12. l. 2. *a peasant.* This is Atlante, disguised.

13. ll. 6–8. i.e. Atlante's palace of illusions.

16. ll. 3–6. cf. XV. 14.

24. ll. 2–5. cf. IV. 45 et seq.

ll. 5–6. cf. X. 66–8.

ll. 7–8. cf. X. 69 et seq.

25. cf. XI. 1–15.

27. ll. 1–3. cf. VIII. 17–18.

ll. 4–5. i.e. Alcina.

ll. 6–8. cf. X. 66–8.

30. l. 8. The knight is Bradamante; cf. XXIII. 10 et seq.

35. ll. 4–5. Ruggiero I and Ruggiero II, grandfather and father of
the Ruggiero in question, are revealed to him as having been
Christians in XXXVI. 3–4 (Vol. II of this translation).

36. ll. 3–6. Vallombrosa is a fictitious abbey. Ariosto may have had
in mind the abbey of that name near Florence, founded in the
eleventh century. The lines by Ariosto are written up on the
wall by the abbey gate, not quite legitimately.

38. l. 8. *A youth.* Ricciardetto.

39. l. 1. *a gentle maiden.* Fiordispina.

47. l. 4. *Ponthieu.* The domain of the Maganza family, to which
Pinabello belongs.

49. l. 8. *a cavalier.* Zerbino.

50. l. 2. *agèd crone.* Gabrina (XX. 106 et seq.).

68. l. 1–2. cf. II. 55–6, and VIII. 11.

71–72. cf. II. 69–76.

82. l. 3. cf. VIII. 10, and X. 50.

ll. 4–8. cf. X. 110, and XI. 1–15.

91–2. As Orlando cast the unchivalrous cannon into the North Sea, so Ruggiero casts the unchivalrous magic shield into the well.

94. ll. 7–8. *The lady*. She who brought him to Pinabello's castle and whom he has carried away with him.

CANTO XXIII

3. l. 2. i.e. in Merlin's cave; cf. 11. 75–6.

9. l. 4. cf. XIII. 75–9.

10. l. 4. *her cousin*. Astolfo's father (Otto) and Bradamante's father (Aymon) are brothers.

13. ll. 3–4. cf. IV. 16 et seq.
 ll. 7–8. cf. IV. 47–8.

15. l. 6. *The son of Galafrone*. Angelica's brother Argalia, to whom the magic lance belonged in Boiardo's *Orlando Innamorato*; cf. VIII. 17.

18. l. 8. cf. XXII. 71.

20. l. 8. Bradamante has five brothers: Rinaldo, Ricciardo, Ricciardetto, Guicciardo and Alardo, and a half-brother, Guidone.

21. ll. 7–8. i.e. the baptism of Ruggiero, which must precede their betrothal.

26. l. 6. *Charles de Gaulle*. 'Il signor Gallo' in the original, i.e. Charlemagne. (A private joke of Ariosto's, perhaps.)

33. l. 3. Rodomonte is in search of Doralice and has sworn to take the first horse he finds. Dame Discord has arranged for him to come upon Ruggiero's horse (XVIII. 36–7).

54. cf. XII. 91–4, and XIII. 11 et seq.

70. This meeting between Mandricardo and Orlando has already been mentioned (XIV. 64).

71. cf. XII. 69 et seq. and XIV. 34.

79–80. Orlando killed Agricane, the father of Mandricardo, at Burgundy in a fair duel, as narrated by Boiardo (*Orl. Inn.*, 1. vi–xix).

85. ll. 7–8. Antaeus, the giant, drew strength from his mother, Gaea, the earth. The only way in which Hercules could kill him was to hold him suspended in mid air and strangle him. Ariosto has previously compared Orlando with Antaeus (IX. 77).

108–9. An early antecedent for this inscription by the grateful lover is to be found in the thirteenth-century French text *La mort le roi Artù*, in the Arthurian Prose-Vulgate, where King Arthur visits his sister, Morgain la Fée, in her castle and in a bedroom

sees the paintings in which Lancelot has depicted his deeds of
prowess and his adulterous love for Queen Guinevere, with
inscriptions beneath which make their meaning only too clear.
(cf. edition by Jean Frappier, Textes Litteraires Français,1954,
par. 48–54.)

110. Ariosto has already said that Orlando has a fluent knowledge
of Arabic (IX. 5).

120. ll. 7–8. This is the bracelet, a gift from Orlando, with which
Angelica rewarded the shepherd (XIX. 37–40).

134. l. 5. *scramasaxe*. A two-handled axe.

136. The madness of Orlando, continued in XXIV (Vol. II. of this
translation), occurs at the very centre of the poem.

INDEX OF PROPER NAMES
(CANTOS I–XXIII)

MORE ABOUT PENGUINS
AND PELICANS

For further information about books available from Penguins please write to Dept EP, Penguin Books Ltd, Harmondsworth, Middlesex UB7 0DA.

In the U.S.A.: For a complete list of books available from Penguins in the United States write to Dept CS, Penguin Books, 625 Madison Avenue, New York, New York 10022.

In Canada: For a complete list of books available from Penguins in Canada write to Penguin Books Canada Ltd, 2801 John Street, Markham, Ontario L3R 1B4.

In Australia: For a complete list of books available from Penguins in Australia write to the Marketing Department, Penguin Books Australia Ltd, P.O. Box 257, Ringwood, Victoria 3134.

DANTE: THE DIVINE COMEDY

PART I: HELL
Translated by Dorothy L. Sayers

Dante (1265–1321) is the greatest of Italian poets and his *Divine Comedy* is the finest of all Christian allegories. In the *Inferno*, the first of its three parts, the poet is conducted by the spirit of the poet Virgil through the twenty-four great circles of Hell on the first stage of his arduous journey towards God. All Dante's qualities – sublime, grim, intellectual, humorous, ecstatic – are brought out in this fresh, vigorous translation of what Dorothy Sayers calls, in her excellent introduction, this 'drama of the soul's choice'.

PART II: PURGATORY
Translated by Dorothy L. Sayers

Of the three parts of *The Divine Comedy*, *Purgatory* (as Dorothy L. Sayers remarks in her comprehensive introduction) is 'the least known, the least quoted, and the most loved'. In her fine translation Dante can clearly be seen as the universal poet. In contrast to the *Inferno*, this canticle deals with the roots instead of the fruits of sin, as Dante struggles up the terraces of Mount Purgatory on his arduous journey towards God.

PART III: PARADISE
Translated by Dorothy L. Sayers and Barbara Reynolds

Still inspired by the memory of Beatrice, Dante (1265–1321) completed the *Paradise* shortly before his death. In this third and final part of the *Divine Comedy* the poet, after his passage through hell and purgatory, is still not fully prepared for what he finds in heaven. His journey through the circling spheres towards the abode of God is a long progress of understanding.

Barbara Reynolds has brilliantly completed the fine verse translation which Dorothy Sayers left unfinished at her death, and the whole spirit of the *Divine Comedy* can now be grasped by a wider public than ever before.

THE PENGUIN CLASSICS

A Selection

THE PSALMS
Translated by Peter Levi

Balzac
SELECTED SHORT STORIES
Translated by Sylvia Raphael

Flaubert
SALAMMBO
Translated by A. J. Krailsheimer

Zola
LA BÊTE HUMAINE
Translated by Leonard Tancock

A NIETZSCHE READER
Translated by R. J. Hollingdale

Cao Xueqin
THE STORY OF THE STONE VOLUME TWO:
THE CRAB-FLOWER CLUB
Translated by David Hawkes

Balzac
THE WILD ASS'S SKIN
Translated by H. J. Hunt

Cicero
LETTERS TO ATTICUS
Translated by Shackleton Bailey